I0754188

HARRINGTON:

A STORY OF TRUE LOVE.

Wm. Douglas O'Connor.

BY THE AUTHOR OF "WHAT CHEER," "THE GHOST: A CHRISTMAS STORY," "A TALE OF LYNN," ETC.

"Herein may be seen noble chivalrye, curtesye, humanyte, friendlyenesse, hardyenesse, love, friendshype, cowardyse, murder, hate, vertue and synne. Doo after the good, and leve the evyl, and it shall brynge you to good fame and renomme."—SIR THOMAS MALORY: *Preface to Morte D'Arthur.*

BOSTON:
THAYER & ELDRIDGE,
114 & 116 WASHINGTON STREET.
1860.

W. H. Tinson, Stereotyper.

I DEDICATE

THIS BOOK

TO MY WIFE.

CONTENTS.

HARRINGTON.

PROLOGUE.

I.

As hot a day as ever blazed on the lowlands of Louisiana, blazed once in mid-April on the plantation of Mr. Torwood Lafitte, parish of Avoyelles, in the Red River region. Perhaps it was because the heat was so unseasonable that it seemed as if never, not even in midsummer, had there been so hot a day. One might have been pardoned for imagining that heat not of this world. Mr. William Tassle, overseer to Lafitte, was a profane man, but he might have been considered as only a profane poet aiming at the vivid expression of a mystical dark truth, when, speaking of the day, he said it was as hot as Hell.

It was the Sabbath, but an active fancy, brooding over the general condition of man and nature on Mr. Lafitte's plantation, might have thought it rather the Devil's Sabbath than the Sabbath of the Lord. Through the vaporous atmosphere, simmering with the heat, swarming with insect life, and reeking with the dense, sickly sweetness of tropic plants and flowers, the fierce sun poured a flood of stagnant, yellow light, which lay in a broad and brassy glare over the low landscape. Veiled by the cruel radiance, rose afar in the west and north the Pine Woods of Avoyelles, and in the southern distance the solemn masses of gloom formed by the cotton-woods, live-oaks and cypresses of the Great Pacoudrie Swamp. The eye wandering backward from the depths of the morass, saw the smouldering fire of the atmosphere envelop the enormous trees, draped everywhere with long streamers of black moss, and kindle the broad palmetto bottoms, and the multi-colored luxuriance of tropical vegetation, which sprang into ranker life beneath the vivid and sullen ray. The sluggish tide of the bayou basked with snaky gleams in the quivering lustre ; the red marl of the plantation where mules and negroes were toiling painfully under the oaths and blows of the drivers and overseer, darkly glowed in it ; the bright, rank green of the lawn before the mansion was aflare with it ; and the mansion itself, with its rose and jasmin vines drooping around the posts of the veranda, looked scorched to a deeper brown in the hot, thick, yellow, intolerable glare.

Shadows that day were the demons of the landscape. Shadows of intense and peculiar blackness, so compact that they seemed to have a substantial being of their own, lurked in the yellow light around and beneath every object. A dark fancy might have dreamed them a host of devils, disguised as shadows, and mustered to prevent the escape of a soul from Hell. Black with a strange blackness, shaped to an ugly goblin resemblance of the thing they accompanied, they were scattered like a host of demon sentries all over the scene, and had watch and ward of everything. The gaunt, stilted bittern standing motionless near the water, had his black goblin duplicate beneath him on the glistering clay. The mud-hued, warty-hided, abominable alligator, as he raised himself on his short legs, had his black, misshapen, shadow-caricature to lumber up with him on the trodden mire, and it went with him as he took his lumpish plunge into the foul bayou. Every plant or shrub had its scraggy imp of shadow sprawling beneath it, and darting and dodging as if to catch it whenever it moved. Every tree—cypress, live-oak, sycamore, cotton-wood, or gum, all solemnly draped with black moss—had its scrawny phantom to toss and flicker fantastically with the tangled motion of a hundred darting arms, if the branches or their streamers swayed in the furnace-breath of the light wind. Every fallen trunk, or log, or stump, or standing post had its immovable, black sentinel shape of shadow projected beyond it, or crouching by its side. Along the running fences on the plantation ran black, spectral bars on the red marl. In the fields, among the new-sprung corn, sown with the pain and sweat of slaves, a demon-crop of shadow mocked with its ugly color and fantastic shape the green beauty of the pennoned grain. The reeking mules, panting and straining, with drooping heads, as they dragged the groaning ploughs through the soil of the cotton fields, or pulled the clanking harrows over the furrowed rows, had their monstrous jags of sooty shadow, like the malformed beasts of a devil's dream, jerking along with shapeless instruments beside them. The black drudges, men and women, plodding and tottering in the sweltering heat, behind the ploughs, beside the harrows, or dropping seed into the drills, had hunched and ugly goblin dwarfs of shadow, vigilantly dogging their footsteps, and bobbing and dodging with their more active movements. The burly overseer on horseback had his horsed demon of lubber shadow, which aped his every gesture and movement, ambling fantastically with him hither and thither among the rows, and grotesquely motioning into squirms of phantom glee the shadows of the writhing slaves on whom his frequent whip-lash fell. Up around the planter's mansion, shadows as fantastical, as black and demoniacal as these, wavered or lay in the fierce, yellow glow. And among them all there was none uglier or more seemingly sentient than one within the room opening on the veranda—a black, hellion shape which floated softly as in a pool of oil, on an oblong square of sluggish sunshine shimmering on the floor, just behind the chair of Mr. Lafitte.

Angry words had been uttered in that room within the last few minutes—angry at least on the part of Madame Lafitte, who sat away from the sunlight, opposite her husband, with a table laid with fruit and wine between them. She was of the superbest type of southern beauty—and there is no beauty more exquisite; but now her lovely olive face was dusky white with fury and agony—its pallor heightened by contrast with her intense black hair, which she wore in heavy tresses drooping almost to the broad gold ornaments in her ears. Silent at present, she sat with her white arms tightly clasped below her bosom, which convulsively rose and fell beneath its muslin folds, and with dilated nostrils, and pale lips curved with hate and grief, kept her dark eyes, lustrous with passion, fixed on the evil visage of her husband.

"You are well named," she broke forth again, her voice, a rich contralto, trembling with vehemence; "but you are worse than your pirate namesake. Worse than the worst of that Baratarian crew. Lafitte! Lafitte, indeed! You are worse than he. Worse than Murrell. Worse than anybody. Devil that you are!"

She paused again, speechless with fury. The tornado which many thought the brassy flare upon the landscape portended, had its proper fulfillment in the raging whirl of passions within her. Mr. Lafitte sat at ease, slowly tilting his chair to and fro, the jewelled fingers of his brown left hand clasped around the stem of a crystal goblet on the table, his right hand carelessly thrust into a side pocket of his white coat, and regarded her with a sardonic smile on his dark visage, while slipping to and fro in the sluggish pool of light upon the floor, his shadow, like a black familiar, moved with an oily motion behind him.

"Anything more, my angel?" he asked in a soft, smooth, courteous voice, habitual with him: "any more epithets? Pray continue. Go on, light of my life, go on. Indulge your own Lafitte—your pirate lover. He loves to hear you."

Maddened by his calm mockery, she did not reply, but kept her blazing eyes fixed upon his face. A weaker man than Mr. Lafitte might have shrunk from that gaze. But its burning fire was wasted on his eyes as flame upon asbestos. Strange eyes had Mr. Lafitte—true tokens of the nature which else his other features might have betrayed less surely. His form was muscular and manly, and his face, though dark and sinister, might have been justly called handsome, if only for the richness of its brunette complexion. Dark, wavy auburn hair, which he wore long, and a thick moustache of the same color, drooping over the mouth, conferred a certain lordly grace upon the countenance. The nose, not finely cut, was bold, aquiline, and deeply curved in the nostrils, and the line of the jaw and chin was vigorous and masterful. In the full visage, suffused with the dense and sultry glow of a highly vascular organization, tropic passions basked in strong repose. But the motor passion of all was evident in the eyes. Large eyes which at a yard's distance might have seemed grey, but nearer were tawny and flecked with minute blood-specks. Steadfast, watchful, glossy, unwinking eyes—without depth, without sympathy—obdurate, rapacious and cruel—they confirmed the expression of the receding brow above them, which, broad and full, with a marked depression down its centre, was thus divided into two lobes, and bore resemblance to the forehead of the tiger. A physiognomist, looking at that face, would have declared Mr. Lafitte a man organized for ferocity as the beast he resembled is organized. A believer in the doctrine of transmigration might have held that the spirit of a tiger dwelt in his frame, and looked out of those tawny, blood-specked orbs.

It looked out of them now as with a feline playfulness he spoke his smooth taunts, meanwhile swaying slowly to and fro in his chair, as though balancing for a spring.

"Go on, my beautiful one," he continued. "Favor me with more of those choice similitudes. Choice? And yet—as a matter of taste, my angel, purely as a matter of taste—that phrase—pirate, though bold and graphic, I admit, might be artistically improved. Corsair, now. What do you think of corsair? Is not corsair better, more poetical, more Byronesque? Yes," he went on reflectively, as though the proposed change were a matter of vital seriousness, "yes, corsair is a finer word. Soul of my soul, let it be corsair. Suffer Lafitte to be your Conrad; you shall be his Zuleika. Have I 'one virtue,' my Zuleika? You will readily concede me the 'thousand crimes,' I know, but have I the 'one virtue?'"

"Why," she wailed passionately, taking no heed of his badinage; "why am I treated thus! Why am I kept here on this hateful plantation, in this remote parish, without life, without society, without pleasure of any kind. Nothing but this routine of dull farm life. No faces but your servants' and your overseer's around me. No company but these planters, these planters' wives, these planters' daughters, these people that ride over here sometimes, that I fatigue myself with visiting, that I care nothing about, anyway. Bad enough to come here once a year for the hot months—but three years, winter and summer, have I spent here. Three, Lafitte. Not once have I been in New Orleans for three years. Not once near the house where seven years of marriage with you were endurable with friends, with society, with life, with pleasures, with things I cared for, and which diverted me. Cut off from them all. You go when you please. Weeks, months, you are away, and leave me here sick, mad, frantic with ennui. Here, up the river, alone, what have I here to enjoy?"

"Here, my Josephine," he replied, in an unruffled voice; "here, do you ask? What have you here? Here you have books, novels, without end, music in reams, your guitar, your piano, this elegant simplicity, this charming country prospect, your own sweet thoughts, the pleasures of imagination, the pleasures of memory, the pleasures—yes, even the pleasures of hope. And then, too," sinking his voice to a softer tone, while his smile became a shade more sardonic and his eyes more cruel, "then, too, you have me."

"You," she raved, her pallid face convulsed with the refluent fury, and her eyes flashing. "You! Yes, I have you. Whom I hate, whom I loathe, whom I abhor! Yes, I have you; you who torture me."

"I who torture you?" interrupted Mr. Lafitte blandly. "And yet, my angel, they say we are a model couple. They are never tired of talking of my unvarying gallant courtesy to you. You, yourself, could not name this moment in a court of law one word or action that would seem incompatible with the tenderest affection for you."

"I know it," she moaned. "Yes, that is the misery of it. I am insulted, I am profaned, I am outraged, I am tortured till I could go mad, or kill myself; and it is all done—my

God! I know not how. Done with smoothness and calmness and courtesy; done with civility; done with sweet stabbing words. Others could only see the sweetness; none but I can feel the stabs. But they kill me daily, and you know it. Subtle and sweet is your cruelty to me—cruel, cruel devil that you are! Cruel to me, cruel to your slaves, cruel to everyone."

"Cruel to my slaves, eh," said Mr. Lafitte, tranquilly, his voice still equable, his face still wearing its sardonic smile: "Cruel to you and cruel to my slaves. Antony, for example."

"Yes, Antony," she replied, speaking in a calmer voice, as of one whose sufferings, whatever they might be, were remote from her, or as nothing to her own, "Antony is one. I saw the wretch just now, as I went down to the cabins. There you have him bucked in this scorching heat, his head bleeding where you and Tassle beat him with your whipstocks, and the flies tormenting him. Is there another planter in the parish that would treat that boy so? No wonder he ran away, like his brother before him. He might as well be in Hell as on this plantation. They might all as well be in Hell—as they are. Sweltering in the cotton-field, on a Sunday, too, there they are, fifty miserable wretches—hark, now! Tassle is laying it on to some of them. That is the howl of some of the wenches. Listen to that!"

Softened by the distance, but heard distinctly in the sultry stillness, came up from the cotton-fields a confusion of dismal screeches. Madame Lafitte sullenly listened, till they wailed away, the planter meanwhile calmly drinking his goblet of iced claret, and then filling the glass again from a slender bottle standing in a cooler on the table.

"These are the sounds I have to listen to, day after day, and year after year," hoarsely murmured Madame Lafitte, her bosom heaving convulsively above her clasped arms, and her eyes burning with dark fire in the pale gloom of her face. "Every hour in the day they come from the field. All through the evening from the gin-house. Day and night, night and day, the yelling of those unhappy creatures is dinned into my ears. That is my music."

Mr. Lafitte, who had resumed his former attitude, and was still tilting his chair, paused, with his eyes fixed upon his wife, and shook with long, silent, devilish merriment, his black familiar wobbling meanwhile in the pool beneath him. Then, in his softest, smoothest voice, he began to curse and swear, if what was rather a flood of profane exclamations may be so described. All names held sacred, grotesquely conjoined with secular names and titles, and poured forth in fluent and rapid succession, composed the outflow of a profanity inexpressibly awful, both from its nature and from the smooth and serene tones in which it found utterance. Madame Lafitte listened to him aghast, for she had never heard this from his lips before, and a dim, blind foreboding that it portended some horrible change in his attitude toward her, filled her soul. Ending it presently in another spasm of chuckling merriment, as if what seemed a mere depraved desire for blasphemy was satisfied, Mr. Lafitte took up the conversation.

"It is positively delightful, Josephine," he remarked, "to hear you lamenting the trouncing of the dear negroes. But, not to dwell upon this touching outbreak of philanthropy, permit me—for I feel refreshingly wicked to-day—permit me to ask you, my angel, if you know what made me marry you?"

She looked at him for a moment with a face of mingled wonder, scorn and loathing.

"What made you marry me?" she repeated, "your love, I suppose—at least, what you call love."

"Indeed, no Josephine," he coolly replied. "It was not love at all. What makes a man keep a mistress? For that was it, and nothing more."

At this atrocious declaration, Madame Lafitte, the very inmost temple of her soul profaned and defiled, as it never had been till then, bowed her head in an agony of shame.

"Yes, Josephine," he continued, "that was it. You were a queen of a girl when I first saw you. Young, innocent, gentle, enchanting, the most beautiful woman then, as I think you are now, that I ever beheld, and though your family was poor, you were accomplished as few of your sex ever become. I wanted you for one of my mistresses, and I got you at the little expense of a marriage ceremony. A strict moralist might say that, at best, you were only my——ah, the coarse word! but in this country you are called my wife. And, *apropos*, do you know what they call this union of ours, contracted on my part from such a motive? They call it holy matrimony."

Mr. Lafitte, with a negrine *ptchih*, went off in a spasm of devilish merriment, keeping his eyes fixed on the bowed and pallid face of the woman opposite him.

"You were in love with young Raynal when I married you," he continued, "and you were bullied and badgered by your amiable family into wedlock with me. Of that, however, I will not speak now. But suppose, Josephine, that you wish a divorce. How are you going to get it? On what grounds? Now *apropos* of my mistresses: by the law of Louisiana, were you false to me, I could get a divorce from you. By the same laws—oh, how I love them!—you could only get that divorce from me if I kept my mistress in your dwelling, or publicly and openly. Suppose you emigrated to another State where they grant divorces on the ground of the husband's infidelity. Could you get a separation then? No. Why not? Because you have no evidence, and I have taken good care that you can have none. Ha! my dear, what do you think of your position?"

"My God, my God!" she moaned, "what have I done that I should be outraged thus! How have I borne this life—how can I bear it! I tell you, Lafitte," she cried, raising her voice, hoarse with anger and agony, into a higher key, and throwing out her arms with a furious gesture, "I tell you that this life is Hell. I know now, what I wondered when I was a child—where Hell is and what it looks like. It is here and it looks like this. This is one of its chambers, and this one of its mansions. These walls, those books, those pictures, this furniture, that fruit, that wine, they all belong to it. Those are its flowers clambering around the windows—this is its light and these are its shadows—this scorching heat is the heat of it, that sun is the sun of it, these slaves swelter in it—I, a slave like them, am tortured in it, and you are the fiend of it, hard, cruel, sensual, heartless, pitiless devil that you are !"

Flinging her arms together again in a convulsive clasp on her bosom, her frame shuddering, her breath coming and going in quick gasps through her clenched teeth, which gleamed behind lips deadly white and tensely drawn, she glared at him with fixed nostrils and flaming eyes, like a beautiful maniac. Save that he had ceased his balancing, that his eyes were a shade more tigerish, and that his form crouched slightly forward in his chair, Mr. Lafitte was as cool and collected as ever, and his face wore the same sardonic smile.

"Now Josephine," he remarked in a tone more nonchalant, serene and soft than before, if that could be, "let me close this delightful conversation by a few brief observations on the value of opportunity. First, with regard to the dear negroes. I am a rich, but I have my little desire to be a *very* rich planter. Therefore I lay plans for a large cotton crop, on which, by the way, I have heavy bets pending. In order that I may have the large crop, which means a great deal of money, and in order that I may win my bets, which are considerable, I make the dear negroes work furiously. But in order that they shall work with due ardor, and lest that tender bond of fidelity and devotion to their master's interests which the good divines up north expatiate so eloquently upon —lest that should not sufficiently inspire them, I get my excellent William Tassle to stimulate them with a plantation whip, and I stimulate them myself with another when I feel like it, which I often do. And they labor like angels—dear me ! how they do spring to it, to be sure ! It is enchanting. Indeed I get a great deal out of them. But in order that I may get a great deal out of them, I must flog them up handsomely at their work, and punish them profusely after their work if their work has not been what the ardent soul of Lafitte could wish. Hence the cruelty, as you harshly call it, my Josephine—hence the floggings, the paddlings, the buckings, hence the howlings that annoy you, my angel, and which, by the way, I really cannot help, since the black beasts will make a clamor—unless, indeed, I could induce some of those cursedly ingenious Yankees to invent me a patent anti-howling machine for their abominable throats. Positively, it is an idea, and I must reflect upon it. But see now. In doing all this, I only avail myself of my legal opportunities. Could I do it if I had not my opportunities? Alas, no. Could I do it up North? Alas, no. I should not have my opportunities. I should have to calculate, and circumvent, and plot and scheme till my poor brain would be fatigued, and then be bothered and baffled with strikes for higher wages, and ten hour systems, and God knows what else. Now here, thanks to our good Livingstone, who was really a fine jurist, I have a code which gives me all the advantages and puts my black laborers completely and comfortably under my thumb. They have no opportunities, and so they work without wages and are well flogged into the bargain. I have my opportunities, which I improve, and hence they work for me. Ha! it is charming! They get their two plantation suits a year, their three and a half pounds of bacon and their peck of meal apiece a week, which is not costly, and keeps them in working order. They are up early and down late, and so profits accrue. Hence the value of opportunities with regard to the dear negroes—my little exactions of whom wound your sensibilities, my angelic Josephine."

He paused to drink his claret slowly and refill his glass, keeping his eyes fixed upon his wife, who sat secretly wondering what he meant by all this devilish frankness.

"Now," resumed the planter, "observe again the value of opportunities in relation to yourself, *ma chère*. I marry you. Good. We live in much elegance, to your soul's delight, in New Orleans. Good again. But one fine day I bring you up here, and here I keep you, where you don't want to stay. Why do you stay, then? Ah! the beautiful social system gives me the opportunity to make you. Could you bring me up here? Oh, no. Could you make me stay? Oh, no. The beautiful social system does not give you that opportunity."

"No," she cried, "it gives me nothing."

"And why?" he continued. "Is it because you are

morally, mentally, or in any way, my inferior? Oh, no. Why, then? Simply because you are a woman. You are less than I by virtue of your sex, my angel. Ha! it is curious. The beautiful social system makes you something like my slave, dear wife. I bring my negroes here, and I bring you here. None of you want to come, but you can't help yourselves, and so come you do. But my negroes cannot bring me here. No. Nor can you bring me here. No. Do my negroes run away? I set Dunwoodie's hounds after them, and run them down. Do you run away? That dear old Mrs. Grundy sets her hounds after you, and runs you down. Ah!"

He paused to drink a little claret, keeping his eyes fixed upon her face.

"Meanwhile," he pursued, "I keep you in perpetual torment, as you say. Try divorce. You have no cause in law, for I take care to give you none. My little, delicate, subtle, intangible, polite aggravations—all my skillful outrages and profanations of your soul and body, which drive you mad, or kill you slowly like poison, are not recognized in law. My courteous, maddening words and actions, which work, it is true, the effect, and worse than the effect, of the most brutal physical cruelty—they are all perfectly legal. It is doubtful whether they could even be stated for the purposes of a divorce suit. They are so subtle, so veiled in good nature, courtesy, kindness, legality, that if they were stated, people probably would laugh at you, and think you dishonest or deranged. At all events, though they slowly madden or murder you, they constitute no breach of holy matrimony."

"They do," she cried. "I do not care what the law says; such matrimony as I live in is not holy. It is"——

"Ah, no, dear Josephine," he interrupted. "Decidedly you are wrong. Go to court—swear that you hate me, loathe me, abhor me—swear that life is insupportable with me, and plead for release, and the blessed old law will tell you that you are living, and must live, in holy matrimony! Go to any southern State—go to South Carolina, and state my refined and delicate cruelty. Why, Judge Somebody or other, in the next State, boasts that it is the unfading honor, as he calls it, of South Carolina, that she never has granted a divorce for any cause whatever. Well, go North—go to New York, for instance. Why, their great Panjandrum up there, the 'Tribune' man—what's his name—Greeley—he will tell you that you are living, and must live, in holy matrimony. Bless him!" said Mr. Lafitte, piously. "I love him. I love him well. I hate him for his Abolitionism: I love him for his views on holy matrimony. I hate him because he tries to weaken my power over my slaves: I love him because he tries to strengthen my power over you, my angel. So do the rest of them. Go to any State you like, and they will all tell you that you are living, and must live, in holy matrimony. Every one, except that naughty, naughty Indiana. Ah, the bad State! The wicked, wicked State, that says a discordant marriage is hell, and saves people from it at the expense of holy matrimony! But you couldn't go there even with your complaint of cruelty, for you haven't a single witness—not one; and if you had, you wouldn't go there, and presently I'll tell you why. Meanwhile, the result is, that there's no help for you anywhere. As for alleging any little infidelities on my part, that is clearly absurd. Thanks to our good Edward Livingstone's code, you can get no testimony from the yellow girls, for slaves are not witnesses, you know, in law; and as for getting any legal testimony on that point, that I take care you can't get, and your convictions are not evidence, my angel. Then, too, observe how the beautiful social system favors me. My little gaieties are reported, for instance, in New Orleans. Well, society does not taboo me. Mrs. Grundy smiles blandly upon me still. The men laugh, and say, 'Ah, Lafitte, you gay dog!' The women are soft as cream, and sweet as sugar. Whereas you—suppose even a whisper of that sort about you—even an idle rumor—ah, what a fine howl! You are quite finished at once, my dear."

He shrugged his shoulders, and elevated his eyebrows with a grimace of mock pity, keeping his carnivorous eyes still fixed upon the raging silence of her face.

"And now," he went on, "why do I keep you here? Why do I torture you daily? I answer—are you listening, my cherished one?—I answer that it is my little vengeance. Harken, Josephine. You and that handsome young Raynal were in love with each other when I first saw you. You were both poor. Raynal has got rich since, but he was then poor as charity. I, on the contrary, was wealthy, and your family wouldn't let you marry Raynal, but were anxious that you should marry me, for they wanted to make a rich match for you. You liked me well enough then, for you only knew the best side of me, which the ladies say is charming; but you did not love me. I pressed my suit, however, and your family worried and drove you—poor young girl of fifteen, that you were—till, unable—for I will be strictly fair to you, Josephine—unable to resist longer, you yielded, and I got you."

"Yes, you got me with a lie," she passionately cried. "Never would I have yielded, had you and they not lied me into believing Raynal had abandoned me and engaged himself to another."

"Oh," returned Mr. Lafitte, with a leer, "you have found that out, have you? No matter. I got you, and you discovered your mistake in yielding as time passed on. Then, the year before I brought you here, when you were in much suffering—for I will be just to you, Josephine—you and Raynal had a little correspondence. Ha! you thought I did not know it! But I found it out. Your treacherous young Creole wench sold me your secret, and I took copies of every letter you wrote before I let her carry them to Raynal. I took copies also of his before they went to you. They are all eloquent, and I love to read them. And they put you both in my power, my lady!"

He saw that the blow struck home. She sat mute and still as marble, but all expression had gone from her face; the fire had faded from her eyes; her arms, still clasped on her bosom, were relaxed; and her bosom had ceased to heave. The planter watched her with an infernal smile on his dark visage.

"With those letters in my possession," he continued, "you could not seek release even in Indiana. For writing them, you have to be tortured most exquisitely till you die, as before you wrote them, you had to be tortured for having loved Raynal. And yet, Josephine, I believe you and Raynal to be people of honor, and, though you loved, to have written those letters with innocent hearts. You were in loveless suffering, and you wanted the consolation a friend could give, and which Raynal gave. See how justly I state it! I will go further—I will admit that the letters are such as two friends might have written to each other. There is really nothing wrong in them. But they are full of passages which are too equivocal to be read in a court of law. There innocent words are made to seem guilty. And those letters, without much twisting, would convict you of conjugal infidelity, my beloved Josephine."

He looked at her with fiendish enjoyment, but she sat still, and her face did not change.

"Ah yes, *ma chère!*" he observed after a long pause, slowly beginning his rocking again, and thus setting in motion the lurking shadow beneath him—"you and that dear handsome young Raynal are certainly compromised. Still there is one consolation for you, Josephine. Really a great consolation. Namely, that you are reputably married. You have the honorable position of a legal wife, my dear. Is it not consoling?"

He sat for a full minute sardonically smiling at her. She did not turn away, nor did her face lose its blank immobility.

"That is your consolation, sweet wife," he continued. "It is the——Hallo, there! Tassle, is that you? Come in."

He had the ear of a cat to have heard the steps of the overseer coming up the grassy lawn. It was a full half minute before the heavy sluff of boots was audible to an ordinary ear. Then came their lazy thud on the veranda, and the overseer lounged in. A short, stocky, burly man, with heavy, sallow, stolid features. He had a broad, straw hat set back on his head, was dressed in coarse, light clothes, and was revolving tobacco in his open mouth.

"Ha!" said Mr. Lafitte, "it is he. Good William Tassle. Faithful William Tassle. Excellent William Tassle."

The overseer, with his dull eye fixed on the planter, stopped chewing, and closing his mouth, slowly smiled.

"It is hot, my Tassle," blandly observed Mr. Lafitte.

"Hot as—beg pardon, madame"—said Mr. Tassle, checking himself in a torrid comparison, with a rude gesture of deference to the planter's wife, who took no notice of his presence. "It singes a man's nostrils to breathe it, Mr. Lafitte."

"Yes?" replied the planter, as if the fact were of great interest. "Then how it must singe that Antony's nostrils, William. That poor Antony. We must have him up here. I must admonish him. Fetch him along, Tassle. And Tassle" —the overseer, who was going, paused—"just bring that iron collar that hangs in the gin-house. You know."

II.

The overseer nodded, and chewing stolidly, lounged out into the yard, where stood the kitchen, smoke-house, and other outbuildings, and going on through the orchard, emerged upon a blinding space where a row of white-washed cabins, with the gin-house hard by, glared in the hot light. A few negro children, half naked, with a lean and sickly old hound, were grouped in the shade of the gin-house. Near them, in the full blaze of the sunlight, a negro man, in coarse plantation clothes of a dirty white, sat on the ground in a squatting posture, feebly shaking his bare head, to keep off the swarm of insects that tormented him. This was Antony. He was bound in a peculiar manner—bucked, as the plantation slang has it. The ankles were firmly lashed together—the knees drawn up to the chest—the wrists also firmly pinioned and passed over the knees, and between the elbow-joints and the knee-pits, a short stick was inserted, thus holding movelessly in a bundle of agonizing cramp the limbs of the victim. This infernal torture—practised by the tyrants of our marine on their sailors—that class whose helplessness and wrongs most nearly resemble those of slaves—practised also on wretched criminals by the tyrants of our jails—Antony had endured from midnight till now, about two o'clock in the afternoon.

Nine years Lafitte's chattel, he had been badly used from time to time, and, of late, dreadfully. He had learned to read and write a little before he had come to the plantation, and a week before the present time he had picked up a scrap of newspaper on which was a fragment of one of those declamations about liberty, which southern politicians are fools enough to be making on all opportunities, amidst a land of slaves. The fragment had some swagger about the northern oppression of the South, which Antony did not understand any more than anybody else; but it rounded up with Patrick Henry's famous "Give me Liberty or give me Death!" which he understood very well; for from that moment Liberty or Death was a phrase which spoke like a voice in his mind, urging him to escape from his bondage. The next thing was to write a pass, make a package addressed to the house of Lafitte Brothers, New Orleans, and with this evidence of his assumed mission endeavor to reach that city, where he meant to smuggle himself into the hold of some vessel northward bound.

Clad in an old suit of Mr. Tassle's, which he had taken from the gin-house, and boldly riding away the night before, on a mare borrowed from Mr. Lafitte's stables, he had been suddenly met on a turn of the road—unaccountably met at midnight—by his master and the overseer, who seized him and found his forged credentials upon him. At once, he had been violently beaten over the head with their whip-stocks driven back to the plantation, reclothed in his plantation suit, securely bound, and left with horrid threats of torment on the morrow. The morrow had come, and here he was in utter misery, half crazy, and more than half fancying that he was in Hell.

Mr. William Tassle, his tobacco revolving slowly in his open mouth, stood and stolidly surveyed him. A pitiable object, truly! His face was bruised and swollen, and from wounds in his brow and cheek, made by the blows of the whip-handles, a dull ooze of blood, thinned by his sweat, had spread its stain over the whole countenance. Around the wounds buzzed and clung greedy clusters of black flies, hardly driven off by the feeble motions of his head, and returning every instant. His dark face, ashen grey and flaccid under the crimson stain, and faint with suffering, wore a look of dumb endurance ; his eyelids drooped heavily over his downcast eyes ; and his breath came in short gasps through the bloody froth that had gathered on his loose mouth. His wrists were cut with the tight cords that bound them, and his hands were discolored and swollen, as were his ankles. Even the overseer felt a sort of rude pity for him.

"Well, Ant'ny," said Mr. Tassle, slowly, pausing and turning his head aside to eject a vigorous squirt of tobacco juice, which lit upon a small chip and deluged a fly thereon, throwing the insect into quivering spasms of torture ; "you're in for it, you poor, mis'ble devil. Yer master's goin' to admonish ye, so he says. Know what that means, don't ye ? It's all up with *you*, Ant'ny."

The dumb, bruised face, with its blood-shot eyes, feebly turned up to his for a moment, then drooped away.

"Come, now," said Mr. Tassle, cutting the negro's bonds with two strokes of a jack-knife, "up with ye."

Antony, suddenly released from his cramped posture, fell over ; then made a feeble effort to crawl up on his hands and knees, tottered, sank down, and lay panting. Mr. Tassle started with alacrity for the gin-house, the black piccaninnies scampering and tumbling over each other in their scramble to get away, and the old hound sneaking after them. Presently he came back with a bucket of water and a gourd. Antony raised himself and drank from the gourd ; then sat up, panting, but relieved.

"Strip," said Mr. Tassle.

Antony tried, and was helped roughly by the overseer, who then dashed the bucket of water over his naked body. It revived him, for he presently began to wipe himself feebly with his trowsers. In the midst of this operation, Mr. Tassle seized him, rolled him over from the wet ground to a dry spot, and began to rub his arms and knees vigorously with his horny hand, chewing and expectorating rapidly as he did so. Soon the arrested circulation began to be restored, and Antony, getting his clothes on, was able to walk up and down in a brisk, tottering walk, the calves of his legs loosely shaking, and his legs trembling with exhaustion.

"That'll do," said Mr. Tassle, at length; "you'll be ready for your floggin' right soon. Here, you dam cuss of a nigger, drink a swallow of this. That'll set you up."

Antony took the proffered whisky-flask—Mr. Tassle's pocket companion—and gulped the liquor. It went to his poor, famished heart like fire, and shot some vigor through his numbed veins.

"Damned if I aint a philanthroper," growled Mr. Tassle. "Lettin' a hell-bent cuss of a sooty nigger drink my whisky. No matter. Have it out o' yer hide, Ant'ny, afore supper time. Now pick up yer feet for the house. Yer master has to settle with yer."

Antony went on to the house, Mr. Tassle following, and contemplatively regarding, as he spat and chewed, the shaking calves of the negro's legs, which he had a chance to do, as the old trowsers, too short in the first instance, were now split up the backs, nearly to the knees, and feebly flapped as the slave tottered on. Antony himself, giddy with his long exposure in the sun, and with the glow of the liquor he had drank, felt his poor mind wander a little, and was conscious of nothing so much as of the queer tattered shadow that bobbed around him, and which he half fancied would trip him up if he were to try to run away now.

An indefinite sense, which fell upon him as he entered the house, and slowly walked through the passage, that this guarding shadow had fallen behind and left him, was succeeded by a sense as vague, that the shadow he now saw lurking in the sunlight on the floor beneath his master's chair, was the same, and that it had gone on before when he came into the passage, and would leap from that place and chase him were he to flee. Dimly conscious of this fancy, he kept his hot eyes fixed upon the shadow—conscious also of a dreadful sullen hatred rising in his heart, and prompting him to spring upon his tyrant and strangle him, though he died for it afterward. Beyond this, he was vaguely aware that Tassle had put something that clanked on the table, and had gone;

and that the madame, as he would have called her, was present, sitting very still, and apparently indifferent to him or anything that might happen to him.

Suddenly he heard the smooth and quiet voice of his master, seeming nearer to him than it should have seemed.

"Well, Antony, so it appears that I have a learned nigger on my plantation. Cousin to the learned pig, I suppose. Did you ever hear of the learned pig, Antony?"

"Never did, Marster."

"Indeed. Then you never heard what happened to him?"

"Never did hear, Marster."

"Ah! Indeed! Well, he ran away, and was caught, and flogged, and bucked, to begin with. Just like you, Antony. After which he was treated so that he wished he was dead, Antony. Just as you are going to be, my learned nigger. Do you understand?"

"Yes, Marster."

In this colloquy, Mr. Lafitte's voice was as smooth and tranquil as though he were promising his servant pleasures instead of pains. Antony had answered mechanically, in a voice as quiet and subdued as his tyrant's, with the slightest possible quaver in his husky tones.

"So you can read and write, Antony," said the planter, after a pause.

"A little bit, Marster."

"A little bit, eh? Yes. Come, now, let's have a specimen. Here's the 'Picayune,' with something that suits your case." Mr. Lafitte took the paper from the table as he spoke. "A little bit of abolition pleasantry that your British friends fling at the South, and this booby editor circulates. Here, read it out."

Antony saw his master's hand extending the paper to him, with the thumb indicating a paragraph. Moving nearer, he mechanically took the paper. The print swam dizzily before his eyes, as, with a halting voice, he slowly read aloud what was, in fact, one of the most pungent anti-slavery sarcasms of the day:

"'From the—London—Morning Advertiser. One million

dollars—reward. Ran away—from—the—subscriber—on the 18th August—a likely—Magyar fellow (Antony boggled terribly over 'Magyar' which he thought must mean mulatto), named—Louis—Kossuth. He is—about—45—years old—5 feet—6 inches—high. Dark—com-plexion, marked—eye-brows, and—grey eyes.'"

"Not a bad description of you, Antony," interpolated Mr. Lafitte. "Quite like you, in fact. Go ahead."

Antony stammered on, losing the place, and beginning lower down.

"'Captains and—masters—of vessels—are—particularly—cautioned—against—harboring—or—concealing—the said—fugitive—on board—their ships—as the—full—penalty—of the law—will—be—rigorously—enforced."

"You see, Antony," again interrupted the planter. "You reckoned, I suppose, on getting off in a ship, when your nice scheme got you to New Orleans. Didn't you, my nigger Kossuth? You'd be advertised though, and caught, just like him. Go on."

Unheeding this sally of Mr. Lafitte's cheerful fancy, Antony went on, losing the place again, and getting to the bottom of the paragraph.

"'N.B.—If the—fellow—cannot—be taken—alive—I will pay—a—reward—of (Antony boggled again over the '250,000 ducats' named, and called it twenty-five dollars), for his—scalp. Terms as—above. Francis—Joseph—Emperor—of—Austria.'"

"Good," said the planter. "Your scalp, you woolly-headed curse, wouldn't bring that in the market, or I'd have it off, and your hide with it. Lay the paper down. You read atrociously."

Antony laid the paper on the table, and without looking at his master, fixed his blurred eyes on the floor again.

"You see," continued the planter, "how runaways get served. You have been told both by Tassle and myself that even if you got North you'd be sent back. We've got a Fugitive Slave Law now for runaway niggers, and back they come. You go to Philadelphia. That good Ingraham—that good Judge Kane—that dear Judge Cadwallader—they send you back. You go to New York. Lord! There everybody sends you back! You go to Boston. That dear Ben Hallett grabs you. That good Sprague—that good Curtis—all these good people grab you, as they grabbed that nigger Sims, and back you come. Yet you try it, you foolish Antony. Your cursed brother got off from me nine years ago, and so you think you'll try it too. Fine fellows both of you. He leaves Cayenne pepper in his tracks, which plays the devil with the hounds, and off he gets. But you've had to smart for him. All you've got since has been on his account. Now you'll get something on your own. I'll teach you to steal my horse and make off for the river with your forged pass and package. Do you see this?"

Lifting his dizzy eyes to the level of his master's hand, Antony saw that it held a heavy iron collar with a prong, on which he read in stamped letters, LAFITTE BROTHERS, NEW ORLEANS.

"My brother had a nigger that wore this collar once," said the smooth, cruel voice, "and now you'll wear it. If you ever get away again, which I'll take care you never will, people will know who you belong to, my fine boy. Kneel down here."

Antony felt the sullen hatred seethe up in his heart, and his brain reeled.

"I won't have that collar on me, Marster," he huskily muttered. "You may kill me, Marster, but I won't have that collar on me."

"You won't, eh?" returned Mr. Lafitte, tranquilly. "Oh, well then, if you won't, you won't. By the way," he pursued, carelessly taking the paper from the table, and fanning himself gently, "do you know how I knew you were going to run away? I'll tell you. I was standing near the gin-house last night when you came there to steal Tassle's old clothes, and I heard you say to yourself—'Now for liberty or death.' Ah, ha, Antony, you shouldn't talk aloud! Tassle and I saw you go to the stable and take the mare, and then we saddled and headed you off, my nigger. That's the way of it. Pick up that paper."

Raising his eyes to his tyrant's feet, Antony saw the folded paper there where it had been dropped. Approaching, he painfully stooped to pick it up, when he felt himself seized, thrown down upon his knees, and the collar, which opened in the centre on a strong hinge, was around his neck! He struggled to free himself, but he was held, and the collar closed. In an instant a key of peculiar wards inserted in one of the cusps of this devilish necklace, shot a bolt into the socket of the other, and Mr. Lafitte, taking out the key, and putting it into his pocket, quietly spat in the face of the man whose neck he had just fettered, and spurning him violently with his foot, hurled him backward from his knees with a dreadful shock over on the floor.

Stunned for a moment, Antony lay motionless on his side. He knew that his master had risen, for as he turned his head, he saw the hideous shadow dart suddenly from the pool, and vanish, as though it had entered the planter. On his feet the next instant, with a dark cloud of blood bellowing in his brain, he saw with bloodshot eyes, Lafitte standing before him, with a calm, infernal smile on his visage, and all the tiger in his tawny orbs. The next second Madame Lafitte swept, like a superb ghost, between him and his revenge.

"Stay, Josephine," yelled the planter, his voice no longer issuing smooth and soft from the throat, but tearing up from his lungs in a loud, harsh snarl—"remain here. This entertainment is for you. You object to the howls of my black curs. I bring one here—into this room—whose howls shall split your ears."

She turned, as he spoke, on the threshold of the room, and advancing toward him, paused. For one instant she stood, imperial in her beauty, her magnificent form drawn to its full height, her haughty brow corrugated, her eyes burning like bale-fires, her outraged blood flooding her countenance with one vivid crimson glow. The next instant she strode forward, and smote him a sounding buffet on the face. Then, without a word, and with the step of an empress, she swept from the room.

Lafitte turned purple and livid in spots, and tottering back, fell into his chair. Struck! By her! Before his slave! Glaring up, he met the blood-shot eyes of Antony.

"Dog!" he yelled; "you are there, are you! Wash my spittle from your face with this!"

For a second, Antony stood holding his breath, with the wine the planter had dashed into his face, dripping from him, and steaming in his nostrils. For a second afterward, he stood unwincing, the fragments of the shattered goblet which followed, stinging his flesh. The next, his whole being rose in a wild, red burst of lightning, and the throat of Lafitte was in his right hand, his left crushing back the hand which had struck at him with a bowie-knife as he sprung. With his right knee set solid on the abdomen of the planter, pinning the writhing form to the chair, he saw the devilish face beneath him redden in his gripe, and deepen into horrible purple, and blacken into the visage of a fiend, with bloody, starting eyeballs, and protruding tongue. Still keeping that iron clutch of an aroused manhood on his tyrant's throat, he heard the mad, hoarse gurgle of his agony, and felt the struggling limbs relax and lose their vigor beneath him. And then yielding to an impulse of compassion his master never knew, and which rose louder than the bellowing voices of his revenge, he unclasped his hold, and saw the body slide flaccid and gasping to the floor.

Away, Antony! The bitter term of your bondage is over, and there is nothing now but Liberty or Death for you! Death? Ay, Death in the land of Liberty for the man who repays long years of outrage with one brave grip on the throttle of his oppressor! Death, when the savage planters muster to avenge their fellow, and drag you down to yon bayou, to shriek and scorch your life away among the sappy fagots of the slow fire! Death like this, or else by gnawing famine, or the beasts and reptiles of the swamp whose beckoning horrors soon must close around you! Liberty or Death—and Liberty a desperate chance, a thousand miles away.

He stood for an instant, panting, with a wild exultation pouring like fire through his veins. Then snatching the heavy bowie-knife from the floor, he sprang from the room, and leaped on the veranda just as the overseer, who had come up again from the fields, had set one foot on the steps to ascend. Flying against him full shock, he threw him backward clear and clean off his feet, and saw his head bounce with a terrific concussion on the grass as he sped on over the stunned body. He did not pause, nor look behind, but flew with the rush of a race-horse for the swamp. The light wind had risen, and the grain in the fields and the scattered trees on either side, and in the skirting woods beyond, and all the lurking shadows, waved, and tossed, and lifted under the sultry vault, as he sped his desperate course, while the hot landscape rushed to meet him, and ran whirling by, closing around and behind him, and seeming to follow as he flew. Across the lawn, its grass and wild-flowers sliding dizzily beneath him—up with a flying leap across the fence, which vanished below him—and down with a light shock on the red plantation marl which rose to meet him, and reeled from under him as he bounded on. Away, with frantic speed, over rows of cotton-plants, bruised beneath his feet, and gliding from under him—away, with a wilder leap, as the loud shouts of the slaves in full chorus struck his ear, and he saw them all, men and women, with open mouths and upthrown arms, stand with the mules and ploughs in the field on one side, and vanish from his flying glimpse as he fled by. Away, with every nerve and sinew desperately strung —with his pained heart knocking against his side—with his held breath bursting from him in short gasps—with the sweat reeking and pouring down his body, and dropping in big drops from his face, to be caught upon his clothes in his speed—with the bright knife, as his last refuge, clutched in his grasp —with the one thought of Liberty or Death burning in the whirl of his brain. Past the plantation now, his feet thudding heavily on a hard, black soil—on, with the swarming hum of innumerable insects, murmurously swirling by—on, with the light and rapid current of the hot south wind cool on the pain and fervor of his face, and swiftly purring in his ears—on, over rushing grass and flowers, and stunted shrubs and butts of trees—up again with a furious leap over a fence that sinks, and down again with a heavy thump on ground that rises—

on and away at headlong speed over a field of monstrous stumps, scattering the light chips as he flies—in now with a bound among the bright-green leaves of a thick palmetto bottom, and on with a rush through the swish, swish, swish of their loud and angry rustle, as he crashes forward to the still gleam of the bayou. Now his feet swash heavily on a grassy turf that yields like sponge, and water fills his shoes at every bound. Now the water deepens, and he sinks above his ankles or midway to his knees, as he splashes forward with headlong velocity, half-conscious and wholly careless in his desperate exultation that black venomous water-snakes writhe up behind him as he plunges through their pools. Now he bounds over a bank of black mire, and swerves in his course as something like a dirty log changes to an alligator, and lumbers swiftly toward him with yawning jaws. And now splashing through the green slime of the margin, he bursts with a plunge into the glistening waters of the bayou, and swims with vigorous strokes, while the gaunt bittern on the bank beyond scrambles away with squawking screams. Swimming till the water shoals, he flounders on again through slime to mire, and over another bog of pools and water-plants and spongy sod, till gaining the outskirts of the dense forest, and reaching a patch of damp, black earth under an enormous cypress-tree, he slackens his pace, stops suddenly, and throwing up his arms upon the trunk, drops his head upon them, panting and blowing—and the first mile-heat of the dreadful race for Liberty or Death is run!

III.

For a few minutes, exhausted with the terrible speed he had maintained, Antony leaned upon his arms with closed eyes, his breath suffocating him, his heart painfully throbbing, his limbs aching and trembling, and the water dripping from his clothes and trickling away on the black soil in small streams. The trees whispered over him as he panted beneath them, and their mysterious murmurs were the only sounds, save his own stertorous breathings, that were heard in the dead stillness. Recovering his breath in a few minutes, he lifted his head and turned around, letting his pained arms fall heavily by his side. He was no longer oppressed with heat, for the plunge in the bayou had cooled him; but his whole body ached not only with the exertions of the last few minutes, but from the previous torture of the bucking, and already his strength, heavily taxed by his long abstinence from food (for it was now more than fifteen hours since he had eaten), and only sustained by the intense excitement he had undergone, began to flag. His brain reeled and whirled still, and his apprehension was confused and dull. Gradually he began to be more sensible of the sore and swollen condition of his wrists and ankles, of the smart of the wounds in his forehead, and the stinging of the fragments of glass in his face. There was one sore spot in his chest just beneath his shoulder, which for a few moments he was at a loss to account for, till he suddenly remembered that his tyrant's foot had struck him there when he had kicked him over upon the floor. At the same instant he felt the chafe of the iron collar on his neck, and raising his hand suddenly, it struck against the blunt point of the prong. Gnashing his teeth with rage as the scene in that room rose in his mind, he seized the collar with both hands, and with a fierce imprecation, strove to rend it asunder. But the lock remained firm, and convulsed with a bitter sense of humiliation, as he thought of that accursed badge of his servitude inexorably riveted to his neck, the miserable man burst into tears.

It was but a brief spasm, and summoning up new courage

to his failing heart as he remembered that his dreadful journey lay still before him, he cast his eyes around into the swamp. Softened by the foliage of the wilderness of gigantic trees, and duskily lighting the long streamers of melancholy moss which greyed their green, the sultry sunlight, slanting athwart the enormous trunks, and tinting with sullen brilliance the scarlet, blue and yellow blossoms of parasitical plants which sprinkled the boles and branches in thick-millioned profusion, glistered on the muddy shallows of the morass, whose dismal level, broken here and there by masses of shadow, and huge bulks of fallen timber, stretched far away, like some abominable tarn of slush and suds, into vistas of horrid gloom. Here and there, stranded on shoals of mire, or basking on pieces of floodwood, alligators, great and small, sunned their barky hides ; while from every shallow pool, or wriggling around drifting logs or trunks of fallen trees, the venomous moccasin-snakes, whose bite is certain death, lifted their black devilish heads by scores, and made the loathsome marsh more loathsome with their presence. Over the frightful quagmire brooded an oppressive stillness, broken only by the mournful and evil whispering of the trees, or by the faint wriggling plash of the water-serpents. Thick, sickly odors of plants and flowers, blent with the stench of the morass, burdened the stagnant air, through whose languid warmth chill breaths crept from the dank and dense arcades of the forest. Vast, malignant, desolate and monstrous, loomed in the eyes of the wretched fugitive, the awful road to Liberty or Death.

His soul shrank from treading it. The fire had faded from his heart, and in that moment death by his own hand, for he would not be captured, seemed preferable to the terrors of the fen. Faint, weak, famished, weary unto agony, his whole body one breathing ache, his spirit all unnerved with the sense of his past and present misery, and nothing but despair before him, how could he hope to go on and live. Yet he could not remain here. Soon the hounds would be on his track—they would cross the bayou he had swam, and strike his trail. He must plunge still further into the swamp to distance them, or he must die here by the knife in his hand.

He turned and looked over the bayou far up the lowland to the plantation a mile away. Suddenly he started, clutching the knife with a firm grasp, his eyes flashing, his teeth and nostrils set, and his manhood once again flooding his heart with fire. Figures near the mansion—figures on horseback, guns, flashing in the sun, in their hands—one, two, three, four, five, six—six mounted horsemen—and, lower down on the lawn, what are those things running in circles? Hark! Far off a long, harsh, savage, yelling bay. The hunt is afoot, and the hounds have struck the trail! Away, Antony, for Liberty or Death!

Eyes flashing, teeth and nostrils set, every nerve and sinew valorously strung, he turned with a leap, and rushed straight into the morass. Before the headlong, desperate courage of his charge, the loathsome tenants of the swamp gave way. Plunging from the floodwood, the affrighted alligator trundled off, and the startled moccasins slipped and writhed from his path at the noise of his coming. Hark, again! Nearer than before the booming yell of the hounds. Speed, Antony! It is the Sabbath of the Lord our God, and we hunt you down. What man shall there be among us that shall have one slave, and if it fly into the morass on the Sabbath day, shall he not set hounds upon it and hunt it down? Speed on, dark chattel! The good Christians of St. Landry and Avoyelles are spurring hard upon your trail, and in the land over which the memory of Christ stretches like the sky, well-doing such as theirs is lawful on the Sabbath as on every other day!

Splashing and swashing on over the slushy surface of the quagmire, now sinking no deeper than the soles of his shoes, now plashing up to his shins, now to his knees, now nearly to his thighs, now bounding upon logs and fallen trunks, or rushing over masses of brushwood and briers, which switched and stung his ankles, he could still hear, at brief intervals, the savage yowling of the hounds. As yet there was no safety, for the dogs could still scent his trail, here and there, on the shoals of mire or clumps of bog over which he had passed. His hope was in reaching deeper water, or arriving at some broad bayou which would effectually impede their course.

Goaded by his imminent peril, for he soon heard the long yells much nearer, and knew that the cruel brutes were rapidly gaining on him—he floundered frantically on, his heart leaping in his throat at every howl, and the sweat gathering in cold drops on his face. Soon, to his great joy, the foul lagoons began to deepen, the water reaching more uniformly above his knees, and at length he came upon a space through which he floundered for more than half an hour, sinking to his thighs at every plunge, and knew by the confused and lessening clamor of the dogs, that he was leaving them. He did not slacken his pace, though the depth of the water made it still more difficult to travel, till at last he entered a horrid grove of gloom, where the pyramidal clumps from which shot up the straight, dark pillars of the cypresses, were submerged in the inky flood, and sinking above his hips, he was forced to move more slowly. Fiercely plunging on through the cold black tarn, over a soft bottom of leaves and moss, which sank loathsomely beneath his tread, like a subfluvial field of sponge, he heard again the harsh yells of the dogs, and they now seemed nearer than before. He strove, but vainly, to move on faster, and his fancy ran riot as he thought of the hounds slopping on through the fen, and coming into sight of him. Already, in his delirious fancy, he heard the wild and savage yowls of that moment, and the exulting halloos of his pursuers. The dogs would leap into the shallow ponds—they would swim faster than he could wade—he would hear their savage panting close behind him—he would turn and feel them flop upon him, and their sharp teeth crush into his flesh—he would strike them with his bowie-knife—he would see the black water redden with their blood—they would overbear him and drag him down with yelling, and howling, and frantic splashing and struggling, while the shouting planters would come riding through the swamp and seize him. Lashed into frenzy by the anticipated drama, he brandished the knife, with a hoarse cry, and staggering forward, suddenly sank to his armpits. An instant of alarm, succeeded by wild joy, for the water had deepened, and striking out, he swam. Clogged by his heavy shoes, now filled with mud, and soaked to an added weight with water, it was hard swimming; but his fear and fury gave him superhuman energy, and nerved with unnatural vigor his weakened thews. He swam for a long time, with the solemn night of the dense cypress dusking his form and shadowing the tarn. At length the dreadful twilight of the grove began to lighten, and far beyond he saw the sunlight illuminating the grey and green of the trees, and the many colored parasites and flowers, and shining on the mud and water of the marsh. Presently he struck bottom, and wading again for a long distance, emerged at length into the sunlight, among the shallows and mud-shoals, and rushed on as before, till at last, as the sun was near its setting, he stood on the banks of an unknown river, which, whispering sullenly past its margin of sedge and water-flowers, moved, with an imperceptible motion, through the solemn and horrible wilderness of forest.

He stood gazing across it with a haggard and mournful countenance. The croak of frogs came faintly from its border, and mingled with the distant quacking of crowds of mallard ducks from the opposite shore, the vague hooting of owls in the swamp beyond, and the occasional plunge of an alligator from the adjacent margin. Dreary and ominous sounds, which yet hardly disturbed the stagnant stillness around him. The wind had lulled, and no whisper came from the bearded trees, which stood like boding shapes on every side. Hope was faint in the heart of the fugitive. Relieved from the engrossment of the immediate peril, his spirit began to come under the sole dominion of the brooding horrors around him, and as he vainly pondered on the dark problem of his deliverance, Death seemed ever gathering slowly toward him, and Liberty lessening in ever-growing distance.

Liberty or Death. The historic phrase came to him again like a voice that urged him forward. He paused only a little longer, to tear a strip from his coarse shirt and tie the bowie-knife at the back of his neck to the iron collar. Then tearing another strip, he pulled off his heavy brogans, shook the mud out of them, and passing the strip through the eyelets, he also secured them to the collar, one on each shoulder. So accoutred, he braced himself anew for effort, and taking up a slender sapling from the ground to beat the pools between him and the bayou—for he now feared the moccasins—in a few moments he was in the water, steadily swimming forward, with the sapling held in his teeth.

Gaining the opposite bank, he stopped on a patch of black mire, to put on his shoes, and then went forward, beating the path before him. Dreadful apprehensions of the beasts and reptiles which inhabited the swamp, now crowded on his mind, while to add to his distress, the sunlight in the forest spaces was stealing rapidly upward from the foliage of the loftiest trees. Quickening his pace, he staggered on through the haunted dusk of the tree-trunks, with the hooting of the swamp owls, the quacking of innumerable ducks, the bellowing and plunging of alligators, the screeching and screaming of strange, semi-tropic birds, the howling of distant beasts, and the multitudinous croak of frogs, sounding on every side around him.

He broke into a heavy run, came at length to a thinner part of the forest, and presently emerged upon a vast open space of quagmire, stretching two or three miles away, with scattered trees standing and leaning in all directions in its broad expanse. Here he paused.

The sun had sunk behind the distant forest, tinging the misty sky far up the zenith with lowering red, and suddenly, as by some fell enchantment, the swamp had become a sullen slough of blood. Shadows of inky blackness stretched athwart the red expanse, and the distorted trees that crossed and intercrossed each other here and there, were giant eldritch shapes of unimaginable things. Lank and hairy—all askew and bristling—clothed as with fearful rags—with monstrous heads ahunch in unnatural places, and shaggy jags of drooping beards, and dusky arms grotesquely forked and twisted, and huge lengths of gaunt body that abruptly splayed and sprawled in malformed feet—they loomed from the fen of murky gore against the angry color of the sky, like some black congress of ambiguous mongrel wizards whose spell was on the scene. All around beneath them, protruding from the red lagoons, huge butts of logs, gnarled stumps, and black knees of cypress, squatted and crouched like water-fiends. Through the dusky air, laden with the damp smell of the swamp, frightful brown bats whirled clacking to and fro in the red light like lesser demons on the wing. From every side came hootings and croakings, screechings and wailings, howlings and bellowings and sullen plunges, like the riotous clamor of devils at some tremendous incantation. A sense of supernatural horror pervaded all, and weighed upon the appalled heart of the trembling fugitive.

He hesitated a few moments whether to cross this dreary expanse, or strike off into the denser forest, but decided to go forward. Whipping a pool before him which did not move, he was just setting his foot in it, when the venomous face of a moccasin rose at him with a dark slapping flash. He sprang back simultaneously, and saw the monster vanish, feeling at the same time a sharp pang just above his ankle. He was bitten! All was over!

Stooping slowly, with a wild terror shuddering through his veins, he looked at the wounded limb. But no, there was no bite. The snake had missed him. In his backward leap, he had struck his leg against the upturned spike of a broken branch which lay behind him. The revulsion in his spirit at this discovery was so great that he broke into a quaver of hysterical laughter, which echoed dismally through the swamp, and woke such an answering chorus of demoniacal hooting and screeching in the adjacent boughs, that he was affrighted, and turning away from the open space, he was about to rush into the forest on his flank, when he saw with a leap of heart, two round glistening balls in the dark foliage of a tree a few yards before him, and something long and dark crouching along the bough. It was a panther! He wheeled at once with a bound, and fled headlong into the red morass.

Recovering presently from his shock of alarm, he trudged along through the inky water, quivering at every step lest he should feel the sting of the moccasin, or the crunching gripe of the alligator. It was a long journey across the open fen. The red light had faded from sky and water, and the full moon, which had lain like a pallid shell in the heavens when he left the forest behind him, had deepened into a lustrous orb of silver, and glistened on the gray water, as he approached the solid sable gloom of the thick-wooded wilderness.

An awful fancy had haunted his mind during his journey across the open fen—quiet, but very awful. A strange man, with a single dog, had followed him, at a considerable distance the whole way. A strange man, silent, with a silent dog, and plodding just at that distance, without coming, or trying to come, any nearer him. He knew that this was so, though he did not dare to turn his head to see if it was so. He knew too just how the man looked—a dark figure with a dark slouched hat, and the dog, also dark, by his side, just a little behind him. Oh, God!

The fancy fell from him as he came under the black trees again. Staggering on through thick darkness, broken only here and there by an uncertain glimmer or a pale ray of moonlight, or the blue flicker of a dancing and vanishing fen-light, he found the water still ankle or knee deep, and the walking difficult and dangerous, with logs and fallen trees and stumps and masses of bushes and briers, and with the deadly tenants of the pools. The fen seemed alive with the latter, and all about him, and in the branches overhead, there were such plungings and crashings, and such a clamor of flutterings and hootings and screechings, that his blood ran cold. He held his course, however, hoping to come upon some dry spot in the great swamp where he could stop and consider what to do to escape from this dreadful region. Rest he must have soon, for his body was giving way with hunger and fatigue. He was drenched from head to foot, and spite of the exertion of walking, he shivered with cold. His vitals were weak and aching for want of food; his head was light with sleeplessness; and insane fancies ran riot in his terror-goaded and horror-laden mind. One was that his legs, which felt numb and seemed heavier every time he lifted them, were slowly changing to iron, and that he would soon be unable to raise them for their weight, and would be obliged to stand there in the quagmire. Then in the glimmering darkness the moccasins would rise from the pools and surround him in a circle. They would gather in from all the swamp around, and pile on top of each other, till they made a high, high writhing wall about him of devilish serpent faces, swaying and bristling, and above them in the branches all the panthers would gather, savagely grinning at him, and every one would have the visage of Lafitte. Then all at once the writhing wall of snakes would sway forward, and strike him with a million fangs, and rebound and strike again with a regular and even motion, while his body would slowly swell, and his shrieks would ring in the darkness, and the panthers would look on with the face of his master, and laugh softly with the smooth voice of his master. And the writhing wall would dilate and expand till every snake was vaster than an anaconda, and the mass together would fall away at every rebound to a horrible distance, and reach up to the sky, and his body would swell at every million-fanged stroke till its monstrous bloat filled the dark world, and his shrieks would rise and resound through space, and the panthers and the tigers would dilate with the rest, and look on with enormous faces like his master's, and their smooth laughter would grow louder and louder into smooth thunders of laughter, and the bristling and the striking and the swelling and the shrieking and the roaring mirth, would go on increasing forever and forever.

"Lord God Almighty help me! I'm going crazy!"

The words burst from him suddenly, as he felt the horrible fancy rush upon him with dreadful reality, and almost master him. All aghast with a new terror at the foreign and incongruous effect of his own tones in that haunted darkness, and amidst the unhuman voices around him, he was utterly appalled and confounded the next instant at the frightful clamor which rose with a simultaneous outburst, volleying tumultuously around him on every side like the multitudinous rush and uproar of devils when the silence of the magic circle has been broken and the enchanter is to be torn to pieces. Whooping, hooting, screaming, wailing, yelling, whirring, flapping, cackling, howling, bellowing and roaring—all rose together in a long continued and reverberating whirl and brawl, filling the darkness with a deafening din. Staggering madly forward, the terrified fugitive broke into a blind and frantic run, feeling as in a horrible dream, that the pools had changed to ground which was sloping rapidly up to strike him in the face and stop him; till at last with a sudden lightening of the darkness, something caught his feet and threw him headlong, and with an awful sense that he was seized, and with the hideous tintamar swirling downward like the gurgling roar of water in the ears of a drowning man, he swooned away

IV.

Slowly that sluggish sea of swoon gave up its dead, and life revived. How long he had lain in that blank trance, he knew not. He felt that he was lying on bare, damp ground, and that the moonlight was around him. The din had sunk into confused and broken noises, sounding and echoing distantly through the darker depths of the moonlit forest, and the air around him was desolate and still. A clear, cold, remote stillness filled his mind. Gradually a dim sense of the former terror, mixed with consciousness of all he had passed through, and of the place he was in, began to invade the silent vacancy, and crept upon him as from afar. Shuddering slightly, with icy thrills crawling through his torpid blood, he slowly raised himself to his knees, and looked around him. With a vague relief, which was almost pleasure, he saw that he was kneeling on dry ground—a low acclivity sloping from the morass, clothed with giant trees, and barred with large spaces of grey moonlight and sable shadow. Behind him was the tough cordage of a ground-vine, in which his foot was still entangled. Disengaging the limb without rising from his knees, he continued to gaze, gradually yielding to an overwhelming sense of awe, as he took in more fully the dark and dreadful magnificence of the forest which loomed before him, like the interior of some infernal cathedral. Far away, through immense irregular vistas, diminishing in interminable perspective, the ground stretched in vast mosaics of sable and silver, bunched and ridged with low flowers and herbage and running vines, all moveless and colorless in the rich pallor of the moonlight, and in the solemn shadow, as though wrought in stone. Upborne on the enormous clustered columns of the trees, every trunk rising sheer like a massive shaft of rough ebony, darkly shining, and fretted and starred with the gleaming leaves and flowers of parasitical vines—masses of gloomy frondage, touched here and there with sullen glory, spread aloft and interwove like the groined concave of some tremendous gothic roof, while from the leaf-embossed and splendor-dappled arches, the long mosses drooped heavily, like black innumerable banners, above the giant aisles. The air was dank and chill, and laden with thick and stagnant odors from the night-blowing flowers. Fire-flies flitted and glimmered with crimson and emerald flames ; fen-lights flickered and quivered bluely down the arcades in the morass ; and all around from the bordering quagmire, and from the crypts and vaults of the shadows, the demon-voices of the region, sounding from above and below, and rapidly swelling into full choir, chanted in discordant chorus. Listening to their subterranean and aërial stridor, which rose in wild accordance with the ghastly pomp, the horrible and sombre grandeur of the scene, a dark imagination might have dreamed that some hellish mass in celebration of the monstrous crime against mankind which centered in this region, was pealing through the vaulted aisles and arches of a church whose bishop was the enemy of human souls. Here, to this dread cathedral, might gather in his wide and wicked diocese—the millions callous to the woes and wrongs of slaves—the myriads careless of all ills their fellows suffer, while their own selfish strivings prosper, and wealth and sensual comforts thrive around them. Peopling the vast and drear nocturnal solitudes, under the moonlit arches, here they might come, while the screaming, hooting, bellowing chant resounded, and kneel, a motley and innumerable concourse of base powers, in fell communion. Statesmen who hold the great object of government to be the protection of property in man, and wield the mighty engine of the state for the oppression of the weak ; placemen who suck on office, deaf and blind to the interests of the poor ; scurvy politicians, intent on pelf and power, who plot and scheme for tyranny, and legislate away the inalienable rights of men ; Jesuit jurists, mocking at natural law, who decree that black men have no rights that white men are bound to respect ; scholars, bastard to the blood of the learned and the brave, who prate with learned ignorance of manifest destiny and inferior races, to justify against all human instincts the cruel practice of the oppressor; hide-bound priests, who would turn the hunted fugitive from their doors, or consent that their brothers should go into slavery to save the Union ; traders and slavers, an innumerable throng, mad-ravening with never-sated avarice, and furious against liberty and justice as lesseners of their gains ; these, and their rabblement of catch-poles, and jail-birds, and kidnappers, and men-hunters, and slave-law commissioners—here they might assemble to pray that their conspiracy against mankind might prosper, and love and reverence for the soul die down in darkness, and man degrade into the brute and fiend. Fit place and time, and fit surroundings for such rites as these ; fitter far than for the trembling murmurs of a solitary slave, kneeling in the dreary moonlight, and pouring out the forlorn agony of his spirit in prayer to the God of the poor.

Some dim association of the aspect of the forest with the cathedrals he had seen many years before when he was a slave in New Orleans ; some dim sense that he was on his knees in the attitude of supplication, had mixed with the overwhelming consciousness of his helplessness, his wretchedness, and his danger, and impelled him to pray. Fervently, in uncouth words and broken tones, he poured forth the mournful and despairing litany of a soul haunted with horror, encompassed with perils, and yearning for deliverance. The demoniac clamor of the forest rose louder and louder as he went on, breaking his communion with God, till at length, appalled by the unhallowed din, he ceased, and rising to his feet, uncomforted and terrified, staggered weakly on his way.

He was very feeble now, and his strength was so nearly gone that he tottered. His setting forward again was a mere mechanical action, but it continued for some minutes before the dull thought came to him that his movement was useless. In his agonizing desire for sleep, he tried to climb a tree, where, lodged in a fork of the branches, he thought he would be safer and more comfortable than on the ground ; but even with the advantage of the parasitical vine which covered its trunk, his strength was not equal to the effort. He was in the last stages of exhaustion.

Sitting upon the ground, he resolved to keep awake till morning, when there would be less danger of wild beasts, and he might dare to repose. He sat for a long time shuddering with cold, and watching intently all about him, lest some panther should spring upon him unawares. Once or twice, with a start of terror, he caught himself nodding ; and at length, affrighted at the possible consequences of his dropping off into slumber, he strove to occupy his mind by observing minutely the various details of the scene before him. He had been busy at this for some time, when he became suddenly and quietly perplexed with the feeling that there was something he ought to take notice of, but was unable to remember or define what it was. All the while he was vacantly gazing at the bole of a gigantic cypress rising from a dense clump of dwarf palmettoes, slightly silvered by a faint ray of moonlight, and from time to time he saw, without receiving any impression therefrom, a dim vapor glide athwart the palmetto leaves. Suddenly but quietly it came to him that what he ought to have noticed was a peculiar odor, and startled a little, he strove to shake the torpor from his mind, and think. What could it be ? As suddenly and quietly as before it came to him, and at the same moment his eye took in the meaning of that curious mist gliding over the palmettoes. It was the smell of smoke, and yonder was its source. Thoroughly roused now, and vaguely alarmed, he scrambled up on his feet, with a little strength returning to his body, and gazed in stupefaction at the misty ringlets lazily stealing across the leaves. It certainly was smoke ; he smelled now very distinctly the dry scent of burning wood. Who could have a fire in the heart of the swamp at this time of night ? At first, superstitious fancies rose in his mind, for the thought that any person could be here with him was inconceivable. But gradually recovering self-possession, he resolved, for he was naturally courageous, to go forward and solve the mystery ; and taking the knife from the back of his neck, he cautiously approached the palmettoes, his blood thrilling, and his heart beating, and all the forest resonant around him. Peering through the leaves, he saw with amazement a pile of smouldering embers duskily glimmering in front of a large hole in the trunk. The tree was hollow. A sort of fright fell upon him, and he retreated ; but recovering instantly, he again advanced, and nerved to desperation, spoke in a voice faint both from weakness and trepidation :

"Ho, there ! Ho, you in there ! You there, whoever you are !"

There was no answer, nor movement, but at the sound of his voice, a tremendous uproar burst forth again in the forest. Desperate at this, he again spoke in a louder tone :

"Ho, now, you in there ! You just say who you are. I'm coming in now !"

No answer, but the uproar in the branches and from the swamp increased like a tempest. Strung up now to his highest pitch, Antony clutched his knife, and setting his teeth hard, plunged in through the hole.

It was densely dark within. The immense cypress was completely hollow, as he could feel, for stretching out his arms he encountered nothing. He began to grope about, but stopped suddenly, thinking it better to get a light. Quite overcome by the strangeness of his discovery, and by the novel circumstance of a fire being found smouldering before an empty tree, he stooped down through the low entrance to the brands, and blowing upon one till it flamed, withdrew himself again into the tree, and looked around. Suddenly, with a hoarse gasp of horror, he tottered back, falling from his squatting posture over upon the ground, and dropping the brand, which at once went out, leaving him in utter darkness. In that instant he had caught a glimpse, by the fitful flame, of a lank figure, duskily clothed, lying on its back, with a mop of thick white hair, a leathern face hideously grinning, and glassy eyes which had met his; and he felt like one who had entered the lair of a fiend.

So paralyzed was he with affright, that instead of scrambling out of the tree, he sat motionless, leaning back on his hands, with his blood curdling, and cold thrills crawling under his hair. A wild fancy that he would be instantly sprung upon by this thing, held him still and breathless. But all remained silent and moveless, and at last, venturing to stir, he got up on one knee, and pressed his hands on his heart to stop its mad beating. By degrees his courage came back to him, or, at least, his dreadful fear became blended with desperation. Then came wild wonder at the horrible strangeness of that figure, and slowly this melted into a savage and frenzied curiosity. Seizing the smoking brand from the earth, he backed out through the hole (for he absolutely did not dare to turn his back to the dread tenant of the cavern), and, once outside, blew upon the stick till it reflamed. Waiting a moment till the light burned strongly, he thrust it through the hole, and holding it above his head, glared with starting eyes upon the face of the figure.

He saw in a moment that it was nothing unearthly—only the form of an aged woman, and of his own race. Instantly it struck him that she was a fugitive, probably a dweller in the swamp. Reëntering the tree, he approached and held the blazing brand over her countenance. With a terrible sensation of awe he saw that it was the countenance of the dead. She lay on a couch of the forest moss, her gaunt figure decently composed, with the hands crossed, as if she had known that she was dying. She was apparently very old; the woolly hair was white ; the black face was deeply wrinkled, and much emaciated ; the mouth was open, and had fallen back, showing the white teeth, which were perfectly sound as in her youth ; and the glassy eyes were unclosed and fixed aslant with that look which had so terrified the fugitive. He felt no terror now, however, only awe ; for with the discovery of the truth, the hideousness of the face was gone. Bending down, he touched the cheek. It was still tepid—almost warm ; the life had not been long extinct, a fact of which the smouldering brands of the fire she had kindled was another evidence. Poring upon the features, a confused feeling gathered in his mind that he had seen them before, and he strove to resolve it into certainty. Suddenly, as the flickering of the burning brand he held brought out a new expression on the dark, withered lineaments, it flashed upon him that this was old Nancy. She had been a slave on Mellott's plantation, near Lafitte's, and had disappeared five or six years before, after a terrible whipping. They had hunted the swamp for her without avail, and it was supposed that she had perished. Here she had lived, however, and here she was now, all her earthly troubles over.

Turning away from the body in wild wonderment, the fugitive looked around him. The space within the tree must have been at least six feet in diameter. It had been hollowed out by time in the form of an upright cone, the apex of which was at least a dozen feet above the ground. The bole had probably been eaten out by a sort of dry rot, or perhaps by insects, for the wooden walls were not damp, nor was the corrugated floor. The only furniture was the couch of Spanish moss on which the body lay, a block of wood fashioned for a seat out of the butt end of a log, and a long paddle, bladed at both ends, which leaned upright against the wall. Looking around further, Antony noticed some little niches cut in the walls, with the handle of a hatchet sticking out of one of them. On the blade was a parcel wrapped in cotton cloth, in which he found three or four corn-cob pipes, a bundle of dried tobacco-leaf, bunches of matches, and two or three knick-knacks of no great use. Evidently Nancy had made occasional excursions from her hiding-place, for these things must all have been borrowed from the race of the taskmasters. This was still more evident as Antony pursued his observations. In another niche, he found at least half a peck of corn done up in a cloth, and in a wooden quart measure there was some more, parched. His hunger rose so suddenly and fiercely at sight of the food that he at once crammed a handful of the parched corn into his mouth, and with the measure in his hand, continued to crunch, although his throat was so swollen with his long fast that he could scarcely swallow. Continuing his search while he ate, he found in a third niche an oblong tin pan and a gourd, but in the pan, to his astonishment and delight, there was a dead opossum and a small fish. They were both fresh—Nancy must have captured them that very day. She had lived a woodman's life in the heart of the morass, setting her fishtraps on the bayou, and catching the smaller animals in the forest. Forgetting to pursue his search further in the desire to appease his ravening hunger, Antony only paused to lay one of the pieces of cotton cloth over the face of the dead, and then set to work to rake the fire into a bed of coals, and hastily dressing the meat with his bowie-knife, broiled it, and ate with the eager voracity of a man half starved.

A mad repast, not given to appetite, but famine, and void of all enjoyment. Not himself, but his hunger as a thing apart from himself, was fed by those gross gobbets. Kneeling before the embers, in the dusky glimmer, he hurried down the half-cooked food, tasting of smoke and cinders, as to some wild wolf that gnawed his vitals. In the darkness behind him lay the swart corpse, and the thought of it was a quiet horror in his mind. Blent with that horror, and with his raging famine, was a dull, stupefied sense of the chafe of the collar on his neck, the swollen pains and weakness of his limbs, the steady suck of the sleeplessness in his jaded brain, the tepid clinging of his wet clothes, the filthy smell of the muck and slime that covered him, and all was mixed confusedly with a dimmer apprehension of the smoky warmth of the cavern, the sullen smoulder of the embers, and the resonance of the vast drear forest.

His meal ended, he still knelt in the murk contraction of all his sensations and apprehensions, before the dull fire. The fierce gnawing at his stomach had changed to an uneasy distention, as if something huge and bloated lay dead within him. His horror of the corpse had grown stronger even than the heavy weariness and frowsy misery of body and spirit, and he now begun to consider what he should do with it. It ought to be buried, he felt, but in his utter torpor of fatigue, he shrunk from the labor of making it a grave.

Slowly his inertia yielded, and he set to work with the hatchet, chopping out a burial-place in an oblong space near the tree between the palmettoes, and scooping up the soft soil with his hands. It was a long and painful task for his weak and sore body ; but at length it was ended, and bringing out the corpse, he laid it in the cavity, heaped the earth over it, and left it to its rest.

The forest was still resounding with the unhuman noises when he entered the cypress hollow again. He heard them dully, with torpid indifference. The tree seemed strangely empty to him now. He sat for a moment on the block, watching, with an utter prostration of heart, the dusky glimmer faintly lighting the smoky gloom. Rising presently, he arranged the embers so that they would outlast the night to keep away the wild beasts ; and then throwing himself upon the heap of moss where the corpse had lain, he sank away in a dead slumber. Soon the hooting and flapping, the screaming and the howling sunk away also, and the vast forest lay still and weird and desolate in the pallor of the moon.

V

He woke with the feeling that he had dropped off and slept a minute, but at the same instant gazing with stiff and smarting eyes through the brown dusk of the hollow, he was confused at seeing the palmetto leaves at the entrance plainly visible, and of a deep, cool green. He knew now that it was broad day, and that he had slept long. Raising himself suddenly, a mass of cramping stitches wrenched his frame, and made him gasp with pain. He remained for a minute supporting himself on his hands, and then slowly and painfully arose. Refreshed in mind by his slumber, he was even worse off in body than when he had lain down. His limbs were stiff, and every joint and muscle ached. His wrists and ankles were much swollen where the ropes of the bucking had cut them. He felt as if he had been switched all over with nettles, from the stings and scratches of the thorns and briers through which he had travelled. His face pained him especially, the atoms of glass still smarting in the cuts, and all its wounds and bruises sore and burning. Worse than all to his sense at that moment were the weight and chafe of the accursed collar. His flesh was raw with it. It hurt him so much that almost the first thing he did was to tie one of the pieces of cotton cloth around his neck for the edge of the iron to rest on. Relieved somewhat by this, he began to limp to and fro, gasping and panting at every step with pain.

After a few minutes of this exercise, he felt a little easier, and stopped walking to examine the paddle. It convinced him that Nancy must have a boat somewhere, and the pilfered articles he had found in the hollow confirmed his belief. To get away from the swamp was his fixed purpose, and in that land of streams, if he could only find Nancy's boat, he might avoid the loathsome and dangerous journey across the morass.

Nancy's boat, he thought, must be a periagua, and the question was, where did she keep it. Crawling out of the tree to commence a search for it, he saw it right at the base of the trunk under the palmettoes. But Nancy's periagua was a canoe! A canoe of buffalo hide on a frame of slender wattles. Had she purloined it from the Indians in the Pine Woods of Avoyelles, and had it been a present to them from some visiting tribe from Texas or the Indian Territory? For all the boats Antony had ever seen among them were periaguas. At all events here it was, and elated with its discovery, the fugitive instantly brought forth the paddle, the hatchet, the bowie-knife, the corn, the tin pan, and the matches, and placed them in it. Going in again to see if there was anything else that might serve him in his flight, he saw an end of dyed cotton cloth hanging out from the couch of moss. With a pull out it came—an old blue cotton gown. Turning over the moss, he uncovered an old blue flannel shirt, an old pair of grey trowsers, a jean jacket torn up the back, a slipper and one stocking. Rejoiced that Nancy's purloinings had furnished him with a change of clothes, he put the gown, shirt and trowsers into the canoe, and lifting the latter, plunged out through the palmettoes into the forest.

A thrill of alarm shot through him as he saw by the sunlight that it was late in the afternoon. So accustomed had he been in the enforced habits of plantation life to rise at daybreak, that on waking in the hollow he naturally thought he had awakened at the usual morning hour. He shuddered now with the consciousness that so much time had been lost, when the dogs, guided by some professional expert at man-hunting, might be coming straight toward him. That Lafitte would, in his burning lust for vengeance, hunt the swamp for weeks to find him, he had no doubt, and he must at once speed away.

He stood for a moment debating which direction to take, when looking down he happened to see a spot where the earth had been harrowed by the claws of some wild beast, and upon the scratches was the distinct imprint of a naked foot. It came to him at once that this was a footmark Nancy had made going up from the water, and he at once resolved to pursue a track, in a bee-line from the heel of the print. Limping along painfully with the canoe on his shoulders and cautiously, for by the sudden slipping and rustling in the grass and herbage he knew that snakes were around him, suddenly his heart and blood jumped, and he sprang backward with a leap that shot a flood of wrenching pangs through his whole frame. He had nearly stepped upon a rattlesnake which lay in a faint glimmer of sunshine on a strip of thinly tufted earth. The sluggish reptile quivered slightly throughout its mottled length, and lifting its head with venom in its sparkling eyes and devilish yawning jaws, sounded its rattle and swiftly slid from view. Antony shuddered, and the old dark fancy that he was in Hell flickered through his mind. Trembling in spite of himself at every buzzard that flew from his path, or small animal that crossed it, and feeling that everything was watching him, and that the multitudinous chatter of the birds that filled the forest was concerning him, he went on his way. Soon he came to the pools, and beating the moccasins from his path, arrived at a shoal of black mire, and a narrow bayou. A fallen tree lay with its branches dipped in the stream, half way across; a rotten log floated in the water; stumps and snags projected here and there ; waifs of moss, slivers of branches, broken boughs, leaves, flowers, and bits of forest debris floated idly on the shining surface or among the shadows.

Hurriedly casting off his foul rags, the fugitive washed himself with the old gown, and put on the shirt and trowsers. Then laying the canoe on the water, where it lightly danced, he cautiously got in, grasped the paddle in the middle, and plying the blades first on one side and then on the other, shot slowly off with a beating heart up the dull stream.

Heading northward, the brown skiff yawed from right to left, and darted with an uncertain forward motion, trembling beneath him like a living thing that shared his agitation. Black banks of mud, pierced here and there with alligator holes, swamp grass, and pools, and luxuriant clumps and masses of strange many-colored flowering verdure, fallen trees and trees leaning to their fall, and trees uptowering in leafy pride, and the vine-enwreathed and flower-gemmed wilderness of massive trunks uplifting their vast moss-bearded and leaf-laden branches, spread and loomed in solemn and splendid confusion on either side as the boat lightly darted on its sinuous course. Alligators swam through the bayou, or plunged from floodwood, or raised themselves with brutal bellowings on the margin as it glided on. Cranes and bitterns fled away from the banks squawking and screaming ; strange birds of gorgeous plumage flew rustling through the branches ; scarlet-gilled black buzzards rose and soared with broad and steady wing ; myriads of ducks and water-fowl of many kinds flapped and swam away continually before it. Paddled steadily forward, now on one side, now on the other, on sped the brown canoe, while the shadows grew inkier on the sombre water, and again under the red reflection of the sky, the dull bayou became a stream of blood.

Awed by the solemn desolation of the scene, the gloomy color of the water, the gathering darkness of the wooded fen, the motions and the voices all around; troubled at the thought of the long and perilous distance that stretched between him and his far bourn of safety; yet with a fearful joy and a sustaining hope within, the fugitive oared his swift darting skiff at length into the river he had swam last the day before. The red glow had died from sky and water, and the moon silvered greyly the stream as he paddled on between the black forest on either side. Heading his prow to the east, and plying his paddle vigorously, he flew lightly up the stream. Voices of bird and beast called and answered weirdly in the darkness of the black shores; trees towered and leaned in ambiguous sable shapes over the dusky stream, and watched him as he shot swiftly by; the solemn sky spread far above him like a doubtful thought, half-boding, yet clearing slowly into deep-withdrawn tranquillity, in the increasing lustre of the tawny moon. Overarched and palisaded by the phantom sentience of the hour, his dark skiff, gliding and darting with light tremors and waverings still held its way like a dumb intelligence over the mysterious water.

Hours went on, and save the scattered hooting and screeching of owls in the forest, and the occasional clacking of some vagrant bat whirling by, the moonlit night was still. Only once the fugitive oared his canoe in to the shore, where on a low projecting bluff under a great tree, he lit a small fire, and hastily parching some corn in the pan, ate a hurried meal. Then slaking the fire, he entered the canoe again, and paddled on.

An hour or two later he turned the skiff into a narrow bayou which debouched into the stream, thus changing his course to the north. His object was to gain the Red River, where he hoped to smuggle himself on board some steamboat, and getting to New Orleans, escape from the steamboat, and hide himself in the hold of some northern vessel. It was his former plan, and he still clung to it with tenacity, bitterly aware of its hazards and dangers, yet unable to think of a better. The bayou he was now in was very narrow, hemmed in on either side by the forest and the fen, and much obstructed by stumps, snags, fallen trees and lodgments of logs. To steer his course through these in the uncertain darkness, for the branches almost shut out the moonlight, was difficult, and several times he was obliged to clamber on the fallen timber, and pull the canoe over, or shove aside the huddled floodwood to clear a passage. But his efforts brought him at length to a sluggish stream, which he judged to be the Pacoudrie—the stream he had swam first in his escape the day before, but at a point several miles below the Lafitte plantation. He was now approaching dangerous ground, and his heart began to beat faster. Turning his prow eastward again, he paddled down the stream, looking for another debouching bayou. He soon came upon one, into which he turned, heading north, and through which his passage was as dark and impeded as before. He exerted himself to the utmost, and at last, heated and panting, he saw that he was leaving the morass, and that the moonlit ground, thinly scattered over with trees, and thickly covered with verdurous underwood, was gradually rising on either side of him. The bayou, too, grew deeper and less impeded, and presently he saw on his left, beyond a cluster of huge trees, the grain of a plantation, and further up, a mansion with outbuildings. Who lived there he did not know—he only knew that he was again in the region of his enemies. Light thrills shot through his heated blood, and the canoe yawed and trembled beneath him, as if conscious of danger. Paddling forward, he saw before him in the clear moonlight, for the trees on either side were thinly scattered now, a huge trunk fallen sheer across the stream, sloping down obliquely, with its crown of branches dipping in the water, and barring half the passage. From the other side, crossing the first trunk, a leafless tree, withered or blasted, had also fallen, and lay, dipped in the water, half way across, with its broken boughs sticking upward like jagged spikes or horns. Steering to the left of these, with the intention of shooting through the space under the large trunk, he gave three or four vigorous strokes of the paddle on either side of the skiff. The canoe darted forward, quivering with the impetus of the strokes—stopped suddenly with a tearing and griding shock, and yawed around, with the water welling up swiftly through its bottom. Antony, who was kneeling on one knee, had just time to spring up, catch at the trunk before him, and lift himself up on it. When he turned, the rim of the canoe was settling in the water. It had struck one of the jagged spikes just below the surface, which had ripped its bottom, and it had gone down forever.

Sitting on the tree, stupefied at this unexpected accident, Antony watched the circling ripples on the moonlit water where his boat had sunk, and thought with bitter regret that he was now without a single weapon to fight his way against any opposing white man, or to end his own existence, should the odds be against him. His hatchet had sunk with the boat, and his knife also. With a fierce imprecation, he rose, ran up the trunk, sprang ashore, and pausing only to wrench off a branch, and strip it of its leaves for a club to defend himself, rushed on through the underwood.

Heading to the northeast, he gained the plantation, and running over rows of corn and springing cotton-plant, pale in the paling moon, he struck upon a fenced road lying between the plantation, with another road diverging from it in the course he was travelling. Into the latter he turned, but afraid to take the open path, he kept within the fences and hedges skirting its side, ready if he saw anybody in the distance to hide in the rows, or if anybody came upon him, to fight till he was killed.

Rushing on, haggard with apprehension and desperate resolution, with his teeth set, his large nostrils dilated, and his glaring eyes roving warily about him, he came to a plantation divided from the one he was on by a hedge of the osage-orange, and with a similar hedge skirting the road. To break through this would be difficult, so he took the road and ran on, with the fresh wind of the coming morning blowing upon him, and increasing his fear with the thought of the new dangers the daybreak would bring. It was a large plantation, and it took him some time to arrive at its terminus, at which a road diverged from the one on which he was journeying. He reached this road, and there, clad in shabby light clothes, and coming down the path, not three yards distant from him, was a man!

Antony swung up his club, and stood with opened nostrils and glaring eyes, his black face alive with fierce courage. The man halted, and looked at him with a sullen scowl. In the blank pause all life seemed to have died from the air, and the moon lay faded in a vacant sky, ghast and grey in the pale light of the morning. The man was a large, gaunt fellow, with a harsh and sallow taciturn face, but to the dark, half demented fancy of the fugitive, he dimly seemed a devil, and the place was still vaguely Hell.

"See here, nigger," he said, in a stern, strident voice, "yer a runaway. There's their name as owns yer on yer collar, and I know Lafitte Brothers, New Orleans, want yer. I'm goin' down in the first boat, and yer comin' with me, right away, and no fuss. What yo' say, nigger?"

He drew a revolver from his breast, and held it idly, watching the fugitive with a scowl. Sense flickered through the mind of Antony. Here was a chance to get safely down the river—beyond, a chance to give his captor the slip when he reached the city. He flung his club away.

"I'll go with ye, Marster," he said, sullenly.

The man put up his pistol.

"What's yer name, boy?" he asked.

"Bill, Marster."

"Bill, eh? You're the Fugitive Slave Bill, I suppose," said the man, with a dull grin.

"Yes, Marster."

"Well, Bill, I collect bills for a livin', and I reckon I've collected you, Bill. Hope I'll collect something on yer, too. Come along."

Antony followed him. Not a word further was said on either side. Meanwhile, around them the pallor of the sky lightened into daybreak; horns sounded over the plantations; the black gangs were coming forth into the fields on every side; the birds darted and sang; the fragrant wind blew freshly from the east, and the life of day began anew.

Weary, and sore, and aching, with insane fancies flitting through the horrible lethargy which was creeping on his mind, Antony followed his taciturn captor, and just as the rising sun shot a low, broad splendor over the landscape, they came

3*

to a solitary landing-place, with a shanty and a wood-pile, on the border of the wide, gleaming river.

It was all a dim, dread dream. In it came a huge monster, puffing, and snorting, and clanking, vomiting clouds of black smoke, and lifting and washing back the drifting trees and logs and refuse on the shining surge. Then a dream of hurry and tumult, a great heaving mass, a swarm of people, an air blind with light and heavy with smoke, a roar of voices laughing, and talking, and hallooing, the clanging of a bell, piles of cotton and goods of all sorts, the clank of engines, the wallowing of water, ponderous snorting, and heaving, and surging, all mixed together in inextricable confusion, and he who dreamed it vaguely knew that he was sitting, like one drugged, on a heaving deck, with heaps of merchandise around him. Gradually he sank away into a still heavier lethargy, in which everything became even more dim and distant, and from thence he slid into a blank and stupid sleep.

Once again the dream seemed to swim heavily into that death-like slumber—a vague, spectral dream, in which some one gave him a hunch of corn bread, which he ate slowly in a glimmering light, remotely conscious of a dark figure standing near, of distant voices, a far-off snorting and clanking, a shuddering motion beneath him, and formless bulks around him. Presently it drowsily dissolved into darkness and silence.

Like one who dreams of awaking, he awoke again, and stupidly strove to remember where he was and what had befallen him. In the dull gleam of a hanging lantern, he saw masses of bales and boxes, casks and furniture, and miscellaneous merchandise, lying in murky gloom. A few dark, uncouth forms of sleeping men, heavily breathing, were strown about in various grotesque attitudes on the piles of cotton. In the stillness, he heard the regular snort and clank of the engine, the rushing of the water, and felt with a dull giddiness the floor rocking and swaying in long, regular undulations.

Somehow, a minute afterward, he found himself out on the edge of the deck, sick and dizzy, steadying himself against a heap of bales, and looking out on a broad, dim river, rolling in mighty, languid surges under a large, low, yellow moon. Logs and trees and masses of chaff and refuse lifted blackly in the tawny light on the long swells. All around the water fled by, churned into a mill-race of seething froth and foam. Beyond was a huge steamboat; black smoke trailing from its double funnels; fire flaring from them and from its escape-pipes; balls of light gleaming from hanging lanterns here and there; light streaming out from the rows of oblong windows, and from every hole and cranny; the strong current beaten up into a flood of foam beneath its wheel; and the darks and lights of an inverted phantom steamboat hung below it in the water. Far away were low, black shores, with here and there a gaunt spectral tree, and dull lights glimmering. He was on the mighty tide of a river which ran through Hell.

Sick and dizzy, and with a horror on his mind, he staggered back with the heavy drowse on all his faculties, through the tortuous lane of cotton-bales, and sinking down on one of them, fell into his former lethargy.

He did not sleep through the night, but lay in utter torpor, thinking of nothing, fearing and hoping nothing, only vaguely conscious of where he was, and of the forms around him. Overstrung for many years with the unnatural toils of a slave, and still more tensely overstrung with the terrible labors of his journey through the morass—overstrung both in body and spirit, as few but slaves ever are—he had sunk back, now that a season of relaxation had come, into lassitude as excessive as were the fatigues and agitations of which it was the reaction. Safe for the present, with no immediate stimulus to urge him into activity, he lay, body and spirit, as in the sentient sleep of the tomb.

Toward morning he sank away again into a heavy, dreamless slumber. Once during the day he dreamed that he was aroused by some one whom he did not recognize, and bidden to come along and get something to eat. In his dream he tried to shake the stupor from his bleared eyes, which even the dim light among the bales pained, and to obey. But the drowse was heavy upon him, and he could only mumble out that he didn't want to eat, and the dream instantly dissolved in oblivion. He was left undisturbed, for his captor was not without pity for him, and saw that he was terribly fatigued.

But late that night, when midnight was two hours gone, and the moon was westering palely from the sky, the trump of Liberty or Death sounded again in the ear of the fugitive, and his spirit arose from its tomb. A hand shook him, a voice shouted in his ear that they were near the city, and instantly springing to his feet, with fresh blood leaping through his veins, with new pulses throbbing in his heart, and all his faculties awake and alive, and armed with their utmost cunning, their fullest courage, and their most desperate resolution, he followed his captor out on deck. The boat was within a mile of the city, which lay beyond a forest of masts and hulls, and scattered lights hung in the rigging, or glimmering on the levee, dark and silent, with its roofs and spires massed against the purple sky, and glittering in the moon. The night was hot and still, and a heavy languor hung over the great breadth of regular rolling swells. Ships lay at anchor all about the stream, lifting with the lifting of the surge, and here and there a flat-boat with lights on board, and the men plying their long sweeps, lazily steered its way on the drift between the hulls. Antony watched the scene, with his heart fiercely beating at the thought of the coming trial.

Meanwhile the boat, with her bell ringing, was slowly clanking and snorting on through the foaming and brattling flood around her bows and wheels, and the passengers were pouring forth, men, women and children, on her decks. The fugitive stood silently by his captor, on the lower forward deck, amidst the tumult and crowding of the risen multitude, biding his time. The moment the boat touched the levee he was determined to quietly slip aside from his companion and lose himself in the crowd. To this end he stood a little to one side of him, watching his every movement.

Suddenly the clatter of conversation and the trampling of feet were stricken still by a wild yell, above which was heard the slow, impassive snort and clank of the engine, and the brattling wash of the water. Then burst forth a shrill clamor of cries and screams from the after deck, followed by a trampling rush which threw all forward, as by a galvanic shock, into mad confusion ; then behind the pouring crowd, suddenly lightened a red flare, followed by a tremendous volume of black smoke, and at once, amidst terrific disorder, uprose a dreadful storm of yells and screams from the horror-stricken multitude. The next instant the uproar of voices was stifled in a multitudinous choking and gasping, as the thick, poisonous smoke swept over the decks, and presently up shot a sheeting burst of clear flame, with shrivelling ringlets of black vapor writhing and vanishing away in it, lighting the ghastly pallor of the hundreds of terrified faces, all turned one way, and throwing its lurid glare on the churning froth and the lifting swells, and on the myriad masts and spars and rigging of the surrounding vessels, which started out suddenly in lines and bars of tawny splendor against a background of gloom.

Even in that awful moment Antony did not lose sight of his captor. With his whole soul fiercely bent on getting away from him, he saw him start back and shout with terror. With his eye fixed upon him, he heard the rapid jabber of a terrified man behind him shrieking out that a lantern had fallen and broken, setting fire to a pool of turpentine which had leaked from a barrel on the after deck, and the fire spreading at once to the barrel, it had burst and flooded the boat with flame. Still watching him, he heard the screamed order to reverse the engines, and amidst howls and cries of anguish and despair, and cursing and praying, and the heavy thump of men and women falling in swoon upon the deck, or trampling and fighting over each other in their frantic desperation, while the advancing flame leaped and writhed, crackling and bristling and roaring furiously on—amidst all the horror and Bedlam confusion of that minute—for it was but one—standing still, with his eye riveted on his captor, he heard thepond erous clank, the long wash and wallow, and felt the boat drift backward to gain the middle of the stream. That instant he sprang backward, and rushing through the crowd, kicked off his shoes, and leaped into the river.

He emerged presently from his plunge, amidst a shower of

fiery cinders, with the lifting surges all aglare around him, and struck boldly forward for the levee, seeing at a glance the burning mass drift behind him, and all the illuminated ships at the piers and in the stream suddenly alive with shouting figures. Turning for an instant, and treading water, he saw the boat clanking backward, with her black funnels rising from a leaping and coiling mountain of smoke and flame, her passengers all huddled forward in a dense, shrieking mass, black against the fiery glow, and figures jumping into the water—which was already dotted with dark, swimming forms, and looked like a turbulent sea of flame ignited from the spectre of a burning boat below its surface. Among the swimming figures there was, perhaps, not one but was his enemy—not one who would not hale him back to the bondage from which he was struggling away. Turning again, he swam on, heading against the ponderous current which would bear him down past the city and out to sea. Boats were putting out in all directions from ships in the stream, and from the shore, to pick up the swimmers, many of whom were swimming in front of him, or clinging to pieces of drift-wood or furniture. To avoid being picked up by any of the boats was a necessary part of his task, for they, too, were manned by his enemies. Reaching a large brig anchored in the stream, with a few sailors standing on the bulwarks and in the rigging, watching the burning vessel, he resolved to cling to its rudder a few moments to recover breath, and as he approached it, looking up through the shadow, made luminous by the wan light of the moon, and the reflected glare of the water, he read on the stern, in white letters, the words, "SOLIMAN, BOSTON." His heart throbbed wildly, and clinging to the rudder under an overhanging boat, he listened to the talking on the deck above him, and presently heard a voice say :

"Devilish lucky we weren't set afire, Jones, and we just ready to sail."

Just ready to sail ! He heard those words with his brain aflame. His chance had come. Setting his knees to the slippery rudder, he began to climb. It was hard work, for the helm was coated with sea-slime, but at length he got his toes upon the slight projection of one of the iron clamps that bound the wood together, and scrambling upward, laid hold of the boat swinging astern, and softly clambering in, remained still, and listened. He had not been discovered. The talking above him was still going on, and presently he heard the tramp of the two men as they moved away forward. Raising himself in the boat, he cautiously peered in at the cabin window. A swinging lamp was burning within, and all was quiet. He put in his head, looked around him for a moment, and then stealthily got in. Going to the cabin door, he peered out on the deck. Everybody was at the bows, standing on the bulwarks and in the rigging in the wild glare, watching the steamboat, which was now one mass of leaping flame, half a mile away up the river. Cries and screams and shouts were resounding from the water in all directions. Looking at the deck, he saw that the hatch nearest him was open, and nerved to desperation, and almost choking with excitement, he went lightly forward, his bare feet making no sound, and, unseen by any one, so intent was the general gaze on the conflagration, stooped and dropped into the hold.

He fell on a cotton-bale, three or four feet from the top, and lay in the thick darkness, reeking with sweat, and listening, with a wild jumping in his throat, for any sound that might tell him his entrance had been observed. He heard none. The talking went on above him, and it was all about the burning steamboat. He knew that he must not remain where he was, for there he could be seen, and in a moment he began to grope for a hiding-place. He was in a sort of square well, formed by the cotton-bales around him. Above them was a horizontal space under the deck, and clambering out of the well, he wormed himself into this, a few feet forward, and lay, panting and fatigued, hot, wet, hungry and thirsty, half stifled by the foul and musty air of the hold, and by the smell of the bilge, but safe for the present.

He lay in a sort of stupor, and gradually heard all sounds die away. For a little while his mind was filled with strange recollections of the passions and events of the last hour; then lying prone in the foul and musty darkness, he lapsed into a sleep haunted with dreams, in which he was again rushing through the swamp, which somehow changed into rolling water on which a steamboat was burning, and he was holding up *Madame Lafitte*, who suddenly turned and bit him on the hand. Starting up in the thick darkness, he struck his head against the deck, and then remembering where he was, lay still. The hatch had been closed. In the darkness he heard light scampering and squealing, and felt the ship shuddering beneath him.

He forgot his dream in the wild whirl of emotion with which he became aware that the vessel was on her way. Presently he felt a sort of pricking in his hand, and touching the spot, found that it was wet, and, as he again heard the scampering and squealing, he knew that a rat had bitten him. Startled a little at the new danger of being set upon by these vermin, and suspicious of poison, he sucked the wound, resolving to keep awake now as long as he could. He did not know how long he had slept, but he could hear the incessant snort, snort, snort, of a steamboat, with the long unbroken wash of the vessel, and knew that the brig was in the tow of a steam-tug, and so not yet out of the river.

At length there was a change in the noises. Orders were shouted above, heavy feet were rushing about, there was a bustle of pulling and hauling, griding and flapping, thudding of ropes on deck, chanting of sailors, amidst the receding snort of the steam-tug, and in the darkness, Antony felt the vessel lean and roll and stagger with a sound of swiftly rushing water, and knew that she was standing out to sea.

Who'll send me back after all I've gone through? Who'll be mean enough to do it? That was his constant thought now, and it came in those words to his mind. He knew the penalties imposed on any captain who took away a fugitive in his vessel. He had thought of them before, but dimly; now they came to him vividly, and he trembled. He was resolved to remain in the hold as long as he could, but he knew the time would come when he must leave his hiding-place, and face the captain. His plan was to tell him all he had suffered, to show him his wounds and scars, to beg him on his knees not to send him back to the Hell he had escaped from. Who would do it? Who'll send me back after all I've gone through? Who'll be mean enough to do it?

Soon the motion of the vessel threw him, already sickened by the horrible smells and closeness of the hold, into agonies of sea-sickness, and he lay on the bales vomiting violently, and feeling as if his soul were rending his aching body asunder. By and by, he crawled down into the well-like cavity under the hatch, where there was a little more room to breathe in, and there he lay without food, without drink, almost without air, for three days.

Days of sickness too loathsome to be described, too dreadful for permitted language to convey. Days of utter prostration, of griping pain, of wrenching convulsions, of horror indescribable, of tortured death-in-life. Days when the ropy and putrid air was sucked into the feeble lungs as if it were some strangling substance; when the oppressed heart beat slowly with dull knocks as though it would burst the bosom, and the bosom labored as though it were loaded down with tons of iron. Days when sleep came down like a weight of lead upon the brain, and struggled with infernal dreams, and was broken to fight off an ever-returning swarm of rats—invisible vermin that swarmed over his invisible body when it lay still, and were heard squeaking and pattering off in the sightless darkness when he feebly flung about his limbs to beat them away. Days whose mad, disgustful horror was desperately borne for the hope of liberty, for the hatred of slavery—borne till he could bear it no longer, and he resolved to beat upon the hatch and cry aloud to let those above him know what a hell of agony raged beneath their feet.

How long he had been immured he did not know. Count time by anguish, and it might have been centuries. Fearful of discovering himself till he was too far from the land from which he had fled to be returned, he had resolved to endure till endurance became impossible. For this he had clung to life, for this he had silently borne the horrors of his tomb, for this he had striven a hundred times against the desire to end his imprisonment by shouting aloud to those above him.

Now when heavy torpor and gradual giddiness were stealing upon him, and the instinct of his soul told him death was drawing near, he roused himself for the long deferred effort.

The ship was staggering heavily, and he heard the trampling of feet on the deck, as, with dizzily reeling brain, he feebly and slowly crawled up on his hands and knees. His strength was almost gone. An infant newly born could have been hardly more helpless than he found himself. He slowly lifted one hand to lay it on the bales beside him—lifted it a few inches like something over which he had no command—and it fell heavily, and losing his balance he tumbled down on his side. An awful feeling stole across his mind that he had delayed too long—that his resolution had outlived his physical powers. Turning over on his back, feebly panting, slowly suffocating, he drew in his breath for a wild cry for help. It rushed from him in a hoarse whistling whisper. His voice had left him!

He lay still now, painfully breathing, but resigned to die. Quietly—quietly—the fears and desires of the present, the hopes of the future withdrew, and the vision of all his past floated softly through his tranquil brain. It faded, and he lay rushing on a fast-rushing tide, and dilated with a wonderful and mystic change. Power and beauty and joy ineffable began to glow and spread divinely through his being with the vague beauteous glimmer of a transcendant life afar. All fierce and dark and sorrowful passions and emotions gone—all sense of pain and horror and disgust fled forever—himself happier, greater, nobler than he had ever dreamed—he lay swiftly drifting to the last repose.

What sound was it that jarred so dully on his failing ear? What sudden light was it that fell upon him? What faces were those that looked on him so strangely from above, and vanished with cries that brought down darkness and silence on him once more?

O blue sky of the nineteenth century, what is this? O pale, fresh light streaming into the noisome hold, what is this? O wonder-stricken, silent faces, gazing aghast upon that swart and loathsome figure lying in the shallow well, with an iron collar on its neck, what does this mean?

The men stood staring at the motionless body on the bales below them, and then, lost in a trance of wonder, stared at each other. Their wild amazement at the sight which met their eyes when they had unbattened the hatch, had burst forth in one cry, and then left them still and dumb. Presently there was a sound of heavy, hurrying feet, and the captain, a short, powerfully-built man, came flying over the deck, with strong excitement working in his sun-burnt face, reached the hold, looked in, turned livid with rage, slapped his straw hat down on his head with both hands, and rushed away cursing and raving like a madman. It was highly natural. A commercial Christian of the nineteenth century breed, the captain had been educated to think of nothing but his ship and trade, and his special reflection was of the penalties that would ensue if it became known that he had carried away a slave from New Orleans.

Recovering from their amazement, the sailors, with uncouth and profane ejaculations of horror and pity, lifted the inanimate body of Antony, disgusting even to their rude senses, and touching even to their rude sensibilities, out of the hold. They had hardly laid it on deck when the captain came rushing back again, shouting with oaths an order for a look-out up aloft, with the hope of meeting some vessel bound for the city he had left that would take the slave back. Then giving the prostrate body a furious kick, he rushed away again, storming and stamping and swearing.

At the direction of the mate, the sailors took the faintly-breathing body of Antony forward to the galley, where the black cook busied himself in reviving the fugitive. Half a dozen times a day the captain came to the spot where the feeble man reclined, and glared at him without saying a word. On the third day, Antony being then weak but able to stand and talk, the captain demanded him to give an account of himself.

Feebly standing before him, with all the vigor gone from his emaciated form, and with the deep marks of awful suffering graven on his wasted lineaments, Antony told his story.

As he finished, imploring the captain in earnest and broken tones not to send him back, the mate, who stood by, turned away with his mouth twitching, saying it was a damned shame. The captain burst into a fit of passion, and stamped on the deck, gesticulating with clenched hands.

"A damned shame, is it, Mr. Jones ?" he roared, perfectly livid with rage. "I should think it was ! Rather ! A blasted nigger to smuggle his ugly carcass aboard my brig —what d'ye think they'll say about it at Orleans, and what'll they do about it, Mr. Jones, and what'll Atkins say when he hears of it, Mr. Jones, and a load of cotton aboard from the very house whose junior partner owns this dingy curse, Mr. Jones ! Look at the name of the house on his neck, man. Blast ye," he howled, turning upon Antony, and shaking both fists at him, "I'd send ye back, you beggar, if they were to fry ye in your own black blood when they got ye ! Send ye back ? If I don't, may I be eternally "——

He finished the sentence by a gasp, and dashed both clenched fists into the haggard and imploring face of the fugitive, who fell to the deck, covered with blood. Shouting and cursing, the infuriated captain leaped on him, and seizing him by the hair, beat his head against the planks ; then jumped to his feet, capering like a madman, and brandishing his clenched fists. The mate stood looking away to the horizon, with a mute, flushed face, and two or three of the sailors standing not far distant, dumb witnesses of this brutal scene, glanced at each other with mutinous brows. Striding off a dozen paces, the captain turned again, bringing down his clenched fist with a slap into the palm of his hand, and stamping with his right foot on the deck as he shouted :

"Keep a sharp look-out, Mr. Jones ! The first vessel that heaves in sight for New Orleans shall take him if it costs me a hundred dollars. And if he gets to Boston, I'll tie him hand and foot, and send him or fetch him back the first chance, or my name's not Bangham !"

He foamed off into the cabin. Who'll send me back after all I've gone through ? Who'll be mean enough to do it ? Antony had received his answer

CHAPTER I.

THE REIGN OF TERROR.

If, on or about the twenty-fifth of May, 1852, a fugitive from Southern tyranny were to arrive in Boston, he would probably very soon discover two things—first, that he must seek refuge with the people of his own color, in the quarter vulgarly known as Nigger Hill ; secondly, that though they had once lived there in safety, neither he nor they could live there in safety any more.

There were, at that period, about three thousand colored people, a large proportion of them fugitives, residing in Boston, and the greater part of them lived in the quarter above mentioned. It was on the slope of Beacon Hill—one of the three hills which gave to the town its old name of Trimount. On the crown of the hill towered the domed State House ; behind and around it rose, street on street descending, the dwellings of the aristocracy ; and behind them, a deep fringe of humble poverty, rose, street on street, the dingy dwellings of the fugitives. There was a maxim of statesmanship then current : "Take care of the rich, and the rich will take care of the poor." It had been acted upon. The rich had been taken care of, and they had taken such care of these poor, that at that period there was no safety for them, as for two years previous there had been no safety for them in the city of Boston. Sidney's Latin blazed in gold on the walls of that State House : *Ense petit placidam sub libertate quietem*—The State seeks by the sword the calm repose of liberty. But the holy legend was dim, and not with the sword of Sidney, nor with the sword of the Spirit, sought Boston the calm repose of liberty for the poor fugitives who had fled from the meanest and the vilest tyranny that ever blackened the world.

Yet it was the city of fugitives, and fugitives had laid its old foundations down in pain and prayer. Winthrop and Dudley, Bellingham, Leverett, Coddington, the star-sweet Lady Arabella, with their compeers, men and women of true and gentle blood, and fugitives all, had reared it from the wilderness. Fugitives who taught a tyrant that he had a joint in his neck, had fled thither when the reborn tyranny again arose in their own land. Fugitives dwelling there who remembered in their own sufferings the sufferings of others, had helped frame the noble statute of 1641, welcoming to State and city any strangers who might fly thither from the tyranny or oppression of their persecutors. Fugitive hands—the hands of the Huguenot Faneuil—had dowered it with the cradling Hall of Liberty named with his name. Over it all, and through it all, and tincturing its history in the very grain, was the tradition of the fugitive. Still, in modern days, fugitives fled thither from the broken hopes, the baffled efforts, the lost battles of continental freedom. German fugitives, Italian fugitives, French fugitives, Irish fugitives, flying from their persecutors, arrived there and nestled under the broad wing of the old statute. At that period, too, the great Hungarian fugitive, Kossuth, had come, with a host of other Hungarian fugitives at his back, and the town, like the land, had roared and blazed in welcome. All these fugitives, of whatever nation, were safe in Boston. No tyrant could molest them. But the fugitives from the South—the black Americans, men and women, who had fled thither for protection from a tyranny in no wise different from any other, save in its sordid vileness and abominable excess of cruelty and outrage—there was no safety for them.

They were, for the most part, humble people—their souls crushed and bruised, as Plato says, with servile employments. Their lives had been obstructed by slavery ; slavery had nurtured in them some vices, had dwarfed and crippled in them many virtues. They were, in the mass, uncouth, grotesque, ungainly, repulsive to the eye ; they were degraded, imbruted, low, ignorant, weak and poor ; and, therefore, the heart of every gentleman should have leaped, like Burke's sword from its scabbard, to avenge even a look that threatened them with insult. Yet, on the other hand, there were many among them too comely and noble to need the defence the hearts of chevaliers fling around those to whom Man and Nature have been unkind. "In the negro countenance," says Charles Lamb, "you will often meet with strong traits of benignity. I have felt yearnings of tenderness toward some of these faces, or rather masks, that have looked out kindly upon one in casual encounters in the streets and highways. I love what Fuller beautifully calls—those 'images of God cut in ebony.'" The gentle Londoner could have said it all, and more, of the negro faces one met in Boston, and he might have added a far prouder word for the character that matched the faces. For all that is manliest in manhood, all that is womanliest in womanhood, rose here and there, with tropic energy, uncrushed by the load of past slavery and present social wrong, among those people. Piety, rude and simple, it may be, yet fervent and mighty as ever clasped with tears the Savior's feet, or rose through eternity to faint in the raptures of prayer before the throne of Jehovah; love, none more loyal and tender, for the father, the mother, the husband, the wife, the child, the home, the country; compassion, quick and strong for mutual succor; flush-handed hospitality; courtesy born not of art but nature; patience; cheerfulness; self-respect; laborious industry; ambition to rise and to excel, despite of fettering disabilities and thick-strewn obstacles; heroic bravery and endurance, such as blanch the cheeks and shake the hearts of those who read or hear the pains and perils negroes have dared for their own freedom, and nobler still, the freedom of their fellows—these, and many other virtues, bourgeoned and blossomed in the hearts and lives of the black fugitives. For these people, whatever pro-slavery snobs and sciolists might say of them, or however they might prate of their inferiority, were, nevertheless, of worthy blood. Take as one sure proof of the negro's native elegance and gentility of soul, his love and talent for music. The old genius of Africa which taught the lips of Memnon those weird auroral tones which enchanted the valley of the Nile, still haunts the broken souls of the race on this continent. America has no distinctive music but her negro melodies. Listening to those merry rigadoon tunes, wonderful for their jovial sweetness and facile celerity of movement, or to those melancholy or mournful chants, ineffable in pathos, which thrill the spirit with their wild, mysterious cadences, he would have little wit who could deny the spiritual worth of the race whose fugitives at that period found no safety in Boston.

No safety. None at all. Yet Boston had it to remember that one of the first five martyrs of her freedom and of the freedom of America, was a negro—Crispus Attucks. But Boston's remembrance of that fact seemed at that time to be almost confined to a certain literary slop-pail who periodically emptied himself upon the fame of the hero whom John Hancock and Samuel Adams had thought worthy of funeral honors. Boston had, for many years, paid her debt of gratitude to Attucks by treating the men and women of his race something after the fashion that Jews were treated in the Middle Ages. They had their Ghetto at the west end of the town; there they lived by sufferance, despised, rejected, borne down by a social scorn which, to the noblest of them, was daily heart-break, and which the lowliest of them could not bear without pain. They had a narrow range of humble employments and avocations, such as window-cleaning, white-washing, boot-blacking, cab-driving, porterage, domestic service, and the like; keeping a barber's shop or an old clothes shop, was perhaps the highest occupation open to them; and these they pursued faithfully and industriously. They were shut out of the mechanic occupations; shut out of commerce; shut out of the professions. They were excluded from the omnibuses; excluded from the first-class cars; excluded from the theatres unless the manager could make a place for them where seeing or hearing was next to impossible; excluded from some of the churches by express provision, and from most, if not all, of the others, by tacit understanding; excluded from the common schools, and allotted caste-schools where to learn anything was against nature; excluded from the colleges; excluded from the decent dwellings; excluded from the decent graveyards; excluded from almost everything. They were, however, freely admitted to the gallows and the jail. But these, somehow or other, saw less of them than of the race that despised them.

For all the years anterior to the period under notice, these people had been, speaking in a general way, safe in Boston. There had, to be sure, been occasional instances of private kidnapping, little known ; and there had been an abortive attempt to legally clutch into slavery one negro, Latimer. Still, Boston cherished, sentimentally, at least, free principles, and the New England traditions and laws, all favoring liberty, had been strong enough in her borders to protect the fugitives. Moreover, the caste prejudices against them had for twenty years or so preceding been slowly breaking down. During that time, thanks to one heroic saint, Emerson—thanks to one saintly hero, Garrison—the dawn of a new era was broadening up the northern sky, and all things had begun to come under the sovereignty of reason. Emerson had shed the new and free disclosing light of a poet's soul and a scholar's mind on the great problems of spiritual and secular life : straightway the primal soul held session ; the old decisions were unsettled ; everything was to be reëxamined ; thought awoke ; the breeze streamed ; the sun shone ; the Dutch canal fled into a rushing river ; all that was generous, all that was thoughtful, all that was intrepid in New England uprose from lethargy ; and while he—

—— "with low tones that decide,
And doubt and reverend use defied—
With a look that solved the sphere,
And stirred the devils everywhere—
Gave his sentiment divine," ——

the contest of reason against authority and precedent began, and amidst much theological mud-flinging and unable-editor jeering, continued from year to year, awakening the distinctive intellectual life of America. On the other hand, Garrison had impeached Slavery before the nation, as the giant foe of civil and political liberty, democracy, society, humanity, in a word, civilization ; and amidst a roaring storm of rancor, and the howls of slavers and traders, that tremendous trial also began, and continued from year to year. At the outset, Boston merchants, convulsed with sordid fear lest their southern trade should suffer by this arraignment of the oligarchy, gathered in a mob to hang the gallant citizen—had, in fact, the rope already around his neck, when the Mayor put him in jail, as a dastardly way of saving him. At the outset, too, the gentle Governor of Georgia issued an official proclamation offering five thousand dollars reward for his assassination. Happy; free America! But Garrison had in his heart all that made patriots and Puritans, and amidst a tempest of persecution unequalled since the Dark Ages, dauntless with pen and voice, he held his course against Slavery like the thunder storm against the wind. To his aid gathered a little group of gentlemen and gentlewomen, writers and orators of marked power. Abby Kelley, fair and eloquent for liberty as ever the Greek Hypatia for science: Lydia Maria Child, whose generous and exquisite literary genius all know: Mrs. Chapman, her thought shining in a terse, crystalline diction, like gold in a mountain stream: Angelina and Sarah Grimke, Carolinians, who knew what Slavery was, and knew how to flash the heart's light upon it: Beriah Green, a master of the old ignited logic: Theodore Weld, a resplendent and indomitable torrent of brave speech: Edmund Quincy, wit, humorist, satirist, gentleman, with the best spirit of the days of Queen Anne in his thought and style: Wendell Phillips, with a fiery glory of classic oratory, strange, but for him, to the air of America: Burleigh, Francis Jackson, in later years Theodore Parker, these, and a score of others gathered around Garrison, sacrificing name and fame, genius, scholarship, wealth, everything they had to sacrifice, to the heroic task of redeeming their country from its shame and wo. Outside of this organization was Channing, with words like morning: John Quincy Adams, too, during those years, fought the battle of free speech in the halls of Congress: Webster, also, poured the lightning and thunder of his mind against the extension of slavery, though never, save in the abstract, against slavery itself: the Whig party backed him; the men of the Liberty party, and in later years the Free Soil party, came to the side issues of the war. But these were not the Abolitionists proper; the Abolitionists were those who stood with Garrison, and their work was with Slavery itself. Against it they reared Alps of testimony and argument; they exposed it utterly; they bent every energy to the task of rousing the nation to its annihilation. Part of their task was the elevation of the fugitives in Boston, and it was owing to their efforts that the caste prejudices were breaking down. The comparative triumph of the present time, whose signal is that the black child sits on equal terms in the Boston schools with the white, was not then achieved, but still, at the period under notice, much had been done. The cars were open to the negro, the omnibuses, the decent dwellings, some mechanic occupations, some of the churches; and one or two colored lawyers had been admitted to the Boston Bar. The theatres still held out; the "respectable" churches, of course—spite of the black bishops of the days of Paul and Augustine; commerce, also; the schools and colleges, likewise; but the Abolitionists were battering on the wall, and it was breaking, breaking, breaking slowly down.

Suddenly over these struggling tides of light and darkness swept the black refluent surge of barbarism. In the year 1850, Congress passed the Fugitive Slave Law. The great Humboldt justly called it "the Webster law"—for with Webster against it, it either could not have passed, or having passed, it never could have been executed. Webster hostile to it, and the North would have risen around him as one man. But the time had come for the Presidential candidates to make their game, and on the seventh of March, 1850, Webster made his game. The draft of a speech for freedom lying in his desk, he stood up in the Senate, spoke a speech for slavery, which was at war with every other speech of his previous life, and his game was made. He made it, played it, lost it, died, and lies cursed with forgiveness, and buried in tears.

A cold, hard Southern tyrant, Mason of Virginia, created the black statute; a sleek, pleasant Northern traitor, Fillmore of New York, then sitting in the Presidential chair, unleashed it, and it burst forth in mischief and ruin, upon the homes of the poor. Such a law! The fugitive to be haled before a Commissioner; no Judge, no Jury; his former slavery sworn to by any unknown claimant, he was to be sent into bondage; five dollars to the Commissioner if he set him free, ten dollars if he made him a slave. Six months imprisonment, and fifteen hundred dollars fine to any person who gave a fugitive food to eat, water to drink, a room to rest in. Happy, free America!

At first Boston was horrified at the law, and aghast at the course of Webster. But the first shock over, Boston became filled with patriotic ardor, and the black statute not only rose in favor, but slavery itself became the theme of eulogy. It was about that period that an eminent Philadelphia surgeon rushed one morning, with a glowing face, before the college-class, and holding up a horrid mass before their astonished eyes, screamed, in a voice trembling with passionate enthusiasm: "Oh, gentlemen! gentlemen, what a *be-a-u*tiful cancer!" With an enthusiasm not less rapturous than his, the Whig and Democratic politicians of that period expatiated upon the charms of the obscene and filthy oligarchic wen which hung from the neck of the South, and the black, accursed conglomerated pustule of a Fugitive Slave Law, which inoculated from it, now deformed the whole face of the North. Slavery was a perfectly paradisaical and divine institution; agitation against it must cease: the Fugitive Slave Law was instinct with the purest and noblest patriotism — the fugitive men, women and children must be hunted down by it with alacrity, or the South would dissolve the Union. To this effect the beautiful emasculate eloquence of Everett moved forth in balanced cadence; to this effect raved rancorous in Bedlam beauty, the intervolved, inextricable, splendor-spotted snarl and coil of Choate's bewildering orations; to this effect, all up and down the land, for two years, rolled Webster's dark and orotund malignant thunder. Everywhere in their train a host of blatherers and roarers spouted and bawled—stop agitation—execute the Slave Law—save the Union! It was a period of absolute insanity. The Union was not in the slightest danger—proof of that, the stocks never fell.

The South would no more have dared to dissolve the Union than a man would dare to swim in the Maelstrom. But the Southern insanity of tyranny demanded the North for its man-hunting ground; the northern insanity of avarice yielded the demand to get southern trade; between the slaver and trader, the politicians' insanity of power made its game; and the pretext for all was the salvation of the Union. Millions of the people cried, "Save the Union!" A thousand presses reëchoed the cry. An immense majority of the clergy echoed it again from their pulpits. The things ministers said in defence of slavery and its black statute were only less incredible than the manner in which they were received. For instance, the Rev. Dr. Dewey, an eminent divine, was reported to have declared in a public lecture that he would send his own mother into slavery to save the Union; a storm of rebuke at once burst upon him from the anti-slavery people, and this sentiment was not considered satisfactory even by citizens of the highest respectability: whereupon Dr. Dewey explained that he had not said he would send his own mother into slavery to save the Union, but that he had said he would consent that his own brother or his own son should go into slavery to save the Union—and the citizens of the highest respectability considered *this* sentiment as highly satisfactory! So amidst such talk and such applause as this, the pro-slavery furore pothered on, and the North was incessantly urged to enforce the black statute as the price of safety to the nation, and incessantly reminded of the priceless privileges the Union secured to us. Perhaps it did—but not least prominent among them was the priceless privilege of paying the debts of South Carolina, and the other priceless privilege of hunting men and women on the soil of the old patriots and Puritans.

Meanwhile the Reign of Terror had begun, and the hell-hound of a law was ravening on its victims. It raged chiefly in the great cities, and from these the fugitives, their years of safety over, were flying by thousands to the wild Canadian snows. But the Abolitionists were upon the law. Upon it Theodore Parker dashed the bolted thunder of his speech. Upon it burst the inextinguishable Greek fire of eloquence from the fortressed soul of Wendell Phillips. Upon it, in a word, all the men and women, the Britomarts and Tancreds of the glorious minority, hurtled like a storm of swords. The Free Soilers, too, were up, and did gallant service. Giddings, Seward, Wilson, Burlingame, Mann, Sewall, Chase, Sumner, all the gentlemen and chevaliers of that league, were in the field. Charles Sumner shook Faneuil Hall with words that beat with the blood of all the ages. In New York, Beecher burst upon the monster with tempests of generous flame, and the Hebraic speech of Cheever fought with the prowess of the Maccabees. All over the North, in country towns and in some city pulpits, there were valiant clergymen, whose souls went forth in arms. The Free Soil presses everywhere, became catapults and mangonels, showering a hail of invective and argument upon the law. But the monster, panoplied in legal forms, and girt with a myriad of defenders, was hard to kill. Beaten from some places, crippled sorely, it still lives, and even at this hour, in New York, in Philadelphia, and in other cities, drags down and devours its victims. At the period under notice, its power was strong in Boston. Boston, in the branding phrase of Theodore Parker, had gone for kidnapping. Her Webster, her city officers, her aristocracy, her courts, her prominent newspapers, her traders and her rabble, were all hostile to the unhappy fugitives. That law, however, was doing the most powerful anti-slavery service ever done in America. But its results—for it broke up the Whig party, sowed death in the bones of the Democratic party, sent Charles Sumner to Congress, made the Republicans a power in the land, and taught the people a detestation of slavery which they had never known before—its results were not then fully deposited, or at least clearly seen ; they were still operant to their end ; and all noble hearts were bowed in sickening sorrow, for it seemed as if liberty, humanity, civilization, all, were going down forever.

It was, then, this hell-dog of a law that had made it no longer safe for the fugitives in Boston. And who is he who shall undertake to paint the agony of those men and women ? He must dip his pencil in the hues of earthquake and eclipse who aims to do it. Their years of security were over. The first news of the passage of the law drove scores of them to Canada, and day by day they were flying. Numbers of their people had already been taken from other cities into slavery, when the first slave case, that of Shadrach, occurred in Boston. Ten or twelve gallant black men burst into the court-room, and took Shadrach from his foes. Boston howled. Soon another fugitive, Sims, was dragged before the Commissioner. No rescue for him; the court-house was ringed with chains, under which the Chief Justice of Massachusetts, and other Judges, crawled to their seats; the cutlasses and bludgeons of the Government begirt the captive, and fifteen hundred Boston gentlemen offered to put muskets to their shoulders, if desired, to insure his being taken into bondage. "The Fifteen Hundred Scoundrels," Wendell Phillips christened this brigade of wretches, praying that bankruptcy might sit on the ledger of every one of them. Nine days the Abolitionists and Free-Soilers fought the case, impeded the Jedburgh justice—the bitter mockery of that infamous trial; then Sims was environed with cutlasses and pistols, marched, at early dawn, to the vessel a Boston merchant volunteered for his rendition, and sent into slavery. The only news of him after that, was that he had been scourged to death at Savannah. His capture and murder completed the ghastly alarm of the Boston fugitives. From that hour they lived in an atmosphere of unimaginable fear and gloom. Frequent reports that kidnappers were in town, harried many of them off to join the thirty thousand fugitives who had fled from the tender mercies of America to seek refuge in the bleak wilds or towns of Canada. Churches were suspended; business arrested; families were broken up; wives and husbands separated; fathers had to leave their sons; sons their fathers; parents their children; for the peril was often immediate, and there was no time for delay. At every fresh rumor that kidnappers were in town, the colored people would hurry up from their occupations to their homes—some to fly, aided by their richer brethren, or by the compassion of the anti-slavery people—others to gather in the streets in excited discussion—and others, with that desperate and splendid courage which is one of the distinctive virtues of the negro, to fortify their dwellings, and prepare for a death-grapple with their hunters. Thick-crowding cares and fears, distress, alarm, foreboding, agony, few friends, a thousand foes, this was their bitter portion.

Such, briefly and faintly sketched, was the state of affairs among these poor people in the City of the Fugitive at that period. What wonder men of heart desponded? It was not a despised Abolitionist, but an Abolitionist whom none despise—the Lord of Civilization standing calm above the ages, he whose spirit slowly wins the world from wrong; it was Francis Bacon of Verulam who said that when Commerce dominates in the State, the State is in its decline. Commerce dominated then. Science, arts, laws, religion, morality, humanity, justice, liberty, the rights, the hearts of mankind—all must give way to it. Rapacious and insolent, it ruled and flourished over all.

Yet there were rays of hope and auguries of better days in Boston even then, and the new was stirring in the old. Emerson was saturating the intellectual life of the city, and through it the mind of America, with the nobleness of his thought. Theodore Parker, gigantesque in learning, courage, devotion to mankind, less a man than a Commonwealth of noble powers, was in his pulpit, with a strong and growing hold on the minds and hearts of the people. The Abolitionists were toiling terribly with all their splendid might of conscience, their genius and their eloquence, to rouse the North to a settlement with the Slave Oligarchy. The Free-Soilers were indefatigably laboring to prevent the base and brutal Democrats from crowding out free American labor from the Territories and incoming States with the labor of Congo and Ashantee; and laboring also to get the Government out of the control of the Slave Power. In a word, Liberty was fighting her battle with Trade, and even the defeats of Liberty are victories.

Add to all that a fair ray of hope and promise still lingered at that period in the air of Boston, cast from a little society of Socialists, under the leadership of William Henry

Manning, which had been dissolved about two years before. They had lit their torch from the old faith that Human Life has its Science, discovering which we rear earth's Golden Age. It was the old idea of Plato, Aristotle, Pythagoras; it was the dream of Campanella and More; it was the divine and deathless purpose of Bacon, and the holy labor of Fourier. The Socialists in Boston had made a limited but profound impression with it, which had outlasted their dissolution. The light of the torch still lived when the torch itself was extinguished; and amidst the sordor and selfishness and cruelty of the period, it showed that the tradition and the promise of the Good Time Coming were immortal.

CHAPTER II.

THE FENCING SCHOOL.

Among other things in Boston at that period there was a fencing school and pistol gallery, kept by an old soldier of the First Empire, Monsieur Hypolite Bagasse. The way to it was up a long, narrow boarded alley which led out of Washington street, ran straight for about twenty steps, and then with the natural disposition of every street, avenue, alley, lane or court in Boston, made an effort to achieve the line of beauty and of grace by slanting off to the left, in which bent it was followed by the blind, brick walls, covered in one spot with a patch of theatre posters on the left hand side of it, and by a large dingy old brick building, preternaturally full of windows, on the right hand side of it. In this building was the fencing school.

A large, long, dim, unfinished interior, lighted on one side only by a row of windows looking on the alley, clap-boarded all around on the other sides, and with rafters overhead. Cool and dry, with a faint acrid smell of powder-smoke pervading its musty atmosphere. One section of the oblong space, to the left of the door, unwindowed, and lying in complete shadow. Three or four square wooden posts, down the long centre, supporting the raftered ceiling. On the left hand, under the windows, the pistol gallery—a fenced lane, with a target at one end, and a bench, with arms and ammunition on it, at the other. Near this a wooden settee with a tin can of cheap claret wine upon it. Opposite, hanging on the boarded wall in the rear of the pistol bench, and in the range of two or three of the windows, rows of foils and yellow buckskin fencing-gloves, black wire masks for the face, leathern plastrons for the breast, and a few single-sticks and blunt broadswords. No other furniture, save three or four old chairs, scattered here and there about the room.

It was about half-past seven o'clock in the morning of the twenty-fifth of May, and Monsieur Bagasse was waiting for pupils to arrive. John Todd, a young fellow about fifteen or sixteen years of age, was at the bench, absorbed in cleaning pistols. Monsieur Bagasse himself, slowly shuffling up and down in front of the fencing implements, with a halt in his step, occasioned by one leg being shorter than the other, was absently smoking a short pipe, which he held to his mouth by the base of the bowl. He was a figure fit for the pencil of Callot or Gavarni. Sixty years old, but not looking more than a weather-beaten forty ; of middling stature, brawny, round-shouldered, slightly bow-legged, with large splay feet, cased in shambling shoes, with an old cap on the back of his head, and his coarse, black hair, dashed with grey, showing under the crescent-shaped visor above his low, broad, corrugated forehead ; with a dilapidated, old-fashioned stock around his neck, a slate-colored worsted jacket buttoned with horn buttons up to his throat, the sleeves of a red flannel shirt showing at his wrists, and coarse, dark, baggy trowsers on his lower limbs. His visage swarthy, ferruginous, picturesquely ugly, but suave and kindly, with a constant expression of curious interrogation upon it—an expression to which the ever upturned jaw contributed—to which the mouth, shaded by a rusty black moustache, and always inquiringly open, contributed—to which the eyes, one bleared and the other bright as a darkly-glowing coal, and both surmounted by shaggy eyebrows, contributed—and which had its contribution from the horn-rimmed goggles worn half way down on the bold aquiline nose, above which the eyes looked from the upturned face as though they were sighting at a mark along a cannon. Wrinkles, of course—wrinkles, and seams and crowsfeet in profusion ; two noticeable fissures sloping deeply down the cheeks from the big nostrils ; and on the right cheek a dim red scar—the record of a Frenchman's last service to his Emperor at Waterloo. Add to all a general association of tobacco, snuff, and garlic, and you have the idea of Monsieur Bagasse.

A step on the stairs announcing the approach of a visitor, Monsieur Bagasse halted, took his pipe from his mouth, and stood in a habitual attitude, his arms hung stiffly, his palms turned outward, his big feet also turned outward and visible from heel to toe, and his face sighting with curious inquiry at the door. The door opening presently, in came a young man of seven or eight and twenty, rather boyish-looking for his years, modishly, though tastefully, attired, whose name was Fernando Witherlee.

"Good morning, Monsieur Bagasse. How de do," he said, touching his moleskin hat with a kid-gloved finger, as, smiling constrainedly, and cringing into a super-elegant bow, he came forward. "Whew ! how you smell of powder in here."

"Ah ! good monning, good monning, Miss'r Witterlee," rejoined the old Frenchman, politely, with a quick salute of the hand.

Privately, Monsieur Bagasse had a supreme contempt for his visitor. Nobody could have guessed it, however, who saw the bland suavity on his grotesque visage, as he curiously scanned the face before him. A plump, smooth, colorless, bilious face, handsome in its general effect, subtle, morbid, fastidious, supercilious, reticent ; but with all its traits masked in a cool assumption of impassibility. With thick, brown hair gracefully arranged; handsome, expressive brown eyebrows; brown eyes, with a restless glitter on them when they were in motion, and a perfect opaqueness in them when they were still ; lips which were rigid in their contour, usually slightly parted, and which moved but little in their speech. Primarily, the face of an epicurean and a dilettante ; a face, too, that bespoke cynicism, conceit, arrogance, and indescribable capacity of aggravation and insult. Such was the face which Monsieur Bagasse smilingly and suavely interrogated.

"Where are our friends this fine morning ?" Witherlee asked, carelessly, with an affected elegance of utterance, which was a cross between mincing and drawling. "Not arrived yet ? The lazy fellows ! Perfect sloths, both of them."

"Lazee ? Oh no ! It is vair early yet," returned Monsieur Bagasse. "Miss'r Harrin'ton an' Miss'r Wentwort' are not lazee yet, Miss'r Witterly."

"Oh, they're up early enough, I know," replied the other, "for I met them an hour ago, idling along Temple street with some ladies."

"Maybe zose ladee was zere sweetheart. Ah, Miss'r Witterly, pardon me, it is not lazee for ze young men to promenade wis zere sweetheart—*sacre bleu*, no !"

Witherlee laughed—a chuckling laugh, as though his throat was full of turtle.

"I was struck with the contrast," he remarked. "Wentworth was dressed in his dandy artist rig—spruce as Beau Brummel, and Harrington wore those superannuated old clothes, looking for all the world as if he had just been let out of the watchhouse. Splendid girls they were with too. Wentworth beside one of them was like a bizarre creature, of some sort or other, walking with a princess, and Harrington like a strapping young rag-picker along side of a queen."

"Ah, zey is vair fine young zhentilmen," tranquilly replied Monsieur Bagasse. "Vair fine."

Witherlee made no reply, but slightly elevated his handsome eyebrows in expressive disparagement.

"You know zose ladee, Miss'r Witterly ?" inquired the old Frenchman.

"Oh yes, very well. I walked along with them this morning. One is a Miss Eastman—she lives in Temple street with her mother. Quite rich. The other is a Miss Ames, who is visiting the Eastmans. Her family are all rich. They live at Cambridge."

"Vair fine ladee? Wis beautee—wis dollair, eh?"

"Oh yes, indeed. Very much sought after too, both of them. With crowds of admirers, I assure you."

"Ah, Miss'r Witterly, I am so glad for zat. It please me vair mush that Miss'r Harrin'ton and Miss'r Wentwort' sall marry zose vair fine ladee."

"Hoity, toity, my dear Monsieur Bagasse, what in the world are you thinking of? Your pupils are not so lucky as that yet. Wentworth might have a chance, for his father's rich, and in good standing, though I judge from the way things go on lately that Miss Ames cares precious little for him. But Harrington—why he's as poor as a church mouse, and doesn't move in good society at all. How Miss Eastman tolerates his visits, *I* can't imagine. I suppose it's her kindness though. Seems to me Harrington must have a great deal of assurance to visit her at all. As for marrying her, why it's perfectly absurd! She'd as soon marry a man out of the poor-house. Good gracious! look at the old coat the fellow wears! Why the lady belongs to our first society—a su-pairb person—perfectly dis-t-a-nguay."

Monsieur Bagasse grinned broadly, possibly with rage, possibly at the affected drawl with which Witherlee had pronounced the French word *distingué*, and then growing grotesquely serious, burst forth in orotund, hoarse, fluent tones, very politely, but with great earnestness.

"Pardon me, Miss'r Witterly," he said, "but why is zat so odd zat ze vair fine *distingué* ladee sall lof Miss'r Harrin'ton? Ah, Miss'r Witterly, you make one vair big mistake. You zink ze pretty girl all so fond of ze dollair—ze rank—ze grand posetion, eh? Bah—no! I tell you, no. Ze duch-ess—ze count-ess—ze great vair fine ladee—zey lof so offen ze wit, ze brave heart, ze gallantree, ze goodness wis ze old coat over him. *Ouf!* Look now. Attend. Was I great vair fine ladee, what sall I do wis myself? I tell you. I see Miss'r Harrington lof me. I make vair sure. Zen I say—here, you brave, good man, so kind, so handsome, so gallant, so like ze superb chevalier of ze old time—look—I lof you! I lof you wis you old coat! I lof you old coat, too, for it covair you so long. Come—I marry you—you take my fine house—my dollair—you take me—all, for evair and evair. *Sacrebleu*, Miss'r Witterly, zat is what I say to Miss'r Harrin'ton was I vair fine ladee."

To this outburst, which was delivered with great vivacity and many shrugs, grimaces, and odd gesticulations, Witherlee listened with opaque eyes and parted lips, and an expression of perfect immobility on his colorless, plump, morbid countenance. At the end, he lifted his expressive eyebrows, slightly curled a contumelious nose, and curved a supercilious lip, with an insolence at once so delicate and so intense, that Monsieur Bagasse, with the most suave smile again on his uncouth visage, felt a strong desire to deal him a thumping French kick under the chin.

"I have no doubt, my dear Monsieur Bagasse," was the rejoinder after a pause, "that you would do as you say if you were the lady in question. But you're not, you know, which makes the difference. However, I won't discuss the point with you. Harrington is not quite so great a fool, I hope, as to expect any such good fortune. As for Wentworth, if you could have seen his face this morning when Emily—that is Miss Ames—gave Harrington a bunch of violets, you would have thought that his hopes, like his prospects, were rather down."

"Eh, what was zat?" inquired the old Frenchman, curiously.

"Why you see," replied Witherlee, with a spirting chuckle at the remembrance, "after the walk we were in the parlor, and Miss Ames went into the conservatory and came back with a little bunch of violets. She was at a table in the further end of the room, dividing the violets into two nosegays, and, just for a joke, I went over to her and whispered that Wentworth would be delighted to receive a true-love posy from her. I don't know what made her color, but she did, and instantly tied up all the flowers in one nosegay, with a piqued air, and went over to the two fellows. You should have seen Wentworth's mortified air when she sailed past him, and gave them to Harrington. He walked across the room, trying to look indifferent, but it was no go. Miss Eastman went out and came back with another bunch of violets which she gave him with her most gracious manner, but I guess she couldn't console him for that rebuff. He made his adieux to Miss Ames stiffly enough, though he was extra cordial to Miss Eastman, at which Miss Ames looked colder than ever. Altogether, for a little matter, it played the deuce with Wentworth everyway."

"Pardon me, Miss'r Witterly—ex-cuse me, sir, please," interposed Monsieur Bagasse, with immense civility of manner, and deprecating grimaces: "Zat was not well—*sacrebleu*, no. You make zat mischeef—ex-cuse me—you vex zat ladee and you wound Miss'r Wentwort' wis you littel gay talk. Ah, you was not right—no indeed. You make maybe littel miff wis zose young peeples—it grow, grow, grow evair so big maybe, and zey nevair, nevair, come back togezzer. You duty sall be to make ze amende honorable—ex-plain—yes indeed, Miss'r Witterly. You tell Miss'r Wentwort' what you say—zen he know, zen it is again right."

"Not at all," replied the mischief-maker. "I don't think so. I only made a playful remark. If Miss Ames chose to act as she did, that is not my affair. I said all I could to console Wentworth. I told him I was truly sorry that Miss Ames had treated him so rudely—very sorry indeed."

"*Mille tonnerre!*" exclaimed the Frenchman, grinning and grimacing desperately: "you say zat to Miss'r Wentwort'!"

"Of course I said it," coolly replied Witherlee. "What less could I say? It didn't console him much, though. He tried to look indifferent, thanked me coolly enough, and remarked that it was of no consequence."

Monsieur Bagasse gave a sort of snort, still grinning and grimacing. The whole proceeding was quite in Fernando Witherlee's style. A piece of boyish malice, perpetrated with mischievously subtle talent—with an expressiveness of manner which had injected the words and action with a wicked meaning not purely their own; afterwards foolishly tattled of, and defended with pig-headed perversity.

"I am very sorry the thing happened," resumed Witherlee, in a cool, sympathizing, soliloquizing tone, looking, meanwhile, at the wall with his opaquest gaze. "And I'm still more sorry to notice that Wentworth and Miss Ames are not so intimate as they were a short time ago. It really seems as if they were becoming estranged. It's odd to see how attentive Wentworth is lately to Miss Eastman, though I'm sure he only cares for her as a friend. Then Miss Ames, on the other hand, is very agreeable to Harrington, which galls Wentworth, I know. 'Pon my word, I believe he is getting jealous of Harrington, and I shouldn't wonder if those two fellows had a falling out presently. It's dreadfully absurd of Wentworth, for I'm sure that if Harrington cares for either of them, it's Miss Eastman."

The case was pretty much as Witherlee had stated it, but the explanation was, that he had been lifting his eyebrows and modulating his tones and dropping his intangible innuendoes to Miss Ames with regard to Wentworth, and the result was, that she had become filled with indeterminate suspicion and distrust of her lover, and had almost alienated him from her by her manner toward him.

"Miss'r Witterly, you are ze friend of zose young men," placidly observed Monsieur Bagasse. "See, now, suppose you tell Miss'r Wentwort' zat he sall not be jalous of Miss'r Harrin'ton—zat Miss'r Harrin'ton haf not lof Mees Ame nevair. Zen you make zem fine young zhentilmen still good friend of ze ozzer. You say zat now to Miss'r Wentwort'."

"Dear me, no; that wouldn't do at all," was the reply. "It's not my business, you know, and I might only make trouble. Better let them alone. It'll all come right, I guess. Wentworth's in no danger from our negro-worshipping friend, and I guess the best policy in this case, like the national policy in regard to Kossuth, will be non-intervention."

"Neeger-worship friend? Who is zat you mean?" inquired Monsieur Bagasse, with grotesque perplexity.

Witherlee laughed his turtle-husky chuckle.

"I was only joking," he returned; "I meant Harrington. You know he's a furious Abolitionist."

"Ah, Miss'r Witterly," said the old Frenchman, with a deprecating shrug and grimace, "zat is not good fon. Miss'r Harrin'ton is vair fine young zhentilman. If he worsheep ze neeger, *pardieu*, Hypolite Bagasse worsheep ze neeger wis him. Zat is only what you call ze attachment zoo libertee. Ah, Miss'r Witterly, zat Miss'r Harrin'ton, so kind, so strong, so good, he is friend of ze neeger, of ze Iris'man, of ze Frenchman, of ze poor fellow, of ze littel child, of ze small fly on ze window, of ze vair old devail himself, of evairybody. See, now. Attend. I was seek—vair seek wis fever in ze winter. Nobody come to me—of my pupeel not one. Zat Miss'r Harrin'ton he come. He find John Todd, and inquire where I live, and he come. He breeng ze doctor—he breeng Miss'r Wentwort', he breeng ze littel jellee, ze grape, all zem littel ting zat he say ze vair fine ladee give him for ze poor old vair seek Bagasse. *Sacrebleu*, he nurse me; he sit up wis me in ze night when my wife tire herself out wis me, and go sleep; he get me well, and zen he go zoo ze pupeel and make ze subscripsheon for zere old fencing-mastair. Feefty dollair—dam! it is sub-lime! Ze wolf he cut off from ze door of Bagasse so queek as his dam leg will trot! Zen Miss'r Harrin'ton he advise Madame Bagasse zoo keep ze boarding-house. Ah! it is grand. She accept—ze boardair come—ze French, ze Italian, ze German man zey board wis me. Hah! zat Miss'r Harrin'ton he set me up on my leg, wis my heart big wis gratitude. You make mock of zat old coat, Miss'r Witterly. Bah! He wear zat old coat zat so many poor devail sall wear any coat at all. *Sacrebleu!* was I ze great Nap-oleon, I sall put ze grand cross of ze Legion—ze Legion d'Honneur—on ze breast of zat old coat for evair."

There was such emotion in the deep, hoarse rolling tones—such a dark glow on the grotesque, brown, wrinkled visage—such fire in the one eye under its shaggy eyebrow—such martial energy in the uncouth, shabby figure, that Witherlee felt the danger of pursuing any further his detraction of Harrington. At the same time, he felt an envious itching to continue it. To hear anybody or anything praised, and not be roused to oppositiveness, was not in the organization of Fernando

Witherlee. A peculiarly aggravating rejoinder was in his mind, and the temptation to utter it was prodigious. 'While he hesitated between the temptation and the imminent prospect of having a quarrel on his hands with Monsieur Bagasse, steps and loud talking on the stairs, announcing the approach of pupils, at once decided and relieved him, and he sauntered away to a chair, sinking into which and tilting it back against the wall, he proceeded to select, light and smoke a cigar.

CHAPTER III.

QUARTE AND TIERCE.

Monsieur Bagasse, meanwhile, resuming his equanimity, stood sighting beyond the muzzle of an invisible cannon, as if the door was the mark, looking very much like some slovenly, awkward old artilleryman, of an uncouth pattern, and not at all like a fencing-master. The door flew open presently with a bang, letting in two smart young men not yet out of their teens, who swaggered forward with a very rakish, gasconading air. Milk street clerks—Fisk and Palmer by name—snobbish in dress and rude in manners.

"Bon swor, Monsoor," said Palmer, loud and patronizing. This address, couched in a purely domestic French, was intended both as an elegant recognition of the nationality of Monsieur Bagasse, and as a way of bidding him good morning. The old man, who with ready politeness had silently saluted the new comers upon their entrance, surveyed the speaker over the rims of his round goggles, with open mouth, and an odd smile on his upturned visage.

"Ha, Miss'r Pammer," he said with vivacity, "you zink ze day is gone, eh?"

Palmer, who was taking off his coat, stopped and stared.

"I don't understand you, Monsoor," he rejoined; "I'm going to take my lesson."

"Hah! Zat is well," said the old man. "But you say, *bon soir*, Miss'r Pammer. Zat is, good night. You intend *bon jour;* zat is, good day."

Palmer, seeing the grotesque, good-natured face of the fencing-master smiling at him, and beginning to comprehend what his domestic French had meant, grinned rather foolishly, and turned off. His companion, who stood in his shirt-sleeves with a wire-mask already on his face, burst into a rude guffaw at the blunder, and slapped him on the back with a fencing-glove. It may be mentioned here that these young cubs, in process of getting their taste for the wolf's milk of trade, had come upon the heady wine of Dumas' "Three Guardsmen"—which admirable romance had so intoxicated their ardent fancy with excited day-dreams of D'Artagnan and Porthos, that, filled with the spirit of the sword, they had resolved to take fencing-lessons of Monsieur Bagasse. This practical recognition of the literary genius of the great French mulatto, was one incident in their joint career. Another, not so creditable, was their participation in a mob of clerks and salesmen, who not long before had brawled down an orator of Dumas' own color—Frederick Douglass—at the Thompson meeting in Faneuil Hall. It is to be feared that the gallant Alexandre himself would have fared no better at their hands, or their employers' either, had he ever been fool enough to leave the democratic streets of Paris, for the color-phobic pavements of Boston.

Monsieur Bagasse put away his pipe and spectacles, shuffled across the room to shut the door which the cubs had left open, and returning took down a foil and glove to give the lesson. Fisk was buckling on Palmer's plastron, as the leathern breast-plate is called, an operation rather hindered by his sense of the supercilious smile with which Witherlee regarded his efforts from his chair against the wall, as well as by the circumstance of his having his face incased in the wire mask, and his arms hampered by the heavy leather gloves which he was holding with his elbows against his sides. While Monsieur Bagasse waited, standing in an awkward drooping posture, with the foil in his gloved hand, a firm step was heard bounding up the stairs, the door flew open, and, with a light, springing tread, a young man, flushed and smiling, and so handsome that any one would have turned to look at him, darted in, bringing with him a warm gust of fragrance into the chill musty pallor of the room. An odd, fond smile shot at once to the visage of the fencing-master.

"Ha, good monning, good monning, Missr Wentwort'," he chirruped, returning with a military salute the quick gesture of gay cordiality the young man made on entering. "How you feel to-day?"

"Capital! most potent, grave and reverend seignior! My very noble and approved good fencing-master, how are you? Hallo, Fernando," his eye catching sight of the equably-smoking Witherlee: "here you are again, old fellow?"

"Just so, Heliogabalus," coolly drawled the bilious-cynical youth from his chair. "Say, Heliogabalus—do you know how to get that smell out of your clothes? Bury 'em!"

There was a decided flavor of verjuice in the manner of Witherlee, as he let fly this borrowed jest at the perfumed raiment of the other. Wentworth, though he took it as a jest, could not help wincing a little at it, and was made even more uncomfortable at the application to him of the name of one of the most bestial of the Roman Emperors.

"Well, Fernando," he returned with a smile, "if ever there was a prickly cactus, you're one. You're a perfect Diogenes. Get a tub, Fernando, do."

"Quarte and tierce, Heliogabalus," responded the cool Fernando, with his turtle-husky chuckle.

Wentworth turned away, and met the smiling look of admiration and fondness on the upturned visage of the old man-at-arms. A handsome young fellow, in the very flower of youth and May, elegantly dressed—who could look at him without admiration and fondness? An artist—one could have told that at the first glance. Long auburn locks curled in a thick cluster under his dark Rubens hat, and around his florid cheeks. He had a gay, electric, passionate face; bright blue eyes; a fair complexion; red lips, shaded by a light brown moustache coquettishly curled up at the ends, and quick to curve into a proud, brilliant smile. His figure was compact, well-knit, shapely, of middle-height, and seeming taller than it was by force of its gallant carriage. The quality of his face was in his voice—so quick, lively, clear and ringing.

"Ah, Missr Wentwort'," said the old man, in hoarse tones, which were yet soft and facile, "you bring me back ever so far—you look so gay! You look as I sall feel wis my young blood tirty, tirty-five years ago. We marsh zen wis ze great Nap-oleon dis mont', all so proud, so gallant, for zat dam Waterloo. Hah! I feel zen jus' like you. So young—so gay! Wis my littel flower like zat at my bouton—ze flower zat ze pretty girl haf give me. Jus' so."

He touched a nosegay of violets in the young man's button-hole with the hilt of the foil as he spoke. Wentworth laughed lightly, taking out the nosegay.

"Jupiter! Bagasse," he cried, "you shall have the flowers for the sake of the memory. What are you grinning at, Fernando!" This to Witherlee, whose cynical grin changed into a cool lift of the eyebrows. "Now, Bagasse," resumed Wentworth, "I'll give them to you since they remind you of old times. Here, let me fix them in your jacket. There now—guard them well against every foil. Violets, you know, Monsieur Bagasse! Worn in remembrance of Corporal Violet—the great little corporal!"

The old man bowed low, with the violets on his breast. With the rush of thrilling souvenirs which the pet name of the beloved Emperor revived, a dark glow came to his rugged visage, and the one bright eye grew suddenly dim, leaving the face blind. Wentworth saw that he was touched, and with a quick regret that he had brought a tear to the old heart, turned away, humming an air.

"But where's Harrington, I wonder?" he burst out, whirling around again. "He said he'd be here before me."

"He will come pretty soon, I zink, Missr Wentwort'," replied Monsieur Bagasse. "You haf seen him dis morning?"

"Oh, yes. I found him, as usual, pegging away at the books, and we walked out together. Afterward we went with him, Witherlee and I, to his room, and then started out again to come here. He left us on the way, saying he'd be here before us, and I left Witherlee on the way, saying I'd be here before him. Two promises of pie-crust, those. I'll bet a denier, Fernando, that dog has something to do with his absence," and the young artist laughed.

"No doubt," returned Witherlee, smoking, with a sarcastic smile. "Perhaps he's commencing his education—developing, on Kant's principle, all the perfection of which the doggish nature is capable."

"Dog?" inquired Monsieur Bagasse, curiously.

"Oh, it's a dog we passed this morning," explained Wentworth; "a miserable old vagabond white cur, with just about life enough in him to crawl. Some Irish and negro boys were lugging the poor old devil along by the ears and tail, and whacking him with sticks, as we came along, and Harrington, of course, stopped to order them off."

"Bright in Harrington," put in Witherlee, with a sneer; "as if they wouldn't be at him again before we'd gone twenty yards!"

"Yes, by Jupiter, but before we had gone twenty yards, Fernando, you and I went into the shop, you know, where you bought the cigars, and it was there that Harrington said he had to go back to the house for something, and made off with himself. It never occurred to me till now—but I'll bet a franc he went back to those boys!"

He burst into a peal of laughter at the idea.

"I'd give something to know what Harrington did with the old cur," he said in a moment.

"Took him off to the butcher's perhaps, and sold him for sausages," suggested Witherlee.

"Ah, Missr Wentwort'," said the old man, grotesquely serious, "you friend, Missr Harrin'ton, is vair fine, vair mush humane, vair fine zhentilman. I feel vair mush warm to him."

"Rather too much of the Don Quixote order, though," drawled Witherlee, affectedly, giving the Spanish pronunciation to the 'Don Quixote' and calling it Don Kehoty.

"O you be hanged, Fernando," burst in Wentworth. "He's no more like Don Kehoty, as you call it, than you're like Sancho Panza. He's the grandest fellow that ever lived, and makes me ashamed of myself every day of my life. Hallo, I guess he's coming."

Witherlee, biliously pale with spite at the double injury of his pronunciation of "Don Quixote" having been mimicked, and Harrington having been so warmly praised, busied himself with adjusting the loosened skin of his cigar, while Monsieur Bagasse and Wentworth turned to the door, which voices and trampling feet were nearing. Presently the door opened and a group of seven or eight poured in with a confusion of salutations. Four or five of them were young mercantiloes, and instantly swarmed around Fisk and Palmer, who were still fussing over the plastron. One was a heavy, taciturn man—a Pennsylvania Dutchman—with blue, fishy eyes, a sodden face and a yellow beard. His name was Whilt, and he kept a wine-cellar, and boarded with Monsieur Bagasse. With him was another of the fencing-master's boarders—a tall, slender, handsome, swaggering young man, half-soldier, half-coxcomb in his bearing, with bright dark eyes, brilliant color, long black hair, well oiled and curled, and a long, slim, black moustache, shaved into two sections, and clinging to his upper lip, and curving around his moist, scarlet mouth, like two flaccid leeches. He was fancifully clad in bright blue, tight-fitting trowsers, a short, rakish coat, gay vest and neckerchief, wore his falling collar open at the throat, and had a Kossuth hat, with a black plume, set smartly on his head. This was Captain Vukovich, a young Hungarian officer, who had come over in the train of Kossuth. Though it was only eight o'clock, he and Whilt had a strong smell of Rhine wine about them, which they diffused through the room upon entering.

"How are you, Whilt," said Wentworth, carelessly nodding. "Captain, how are you? I thought you had gone on to New York with Kossuth."

Wentworth had the Kossuth furor, prevalent about that time, and saluted Vukovich with a touch of enthusiasm.

"No," responded the Hungarian, in a soft voice, conceitedly

fingering his moustache, and swaying on his shapely legs as he spoke. "No, I stays. Se Gofernor go on, an' I stays back. I sink to keep cigar shop in Bosson pretty soon. So I stays. Goot tay, Mossieu Bagasse. How you feel?"

He begun to talk in French to the fencing-master, and Wentworth, full of fiery sentiment for liberty and Hungary, moved away to the foils, humming the Marseillaise. Presently, Palmer and Fisk were ready, and Monsieur Bagasse, after much preliminary effort to get Palmer into strict position, began to give him his lesson.

Both Witherlee and Wentworth were very sensitive to all forms of artistic beauty, and they now saw, with strange pleasure, as they had often seen before, the wonderful transformation of the fencing-master's awkward, sloven figure. Looking at him in his ordinary aspect, nobody would ever have imagined that he was cut out for a pillar of the school of arms. But now, as he threw himself into the noble attitude of the exercise, every deformity seemed suddenly to have dropped from his face and figure, and vanished. The head erect and proud—the lit face turned square in rugged, grand repose, with the visor of the old cap looking now like the raised visor of a helmet—the one eye firm and jewel-bright, fixed on his adversary's—the left arm thrown up and out behind in easy balance—the body set in perfect poise on legs as strong as iron, as flexible as steel—and the lithe foil gently playing from the extended ease of his right arm over the stiff guard of his antagonist, like a line of living light—so, with every trait and outline of his figure blended into an indescribable ensemble, he stood, an image of martial grace, superb and invincible. For one instant, the two young men drank in with eager eyes the beauty of that military statue—the next, Palmer's blade lunged in swift and stiff—was parried wide aside with a light, almost imperceptible, deft motion, and a flashing clash—and the figure of Bagasse had changed into another statue of martial grandeur, the left arm down aslope with the left leg, the body heaved forward on the bent right knee, the right arm up and out in strong extension, and the foil, a gleaming curve of steel, with its buttoned point on the breast of the adversary.

Only a second, and while murmurs of applause ran round, the first position was resumed.

"You see now, Miss'r Pammer," politely said the fencing-master, breaking the spell, "I hit you zen, be-cause you longe off you guard. Now see—I show you how."

He dropped his point, and explained to Palmer where he had done wrong, showing him with his own foil the way the pass should have been made. Palmer promised to remember, and the lesson went on.

Presently, while they were on guard, Palmer was wrong again—this time in his position. Bagasse, smiling politely, lowered his point ; whereat, Palmer, with immense haste, lunged in, and triumphantly bent his foil on the breast of the fencing-master, who, of course, made no effort to ward. The young mercantiloes, delighted with this evidence of their friend's proficiency, set up a cry of bravo. Witherlee sneered to himself, and Wentworth laughed and exchanged glances with the surprised Hungarian, and the imperturbable Whilt. As for Monsieur Bagasse, he stood, with upturned visage, smiling with grotesque placidity, then made a grimace, and limping off to the claret-can, gulped a mouthful, and came hurrying back. Palmer instantly threw himself on guard, thrilling with vanity, and confident that he was getting ahead of his fencing-master.

"See, now, Missr Pammer," said the old man, with great vivacity, smiling good-naturedly as he spoke ; "you parry, now—it is simple quarte and tierce—vair, vair easy. Hey, now! Hey, now! Hey, now! Hey, now! Four."

Quietly, at every exclamation, Monsieur Bagasse, without effort, bent his foil almost double on the breast of his antagonist. Palmer could no more parry the deft lunges than he could fly. Bagasse stood grinning good-naturedly at him, and lowered his point. Palmer instantly made a desperate lunge at the unguarded breast, and the same instant found that his foil had flown out of his hand, and that the blade of Bagasse was resting in a firm curve on his bosom.

All present, Palmer included, burst into a roar of laughter. All but the master, who stood silent, with his curious, good-

5

natured smile on his upturned visage. It was quite plain to the pupil now, that he could not touch Monsieur Bagasse on or off guard, unless the latter chose to let him.

Suddenly, like a light magnetic shock, a silence fell upon the uproarious mirth, as with a surprised and startled feeling, all present recognized a new figure, serene in youthful majesty, standing quietly at a little distance near them, in the full light of the windows. It was Harrington. They all knew him, but somehow the unexpectedness of his appearance gave him the momentary effect of a stranger. He was a young man of about twenty-five, tall and stalwart, and of regnant and martial bearing. His face, looking out from under a black slouched felt hat, was long and bearded, singularly open and noble in its character, firm, calm-eyed, straight-featured, broad-nostrilled, and masculine, but very pale. The beard was light-brown, and the hair, chestnut in color, and darker than the beard, curled closely, and was worn somewhat long. A loose, dark sack, with large sleeves, buttoned with a single button at the throat, showed the spread of his chest, and added to the commanding grace of his figure. This was the coat which had been so opprobriously celebrated by the esthetic Witherlee. It was an old coat certainly, but it was not the less a well-chosen and graceful garment, and it is questionable whether if it had hung in tatters, it would have diminished the effect of a presence in contrast with which the others seemed common-place and inferior. Witherlee himself, set in comparison with Harrington, looked unmanly and contemptibly genteel. Whilt was nobody, Vukovich a simpering fop, the mercantiloes simple snobs. Even the handsome and gallant Wentworth seemed of a lower order beside him, and Bagasse, in his uncouth and shabby grotesqueness, though not degraded by the contrast, was so removed by his essential unlikeness, as to be out of comparison altogether.

Wentworth was the first to recover from the momentary ghostly trance into which they had all dropped on discovering Harrington in the room.

"Jupiter Tonans!" he exclaimed: "How—when—where—in what manner did you arrive, Harrington!"

"Well," returned Harrington in a sweet and cordial baritone voice, affably saluting the company, "I didn't exactly step out from behind the air, though you all look as if you thought so. I came in just now prosaically at the door—not stealthily either, for John Todd, there, both heard and saw me. But you were all in such a tempest of merriment that no one but Johnny noticed me. Come—go on with the fun. Tell me what it's all about, that I may laugh too."

"O, I just disarmed Monsoor—that's all," said Palmer.

This quip, though slight, was sufficient to set the group off again in a confusion of jests and laughter, in the midst of which Harrington wandered over to the pistol bench, and began to chat with the young fellow while the bout between Monsieur Bagasse and his pupil went on. In a few minutes Monsieur Bagasse came over to the claret-can in that region, drank, and took the opportunity to shake hands with Harrington, and ask for his health.

"O by the way, Mr. Bagasse," said Harrington, after due replication to the old Frenchman's polite inquiries, taking from his breast pocket as he spoke, a bunch of violets inclosed in a funnel of stiff white paper, "here's a May gift for you. I thought of you and your Corporal Violet so instantly when I got this bouquet, that I resolved to present it to you. Hallo, though! you've got one already."

He had just caught sight of the nosegay in the old slate-colored jacket. Like his own, it was tied with a pink string. A comical look of surprise came with a slight flush to his frank, pale face, and his eye glanced quickly at the young artist who, he saw, was eagerly watching him from the other side of the room. At the same instant he saw Witherlee looking with opaque eyes over in his direction, very intent upon the iron vice on the bench near by, and with a face entirely discharged of expression. Harrington's intelligence was almost clairvoyant, and he felt that Witherlee was watching him and not the vice—felt also that Wentworth's gaze meant something connected with his present action. With the feeling, which was as instantaneous as his glance had been, he caught sight of the eye of the old Frenchman, roguishly twinkling at him. Harrington was puzzled.

"Ah, ha, Missr Harrin'ton," said Monsieur Bagasse in a bantering whisper, "zere are two ladee zat gif ze vilet, an' two zhentilmen zat gif ze vilet too! Eh, now, zem zhentilmen sall not bé so vair mush fond of zem ladee zat zey gif away zere littel bouquet! Ha?"

"Two ladies!" exclaimed Harrington. "How do you know there are two? I didn't say so."

Monsieur Bagasse was caught, and shrugged his humpy shoulders with an odd grimace. A feeling of honor withheld him from saying how he came by his information, since that would involve the exposure of the blabbing Witherlee. Witherlee, meanwhile, fully conscious of the ridiculous impropriety he had been guilty of, in tattling about his friends' affairs to any person, much less the old fencing-master, and momently expecting to be subjected to the rage of Wentworth, and the rebuke of Harrington, stood nervously dreading the reply of Bagasse, and looking pale in spite of himself. Wentworth, for his part, taking a true-lover's stand-point, was considerably amazed to see Harrington, whom he thought the secret lover of Miss Ames, so coolly bestowing her nosegay on the old Frenchman. As for Harrington, he was divided between wonder at Wentworth, for having not only given to the old Frenchman the flowers he had received from Miss Eastman—whom he in turn thought Wentworth secretly loved—but having also, as he naturally supposed, made the old Frenchman his confidant, at least to the extent of telling him of the two ladies and of their gifts. Fisk and Palmer were at it, quarte and tierce, with the foils. Meanwhile, there was a game of quarte and tierce of another sort begun between four, all against each other, and Monsieur Bagasse had just been buttoned.

Harrington smiled good-naturedly, and silently gave the violets to the fencing-master, who took them and bowed without a word. Just then Wentworth approached with a composed air, which was so evidently assumed that Harrington began to laugh. Wentworth's florid color had paled a little, but he answered Harrington's laugh with a constrained smile, looking meanwhile in his face.

"Well, Harrington," he said, with an unsuccessful attempt at carelessness, "what the deuce is there in my giving Bagasse the violets, to make you show your maxillary muscles and the teeth under your beard so delightedly? Hanged if I see anything to laugh at."

The maxillary muscles, which were unusually developed in Harrington's cheeks, and always wrinkled them when he laughed, relaxed at this, but his white, regular teeth still showed in a curious, half-sad, half-absent smile, as he fixed his clear, broad gaze wistfully on the face of his friend. Wentworth, nettled at the mystery of a look he could not fathom, became peevish, and began to twirl his moustache, half smiling, half irritated.

"Don't be vexed, Wentworth," said Harrington, throwing his long arm affectionately around the latter's shoulder, and moving away up the room with him, while Bagasse shuffled off to his pupils. "I laughed thoughtlessly—but, frankly, I was somewhat surprised to see that you had given away the violets. That was all."

"All!" exclaimed Wentworth. "And why shouldn't I give them away? They were mine, weren't they? Why, you gave yours away too, didn't you?"

"To be sure," replied Harrington, with a bothered air, adding tranquilly, "Emily gave them to me, and I gave them to Bagasse."

"Well," retorted Wentworth, "Muriel gave them to me and I gave them to Bagasse also. What of it?"

Harrington, who could not see into this matter at all, was silent, and stroked his beard with his hand, a habit of his when he was very much puzzled.

"No matter—it's a trifle," he said lightly, after a pause. "Only, Richard, to be very plain with you—I hope you'll not think me intrusive—well, I thought it was—odd—that you should have given away the flowers Muriel gave you."

He spoke these words with marked, but delicate significance—stammering and hesitating a little in his speech, which was unusual with him. It was the first allusion he had ever made to Wentworth's supposed love for Miss Eastman. Loving her himself, it was not made without a pang. If Wentworth had been cool, he could not but have understood it. As it was, it only put him in a rage.

"Well, if I ever heard the like of this!" he sputtered. "To be very plain with me—what in thunder—blast it all, Harrington, what are you driving at? Why, I was struck all of a heap at the oddity of your giving away Emily's nosegay, and here you turn upon me and tell me it's odd—yes, odd, that I should give away Muriel's! What's the difference, I'd like to know? Now, just tell me!"

Harrington was silent, and again stroked his beard, wondering what sort of cross-purposes they were playing at. Wentworth stood for a moment with flushed face and passionate eyes, angry with Harrington for the first time in his life, and then walked away in great exasperation.

Perplexed and amazed at this state of affairs, and grieved to think he had, however unwittingly, angered his friend, Harrington stood looking after him, irresolute whether to follow and attempt an explanation now, or wait till his fume was over. Presently, he resolved to wait, and sadly musing, began to pace to and fro at the upper end of the long room.

On his way down to the fencing-ground, Wentworth was met by Witherlee, who had been watching the conference, and though he could not catch a word, knew well enough by Wentworth's excited tones then, and by his flushed cheeks and sparkling eyes now, that there had been some difference between the two.

"What's the matter, Richard?" he asked, kindly.

"O nothing, nothing!" fretfully replied the vexed Wentworth, taking off his Rubens hat, dashing back the thick curls from his handsome, sloping forehead with a hasty hand, and passionately slapping on the hat again.

"I am very sorry, very. Harrington is really very aggravating sometimes," ventured the kind Fernando.

At any other time Wentworth would have resented this insidious speech, as a slander upon the gentle Harrington. But now—

"He's the most aggravating fellow I ever knew in my life," was his hot answer.

"Well, I wouldn't go so far as that," returned Fernando, with mild moderation. "By no means. Harrington has fine qualities, you know. You should remember that the best of us are apt to be a little forgetful when our own personal interests, or wishes, or affections are involved."

Blandly and kindly said, with just a shade of hesitating emphasis on "personal" and "affections"—just a shade.

"What do you mean by that, Fernando?" asked Wentworth, almost choking, and catching at the insidious hint, which the good Fernando had made almost impalpable by throwing it out with the easy manner of one uttering a mere generality.

"Mean?" he asked, with a delicate shade of bewilderment, "why nothing particular, that I know of."

But he smiled slightly and lifted his handsome eyebrows very slightly, and then lapsed into an expression of soft compassion.

"Yes, I understand," said Wentworth, walking away in passionate misery.

What particular meaning the good Fernando's vague words and mysterious looks expressed, nobody could have told. It was their especial beauty, perhaps, that they really expressed nothing definite at all, and were merely random spurs to the imagination of the listener, goading him on the path he happened to be pursuing. Wentworth's path at that moment was the vague suspicion that Harrington was selfishly supplanting him in his relation to Emily. It was a path out of which he had turned several times, urged by his strong sense of Harrington's perfect nobility, but he was now in it again, and with the talented Fernando's last bunch of thorns insidiously tied to his galloping fancy, and stinging it on, he was going at a headlong pace for mad jealousy and outright hostility, and would soon be there.

Witherlee, meanwhile, highly gratified at the success of his insinuations with Wentworth, was enjoying the young artist's distress when he caught sight of Harrington standing at the upper end of the room, and looking at him. It was embarrassing, and he was about to avert his eyes, but at that instant Harrington beckoned to him. He hesitated, and then with considerable trepidation, for he did not know what was coming, he walked up the room.

Harrington's face was introverted and sad, and his eyes were fixed on vacancy. Witherlee felt glad that the broad gaze did not rest on his face, for he feared its inquest.

"Fernando," said Harrington, calmly and kindly, though with evident embarrassment, "I want to speak with you on a very delicate subject. You have known Miss Eastman and Miss Ames a long time—much longer than I have. You"—

Harrington paused for a moment. Witherlee's heart beat an alarmed tattoo, though his colorless face was perfectly impassible.

"Richard is in a strange state lately," resumed Harrington, smiling vaguely. "You must have noticed it, Fernando. Just now, he spoke to me in a manner which I do not understand. Something frets him. Have you any idea what it is?"

"Not the least, though I've noticed it," returned the imperturbable Fernando.

"Well, I haven't either," said Harrington. "But see here. You remember what you said to me at my room about a week ago. Previous to that conversation, it was my own fancy that Richard was very much attached to Miss Ames. You surprised me very much when you told me you thought his feeling was for—for Muriel. I never should have guessed it. You astonished me still more by what you told me after that. But something Richard said just now made me fancy that you may have been mistaken, and I want to ask you if you are perfectly sure of what you saw."

Harrington paused again, nervously twitching his beard with his large shapely hand. Before Witherlee could reply, he went on again.

"Let me recall that conversation," he said. "You sat in my arm-chair smoking, and you were praising Muriel, which was pleasant for me to hear. Presently, you remarked, 'she'll make Wentworth a superb wife,' and then you quoted from

Tennyson's 'Isabel'—'the queen of marriage, a most perfect wife.' I was, I own, amazed. 'Why, Wentworth?' I asked. You looked surprised, and said, 'Why not Wentworth?' Then you added—'When people love, don't they marry?' 'Certainly,' I returned, 'but you are mistaken, I think.' 'I think not,' you replied, with a manner so cool and positive, that I was, to be frank with you, a little annoyed. I was about to drop the subject there, for it seemed to me hardly fair to canvass such a matter, when you remarked, 'In fact, I *know* I'm not.' I replied, 'It is quite impossible that you should *know* it, Fernando, though you may have what seem to you strong reasons for believing it.' You answered, rather unkindly it appeared to me—'Do you doubt my word?' 'Not at all,' I said. 'How can you think so—it's not a question of veracity at all, but of judgment? 'Well,' said you, 'I have proof—ocular proof—I wouldn't say it if you didn't put me to it.' And then you told me that you visited the house the previous afternoon, and as you were entering the parlor, you saw Richard and Muriel standing together at the other end of the room, with their arms around each other, and saw them kiss each other. You drew back instantly, you said, without having been perceived by them, and made a clatter in the hall before you entered again. I could hardly forgive you at the time for having told me what you saw, or myself for having listened to you, for it was not a thing to be either told of or listened to. But I grant it happened naturally enough in the heat of the moment, and after all, I am glad to have known of an occurrence, the knowledge of which may prevent misunderstanding and trouble."

Harrington paused once more, with vague emotion struggling in his features and his eyes fixed sadly on vacancy. The truth of the matter was this: Witherlee had seen on the occasion referred to, two persons in the attitude described, one of whom was Wentworth, and the other a young lady who, at the first glance, he thought was Muriel, inasmuch as she wore a lilac dress such as Muriel wore at times. He had, as he had said, retreated instantly—quite astounded too, for he had made up his mind that Emily was Wentworth's sweetheart. But on entering again, he saw that he had been mistaken, and that the lady with Wentworth was not Muriel, but Emily. The illusion, however, made a strong impression on his fancy, and his mind teemed with tempting imaginings of Wentworth and Muriel in the Romeo and Juliet tableau. It was an easy step in his controversy with Harrington, begun simply for aggravation and continued with an obstinate desire to establish what he had so impudently assumed, to present his fancy as a fact, and insist upon it. This was a fair specimen of one of the good Fernando's lies, which were rarely sheer inventions, but generally had a basis of truth in them.

"Now, Fernando," resumed Harrington, "I want to ask you whether it is possible that you could have been mistaken? Are you absolutely sure that it was Muriel you saw with Wentworth, and not Miss Ames?"

Fernando's drowsy conscience awoke just enough to give him a lethargic pinch, and dozed off again.

"I do not see, Harrington," he replied with an injured air, "how I could be mistaken. There was nobody else in the room but Wentworth and Muriel when I first looked in. Emily was coming in through the conservatory door at the end of the parlor as I entered, but she was not there before."

This was an ingenious transposition of the fact. It was Muriel who came in at the conservatory door, and not Emily. But Fernando had covered his position famously. In the event of the truth coming out, he could swear that in the confusion of the moment he had mistaken one lady for the other, apologize profusely, and make the explanation seem plausible.

"It was certainly Muriel," he resumed. "Still the affair may be susceptible of a different interpretation. You must concede at least that Muriel and Wentworth like each other very much, and they might kiss each other and still be only friends."

"No," said Harrington, firmly—"that is not possible. That is not like Muriel. I know her too well to suppose that for a moment. If she kissed Wentworth, she loves him. I do not doubt you, Fernando. Their present close intimacy with each other confirms your story, I own. But something Richard said just now shook my belief—made me think, in fact, that you were in error, and I wanted to be doubly sure that you were not. Let me only say that I have a better motive for this inquiry than curiosity—and now let all this be forgotten. Never mention it again, I beg of you, to any person. Let it all pass forever."

Witherlee's conscience smote him terribly, and he felt maddened at his meanness, as Harrington strode away. But he was fully committed to his course, and to own his fault was impossible with him.

Wentworth, meanwhile, was standing apart with a gloomy face, listlessly watching the fencing. His fancy was still galloping furiously with him to the goal of the jealous lover, but it began to swerve from the track in spite of him, as he saw Harrington coming down the room. Harrington's mere presence was a constant demand on every person for the best that was in them; and before the conquering sweetness of his smile, Wentworth's jealous doubts and suspicions at once scattered and fled, and his nobler feelings rushed forward. The tears filled his bright eyes as Harrington came straight up to him and caught his hand. He tried to speak, but his lips faltered.

"Richard, I ask your pardon," said Harrington. "I am sorry to have annoyed you ; but it was entirely unintentional. I want to have a talk with you, that we may understand each other better. Not now—another time. In the meantime, let us be friends."

Wentworth wrung his hand, wholly vanquished, and unable to say a word.

"Come," said Harrington, gaily, with the muscles in his cheeks wrinkling again, and his teeth gleaming in his beard, with a rich smile—"come, that was only a zephyr. Let's go fence."

No more was said, and they went over to the fencing-ground, where Fisk was being punched and poked and interjected at and admonished by Monsieur Bagasse, to his utter bewilderment. In a few minutes, the master got through with him, and set him and Palmer to practise against each other He then turned to Wentworth, who had taken off hat and coat, and was chattering like a mercurial magpie, with his handsome face enveloped in a mask.

"Come, now, Missr Wentwort'," said Bagasse. "You pink zat ozzer vilet if you can. *En garde.*"

Wentworth laughed, and, crossing blades, they fell to. The young artist fenced briskly and well, though somewhat rashly. Once he contrived to touch the fencing-master on the arm, for which lucky stroke he got paid with half a dozen in succession on his breast.

"Thunder!" he exclaimed as he got the last, "what's the use of fencing with you, Bagasse? Nobody can touch you, and you're as light on your pins as though you were twenty."

The old man chuckled grimly, relapsing into his clumsiest and most ungainly attitude.

"Light!" put in Witherlee. "I guess he is. His legs are made of caout-chouc, I should think, judging by the way he can kick."

"Oh, yes, I can keek," returned Bagasse. "I haf my leg pretty su-ple."

He turned toward the post against which Witherlee was leaning, and laid his grimy finger on a notch a little above his own head. Witherlee stood aside, and every eye followed the fencing-master. Suddenly, rising on one foot, he dealt the notch a furious kick, amidst cries of "good" and "bravo." Sure enough, the leg had flown up to the mark, like a leg of india-rubber.

"Ha!" he exclaimed, complacently, "you do zat, you young men. Try now—evairy one."

Wentworth tried first, kicked high, but did not come within a foot of the mark. Whilt came next, stolid and taciturn, kicked, and tumbled over, amidst general laughter. Vukovich lifted his shapely leg, kicked within half a foot, and split his blue trowsers, at which he looked grieved, and swore softly in Hungarian, while the rest laughed at him. Then came Fisk and Palmer and the others, with poor success, and amidst much merriment.

In the quiet that followed, Whilt, who had been as dumb as a skull, suddenly began to shake and whinny so with guttural mirth, that everybody looked at him with surprise. It came out, after some inquiry, that he was laughing at Vukovich for having torn his trowsers, an incident which had just touched his sense of the ludicrous when everybody else had almost forgotten it. Of course there was another obstreperous roar of merriment, and Witherlee told Whilt he laughed too soon—he ought to have waited till next week—with other sarcasms of the same nature, which the slow Dutchman took into sober consideration.

"Come, Harrington," said Wentworth, "you try."

Harrington had stood apart, smiling amusedly, through all this clatter.

"Ah, Missr Harrin'ton, he can keek wis me," exclaimed Bagasse. "He keek sublime."

Harrington laughed, and advancing, took up a bit of chalk from the floor, and marked a line on the post, as much above his own head as the notch had been above the fencing-master's. Then poising a second, he threw up his leg, and brought away chalk on his boot. There was a general burst of acclamation.

"Ah, ha! it is grand—it is superb!" cried Monsieur Bagasse. "Missr Harrin'ton, he can keek wis me, he can fence wis me, he can shoot wis me, he can engage wis me in ze broadsword—ze single-steek, he can do everysing so I can. It is his talent. *Sacrebleu!* He is for-r-mi-dabble."

Harrington laughed, with an expression and gesture of deprecation.

"How many men could you fight together, Monsoor?" asked Palmer.

"Me? I fight you all. Evairy one. Togezzer," replied the Frenchman.

"Mawdoo!" ejaculated Palmer. "Isn't he a trump!"

"Come, Bagasse, that will do for the marines," said Wentworth. "You can't do it."

"Ah," replied the fencing-master, "you zink not? Bah! Come, I show you."

In a minute he had seven or eight of them, Wentworth, Vukovich, Palmer and Fisk included, masked and foiled. Then putting his back to the wall, he directed them to set upon him. It was agreed that if he was touched the contest was to end there. On the other hand, every combatant touched was to withdraw.

"Pardoo! It is splendid!" exclaimed Palmer.

"Mawdoo! It is fine!" returned Fisk.

The domestically-pronounced French oaths which prefixed these asseverations, were, of course, borrowed by Messrs. Fisk and Palmer from the "Three Guardsmen," and figured extensively on all possible occasions in their general conversation.

"Come, Harrington, you too," cried Wentworth.

"No, no—ex-cuse me—pardon," interrupted Monsieur Bagasse, smiling, grimacing and bowing all at once; "not Missr Harrin'ton. Zat will be too mush—vair many too mush."

Harrington colored slightly, and laughed. Monsieur Bagasse put on a mask, threw himself on guard, and stood girt with antagonists, with his foil playing like a pale gleam, menacing them all. Suddenly it darted—there was a brisk clatter of parries—and Vukovich was touched. It was a compliment to the skill of the gallant captain that Bagasse had got rid of him thus early in the game, and he came off simpering, and stroking his moustache complacently.

"He keel me fery queek, Meeser Haynton," he observed to the young man, who stood attentively watching the contest.

"Ah, Captain," returned Harrington gaily, addressing him in French, "but your ghost can fence better than most of us still."

The captain's vanity was evidently flattered by the compliment, for he swelled a little with an air of increased complacency, though he made no reply. Witherlee, who was standing behind him, a silent observer of the sport, glanced at him with a bilious sneer. Meanwhile, amidst shouts and laughter, and noisy appels and glizades, the young men were assailing Bagasse, trying all sorts of feints and tricks to penetrate his guard. Harrington watched him admiringly—so statue-still in the tumultuous press, his awkwardness and shabbiness gone, the wire globe of the mask giving a weird look to his head, his bent arm holding his assailants at bay, and the pale gleam of the foil glancing nimbly all about the arc of the ring. Presently the guarding foil whisked and rattled with a confusion of brilliant coruscations, playing like elfin lightning all around the semi-circle—the bent arm of the invincible figure at which all were lunging, straightened and darted thrice, rapid as a flash—and amidst mock groans and cries and laughter, Wentworth, Fisk, and Palmer withdrew. They came away vociferously mirthful, and before they had well got the masks off their flushed faces, the others were all touched and followed them, leaving Monsieur Bagasse standing alone, erect and martial, his one eye glowing like a coal in the proud grotesque smile of his swarthy visage, his left arm akimbo, holding the mask on his hip, and the victorious foil held aloft in his right hand, and quivering above his head like a rod of wizard lustre.

There were loud bravos and clapping of hands. The next instant the statue of military triumph dropped into the clumsy, sloven figure of Bagasse, and hobbled off to the claret-can. He came hurrying back presently with the foil and mask in one hand, and stood, the centre of a great smell of garlic, grinning curiously at Fisk and Palmer, who, in an ecstasy of excitement from their recent engagement, were playing they were D'Artagnan and Porthos, and poking furiously at each other with all the "Guardsmen" oaths and epigrams in full ventilation.

"Well, Missr Wentwort', what you zink now?" he asked, triumphantly.

"What do I think? I think you could have let Harrington come on too, and then have beaten us all," was the gay reply.

"Ah, no," returned Monsieur Bagasse, "not wis Missr Harrin'ton."

"Come, Meeser Haynton," said Vukovich; "you an' Mossieu Bagasse. Oblise me and dese sentilmen."

At once there was a clamor of beseechings, to which the

parties addressed presently yielded. Witherlee, who hated to see Harrington fence, because he fenced so well, quietly slipped away from the room. Fisk and Palmer stopped, and gathered with the others around the fencing-place. Meanwhile, Monsieur Bagasse took the violets from his jacket and laid them away ; then put on a plastron—an honor he had not paid to any other of his pupils that day, and resumed his mask. Harrington took off his coat and vest, and arrayed himself also in mask and plastron.

They took their places, and after performing the beautiful elaborate salute of the exercise, fell upon guard. Every eye was riveted on the stalwart grace of Harrington as he crossed blades with his antagonist. As for the French gladiator, excited by the coming contest with one who could call into play all his powers, his attitude was superb, and his transformation more complete than before.

The contest was begun by a feint, quick and light, on the part of the fencing-master, and in a second it was pass and parry with a rapturous flash and clash of steel. Presently the right foot of Bagasse beat the floor with the loud rat-tat of the appel, and foot and arm and body sprang forward with a terrific lunge. Harrington, immovable as a pillar, met it with a swift twirl of the wrist, and the next second both combatants were still, with their foils locked in a complete spiral from hilt to point.

Disengaging presently, the combatants saluted amidst suppressed murmurs of applause, crossed blades once more, and stood with each point seeking an opening. In a moment or two, Bagasse feinted again, and lunged in tierce. Harrington parried in seconde, letting his point fly up and his arm extend in the parry, and pushing home, his foil became a curve with the button resting on the bosom of the fencing-master.

It was the first hit, and everybody hurrahed. Presently the hurrah burst forth again for Bagasse, who had hit Harrington. In less than five minutes the combat grew almost as exciting as a duel with swords. To follow the dazzling rapidity of the lunges and parries became impossible. The gazers could only see a nimble play of rattling light between the two

–the lines of the foils lost in curves and gleams of brilliance —and the gloved sword-arms of the antagonists flying like twirling and darting shuttles above the clashing coruscations. The interest now centred in the aspect and expression of the combatants. Bagasse, throwing his whole fiery nature into the soul-entrancing action of the duel, was in an ecstasy of martial joy, and lunged and parried with exulting shouts and cries—a darting, swaying figure, terribly alert and alive, with the spring and strength of a fury. Harrington, on the contrary, was silent as death, impassible, elastic, swift—a regnant form of muscular grace poised in superb aplomb, that fell to half its height in the long lunges, and rose magnificent in the quick recoils. An atmosphere of fiery ether seemed to envelop the combatants, spreading its glorious delirium through the veins of the gazers, and kindling the delight of battle in their eyes. But as the combat continued, the wild passion of the action became so intense and real that the heroic glow began to pale and mingle with a cold affright, and Wentworth, beginning to feel his agitation master him, was on the point of shouting to Harrington to stop, when there was a sharp snap, followed by sudden silence, and the combat was over. Bagasse stood panting through his mask with a broken foil in his hand. Harrington breathing audibly in long, regular breaths through his, remained in attitude with his point lowered, like one awakened from a dream. The next instant, Bagasse broke the silence with a wild shout, and throwing away mask and foil, flung his arms around Harrington in a joyful embrace, and bursting away, vented the remnant of his joy by dealing the high notch on the post a kick that might have brought the roof down.

There was a ringing hurrah, followed by a burst of hearty laughter, congratulations, and shaking of hands all round.

"But, by Jupiter," cried Wentworth, "I'm glad its over, for, upon my word, I began to get frightened. Blessed if I ever saw you two have such a bout before! Bagasse, you old reprobate, I believe you were in earnest."

He turned with a peal of laughter upon the old man, who stood exhaling garlic, and wiping his hot face with a snuffy old red pocket handkerchief. Bagasse grinned good-naturedly, gave his old moustache a dab with the handkerchief, and thrusting out the latter with a joyful gesture, replied:

"I was teepsy, Missr Wentwort'—daid-drunk wis ze joay of ze beautifool en-countair. Hah! by dam! 'zat make me feel young."

"I should think so, you blood-thirsty old rapier!" bawled Wentworth. "And you," he continued, turning upon Harrington, "you were in earnest, too, I verily believe, and bent upon taking your fencing-master's life. A nice pair, both of you, for a peaceable young man like me to meet in a dark alley going home late."

Harrington, who was leaning against the wall, getting his wind, as the saying goes, laughed without replying. His usual pallor had given place to a faint pink, and his broad winged nostrils were lifting with his deep breaths under his lighted eyes and white forehead, on which the brown locks lay damp. Wentworth thought he had never seen him look more princely.

"But no," Wentworth rattled on, "I don't believe it of you, Harrington. For you're what Kingsley calls a muscular Christian. As for Bagasse, he's a muscular pagan, who lives on raw meat, gunpowder and brandy, and there's nothing too bad for me to believe of him. Is there, Bagasse?"

He patted the old man on the shoulder as he said it, looking smilingly in his face. Bagasse gazed with grotesque fondness at the handsome and gallant countenance, as on that of a privileged pet, and continued to mop his glowing visage.

"What's the time, Richard?" asked Harrington, beginning to dress himself.

"Quarter of ten by all that's good!" exclaimed the other, looking at his watch. "Time for me to be at the studio, and you at the books. But I won't say that, for upon my word, Harrington, you study too hard. The Pierian spring will be the death of you, young man."

"O, no," replied Harrington, laughing gaily. "I'm in good health. The daily bout with the foils or broadswords balances the hours at the books."

"Nevertheless you look rather Hamletish in your pallor," returned Wentworth. "Though to be sure the pale prince was a special good hand at the rapier, in which, as in other respects, you resemble him. 'The scholar, soldier, courtier's eye, tongue, sword—the expectancy and rose of the fair State' of Massachusetts—that's you, Harrington."

"Seems to me, Richard, the quotation bung and the head of the soft-soap barrel are both out together this morning," bantered Harrington.

"'I paint you in character,'" returned the mercurial Wentworth, with another Shaksperean reminiscence. "Being a member of the Boston Mutual Admiration Society, and this being Anniversary week, soft-soap is perfectly in order. Therefore, I affirm that you are of the Hamlet order plus Crichton, plus Raleigh, Sidney, Hatton, Blount, Southampton"——

"Shakspeare and Verulam," jeered Harrington.

"Together with Shakspeare and Verulam. And now that I have made a clean breast of it, and as you are dressed, suppose we depart. Young Mephistopheles, *alias* Witherlee, has gone already, I notice. Our mercantile friends are off, too, and a proper rowing they'll get for being late at the store this morning. Oh, Bagasse, Bagasse! you've much to answer for—corrupting the mercantile youth of this realm by traitorously erecting a fencing-school! Apropos of fencing, it's more than a week since we've had a bout with our dear fairy prince. By Jupiter! what a pleasure it is to see Muriel at the foils! I'm so glad you persuaded her to learn"——

"Oh, you're wrong there," interrupted Harrington. "It was she persuaded me to teach her. Muriel has a passion for liberal culture, and fencing is part of her programme."

"Isn't she glorious!" cried Wentworth with enthusiasm. "A woman?—a young goddess rather! By Jove! the best swimmer of all the girls last summer at Gloucester. The best skater last winter on Jamaica pond. Climbed the mountains in October with the best of us. Runs like Atalanta. Dances like Terpsichore. Sings like a seraph. Talks in a voice like Israfel's. Studies almost as hard as you do, Harrington. And now she fences like an angel. I declare she's a perfect young Crichtona. And yet how womanly withal! Not a touch of the masculine about her. Gay, free, strong, sweet—oh, fairy prince, there's none like you, none."

Harrington listened to this ardent celebration of the charms of her Wentworth called the fairy prince, in perfect silence and with a secret astonishment in his pale, controlled countenance. He believed Wentworth loved Muriel, but for the life of him he could not reconcile this lavish panegyric with that belief. For love is reticent, and we let expressive silence muse the sweetheart's praise. How then could Wentworth thus blazon his beloved? Harrington was puzzled.

"There's a curious element of surprise in Muriel, too," resumed Wentworth, with a musing air. "She is so gentle, so reposeful and graceful, that when she flashes out in these courageous physical accomplishments I always feel a little astonished. Don't you, Harrington?"

"Oh, no," returned Harrington. "She has a rich, versatile, inclusive nature. You know that this union of feminine gentleness and manly spirit is not so uncommon. There was the Countess Emily Plater, for example, the heroine of the Polish Revolution; yet with all her bravery, she was peculiarly tender and gentle. There, again, was the Maid of Saragossa, who fought for her country over the body of her lover; but Byron, who saw her often at Madrid, says she was remarkable for her soft, feminine beauty. Muriel is a woman of the same style, I suppose. Come, Richard, let's go."

They saluted the old Frenchman, who stood with the Hungarian at the pistol bench, and left the room.

CHAPTER IV.

MURIEL AND EMILY.

TEMPLE street slopes steeply down Beacon Hill, an aristocratic street of the aristocratic quarter.

In Temple street lived Muriel with her mother. Mrs. Eastman was a widow. Her husband, a young scholar, primarily a lawyer, had died three years after their marriage, when Muriel was but two years old. The effect of his death on his wife was peculiar. Fitly named Serena, so gentle and lovely was her nature, his death had not made her unhappy, but it had breathed a deeper quiet into her gentleness, and her life had been, since then, as calm as evening. She had been a poet—some of those exquisite little anonymous lyrics, of which America produces so many, and which float about through the press, scattering delight but winning no fame, were hers. But his death had stilled her muse forever. It seemed to have cloistered her spirit from the world. Never very fond of company, his decease had made her in love with solitude, and she spent much of her time in her own chamber, alone.

She was wealthy, having inherited from her husband a considerable property. Muriel, too, was rich in her own right; Mr. Eastman's brother, who had a great affection for her, having died a bachelor four or five years before, and left her a handsome fortune.

It was a large, sumptuously furnished house they lived in. Into its library, the fresh spring light, which lay so palely in the long, musty, powder-scented fencing-school, streamed that morning through crystal and purple panes, and filled the perfumed air with a gold and violet glory. The library was rich and dark in color, with walnut bookcases, deep-toned walls, and violet-velvet furniture. Its prevailing sombrous hue seemed to confine and intensify the cheerful radiance which filled it, like some ethereal lustrous liquid in a cup of ebony, touching the dim gilding of the picture-frames, the delicate ornaments here and there, and resting on a distinctive feature of the apartment, a large parlor organ, of dark oak and gold.

But the library's chief ornament that morning was Muriel —as lovely a blonde as ever grew to the gathered grace and vigor of twenty summers, and with that pervading glimmer of natural elegance and fine courtly breeding in her loveliness, which we express in the word debonair. She was standing very still, rapt in deep musing, with an open volume of Dante held in her left palm, and her white, nervous right hand resting on the page. A lilac dress of some soft tissue, stirred only above the light pulsations of her bosom, flowed in graceful folds, as she stood with one arched foot advanced and partly visible at its margin, and revealed the enchanting harmony of her tall and stately figure. The dress came quite up to the neck, flowering over there in a charming ruffle of lace, above which bloomed her exquisite countenance, virginal and gracious as the morning, as dewy-sweet, as fresh, as spiritually pure. The complexion, fair and clear as a pond-lily, was radiant with perfect health. Color, faint as the dawn, tinted the oval cheeks, and the sweet, curved mouth wore the hue of the wild-brier rose. The large grey eyes were softened with a golden sheen. Amber hair, with a tint of gold in it, parted over the serene and open brow, and rising from the head, as we see it in the Greek statues, rippled down in wavy tresses around the delicate ears, to gather behind in soft, thick loops of antique beauty. Noble and debonair from head to foot, and all imparadised in charm, so on that morning stood Muriel.

Who would have dreamed that the reverie in which she was absorbed was too solemn to have grown upon her spirit from the mighty Tuscan page before her? Who could have imagined, gazing upon her calm loveliness, that a great and awful, though silent, struggle had shaken her heart? Yet it was so. The event which can most convulse a woman's life had come to her. She loved Harrington, and it had dawned upon her that he loved her friend Emily.

She had met it bravely. With that revelation her heart had risen to the level of heroic story, and in the spiritual strife which makes life tremble to its centre, she was the victor. She knew that the world lay lonely and disenchanted before her, but she was calm. She knew that life's fairest hope was unaccomplished, life's loveliest dream dissolved, but she was strong. She saw afar the dark battalia of the coming years of sadness, and her heart rose to meet them with the pulses of Marathon. It was love's crowning hour with her—the hour of sacrifice, renunciation, the high soul's rapture of martyrdom—the hour of bravery and sad, generous joy.

But now the immediate strife in her spirit was over, and in

the deeps of her reverie, she saw, strangely distinct as in a dream, the phantom face of Harrington smiling palely upon her from an illimitable distance. It had never before been so vivid in her vision, nor had it ever come to her with such a sense of being mystically far-removed. As she dreamed upon it, its visionary remoteness seemed less a symbol of the distance of unanswering love than of love immortal withdrawn by death to smile upon her from the depths of Eternity. But it was Love, not Death, that had divided them: he had receded from her to love her friend. She was resigned that it should be so—happy still, though lonelier, that it was so. Hers was the true love which gives and needs, but asks not; and aspiring only to the happiness and good of the beloved one, willingly, for that, resigns all that makes life most precious and finds a sad joy in the sacrifice. It was her loss, but another's gain. There was joy still in the belief that he was happy in his love for her friend—in the faith that she was worthy of that love—in the trust that the lofty purposes for which spirits work on earth in wedded lives would be achieved by them.

Calm, tender, solemn and regal flowed her reverie, haunted ever by the phantom face that was never to be near her again—never to smile henceforth in her dreams save at this visionary distance, which seemed to her prescient spirit ever less and less the distance of unanswered love, ever more and more the distance of love responding from the serene depths of Eternity.

"Muriel!"

A hushed, wondering voice spoke her name. A figure stood before her at a little distance. Voice and figure were alike remote and dim to her tranced mind.

"Muriel! Good heavens! Muriel!"

It was Emily. She saw her standing before her, astonished—she herself tranquil, clearly cognizant, and utterly unsurprised. A superb brunette, attired in rich brown silk, with a brilliant scarlet scarf on her shoulders, admirably contrasted with her dark hair, and the sunny gold and rose of her complexion.

"Why, Muriel, you frightened me! I spoke, and yet you

did not hear. What a strange, still shine there is in your eyes! One would think you were a somnambulist."

The happy and noble face smiled at her as she spoke, and two bright tears flowed upon it. A moment, and the book fell to the floor, and embracing Emily, she kissed her crimson mouth, and fondly gazed into her countenance. At the pressure of the soft bosom against her own, at the touch of the fragrant and dewy lips, Emily's spirit rose in fervent affection, and in that moment her heart clasped Muriel like her arms.

"I was a dreamer, and not a somnambulist, dear Emily," said Muriel. "I was lost in a reverie, deeper than I have ever known, and it gave me the peace of a holy thought."

"What was the thought, dear Muriel?" asked Emily.

"One that you can appreciate, dear lover," was the tender and gay reply. "The thought that life is truliest life in the greatness and sweetness of love."

A refluent jealousy vainly strove at that moment to enter the heart of Emily. The charm of her friend's gracious countenance, and of her mellow silver voice, was strong upon her. But the rich color came to her golden face and over her broad, low brow to the roots of her hair, and her lustrous brown eyes wandered into vacancy.

"Yes, Muriel," she answered, after a moment's hesitation, "I agree with you. Life is truliest life in loving and being loved."

"No, that is not agreeing with me," said Muriel, with a frank smile. "Life is sufficiently life in loving. To love is enough.—But come, dear Emily, your chocolate voice shall not be used in discussion, but in confession. We must talk this morning, for I fancy you have some little grudge against me, and it is time for us to understand each other, like good friends.

Emily colored again, and the tears were very near her eyes. She loved Muriel, yet could not help being jealous of her, believing, as she did, that she was her rival for the love of Wentworth. But she laughed lightly, dissembling her emotion, and asked:

"Why is my voice a chocolate voice, Muriel? That is an odd epithet."

"A very good one, dear," replied Muriel, laughing, and picking up the Dante from the floor. "Your voice is a contralto. Sounds, you know, have their analogical colors, as Madame de Staël knew when she said the sound of the trumpet was crimson. Now the analogue of contralto is brown. Chocolate, too, is brown. Hence your voice is chocolate."

"Well done, Muriel! Come, now, that is really ingenious."

Muriel laughed her clear and mellow silver laugh, and looked playfully at Emily.

"Thank you for the compliment, *mignonne*. I shall make it over to the gentleman from whom I stole the idea."

"Stole? It's not yours, then?"

"O yes! It's mine, because I stole it."

"And who from? Harrington?"

"Guess again, dear! But *n'importe*—no matter. Come and sit here with me."

Muriel moved smilingly away to a couch of violet-velvet, and sinking upon the cushioned seat, waved her hand to her friend. Emily stood unheeding, in an attitude of sumptuous repose, with her rounded arms folded, a faint smile on her face, and her lustrous and lambent eyes half-veiled by their long lashes. The damask color was bright on her cheeks and on her parted lips, and with every slow breath, her bosom slowly lifted and fell, stirring the rich and heavy attar-of-rose odor which brooded slumberously about her form.

"Thou gorgeous queen-rose of Ispahan, why dreamest thou?" said Muriel's voice of silver mockery. "Didst thou not hear me call? Come, I say!"

The beautiful brunette did not obey, but raised her proud patrician head from its drooping curve, and vaguely sighed. Muriel rose, lightly glided over to her, clasped her waist with both arms, and standing a little on one side and bending forward—a fresh and full-grown lily—a fair, gay woman, with the grace and glimmer of a bewitching child in her womanhood—looked with a naive and radiant, half-mocking, half-serious smile, into the face of her she had called the gorgeous queen-rose of Ispahan. Presently she began to lead her to the couch. Emily held back, but Muriel's clasp tightened, and yielding to the firm, fairy strength with which, though strong, she was unable to cope, Emily suffered herself to be conducted to the seat.

"Ah, stayaway," blithely said Muriel, sitting beside her, and playfully shaking a finger at her in sportive reproach, "who is the stronger now? You are fairly captured, and I hold you my prisoner until peace is concluded."

Emily, amused by this pleasantry, showed the pearls of her red mouth in a brilliant laugh over her indolently folded arms.

"And if you could only fence," continued Muriel, in the same tone as before, "I would conquer a peace at the point of my rapier. Can't I persuade you to learn, for that especial purpose?"

"Indeed you can't," said Emily. "It's not in the line of my accomplishments, though you have included it in yours. Bless me! Muriel, what will you be learning next? Dancing on the tight-rope, I suppose, or standing on one toe on the back of a galloping horse, like a circus girl."

"That would be fine, dear, wouldn't it!" returned Muriel. "Decidedly, I never thought of the tight-rope or the circus horse before. It is really an idea! But let us cry truce to this nonsense, for indeed I have something to say to you."

Moving a little nearer to Emily as she spoke, her frolic manner vanished, and her face grew sweetly serious.

"When you found me so entranced this morning," she said, after a long pause, "I was thinking of you, dear Emily—in part of you. You know how much I love you. We grew up together from girlhood, and among all your friends there is none whose happiness is more closely entwined in yours than mine."

Emily's heart beat fast, and the moisture gathered in her down-dropped eyes. She did not look up, but she felt that the clear eyes of Muriel were fixed on her face.

"We have had many happy hours together, Emily," murmured the low, sweet voice; "and when you came here two weeks ago, on this visit, it seemed that the happiest hours of all, both for you and me, were beginning. Happiest for me because I thought that what makes life sweetest to us all had come to you—here—in this house."

There was another pause, in which Emily bowed her head, with an inexpressible sense of passionate sorrow.

"And it has come to you, Emily," continued Muriel. "You did not tell me—you kept your heart's secret closely—but I saw it—I felt it—though I so strangely mistook its object. I did not think my intuition could so mislead me, but it did. For I thought your feeling was for Richard and his for you."

Emily smiled serenely, but under the serene smile her wild grief raged.

"How could you think so, Muriel?" she lightly asked.

"I judged so from his manner toward you, and yours toward him," replied Muriel.

Emily laughed gaily.

"I cannot imagine," she answered, "how you could think his attentions meant anything more than the ordinary reckless gallantries it is his nature to lavish on young women. And as for myself, I should indeed be weak to love such a person as he."

She said it with the most bland and tranquil indifference of voice and manner—grief and scorn and the wild resentment of slighted love all hidden and raging in her heart.

"Emily!" The silver voice was raised in mild reproach, and she felt the nervous hands suddenly clasp her arm. "How can you speak so of Richard! Indeed, you do him great injustice. I know him better than to think that of him. Emily, you amaze me! Why, how can you imagine him such a person!"

Emily smiled blandly. She may well defend him, was her thought, for she loves him. Calmly lifting her lustrous eyes, she saw Muriel's wondering face all suffused with generous color. Yes, she thought, it is her love for him.

"Why Muriel," she remarked quietly, "everybody knows

he is a handsome young flirt. It is his general reputation. His words, his looks, his manner toward women are proof enough of it, I'm sure. Nobody thinks more highly of him than Fernando, but even Fernando, spite of his friendship, says it is the great fault of his character."

Muriel laughed suddenly, then looked very grave.

"I'm afraid, Emily," she said quickly, "that it is Fernando who has put this strange and ridiculous idea into your head."

"Not at all," quietly responded Emily. "Fernando only corroborates my own judgment. But if you cannot trust the opinion of a man's intimate friends and associates, what can you trust?"

"I would not trust Fernando's opinion of anybody," said Muriel.

"Why?" asked Emily, coolly.

"Why, dear? Because our good Fernando is nothing if not critical," piquantly answered Muriel.

"Do you think him false?" said Emily.

"Hum!" Muriel looked doubtful—then laughed. "To tell the truth, *mignonne*, I think he is, on a small scale, the Iago of private life."

"You are witty, Muriel, but you are not just," was Emily's cold reply.

Muriel was silent for a moment.

"Never mind," she resumed. "We will not discuss Fernando. You will yet think better of Richard, I am confident, but as you are not in love with him, it's no matter."

As I am not in love with him! thought Emily. She could hardly keep from shuddering with the flood of conflicting passion that shot through her. The wild impulse to tell Muriel that she had cast her life upon him, burst into her mind. What? Tell her that she loved him, and that he had slighted her love; that he had won her heart from her; that once, in one electric moment, his arms had enfolded her, his lips had pressed hers, and then, his whim gratified, he had left unspoken the words her soul panted to hear, and coldly alienated himself from her! Tell all this to her, whom he was now wooing, and who loved him! Passionate pride arose, and held the impulse down.

"Yes, I own that I was mistaken," pursued Muriel, "strangely mistaken, in dreaming that you and Richard were lovers. Still, there was love. It is my joy to think that you love another dear friend of mine, and that he loves you. And my joy is all the greater to feel that you are above our social prejudices—that you are great enough to love one whose wealth is in his manhood. You and Harrington"——

Emily turned quickly, her face calm, but all aglow with rich scarlet, and lighted with an indefinable smile. Muriel, pale with love and sacrifice, her clear voice trembling, and her eyes humid, stopped as she met that singular look, and changed color.

"Forgive me, dear Emily," she said quickly. "I would not speak of it—I would not touch a subject cloistered even from me—but for one reason, which I will tell you presently. But first let me say that I was again surprised when I read in your mutual attentions for the last few days—yours and Harrington's—the tokens of your love. For I had thought Harrington's heart was not free—that he loved another. Now let me"——

"Who?" interrupted Emily. "Who did you think he loved? Tell me. I am curious to know."

"Nay, dear," replied Muriel. "It would be unnecessary to tell that. Since I was wrong, is it not better to let it go unmentioned? Surely it is."

Perhaps Emily might have guessed who it was, had she looked then at Muriel's face. But her eyes were downcast, and she was vainly striving to imagine who Muriel could mean. Then the remembrance of how constant and reckless had been her recent attentions to Harrington, and, though paid only to abate Wentworth's supposed triumph by convincing him that she cared nothing for him, how good a ground they afforded to Muriel for her present belief, came into her mind, and she almost groaned. But what would have been her grief had she dreamed of the effects of her conduct on Muriel?

"Now, dear Emily," resumed Muriel, "let me come at once to the only sad thing in all this—in a word, to the reason which compels me to speak thus frankly to you for the sake of our friendship, which I cannot bear to see disturbed even for an hour. You know I have known John for a long time, and that he is my best, my most cherished friend. I cannot tell you how much he has been and is to me—with how many noble hours he is associated. Since I have thought you loved him, I have been conscious—painfully conscious—that your manner has not been what it once was to me—that you have felt our communion—his and mine—as something that interfered with your relation to him."

Muriel paused, earnestly gazing in the face of her friend, to be certain that she was not offending her. The hot color suffused Emily's face, but she was calm and even smiled. Yes, I am jealous of her, was her thought, but it is because she loves Wentworth and he her. And she thinks I love Harrington! Then came the impulse to undeceive Muriel in this regard. Pride arose on one side, taunting her to confess that she had paid court to a man she did not love. Shame arose on the other side, urging her to conceal the thoughtless folly of having lured that man to love her. Both together held the impulse down.

"Dear Emily," pursued Muriel, in tender and pleading tones, "do not let this be so. Do not think of me as your rival because I am your lover's friend. There cannot be in our relation—his and mine—anything to weaken his faith to you. Oh, believe that, and let there be no discord between you and me! There, I have said all. I might have waited till he or you told me that you were lovers. But I could not bear to see you tortured with the feeling that there was rivalry between us, or to see our friendship in any way impaired. Forgive me for my haste—for my brusque plain-speaking; and love me truly as I love you."

Leaning over to her, as she ended, Muriel, the bright tears welling from her eyes, embraced her tenderly. Emily, smiling wanly, her brain whirling with affection, with self-scorn and passionate despair, clasped the loving form to her breast, and held it there. In a few moments Muriel disengaged herself, her happy and noble face radiant, but wet with tears, smiled at Emily, and smiling, rose and glided from the room.

CHAPTER V.

LA BOSTONIENNE.

Emily covered her face with her hands, and for more than fifteen minutes sat in silent stupor where Muriel had left her. At length she sprang up, throwing her clenched hands from her in agony, and walked the library. Her eyes were hotly lustrous, her damask cheeks vivid with heightened color, her parted lips wore an unnatural bloom, and the flush of fever deepened the sunny gold of her complexion. Slowly, with measured steps, to and fro, up and down, she paced the room, with rustling robes, like a doomed Sultana.

"Great Heaven!" she murmured, stopping suddenly in the centre of the floor, and clasping her hands; "to know that it has come to this! She thinks I love Harrington. How shall I undeceive her! How shall I undeceive him! How extricate myself from this maze! O, for a friend, a counsellor! Richard, Richard, how can you treat me so basely! To turn from me—and in my very sight to turn from me to her! O, that I could die, that I could die!"

Wringing her clasped hands, a wild heart-break in her face, she heard a light step in the passage. The door opened, and Muriel reappeared, gay and elegant as usual, and bending into a graceful courtesy, half playful, half unconscious, as she came forward. As for Emily, no one could have discovered a trace of emotion in her. At the sound of Muriel's footsteps, she had dissolved into a sumptuous beauty, with a rich, indolent smile on her brilliant-colored face, her bare, rounded arms folded on her bosom, and her figure in nonchalant and queenly repose.

"Ah, neglectful one," said Muriel, shaking a finger at her, "to let your moulding drop to pieces for lack of a little water! I told you yesterday that you ought to wet the clay. Just now I looked into the studio, and saw the poor Muriel almost crumbling. Thou naughty girl!"

"I declare I forgot it," replied Emily. "I meant to water the bust yesterday, and it slipped my mind. I will see to it presently."

"If you don't, I'll never give you another sitting," returned Muriel. "So take notice."

All sorts of studies and arts were pursued at the house in Temple street. Muriel, amidst her botany, drawing, moulding, music, Latin, French, German, Italian, miscellaneous reading, and her vigorous calisthenics, had for a year past interpolated the art of fencing, which Harrington had taught her, and which was at present her grand passion. Emily, who had been absent at Chicago for the last ten months, had previously learned from Wentworth and Muriel how to mould in clay, and upon her return, urged on chiefly by him, had resumed this crowning accomplishment of hers, and began to develop in it unusual talent.. The bust referred to was one of Muriel, which she had been working on. Lately, the check she had received in her love for Wentworth, had sadly damped the ardor of her passion for sculpture, and the bust had been neglected.

"Don't let your belief in Wentworth's flirtations interfere with your pursuit of the fine arts, *mignonne*," continued Muriel, gaily.

"Dear me, no!" languidly returned Emily. "His flirtations are nothing to me."

"Certainly not," said Muriel, sportively patting her on the shoulder. "And as you owe the bad boy a debt of gratitude for showing you how to mould, be civil to him, I pray."

"Civil? And am I not civil to him?" returned Emily, smiling with lazy serenity.

"Ah, wicked one, no," said Muriel, silverly murmuring the words into Emily's ear, as she stood behind her with her arms around her waist, and her face looking jestingly over her shoulder. "Not a bit civil. Didn't I see that freak of the violets this morning! I know that hurt Richard's feelings. Not because you did not give them to him, but on account of your manner, which was indescribably disdainful. I verily believe Fernando had something to do with that transaction. What was it he said to you at the table when I saw you color?"

"Oh, nothing," replied Emily, blushing. "It was something he meant for a joke, though I thought it rather impudent. To tell the truth, Muriel, I did intend to share the violets between Harrington and Wentworth, when Fernando observed to me that Wentworth would be delighted to receive a true-love posy from me, or something of that sort. Now that provoked me, and I knew Wentworth had put him up to say it, for I saw them whispering and laughing together just before, and I"——

"My dear Emily," said Muriel, in a beseeching tone, coming around in front of the speaker, "how can you be so unreasonable as to jump to such a conclusion?"

"Oh! I know he had something to do with it," returned Emily, obstinately; "so I just punished him by giving all the flowers to Harrington. I know it piqued him, and I'm glad of it."

Muriel sighed, and then laughed, feeling painfully the littleness of this conduct, yet excusing Emily out of her sense of the provocation of Witherlee.

"*N'importe*, Emily dear," she said lightly, after a pause. "It matters not. But I blame Fernando for it all. I am not unjust to him, for I appreciate his power and talents, and very often find him agreeable enough. But I do not like his carping and cavilling and the envious spirit of him, and I cannot help thinking that he is untruthful, and given to mischief-making. What he said to you was really impudent—and, by the way, it was quite matched by the impudence of his joining us this morning, uninvited, and so coolly walking into the house with us unasked. If I had not been amused at it, I should have been indignant. It was a cool proceeding, faith, —positively arctic."

Muriel paused to laugh delightedly at the drollery of the recollection.

"However, let it all go," she continued. "Only, Emily, beware of being influenced by Fernando. That's good counsel. For my part, if I catch him at any of his tricks, we shall quarrel outright. I believe I never quarrelled with anybody in my life, and perhaps the experience may be refreshing. But come—business before pleasure. What are you going to do to-day? I must go on a tour—will you come with me?"

"Where are you going?" asked Emily.

"First and foremost, I am on a Pardiggle excursion among two or three families of my parish," replied Muriel.

Dickens' "Bleak House," was coming out in serials at that period, and Muriel, with the rest of the town, was full of it, and was particularly delighted with Mrs. Pardiggle, to whom she jestingly likened herself when she made visits of charity.

"The Pardiggle path will first lead me to poor Mrs. Roux," continued Muriel. "Mrs. Roux, in Southac street, the wife of the colored man who was here the other day to white-wash the studio. She had another child born a couple of months ago—did I tell you?—and we must take care of the black babies as well as the white ones, you know, and the black mothers, too, as well as the white mothers, most gorgeous honey-darling."

Emily smiled at the pet name Muriel bestowed upon her, admiringly gazing meanwhile at the fair face, half arch, half serious, which looked at her over the lace ruffle.

"Poor Roux was very sick in March," continued Muriel, "and has only got to work again recently—so as times are hard with them, mother and I have taken them under our wing."

"How did you find them out, Muriel?" asked Emily.

"Oh, through Harrington;" answered her friend. "Harrington is the general repository of the grievances and troubles of everybody he falls in with, and when he can't help, he tells us, and we help. We are a Pardiggle society. He is the President, and mother and I are the Board of Directors."

"I have a mind to become a member," said Emily, smilingly. "But where next?"

"Next," answered Muriel, "I am going to make a call on the Tenehans. That's an Irish family in North Russell street. Then there is Judith, the sempstress, for whom I have some sewing. Let's see—that's all to-day, I believe. Then I'm going to see Captain Greatheart."

"Who's that?" interrupted Emily.

"Mr. Parker, of course."

"Mr. Parker? Pray what entitles a lawyer to that Bunyanesque"——

"A lawyer! Bless me, Emily, where are your five wits! It is *the* Mr. Parker I mean—Theodore Parker. And is he not a model Captain Greatheart? The nineteenth century Apollyon has reason to know him in that character, at all events. So too have the poor Christians and Christianas, for whom he is guarding shield and smiting sword."

Emily bowed her head in assenting abstraction.

"I'm going to see if he has in his library a book I want," continued Muriel. "Then, perhaps, I'll go to the Athenæum, and refresh my art-sense—no I won't either, for I remember Fernando said he would be there, and I can't enjoy pictures with his everlasting cavilling in my ears."

"Fernando has exquisite tastes," said Emily, musingly.

"Fernando has exquisite *dis*tastes," returned Muriel, piquantly. "Which I shall not enjoy this morning. So instead of the Athenæum, I'll go to the Anti-Slavery Convention at the Melodeon. Uncle Lemuel was here last evening, you know, talking up Union-saving and the Fugitive Slave Law, and Mr. Webster, and all that sort of thing, and I shan't feel right again till I hear the voices of the Good Old Cause from the platform of the Garrisonians."

"Well, Muriel, you are the most astonishing Bostonienne I know," said Emily, laughing. "I should just like to analyze your mélange. Let's see now. In the first place, you defy fashion, and insist on wearing dresses that show your shape, when all the rest of us are swaddled in half a dozen starched petticoats, and are pining in secret for the hoops of our grandmothers to come into vogue again. You"——

"How many have you on, honey-bird? Come, ''fess,' as Topsy says," demanded Muriel, mischievously.

"I? Oh, I'm moderate," returned Emily. "I only wear six."

Muriel put up her hands, orbed her mouth, and opened her large eyes in mock horror.

"Goodness me!" said Emily, laughing and smoothing her bounteous skirts, "Six is nothing. Why everybody wears seven. Eight and nine are not uncommon. And there's Bertha Appleby wears twelve."

Muriel burst into low, silver laughter, in which she was joined by her friend.

"To resume," continued Emily when the mirth had subsided, "you won't wear low-necked dresses at parties. You don't waltz. You don't flirt. You don't care to be admired. You don't run after the lions. You pay court to all the taboo people, visit those who are voted out of good society, ask them to visit you"——

"And cry 'à bas la Madame Grundy,'" put in Muriel, with a free and frolic toss of her arm.

"Yes, and cry, 'down with Mrs. Grundy,'" continued Emily. "Then you cultivate the most miscellaneous and outlandish set of characters—authors and actors, and actresses, and reformers, and clergymen, and musicians and comeouters and people respectable and disrespectable all meet here, higgledy-piggledy, in the most heterogeneous mixture—the most chaotic"——

"O no, Emily dear, not chaotic," interposed Muriel, "not chaotic but cosmic. I accept them all as Nature accepts them all. Down with the walls! That's my principle. No castes—no factitious distinctions. Let fine people of all sorts come together and learn to know each other. Democracy forever!"

"Yes, indeed—but doesn't good society get horrified at your doings!" laughingly exclaimed Emily "Doesn't the whole neighborhood hold up its hands at you? Why, your aristocratic acquaintance look at you with perfect horror."

"Well," rejoined Muriel, with nonchalant gaiety, "you know what Mercutio says: 'Their eyes were made to see and let them look.'"

"And then your studies," ran on Emily. "Perfectly omnivorous. French, German, Italian, Latin, music, drawing, painting, moulding, science, poetry, history, oratory, philosophy, Shakspeare, Bacon, Dante, Plato, Goethe, Swedenborg."

"And Fourier," interpolated Muriel. "I've added him to my list, you know, and Uncle Lemuel says I ought to blush to own that I read him. The poor man thinks Fourier had hoofs and horns and a harpoon tail."

"Yes, I know," rejoined Emily with a laugh. "He says such works loosen the foundations of society and are fatal to the interests of morality," she added, mimicking Uncle Lemuel's stock phrases, which he used in common with a great many people of the highest respectability. "But to resume, Muriel: there are your muscularities. You skate, you swim, you climb mountains, you ride horseback, you walk ten miles on a stretch, you saddle or harness your horse like a stableman, you catch up your horse's feet, and look at the shoes like a blacksmith, you dance, you row, you lift weights, you swing by your hands, you walk on the parallel poles"——

"And fence," suggested the amused listener. "Don't forget the fencing!"

"Yes, and fence with Wentworth and Harrington, besides turning the studio up-stairs into a gymnasium. Then you go on these tours, as you call them. You have a regular parish of negroes and Irish people, and all sorts of forlorn characters, on whom you shower food, and clothes, and books, and goodness knows what else. And you go to theatres, circuses, operas, lectures, picture-galleries, woman's rights conventions, abolition meetings, political gatherings of all sorts at Faneuil Hall, with the most delectable impartiality. Then you used to attend church at William Henry Channing's, which our best society thought horrid."

"And now Theodore Parker's" ——

"Yes, and now Theodore Parker's, which they think worse still. And you have harbored fugitive slaves in your house, and helped them off to Canada. And you swallow Garrison and Parker Pillsbury"——

"And adore Wendell Phillips."

"Yes, and adore Wendell Phillips. And subscribe for the 'Commonwealth' newspaper, which your uncle says ought to be put down"——

"And the 'Liberator.'"

"Yes, and subscribe for Garrison's 'Liberator,' which is your uncle's *bête noire*. In short, Muriel, I wonder how you keep your popularity. I'm sure I couldn't do all that you do, and have these cozy old citizens, these formal and fashionable mammas, these mutton-chop whiskered, English-mannered gentlemen, and Beacon street belladonnas, so fond of me as they are of you. But then, I suppose they don't know the extent of your heresies."

"My dear Emily," returned Muriel, "please to remember that you're from the rural districts. You live at Cambridge half the year, and you've been off there in Chicago for the last ten months, so you don't know how many Boston ladies do all, or nearly all, that I do. I'm not half such an original as you imagine. But see here, bird of Paradise, time passes. Are you going with me, or not? I'll go anywhere, or do anything you like, after the Pardiggle excursion is over. That must be attended to, anyway."

Before Emily could reply, the door opened, and Mrs. Eastman came in. A beautiful, fair-complexioned, gentle lady, of middle age, with silver-grey hair falling in graceful tresses beside her face. As beautiful in her waning day as Muriel in her matin prime.

"Not gone yet, dear," she said, with a bright smile.

"Just going, mother."

"Well the carriage is below, and here is little Charles come to say that Mrs. Roux is rather poorly. And he says, dear, which I hope is not true, that some of those dreadful men are in town."

Muriel's face grew grave, and she flew to the door.

"Charles!" she called. "Come up-stairs, Charles."

"Yes, Miss Eas'man. Comin' right up, Miss Eas'man," chirruped a shrill, smart voice, from below, followed by the softened bounce of feet on the carpeted flight, coming up two stairs at a time.

"What is it?" asked the wondering Emily.

"The kidnappers," returned Muriel. "Come in, Charles."

A most astonishing fat negro boy entered, cap in hand, ducking and bowing, with a scrape of his foot, and showing a saucy row of splendid white teeth in the droll grin which expanded his big mouth and nostrils; his great eyes meanwhile revolving rapidly around the library, and momently vanishing in their whites with a facility curious to behold. His face, surmounted by a mass of ashen-colored wool, parted on one side into two great shocks, was exactly the shape of a huge d'Angouleme pear, the great blobber cheeks making the forehead, which was respectably large, seem small. His complexion was a clean, warm, dark grey. He was not tall for his age, which was about ten years, but he was broad. Breadth was the characteristic of his figure. His short arms were broad; his short legs were broad; his body was broad; and he broadened his face at present with a grin. He had big feet, clad in battered old shoes; and big hands, which just now played with his cap. He wore a grey jacket thrown back from his fat chest, which was covered with a blue and white small-striped shirt; and his legs were incased in grey trowsers. Grey, in fact, was the prevailing color of him all over. The face was intelligent, and full of precocity, assurance, and supreme self-importance, with what people call a little-old-man-look pervading it all, though this was only seen when he was in his grave moods, and now was not visible.

"What is it, Charles?" anxiously asked Muriel.

"Please, Miss Eas'man," he began, suddenly stopping his grin, and looking preternaturally demure, with a portentous roll of his saucer eyes, "please, Miss Eas'man, I jus' run up here like a bob-tail nag for to say—to wit, that Brudder Baby is fus' rate; so is Josey; so is Tom; so is I; so is father; and mar isn't not nearly so well, an' she feels right bad lest father should be took off, an' them kidnappers is in town, an' we'll all be took off, jus' so sure's my name's Tugmutton, Miss Eas'man—yes, Miss Eas'man, there aint no sort of a chance for us anyway, jus' so sure as you're born."

Having delivered himself in shrill, fluent tones, to this effect, the young imp grinned cheerfully, and stood rapidly twirling his cap on his hand like a pin-wheel, and rolling his eyes at the three ladies. Muriel looked at him with a still face, but Mrs. Eastman smiled, and Emily, who had seen him once before, laughed amusedly.

"What an odd creature he is," said the latter. "To think of his preferring to be called by that droll name? Don't you like to be called Charles?" she asked, addressing the boy.

"Like it extrornerly, Miss Ames—never git done likin' that name noways, Miss Ames," he asseverated, with great earnestness. "But you see, Miss Ames, 'taint so familiar like as Tugmutton. Father calls me Tugmutton, an' mar, an' Josey, an' Tom, an' everbody, since I was knee-high to a toad, Miss Ames. Tugmutton 's my Christian name, Miss Ames, and Charles 's my given name as Miss Eas'man give me, Miss Ames."

"Look here, Charles," said Muriel, suddenly, "are you sure the kidnappers are in town?"

"Dead sure, Miss Eas'man—jus' as sure as can be."

"How do you know? Who told you?"

"Laws! Miss Eas'man! Why it's in the newspaper!" blurted out the imp, rolling up the whites of his eyes at her with a look of amazed reproach.

"O, no, Charles! It's not in the newspaper, for I've read the papers this morning," said Muriel, smiling, and shaking her finger at him.

Tugmutton looked demure for a second, then smiled sheepishly, furtively rolled his eyes one side at the wall, and fidgeted on his feet, and with his cap and jacket.

"Laws, Miss Eas'man! it's goin' to be in the paper. Paper 'll be chock full of it to-morrow."

"O, I guess it's not true," said Muriel, slowly, with a relieved smile. "It must be a false alarm, Charles."

"My gosh, Miss Eas'man, I don't believe there's one word of truth in it," said Tugmutton, puckering out his great lips with an air of precocious contempt, and whirling his cap on his hand. "Never *could* make me believe one word of that story. It's jus' nothin' but a weak invention of the enemy."

The phrase, which Tugmutton had picked up from somebody, was so odd in his childish mouth, and so oddly expressed, that Emily burst into a fit of laughter, and threw herself into a chair, while both Mrs. Eastman and Muriel smiled. Tugmutton grinned delightedly at the effect of his speech, and then looked awfully demure and dignified.

"Anyhow," he continued, "all them foolish colored folks are believin' that story. Them folks has jus' got no gumption, anyway. Talkin' about that story in the street, now—millions of them."

"Are the colored people out in the street, Charles?" asked Mrs. Eastman.

"In the street? Laws, Missus Eas'man, Southac street's full of 'em," returned Tugmutton.

"There may be something in it, after all, mother," said Muriel. "I'll go."

"Bless me, Muriel, are you not afraid?" exclaimed Emily.

"Afraid! Not at all. What possible danger is there? Besides, I want to see what's going on. Come, let's go."

Emily rose and followed Muriel, who left the room for her bonnet.

"Come, Charles," said Mrs. Eastman, moving to the door; "come down-stairs, and I'll give you something to eat. Little men like you are always ready for pie."

Tugmutton, with the prospect of pie in his delighted vision, flashed into a huge grin, which displayed all his ivories, and lit his blobber-grey face; and checking the impulse which prompted him to execute a shuffling breakdown on the spot, he dodged out at the door after Mrs. Eastman.

CHAPTER VI.

AN EPISODE OF THE REIGN OF TERROR.

In a few minutes the two young ladies, cloaked and bonneted, came out into the sunlit street, where stood the carriage, which Patrick, the inside man, had brought up from Niles's stables. Emily, characteristically indifferent to the driver, swept in and took her seat. Muriel, on the contrary, who was on friendly terms with everybody, courteously bent her head to him as she passed. The driver took off his hat to her, and stood waiting for orders.

"Wait a minute, please," said Muriel.

Presently, Patrick, a grey-haired, decorous old Irishman, came out with a basket, covered with a white cloth, which he deposited on the seat of the carriage.

"Bless me, what's that!" exclaimed Emily, laughing.

"Pardiggle tracts for the poor," said Muriel, jestingly. "Patrick, tell Charles to hurry."

Patrick went in and soon returned with Tugmutton, who jumped down the steps, and scrambled into the carriage. Tugmutton's fat face was all agrin and shining like satin-wood. The happy youth had devoured a whole pie, and was in a state of supreme exhilaration. His repletion, however, did not prevent him from ogling the basket by his side, and he would have liked nothing better than to make his dessert on its contents.

Muriel gave the driver his directions, and the vehicle started off down Temple and into Cambridge street to the corner of Garden. They were turning up Garden street, when Tugmutton opened his great eyes, and said.

"Well now, I declare! If there ain't Mr. Harrington!"

Muriel leaned forward, and caught sight of the noble soldier-figure of Harrington striding up the street before them.

"Hullo! Mr. Harrington! I say!" screeched Tugmutton.

Harrington turned, with the sun on the martial lines of his face and beard. He caught sight of the inmates of the carriage instantly, and signaling to the driver to stop, he came down the street, to the side of the carriage.

"What is it, John?" asked Muriel.

"Nothing," he replied, smiling, and bending his head to Emily. "It's a false alarm, I find. But these poor people are very much excited, and I was going up to quiet them."

"Come in. We're going to Roux's," said Muriel.

Harrington entered, sat in Tugmutton's place, taking him on his knee, and the carriage went on till it reached the corner of Southac street, where it stopped.

"There's considerable of a crowd here," cried the driver.

They all looked out at the carriage window upon the squalid neighborhood. Only a Dickens or a Victor Hugo could fitly describe the strange and picturesque scene which met their eyes. Huddled together in excited groups, or moving hither and thither in straggling masses, hundreds of colored men and women, clad in every variety of costume, and lawless and unhuman in aspect, swarmed over the street with a loud, dense inarticulate confusion of voices, the bright sunlight bringing out their motley forms and bronze faces in grotesque and vivid salience. So uncouth and various were the costumes—coats and hats of extinct styles and patterns, frowsy and shabby raiment of every fashion within the last half century, intermingling with the many-colored gowns and head-dresses of the girls and women—that but for the heavy-lipped, sombre faces, with their flashing teeth and wild-rolling eyes, and the menacing gestures and threatening hum of the multitude, it might have seemed some masquerading mob, arrayed in the garments of the old clothes shops. Protruding from every window in the dingy and dilapidated houses on either side of the street, big clusters of heads, mostly those of women and children, some with great shocks of wool, some bullet-shaped and closely shorn, some wearing white mob caps and red and yellow bandanna kerchiefs, were bobbing restlessly over the excited multitude below. Up and down cellar-ways, and in and out of numerous alleys and yawning doors, uneasy shoals were constantly pouring, passing from or mingling with the mongrel and fantastic concourse in the street, which continually moved in the sunlight with a hoarse, turbulent, swarming undertone, like the far-off roar of insurrection.

A deep flush came to the broad-nostrilled face of Harrington as he gazed.

"What a sight for Boston in the nineteenth century!" he exclaimed. "Vaunting her civilization while terror invades the refuge of her poor!"

Emily, deathly pale, leaned back in the carriage, and shuddered.

At that moment, a portion of the crowd, seeing the carriage, set up a clamor of cries, and surged down toward it. Two or three stones were thrown, which rattled on the pavement around the vehicle, and the horses began to plunge and rear. Instantly Muriel flung open the carriage-door, and springing into the street, calm and fearless, held up her hand. Harrington quickly leaped out after her.

"Halloa, there!" he shouted, with a commanding voice, which, like Muriel's gesture, fell like magic upon the thoughtless assailants. He was well known in the quarter, and the negroes recognizing a friend, set up a cheer of welcome. Tugmutton meanwhile had pounced from the carriage upon the boys that threw the stones, and assaulted them with a shower of cuffs and kicks. He came back, presently, full of victory, his blobber cheeks puffed out with rage and self-importance.

"Them miser'ble young niggers haven't got no more gumption than just nothin' at all," he spluttered. "Guess they'll mind now, though. Gosh! I lit on 'em like a duck on a June bug. When I fall afoul of 'em guess they think it's General Washington and the spirit of seventy-six. Miser'ble young bloats!"

Harrington could not help smiling as he looked down on

the fat imp, who was delivering himself in these figurative terms, with an indescribable swell and swagger. The horses were still pawing and trembling, and Muriel went to their heads, and stood with one gloved hand grasping the reins, and the other patting and stroking the cheeks and noses of the alarmed animals. The driver, who sat on his box, white as a sheet, firmly holding the reins, looked down admiringly on the fearless and graceful sunlit figure, and the negroes standing around, stared with delighted awe.

Harrington, meanwhile, was at the carriage door, assuring Emily, who protested that she was not afraid, as indeed she was not, for she was naturally courageous. Presently Muriel came around to the carriage door, her face bright and calm.

"Now," she said, "I will go on to Roux's. The carriage had better stand here. Emily, will you come with us?"

"But you're not going through that crowd, Muriel!" exclaimed Emily.

"Why certainly," replied Muriel, laughing. "I wouldn't miss the chance for the world. Going through that crowd is part of my culture. Besides, dear, the crowd won't eat us."

"I think I will stay here," returned Emily. "I am not afraid, but this scene is terribly painful to me, and I could hardly bear to go among the poor people. Do you think this will drive some of them off to Canada, Muriel?"

"I fear so," replied Muriel, with a wistful glance at the concourse.

Emily colored, and her eyes filled with tears.

"Let me give something for them, Muriel," she faltered, taking out her porte-monnaie. "You may know some of them who want means, and if you do, give them this."

She held out a little roll of bills—fifty dollars. It was money she had intended for shopping, and it was all she had with her.

"But, dear Emily," said Muriel, looking at her with humid eyes, "I do not know that I shall meet with any one who will need it."

"No matter," replied Emily; "take it with you in case you should. I wish I could help them all."

Muriel took the bills with a tender smile, and Harrington caught the profuse hand, and looked fervently in the face of the giver. At that look Emily cowered, for she thought it the look of love she had wickedly evoked, and her soul quailed in grief and shame. Muriel, too, misread the look, and her spirit rose in generous feeling at the token of a lover's happiness in his beloved one.

"Ah, thou noble one!" she said, with playful sweetness. "Thou rose of the rose-garden! Well, it shall be as you say. Come, Charles; you can carry the basket. John, you will stay here to keep Emily company."

Before Emily could reply, Muriel moved away, followed by the triumphant Tugmutton with the basket on his arm. Presently she was passing through the parting concourse, bending her head in acknowledgment of the bows, and curtseys, and doffing of hats which saluted her. The negro in his lowest estate is a gentleman in his courtesy, superior in this to many a white of high and low degree. The weight of social wrong had crushed out or bruised down many an excellence in these humble people, but politeness was one which society could not destroy in them. As Muriel went on through the swarming hum, the clatter of voices would cease, the men and women would step aside from the path, the hats would be taken from the heads with a courteous recognition of her presence, which a snob might not have the wits to honor, but which Philip Sidney's pulse would surely have quickened to behold. Low Irish, in their place, would have stood stolidly and gazed. Low English would have shambled aside with clownish loutishness. Low Americans would have stared and leered, and perhaps spat tobacco-juice on her skirts as she passed them. The low negroes were civil as Frenchmen.

In the heart of the grotesque and motley throng, Muriel came upon a black man whom she knew—an erect and stalwart figure, straight as an Indian, with a fine, masculine face, and the full swart negrine features. He was standing in a doorway in his shirtsleeves. Instantly bowing low, and taking off his felt hat when he saw her, he came forward in courteous posture as she stopped. Muriel smiled graciously, and gave him her hand as freely and firmly as she would have given it to her most aristocratic friend. He took it reverentially, yet without bashfulness, while all the black people around stared.

"Have you heard the news, Mr. Brown?" she asked.

"Yes, madam," returned the negro, bowing low. "It's sad news, too, madam. As yet we don't know which of us they're after, but I was just going down town to see the Vigilance Committee, and find out about it."

"I am happy to tell you that it's a false alarm," replied Muriel, smiling. "Mr. Harrington says so, so you can be at ease. Won't you please to spread the news among your people here, so that they may be relieved."

The news was spread already, for she had no sooner said it, than it was taken up and passed from lip to lip with joyful confusion. Presently it reached the depths of the crowd, and instantly there was a straggling shout, followed by a surge of the whole concourse toward the direction from whence the information had proceeded.

"Stand back," roared the negro in a tremendous voice. "There's a lady here. Don't crowd the lady."

Instantly the cry, "don't crowd the lady," was taken up, and the dense masses surged back, every man turning upon his neighbor, and shouldering him away in officious zeal, till there was a great bare space left around Muriel and her companion, with a circular crowd around its border, and further behind in the throng, negroes jumping up and down, to catch a sight of "the lady."

Muriel laughed, and at once the negroes in front laughed, and the laugh spread till it became a universal, jovial guffaw, while some of the lighter spirits threw themselves into grotesque contortions, and capered and stamped up and down in extravagant glee. Presently a conviction came to the crowd that they were at an unnecessary distance, and at once there was a forward movement of the whole mass to within a yard of Muriel, every one nervously ready to turn again upon his neighbor, and crowd him off, at the slightest hint that they were too near, and some of them looking anxiously at Tugmutton, who, taking upon himself very important airs by virtue of his attendance upon Miss Eastman, stood holding the basket, with his blobber cheeks and big lips puffed out in ludicrous dignity, as wondering at their impudence.

"I trust, Mr. Brown," continued Muriel, "that none of the poor people will be frightened by this, into going to Canada."

The negro looked sombrely into vacancy for a moment before answering. He was one of the influential men of the quarter, and knew pretty much all that went on there. Brave, faithful, generous himself, he added to his good qualities that of keen sympathy for his people.

"I'm afeared, madam," he said, "that this affair will scare off some of them. I advise every one to stay that can, and fight it out. I don't go myself, and I wouldn't give two cents for the chance of taking me, so long as I have this."

He opened his waistcoat as he spoke, showing a huge sheathed bowie-knife in a side-pocket of the garment.

"I carry this, madam, night and day," he continued. "Whenever they want me, they'll find me ready. But there's a lot of folks here that ain't up to my way, and the poor cre'turs go. There's two boardin' with me now that have about made up their minds to git away right off, and as they're bent on it, I shall have to help them all I can, though cash is rather low with me just now. Then I've been told that old Pete Washington is goin', too, with his folks. Pete's proper scared, and thinks he's sent for every time he hears kidnappers are in town. I haven't heerd tell of no more."

He said it with a kind of mechanical sadness, fumbling slowly as he spoke with the handle of the knife under his waistcoat, his eyes roving absently, meanwhile, over the gaping faces of the motley crowd.

"Mr. Brown," said Muriel, "here are fifty dollars, which I want you to divide at your discretion among those that need means to get away. It is from a lady who is sitting down there in my carriage. She wanted it given for this purpose. If you need any more, come to my house at any time. And if I can do anything, please to let me know, for I want to help if I can."

He took the money quietly, put his large black hand over his mouth, and bowed low. Then throwing back his head and shoulders, and extending his brawny arm with the bills in the hand, he suddenly fronted the crowd.

"Ladies and gentlemen," he said, with a grandiose manner, pouring his tremendous bass into the concourse, "a lady in the carriage gives fifty dollars to help the brethren that are leaving us for Canada. The lady here has often helped us, and will help again. In my humble opinion, they're both of 'em God's ladies, and"——

The great voice broke. Muriel, astonished by this unexpected outburst, was yet so overcome by the electric passion of the negro's speech and manner, that she lost her self-possession, and knew not how to interpose.

"Three cheers," screeched Tugmutton, at this juncture, thinking that some cheering would be highly appropriate.

Three? They cheered till they reeled! Roar on roar went up in solid volume, till the sky seemed to swoon above them. Muriel, disconcerted for once in her life, turned to Brown, who stood grimly smiling, and begged him to quiet them and get them to disperse. He put out his hand, and at once the tumult immediately around them dropped, though broken shouting still went on in the rear. Turning to the fat squab who had given the word for this ovation, and played fugleman with cap and voice to it all, Muriel silently beckoned him to follow, and hurriedly bowing and smiling to the calm negro, went on.

CHAPTER VII.

ROUX.

She had not gone half a dozen paces, before some one came striding to her side. It was Harrington, and she instantly put her arm in his, with a gesture so sudden and joyous, that the young man thrilled.

"I am so glad you have come," she said.

Emily had insisted on his leaving her, and attending upon Muriel, Harrington remarked.

"But you are pale," he pursued, looking into her face, which colored and smiled under his kind and searching eyes.

"And now you are not pale," he added, laughingly.

Muriel laughed silverly, and told the reason of her momentary agitation, which amused Harrington vastly.

Presently they reached the dingy alley in which Roux lived. It was a corner house, inhabited by several families. A flight of wooden steps led up to the second story, in which Roux had two rooms.

Roux was a white-washer, window-cleaner, boot-black and what not by occupation. He had come up from his little shop in Water street, down in the heart of the city, at the rumor which Tugmutton had brought him, that kidnappers were in town; for he was a fugitive, and since the passage of the Fugitive Slave Law he had never felt safe in Boston, where he had previously passed nearly nine secure years.

He was sitting on an old chair, in an attitude of deep dejection, crooning to his babe, which he held in his arms, with his other two children, a boy and girl, sitting on either knee. The baby was a pretty little boy, with negrine features, clear saffron skin, and glittering dark eyes. Josey, who sat on his right knee, was a slender, bright-eyed, brown-skinned little girl, six years old. Tom, sitting on the other knee, was like his sister, and four years of age. They were both pretty children, neatly dressed in clothes which Muriel and her mother had provided for them. Roux himself was a good-looking negro, athletic in build, dark-complexioned, with short, woolly hair, and heavy eyebrows. He was attired in an old sack coat and blue overalls, specked with white-wash, for he had come up to the house in his working clothes. The room in which he sat had received a touch of his art, as the yellow-washed walls and white-washed ceiling testified. It was a poor, low-browed apartment, but neat and clean, though pervaded by that frowsy odor which one often scents in the dwellings of the poor. The floor was bare. Three or four cheap colored prints hung in veneered frames on the walls. There was a trundle bed in one corner for the children; a small cooking-stove near the fireboard, with an immense deal of gawky funnel zigzagging up to a hole in the wall near the ceiling; a small clock ticking faintly on the mantelpiece, with some gaudy ornaments near it; a table, and half a dozen old-fashioned, second-hand chairs. Behind the family group was an open door, giving a view of another room, with a rag-carpet on the floor, a bureau, and a bed, on which lay, in her clothes, a mulatto woman, Roux's wife.

Roux ceased his crooning as the broad-limbed, blobber-cheeked squab of a Tugmutton threw open the door, grinning from ear to ear, and lumbered in with the basket, which he deposited in the middle of the floor.

"You ain't goin' to be took back, father, this time," bawled the cheerful youth. "It's a false alarm. Gosh! I knew it wasn't nothin' but a false alarm. There ain't no kidnappers in Boston, an' never will be neither."

"Tugmutton, what's that?" demanded Roux, eyeing the basket.

The imp drew up his chunky figure with severe dignity, and rolled his saucer eyes and jerked his thumb over his shoulder. At the same moment Muriel's courtly face and figure appeared at the door, with Harrington's countenance smiling over her shoulder. The poor room was suddenly adorned by these fair, strong presences, and its frowsy air was sweetened and softened with delicate fragrance. Roux's children scrambled down at once to run over to their smiling angel, who entered with affable and cordial grace, and stooped to fondle and kiss the little ones, while Roux himself rose, with the baby on his left arm, bowing confusedly, and smiling with considerable pompousness of manner, as of one who thought himself highly honored.

"How are you to-day, Mr. Roux," said Harrington, coming over to the delighted negro, and shaking hands with him. "And how is your wife? And this little one," he added, putting his large hand on the head of the staring baby.

"All right, Mr. Harrington," returned Roux. "Though the madam's not as well as she might be, sir," he continued, in a grandiloquent tone. "She got a sort of a shock, Mr. Harrington, when this news come, and went right off into spasms. Clarindy's awful scared lest some of these here days old master should send for me, and I'm right skittish myself, sir, in view of that catastrophe."

Another person might have smiled at Roux's half-anxious, half-pompous tone, but Harrington looked at him with a kind and concerned face, knowing how much real apprehension and distress his words covered.

"I am extremely sorry that your wife should have been alarmed," said the young man. "But it's true, as Charles said, that this is a false report."

"Yes, Mr. Roux," added Muriel, coming forward from the children, and giving him her hand, "it's nothing but an idle rumor, so keep a good heart."

"Thank ye, Miss Eas'man, and I am extrornerly rejoiced at the reception of this unlooked for intelligence," returned Roux, bowing reverentially, while his manner grew more pompous, and his language more grandiloquent. "And the madam," he continued, "will hear the glad tidings with great joy, likewise, Miss Eas'man. I heerd the shoutin' and hoorawin' in the street, though I wasn't able to spekilate with any certainty as to its cause, an' with the chil'ren here, an' Clarindy a-lyin' on the bed, feelin' ruther weak, I found it on the whole, inexpedient to go out and see what was a goin' on."

He addressed the last sentence of this speech to Harrington. Muriel had gone into the other room, and was leaning over Mrs. Roux, speaking in a low, soothing voice, with her hands on the sick woman's head. The children were prattling with each other, and Tugmutton was standing apart, with his short arms akimbo, the hands spread on his hips, and an expression of ineffable scorn on his fat, grey face, which was turned toward Roux.

"Now, father," said the squab, taking advantage of the pause, "ain't you ashamed? My gosh! I'm goin' to blush at ye, father."

"What's the matter, Tugmutton," asked Roux, with comical deprecation.

"What's the matter? That's a pretty question!" was the reproachful reply. "There you stand, and never ask Mr. Harrington to take a chair. That's the matter. Do you call *that* doin' the honors of the establishment?"

Roux looked abashed, while Tugmutton, with his face puffed out, and his eye sternly fixed upon the offending party, brought forward a chair, dumped it down under Harrington's coat-tails, and retreating a couple of paces, put his arms akimbo again, still sternly regarding Roux.

The whole proceeding was so ineffably droll, that Harrington, sinking into the chair, with a hand on each knee, laughed heartily, though quietly, with his eyes fixed on the fat pigmy. Roux, who was very fond of Tugmutton, and submitted meekly to all his odd humors, regarding him, indeed, with an absurd mixture of puzzled curiosity and reverential awe, such as the good-natured Welsh giant might have bestowed upon Jack the Giant-killer, stood now, with the baby on his arm, uneasily eyeing his chunky mentor, and smiling confusedly. Nothing could be more amusing than the relation Tugmutton occupied toward him, and the rest of the family. They were all under the domination of this small, fat chunk. Tugmutton's grand assumption of importance, and his authoritative airs, conjoined with his genuine affection for them all, which took the form of perpetual wardenship, had prevailed over the age and experience of both Roux and his wife. He was so old-fashioned, so queer, so mysterious and inconceivable a creature to them, that they looked upon him almost as a superior being, and petted and humored him in all possible ways.

"Just look at you, now," continued the irate fat boy. "Do you call *that* the way to hold a baby? With his head hangin' down, and every drop of blood in his body runnin' into it! My gosh! that child'll never have one speck of hair, father, an' water on the brain, beside."

Without feeling any apprehension of the capillary and hydrocephalous catastrophe thus ominously predicted as the inevitable consequence of his way of holding the baby, Roux glanced at the little one, whose head was drooping back over his arm, and whose fat, yellow fists were contentedly inserted in its mouth, and then gently shifted the position of the child, so as to rest its head on his shoulder.

"Just you give me that baby, father," blurted out the fat boy, starting forward, and receiving in his short arms the infant which Roux readily abandoned to his charge. "There's nobody knows how to take care of this poor child but me," he indignantly continued, bearing off his burden, and sitting down with it in a short chair near the wall. "Lord a mercy! If it wasn't for me, I don't know what'd become of this family! Chick-a-dee-dee—chick-a-dee-dee—honey—honey—pretty Brudder Baby," he chirruped, showing all his ivories in a jovial grin to the infant, and dancing it up and down in his short arms.

"Tugmutton's great on takin' care of the chil'ren," remarked Roux to the smiling Harrington. "There aint no better boy than Tug nowhere, Mr. Harrington. He helps Clarindy a mighty deal, an' he's a reel comfort, I tell you."

"Why, yes, Mr. Roux, so I see," smilingly returned the young man. "And he learns the lessons I give him, very well. I shouldn't wonder if Charles came to be a great man one of these days. He says he's going to be a lawyer like Robert Morris."

Robert Morris was a colored man, who had fought his way up against the prejudice of the many, and with the aid of a few, to an honorable position, which he then held, at the Boston Bar.

"Tell you what, Mr. Harrington," said the proud Tugmutton, "Danel Webster won't be nowhere when I come on the scene of action. I'll make him stand round. Fugitive Slave Law's bound to go then, an' all the kidnappers 'll be hung right up."

At that moment steps were heard, and Emily appeared at the door, coloring with the novelty of her situation, and followed by a short, thick-set man, in a straw hat, with his head bent sideways.

"Why, Emily!" exclaimed Harrington, starting up. "And with the Captain! Miss Ames, Mr. Roux. Captain Fisher you know."

The superb beauty curtseyed low, with a sweeping rustle of silks, and Roux, fluttering at heart in the presence of the aristocratic lady, bent himself as if he had a hinge in his back. Harrington handed Emily a chair, into which she sank, smiling and nodding to the enchanted Tugmutton, and Muriel came floating out from the inner room with her natural urbane curtsey.

"Why, Emily!" she exclaimed, shutting the door behind her. "You too. Good morning, Captain Fisher.

"It's my doin's, Miss Eastman," said the Captain, in a cheery voice, looking at Muriel with his head on one side, and his hat on, as he shook hands with her. "Comin' along, I see Miss Ames in the hack, and she said you was here; so I said, why not go too, and she took my extinded arm, and up we come together."

He held Muriel's hand as he made this explanation, and dropping it when he had concluded, stood looking intently at her, as though some reply was expected. He was a short man, with a round face, yellow and rosy, like a winter pippin; round, dark eyes, which never winked; a short nose, shaped like a beak; and he had a way of bending his head sideways, and looking at you like some odd bird. There was a general aspect of the sea-faring man about him, and he had been for many years the skipper of coasting vessels, in which occupation he had amassed some property. He now lived in the same house with Harrington, for whom he had a great affection, and did a little business in collecting rents for a number of house-owners.

"I just came up to let the folks here know," he continued, "that there's no sneakin' soul-drivers come to Boston this time. I was told there was some of a crowd here, but they're all scattered now, and I met Brown, who said he'd been informed 'twas a false alarm. No danger, I hope. The Vigilance Committee keep a sharp look-out ahead, and we're pretty sure to know what's goin' on."

In those dark days, when Boston had gone for kidnapping, there was an organization, composed of the leading Abolitionists, with a few anti-slavery people, young and old, who made it their business to keep a watch for Southern man-hunters, to warn fugitives of their danger, to assist them in their flight with money and arms, and in every practicable way to baffle the kidnappers. This was known as the Vigilance Committee, and its existence and efforts were among the few bright rays which lit the dark insanity of Boston at that period. Captain Fisher was a member of it, as was Harrington.

"I got here before you, Eldad," said Harrington, smiling. "Charles came to the house with the rumor, and I ran down town at once, and found there was no truth in it."

"Trust you for bein' on hand, John," returned the Captain. "You're spry as a tópman. When Gabriel toots that horn of his, you'll be the first one up out o' your grave."

The Captain wandered over to Roux, and laying his hands on the negro's shoulders looked at him steadily with his head curved sideways, then shook him gently to and fro, then got round to one side of him and took another look, and then punched him with his forefinger in the ribs.

"Roux, how are you?" he chirruped in conclusion, as the negro squirmed away from the fore-finger, good-naturedly smiling.

"Firs'-rate, Captain," answered Roux. "Got scared though at that story."

The Captain stood oblivious of his answer, looking at Tugmutton who, swollen with pride, was exhibiting the baby to Emily. Roux became absorbed in admiring awe at Tugmutton's complacent familiarity with Miss Ames. Tugmutton was in one of his lordliest moods, proud of his exclusive aristocratic acquaintance, and conscious that Roux and the two children, who stood timidly at a distance, were following him with reverent eyes.

"It's a very pretty baby," said Emily graciously, turning to Roux, who hastened to smile and bow. "But, Mr. Roux, these three children do not resemble Charles at all."

"Different style of beauty," remarked Tugmutton, with preternatural gravity, rolling his great eyes up at Emily.

Emily laughed aloud at this oracular suggestion, and Harrington and Muriel looked at each other and smiled, while the Captain fixedly surveyed the squab with mute admiration.

"You know, dear," said Muriel to Emily, "or rather you do not know, that Charles is only an adopted child of Mr. and Mrs. Roux."

"Oh!" returned Emily, suddenly enlightened, "that accounts for the different style of beauty."

"Yes, madam," said Roux elaborately bowing, "that accounts for it."

Emily smiled at the simplicity of the reply.

"And how did it happen that he got the name of Tugmutton, Mr. Roux?" she inquired.

"Well, Madam," replied Roux, quite seriously, "it was a sort of accidental. When I firs' got to Boston, Tug's father and mother treated me right handsome. I was ruther bad off, an' they took me in till I got somethin' to do. They was very fat folks, both of 'em, an' Tug was an uncommon fat baby. Somehow his father and mother never could fix on a name for him, so he growed along without none. Bimeby when he was three year old, his father died, and bimeby when he was five, his mother died likewise. I was married to Clarindy when that catastrophe happened, so feelin' right grateful to Ezek'el and Sally Pitts—that was Tug's father and mother's name, madam—I took Tug in. That day we had a chunk of baked mutton, wich you couldn't bite, madam, it was so tough, an' after dinner we missed Tug all on a sudden. We got ruther skeered at not findin' him, an' went lookin' round the streets, but couldn't git no news of him. Long toward evenin' we heerd a stir under the bed, an' lookin' under, there he was tuggin' away at that chunk of mutton, and there he'd hid himself all the afternoon. I'm a miser'ble orphan, says he, the minute we sot eyes on him, never leavin' off tuggin' at the meat. You're a young Tugmutton, an' that's what you are, says Clarindy. Then we larfed, and so after that we got to callin' him Tugmutton, an' he took to that name astonishin' That's the way of it, madam."

Muriel and Harrington, who had heard this story before, listened to it now smiling, while Emily and the Captain, vastly amused during its repetition, laughed heartily as Roux ended. Tugmutton, meanwhile, sitting in the low chair with the baby, grinned sheepishly at the revival of this reminiscence of his miserable orphanage.

"Are you—that is, did you—escape from the South, Mr. Roux?" inquired Emily, hesitatingly, after a pause.

"Yes, madam, I did," replied Roux with another elaborate bow. "It wouldn't be well, madam, to have it mentioned roundabout, lest"——

"O never fear, Mr. Roux," she rejoined hurriedly. "I wouldn't speak of it for the world."

"In fact, madam, I believe I never told any one about it," continued Roux, falteringly, "with the especial exception of Mr. Harrington and Miss Eastman. But I did git away from the southern country, way down in Louzeana, nine years ago. And I've got a brother still there, madam, leastways if he's alive, wich is not certain, seein' that he was with an uncommon bad master, madam—in fact, one of the worst sort of masters, madam."

"Why didn't he run away with you, Mr. Roux?" inquired Emily.

"He was ruther scared at the resks, madam," replied Roux, "Says I, Ant'ny—his name was Ant'ny, madam—Ant'ny, says I, Master Lafitte—Lafitte was old Master's name, madam—Master Lafitte'll be the death of us, Ant'ny. We'd better try to git away to that Boston we've heerd tell of.

Ant'ny, says I, I've got three pounds of kian, Ant'ny, says I"——

"Of what?" asked Emily.

"Of kian, madam—kian pepper, you know."

"O, yes. Cayenne pepper."

"Yes, madam. Wich we can leave on the track, Ant'ny, says I, and that'll throw off the hounds, I'm a thinkin'."

"The hounds!" ejaculated Emily, knitting her brow with horror, and looking at the still face of Muriel and then at Harrington.

"Certainly," said the latter, tranquilly. "In this free and happy country, they hunt men and women with hounds. When hounds fail, they try Fugitive Slave Law Commissioners."

"And were you hunted, Mr. Roux?" asked Emily, shuddering.

"Yes, madam," replied the negro, naïvely. "Ant'ny was afeared to try it, and then I thought I wouldn't nuther, for he was my brother, and we'd been brought up together on old Madam Roux's estate in New Orleans, and I was very fond of Ant'ny, madam. But next day, you see, madam, I was feelin' ruther sick, and fell short in the pickin'—cotton-pickin', you know. So when night come, Master Lafitte he flogged me awful, and then hung me up in the gin-house—hung me up by the wrists, an' left me to hang overnight."

Roux, hearing Captain Fisher muttering, paused. The Captain, with his head very much on one side, was swearing awfully in a low undertone at slavery and slaveholders in general. He usually contented himself with such mild oaths as "by the great horn spoon"—as people who leave off chewing tobacco supply its place with spruce gum. But as the spruce-gum chewers sometimes backslide into tobacco again, so the Captain, when he got excited, which was seldom, would backslide from his mild profanity into such swearing as sailors, who swear with genius, know how to express the passion of their souls withal.

"Bimeby, madam," resumed Roux, still addressing Emily, who sat looking at him with a flush of fiery indignation on her beautiful countenance, "I sloshed about, an' the rope broke an' let me down. I jus' got out of that gin-house mighty quick, I tell you. Then I went down a piece to the hollow stump, where I'd hid the kian an' a carvin' knife, which I'd took one day from the kitchen. I got the kian an' the knife, an' put off hot foot for the north. Jus' about sunrise, I heerd Dan Belcher's hounds a-comin' after me—two of 'em, yellin' awful. I was proper skeered, madam, but I jus' made a hole in the paper of kian, an' run on, holdin' the paper low down on the trail, so's to let the kian drop out along, you know. Then when the kian was all gone, I got skeered, an' I run on a piece, an' shinned up a live-oak 'way into the thick of the leaves, an' lay still. 'Fore long, I see the hounds comin', an' Dan Belcher an' old Toler an' Master Lafitte ridin' after 'em. I got so skeered I like to dropped, but I lay hush, an' right soon I saw the dogs run up, an' poke their noses into the kian. Ki-yi-yah," cachinnated Roux, overcome with the reminiscence, "you ought to have seen them dogs, madam. They jus' acted as if they'd got religion! They flopped down an' rolled over, yellin' like mad, an' rubbin' their noses into the kian, an' rollin' agin, an' hollerin'—hi! Never saw nothin' out of camp-meetin' act like them cre'turs. 'Fore long up come old Master an' Dan Belcher an' Toler, an' looked at them dogs. I couldn't hear a word they was sayin', but I spekilated they was wonderin' what had got into them dogs. Then Dan Belcher, he got down, an' dragged off the hounds, an' poked his nose into the kian. Hi! I reckon he got a smell, for he jumped up rubbin' his nose, an' stampin' round awful."

Tugmutton, with the baby in his arms, burst into a screech of eldritch laughter, kicking up his feet from the low chair in which he sat, in phrenetic glee. All the others were silent, with faces intent on Roux.

"Bimeby," resumed the negro, "Dan Belcher he laid a hold of the dogs, an' dragged them on a piece to find the trail with no kian on it. 'Twasn't no use, for the dogs didn't do nothin' but snuff an' yell an' roll over. So'n about a half an hour, I reckon, they all went back, an' I lay hush in the tree all day. Along towards evenin' I got down, an' run on agin. Bimeby I come plump on a man. 'Where's your pass?' says he. 'Here it is,' says I, givin' him a dig with the carvin'-knife. 'Ugh,' says he" ——

Everybody burst into a peal of laughter at the nonchalant, matter-of-fact simplicity with which Roux said this. Roux himself was rather amazed at the interruption, and stood, faintly smiling, with his whitewash-stained dark hand fumbling over his mouth, and his eyes uneasily roving over the laughing company.

"Well done, Roux," said Harrington, jumping up, and slapping the negro on the shoulder. "'Ense petit placidam sub libertate quietem,'" he continued, quoting the legend of the Massachusetts State-arms. "And you sought the tranquil rest of freedom with a carving-knife."

"Yes, quietem was the word, and you did quiet him," chuckled the Captain, punning upon the Latin. "Sic semper tyrannis, is another bit of that lingo, an' I guess old tyrannis *was* rather sick when he got a touch of Roux's carving-knife. By the great horn-spoon, that's the richest thing I've heard lately!"

"But what did the man do then, Mr. Roux?" asked Emily.

"Ugh, says he, madam, and then he doubled himself up, an' I run on," replied Roux, simply. "Bimeby I come to the Red River, and I swum over. Then I run on agin, till I come to the Mississip, an' hid in a wood-pile. Long toward mornin' a flat boat came up the river, and hitched. Then I heerd the Captin say, says he, argufying with another man, and gittin' mad with him, I'm Ohio, says he, and my men are Ohio, an' we don't care a damn for slavery, says he. Tother man went off, an' I run out, an' says, Captin, says I, I've run for my freedom, an' won't you take me with you, I says. Step right aboard, says he, an' I'm damned if I don't wish I'd a load more like you, says he."

"Bravo," cried Muriel, clapping her hands. "Good for Ohio!"

"Hooraw for Ohio!" piped Tugmutton, bouncing up, and

flourishing the baby. "Chick-a-dee-dee, Brudder Baby, pretty little birdy," he added, with a sudden change of key, wagging his bushy head and grinning blobber cheeks over the complacent infant. "Send him right down to Ohio. Kidnapper come to fetch Brudder Baby, won't have no more chance than a bob-tail horse in fly-time when he gits to Ohio."

Alas! poor Tugmutton!—the dark days could come even to Ohio! Broad and strong and generous the hearts of Ohio, mighty in noble impulse, mighty in love and bravery, mighty in truth to liberty and tenderness to man. But the rampart of Ohio hearts prevailed not in the black hour when Margaret Garner, with the hell-dog statute and the hunters upon her, sublimely slew her children to save from slavery the souls Ohio could not save.

"And so you escaped, Mr. Roux," said Emily.

"Yes, madam," returned Roux, "the captain took me all the way up to Cincinnati. Where are ye goin' now, William, says he. Boston, says I. Men, says he, let's give him an Ohio lift. Wich meant takin' up a collection, madam," explained Roux, bowing. "An' the collection was fifteen dollars and thirty-three cents, madam, together with a suit of the captain's clothes, an' some vittles in a paper bag. Captain, says I, my gratefulness will never fail. William, says he, just hold on to that carving-knife, an' don't let yourself be taken. Captain, says I, if I ever git to heaven, I'll make the Lord acquainted with all you've done for me. William, says he, don't you never acquaint anybody but the Lord with it, or I'm a gone coon. An' now make tracks, says he. So I made tracks, an' come on safe to Boston."

"Well, I declare!" exclaimed Emily, drawing a long breath, and looking around her. "It makes my blood boil to think that men are treated so in this country. And you never heard from your brother, Mr. Roux?"

"Never, madam. But I don't think he's alive. I'm afeared that Master Lafitte would kill him to be revenged on me, and that makes me feel, sometimes, as if I'd murdered my own brother."

He said this in low, ghostly tones, with a sudden agony and

horror convulsing his dark face. It is impossible to describe the shock of awful emotion which his words gave to Emily. There was a moment of solemn silence, in which Roux stood faintly gasping, with his swart visage ashen and distorted with overmastering anguish, and she, gazing on him with a blanched countenance, felt as if her very soul would die with pity.

"Couldn't he be bought?" she timidly stammered, at length, half feeling that she was proposing an absurdity. "That is—I mean if he is—if he has not—died."

Roux despairingly shook his head.

"If I had the money, madam," he hoarsely faltered, "I'd try to buy him. But that'll never be—never."

"I'll engage to furnish the money," said Emily, vehemently, the generous color flooding her face like fire. "I will," she added, stamping her foot as she sat. "If it costs me two thousand dollars, or twice two thousand, it shall be done."

A dead silence ensued, in which she gazed at their mute faces. It was the brave New England scholar who did sweet service to liberty when the guns of tyranny stormed on Rome—it was Margaret Fuller who once gave away all her little property, five hundred dollars, to a poor exile, a stranger to her, whose distresses had touched her heart. Born of such an impulse, and kindred to that splendid generosity, was this act of Emily's.

"Why do you all look so?" she continued. "I mean what I say."

Harrington and Muriel, to whom she lifted her flushed face, were standing near each other, Muriel's face still, solemn, and turned toward the window, Harrington's noble countenance rigid, and bent upon the floor. The Captain stood looking at Emily with his head bent on one side, and his features all atwist. As for Roux, his black visage was wildly lighted with hope, joy, awe, and startled amazement, while Tugmutton sat in the low chair, with the baby in his arms, his mouth open, his huge eyes staring, and the big shocks of wool on his head seeming bigger than ever in his astonishment.

"It shall be done, I say," declared Emily. "Harrington, I depend on you to show me the way."

Harrington looked blank—like one who did not know how to answer her; then furtively glanced at Roux, and then at the floor.

"You are the soul of generosity, Miss Ames," he said, after a pause, smiling constrainedly. "I should be happy to help you. We will see what can be done."

Roux clasped his hands and bowed his head. In that instant, Harrington flashed a lightning glance at Emily, so stern, so menacing, so agonized in its look of warning and entreaty, that Emily was confounded. The next second, Roux's face was raised, and Harrington's wore an expression of such bland indifference, that Emily could hardly believe she had seen the other.

"We will speak of this another time," said Harrington. "At present, I think I must go. Shall I see you to the carriage, ladies, or do you remain longer?"

Roux threw himself on his knees, and bending, grovelled at Emily's feet. Then raising his black face, convulsed, and streaming with tears, he faltered out the broken words of his gratitude.

"I'll pray for ye, forever and ever, Miss Ames," he said. "I'll pray to the Lord for ye, Miss Ames. And the blessing of the Father and of the Son and of the Holy Ghost, be on ye, Miss Ames. I've had a good deal of kindness, but there's never been no kindness like yours, Miss Ames, an' I don't want ye to give away all that money, madam, for it's a mighty deal of money, though it's for my brother, Miss Ames, and I'd clean give my life to see my poor brother, madam. And oh, if Master Lafitte will only sell him, if he's alive, madam, I'll pray for him too, and for everybody, forever and ever, amen, an' for you more especial than anybody, for there never was such kindness as yours to a poor, miser'ble, forsaken black man —no, never, never."

Uncouth words poured forth rapidly in a weak, broken voice, with sobs and tears; but words that blanched the gold and roses of the face that bent with swimming eyes over the bowed and weeping figure on the floor. In the cold, succeeding silence, there was no sound but the dim sobs of Roux. The Captain stood with his features screwed into a hard rigor, gazing at the abject form beneath him. Harrington's face was wan and rigid, and fixed on vacancy. The two little ones, frightened and almost crying, clung around the stupefied and staring Tugmutton, who sat holding the baby, with the big whites of his eyes glaring at Roux from the ashy pallor of his fat visage.

"Mr. Roux."

At the gentle, silver tones of Muriel, at the firm touch of her hand on his shoulder, the negro lifted up his bowed head from his breast, and gazed with a haggard, beseeching face, all wet with tears, at the benignant countenance that bent above him. For an instant only, and then rising to his feet, ashamed of his emotion, yet unable to repress it wholly, the poor fellow stood awkwardly wiping away his tears with his rough sleeve, with his breast heaving, and the stertorous sobs still breaking from him.

"It will all be well," said Muriel, gently. "Do not grieve, Mr. Roux."

"Yes, Miss Eas'man, I wont; indeed I wont grieve. But sometimes I git desperate, Miss Eas'man," he faltered. "'Pears sometimes as if everybody was against us colored folks, Miss Eas'man."

"Cheer up, Roux, we are all your friends here."

It was the strong, sweet baritone of Harrington that sounded now. Roux looked up, smiling mournfully, into the masculine, calm features, which strangely comforted him.

"Yes, Roux, cheer up's the word. 'Tan't always goin' to be slavery and slaveholders in this free and happy country, mind that, my man."

Thus the Captain, shaking a fore-finger at the negro, and then cheerfully punching him in the ribs with it.

"An' if I catch any kidnappers round this establishment, I'll heave a brick at him," screeched Tugmutton, in a rage, glaring with rolling eyes at everybody over the baby.

Emily, who had risen, and stood wiping her eyes with a cambric handkerchief, burst into laughter, in which Muriel and Harrington joined. Tugmutton looked awfully irate for an instant, and then grinned sheepishly.

"Come, come," said Muriel, "we must be going. Where's the basket? Oh, there it is on the floor. Mr. Roux," she continued, stooping down to it, and unpacking, "I won't go in again to your wife—by the way, I hope our talk has not disturbed her—but here are some baby-clothes which I wore myself when I was a baby—old things which I found yesterday, but they'll do for the little boy. And here's some nice beef and a pie, which my mother had cooked expressly for your dinner to-day. And here's my copy of 'Uncle Tom's Cabin,' which you told me you hadn't read. When you and your wife are done with it, Tugmutton, as you call him, can bring it up to the house, with the plates and napkins."

The famous Uncle Tom had recently issued from the Boston press, and begun its illustrious journey through Christendom. Muriel handed the two volumes to Roux, who took them timidly, with a low bow, immensely gratified. The napkined meat and pie, she had already laid on the table, with the package of baby-clothes.

"And that's all," said Muriel, arranging the remaining contents of the basket under the fond eyes of Harrington. "The other things are for our Irish cousins in North Russell Street. You, John, shall carry the basket out to the carriage. Now let's go."

"Miss Eas'man," said Roux, "I'm so much obliged"——

"Never mind, Mr. Roux," interrupted Muriel, smiling gaily, "I see all that. Good bye."

She stooped to kiss the children, then with a curtsey, glided from the room. Roux, timidly rubbing his hands one within another, bowed after her, almost servile in his reverence. Tugmutton, severely dignified, and swelling like the frog that tried to be an ox, with the proud consciousness that something great had been done, and that it was all due to him, stood in the centre of the floor, with the baby clasped against his shoulder, and serenely waved his big paw in token of his distinguished consideration. Emily smiled at him, and bowing to Roux, swept with a rich rustle of silk after Muriel, followed by Harrington with the basket. The Captain lingered to bounce up Tom and Josey once apiece to the ceiling, and to poke Roux in the ribs with an anti-slavery forefinger, and then, shaking his fist at the grinning Tugmutton, departed also.

CHAPTER VIII.

THE SHADOW OF THE HUNTER.

Muriel and Emily were sitting on the back seat of the carriage as the Captain came down Roux's steps, nodding as he passed, and went down the street alone.

"Driver, North Russell street, and walk the horses," said Harrington, leaping in on the front seat, beside the basket.

The carriage immediately set off as directed, and Harrington, leaning forward, took Emily's gloved hands in his, and looked fervently into her beautiful face. Emily did not turn away this time, but forgetting that she thought him her lover, in her perception of an expression which recalled the look he had flashed at her in the room a few moments before, gazed anxiously with a vague tremor into his countenance, in which the winged nostrils were lifting.

"What is it, Harrington?" she faltered; "I'm afraid I have done something wrong, though"——

"No, dear Emily," interrupted Harrington; "nothing wrong Only unfortunate. You spoke from impulse; but it would have been better not to have said what you did before Roux."

"I understand," she replied, hurriedly. "I have raised hopes which may never be gratified. Heaven forgive me! O how thoughtless it was!"

Muriel put one arm around her, and looked into her face, with tender sympathy.

"You will think me ostentatious," faltered Emily, tears wetting her long lashes; "but, Harrington, it is not so. The poor man's distress touched me so keenly, that I could not forbear saying what I did."

"No, Emily," warmly returned Harrington, "you mistake. I do not think your offer was made in ostentation. Don't think me insensible to the splendid generosity that would give so large a sum to bring joy to the home of a poor, despised negro, and he a stranger to you. It is not a common heart that could enter into the depths of his sorrow, and so promptly seek to relieve it. But, listen, Emily. Muriel and I have a secret to tell you."

He released her hands to take a wallet from his breast-pocket, from which he drew a letter.

"God knows," he resumed sadly, "it is at best a noble folly to give away wealth, as you would do, to ransom one man from that dismal pit of slavery when nearly four millions with as strong a claim on our hearts must be left behind. And yet these individual cases come to us so like special claims, that we cannot deny them. See now—in this noble folly there was another heart before you. Yes, Emily, Muriel, too, was touched to the ransom of Roux's brother."

"Muriel!" exclaimed Emily.

"We said nothing to Roux," continued Harrington, "for the result was doubtful. And we had to proceed with caution lest this Lafitte should seek to capture him. I wrote a letter, which I had mailed from Philadelphia. Here is the fiend's answer, received two months ago. Don't read it unless you have strong nerves."

Emily eagerly snatched the letter from Harrington, and looked at the envelope. It was postmarked from Marksville, Louisiana, and directed to John Harrington, Esquire, care of Joseph House, Esquire, Philadelphia, Pennsylvania.

"Jo House is a young literary friend of mine—an editor," observed Harrington. "I explained the matter to him, telling the reason for secrecy, and got him to mail the letter for me, and transmit the answer. And by the way," he continued, "to give you an idea of the risk of dealing with such a man as Lafitte, let me tell you that since this letter was received, Lafitte has been up to Philadelphia, and called on Jo for my address, desiring, he said, to enter into negotiation with me for the sale of Antony."

"Good Heavens!" exclaimed Emily, with sudden alarm, "I hope your friend did not tell him where you were."

Harrington laughed.

"Not a bit of it," he replied. "What do you think Jo told him? He told him with the utmost gravity that I resided in London. And when Lafitte looked incredulous, the jolly young Bohemian produced a London Directory he happened to have, and showed him my name among the Harringtons, offering to copy the address for him."

Emily laughed delightedly.

"That was a brilliant fib, I declare," said she. "What did Lafitte say?"

"Jo wrote me that he looked as blank as a board, declined the offer, and went away. I can imagine that Jo's perfect soberness—for he's an awfully solemn-looking fellow—together with the circumstance of the London Directory being in his possession, convinced Lafitte of the truth of the statement, and I'll be bound he thinks Roux is on the other side of the Atlantic with my namesake."

Harrington laughed, but his laugh ended in a deep and weary sigh. Emily took the letter from the envelope, opened it, and began to read, while Muriel looked with sad tranquillity out at the carriage windows. The letter, read slowly in the swaying carriage, ran thus:

LAFITTE PLANTATION,
Parish of Avoyelles, Louisiana.

JOHN HARRINGTON, Esquire:

MY DEAR SIR: Your letter (appropriately dated the 7th of March—a souvenir of dear Mr. Webster—bless him! I can't think of that great speech without emotion—it was so noble) came to hand. In reply I beg to say that the dear Antony is alive and well, and, vicariously, sends his love and this little bunch of his wool to his beloved brother, whom you do not mention, but who is undoubtedly under your wing. So penetrated was the dear boy with a refluent sense of his brother's beastly ingratitude in leaving me, his affectionate master, that he was really unwilling to part with the wool, which I finally tore with loving violence from his black pate, and send in his behalf to your charge for the wicked William. As for Antony, the dear boy loves me so much that no money could persuade him to leave me, and for my part, I am so fond of him, that millions would not induce me to part with him. Thus, my dear sir, you will perceive that Antony is not for sale at any price.

I may add that dear Antony is a devout believer in the doctrine of vicarious atonement, and was so overcome with a new conviction of his brother's wickedness in leaving me, that he insisted on being trussed up and receiving fifty lashes, which I administered with my own hand, of course with tears in my eyes. I am sure that if the depraved William could have heard dear Antony's howls, he would have been stricken to the heart with a sense of his own unworthiness, and of the grandeur of this atoning love. To be frank with you, I am concerned lest Antony should carry his vicarious notions to the extent of demanding to be crucified for William's sins. In which case, I should feel compelled to oblige him. It would be difficult to carry out this sublime design; but, at a pinch, I could send away my overseer, and ride with Antony into the swamp, where we could readily extemporize a Calvary.

Give my love to Mr. Joseph House, *who does your Philadelphia mailing*, and believe me, dear sir,

Affectionately yours,

TORWOOD LAFITTE.

March 15th, 1852.

Emily turned white as marble over this insolent and horrible epistle, and, with her lips colorless, looked at Harrington, who took the letter from her hand.

"Charles Sumner has been in the Senate for six months, silent," remarked Harrington. "I have a mind to send him this letter."

"Now, John," said Muriel, smiling, "I won't tolerate any reflections on my neighbor. Every time I pass his house in Temple street, I think that he has not gone to Washington for nothing. Wait a little, and you shall hear the leap of the live thunder. In the meantime, as the knight Durindarte said to the weeping queen Belerma, 'patience, and shuffle the cards.'"

"You are right, Muriel," returned Harrington, with a faint smile, "we talk of his silence now, but we shall yet talk of his speech. Yes, the heart lives that shook Faneuil Hall for liberty, and we must not be impatient. But sometimes I despond, for it seems the destiny of our best men to lose power and purpose when they get into Congress."

"No matter," replied Muriel. "As King Pellinore said to Merlin, 'God may foredoo well destiny.'"

Harrington bent his head abstractedly.

"But to return," said he. "You observe, Emily, that the only result of my letter was to bring torture upon poor Antony. In the letter was a bunch of the poor fellow's hair, which this moral idiot tore from his head. You see, too, he flogged him in mere wantonness of cruelty. From all Roux tells me of the character of this man, I fear that he will end by killing Antony; and it is not too much to suppose, that with the opportunities the slave system gives him, he may even do it in the manner he suggests. Murders as dreadful take place on those obscure plantations, as escaped slaves tell us. Just see the infernal nature of a system which gives a fiend like this absolute, irresponsible control over his fellow creatures! Here is this pirate, with a pirate's name and a pirate's disposition; and the law of Louisiana, as of every Southern State in the Union, entrusts to his care as many men and women as he may choose to buy; and while it sanctions, by express statute, various degrees of cruelty toward them, makes it impossible to hold him to account for the most merciless torture and murder, by excluding the testimony of slaves."

Emily listened, with a countenance deathly pale.

"I declare, Harrington," she said, "when I read that letter I felt as if the earth had cracked and shown me a glimpse of hell. Is it possible that there can be such men as this? Are there many of them at the South?"

Harrington did not reply for a moment, and sat sadly looking into vacancy.

"It is not Southern nature," he said, at length, "it is human nature. It is human nature depraved by a tyranny, and licensed, practically licensed, even in its wildest excesses, by a tyrant code. Read Shakspeare; there you have in representative figures, the scientific account of man. Here is Shakspeare's Chiron, Demetrius, Iago, Cloten—a moral monster with statutory power to hold slaves, and treat them at his pleasure. But the blame is less with him than with the polity from which he sprang—which organized him and reared him. Bating for their life-long education in despotism, Southern men are no worse than Northern men. Put the code of Louisiana over Massachusetts, and you shall have the self-same results. Look at our Northern marine—that blot on our democracy; how does the despotism of it work on our captains, even with some sort of a legal check upon them? Read the criminal reports, or talk with seamen, and learn how Northern captains can maltreat the men under their command. No—human nature is no more incapable of degeneracy in Massachusetts than in Louisiana. If people are better here, it is because conditions are better."

"Such men as this Lafitte are more to be pitied than blamed," said Muriel, gently. "I wish we were great enough to feel so."

There was a moment's silence, in which nothing was heard but the slow rattle of the carriage-wheels over the paving-stones.

"You see, Emily," said Harrington, sadly, breaking the pause, "that your promise to Roux cannot be fulfilled. It is now our painful problem how to destroy his new hope, without giving him the anguish of an explanation. We are in a very difficult position."

"Oh, if I had only known of this!" cried Emily, in bitter distress. "As long as Roux expected nothing, he had only his ordinary pain. But I have lifted the poor man to this height only to dash him into a pit of despair."

"Hush, dear Emily," said Muriel, tenderly. "Do not reproach yourself. You could not have imagined that an effort had been made to buy Roux's brother. So don't feel badly about it. We will devise some means of escape out of this dilemma. What I am most afraid of is, that Lafitte may, after all, find out Harrington, and get on the track of Roux."

"In which case," said Harrington, tranquilly, "it would be a good idea to take him to Southac street and show him Roux's house."

"Harrington!" exclaimed Emily, almost shrilly.

"Yes indeed it would," said Harrington, quietly. "But before I showed him the house, I would say two words to Elkanah Brown. I'll engage that he would hurry back to the pirate civilization that spawned him, resolved never to set foot in Boston again. The negroes here would sound a roar in his ears that he would remember to his dying day."

"Good Heavens, Harrington," cried Emily, "they would kill him!"

Harrington's face was calm, but his blue eyes gleamed, and his broad nostrils lifted with passionate emotion.

"And if I were an American patriot, pure and simple," he replied, "I would answer that it would be no matter if they did, and that Bunker Hill is near enough to keep tyrannicide in countenance. You remember what one of our leading Whigs said in convention many years ago—in the time, when to be a Whig was not to be a Webster Whig, with a fine speech for kidnapping. 'Why, sir,' foamed a slaveholder, 'if your doctrines obtain, our slaves would cut our throats for us.' 'And in God's name,' said our Whig friend, tossing the words over his shoulder—'in God's name, why shouldn't they!"

"Oh, Harrington, Harrington," said Emily, shaking her head, "is this you? I did not think John Harrington had the heart to hate any man—not even Lafitte—much less kill him, or see him killed."

"Nor has he," said Muriel, quickly.

"You are right," said Harrington, calmly; "at least so far as the hating goes. It may be a defect in my organization, but I have never known what it is to hate anybody. I hope I never may. As for killing men, or seeing them killed, that is another matter. I believe that I could do both the one and the other without a pang. This Lafitte—a man in whom there is not one trait worthy to be called human—I could kill him or see him killed without the least regret. It is not his death but his life that should be regretted."

"But, Harrington," said Emily, "this is impossible. How could you beat a man, much less kill him, without hating him?"

"Christ beat the money changers in the temple: Was that hate?" answered Harrington.

Emily smiled vaguely.

"Well," she continued, "that is ingenious—but not conclusive. Besides, to beat men is not to kill them. You could hardly kill a man without hating him."

"Xenophon says Socrates shore down a soldier in the battle, and blessed him as he died: Was that hate?" answered Harrington.

Emily colored slightly, and looked up smiling into the calm countenance of the speaker.

"Death is not the worst fate that may befall a man," continued Harrington. "If to kill a man were to end his life, we might well hold our hands. But the soul survives the blow that slays the body."

"And to kill a man is only to shell him, Emily," said Muriel with a smile.

"Mercy!" exclaimed Emily, laughing, "what a couple of Robespierres!"

"Seriously, now," said Harrington, "I think Muriel is right. A killed man is a shelled man, and not a dead man. 'Where shall we bury you?' asked the friends around the dying Socrates. And the escaping soul replied, 'Wherever you please, if you can catch me.' But with regard to this matter. If I believed in free will and moral responsibility, and all the doctrines professedly accepted by the mass of my fellow-citizens, I should hold that, on the principle of justice, we had a right to terminate the life of a man who was willfully using it to the injury of his fellow-creatures. For I agree with Lord Bacon that men without goodness of nature are but a nobler kind of vermin. But, as I happen to think that such men are the necessary product of an unscientific order of society, and that society is responsible for them and their misdeeds, I could only kill them at the cry of a terrible expediency, not to punish them, but simply to arrest their mischief. At the same time I go with Shakespeare, rather to 'prevent the fiend' than to kill the fiend. I would not kill a rattlesnake lying harmlessly in the sun, simply because he is a rattlesnake, and may bite to-morrow. But if he coils to strike, I slay him, purely as a measure of safety, not in hate, not forgetting that forces external to him organized him for malice and venom. So, too, with the nobler vermin—the human reptiles. I do not hate them ; I pity them. I do not forget that they are a consequence, and not self-caused. But I cannot let them flesh their fangs in the innocent, when the saving mercy of a death-blow can rescue their blameless victims to lives of human use and accomplishment. When such men as Lafitte come here to hunt the poor, I baffle and drive them away if I can, and, as a last resort, I kill them. That is not hate—it is love. It is stern love, but it is love. Wo to the civilization that makes it necessary! Wo to the state that suffers an injury to be done to the humblest man or woman, or leaves his or her protection to the chance charity of the private citizen! And treble wo to the government that gives despotic power to ruffians, and arms and guards them in their crime against mankind with the prestige and forms of civil law !"

Harrington ceased, and they all sat in silence with brooding faces.

"Well, I trust that this wretch may never trouble Boston," said Emily, at length, with a sigh.

"I trust not," replied Harrington. "He is shrewd and subtle though, and I have, I own, an anxious foreboding that he will come this way. I am sorry I wrote that letter. You observed the underlined sentence in his reply, didn't you ? It is curious that he should have so readily conjectured that the letter was sent to Jo House to mail."

"Very curious," responded Emily.

"Here's North Russell street," said Harrington. "I'll leave you, and rush home, for I have my article to finish."

"Harrington—whisper," said Muriel, bending her face toward him with a charming smile.

Harrington, who was just putting out his hand to unfasten the carriage door, leaned forward, while Emily turned away. The young man felt, with a delicious thrill, the balmy breath of Muriel on his cheek, and her soft lips touch his ear, and the hot blood flew to his face before she had spoken a word.

"John," she whispered, "you write your article to make some money. Hush, now! Let it go, and let me supply you—just for once now, pray do. Don't be proud and foolish, but let me make you a present, for I have plenty, and come with us and have a day of recreation, for you are pale with work and study—now, John."

"Now, John," was said aloud with arch reproach, for Harrington had drawn back, flushed and laughing, with a gesture of negation.

"Not a bit of it," he answered, gaily. "Did I ever?"

"No, you never did, bad young man that you are," returned Muriel, aloud, with a face of playful reproach. "But see here, John"—she bent forward again to whisper, her face so sweetly pleading that it was hard to resist giving the besought audience.

"I won't—that's flat," said Harrington, laughing and blushing, and putting out his hand to the hasp, for he felt that Muriel's entreaty was getting dangerous.

"Very well," she said. "That's settled. But come up to tea this evening—come up early, if you can, and we'll have a fencing lesson, and then, after tea, we'll go to the Convention, trusting our luck to hear Wendell Phillips. How will that do?"

"Capital," replied Harrington. "I'll come."

"And bring Wentworth with you."

"Yes. Good bye. Good bye, Emily."

Emily turned and nodded, with her face scarlet at the mention of Wentworth's name. She had been living in broader life for the last hour, and now her heart was painfully sinking back to its private love and sorrow.

Without stopping the carriage, Harrington opened the door, sprang out, and walked for a moment between the wheels to refix the hasp, then stepped back, touched his hat, and was gone.

Muriel turned and watched from the oval window in the back of the carriage his martial figure as it strode up the street.

"There goes a chevalier," she said, gaily, as she turned away.

"Yes," replied Emily. "First in war, first in peace"——

"And first in the hearts of his countrywomen," concluded Muriel.

They laughed merrily, and the carriage went on.

CHAPTER IX.

SCHOLAR AND SOLDIER.

Harrington lived in Chambers street, not far from where he had left the carriage, and strode on over the pavement of Cambridge street to his house, drawing in deep breaths of the delicious, cool, spring air, and thinking with a rapt heart of Muriel.

It was a perfect day. The long thoroughfare sloping gently, and narrowing away into distance, with its descending row of irregular, motley buildings of brick and wood, and its lines of passengers, was fresh and salient in the morning sunlight. Blown from the country, wafts of woodland odors, balmy as the breath of Muriel, floated softly to his sense. Flowing out of the west, the morning wind, light as the lips of Muriel, touched his cheeks, and the young man's heart and blood were full of love and spring.

O, blessed magic of one little moment, which had repaired what hours and days undid! Her breath had breathed upon his sense, her lips had met his cheek, and therefore, all thought that she loved another, all evidence that her soul was not in secret, firm alliance with his own, had vanished in the flash of rapture which filled his being. And more—the phantoms which surrounded him had vanished too. Born servant and soldier of mankind, he was often made to feel how powerless he was in the great social war of the many against the one; and at such times, to his spirit, as to that of many a lover of men, came gloomy spectres from the world of complicated wo and wrong. From the grim-grotesque, sad, turbulent scene of the morning street; from the low room of the fugitive's humbleness and anguish, and the futile generosity of the patrician girl; from the cloud on the horizon of his soul, where glimmered the image of the coming hunter; from the whole dark consciousness of a social order leagued against the poor and weak, the invading phantoms had poured like midnight ghosts around him. But they were all gone, and again there was strength and morning in his soul. The spring day was sweet and beautiful; perfume and victory coursed through his veins; the noble face of his beloved bloomed in his heart; her wild-rose mouth had touched him like the envoy of a costly kiss; her fragrant breath had shot his blood with ecstasy; and past and future melted into the rich passion of the present hour, which had renewed his manhood and left him with the pulse and thews of a Crusader.

Flushed and throbbing with the bliss of his thought of Muriel, he reached his dwelling. It was an old, three-storied, quaintly-fashioned brick house, with green blinds, windows and window-panes smaller than those of modern date, and in the centre, up three stone steps, a door with a brass knocker, and a brass plate below it, on which was engraved the name, E. Z. FISHER. The house breathed in an air fragrant with lilacs, whose clumped green and purple bloomed pleasantly over the top of a close board fence, with a gate in it, which extended from the left hand side of the tenement to the blind side-wall of the adjoining dwelling, and inclosed a yard within which abutted from the main building a wing of two stories. In this wing dwelt Harrington; the rest of the house was occupied by the Captain and his family.

He opened the gate and entered the yard, which was in fact a small garden. A planked footway led from the gate to the two wooden steps of the door in the wing, and a similar footway crossed this, and crooked around the side of the abutment. Lilac bushes were planted against the fence and the blind wall of the dwelling on the left, and there were shrubs and flowers on either side of the door, and around the wall of the wing. It was a pleasant spot, full of fragrance and retiracy.

Without pausing, Harrington unlocked his door and entered his study. It was a square room, cool and quiet, lit by two green-curtained front windows which looked on the garden, and containing several hundred volumes on shelves, row above row, on three sides of the apartment. In the centre was a table loaded with books and papers, and an arm-chair. Four or five choice engravings hung in spaces between the book-shelves, and on one side, on a pedestal, was a noble bust of Lord Bacon. A set of foils and masks hung across the mantel, and a huge pair of dumb-bells lay on the floor in a corner. A carpet of green baize, an old sofa between the windows, and a few chairs, completed the furniture of the room, whose only other noticeable feature was a slanting step-ladder on one side, leading up by a trap in the ceiling into Harrington's bed-chamber.

Throwing himself into his arm-chair, the young scholar took from a drawer, and pressed to his lips, a little bunch of withered herbs, which Muriel had held in her hand one evening two or three weeks before, and given him at parting. Their dry balsamic odor stole softly to his brain, freighted with the thought of the white hand that gave them, and closing his eyes, he abandoned himself to ecstatic dreams.

In a few minutes, a barrel-organ began to play outside his gate. It was a peculiarly sweet instrument—some people in the region of Beacon Hill may remember it as the one they used to follow from street to street on balmy summer evenings, so loth were they to part with its melody. Harrington was fond of all barrel-organs that were at all melodious—the poor man's opera, he used to call them, associating them with the delight they gave to little children and the dwellers in poor houses, and always pleased to have them bring Italy into the street, as some one has felicitously phrased it. The organist, sure of his reward whenever his patron was at home, came often to the house. On this occasion, Harrington had no sooner heard the first notes, than he twisted up some change in paper, and opening the door, tossed it over the gate. The instrument stopped in the midst of the tune, and while the man was picking up the largesse, Harrington opened his windows, and resumed his chair to enjoy the music.

A rich light gush of lilac fragrance which seemed to blend

with the brilliant melody of the polacca the organ played, poured in at the open windows, and melted into his mood. He sat softly beating with his hand the dance of the tune, with the debonair image of Muriel floating in melody through his fancy. She came again, expressed in a tenderer mood, as the music changed to a strain of yearning and dreamful sweetness, like a poem of deep love. Then followed one of the negro melodies of the day, a simple and mournful air, with notes of anguish, and still she was present in his mind linked with a shadowy remembrance of the wrongs and sorrows of the race to whose low estate her heart stooped so often to help and console. Soul in soul, he moved with her through the rich and melancholy maze of the succeeding music—a sombre and sumptuous Italian romanza, crowded with slow passion and tumult, with notes that swelled and poured athwart the central theme, like some dim innumerable host of love and sorrow gathering and forming, and dividing again in baffled and harmonious disorder. Air upon air came after, and sinking away, the listener lost for awhile their melody and meaning, and only knew that they were sweet and sad; till rising from reverie he heard the last of a solemn and tender strain like some delicious psalm of death and life immortal.

It ceased; there was a pause, and the world's hopes and struggles surged in upon his kindled spirit, as the organ rolled forth in golden sweetness the martial and mournful andante of the Marsellaise. The French hymn of liberty, whose sombre and fiery tonal morning burst once on the birth-throes of Democracy, like the light of God upon the chaos of the globe! He never heard it without emotion, and now it rushed into his soul, dilating and expanding into vast orchestral harmonies. His eye gleamed and bright color lit his face as he listened to the triumphal terror and glory of the thrilling strain. On and on it swept in cadences of tears and fire; down and down it darkened in weird and burning melody, fraught with the passion of all human wrongs; and rising into the pealing cry of the battle-summons, and flowing into the proud, heroic tones of mournful rapture which seem to exult for the dead who die for man, it melted away.

Harrington sat, flushed and throbbing, in the fragrant silence of the room. The organ had ceased and gone, and he was alone. Gradually the tumult of his spirit sank into golden calm, and with the charm of the music still lingering in his mind, he put the faded herbs into the drawer, and prepared to begin his tasks.

His unfinished article was the first thing to be attended to, and he got it out and set to work upon it. The article, as Muriel had said, he was writing for money, for Harrington's means sometimes ran low. His mother dying six years before, when he was nineteen, had left him her little property, including this house. The house he rented to Captain Fisher, and this rent, added to the interest of the money his mother had left him, gave him a yearly income of about six hundred dollars. An economical and selfish man might have got on well enough on these receipts ; but Harrington, though economical enough, was anything but selfish, and between his own expenses and his pecuniary outlay for others, he sometimes found himself in want of money. On these occasions he was wont to interrupt his studies to write for certain periodicals till he wrote himself into funds again. What he wrote sold well, and his pen was in demand ; but philosophy, Hegel said, has nothing to do with dollars, and Harrington evidently thought scholarship had not either, for when he had once filled the gap in his finances, back he went to his studies, and the magazine editor did not live who could tempt him from them into another contribution.

For he was a scholar born, and in this room he kept alive the traditions which have made the name of Harrington dear to scholarship and man. It is a shining name in literature and history, and bears the recorded honors due to names linked with the memory of human pleasure or the cause of human service. There was one Harrington in the days of the Eighth Henry—a polished poet, who surpassed the verse of his time. There was another, his child, the darling of Queen Elizabeth, a sprightly wit and poet, who sunned his muse in the brightness of the bright Britannic days, wrought well for belle-lettres and history, and gave his country her first English version of the fun and fire of Ariosto. There was still another, the Oxford scholar of a later age, of whom the chronicle records that he was a prodigy in the common law, a person of excellent parts, honest in dealing, and of good and generous nature. There was one more, loftier far than these, whose mighty pulses beat for liberty and justice, the brave Utopian of Sidney's time, who aimed to lay the deep foundations of the perfect and immortal state—James Harrington, the author of Oceana. And among the rest, skilled or famed in law and science and poetry, there was yet another, James Harrington's true brother by a closer tie than that of blood—the stout jurist of Vermont, who spoke the decision of her Supreme Court on the demand of a slave claimant, decreeing that his title to a man was not good till he could show a bill of sale from the Almighty God. That was Judge Harrington, and by that decree he earned his right to a statue from mankind.

Whatever was best and greatest in the works and days of the ancestral Harringtons, seemed likely to be renewed and excelled by the young scholar who bore their name. Primarily, he was a Baconist. There stood the bust of Bacon on the pedestal in his library, and to him it was the treasure of treasures. Wentworth used to say jestingly, that Harrington was a heathen and worshipped an idol. For the idol, however, Wentworth himself, with Muriel, was responsible. Harrington had been sadly disappointed in not being able to find any bust of Verulam at the statuary's; so Wentworth and Muriel had collected the various portraits of the great Chancellor, moulded from them a bust in clay, somewhat larger than life, cast it in plaster, and one day Harrington, entering his study, was astonished and enraptured at finding the bust there on its pedestal. It was a magnificent success, and well embodied the noble sagacity, the tender and gentle sweetness, the regal compassion and calm, massive intellectuality, which appear in Bacon's enormous brow and face of princely majesty, as the painters of his time have pictured him.

Harrington now loved Bacon with tenfold ardor, and Harrington's love for Bacon was something wonderful. It was absolutely a personal attachment, and there was no surer way to rouse him than to speak disparagingly of Verulam. He put him above all authors or men. He spoke of him as the flower of the human race. He resented any imputation on his fame, scouted at the modern aspersions upon him of Lord Campbell, Macaulay and others, as baseless and infamous slanders, and altered Pope's epigrammatic line, which he thought the seed-cone of the whole modern libel, to read "the wisest, brightest, *noblest* of mankind." With a standing promise to his friends to put the evidence together some day in demonstrable form, having already, he said, begun to make notes to that end, he meanwhile rested in the broad assertion that Bacon's downfall was the work of the conservatism of his time—that the conservators of social abuses had smelt out his concealed democracy and socialism, trumped up the charge of malfeasance in office against him, ruined and defamed him in his life and flung the mire of a traditionary calumny on his tomb. It was another of Harrington's heresies that Bacon in the seventeenth century aimed to do for the world what Fourier aimed to do in the nineteenth. This, he insisted, was the key to his works and life—this the torch by which they were to be read and interpreted. It was evident that Harrington had a very pretty affair on his hands, should he ever venture to publish an idea so heretical. The sin of connecting the world-honored Verulam with the man whom modern society has endowed, as Muriel said, with hoofs and horns and a harpoon tail, and of asserting that either or both had meant to bring the kingdom of God upon the earth, would be only less than the effort of both or either to so interfere with our highly respectable institutions.

However this may be, Harrington's heart was anchored on the idea, and with this faith in him, he studied his Bacon, together with Montaigne and Shakspeare, who, he thought, or seemed to think—for on this point he was mysteriously non-committal—were in the interest of the Baconian design. Possibly, he might yet come to different conclusions, for he was young; and, like Sterne's Pilgrim, had just begun his journey, and had much to learn.

Meanwhile he pursued his studies, though with the full conciousness that there was no accredited career open to him. To a man who held unpopular convictions as he did; no more a Christian of the modern sort than Christ was; no more a patriot of the modern sort than Sidney was; no more a believer in the modern order of society than Bacon and Fourier were; despising the Government as an engine of force and fraud; refusing assent to the Constitution, and allegiance to the Union, because in his view they legalized and fortified the crime and ruin of Slavery—to such a man the church, the bar, the bench, the senate, the official station of any kind were all closed. But Harrington had a solemn instinct at his heart, that the time was coming when his country would rise against slavery and social wrong and call upon her outlawed sons for their best service. Against that day he prepared himself to do his part, whatever it might prove to be. In his conception of it, the utter annihilation of slavery was first in the programme. This involved the possibility of civil war. It might come between the dark millions of the South and the Government. It might come between the Government's pro-slavery liegemen and the freemen of the North. In either case, Harrington was pledged to serve liberty, and that his service might be efficient, he had begun the study of military science, and had the best text books, such as those of Mahan, Kinsley, Thiroux and Knowlton, together with the chief standard works relating to warfare, from the Commentaries of Cæsar to the volumes of Durat-Lasalle To this end also went his varied practice with Bagasse in the school of arms, with rifle practice elsewhere. Hoping, too, that the period of social reconstruction would come in his own time or follow hard upon it, he was preparing to add his thought to bring it on, or shape his thought to guide it when it should come, and to this end were his scholastic labors. His shelves might have hinted as much. There were the works of the masters of law and government, and of those who have studied and schemed for society, Plato, Aristotle, Pythagoras, Cicero, Justinian, Grotius, Burlamaqui, Vattel, Puffendorff, Heneicius, Milton, Sidney, Harrington, Pothier, Montaigne, Machiavelli, Bacon, Montesquieu, Bentham, Burke, St. Simon, Fourier, Compte—legists, jurists, scholiasts, works of practice and theory, statements of codes, and books that are the seed of codes. With them works of exact science in all its branches, and works of history, biography, poetry, travel and fiction, classic and modern—for it was Harrington's design to grasp the thought and life of all the ages.

So toiled he. No dilettante litterateur; no student forgetful of his time and kind, or gaining lore to fortify or gild oppression;—but kinsman to the golden blood of the gallant scholars to whose graves the heart brings its laurels and its tears. No scholar, either of the modern sort, which stores the brain and saps the arm—but of the large Elizabethan type, training his body in every manly exercise, training his mind in equal skill and power. Such was the budding promise of Harrington.

CHAPTER X.

CONVERSATION.

In the young man's kindled mood, composition was easy, and by two o'clock his article was done.

He was leaning back in his chair, enjoying the consciousness of eighty dollars earned, when the door opened, and in came the Captain, with his head very much on one side, and an ominous gravity on his quaint features. He did not remove his straw-hat, but stood surveying Harrington with a critical eye, like a marine raven. A slow smile twinkled around the young man's bearded mouth, for he instantly divined what the Captain had come for.

"Well, Eldad," he said, "it's the rent, I know. I see rent written in every lineament of your ingenuous countenance. Come, sit down."

The Captain slowly lifted his clenched fist and shook it at Harrington, then lounged about, seated himself on the sofa under the windows, and cocked up his eye at the trap in the ceiling.

"Could I smoke, John?" he asked, suddenly dropping his glance at the young man.

"Certainly. Light up, and smoke away."

Keeping his head on one side, and his round, bright eyes intent on the smiling Harrington, the Captain produced a short pipe and a match from the hollow of his left hand, and putting the pipe in one corner of his mouth, lit the match on his sleeve, and igniting the tobacco, began to blow a cloud.

"And why didn't you come to dinner?" he blandly demanded, opening the war.

"Dinner! I declare I never thought of it till this minute," exclaimed Harrington, coloring a little.

"It was a brile to-day, John," pursued the Captain, contemplatively, smoking. "Briled steak, potatoes, spinach, with a top off of bread puddin' and coffee," he continued, pensively enumerating the components of the meal. "Together with bread and butter, and apple-sarce. Joel James eat till he thought his jacket was buttoned. Hannah says, 'I wonder where John is?' Sophrony answers, 'he's in his room, for I see him go in at eleven o'clock.' 'Better call him,' says John H. 'Better not,' says I, 'or you'll scatter some of his idees.' So we didn't."

Harrington listened attentively to this account of the family colloquy on his absence from the dinner-table. Joel James was the Captain's son, a sturdy schoolboy of ten. Sophronia was his daughter, a girl of fifteen. John H. was the youngest son, named after Harrington. Hannah was the Captain's wife.

"John," said the Captain, changing the subject, "two hundred and fifty's not enough. I'm goin' to raise it to three hundred."

"Good!" exclaimed Harrington, with a jovial air. "I knew it was the rent! Eldad, this rent is our standing grievance. Well, I'm going to lower it to two hundred."

"In which event, I'm going to move, bag and baggage," retorted the Captain.

Harrington laughed aloud, and sat smiling at the Captain, whose quaint features were screwed into a grin, and momently lit in little flashes of red from the bowl of the pipe near his cheek.

"Eldad," replied Harrington, "if I had my way, you should have the house rent free."

"Which I wunt," said the Captain.

"Of course you won't," continued Harrington; "but, Eldad, you were mother's mainstay, and have been like a father to me since she died, and it grates on my feelings to have you paying me money. Well, no matter. Let it go. But I'll be even with you one of these days."

"Well," returned the Captain, "it's settled then?"

"Yes, I suppose so."

"Three hundred, you say."

"O no, Eldad. Two fifty.

"Three hundred."

"Two fifty."

"Three hundred dollars."

"Two hundred and fifty dollars, Eldad. Not another stiver. I'm resolved now."

The Captain sighed, and smoked pensively.

"I lost a customer to-day, John," he remarked, after a long pause.

"Indeed! Which induced you to increase your expenses, by raising the rent," bantered Harrington.

"Collected for him these six years back," continued the Captain, pensively. "Lem Atkins, you know."

"Lemuel Atkins!" exclaimed Harrington, leaning forward. "Why that's Mrs. Eastman's brother."

"Certain. Cotton merchant on Long Wharf, and a black sheep he is too. Webster Whig—pro-slavery up to the hub—reg'lar aristocrat every way. He was one of the Fifteen Hundred Scoundrels, as Phillips called 'em. Ruther guess all the bad that ever was in his sister and niece was drawn off before they were born, and bottled up in him."

"And how came you to lose him?" interrogated Harrington.

"Well, I'll tell you," replied the Captain. "You see, I've collected the rents of eight of his houses for six years back—

some of 'em went ruther aginst my grain, too. Poor houses, scacely fit for human bein's to live in, two or three of 'em, and sech as no decent man would own or let out to anybody. Howiver. He gave me the memorandums of three more about a week ago. Mighty big rents Atkins gits for these dwellin's, thinks I to myself, as I entered them on my book. Spoon o' horn! I niver guessed it till I went down there yesterday, an' found out what sort of houses them are for which Atkins gits his big rents."

"That's fine in Atkins," remarked Harrington. "Always talking about the duty of citizens to obey the laws, right or wrong, and here he violates the statute against letting houses for such purposes. But perhaps he didn't know who his tenants were."

"*He* know? Lord! he knew fast enough," replied the Captain. "Laws? All the laws he obeys are the laws that go for his money. There's lots like him. They go for every money law, from the Fugitive Slave Law upward, for I ruther guess there ain't no downward from the Fugitive Slave Law. Why, there's a Massachusetts law aginst over usury. Who don't keep it? Who lets out money for ten per cent., twenty per cent., any per cent. they can git? Them very sort o' men that's always blatherin' about obedience to the laws, right or wrong. Ony when a man's libaty's consarned, and the law goes for takin' it away from him, then they're awfully law-abidin' citizens. By the great horn spoon! I'd just like to have the stringin' up of them law-abiders with a copy of the Revised Statutes round their necks!"

Harrington leaned back in his chair, with his hands clasped, and his brow knitted.

"Well, as I was sayin'," resumed the Captain, "I went into one of them houses. 'Young women,' says I, leavin', 'you'd better repent, for the kingdom of heaven's at hand.' I tell you I was mad when I found a similar state o' things in the tother two, and I just bounced out, and went right down to Lem Atkins. 'Mr. Atkins,' says I, 'you'd better employ your former agent for them houses.' 'What's the matter, Fisher,' says he. 'Matter is,' says I, 'that I guess you don't know what sort o' callin''s followed in them tenements.' 'It's not my business, Mr. Fisher,' says he, 'to busy myself with the occupation of my tenants. How dare you speak to me in that manner.' I looked him right in the eye. He swelled up like a turkey-cock, but he didn't look at me a second. 'Mr. Atkins,' says I, 'no offince, but as I've got sons and a daughter, the occupation of your tenants is a consarn o' mine, and you must get another man to collect them rents, for I wunt do it, an' I pity the man that will.' He turned off to his desk. 'Mr. Fisher,' says he, 'you wunt do any more collectin' for me, so just send up your accounts, and we'll be quits.' 'Very well,' says I, and I left with his collectin' off my hands for good."

"Bravo, Eldad! That was done like a man!" cried Harrington.

"If it wasn't for bringin' disgrace on his sister and that splendid daughter of hers," said the Captain, rising, with his pipe in his clenched hand, "I'd just let the thing be known around town, I would. Say, John, she's a beauty, though, ain't she? John, she's the ony lady I know that's good enough for you."

Harrington colored deeply, in spite of himself.

"Well, the other one's splendid, too," said the Captain, as if in answer to a private thought of the young man, scrutinizing his countenance meanwhile, with his own head all awry. "Yes, she's a regular clipper. I never was so took aback by any human action as by that offer to buy Roux's brother. That was ginerosity such as we read of—ony it's a pity she didn't know the harm she was doin'. Yes, she's a glory, and that's a fact. Still, I wish it was tother one."

"Why, Eldad," said Harrington, laughing and fiery red, "you're all at sea. Surely you don't think I'm in love with Miss Ames?"

The Captain looked hard at him.

"Well, so I've ben told, John," he replied.

Harrington puckered up his mouth in wonder.

"Bless me, how people will talk!" he exclaimed. "Why there's not a word of truth in it. Of course I like Emily very much"——

"And she you," interposed the Captain.

"And she me? I declare! I shall hear next that she is in love with me, I suppose!" exclaimed Harrington.

"Well, so I've ben told," coolly responded the Captain; "dead in love with you."

Harrington stared at him, but the color ebbed away from his countenance, and a flood of dreadful confirmations over-swept him. Her recent sudden preference for his society, her lavish attentions to him, the fervent and sumptuous fondness of her manner, rushed in new light upon his consciousness. Purblind fool that I am, he thought; I mistook it all for friendship, and it meant love! For a moment, poor Harrington felt as guilty as though he had known and encouraged Emily's passion for him. But no, he thought, this is all a mistake; it cannot be.

"Eldad," said he, "this is rather a serious matter; more serious than you may imagine. Come, now, be frank with me. You say you've been told Miss Ames is in love with me. Now who told you!"

The Captain, with his head all atwist, scanned him curiously, slowly rubbing his chin, meanwhile, with the palm of his brown hand.

"Well, John," he answered, slowly, "I was asked not to mention it. Howiver, I guess I will. That young Witherlee told me."

"Oh!" said Harrington.

"Yis, John," continued the Captain. "I come in here one day about a week ago, I guess, an' found him sittin' in your chair, smokin' his cigar. He said he was waitin' for you, an' we had a chat. In the course of the conversation, he let that out. I ruther thought he was tryin' to pump somethin' out of me on that subject, but I didn't know nothin', an' if I did, he wouldn't have been the wiser, I guess."

"What did he say?" asked Harrington.

"Well, not overmuch," replied the Captain. "Seemed to know all about it, howiver. Talked as if he was in your confidence. Asked when you were goin' to be married. Well, now, he didn't exactly *say* it, you know, but he somehow gave me to understand that you were in love with Miss Ames, an' she likewise with you ; an' thought her family wouldn't make no objections. That was about all."

Harrington, with a look of pain, reddened while the Captain was speaking, and his nostrils quivered.

"I am shocked and grieved that Witherlee should talk in this way," he said, sadly. "I shall certainly call him to account for this."

"John, you musn't mention it," said the Captain, anxiously. "He said he thought I knew all about it, or he wouldn't have alluded to it, and he made me promise not to speak of it. It won't do, John. Fact is, I oughtn't to have said a word."

Harrington leaned his elbows on the table, and for a moment buried his face in his hands. He had a clear glimpse into the method of the good Fernando.

"Very well, Eldad," he said, calmly, leaning back in his chair. "Let it go, I won't speak of it. But I assure you there's not a word of truth in this statement, so far as I'm concerned, and I hope there is not in regard to Miss Ames !"

The Captain did not answer, but lounged away, and during the long silence that followed, walked up and down with a ruminating air. At length he stopped and fronted the young man, who was absorbed in musing.

"John," said he, "to-day's the day, you know."

Harrington, knowing what he meant, bent his head, looking with half-absent sadness into vacancy.

"Twelve years ago to-day, John, the good ship Contocook went down," continued the Captain, in a hushed voice, with a half-soliloquizing air. "All the women an' children saved. That was a comfort, John."

Harrington again bowed his head silently. Every year, on the twenty-fifth of May, he was accustomed to hear the Captain speak of this.

"And all the men saved, John," continued the Captain. "That was another comfort. All but one, John."

The Captain paused, solemnly, and took off his hat.

"As good a seaman as ever trod the deck," he resumed.

"As fine a man as ever breathed the breath of life. Captain John Harrington, aged forty-two. Blessed are the dead who die in the Lord!"

There was a long silence.

"And he died in the Lord, John, continued the Captain." I don't know as he ever got religion. But he died in the Lord."

The Captain paused once more, muttering the last words below his breath.

"Yes, John," he continued, "that's the way he died. I've been thinkin' of it all day. It's been comin' to me how that rollin' iceberg tumbled through the thick fog, in the dead of night, and struck the ship, and stove in her bows. 'Back from the boats,' he shouts, catchin' up the hand-spike. 'The first man that touches a boat I'll brain. Women and children first, men.' 'That's the talk,' sings out some of the sailors, an' them that was goin' to take the boats fell away. 'Now, then, the women and children,' says he. Over the side they went, one by one; he standin' by with the handspike. 'Now the other passengers,' says he. Over they went too. 'Now, men,' he says, 'there's room in that boat for some of ye, and the rest of us 'll go into the other. Over they went, likewise, till only he and the black cook was left. 'The boat's full, captain,' says John Timbs, the first mate, 'but I guess she'll hold another.' 'Jump in doctor,' says Captain Harrington to the darkey. 'No,' they hollered, 'white men before niggers, captain, and we'll have you.' 'I'll stay, captain,' blubbers cook, 'No you won't,' says he. 'Men,' he says, 'it's a favor I ask. Don't deny me, or you'll never know peace. In with you, doctor,' an' he slung the cook over the side. 'Try now, captain,' says they, all beseechin' together. An' he let himself down by the rope till he stood in the boat, an' the sea begun to come over the gunnels. He was up into the ship again in a minute. 'It's no use, men,' says he, 'push off. Timbs,' says he, 'give my love to my wife and boy, if I never see 'em again. God bless ye, men.' And then the ship lurched for'ard, an' they pushed off, cryin' like babes. Last thing they saw through the fog was the captain flingin' a hatch overboard, and jumpin' after it. But that sea was too cold for a man to be in long. Then when they lost sight of him, they heard the wallow, an' saw the lazy swells lift up round the boat, an' knew that the ship had gone down."

The Captain paused, wiping away with his sleeve the salt tears which the simple epic of a brave man's death brought to his eyes.

"That was the story, and them was the last words Timbs brought home to your mother, John," he continued. "An' that's the way he died. Women and children saved. That's a comfort. An' all the men saved, includin' the poor old moke of a doctor. That's another comfort. But he died. An', somehow, I kinder feel that's a comfort too, John. For he died in the Lord."

The light lay softly on the pale and kindled features of Harrington, and the fragrance of the garden floated through his brain like incense.

"It was a manly way to leave the world," he said. "Life is sweet to me with the memory of such a father."

"You think of him often, John," murmured the Captain.

"Often, Eldad, often. Never as one dead. Always as one alive and well."

The Captain moved his head up and down, two or three times, in token of assent, and moved away to the door.

"Well, good bye, John," he said, suddenly.

"Good bye, Eldad," returned the young man, rising and following him to the door.

The Captain departed, and Harrington, closing the door after him, folded his arms, and began to pace to and fro in deep musing. The sweet and solemn feeling which the anniversary of his father's death brought him, gradually melted away in feelings of sadness and pain, as the torturing thought came into his mind, that in his free and frank friendship for Emily he might have won her to love him. The more he reflected upon it, the more terrible grew the confirmations. His conviction of a fortnight before, that she and Wentworth were lovers—how could he have been so deceived!

The spell of the magic moment that had filled his soul with morning, was disenchanted now, and darkness gathered upon him. Darkness that was not without light, for he again believed that Wentworth and Muriel loved each other, and he felt a sorrowful and generous gladness in their happiness. His heart yearned to Wentworth—yearned to make him rejoice with the assurance that he was not his rival—yearned to them both in love and blessing.

He paused in his walk, as through his joy for them struck the sharp pain of the consciousness that the costly treasure of her love was not for him.

"Heart of my heart, soul of my soul," he murmured fervently, "I love you, though I lose you. All that is divine and human is dearer and lovelier to me because I love you, though you are lost to me. Lost, lost to me forever."

His head sunk upon his breast, and his eyes closed. The lilac fragrance floated in and reeled in a warm gust upon his throbbing brain. Some silent spirit seemed near him in the sunlit room, and strange comfort stole upon him like the bliss of a dream.

"Farewell, Muriel," he murmured, his blue eyes unclosing, dimmed with a mist of tears, "farewell, farewell. It is one hope the less, and life calls me still."

He sunk into his chair, and striving to banish her image from his mind, began to think how he should deal with Emily. In a little while he resolved that, however difficult and delicate to do, he must frankly tell her of what he had heard, and let her know his true relation to her.

His conclusion made, he still sat musing, his spirit clouded with sadness and anxiety. Suddenly he heard the gate fly open and slam to, and a firm tread rush over the planked walk, then the door opening, in darted Wentworth, flushed, electric, panting, furious with rage.

CHAPTER XI.

NORTH AND SOUTH.

THE family of the Mr. Lemuel Atkins, of whom the Captain had spoken, belonged to what is called Good Society ; but let no one suppose that they constituted a specimen of the Boston aristocracy, with its men, too often, indeed, cold and careless in the interests of mankind, yet always polished gentlemen in instinct and education, and with its women, cultured and noble, patrician from brow to foot, and many, very many of them, angels of compassion and succor to the weak and poor. The Atkinses were only of a large and dominant moneyed class, vulgar mushrooms—no, toadstools—who spring up thickly in the aristocratic quarter and call themselves Good Society!

These fine people were expecting a guest to dinner that afternoon, who would have been a skeleton at any possible banquet of Harrington's, could he have known that such a guest was in town. Mr. Atkins's usual dinner hour was two o'clock, but on this occasion it had been postponed to four, while the merchant was showing the guest a few of the lions.

It was within an hour of the dinner-time, and the servants in the kitchen were sweltering over the preparation of the meal in the hottest possible hurry, and the greatest possible trepidation, lest anything should be overdone or underdone, or in any way done wrong. For they had been duly impressed with the magnitude of the occasion, and they were trembling lest the magnitude of the occasion should be disgraced by their humble efforts.

Meanwhile Good Society was filled with soft tremors in the drawing-room above. He had not come yet, but he was coming. Anxious eyes glanced occasionally out at the front windows on Mount Vernon street, to see if he was approaching. Eager ears listened momently for the slightest intimation of a pull at the bell-wire. Palpitating hearts leaped at every footfall in the highly respectable street, and Good Society was in a steady flutter of delicious expectation.

Good Society, then and there represented by Mrs. Atkins, Miss Atkins, Miss Julia Atkins, Mr. Thomas Atkins, and Mr. Horatio Atkins ; and elsewhere represented by the highly respectable father of this highly respectable family, Mr. Lemuel Atkins, was not so honored every day in the week—by no means. Distinguished gentlemen had come there to dine with us ; Count Blomanosoff, when he was in Boston, had come there to dine with us ; Lord Hawbury and Lord Charles Chawles, when they were in Boston, had come there to dine with us ; and eminent clergymen, and able lawyers, and distinguished senators, and even a Massachusetts Governor, had come there to dine with us. But a rich Southern gentleman—oh ! A child of the sunny South—ah ! A gallant and chivalrous son of Louisiana, who owns an immense plantation, and nobody knows how many of his fellow creatures—decidedly, it is the next thing to having Mr. Webster to dine with us.

The drawing-room in which the so highly honored family were assembled in eager expectation, was a large oblong square, papered with purple and gold-spotted paper, and full of gaudy furniture. There were two chandeliers hanging from the ceiling, all gilt and glitter ; gilt sconces, with cut glass globes, on the walls ; a profusion of gold-framed pictures and engravings ; large mirrors over the mantels and between the windows ; red velvet, and blue velvet, and green velvet arm-chairs and sofas, all around ; a huge piano ; vases ; ormolu tables ; tables of sienna marble ; statuettes on brackets ; a bust of Mr. Webster on a pedestal; divers ornaments in all directions ; a vivid, huge-figured Brussels carpet on the floor ; and yellow and purple curtains to the windows. Taste, not in its dying agonies, but murdered outright and horribly stone dead, was the prevailing sentiment of the entire apartment.

Judged by a rigorous artistic eye, the same estheticide was

chargeable upon the drawing-room's occupants. They were all excessively *à-la-mode* in their general appearance, and evidently of the highest respectability. Mrs. Atkins, the mother—who sat languidly leaning in the corner of a velvet sofa, with her cheek resting on her fingers—was a fair-haired, waxen-faced lady of middle age, with pallid-blue eyes, a snub nose, a rabbit mouth half open, and a receding chin. She was expensively arrayed in full dress of changeable silk, with many flounces; wore a lace cap, and had a general air of weak good-nature and dawdling insipidity, enervating to behold. Miss Atkins, the eldest daughter, who occupied the other end of the sofa, was a yellow-haired, waxen-faced young lady of at least twenty-five; the living suggestion of what her mother had been at her age; with a chin even more receding, a nose as snub, eyes as pallidly blue, the same drooping rabbit mouth, and the same air of mild vapidity and hopeless enervation. She was also expensively attired, in deep blue satin, cut low in the neck, and fitting closely to her full and shapely bosom. Julia, the younger daughter, was an ultra fashionable miss of sweet sixteen; with a bold, saucy face, smooth dark hair, a short, broad nose, hard, black eyes, a prude's mouth, and a great length and breadth of flat circular jaw. The two young men, who were standing like highly respectable caryatides, at opposite corners of the mantel, were snobs of the purest water, both in dress and manner. They were got up in the English style; for, like some of the highly respectable Bostonians, they cherished a noble passion for that sort of Anglicism caricatured by Mr. Punch. Their black trowsers were of the tightest, on legs the slimmest; their black dress coats were close in the body, large in the sleeves, and small in the tail; their vests were very short, their collars high and stiff, and each wore the Joinville neck-tie, a horizontal bar of silk reaching from ear to ear, to the successful adjustment of which, as Punch observed about that time, a man had to give his whole mind. Whatever mind the two young Atkinses possessed, had evidently been wholly given, for the neck-ties were alarmingly perfect, and constituted, in fact, an incontestable triumph of mind over matter. In the solitude of their aspiring souls, the young men worshipped the memory of Lord Hawbury and Lord Charles Chawles, and moulded their whiskers after the style of whiskerage patronized by those eminent nobles. It mattered not that the vulgar rumor had crossed the Atlantic that Lord Hawbury, immediately on his return to his ancestral acres, had been clapped into limbo by a low British tradesman, on account of certain pounds, shillings and pence owed by him the said Hawbury to him the said low tradesman. It mattered not that the still vulgarer rumor had crossed the Atlantic that Lord Charles Chawles, that bright, consummate flower of the British aristocracy, who had deigned to honor our humble homes with his august presence, had got into a row in a theatre just after his return to London—had, in the coarse language of the London newspapers, which love to hawk at merit, got drunk; cruelly insulted a poor ballet-dancer behind the scenes; cruelly beat and trod upon the manager, who had ventured a remonstrance; had thereupon been borne away, roaring and fighting, to the nearest station-house, from whence he had emerged in the morning, to incur the reprimand of a magistrate, and pay a brawler's fine. What mattered such reports as these? mere evidence of the rush and outbreak of a fiery mind of general assault, as Horatio felicitously said, quoting from Hamlet, when the rumor reached him. Whiskers were whiskers still, and so Horatio trimmed the sandy crop which was his own, after the Hawbury model. The result was a scraggy mutton-chop, depending big end down, in tawny, straggling moss of hair from Horatio's cheeks, and between these manly hirsute ornaments loomed a bald, flat, tallowy, superficial face, with an air of sullen emptiness upon it; with short brown hair, parted behind, and on the side, and brushed forward around it; with a low, broad forehead; dull, boiled blue eyes; a strong, short nose; a thin, lineless, resolute mouth; and a great expanse of chin and jaw, bolder than, but like, his younger sister's. Mighty in whiskerage and hair, and on the Lord Charles Chawles model, was Horatio's brother Thomas. Hair, tawny-brown in color, parted on the left, sloping up and off crescendo to fall in a mass on the right side, and bunching off in a round, full tuft of lesser quantity on the other side. This, as the lobsided crown of a puffy face, with the younger sister's chin and jaw. Eyes, close together, hard, black and insolent; short nose, a compromise between snub and straight, with a lift in the nostrils, as if it snuffed offence; mouth, a short, stern, small horseshoe curve, cusps down; and under this, on the broad and long flat chin, a tawny short imperial, and over this, curving down from the centre of the nose and rounding up the cheeks, in a military pothook, the gallant whiskerage of Lord Charles Chawles. Over the whole face an expression of sternly supercilious insolence, inspiring to behold. A fine young man—two fine young men indeed; models of their kind; full of the pride of caste and all its callousness. Destined to be citizens of the highest respectability, when their wild oats—and they were wild—were sown and come to the hard and selfish harvest. Already they had begun, and begun well. Furnished with their father's money, they had their club, their boon-companions, their mistresses, their fast horses, and drank and drove and gamed and revelled in a manner hardly outdone by Lord Hawbury and Lord Charles Chawles themselves. They were, moreover, stanch young Whigs—Union men, Constitution men, Law and Order men, Fugitive Slave Law men, sound on the goose in every conceivable particular. Proof of their devotion to their country, they had only the Saturday before, foregone their customary drive on the Cambridge road, foregone their supper and wine at Porter's, and stayed in town to hear Mr. Webster at Faneuil Hall, and even now, Thomas, the younger and more ardent spirit, was a little hoarse from cheering on that memorable occasion. Proof again of their devotion to their country, which always meant in one form or another the Southern-Slavery part of their country, here they were, nobly sacrificing their customary drive, to muster with the rest of the family and greet the ardent son of the sunny South, the gallant and chivalrous Southern gentleman then expected, and not yet come.

He was coming, though, for while this interesting group, properly stilted for the occasion, were waiting and chatting, a strenuous pull at the bell-wire was heard, with the answering jingle of the hall bell.

"That's him, be Jove!" exclaimed Thomas, straightening up on his slim legs, and adjusting the bows of his neck-tie, while he looked with military sternness at the drawing-room door.

Horatio, who, with the laudable desire to add brilliancy, as was his wont on company days, to the dinner-table conversation, had been diligently storing his memory with the quaint sayings of Charles Lamb—for Charles Lamb is quite the *ton* with the young Boston aristocracy, as Alexander Pope is with the old—laid the book, which he had brought down to study till the last minute, on the mantel behind a large vase, and with a glance into the mirror behind him to see that his neck-tie was all right, assumed a dignified and graceful attitude, with his left thumb inserted in his vest pocket, and his head turned solemnly toward the door. Mrs. Atkins, without moving, cast a glance along her flounces, and made sure in her mind that she was seated so as to be able to rise gracefully when the guest appeared. Her eldest daughter, with a little soft palpitation at heart, for the guest might be a bachelor or a widower, and she was ready to fall in love with any child of the sunny South, or son of the icy North, who had money and social position, also cast an eye at her ample skirts, and a mind's eye at her capabilities for rising. The other daughter, Julia, started bolt upright in her chair, and with her hard, black eyes fixed on the door as though she would look through the panels, listened intently.

Presently they heard Michael shuffling along through the hall, and then the hall door opening.

"Is Mr. Atkins in?" demanded a resonant, loud voice, which was heard in the drawing-room.

A moment's silence, and Michael's reply inaudible.

"Will he be in soon?"

Another silence, and Michael's reply again inaudible.

"Well, I'll wait for him."

Michael was heard this time, explaining in a thin key that Mr. Atkins had company, and wouldn't wish to see him.

"Can't help that," was the bluff answer, followed by heavy feet stamping into the hall, and the dump of a heavy body flinging itself on one of the hall chairs. "It's a matter of business, and he won't thank you if I don't see him. Mind that, my man."

"Humbug!" blurted out Horatio, taking up his book again. "It's not him."

"O fiddlestick!" was the elegant exclamation of Julia, in a pet, "he's not coming at all."

"Hush, my child," said her mamma in a soft, drawling voice, "don't be impatient. Show your breeding, my child, show your breeding."

"Well, be Jove, I'd like to know who *that* is!" exclaimed Thomas, with some vehemence; "coming into the house like the sheriff, be Jove."

Michael meanwhile, having probably stood still for a minute, was now heard shutting the hall door, and presently came into the drawing-room, and closing the door behind him, gave an account of the dialogue.

"Who is the man, Mike?" demanded Thomas in the imperative mood. "What does he look like?"

Michael replied that he looked like a sailor, though he was not dressed in sailor's clothes.

"O it's some of father's people from the wharf," said Horatio. "Better show him up into the library, and not have him sitting there like a scare-crow."

"Yes, Michael, show him up into the library," said Mrs. Atkins, "and tell him Mr. Atkins will be in soon. If it's business, your father will want to see him, for he always sees people that come on business," she added, in a lower tone, as Michael slid out of the room.

They were quiet again for a minute, while the heavy boots of the visitor were heard thumping up over the carpeted stairs into distance.

"Be Jove!" said Thomas, with a fierce air, "that chap goes up like one of Dan Rice's elephants, be Jove! Now then, where's our Southern friend? That's the next question."

"Mamma," said Miss Atkins, in a soft, debilitated voice, with a slight lisp, "do you know if he's married?"

"No, Caroline, I don't know," replied Mrs. Atkins, languidly. "But I think he's not, or he would have brought his wife with him. These Southern gentlemen are so gallant, you know, and they always bring their wives with them."

"Ecod, Carry," blurted Thomas, while Caroline was taking the flattering unction of her mother's astonishing answer to her soul—"if he's got a wife already, it's all up with your chance, me girl. Our Southern friends are the deuce and all among the women, but Louisiana ain't Turkey, you know."

"Now, Tom, I should be ashamed," exclaimed Julia, bridling. "One would think you were never brought up in good society, and I should be ashamed, I should."

"Oh, you cork up, Jule," was the fine youth's exquisite reply. "You girls allow yourselves too much tongue, be Jove!"

"Hush, Julia," interposed Mrs. Atkins, with soft authority, stopping the young lady's angry retort. "Silence, this instant. You musn't speak to your brother that way. It's low, my child—very low, and you must show your breeding."

Julia was silent, but glared spitefully at Thomas. It is noticeable that Mrs. Atkins never reproved her boys. Her girls she kept a check-rein upon constantly.

"Mamma," continued Caroline, perfectly unmoved by her brother's late remarks, "does he own a very large plantation, and how many negroes has he, mamma?"

"Indeed, I can't tell you, Caroline," replied Mrs. Atkins, blandly. "I think he must have a great many of the horrid creatures, for those Southern gentlemen all have a great many, and numbers of the ungrateful things run away, which was the reason why the Fugitive Slave Bill was passed, you know."

"Yes, and I wish the South would just march up back here on Nigger Hill, and lug off the whole pack of them, men, women, and children, for they're a disgrace to the neighborhood, and it's a burning shame to have them staying away from their masters," growled Horatio, looking up from the gentle and human pages of Charles Lamb.

"All I know about him," resumed Mrs. Atkins, continuing her notice of the expected guest, "is what your father said in the note he sent up to the house. Namely, that he belongs to a great cotton-house in New Orleans, with which your father deals largely, and that he owns a plantation, and that he is a splendid fellow, and a real Southern gentleman, and one of the chivalry, and all that, and that we must have an excellent dinner, and treat him with true Northern hospitality, and so forth. All which you saw in the note, and really I don't know any more about him. But of course he is a perfect gentleman, for all the Southern gentlemen are perfect gentlemen, and they are as gallant and chivalrous as gentlemen can be, and as *distingué* as—as Count Blomanosoff, and I'm sure nothing could be more *distingué* than Count Blomanosoff, you know."

To compare anybody to the horrent-whiskered Russ who had dined with the Atkinses on his way to Washington, was the highest compliment Mrs. Atkins could pay. Count Blomanosoff was the god of her idolatry.

"Dear me, I wish he would come!" exclaimed Julia, fidgeting in her chair.

As if in response to her wish, and before her mother could again entreat her to show her breeding, the door-bell rang.

"Here he is, be Jove!" cried Thomas, amidst a general flutter and movement.

Anxious silence succeeded, while Michael was shuffling to the door. Presently, the noise of entering feet, a full, decisive voice saying something, and a soft, smooth, courteous voice answering; then, after a moment's pause, the drawing-room door swung open, and behind the sturdy form of Mr. Lemuel Atkins, the enraptured ladies saw the rich brunette complexion, the long waven hair and thick moustache, and the lordly figure of their Southern guest.

At the first glance they were enchanted. So handsome, so gallant, so chivalrous! Mrs. Atkins rose with a sweeping rustle of flounces, and stepped forward; and there was a general rustle of rising and moving as the two entered.

"Here we are," cried Mr. Atkins, in his rotund, energetic voice, striding in as he spoke, with a smile on his hard visage, and stepping aside to pause and turn with an extended hand toward his guest. "Mr. Lafitte, I have the honor to present you to my wife. My love, Mr. Lafitte, of Louisiana."

Mrs. Atkins curtseyed low as she slid forward with outstretched hand, her waxen face slightly colored, and wreathed with smiles.

"I am most happy to see you, Mr. Lafitte," she softly murmured, "and I am delighted to welcome you to Boston."

"Madam, I am charmed with the honor you do me," courteously returned the Southerner, bowing low with her hand in his, and serenely smiling.

"And this is my eldest daughter, sir," continued the merchant. "Caroline, Mr. Lafitte."

Caroline looked very pretty, as with a fluttering heart, and a faint sea-shell pink on her cheeks and lips, she wafted herself forward, and dawdled down into a low curtsey, with a languishing glance at the rich brunette visage of the Southerner. Mr. Lafitte glided up to her, bowing, pressed her hand in his, and cast into her eyes a momentary ardent look, which threw Caroline into feeble ecstasy.

"I am enchanted to meet you, Miss Atkins," said Mr. Lafitte, in a low, smooth voice, sweeter than music to her ear.

Caroline was so overcome with rapture, that she could only color, curtsey, cast another languishing glance at her adorer, and withdraw a pace or two, while her father introduced Julia. Then came Horatio's turn, and then Thomas's. Horatio did it in the aristocratic Hawbury style—a solemn face, a stiff bend of the back, the thumb of the left hand in his vest pocket, and his right hand clasping Mr. Lafitte's fingers. Thomas came the Lord Charles Chawles—head up, shoulders back, coat-tail jutting out in the bow, legs wide, hand slowly wagging Mr. Lafitte's, horse-shoe mouth agrin, and voice remarking, "Mr. Lafitte, yours—glad to meet you, sir; be Jove, I am!" To which Mr. Lafitte replied, that he was always proud to make a gentleman's acquaintance, especially yours, Mr. Atkins, on this happy occasion.

The introductions successfully over, Mr. Lafitte was invited to take a seat near the hostess, and the rest of the company settled into their respective chairs, Mr. Atkins surveying them all with an air of proud and smiling gratification. He was a strong, sturdily-built man, of good presence, dressed in black, with a purple velvet vest, crossed by a short and thick gold chain. On his little finger he wore a heavy gold seal-ring, with a red stone. His face was more like Horatio's and Julia's than any of the others, but much finer and stronger than either's, for Mr. Atkins's boyhood was cast in the robust life of a country town, and he had fought his way up to wealth and social position in Boston, battling with the forces of trade, and hewing out for himself the character of a self-made man. The black, hard eyes of his younger daughter, and the short, bold nose and large round jaw of her and the sons, were stronglier seen in him than in them. He was smooth-shaven, wore his hair short, and had the blanched, resolute color of a man whose days had been strenuously devoted to money-making. Usually his face was decisive and stern, though now it was relaxed into a proud and gratified smile, as he surveyed his guest and family circle.

"Charming weather you're having in Boston, madam," remarked Mr. Lafitte, addressing his hostess. "Cooler though than when I left Louisiana three weeks ago. We had some of the hottest days there in April that I ever knew. It was positively like midsummer."

"Ah, Mr. Lafitte," sighed Mrs. Atkins, "our climate must seem cold to you, who have come so lately from the sunny South. Is this your first visit to Boston?"

"Yes, madam, it is the first time I ever had the pleasure of visiting your beautiful city," courteously replied the Southerner. "I was sorry not to be able to get here in time to hear Mr. Webster, who spoke, they tell me, in your Faneuil Hall, last Saturday. Dear Webster! I positively love him as if he were my brother. He is doing such a good work for our common country."

"Oh, isn't he splendid!" lisped Miss Atkins, with a languishing air. "So statesmanlike! We were all there to hear him, Mr. Lafitte. Oh, it was beautiful!"

"I can well imagine that, Miss Atkins," replied Mr. Lafitte, smiling blandly at her; "and it was really patriotic in you to lend the grace and beauty of your presence, ladies, to ornament such an occasion. Dear Webster is giving abolition fanaticism its death-blow. By the way, speaking of fanaticism, Mr. Atkins pointed out two of your notorieties to me in the street to-day—Garrison and Wendell Phillips."

"Horrid wretches!" murmured Mrs. Atkins, in a die-away tone.

"Be Jove!" blurted Thomas, "I'd just like to put an ounce of lead into them two. I would, be Jove!"

"Very patriotic," said Mr. Lafitte, with a courteous inclination of his head toward the speaker, "and spoken in the true Southern spirit."

"Those two men ought to be hung," said Horatio, solemnly, emulous of Southern approbation. "They make me think of that anecdote of Charles Lamb, Mr. Lafitte. You remember, sir, a stranger called on Lamb at the West Indy House. 'Are you Mr. Lamb?' said he. 'Well,' said Charles, feeling the grey whisker on his cheek, 'I think I'm old enough to be a sheep.' Now, Garrison and Wendell Phillips," continued Horatio, making the exquisitely felicitous application, "they're old enough to be sheep, and I go for making them dead mutton."

"Ha, ha, capital!" exclaimed Mr. Atkins, with a mild bellow, looking around on the company, with a smiling, open mouth of satisfaction in his son's wit.

"Very good, be Jove!" said Thomas, with a grin.

Mrs. Atkins feebly clapped her hands, and said, "good, good," and Caroline giggled, and softly murmured, "Oh, Horatio, you're so funny!"

What a set of damned boobies! thought Mr. Lafitte; then aloud: "Yes, that's a capital story, and your application of it, Mr. Horatio, is one of the best things I've heard. But I was surprised to see that Garrison is quite a mild, benevolent-looking man. We think of him down South, you know, as a red-faced brawler, and I was struck with the contrast between the original and the fancy portrait. Phillips, too, surprised me still more, for he has the air of a high-bred gentleman. I'll tell you who he reminded me of. You are aware, ladies, that the Mobilians are famous for their polished grace and high breeding. Now, the flower of them all is

Tom Lafourcade. In fact his elegance and dignity of manner and bearing are town-talk down there. Well, if you'll believe me, Phillips, though he has a graver and less pronounced air, actually reminded me of Tom Lafourcade."

"Dear me! how surprising," softly exclaimed Mrs. Atkins.

"Why, yes, madam, very," returned Mr. Lafitte. "It was really odd to come North and have the arch abolition fanatic remind one of princely Tom Lafourcade, of Mobile."

"Oh, he's very handsome," lisped Caroline, pensively. "But so fanatical."

"I tell you, Mr. Lafitte, it's an awful pity about Phillips," broke in Mr. Atkins. "He's very much of a gentleman, a splendid orator, full of ability every way, and belongs to one of our most respectable families. Why, I heard Choate say once that if he'd stuck to the bar, he'd have been the first lawyer in America. Yes, sir. And there's no doubt that if he was in our party he'd be second to no man in the country, unless it was Webster. But he's thrown himself away—positively sacrificed all his influence and wasted his talents by joining that abolition crew."

"In short, Nicodemused himself into nothing, as Charles Lamb says," observed Horatio.

"Nicodemused?" interrogated Mr. Lafitte. "Might I ask the meaning of that phrase, sir? I am so dull, and I confess my unacquaintance with Lamb."

It is not Charles Lamb, but another humorist, who, alluding to the obstructive influence of an ugly name upon its owner's career, and giving parents a quaint hint for the christening, remarks, "don't Nicodemus a boy into nothing." Horatio, who only remembered the phrase for its oddity, and as usual with his quotations, lugged it into his remarks, without much thought of its relevancy, utterly forgetting the context and the meaning, was considerably disconcerted by Mr. Lafitte's question, and reddened slightly.

"Nicodemused, Mr. Lafitte?" he stammered. "Why, you know, sir," he continued, as a happy means of extrication from his difficulty, suggested itself—"you know that the Bible says Nicodemus went to Christ."

"Oh, yes, I see. And lost his influence by so doing," blandly answered Mr. Lafitte, with a furtive smile which nobody noticed. "Yes, yes. That's very clear. Very happily said, sir, and I'm much obliged to you for enlightening my stupidity. So Phillips has Nicodemused himself into nothing?"

"Indeed he has, sir," replied Mr. Atkins. "Just thrown away his talents, and misused his eloquence in denouncing the Compromise Measures, and Mr. Webster, and Slavery, and all the best interests of his country."

"Be Jove, he's a fool, that's what he is," remarked Thomas, caressing his military whiskerage.

"He's worse, Tom," replied his father; "he's a traitor, and ought to be indicted for treason."

"Does he move in good society here, Mr. Atkins?" blandly asked Mr. Lafitte.

"He! Why, sir, he's a rank Disunionist!" exclaimed the merchant. "A Disunionist received into good society! My dear sir, what are you thinking of!"

"Pardon me," politely returned the Southerner, with a courteous inclination of his head, and cherishing in secret, a malicious desire to corner his host, though he must tell a lie to do it—"pardon me, I did not know. You are aware that I am a Disunionist myself. The difference I apprehend to be this: Phillips is for a Dissolution of the Union for the sake of liberty; I am for a dissolution of the Union for the sake of slavery. I state it frankly, for I wish to plainly present the fact that we are both Disunionists, though for different reasons. Now am I to infer that the fact of my Disunion sentiments would exclude me from good society here? For I have letters to some of your leading citizens, and it would indeed be awkward were I to present them where I should not be welcome."

"No, sir, no indeed, sir," replied the merchant with sonorous emphasis. "That is a different case altogether, sir. Entirely different. We honor the spirit of Southern gentlemen in defence of their property, sir, and our first society is always open to them, Mr. Lafitte."

"You Southern gentleman are so chivalrous!" said Mrs. Atkins, with languid playfulness.

"So ardent!" lisped Caroline, with a languishing glance at the Southerner.

"Indeed, ladies, you overwhelm me," returned Mr. Lafitte, gallantly; "and I am glad to perceive the true state of the case, Mr. Atkins. It is curious, however, if we look at it from one point of view, that Mr. Phillips, who, as you say, is very much of a gentleman, one of your most talented men, and belonging to one of your most respectable families—it is curious that he should be sent to Coventry by your first society for his Disunion, and we received so handsomely for ours. But then, he is for liberty, and we are for slavery, which, as you happily observed, makes an important difference. Yes, I see the distinction, and it is both broad and just. An admirable distinction, indeed, and one that does your society great credit."

Mr. Lafitte said all this so courteously—with such flattering and affable sincerity of voice and manner—that his listeners had not the slightest apprehension of the terrific sarcasm which lurked in his words. They took it all as an elaborate compliment, and sat smiling and simpering at him, each after his or her respective fashion. The damned, mean, contemptible, servile curs—tabooing their own Disunionists, and ducking and smiling to ours!—was Mr. Lafitte's irreverent mental reflection, as, softly fingering his moustache, with the most affable of smiles lighting his rich brunette complexion, he equably surveyed them—floods of contemptuous disgust meanwhile raging delightedly in his lordly bosom.

"Oh, Mr. Atkins," said the lady of the house, "I almost forgot to tell you that a—a person called to see you, and is up-stairs in the library."

"A person. Who is he? I can't see persons now. Send up word that I'm engaged," returned the merchant, somewhat brusquely.

"Michael thought he was a sailor," drawled Mrs. Atkins, in her fal-lal voice; "and he said he'd come on business of importance, and that you'd want to see him."

"Oh, business. That's another affair," returned her husband, rising and looking at his watch. "Business before pleasure always. You'll excuse me a few moments, Mr. Lafitte. I'll be right down."

"Certainly, sir, certainly," said the Southerner, blandly bowing.

Mr. Atkins at once left the drawing-room and went up-stairs into the library. The visitor, a short, strongly-built man, with a sunburnt face, who was slowly walking up and down, with his hands in his pockets, came toward him as he entered.

"Why, Captain Bangham! You? How are you?" exclaimed the merchant, smiling, and shaking hands with him.

"All right, Mr. Atkins. How are you, sir?"

"Capital. And so the Soliman's in."

"Yes, sir. Came up this morning. I've been waiting at the office pretty much all day"——

"Indeed. I'm sorry, captain. But, for a wonder, Lafitte came to town, and I've been showing him round."

Captain Bangham started, and slapped his hips with his hands.

"Lafitte in town!" he burst out. "Which one of 'em?"

"Lafitte the younger. Torwood, you know," returned the merchant, taking an easy chair.

"The hell he is!" ejaculated the profane captain, reddening, and thrusting both hands into his pocket. "You don't mean to say he's down-stairs now?"

"Why Bangham, what in the world's the matter with you, man?" said the surprised merchant, staring at him. "Down stairs? Of course he's down stairs. Come to dine with us."

"Well, I'm damned!" vociferated the excited captain. "If this ain't horrid."

He stamped off, with his hands in his pocket, while Mr. Atkins stared at him, as if he thought the man had gone mad.

"Captain Bangham," said the merchant, slowly, "will you be so good as to tell me what you mean by this extraordinary ebullition. What's the matter? Isn't the Soliman all right? Has the cargo"——

"The matter's just this, Mr. Atkins," broke in the sailor,

coming toward him, and flinging himself into a chair. "Soliman, cargo, and all is right. There's nothing the matter with them"——

"Then what *is* the matter?" demanded the merchant, angrily.

"The matter's this, Mr. Atkins," roared Bangham, pounding his knees with his clenched hands. "When we were three days out we found a blasted nigger, half smothered in the hold. And that nigger belongs to Torwood Lafitte, and you've got him down-stairs to dine with you. Yes, sir, I've got the nigger tied up aboard the brig this minute, and you've got his master."

Mr. Atkins turned white, and sat looking at the sailor with rigid lips.

"Yes, sir. That's the matter," continued Bangham. "And matter enough, too, Mr. Atkins. Just think of what Lafitte 'll say if he hears that his nigger got off on your brig. Just think of the row there'll be in Orleans if it gets out. They'll seize me for it, if the brig ever touches the levee again, Mr. Atkins."

"She'll touch the levee again with that scoundrel on board of her," shouted the merchant, with an oath, thrusting his thumbs into the arm-holes of his vest, and swelling proudly. "They shall know in New Orleans that we're law-abiding citizens, Bangham. Back he shall go, and it will redound to the credit of the house when it's known that we sent him back promptly. I'm glad you came to tell me this, Bangham. Just keep it quiet. He shall go back just as soon as the Soliman can get ready for the return voyage."

"All right, sir," replied the sailor. "But, Mr. Atkins, we've got him here now in Boston Bay, and how are we going to take him back without going to law about it? Hadn't Lafitte better bring him before a Commissioner, and have a certificate made out"——

"No," interrupted the merchant, with strenuous emphasis. "I'll have it said in New Orleans that a Boston merchant can show his devotion to the interests of the South without any ridiculous formalities. It'll strike them well, Bangham, and raise our credit there. Besides, if we go before the Commissioner, those infernal Abolitionists will have another long fuss about it, as they had about Sims, and who knows but that they'll rescue him as they did Shadrach. No, I'll make sure work of it. If the black villain were to escape, the effect on my trade would be as bad in New Orleans as if I hadn't done my best to return him, and I won't have my trade injured. Business before everything. I'm not going to have the delay of the law, nor the risks either, in this matter. So just hold on to the black reprobate, Bangham, till we can return him."

"It's rather risky, Mr. Atkins," demurred the sailor. "You know it's illegal, sir, to take off the man without due process of law, and if the Grand Jury gets hold of it, they'll be apt to indict you for kidnapping."

"Indict *me?*" returned the merchant. "Ho, ho, Bangham," he laughed, "you're verdant, my man. There's not a Grand Jury would ever find a bill against me for that, Bangham. Why, bless your soul, Bangham, the Grand Jury's made up of our most respectable citizens—property holders every man of them—Fugitive Slave Law men to the backbone—and do you think they'd indict me for an act in the very spirit of the Compromise Measures, and for the best interests of our Southern commerce? Oh, no, Bangham! There's not one of them that wouldn't wink at it—not one. No fear about the Grand Jury, captain, not the least in the world. But you haven't told me how this black wretch got aboard."

"And I'll be hanged if I know, Mr. Atkins," replied the sailor, with another thump on his knees. "All I know is, that when we were three days out we unbattened one of the hatches to get an axe that had been left in there accidentally, and there was the black beast, almost dead. Lord, how he smelt! It was horrid. And he looked like the very devil himself. Had an iron collar on his neck, with the name of Lafitte Brothers engraved on it. He escaped from the Red River, lived in a swamp with the snakes and alligators, got down the river somehow, and had a horrid time all round. Didn't seem to know, or else he wouldn't tell, how he got aboard the brig. Fact is, the black pig's not more than half-witted now, with all he's gone through."

"Badly treated?" inquired Mr. Atkins, placidly.

"Oh, yes, treated bad enough," carelessly replied the sailor. "Lafitte's a high-binder with his niggers, I reckon. This chap's all covered with scars and marks, and accordin' to his story, and that's true enough, I don't doubt, there's not a worse treated nigger in the whole South than he was. He wouldn't have run off, I guess, if he hadn't been desperate with bad usage. I expect Lafitte 'll be the death of him when he gets him again."

"That's his lookout," said the merchant, calmly. "If Lafitte chooses to maltreat his own property, there's no one the loser by it but himself."

At this moment Michael appeared at the library door with the announcement that dinner was served. The merchant rose, and Bangham took his straw hat from the table and rose also.

"I'll see you to-morrow, captain," said Mr. Atkins. "In the meantime, keep that fellow in limbo, and we'll arrange for his return."

"All right, Mr. Atkins," returned the sailor, lounging out of the room, with a relieved mind.

Mr. Atkins followed him down-stairs to the hall-door, and then turned into the drawing-room, with a smiling countenance.

"Now, Mr. Lafitte," said this manly, humane, high-souled, law-abiding, patriotic American Christian and flower of mercantile morality, addressing the gallant and chivalrous son of the sunny South, "now, if you please, we will go out to dinner."

"Shall I have the honor?" said Mr. Lafitte, rising and offering his arm, with a bow, to the hostess.

She took the offered arm, and they swept out together, the brave and the fair. Bouquet de Caroline streamed in their wake, as Miss Atkins, leaning on the arm of her highly respectable papa, wafted on after them. Millefleurs and pomatum lent their sweetness to the desert air of the drawing-room, as the gallant Horatio escorted out the lovely Julia. Following up the rear, in martial state, and redolent of musk and marrowfat, came haughty Thomas, caressing the whiskerage of Lord Charles Chawles, and sniffing the rich odor of the dinner from afar.

Meanwhile, low Antony, brother of Roux, bought chattel of Lafitte, foodless, filthy, helpless, friendless, despised and accursed, lay bound in the dark and noisome hold of a Boston vessel—a negro with no rights that a white man is bound to respect—with no rights that a Boston merchant might not, and would not, take away, all for the good of party and of trade—a good which, as every thoughtful patriot and Christian will allow, is the chief good of existence.

CHAPTER XII.

STARTLING DEVELOPMENTS.

Harrington lifted his calm eyebrows with some wonder at the furious entrance of his friend, and sat regarding him with a firm mouth and steadfast eyes. Wentworth, out of breath with the speed of his course, and the tumult of his emotions, had flung his hat across the room, and himself upon the sofa, and sat panting, with his handsome face flushed, and his bright auburn curls damp with perspiration.

"Well, Richard, what's the matter?" said Harrington, calmly. "Has the sky fallen?"

"Harrington, see here," panted Wentworth, "Johnny's just been up to the studio."

"Johnny? Who's Johnny?" interrupted Harrington.

"Oh, pshaw! Bagasse's boy, you know. John Todd," fumed Wentworth, stopping to wipe his brow with a white handkerchief.

"Well. Is that any reason for your running yourself into a pleurisy?" bantered Harrington.

"By George!" exclaimed the young artist, "it's a reason for

my running Fernando Witherlee into something else, and that's a broken neck, I'm thinking. Cursed rascal!"

"What's Witherlee been up to now?" inquired Harrington, with sudden interest.

"Impudence," replied Wentworth. "Impudence unparalleled. Listen, Harrington. John Todd says Witherlee came into the fencing-school this morning, and had the atrocious impudence—the abominable—the infernal"——

Wentworth stopped, gasping with rage.

"O Muse of adjectives, descend!" jocosely cried Harrington, lifting his hand in mock-heroic invocation, with his cheeks wrinkled in a rich smile.

Wentworth, thus prayed for, began to laugh, even in the midst of his fury.

"Well, Harrington," said he, "I know it's foolish to get excited about it, but upon my word, Witherlee behaves scandalously. Do you know that he has been telling Bagasse a long rigmarole about Muriel and Emily, and you and me. Bagasse! Now just think of it! Think of his talking of two ladies like those, and in such a connection, and to Bagasse! Yes, of all persons in the world, to Bagasse!"

Harrington's color changed and his face puckered with amazement, while he nervously grasped the arms of his chair.

"Is Witherlee possessed!" he ejaculated. "Why, I never heard of such conduct. So boyish, so foolish, such an outrage against the fitness of things"——

"And so infamously impudent," put in Wentworth. "It's the impudence that strikes me."

"Certainly. It's impudent, too, and I don't wonder you were moved," murmured Harrington, slowly, with an absorbed air.

"Moved!" snapped Wentworth. "By Jupiter, I am moved to give him a sound horse-whipping, and he'll get it, or my name's not what it is. Why, look at it, Harrington. In the first place, Emily's a particular friend of his. Now, wouldn't you think that the commonest respect for her would have prevented him from bandying her name about in conversation with anybody, much less old Bagasse?"

"Eureka! I have it," exclaimed Harrington, bursting from his abstraction. "That accounts for Bagasse's remark about the two ladies that gave the violets."

"What do you mean?" inquired Wentworth.

Harrington recounted what the fencing-master had said that morning.

"You see, Richard," he added, "that set me wondering; for how did Bagasse know that ladies had given us the violets? How did he know but that I had gathered them from my own yard? Then, when I saw your nosegay in his button-hole, I thought you must have told him, and I was astonished to think that you should choose the old veteran for a confidant."

"By Jupiter, Harrington, you didn't think I would do such a thing," exclaimed Wentworth, reproachfully.

"My dear Wentworth, it was absurd in me, and I beg your pardon," returned Harrington. "Certainly, it was not like you; but then, somebody must have told him, and how could I imagine it was Witherlee?"

Wentworth sat silent, thinking with mounting rage of Witherlee's remarks to the fencing-master. If he had been cool and thoughtful, he might have at least suspected, from the sample he had of the good Fernando's nature, that he was at the bottom of Emily's alienation from himself. But Wentworth's vivid temper only threw gleams and flashes on things, and what he saw, he saw in salient points, without observing their connections and relations.

"By George, I'll break his neck!" he foamed, stamping his foot on the floor.

"Now, Richard, keep cool," said Harrington. "You can depend that Fernando has been making mischief all round, and let us just track it out. In the first place, let's hear Johnny's report of what he said."

"Lord! I can't tell you! it's gone from me," fumed Wentworth, running his hands through his curls, as if in search of it. "Let's see. In the first place, he had some snob criticisms on your coat; which, he thinks, is not genteel enough to entitle you to Muriel's friendship."

"Oh, indeed," said Harrington, with grand good-nature. "Well, that's a trifle, anyway."

"He said," continued Wentworth, "that you looked like a beggarman, who had been in the watch-house all night."

"Complimentary," jeered Harrington.

"Wondered how you had the assurance to visit Miss Eastman at all, when your social position was so much beneath hers," pursued Wentworth; "and thought it was very kind in her to permit you."

Harrington burst into a peal of hearty laughter.

"Positively," he said, "this is comic. The only tragic thing about it is, that all this time, Fernando has been pretending that he was the best of friends to me."

"I tell you, Harrington," replied Wentworth, "that fellow's a perfect snake in the grass. The next thing was to pitch into my personal appearance."

"Yours!" exclaimed Harrington, laughingly. "Why, Richard, you're the pink of fashion. You're D'Orsay and Raphael Sanzio, in one."

Wentworth smiled faintly; too angry at Witherlee to be much amused.

"Nevertheless," he continued, "Witherlee poked his gibes at me, too—something about the Anti-Slavery Bazaar. Do they sell clothes there?"

"Not exactly," replied Harrington, laughing.

"Then, I'm hanged if I know what he meant by that," said Wentworth.

"Well, probably he said you looked bizarre; and Johnny, not knowing the word, mistook it for its fellow in sound," remarked Harrington.

"That's it I'll bet," burst out Wentworth, reddening. "Bizarre! The cursed snob! He wants me to cut my hair off, I suppose, and wear a stove-pipe hat instead of my Rubens. I'll see him hanged first."

"Well, go on Richard," said Harrington. "All this is unimportant."

"Then," continued the young artist, fidgeting in his seat like a man who had to deal with an awkward subject, and looking very fixedly at the opposite wall, with his face redder than before, "then he proceeded to give Bagasse a sketch of us two with Cupid's arrows stuck in our bleeding hearts—a regular Saint Valentine picture. O bother, I won't report the stuff! It makes me crawl."

"Oh, go on, Richard, go on," urged Harrington.

"No, I won't. Let it go. Come, Harrington, let's drop it. Upon my word, I can't repeat it, and I won't," said Wentworth.

Harrington saw that it was no use to urge him, and was silent. The fact was, Wentworth did not like to have Harrington think of him as the lover of Emily, and Witherlee's portraiture of him as such was too faithful for exhibition. No man likes to confess that he has been jilted by a woman, as Wentworth thought he had been by Emily, and to say that he had been reputed her lover by Witherlee was certainly an approximation at least to such a confession.

"Very well," remarked Harrington after a pause, "if you don't care to talk about it, let it go. Now, Richard, I want you to leave this matter to me. There's more in it, I'm convinced, than appears, and if you make a quarrel with Fernando we shall never know the whole of it. Just keep cool, say nothing to him of what you have heard, and let me track the fox through all his doublings. Will you promise?"

Wentworth hesitated, but his own suspicions were roused, and he felt the good sense of Harrington's proposal.

"I agree, Harrington," he said at length. "Yes, I promise, and I'll keep dark."

"Good," replied Harrington. "I declare, Richard, I can't help feeling, in view of the serious grandeur of life, that all this is pitifully petty. These pigmy broils and imbroglios seem all the more trivial in contrast with such scenes and passions as I have been in to-day. I wish we could live only in the larger life, unvexed by this buzz and fribble."

"What has happened to-day, Harrington?" asked Wentworth.

Harrington told him briefly of the scene in Southac street, omitting to mention what passed in Roux's house, lest it should lead to questions verging upon the secret which Emily now shared with Muriel, himself and Captain Fisher.

"I wish I could feel interested as you do in these political affairs," said Wentworth, lightly, when Harrington had concluded. "Somehow, I can't though. Of course, I'm for liberty in my own quiet way, and I pity the poor darkeys and all that, but then it doesn't come home to me at all. I'm an artist in the grain, I suppose, and art-life and matters connected with it, leave me no interest for other matters."

"Ah, Richard," replied Harrington, "you must outlive these notions. Art cannot thrive sequestered from life. It may live in the cell, but it will narrow and spire, and it can only branch and broaden into Shakspearean greatness when planted among the ways and walks of men. No man can be a great painter, sculptor, composer, poet, whose heart is not deeply and warmly engaged in the life of his own time. It is the lack of interest and participation in human affairs which makes our modern artists mere imitators and colorists, and so much of modern art weak and pallid—a mere watery reflection of old models and forms of beauty."

"Come, now, that's heresy?" said Wentworth, laughing. "Talk of poets—look at Shakspeare. What interest did he take in human affairs? He kept the Globe Theatre, studied his part by day, played it at night, and wrote his dramas between whiles. That's the way his years were occupied. What participation had he in Elizabethan politics? What in the life of his own time? Why, Ulrici says, in substance, that Shakspeare didn't care enough about the politics of his age to have his mind even colored by them. The critics agree that a more thorough aristocrat or conservative never breathed. Jupiter! according to the critics, he was a perfect despiser of the common people, and a man utterly without patriotism and philanthropy." Your Verulam there, now," pursued Wentworth, looking at the statue, "was patriot and philanthrope. He toiled for his country and wrought for 'the relief of the human estate,' as he phrases it. But the most powerful microscope couldn't detect anything of that sort in William."

Harrington laughed amusedly.

"Now, look here, Richard," he replied. "In the first place, I flatly deny that there is contempt for any sort of people, common or uncommon, in the Shakspearean pages. But let that pass, for what I am going to say will cover it fully. I want to call your attention to the distinctive peculiarity—the uniqueness—of the Shakspearean creations. In the Shakspearean mind you have an unexampled union of the subtlest observation and the profoundest reason. This author observed far more closely than even Thackeray, and philosophized far more greatly than even Plato. But this is not all. He constructed a series of works which show the principles of human action as they lie in the nature of man, and all the complex operation of the human passions. And more, he created a number of figures, which are not characters, but types. That is the grand distinctive Shakspearean peculiarity. Nobody has done that but he. The Don Quixote of Cervantes is a great figure, but it is not Shakspearean. The Greek Prometheus, the German Mephistopheles are immense allegorical creations, but they are not Shakspearean. He alone has made figures which are types—reprèsentative men and women standing for classes. In a word, he alone has given us in a series of models or images, the Science of Human Nature. This it is that makes him solitary, as the power with which it is done makes him supreme, in literature."

"I understand," said Wentworth, "and I agree; but I don't see what you're driving at, mine ancient."

"Wait a minute, and you shall see," returned Harrington. "Bacon wanted this very thing done. Nothing that you can do for the elevation of the world, he says substantially, is of any value, unless this is done. The radical defect in all science is, he says, that it has not been done, and he rates Aristotle sharply for not doing it. He wants a work which will give us the Science of Man, as he is, in order that we may make him what he ought to be—a work, he says, which is to contain the descriptions of the several characters and tempers of men's natures and dispositions to the end that the precepts concerning the culture and cure of the mind may be concluded upon—a work which is also to contain examples in moral and civil life. This is what Bacon wanted done, and the author of the Shakspeare Drama did it. Bacon's requirement is fulfilled exactly in the Shakspeare Drama. Even our critics have got hold of the idea that the Science of Human Nature which Bacon wanted is in the Shakspeare Drama, and the purpose which Bacon intended such a work to accomplish, is in daily process of accomplishment through the agency of those plays. And what is more, Bacon wanted that work to be in the form of poetry—the Georgics of the Mind, he calls it, with a reminiscence of Virgil. The poets, he says elsewhere, are the best doctors of this knowledge ; and again, for the expression of such a purpose, reason is not so perspicuous, nor examples so apt, as the dramatic or poetic presentation. Very good. Bacon wanted it in poetry, and in poetry you have it."

Wentworth looked at Harrington steadily, with so curious an amazement on his countenance, that Harrington smiled.

"Now, Richard, observe," he pursued. "The Shakspeare Drama contains the Science of Man. A Science of Man cannot be formed accidentally, or by the mere spontaneity of genius; it involves design. The author of the Shakspeare Drama knew, therefore, what he was about; and the fact that his figures have the peculiarity of being types, sufficiently proves it. Now, science is preparatory to art, and a Science of Man is a preparation for an Art of Human Life. This makes of your 'aristocrat' and 'conservative' Shakspeare a Socialist of the most daring order—the largest innovator the world has ever known."

"By Jupiter!" exclaimed Wentworth, "it's precious odd that nobody has noticed all this before."

"So it is, Richard," returned Harrington, smiling good-naturedly at him. "About as odd as that Ulrici should have said that Shakspeare took no heed of the politics of his time, when Lear, Coriolanus, and Julius Cæsar are occupied, under the dramatic cover, and in the very face of the military despotism of the age, with the broadest sort of political discussion. About as odd as that you should think Shakspeare had no patriotism, when the historical dramas so overflow with passionate love for England that London theatres, at this day, rise and roar to it when Phelps or Macready gives it voice from the stage."

"Well," said Wentworth, reddening and laughing, "I spoke too fast, no doubt. Besides, there's Brutus—a splendid type of the pure country-lover. But the philanthropy—where's that?"

"So the man who drew up the Science of Human Nature, subtle, vast, exact, complete, the inevitable preliminary to the relief of the human estate that Bacon schemed for, had no philanthropy," bantered Harrington.

"That's you exactly!" burst out Wentworth, coloring again, and laughing. "Thunder, Harrington! that's the way you hook in a fellow. Of course, since I've accepted your first proposition, the rest follows. Well, at all events, you may show philanthropy as the genius of the plan, but I'm hanged if you can name a character that has it in the plays."

"Can't I, then?" retorted Harrington, good-humoredly. "What do you think of Lear? Whose heart folds in poor Tom, the social outcast from the lowest sinks of the Elizabethan wretchedness? Who hurls forth that terrible invocation for the 'superfluous and lust-dieted man that slaves Heaven's ordinance—that will not see because he does not feel?' Who prays for the 'poor naked wretches that bide the peltings of the pitiless storm,' and dwells so eloquently on 'their houseless heads and unfed sides, their looped and windowed raggedness.' Who is it, the impersonation of cold and callous conservatism, that is made, as Burke says, to 'attend to the neglected and remember the forgotten,' and comes face to face with houseless poverty and want to exclaim, 'Oh, I have ta'en too little care of this?' Who demands that the rich and fortunate shall expose themselves to 'feel what wretches feel,' in order that their superfluities may be shared with them, and justice be more the law of social life? And if this is not philanthropy, what is it?"

"Say no more, Harrington, I cave," replied Wentworth, gaily.

"It is true," pursued Harrington, "that the Shakspeare

Drama has no figure of a philanthropist like Howard, no more than it has of a religious saint like Xavier or Monica. But I do not think that such portraitures would consist with the author's design, which, however vast, is still special, having for its end the culture and cure of the human mind, and, as I have said, the reconstruction of society. Ah, but the true philanthropist, the true saint of that Drama is its author! No need to add such a figure to his pages when he himself stands there added to them by our thought, an image of the noblest love that ever strove and suffered for mankind."

They both sat in silence for a few moments, lost in musing.

"It is strange," said Wentworth, at length. "All we know about Shakspeare personally, is in conflict with what you have said—though I admit that his works sustain your view. He seems to have lived a very common-place and vulgar sort of a life. Certainly, his biography does not show that he had large sympathies and designs for man, and it is indisputable that he did not participate in the loftier life of his age."

"I look at it in this way," replied Harrington. "Set aside the evidence we might collect from his writings, and consider only what must inevitably have followed from the nature of his intellect. The complex catholicity—the massive breadth—in a word, the universality of his mind, inevitably involves a corresponding vastness of interest and participation in the public affairs of his time, and all the varieties of its thought and life. Isolation from public life may coexist, and be perfectly compatible, with intensity of genius—with universality, never. Moreover, to be worldly wise, as the plays show their author to have been, a man must follow the rule Bacon insists upon as indispensable—namely, to ally contemplation with action. Deny such a man experience, and you cannot get from him the lessons of experience, as you get them from this author. Isolate such a man from affairs, and his genius spreads aloft into the vast air of the abstract, and you never get in his writings the voices of the street, the camp, the court, the cabinet—in a word, the voices of concrete practical life, as you do in the Shakspeare Drama. Take for example, the man nearest Shakspeare, the many-sided Goethe: the corollary to his many-sidedness is the fact that he was a man of the world, a scientifician, courtier, statesman. So with the author of the Drama. He must have been immersed in public life. He must have held office. He must have administered the affairs of State. It was the inevitable result of his genius, and it was the condition on which the manifestations of that genius depended. Denied public life, and either his development would have been arrested, or he would have become a vast dreamer or abstractionist."

"Upon my word, Harrington," said Wentworth, "that's an astonishing thing for you to say!"

"It's the truth, nevertheless," replied Harrington, smiling.

"But the facts of Shakspeare's life are against you," rejoined Wentworth.

"Well, you must reconcile them as you can," said Harrington. "Meanwhile, there is the indestructible truth. All history, all facts, all reason testify to it. It is so."

"But look here, Harrington," said the amazed Wentworth. "On the one hand, you infer that a man of Shakspeare's genius must have been a statesman. On the other hand, is the plain fact that Shakspeare was nothing of the sort. Now, therefore, we must at once conclude that your inference is wrong."

"Not necessarily," replied Harrington.

"Not necessarily?" Wentworth laughed, and fixed his eyes with a puzzled look upon the floor. "Well, I don't see how you can escape from so obvious a conclusion. Now, let me state it again. In the first place, who wrote the plays?"

Receiving no answer, Wentworth looked up, and saw Harrington gazing with rapt affection on the noble bust of Verulam. For a moment the young artist held his breath in utter stupefaction; then a deep flush burned upon his face, and he laughed immoderately. Harrington colored, but took his friend's merriment, as he took everything, good-naturedly, and sat smiling at him.

"Bravo!" cried Wentworth, at length. "Another sacrifice to the idol! Now, Harrington, I can't swallow the idea, that the idol wrote Shakspeare's plays, but, for goodness' sake do publish it! It will make such a jolly row. By Jupiter! what fun it will be to see all the steady old ink-pots fizzing into vitriol bottles, and foaming over on to your idea! Do publish it."

"One of these days, Richard," said Harrington, gently. "But I don't think Verulam alone wrote the plays. He had help from others—and some of them came from a lower order of mind than his. But in all the great plays his intellect and design are visible. However, let it pass, and in the meantime, say nothing about it to any one, for till it can come with solid proof, it will meet with no favor from the Jedburgh justice of a world that hangs your thought first, and tries it afterward. But for your own sake, I wish you could believe that this great poet could not have been the poet he was, if he had not been concerned in everything that concerns mankind. Especially must he have cherished the idea of political liberty, for without that, poet or artist can be but little."

"Upon my word, Harrington," said Wentworth, "I shouldn't be much astonished if you were to assert that the author of Shakspeare's plays, as you call him, would be, if he was alive, a Garrisonian Abolitionist."

"Well," replied Harrington, laughing in his beard, "you know Montaigne says a man's books are his children, and I'm sure this author's children don't vote with the Webster Whigs or go union-saving or kidnapping with either Whigs or Democrats. And as for Shakspeare being a Garrisonian, it's quite clear to my perverted sense, that the man who makes his patriot, Brutus, cry aloud, as the first demand of political justice, 'Liberty, Freedom, and Enfranchisement,' would not, at any rate, if he were with us, be found in Mr. Ben Hallett's party."

Wentworth, touched at the idea of Shakspeare and Ben Hallett being by any chance thrown together, laughed immoderately, while Harrington, highly amused at his mirth, sat and smiled at him.

"Harrington," said Wentworth, recovering from his merriment, "you almost tempt me to extend my studio among the sons of men."

"That's where the great artists extended theirs," replied Harrington. "Raphael, Giotto, Cellini, Angelo, all those superb artists, were politicians, country-lovers, friends and comrades of their kind. Their human sympathies gave their genius its pulse of life. You young artists ought to blush when you think of Michael Angelo."

"Well, Michael was a trump," returned Wentworth, gaily.

"A trump?" repeated Harrington. "I wish he was a trump that could sound some of you fellows into life. Yes, there was a man behind the artist in Michael, and his works are cryptic with his humanity. By the way, Richard, how comes on the 'Death of Attucks?'"

The "Death of Attucks" was a picture which Wentworth, instigated by Harrington, had begun to paint in illustration of the picturesque scene on that wild March night of the early Revolution, when a black man flung himself on the bayonets for a country which enslaves his race, and has scribes to defile his memory.

"Well," replied Wentworth, with a look of momentary sadness, "I haven't painted much lately—so the picture stands. O me," he sighed, "I see intellectually the truth of all you say about the relation of liberty to art, but somehow I don't get kindled."

"Look here, Richard," said Harrington, "you ought to hear Wendell Phillips."

"So I ought," answered Wentworth, "and I mean to sometime."

"You must," replied Harrington. "He will show you the ideal beauty of anti-slavery. Many a young man has found his eloquence the golden door to a life for liberty. Now Muriel has planned to go to the Convention to-night, and you are to go with us, and I hope you will hear him.

"Who are going?" asked Wentworth.

"We four," replied Harrington.

"You three," responded Wentworth; "I won't go."

"Oh, but you must," replied Harrington. "I promised to bring you there to tea, and my word is at stake."

Wentworth was silent, and sat with his eyes fixed on the

floor, and his face reluctant and uneasy. Harrington watched him, and felt that there was some reason connected with either Muriel or Emily for his desire to avoid going to Temple street that evening. Suddenly the story Witherlee had told him about Wentworth and Muriel flashed into his memory, and with it came the sharp suspicion that Witherlee had lied. Could it be, after all, that Wentworth and Emily were lovers? Harrington's heart trembled, and he determined to question Wentworth on the spot.

"Richard," said he, "why are you averse to going up to Temple street this evening? Is it on account of anything in this talk of Fernando's which John Todd told you?"

"Oh, no," replied Wentworth, coloring. "I don't care—I'll go since you desire it."

"Richard," said Harrington, after an awkward pause, "pardon my rudeness, but I want to ask you a frank question, and I have a reason for asking it. Are you in—well, have you, as Witherlee said, one of Cupid's arrows in your bleeding heart?"

Harrington tossed out the question gaily, but with a flushed face, and his heart beating. As for Wentworth he was scarlet to the roots of his hair, and with his eyes fixed on the floor, toyed with his moustache in great confusion.

"Oh, that wasn't Witherlee's phrase," he stammered evasively. "That was my way of reporting what he said."

"Well," returned Harrington, "but is it true or not?"

Wentworth was silent for a moment.

"Suppose it is true. What then?" was his answer.

"It is true, then?" faltered Harrington.

Wentworth was still for a moment, then nodded affirmatively.

"Good!" exclaimed Harrington. "Richard, I give you joy. But now tell me—pardon my inquisitiveness—tell me which is the one?"

Wentworth felt himself in a corner, and with his face hot as fire, and his heart throbbing furiously, cast desperately about for some evasive answer.

"Is it Emily?" said Harrington hastily, in a voice which he could not keep from trembling.

Wentworth instantly took the tone as evidence of Harrington's love for Miss Ames, and with a bitter feeling filling his heart as the sense of the injury she had done him, swept over him, he became self-possessed and cold.

"Emily!" he repeated, affecting surprise and looking at Harrington's flushed face with desperate placidity, while a faint smile curved his proud lip. "Indeed, Harrington, none of Emily's lovers have a rival in me."

The answer was at once a taunt and an evasion, but to Harrington it seemed decisive, and spoken in plain good-faith. It fell upon him like a death-blow, but his heart, mailed in magnanimity, rose from under it, and he forced himself to smile, lest Wentworth should be pained by perceiving that it gave him pain. As yet, Wentworth had not the least idea that his friend loved Muriel. And, as yet, he did not perceive that he had just given Harrington to understand that he himself was her lover.

So, thought Harrington, Witherlee told the truth after all, and I was not mistaken.

"Richard," he cried, springing from his seat, and crossing over to Wentworth, who instantly rose, startled by his sudden movement, as well as by the strange emotion which struggled with a smile in his lit face. "Richard, I give you joy. I do with all my heart and soul. You should have told me before, that I might sooner have been happy in your happiness. But I am glad to know it now—from your own lips, for I knew it, or all but knew it, before. My love and blessing on you both forever!"

All this poured forth impetuously, his hands grasping Wentworth's, his features convulsed and smiling, his kind eyes shining through tears. An awful feeling swept down, like an avalanche, on Wentworth. Petrified with the suddenness of the revelation, he not only saw that he had inadvertently confessed himself Muriel's lover, but he saw that Harrington loved her! He strove to speak, but his lips refused their office, and no form of words came to his whirling mind. Harrington saw his pallor and agitation, and mistaking them for the signs of a young lover's emotion at being thus brusquely congratulated, wrung his hands once more, and turned away. Wentworth, too much overwhelmed to even think, sank down upon his seat, and leaning his arm on the back of the sofa, covered his hot eyes with his hand.

At that moment a low, piteous whine was heard in the yard. Harrington started and colored and went out instantly.

Wentworth, meanwhile, hearing the noise, and aware of his friend's exit, took no heed of either, but sat trying to compose his mind to think of the new complication in which he found himself.

Presently the deep sense of Harrington's splendid magnanimity in so joyfully giving up the woman he loved, rose upon him in contrast with his own passionate envy and jealousy when he thought him the lover of Emily, and with the tears springing to his eyes, he felt as if he were the meanest man that ever breathed. To go and fling his arms around Harrington, ask his forgiveness, and explain the whole matter, was his first impulse. Then came the consideration that in doing this, he must own that he loved Emily, for had he not said that he was in love with one? and he must own that she had played the coquette with him, and left him with a wounded heart. He could not do it. Pride forbade it. But what should he do? He could not leave Harrington in error, and such an error! Yet how explain that loving one of the two, he did not love Muriel, nor yet Emily. Altogether, Wentworth was in a dilemma!

Vainly revolving the matter for a few moments, he finally came to the desperate resolution so say nothing at present, but wait until he could be alone, and then think what course he could pursue to extricate himself from this embroilment.

The clear remembrance came to his mind how sedulously Emily had been wooing Harrington of late. Acquitting him now of all knowledge or blame in this respect, his censure gathered into a fiercer focus on her. It was plain that, having played the heartless coquette with him, she was trying the same game on his friend. A regular Lady Clara Vere de Vere, he thought, remembering the haughty beauty dowered with manly scorn in Tennyson's poem. Fiery rage at Emily contended in his soul with fiery love for her. Gnashing his teeth with fury, scorning himself that he could love her and she so false and base, scorning himself that he could hate her when he so loved her, he walked up and down the room for a minute or two; then suddenly, with a violent effort, grew cool, and picking up his hat from the floor, went out into the yard.

He did not see Harrington at first, but stepping around the corner of the house, he caught sight of him, and all his passionate agitation faded away in surprise as he became aware of his friend's occupation. Harrington was stooping down in an angle of the garden near a large square box set on end, rubbing away with a gloved hand at the back of an old, weak, white dog, the same Wentworth had seen tormented in the street that morning. Actually, thought Wentworth, he went back to take that forsaken brute home with him!

"What in thunder are you doing, Harrington?" he exclaimed, approaching the scene of his friend's operations.

Harrington started, and turned his glowing face with a half ashamed smile upon Wentworth, then continued to rub the dog's back.

"I couldn't leave the poor old fellow in such a plight, Richard," he remarked, in an apologetic tone, "so, you see, I took him in."

"Why, he's got the mange," said Wentworth, eying the animal with a face of mingled disgust and curiosity.

"That's not his fault," returned Harrington, coolly, dipping his gloved hand into a box of what appeared to be powdered sulphur, sprinkling a handful on the dog's back, and rubbing it in.

The dog, meanwhile, lying on the ground, was devouring with feeble content a plateful of broken victuals which the young man had procured from the house. He was a miserable, weak, red-eyed, flaccid-jawed, dirty-white old mastiff, and, as the young artist had observed, he had the mange. As ugly, forlorn-looking and worthless a cur in his life as that dead dog which, the old Mohammedan apologue says, the Jewish mob derided in the streets of Jerusalem, when a tall stranger of grave and sweet aspect drew near, and paused to cast a look of compassion on the object of their derision. "Is it not a miracle of ugliness!" jeered the crowd. "But see," said the stranger, "pearls are not equal to the whiteness of his teeth!" And then, says the Mohammedan story, the people knew that the stranger was the great prophet Jesus, for none but he would look upon a dead dog with the beauty-seeing eye of love.

"Poor old fellow," soliloquized Harrington, "I quite forgot I had him, till he whined for his dinner."

"How confoundedly dirty he is," observed Wentworth.

"Dirty? Oh, no—that's his color," said Harrington, naïvely. "He's not dirty now, for I washed him."

"The deuce you did!" replied Wentworth, laughing. "Upon my word, Harrington, you're a regular Brahmin. Though it's mighty good in you to take so much trouble for a brute like that. Faith, I'd have left him to his fate."

"Oh, well," replied Harrington, tranquilly, scanning the dog's back, to see if any diseased spot had escaped him, "the poor old thing has something to do in this world, or he wouldn't have been sent, and he has a right here, seeing that he does no harm. There, I guess that'll do, and he'll be comfortable till I get back."

He took off his glove, patted the old dog on the head, and spoke to him. The animal, who had finished his dinner, feebly wagged his tail, and licked the kind hand, then looked up with bleared red eyes into the face of his protector, still wagging his tail.

"Good," said Harrington; "see how grateful he is! Come, Wentworth, it's time for us to go," he continued, rising to his feet. "It's after four o'clock, and I promised to be there early."

Stooping again, he lifted the dog into the packing-case on some old rags of carpeting, put a pan of water near him, laid the tin box of sulphur and the glove on top, and turned away to the house.

"What a good fellow Harrington is," muttered Wentworth, following him. "To think of his rescuing that old brute from the boys, and taking as much care of him as if he was Scott's

Maida! I wonder that I, who admire such things so much, never think of doing such things."

He got into the room just as Harrington was disappearing up the flight of steps into the room above, whither he went to wash his hands and brush his clothes. In a few minutes he descended again, closed the windows, put on his slouched hat, and they set off together arm in arm.

CHAPTER XIII.

THE FAIRY PRINCE.

THEY arrived in a few minutes at the house in Temple street, and were let in by Patrick. Wentworth had been complaining that something was hurting his foot, and sat down in the hall to take off his boot and see what was the matter, while Harrington went up-stairs into the library.

The jewel of the rich room was Muriel, and Muriel lay on a velvet couch, asleep. The young man noiselessly approached her, and stood tenderly watching her beauty in its repose. She lay in a glimmer of light from the western window, and the faint radiance lit her dreamful face, whose beauty was like a hymn of immortal joy. The draped arms lay restfully along her form, with the white hands lightly clasped together, and the expression of the figure was repose. Gazing at her with heavenly sadness, the lover saw her countenance gleam with an evanescent smile, and the lips murmured a word. It was "Richard." A quick pang shot to his heart, and at the same instant Muriel started and awoke.

"John!" she exclaimed, coloring and smiling as she sprang up from her light sleep and gave him her hands, "you here! When did you come?"

"Just come," he replied, holding her hands, and smiling into her face. "Why, Muriel, you looked like the Sleeping Beauty of the fairy tale."

"Oh, John! And you like the fairy prince that woke the Sleeping Beauty up!" returned Muriel, gaily.

"That's a compliment, I suppose," said Harrington.

"Compliment for compliment," said she.

"Oh, but mine was the truth," he replied.

"And so was mine," she answered. "So it's arranged that I am the Sleeping Beauty awakened, and you the fairy prince that awakened me, and now I shall have to follow you through all the world, as she did him in Tennyson's poem."

Harrington's color rose, and he dropped her hands. Muriel blushed too, for she felt that what she had said in thoughtless play had carried some deeper sense to him than she had intended.

"Pardon me, John," she murmured, "I did not mean to offend you."

"You offend me!" exclaimed Harrington, in astonishment. "You, Muriel! Indeed, no."

"Then why did you color?" she asked archly, reassured

"I? Oh—no matter. I was thinking of something."

"Of what? Come now. Be frank, John. I desire—I command"——

Harrington looked confused for a moment. An impulse came to him.

"It is you who must tell me, Muriel," he said in a low voice.

"I? What shall I tell you, John. I will tell you anything you ask."

"Tell me then of the fairy prince who awakened you indeed, and whom you are to follow through all the world. Tell me of him, that I may congratulate you and him together."

Muriel gazed at him in wonder. If he had not spoken with such sweet seriousness, she would have thought he was jesting.

"You said you would tell me anything I asked," said Harrington, gravely. "Tell me this, then."

"I will, John," she replied slowly. "I will tell you of him—when I find him. Not till then."

She turned away, musing. It was Harrington's turn now to look at her with wonder. What did she mean? He had never seen any tokens of duplicity in her, but what was this?

Just then in came Wentworth, smiling. Harrington saw her face light as she went toward him, and wondered if she had understood what he had said to her. That's it, he thought; she could not have understood me.

"Ha, Muriel. Good afternoon," burst out Wentworth in his airy way. "Excuse me for not coming up at once, but I was ransacking my boot. And see what I found. A damson stone. Take it, Harrington, and be happy."

"Come, no nonsense, Richard," said Muriel. "Let's go up to the studio, and fence."

Wentworth darted at her, and she nimbly dodged him, flashed out of the room and flew up-stairs, laughing, followed by the young artist on the run. She vanished into the studio before he could come up with her, and Wentworth turned to wait for his friend, who was leisurely ascending the stairs.

"Lightfoot cannot outrun Atalanta," said Harrington.

"Exactly so," returned Wentworth.

They went up and into the studio, as it was called, together. It was a large, square, sunlit room, the floor covered with a thick, hard carpet, and it had two windows looking to the west, with boxes on the sills, filled with heliotrope and mignionette, which filled the air with their rich and delicate fragrance. Muriel's table, with a small easel, cases of water-colors, and bristol-board, drawing paper, tinted sketches, and other artistic paraphernalia, stood near one of the windows. Not far from the other was a moulding stand, on which stood Emily's bust of her friend, with a box of clay on the floor near it. The walls were a warm grey, and ornamented with three or four of Jullien's crayons, some plaster medallions and bas-reliefs, and a set of hanging-shelves filled with books. Parallel-bars on one side of the room, a pair of large dumb-bells on the floor, several iron weights, with rings for lifting them, near by, and a set of gilded foils and masks on the wall, gave the studio something of the air of a gymnasium. A small piano, with books of music upon it, a low sofa, and a few plain arm-chairs, completed the furniture of the apartment.

The young men had sat talking a few minutes, waiting for Muriel, when Mrs. Eastman and Emily came in, and they rose again to make their salutations. Emily was in her most sumptuous mood, and smiled serenely as she entered and curtseyed down into a chair. Mrs. Eastman gave her hand to the young men, whom she loved as much as if they were her own sons, and standing near Harrington, with her arm in his, affectionately asked for his health.

"You are looking pale, John," she said, with motherly solicitude. "Too much study I'm afraid."

"Not at all, mother," said Harrington, gaily—he always called Mrs. Eastman "mother." "Celestial pale, the student's proper hue, you know; and spite of my paleness, I'm strong and well."

"Nevertheless, I wish you had some of Richard's roses," she said playfully.

"My roses, indeed!" rattled Wentworth. "Why, Mrs. Eastman, I'm so much in love with Harrington's intellectual pallor that I'm thinking of trying some of Jules Hauel's lily-white cosmetic to get my face of the same tint. For what is —hurrah! Here comes the fairy prince!" he cried, breaking off, as the door of a chamber adjoining the studio opened, and a beautiful and brilliant figure came forward into the room.

It was Muriel, transformed by the vivid and gorgeous dress of a fairy prince—such a dress as the artists of fairy books give to Percinet or Valentine; and in it she was courtly and noble as Shakspeare's Rosalind, when Rosalind wore "man's apparel" in the gay greenwood of Arden. A year before when she had resolved to take fencing lessons of Harrington, she had devised this dress, and with a woman's natural disposition to ornamentation, and with her own special wish to throw festal grace and the hues of romance even on her hours of exercise, she had brought to the fashioning of her attire all the richness of her lavish fancy. To wear anything that was ugly even at her gymnastics, or to make her exercise a sober business and not a poetic pleasure, was quite impossible for

Muriel. She must clothe her muscularities with beauty, as Harmodius wreathed his sword with myrtle. So she gilded her foils and masks, and fashioned her garb in fairy magnificence. The dress was a cymar of vivid crimson silk, loosely belted at the waist, and adorned with broidered arabesques of gold. The bodice, cut loose to the form, with large sleeves, ruffled with lace at the wrists, had a frilled ruffle of lace emerging from the bosom, and rising in a sort of fraise around the neck, in exquisite keeping with the refined beauty of the countenance which bloomed above it. A little crimson cap, with a thick, swailing, white plume, rested lightly on the head, and the glorious amber hair was arranged to lie on the back of the neck like the locks of a page. The skirt of the dress, also of crimson silk, broidered with golden arabesques, and deeply bordered with heavy, gold fringe, fell in graceful folds, ending just above the knee, and white silk hose, with crimson satin slippers, completed the poetic and splendid costume. Never had Muriel appeared more fascinating than in this attire, which showed the full perfection of a form, straight, supple, tall and strong, whose every rounded outline was elegance, and whose free strength was harmonized in grace and beauty.

"By Jupiter!" cried Wentworth, "I never see Muriel in that costume, without thinking that the long skirts are a tremendous shame. There's a figure for you!"

"Yes, but please remember," said Emily, "that there are some of us women who are not endowed with such fine forms as Muriel."

"Oh, I'm pretty well," said Muriel, with a light laugh. "But it's mainly due to my life-long muscular exercise, Emily."

"Indeed, Muriel," replied Emily, "nature must have contributed largely in the first instance, to a form like yours."

"Thanks for compliments," said Muriel gaily, doffing her plumed cap and bowing.

"You're inclined to underrate muscular exercise, Emily," said Harrington, laughing.

"Well, perhaps so, John," she replied, with a slow smile.

"And yet," he pursued, "I'm not sure, that to make women

a race of gymnasts, wouldn't be one of the surest ways of securing their social enfranchisement."

"Why, John," returned Emily, laughing, "do you want to make us athletic enough to get our rights by the strong hand ?"

"Oh, no," he rejoined, amusedly. "But men could not help respecting women, if women were on a grander scale, and justice might be born of that respect. And, to make women all they latently are, gymnastics are a very important instrument. I am inclined to think physical training the foundation of all noble culture. You get from it health, strength, beauty of form, grace of carriage, dexterity of movement and action, a very potent safeguard against all diseases, mental vigor, cheerfulness, courage, self-reliance, a spirit that nourishes and promotes self-respect, independence, generosity, moral purity, heroic desires, large sympathies ; in fact, all the virtues. I do not say that gymnastics bestow the great intellectualities and moralities ; but they encourage, develop, and sustain them. You know what Dr. Johnson said—'a sick person is a scoundrel;' and I think a pretty large sermon might be preached from that text, in these days. At all events, I am quite sure that you will see grander and more womanly women, and an increase of social happiness, when a vigorous muscular training is made part of women's culture."

"Bravo !" cried Muriel. "I feel inspired. The foils, Harrington—the foils !"

Harrington—who had been admiring while he spoke, the free, beautiful figure—started and went to the wall to take the weapons down.

"First, some exercise to get the muscles in order," said Muriel.

She threw down her cap, and bounding forward, with the light strong spring of a bayadere, to the parallel bars, put her hands on the poles, and leaped up between them. Then, with a succession of springs, she traversed the whole length, leaping along the bars on her hands ; then, back again to the centre, where she swung to and fro for an instant ; and, as she rose again, vaulted over and alighted in the middle of the room, tossing the air into perfume.

"Bravo!" cried Wentworth. "That's religion, as Emerson says."

"Emerson!" chided Mrs. Eastman, amusedly. "Emerson never said any such thing."

"More shame for him," retorted Wentworth, gaily. "Kingsley says so, at any rate."

"Kingsley!" she replied, in the same amused, chiding tone.

"Yes, *ma mère*," asserted Wentworth. "That's what Kingsley calls muscular Christianity, and I'm going in for some of it."

He bounded forward to the bars just as Muriel was running up to them again. She stopped and stood a little one side, watching him as he swung and leaped forward.

"You don't do it half as well as Muriel," said Mrs. Eastman, very truly.

"Take care now, Richard, that's dangerous," cried Muriel in a warning voice, as Wentworth was swinging, preparatory to vaulting over.

Wentworth laughed recklessly, and flung himself over the bars. Muriel's warning was not without reason, for as he came over, his foot struck the pole, and, with a cry from Emily which proved her interest in him, he pitched head downward. Muriel sprang on the instant, caught him with all her strength, and set him on his feet. Wentworth reddened, and looked dazed.

"Careless boy," she chided, playfully giving him a light cuff on the ear, "you came nigh breaking your neck."

"That he did," exclaimed Harrington; and "indeed he did," exclaimed the others in chorus.

"Saved by a fairy prince," cried Wentworth in a mock-tragic tone. "By Jupiter, Muriel, but you're as strong as you're quick. I wonder how many young ladies there are in the world that could catch a fellow when he's tumbling over neck and heels to destruction. Well, I guess I won't try that again. Thank you, dear fairy prince."

He put her hand gallantly to his lips as he said the last words.

"I declare," cried Emily, laughing, "what would society say

if it could behold these operations! I can't help thinking how our minister at Cambridge, and all my Episcopal friends would stare at you, Muriel."

"Yes, flower of the world," replied Muriel, "we should be awfully scandalized, no doubt. But there's virtue in our games, nevertheless, for health is there, and health is a virtue that beckons the others on. The fencing, however, is the perfection of. exercise."

"Why is that so superior?" asked Emily.

"Because it develops bodily strength and activity more harmoniously than any other," replied Muriel. "So Roland says."

"Roland?" inquired Emily.

"Yes. Roland is the author of the best modern work on fencing," answered Muriel. "Stay, I'll read you what he says."

She went to the book-shelves, and returned with the volume —Roland's "Theory and Practice of Fencing."

"Here it is," she observed, finding the page. "Listen: 'Perhaps there is no exercise whatever more calculated for these purposes (developing and cultivating bodily strength and activity) than fencing. Riding, walking, sparring, wrestling, running, and pitching the bar are all of them certainly highly beneficial, but beyond all question there is no single exercise which combines so many advantages as fencing. By it the muscles of every part of the body are brought into play; it expands the chest and occasions an equal distribution of the blood and other circulating fluids through the whole system. More than one case has fallen under the author's own observation, in which affections of the lungs, and a tendency to consumption have been entirely removed by occasional practice with the foil; and he can state, upon the highest medical authority, that since the institution of the School of Arms at Geneva, scrofula, which was long lamentably prevalent there, had been gradually disappearing.'"

Just then a tap was heard at the door. Muriel dropped the book, and made one nimble spring through the entrance intc her chamber, while Harrington went to the door. It was Patrick come to say that Mr. Witherlee was down-stairs.

"Tell him we're engaged, Patrick, and ask him to excuse us," rang the silver voice of Muriel through the half open entrance of her room.

Patrick departed, and as the door closed, Muriel emerged, laughing, from her hiding-place.

"That was a stroke of policy," she said. "If Fernando were to see me in this costume, it would be town talk to-morrow, and in the papers the day after. Fernando's mind is a perfect colander—all that gets into it runs out of it."

She was more than ever like a fairy prince the next instant as she stood with the light bright foil in her gloved hand, and her face covered by the gilt mask, over which waved a thick crimson plume. Harrington, similarly arrayed, save for the plume, with the golden wires envisoring his features, advanced toward her.

"You have not forgotten your plastron, have you?" he said.

"No : it's under the dress," she replied.

Firm and true as he, she struck guard, and the foils crossed with a clash.

"By George ! this is delicious," exclaimed Wentworth, in perfect rapture.

And so it was, for Muriel was like some unimagined fairy chevalier as she stood in the beautiful attitude of the exercise, the rich crimson lights of her dress glowing, and its golden ornaments tremulously flashing in the sun-ray, and the sumptuous radiance resting on the proud and elegant flowing curves of her figure. Lithe, superb and strong, an image of health and grace, a form of lyric beauty, she might have stood in her armed posture for the spirit of the foil.

Emily had crossed over to the piano, and sitting behind it with her eyes fixed upon the combatants, began to play a low drumming strain of Bacchic fury in the pause preluding the game. Fierce, monotonous and dreamful, a congeries of bass tones swarming grumly from the keys, with low minor notes faintly chirping at intervals between, it suddenly rang up, pierced with one sharp tingling treble, like a cry, as with a loud clash of the foils, the agile and vivid figure of Muriel darted forward in a superb lunge. Harrington uttered a low ejaculation, for the thrust had nearly reached him, and he had parried in the compass of a ring. Muriel stood on guard again, her gold and crimson tremulously glowing and flashing in the sun, and her bright plume dancing, while the dark and furious music, swarming and drumming loudly from the bass keys, sunk away into the low, monotonous and dreamful strain, with the chirping notes still fluttering and sounding in. It did not rise again, but ran sombrely swarming on, as Harrington reached in his long arm in a quick and quiet lunge, which was deftly parried with only a faint clink of the foils, and then, with another splendid flash of glitter and color, Muriel sprang, lunging nimbly home, and clash on clash, with a rapturous clamor of steel, came pass and parry on either side, while the hurrying music rose and rang in whirling riot, like a wild, tumultuous race of Mænads, with heavy bars of thunderous sound striking through the loud, triumphant swarming fury of the melody. Clash and flash, amidst the strumming whirl and anvil blows of the melodious choral, flew the bright foils, and stamp and tramp, advancing and retreating, sinking and rising, low to the lunge, and high to the parry, swayed and darted the lords of the fairy duel—Muriel's crimson feather tossing and dancing in time to the gathering and racing of the music, like a delirious sprite of combat.

Suddenly—snap—jingle—the contest ceased, and the music flittered off into a light and brilliant strain, like the tinkling laughter of elves. Harrington stood with a dazed air, looking at the fragment of the foil he held, the rest of which lay on the floor. Muriel broke into a merry peal of laughter, in which Wentworth and her mother joined, while Emily, still playing, smiled indolently over the piano.

"Plague!" exclaimed Harrington. "That's the second foil I've seen broken to-day. They make these things miserably bad."

"It's the last pair we have, so that ends our fun for this day," cried Muriel, taking the gilt mask from her bright, flushed face. "Serves me right for not always having half a dozen sets on hand, a thing I'll do in future."

"By Jupiter!" exclaimed Wentworth, while Muriel crossed to hang up her mask and foil, "that was tall fencing, while it lasted, anyhow. I'm sorry the foil's broken, Muriel, for I wanted to fence with the fairy prince myself."

"You ought to learn, Emily," said Mrs. Eastman. "Then you and Richard could match John and Muriel."

Emily stopped playing, and glanced at Wentworth with a slight curl of her lip, which did not escape the young artist.

"Indeed, Mrs. Eastman," she said, "it's not in my line, and I should make a poor figure at it, I know."

"But it's as beautiful as dancing," said Mrs. Eastman.

"And a great deal more womanly than waltzing," put in Wentworth, interrupting, to have his fling at Emily, who was very fond of the waltz.

Emily reddened, and fixed her lustrous eyes on Wentworth, hurt and angered by his remark.

"Come, come," interposed Muriel, gaily, "I won't have Emily badgered into doing anything it is not her genius to do. Fencing is not in her line, as she says; but music, dear Emily," she added, putting her arms around her friend, "music *is* in your line, and charmingly you played for us. Your improvisation inspired our battle, and I should fence twice as well if I always had you to play for me."

"Faith, Emily, there's something in that, I believe," remarked Harrington. "But you fence wonderfully, Muriel, for one who has had only a year's practice."

"Are you sure you don't spare her, Harrington?" said Emily, slily.

"Spare her? Indeed I don't. I'd scorn to do such a thing!" answered Harrington, with animation.

"That's right, John," said Muriel in a tone of gay gratitude; "it's always a shame for a woman to be treated like a weak sister, and there's a subtle assumption of our inferiority in the consideration we women get from men in this polite age, which does not please me at all. No effeminate culture for me! What I know or do, I will know or do thoroughly and vigorously, or not at all."

"Bravo, Muriel!" said Mrs. Eastman, rising, "so your

father would say, if he were with us. There's no reason, he used to observe, why girls shouldn't be as vigorously trained as boys, and even supposing woman's sphere to be purely and simply that of a wife and mother, said he, she ought, on the most ultra conservative principles, to have every power and faculty fully developed that she may fitly educate her children."

"Good! Woman's rights doctrine, that," said Wentworth, playfully. "Muriel, do you vote?" he added, with a quizzical air.

"Yes," answered Muriel, so naively, that Wentworth was taken aback. "Do you want to know how? Every election day, Patrick comes to ask me how he shall vote, and I tell him, and he votes. That is my ballot, for my judgment casts it. But what do you think of the good sense of a community that allowing me capable of instructing a man how to vote, will not allow that I am capable of voting myself? What do you think of the good sense of a country that denies to a cultured woman a right which it accords to the uncultured man who opens her street door?"

"Well," returned Wentworth, laughing, "we are not all such fools, Muriel, as to think the arrangement you criticise right and proper."

"Come, children," said Mrs. Eastman, after a pause, "since the play is over, let us adjourn to the library."

And she departed, followed by the others. Harrington, seeing Muriel linger, half-absently, paused near her. Becoming aware that he was looking at her, she looked up from her musing, with a quiet smile.

"Well, fairy prince," he said, lightly.

"Ah," she replied, with pensive playfulness, "you recognize the fairy prince in me, then, do you? And that is the fairy prince I am to follow through all the world."

She had approached him as she spoke, and while he looked at her with an inquiring face, seeking to fathom the riddle of her speech, she passed close by him, with a light waft of delicate perfume, and vanished into her chamber.

He stood for a moment, lost in a sense of some unravelled

mystery lurking in her words and manner, and then suddenly turned and went down-stairs.

CHAPTER XIV.

THE ANTI-SLAVERY CONVENTION.

Transformed again in lace and lilac from a fairy prince to a fairy princess, Muriel joined her friends in the library. Music and blithe talk filled up the hours till tea-time, and after tea they prepared to go to the Convention. Mrs. Eastman had declined accompanying them, and they set out together through the moonlit dusk, Harrington escorting Emily, and Wentworth Muriel.

"Why, how cold it has grown!" exclaimed Emily, surprised at the strange chillness of the air, as she and Harrington walked up the shadowy street.

"Yes, indeed," replied Harrington, "and the wind has changed to the north, I verily believe. After this warm, delicious day, too! But no New Englander has a right to be surprised at the freaks of the climate."

Engaged in conversation, they did not notice, as Wentworth and Muriel behind them did, when they were passing under the walled plateau, on which loomed in the dim moonlight the domed bulk of the State House, two young men who went by considerably intoxicated. The young men were Horatio and Thomas Atkins, who had been drinking juleps in honor of Southern institutions with Mr. Lafitte at the Tremont House, whither they had escorted him after dinner. Thomas had taken so many juleps that his hat was acock, his whiskerage fiercer than ever, and his gait a swaggering stagger, while Horatio was in that state of solemn and stubborn tipsiness in which a man is upon his honor to walk straight. Muriel sighed as she passed them, and all the way across the broad Common, its trees and sward dimly lighted by the moon, and chill in the fresher breath of the keen breeze, while she conversed with Wentworth, her thoughts rested with vague uneasiness on her uncle and his graceless sons. It was altogether the most unpleasant topic that ever entered her mind, and it was especially so on account of her mother. Mrs. Eastman felt her brother's general course, particularly his political course, to be a family disgrace. All the old New England traditions, laws, and habitudes had been at least passively for liberty up to the insane year of 1850 ; and to have her kinsman one of the new brawlers for slavery and kidnapping was a sore reflection for the gentle lady. She had never recovered from the wound he had given her spirit, by enrolling himself as one of the Fifteen Hundred Scoundrels. And on this point, at least, Muriel felt as strongly as she did, particularly since the report had arrived that Sims had been scourged to death at Savannah.

The noise of life thickened around the party as they passed down Winter street into Washington street, the main avenue of Boston. The street was processional, grotesque, and gay under the moon. Vehicles of all sorts dashed and rattled over the pavement, and passengers were bustling and swarming along the irregular vista of lighted shop windows, under the dark, motley buildings covered with their multitude of golden-lettered signs.

Passing up the crowded thoroughfare, they arrived presently at the Melodeon, where the Anti-Slavery Convention was holding its evening session. It was a hall rented most frequently for concerts and exhibitions of one sort or another, but memorable in history as the church of Theodore Parker. There, on every Sabbath, he shook the hearts of thousands with the sacred and heroic eloquence of those sermons which have passed to shine in pulpit literature with the strong splendors of Taylor and Latimer, and a nobleness and courage all their own.

The hall was full as the party entered, and some one was speaking from the platform. They paused, looking over the dense concourse for seats, and seeing none, were about to try their chance in the gallery above, when a party of five left theirs in the centre of the hall, and going down the aisle at once, they took the vacant places. Harrington had passed in first, and leaning over to Muriel, said in a whisper :

"Did you see your uncle as we came in ?"

"Yes," she replied. "Who was that with him, that looked at you so strangely ?"

Harrington turned his head and gazed up to the back of the hall, where Mr. Atkins was sitting, scornfully listening to the speaker. By his side he saw a dark, handsome face, with a moustache, and the face was intently watching him. With a vague thrill he turned again to Muriel.

"I don't know him," he whispered.

"It is strange," she whispered in reply. "I saw by Mr. Atkins's manner that he was telling that person who we were, and I know by the slight start the stranger gave, and the look he cast at you, that my uncle had mentioned your name, and that the stranger had some interest in you."

Nothing more was said, but Harrington felt disturbed even to apprehension, though he could not have told why. In a minute or two, looking around again, he saw the stranger still watching him, and saw his eye wander away with a sinister smile. Turning his face resolutely to the platform, Harrington, with another mysterious tremor, tried to recollect if he had ever seen that face before, and unable to recall it, he dismissed it from his thoughts with a strong effort of will, and set himself to listen to the speaker.

Just then, the speaker ended, and sat down, amidst a rushing rustle of the audience, and some slight applause. There was a minute's intermission, during which Harrington's eye swept over the multitude, seated in rows around him, and filling the gallery, which extended in a horse-shoe curve around the walls of the oblong hall. Both sexes were about equally represented in the concourse, which was dotted here and there with the dark faces of negroes. The platform was occupied by a number of the anti-slavery leaders, men and women. The chairman, who was leaning from his seat in hasty conference with two or three persons, was the gallant Francis Jackson, a wealthy citizen, who, when the "gentlemen" of Boston had broken up an anti-slavery meeting of women, fifteen years before, opened his house to the outcasts, at the imminent peril of having it razed by the mob. But he was resolved to defend free speech, and in this cause, said he, "let my walls fall if they must: they will appear of little value after their owner shall have been whipped into silence." Such was the Roman deed, the Roman word, of Francis Jackson. Near him sat Garrison. The light of the chandelier shone full on the bald head and high-featured, dauntless face of the grand Puritan—a face in which blended the austere gentleness of Brewster with the stern integrity and solemn enthusiasm of Vane. Not far distant was the antique and noble countenance of Burleigh, with its long beard and lengths of ringlets giving it the character of some of the heads mediæval painters have imagined for Jesus. An orator he, whose massive and definite logic ran burning with Miltonian sweep, and could burst, when he so chose, in an iron hail of Miltonian invective. By his side, Harrington saw the domed brow and Socratic features of the mighty Theodore, with the lips curling in some rich stroke of whispered wit, which brought a momentary smile to the face of Burleigh. Behind them was the rugged and salient visage of Parker Pillsbury, a man whose speech rode like the Pounder of Bivar, and smote with a flail. Before Harrington's eye had wandered from him, the chairman rose, announcing a name which was lost in the sudden pour of applause that swept up from the front, and spread from rank to rank with loud cheers, and then at once the whole concourse burst into a surging and tossing uproar of acclamation, as a beautiful patrician figure, dressed in black, came forward on the lighted platform.

It was Wendell Phillips—the flower of the anti-slavery chivalry. Memory recalls the words in which Robertus Monachus describes the leader of the twelfth century Crusaders, Godfrey of Bouillon: "He was beautiful in countenance," says the chronicler, "tall in stature, agreeable in his discourse, admirable in his morals, and at the same time so gentle, that he seemed better fitted for the monk than the knight; but when his enemies appeared before him, and the combat approached, his soul became filled with mighty daring; like a lion, he feared not for his person—and what shield, what buckler, could resist the fall of his sword ?" So might one describe the great Abolitionist. But a poetic heart would take from that rich old world Past a more lustrous figure than even Godfrey to stand as his representative. In England they call Lord Derby the Rupert of debate ; and far more aptly might Wendell Phillips be termed the Tancred of liberty. In his personal appearance, as in the attitude of his life, the nature of his thought, and the style of his rhetoric, there was that which recalled the image of the loveliest of the antique chevaliers. As he stood on that brilliant platform, while the enthusiastic applause swelled and tossed in a tempest of sound and stir—one foot advanced, his hands lightly clasped behind him, his head curved a little to one side, the light bringing out in definite relief a face and form in strange contrast with every other around him, and whose statuesque repose seemed heightened by the tumultuous commotion of the audience—he impressed the eye like a piece of exquisite sculpture when seen among the alien shapes of men. A tall-browed, oval head of severe and singular grace ; long, clear-cut, Roman features ; a keen and penetrant eye ; around the firm mouth a glimmer of feminine sweetness ; the face harmonized with an expression of golden urbanity ; and in the whole aspect the polished ease of the gentleman blended with the lofty bearing of the Paladin. And a Paladin he was—a star of oratoric tournament, proved so by many a hard-fought argument in the chivalrous fields of liberty, where his eloquence, that fiery sword wrought of Justice and Beauty, as his friend Parker has called it, flashed and rang on the armor of the vile, and brought new courage to the war. None listened to the bright and terrible music of his speech unmoved ; no bitterest conservative could hear it without owning its magic. Robbed of his just due of fame by the unpopularity of the cause he championed, even his foes could whisper that he was the greatest orator in America—even the scholars of the Boston "Courier", the representative pro-slavery organ in that latitude, and the deadly enemy of the Abolitionists, could call him, with strange warmth, the Cicero of anti-slavery.

The applause sunk down, and an expectant, breathless hush succeeded. Slowly his lips curved apart, and the clear, persuasive silver of his voice flowed into words. It was a simple and ordinary sentence, and yet what a fascination it had! It was not a sentence—it was something bright that flew into the souls of his audience; and as it flew, the magnetic glance of his eye seemed to follow it, and every one was captive. His address was at once exposition and criticism. The condition of the nation, the aggressions of the slave oligarchy, the recent plunder of Mexico for the extension of slavery, the servility of the pulpit, the pro-slavery scheming of Northern merchants and manufacturers—these were his themes, and how he treated them! He was not in his loftiest lyric mood that night, and his speech only rose now and then from its tone of exquisite impressive colloquy into the long, imperial sweep of the oration; but still, as Thomas Davis said of Curran, his words went forth in robes of light with swords. Shapes of severest crystal grace that moved to Dorian music, an armed battalia, a bright procession, the splendid phrases trooped, with strength to strike and skill to guard for liberty and justice. What language—so finely chosen, so apt, terse, limpid, electrical! What logic—proof-mail of gold and steel around his thought, or a smiting weapon of celestial temper! Now came some metaphor so analogically related to the theme that it flashed on the mind like a subtle argument. And now a sentence shining upon the imagination with the beauty of an antique frieze. Here was an expression that memory would wear like a gem-cameo forever. And here some jewel of classic story re-cut more purely, or some historic picture that glowed sharp, definite, in lines and hues of life, upon the eye of the mind. Now it was the scimitar-glance of wit shearing the floating film of some intangible popular delusion, or lie. Now some homely illustration borrowed from the street, the shop, the farm, yet suddenly interpenetrated with as strange a poetic grace as though it had dropped from the lips of Tully two thousand years ago. Or here again invective, rising above some gloomy wrong, and smiting bright, like the diamond sword of Dante's black-stoled angel. Rhetoric, yet not the artificial, decorative rhetoric of the schools, but an organic growth of the man. Art, but art that seemed like nature, for it was the art that nature makes. One felt, and truly felt, in listening to the orator, that this was his natural normal speech. It was beautiful, it was ornate, it was artistic, but it was of the heart, it was of the life; and everywhere it was the stern, the solemn voice of conscience, of honor, of virtue—everywhere it was terrible and sacred with radiant pity for the poor and weak, flaming scorn for the traitor and the oppressor, burning love for liberty and justice. But who is he that shall so much as hint description of the classic grace, the delicate fiery power of the speeches of Wendell Phillips to the men of Boston? The golden bees that clustered at the lips of baby Plato, must swarm again from old Hymettus to the cradle of the child unborn who shall essay to tell the magic of that eloquence. Say that in an age and land of muck-rakes it was the speech of a gentleman—say that in its tones were heard the ancestral voices from the blocks and battle-fields of liberty—say that it touched with heavenly ardor and lifted to nobler life all uncorrupted hearts, and was light to the blind, and conscience to the base, and to the caitiff whatever he could know of shame; so leave it to worthier and more abundant praise, and to the future.

The applause which had burst forth again and again during the speech, now swelled into a tempest of acclamation as the orator withdrew. Muriel still kept her lit face fixed on the platform, and Emily, kindled into ardent color, leaned back with a sigh. Wentworth, meanwhile, flushed with delight, was splitting his gloves to ribbons with vehement applause, when looking around, his eye fell upon Harrington, and stopping in the midst of his furore, he stared at him, amazed. Harrington's strong face was white, his brow knitted, and his nostrils tensely drawn.

"What's the matter, John?" cried Wentworth, alarmed, and raising his voice to be heard amidst the cheering.

Muriel and Emily both looked at him suddenly, and the young man recovering, smiled like one sick at heart, and rose. They thought him ill, and unheeding the announcement of the next speaker, they left their seats and went from the hall, Muriel and Harrington noticing, as they passed up the aisle, that the seats occupied by Mr. Atkins and the stranger were vacant.

In the vestibule, Harrington paused with Emily on his arm.

"Muriel," he said, "I want to speak with you a moment."

She left Wentworth instantly, and came to him, with a face of inquiry.

"Muriel," he said, in a low, clear voice, taking her hands in his, and looking into her eyes, "I feel a dreadful foreboding. It struck upon me just now who that man is we saw with your uncle."

"Who is it?" she said, quickly.

"Lafitte! I know it is he. I feel it in my soul," he replied.

For a moment she looked at him vacantly, with parted lips and dilated eyes.

"Hurry," she cried, breaking from him; "hurry home. Come, Wentworth. Oh, it's nothing," she said, with a vanishing smile, as she caught the astonished eyes of the young artist. "Ask me no questions, Richard. You shall know hereafter."

And putting her arm in his, they went off rapidly together, followed by Harrington and Emily.

On the way, Harrington told Emily of his conjecture, and they excitedly discussed the matter till they arrived with the other two at the door of the house.

"Now, Emily and Richard," said Muriel, "you go in. John and I are going to walk further. And, Emily," she whispered, "tell mother I shall bring home five people to stop all night. Remember. Come, John;" and taking his arm, they went up Temple street together.

"Well, by Jupiter!" exclaimed the mystified Wentworth, "this is decidedly odd! What does it mean, Emily?"

"I cannot tell you," replied Emily, coldly. "Will you please ring?"

Wentworth, bitterly recalled to her attitude toward him by this frigid reticence, rang the bell, and the door opening presently, they went in.

In the meantime, Muriel and Harrington went up the street together, he vaguely thrilling with the electric energy of her manner. She was silent for a few moments.

"John," she said, suddenly, "I respect an intuition like this of yours, and I think you are right. Roux is in danger. Now this man only arrived to-day."

"How do you know, Muriel," he interrupted.

"Thus," she replied. "On the way home from Mr. Parker's, Emily and I overtook little Julia Atkins, and she said that a gentleman from New Orleans had come to town, to-day, and was to dine with them. I did not ask her anything on the subject, for the conceit of the child's manner was not agreeable, and I changed the subject. But that was the gentleman from New Orleans, I am confident. No doubt, Uncle Lemuel and he thought it would be amusing to visit an Anti-Slavery Convention."

"Yes, and the next thing a warrant will be out for Roux, and we shall have another fugitive slave-case in Boston," said Harrington. "But I shall stop that by taking Roux home to my house, and sitting with him with loaded pistols till the hunt is abandoned."

"Bravo, John," cried Muriel. "But that will never do. Mr. Atkins told that man your name, I know, and you are likely to have an early visit from him. It will not do to have Roux at your house. Roux must be hid where they will never think of searching for him."

"True," he replied. "But, by the way, Muriel, where are we going now?"

"Have you just thought to ask?" she answered, gaily. "Oh, John! But we are going to bring five people home to my house."

"Muriel!" He started as he spoke. The tears sprung to his eyes, as looking into her noble face, he met its proud and laughing gaze.

"We are going to Southac street, you know," she said, "and we shall bring home Roux and his wife, Charles, and the two children. That's five. The baby we don't count," she playfully added.

Harrington was speechless with emotion.

"In Temple street they will be safe for the present," she continued. "Then we can decide on the next step. I think Roux must remove to Worcester, for whatever they may do in Boston, I believe they will never take a fugitive from Worcester. There's good blood yet in the heart of the Commonwealth, the heart of which, moreover, is the heart of Wentworth Higginson."

Wentworth Higginson was, at that period, the gallant minister of the Free Church at Worcester, a man with the Revolutionary soul of fire,. and the incarnate nucleus of that glorious public spirit which is still prompt to defend a man against the kidnappers in the heart of the old Commonwealth.

"Meanwhile," pursued Muriel, "I'll take care of poor Roux."

"Oh, Muriel!" said Harrington, fervently, "there is no nobleness, no tenderness, like yours."

In the wan moonlight he saw her color under his impassioned gaze. She did not reply for a moment, but turning her face away, she laid her hand upon his arm, and its almost imperceptible tremor sent a mystical, sweet agitation through his being.

"It is nothing but a duty," she replied, presently, in a gentle voice. "A clear and simple duty. Life opens plainlier to me every day, and I see that I have wealth and strength and youth, that I may succor and protect the poor!"

No more was said, but tranced in thoughts and feelings too sacred and deep for words, they moved in silence through the dim and solitary streets, vaguely lit by the wan lustre of the moon. There were lights in the houses as they passed, for it was not yet ten o'clock, but save a few boys, white and negro, fantastically playing in some of the streets, and half-dispirited in their nocturnal games by the strange bleakness of the air, they hardly met a person.

Lights glimmered dimly in the windows of Southac street, but Roux's windows were in darkness. Some negro boys, sitting on the wooden steps of his abode, made way for them, and ascending they entered the open outer door, and tapped at the panels of his room. No answer. They tapped louder. No answer still. Harrington, oddly remembering the strenuous snoring of Tugmutton on the nights in March when Roux was sick, and he had watched with him, put his ear to the door and listened for those tokens of the fat boy's slumbers. But no sound reached him.

"Pray Heaven nothing has happened," said Muriel. "Let us try the other door."

Harrington turned to the opposite side of the passage, and knocked loudly. There was an instant stir within, and presently the door opened, and a strange little wizened colored man, not more than four feet high, with a pair of tin-rimmed spectacles on his shrunken nose, and a long coat reaching nearly to his heels, appeared, with a copy of the "Commonwealth" newspaper in his left hand, and in the other a tallow candle stuck in a bottle which he held above his head. Harrington had seen him before, though he had forgotten his name.

"Good evening, sir. Can you tell me where Mr. Roux is this evening?" asked Harrington.

The little man stood still for a moment, gazing past them at nothing, and looking like some fantastic little corpse, set bolt upright.

"Good evening, Mr. Harrington. Good evening, Mrs. Harrington," he said, at length, in a voice like the squeak of a mouse. Then he paused. Muriel smiled faintly at the oddity of being called Mrs. Harrington, and though the wizened creature was not looking at her, he seemed to see the smile, for he smiled also in a slow, fantastic, frozen way.

"Willum Roux's been took off," he at length squeaked in a deliberate tone.

Harrington and Muriel started violently, and holding each other, looked at the speaker.

"Took off!" gasped Harrington. "What do you mean?"

The little man made another long pause, then squeaked like an incantation, "Ophelee!"

A large fat mulatto woman with a red kerchief tied round her head, came from within, rubbing her eyes. Ophelia had evidently been asleep, but she nodded her head, bright and wide awake, when she saw the visitors.

"What has become of Roux?" said Harrington, looking at her with his pale, startled face.

"Oh, they's all been took off to Cambridge," she replied quickly, towering in good-natured bulk above her elvish husband, why stood like one magnetized. "Clarindy Roux's married sister lives thar, Mr. Har'nton, an' her old man come in with his wagon and took 'm all out thar this afternoon. They's to be fotched back to-morrow at dinner-time, so Tug says."

"Thank you," said Harrington. "Good evening;" and "good evening," said Muriel; both too much agitated with the sudden relief that swept over them, to say another word.

"Laws bless you; good evening," said Ophelia; and "good evening, Mr. Harrington—good evening, Mrs. Harrington," squeaked the strange little creature, still standing in the same attitude, as Muriel and Harrington departed.

"Well," said Muriel, with a deep-drawn breath, and then a laugh, as they gained the street; "that was as good a fright as I ever got in my life."

"A fright, indeed," he returned. "I felt as if I should swoon!"

They walked on in silence for a few moments.

"What a singular little kobold that is," she said, as they went into the street.

"Very," replied Harrington. "He's a tailor, and a great Free-Soiler, as you may imagine by the newspaper he had. Now, Muriel, it seems the Rouxs are fortunately away for the night. So they're safe for the present."

"Yes," she returned, gaily; "and my word is forfeit, for where are my five captives! *N'importe.* I'll have them to-morrow."

"To-morrow, at noon, we'll come here together," said Harrington.

"Agreed," she replied. "Punctually, at one o'clock, we'll be here; and, like two fairy princes, carry off the Ogre's victim."

They fell from this into a strain of talk, half-gay, half-serious;

and, satisfied that affairs were in a good state at present, returned rapidly to the house.

CHAPTER XV.

WAR AND PEACE.

After the incidents of the evening, it was not a little discomposing to behold, as they did, upon entering the parlor, Mrs. Atkins, Miss Atkins and Julia, together with Fernando Witherlee. The Atkins family had been there for a couple of hours, making a family call. Muriel was a favorite with them, as with everybody, and they saluted her affectionately ; she responding with her usual affability. Harrington, too, was politely favored ; though Mrs. Atkins (who had been a poor country girl once) and her daughters, also, had their misgivings as to his being of sufficient respectability to deserve the civilities due only to Good Society. But, despite this consideration, no woman could resist the sweet manhood of young Harrington ; and so he received from these ladies as much politeness as though he moved, with mutton-chop whiskers and modish clothes, in fashionable circles—which was unfair.

While Muriel was privately explaining matters to her mother, Harrington joined in the conversation, in which all participated, save Wentworth, who was unusually quiet, and sat a little apart, with a cold and reserved air, the result of his feelings for Emily. The conversation, which had been on topics more or less commonplace, and had hovered frequently about, and several times fairly settled on, the charms and graces of Mr. Lafitte, dipped again to that enrapturing theme, by the will of Mrs. Atkins. Miss Atkins, by the way, though still a devotee of the chivalrous son of the sunny South, had suffered some slight abatement of her rapture ; having learned, by chance, that Mr. Lafitte was already married.

" Oh, Mr. Harrington," continued Mrs. Atkins, after much eulogium of the Southern gentleman who had done us the honor of dining with us to-day, "if you could only meet Mr. Lafitte, you would have such different ideas of the Southern gentlemen."

"Indeed, madam," replied Harrington, courteously; "I should be sorry to have my ideas of Southern gentlemen changed, for I credit them with many fine and high qualities. Don't think that I imagine Northerners and Southerners in the absolute colors of good and evil—black and white; all the white on our side, and all the black on theirs."

"Oh, no, of course not," responded Mrs. Atkins in her fal-lal manner; "but I thought you were so anti-slavery, Mr. Harrington."

"I certainly am anti-slavery, madam," good-naturedly said Harrington, "and if I were living in Hancock's time, I should be on the same principles anti-George the Third. But I hope I should not any the less pay due regard to the Tory gentlemen of that era. As far as their Toryism went, I should of course be their foe, and in like manner I am hostile to the gentlemen of this day who are tyrants."

"But, Mr. Harrington," said Julia, pertly, "you don't like Mr. Webster, and I know you don't, do you? Now do tell me, Mr. Harrington, why you don't like Mr. Webster.

Witherlee smiled furtively at Miss Julia's immature gabble, and lifted his eyebrows in a faint sneer.

"Because, Miss Julia," replied Harrington simply, with a gentle impressiveness of voice and manner which brought a new sensation to the poor child's mind, and made her color, "because Mr. Webster helped to pass a law which has made a great many poor people very unhappy. You yourself wouldn't like a man who made innocent people suffer, would you?"

"Oh, no, of course not," stammered Julia, while Witherlee smiled maliciously, enjoying her confusion.

"Dear me! but they're only negroes, Mr. Harrington," feebly remarked Mrs. Atkins, in a deprecating tone.

"But, Mrs. Atkins, negroes have feelings," said Emily.

"Oh, well, dear," responded Mrs. Atkins, "but their feelings are not the same as ours, you know. That is, they haven't fine feelings."

"You remember the case that was lately reported in the

newspapers. Mrs. Atkins," said Harrington. "The rumor came that the kidnappers were in town with a warrant for a colored man, and his wife fell down dead with alarm when she heard it. I think you must allow that poor woman had feelings, and it is hard to deny that Mr. Webster was responsible for her murder. I saw those poor colored people in Southac street to-day, in wild distress and alarm at the report that a slave-hunter was in town, and no one who sees such things, and realizes them, can like Mr. Webster."

"O Mr. Harrington, indeed I can't agree with you," returned Mrs. Atkins with feeble excitement. "These things are unpleasant, I admit, but Mr. Webster is a great statesman, you know—oh, there never was such a statesman as Mr. Webster! He's perfectly splendid, and I'm sure if he was to have all the negroes in the country killed—the horrid creatures!—I'm sure I would like him just as much as ever. Indeed I would, and so would Mr. Atkins. O if you'd only heard Mr. Webster at Faneuil Hall last Saturday, I know you'd have been converted. He didn't say a word about politics, and he was so majestic, and so venerable and so—so pleasant—oh, it was beautiful!"

And Mrs. Atkins fanned herself in a feeble fluster of admiration for Mr. Webster, whose speech, by the way, had been very decrepit, rambling, and dull, with only a touch here and there of the true Websterian massive power and energy.

"Well, Mrs. Atkins," said Witherlee in his cool, polite, provoking way, "for my part, I don't understand how you can admire Mr. Webster's private life, I'm sure."

This change in the venue, as the lawyers say, and this impudent assumption that Mrs. Atkins had been admiring Mr. Webster's private life, were both highly characteristic of the good Fernando. His remark was not prompted by even the pale esthetic anti-slavery, which he sometimes indulged in, but by the simple desire to say something which he knew would aggravate the lady. And Mrs. Atkins was aggravated, for she colored and fanned herself nervously.

"I don't know what you refer to, Mr. Witherlee," she remarked, pettishly.

"Why, you know what Mr. Webster's habits are, Mrs. Atkins," said Fernando, lifting his eyebrows with an air of painful regret, in which there was also a bilious sneer. "You are aware of his excessive fondness for old Otard. And then his relations to women"——

"I don't care," interrupted Mrs. Atkins, bridling with faint excitement. "I don't care at all, and I think that God gave Mr. Webster some faults to remind us that he is mortal."

This was smart for Mrs. Atkins, and Witherlee, somewhat nonplused, turned pale with spite, and lifted his eyebrows, and shrugged his shoulders with a manner that was equivalent to saying—Oh, if you talk in that way, Mrs. Atkins, there's no use in wasting words upon you. His manner would have been ineffably maddening to most men, but women are less easily transported beyond control, and Mrs. Atkins, conscious that she had the advantage of Mr. Witherlee in her reply, fanned herself equably and took no notice of his insulting gesture.

"For my part," said Harrington, gravely offended by Witherlee's remarks, "I deprecate any reflections upon Mr. Webster's private life. It seems to me that our concern is with his public acts, and not with his personal habits."

"Oh, you're a gentleman, Mr. Harrington," said Mrs. Atkins, in a tone that implied that Mr. Witherlee was not.

Witherlee looked at Mrs. Atkins with parted lips, and still, opaque eyes, white with spleen, but perfectly cool.

"Now, fellow-citizens, what's the row?" blithely said Muriel, approaching the circle with her mother.

"Oh, cousin Muriel!" exclaimed Julia, "how can you talk in that way. It's so low!"

"So it is, dear," archly replied Muriel, "shockingly low, and you must be warned by my example."

Julia looked a little foolish, and smiled.

"We were discussing, Mr. Webster," said Fernando, tranquilly.

"Oh, Mr. Webster," said Muriel; "I used to admire him very much when I was a girl."

"It's a pity you don't now, Muriel," said Mrs. Atkins, "for he deserves to be admired, I'm sure."

"Yes, aunt, but I never recovered from a shock he gave me in my 'sallet days, when I was green in judgment,'" replied Muriel.

"A shock? Dear me! I can't imagine Mr. Webster shocking anybody," drawled Caroline, with weak surprise.

"Nevertheless," said Muriel, "Mr. Webster shocked me, like a torpedo fish, and I'll tell you how. There was a grand party, at which he was present. Mother and I were there, and I, who was a girl of fourteen, had no eyes for anybody but Mr. Webster. My great desire was to hear him say something, for I thought anything he said would be remarkable, and worth putting in an album, so I followed him wherever he went through the crowded drawing-rooms, with my ears wide open, eagerly listening for the golden sentence. But Mr. Webster was in a very silent humor, and wandered about without speaking to anybody. By and by he went up-stairs to the supper room, and I followed him, in reverent admiration and expectancy. He approached the supper-table, bowed solemnly to some ladies near by, took a fork, and began to eat from a dish of pickled oysters. After he had eaten three or four, he paused, with an oyster on his fork, turned his great head slowly and majestically to the ladies, and opened his lips. The golden sentence was coming, and I listened breathlessly. Now what do you think he said?"

"Well, what?" inquired Harrington, after a hushed pause.

"Said he, in his deep, grum, orotund, bass voice, like the low rolling of distant summer thunder, 'What nice little oysters these are!'"

Every one burst into hearty laughter, as Muriel mimicked the tones of the Websterian ejaculation.

"That was my reward for so long waiting," she continued, when the laughter had subsided. "That was my golden sentence, which, of course, never went from the tablets of memory to the album. It was an immense shock to know that great statesmen said such things as common people say."

"And you heard nothing else?" said Wentworth, vastly amused at the anecdote.

"Not another word. He devoured the oyster, and wandered down-stairs again, leaving with me the ponderous sprat which the flavor of the mollusc had conjured from the ocean depths of his mighty mind."

They began to laugh again, when a ring at the door-bell was heard.

"That's papa!" cried Julia.

Papa it was—come for his family. He came in presently, robust and decisive, purseproud, as usual, and smiling, made his salutations with a certain rude courtesy, and took a chair.

"Well, young ladies," he burst out presently, "so you went to hear Phillips harangue this evening."

"Yes, uncle," returned Muriel, sportively, "we had you to keep us in countenance you know."

"Indeed! Well, I'm sorry if my example incited you. Lafitte, our Southern visitor, thought it would be amusing to hear some of the fanatical blather, and so I took him along, and, just by chance, he got a dose of Phillips."

"I hope the dose did him good, Lemuel, and you also," said Mrs. Eastman, with some spirit.

"Oh, I don't deny Phillips's power, Serena," replied the merchant, carelessly. "It's all very fine, and if he were in the Whig party, he'd be a man of mark. It's a pity, as I always say, to see such wonderful ability wasted."

"How did Mr. Lafitte enjoy it, sir?" asked Emily, blandly.

"Oh, he—well, I was rather amused at the way he took it," responded Mr. Atkins, laughing. "It quite upset him, and in his hot, Southern way, he said Phillips ought to be shot. In fact, I thought Lafitte was rather thin-skinned about it, though, to be sure, Phillips's words are enough to try a saint. Anyhow, Lafitte felt 'em rankle."

"He must certainly, to have had so murderous a spirit aroused in him," remarked Mrs. Eastman.

"Murderous? Upon my word, Serena," replied the merchant, bluffly, "I think his spirit was not unworthy of a man of high tone, and I shouldn't blame him at all if he had pistolled your orator on the spot."

"Like the assassin who bludgeoned Otis in Revolutionary times," remarked Witherlee, blandly aggravating.

"Oh, you young men are all tainted with fanaticism," returned Mr. Atkins, reddening. "When you're older you'll know better. I'm always sorry to see young men of talent, like Mr. Harrington here, misled by Phillips's eloquent abstractions. But live and learn, live and learn."

"I hope, Mr. Atkins, I shall not live to learn distrust in the statesmanship that reprobates slavery," said Harrington, urbanely.

"Statesmanship!" contemptuously exclaimed the merchant. "Do you call such incendiary measures as Phillips and Parker advise, statesmanship? Sedition and treason! I declare, Mr. Harrington—and I say this coolly, in sober earnest—that if any one were to shoot down Phillips and Parker in the street, and I were summoned as a Grand Juror to pass upon the act, I would refuse to indict him on the ground that it was justifiable homicide. Yes, sir, justifiable homicide. I have said it a hundred times, and I now say it again. What do you think of that, Mr. Harrington?"

Harrington met the insulting exultation of the merchant's gaze, with a look quiet and firm.

"Since you ask me what I think of it, Mr. Atkins," he replied, tranquilly, "you must permit me to say that I think it atrocious."

"And so do I," said Mrs. Eastman, crimson with indignation. "And you ought to blush, Lemuel, to say that you would give legality to a ferocious murder."

"Ought I?" replied the merchant, coolly. "Well, I don't, Serena. In such a case, killing's no murder. Murder, indeed! Ha! men like those to dare to wage war on the institutions of their country!"

"What institutions do they wage war upon, Mr. Atkins?" asked Wentworth, civilly.

"Well, sir, slavery for one," excitedly returned the merchant. "An institution expressly sanctioned by the Constitution, and on the protection of which the safety of this Union depends, Mr. Wentworth. An institution, sir, which no statesman would think of assailing for a moment. Where can you point to one statesman, worthy of the name, from Webster back to Burke, or as far back as you like to go, that has ever assailed a great politico-economical institution like slavery? You're a scholar, I'm told, Mr. Harrington ; now just answer me that question."

"Mr. Atkins, I am surprised beyond measure that you should ask me such a question," calmly replied Harrington. "The real difficulty would be to name any statesman of the first eminence that has ever defended slavery. You mention Burke and Webster. Why, sir, the whole record of Mr. Webster's life up to 1850, is against slavery. It is only eight years ago since he stood up in Faneuil Hall, and said—I quote his very words, for I have been lately reading them—'What,' said he, 'when all the civilized world is opposed to slavery ; when morality denounces it ; when Christianity denounces it ; when everything respected, everything good, bears one united witness against it, is it for America—America, the land of Washington, the model republic of the world—is it for America to come to its assistance, and to insist that the maintenance of slavery is necessary to the support of her institutions !' Those are Daniel Webster's very words, sir, and yet you ask when he ever assailed slavery !"

"Good ! good !" cried Mrs. Eastman, amidst a general murmur of satisfaction from all but the Atkinses. Mr. Atkins sat dumb, wincing under the crushing blow of the quotation. Their new-born zeal for slavery and kidnapping gave the Boston merchants of that period terribly short memories.

"Faneuil Hall, crowded with Whig merchants, answered those words with six-and-twenty cheers. Have you forgotten them, Mr. Atkins ?" said Harrington. "Now the cheers are all for slavery. Now, in defiance of your own statesman's declaration, you assert slavery to be necessary to the maintenance of your Union. And now, because Phillips and Parker wage war upon slavery, as Webster did then, you would justify their murder."

Still dumb, with his strong lip nervously twitching, the merchant sat, whelmed in utter confusion.

"You mentioned Burke, Mr. Atkins," continued Harrington, "and since you have mentioned him, let me ask if you have forgotten his speech to the electors of Bristol? Listen to the words of the greatest statesman since Bacon—for they, too, are fresh in my memory. 'I have no idea,' said Edmund Burke—'I have no idea of a liberty unconnected with honesty and justice. Nor do I believe that any good constitutions of government or of freedom can find it necessary for their security to doom any part of the people to a permanent slavery. Such a constitution of freedom, if such can be, is in effect no more than another name for the tyranny of the strongest faction.' Those are the words of Burke, sir. If you doubt, Mrs. Eastman will get the volume from the library, and you shall read them for yourself."

"No consequence, Mr. Harrington, no consequence," returned the merchant, abruptly rising. "We will not discuss the matter further, sir. Come, Mrs. Atkins, it is time for us to go home."

"O dear me," drawled Mrs. Atkins, leaving her seat, "you gentlemen are so fond of these horrid politics. Come, children, come."

They all rose, with a flutter and rustle of movement. Presently, while the Atkins ladies, cloaked and bonneted, were moving toward the door, Harrington approached Mr. Atkins, who had gone into the entry for his hat and returned, and now stood, cold, harsh and moody, apart from the rest of the company.

"I trust, Mr. Atkins," said the young man, with grave courtesy, "that you are not offended by my plain speaking on these matters, or at least that you will not understand me to intend any disrespect to you personally."

The merchant glared at him with a sullen and insolent smile.

"Mr. Harrington," he hissed hoarsely, bending his face close to the young man's, "such sentiments as yours find favor with my sister and niece. It is politic in you to adopt them, and so curry favor with the one that you may mend your poverty by a rich marriage with the other."

And with these brutal words, the merchant threw back his

head, glaring at the young man with open mouth, and a frightful smile on his blanched visage, which was at that moment the visage of a demon. Harrington met that glare with a look of such majestic severity, such a stern glory of anger lighting his calm eyes and brow, that the merchant's face fell, and he slunk a pace away. The company had left the parlor, and were talking in the hall, as Mr. Atkins had made his reply, but Mrs. Eastman, who was standing nearest the parlor door, had heard it all, and before Harrington could make any rejoinder, if any he intended, she came quickly in, shutting the door behind her, her silver tresses trembling and her beautiful face flushed with haughty and indignant emotion.

"Permit me to tell you, Lemuel Atkins," said she, confronting her brother, and speaking in a proud and steady voice, "that the sentiments which you have not the wit to controvert, nor the manhood to entertain, were held by Mr. Harrington before we had the honor of his friendship, and let me further say to you that while the choice of my daughter's heart, be he rich or poor, shall be my choice also, I should esteem it the best hour of my life which gave me assurance that she would wed a man worthier of her than any man I know, and dear to me as my own son! Take that home with you, sir, and do us the honor to believe that in this house we value gentlemen for what they are, and not for what they own."

He shrank from the serene and haughty magnetism of her manner, and cowering under her rebuke, slunk away to the door without a word, and went into the hall. Harrington stood like one thunder-struck, the slow thrill her words gave him running through his veins. while she swept across the room to close the door the merchant had left ajar, and turning again, came quickly toward him, her beautiful face pale and wet with calmly-flowing tears.

"Tell me, John," she said, seizing his hands, and speaking in low, rapid tones, tremulous with emotion—"this pitiful insult moved me to anger, and in my anger I have spoken the true thought of my heart—tell me that so dear a hope is not so vain. Oh, confide in me as in your own mother, for no mother could love you more tenderly than I do."

In the spiritual passion of the moment, all cold prudence, all reticence, melted, and fell away. He clasped her in his arms, and with sweet and sorrowful emotion, kissed her fair brow and silver hair.

"I love her, my mother," he murmured, sadly smiling—"I love her, but the love I once thought mine, is not for me."

"You love her—you love Muriel, and she does not love you! I do not believe it—I cannot. John, at my age women are not easily deceived—they do not mistake the tokens of love. Take care that you are sure of what you say"——

"I am sure, mother, I am sure," he interrupted, in a low voice. "Her accepted lover told me of his happiness to-day. Do not ask me his name. They themselves will tell you. Hush!"

The hall-door was heard closing, and the voices talking gaily in the hall. She looked at him wonderingly for an instant, then quickly pressed her lips to his drooping forehead, and glided from his arms to the back-door of the parlor, out of which she passed up to her chamber, as the others came in.

Witherlee had departed as the escort of Miss Julia, his natural impudence perfectly ignoring the rebuff he had received from her mother.

"Where's Mrs. Eastman?" said Emily.

"She went out as you came in," replied Harrington.

"John," said Muriel, coming up to him, and playfully shaking her finger. "You quite discomfited poor Uncle Lemuel, and he went off as cross as a bear."

"What a memory Harrington has!" laughed Wentworth. "To think that he gave him Burke and Webster plump! That was a double-barrelled shot, by Jupiter!"

"Oh, it was capital," chimed in Emily.

"Faith," said Harrington, "it was simply lucky. I happened to have been reading the speeches lately, and so had the passages by heart. But I wonder at Mr. Atkins making such an absurd assertion."

"Oh, he remembers nothing previous to 1850," said Muriel.

"These people are perfectly wild with their Webster and Fugitive Slave Law mania, and they repeat certain phrases until their organs of intelligence are ossified, as Goethe says. Come, Emily, let us have some music."

"Yes, do, Emily," said Wentworth, half absently, and forgetting for a moment, as was frequent with him, the state of affairs between him and Miss Ames.

Emily looked at him with cool serenity, as if she thought his request impertinent. Wentworth, recalled to himself, was maddened by the look and all it brought him, and turning to conceal his anger, wandered away to the piano, humming an air.

"Come, Emily, we must go home, for it's getting late," said Harrington; "so sing us that sweet song of Körner's—the 'Good Night' song—to sooth us to dreams."

Emily smiled with superb languor, and half-reluctant, for she was not in a songful mood, swept over to the piano, looking steadily as she advanced at Wentworth, who was leaning carelessly against the instrument, and regarding her with stern eyes.

"I believe," said she, listlessly, as she sunk upon the music-stool, and with a parting glance of cold hauteur dropped her eyes from the steady gaze of Wentworth, "I believe that the piano is out of tune."

"Do you know why, Miss Ames?" asked Wentworth suddenly, in a voice at once so quiet and so marked that both Muriel and Harrington looked at him.

"Because," he said with bitter and terrible significance, a scowl darkening his features—"because it has been played upon!"

Muriel and Harrington started with a low exclamation, and glanced first at Wentworth, and then at Emily, with mute amazement. A smile arose on Wentworth's face, and mingled with his scowl, as he slowly walked away. Emily rose from her seat, and gazed after him, her form dilated to its full height, her bosom heaving, and her face and neck suffused with an indignant scarlet glow. Turning, Wentworth looked haughtily at her for a moment, and then, utterly reckless, with heart and brain on fire, laughed a bitter and scornful laugh, and moved toward the parlor door. Emily's lip quivered, her color faded to pallor, and bursting into a passionate flood of tears, she covered her face with her hands, and swept by the other door from the room.

Muriel and Harrington had stood transfixed with astonishment up to this moment, but as they saw both Emily and Wentworth leave the parlor, they recovered with a start.

"Stay, Wentworth," cried Harrington, rushing to the door, and "Emily, Emily," cried Muriel, flying after her friend.

But Harrington reached the hall, just as the front door slammed at the heels of Wentworth, and tearing it open, he beheld him running up the street like a madman, while Muriel, bounding up-stairs after Emily, saw her vanish into her chamber, and heard the lock of her door click behind her.

Both returned to the parlor at the same moment, and advancing toward each other, pale, agitated, and almost petrified with wonder at the lightning-like suddenness and inexplicable character of this incident, gazed into each other's faces. The affair was like a flash on a dark landscape, giving a vague glimpse of some mysterious form there, and vanishing before its nature was revealed.

"Good Heavens, John! what does this mean?" exclaimed Muriel, breaking the lonely stillness of the lighted parlor.

"I do not know," he murmured, vacantly gazing at her. "Is Richard mad?"

She put her hands to her bosom to repress its throbbings, and sank into a large chair near her. Both were silent for some minutes, each trying to think, with a whirling brain, what this could possibly mean.

"What a singular day this has been!" murmured Harrington at length, as behind this last incident the tableau of its many-passioned hours rose in his mind.

"Singular, indeed!" replied Muriel, in a low voice, "and how singularly and sadly it ends!"

"Not so," he replied with sweet gravity. "Let it end in our good night, which is always happy with affection and peace. We will dismiss this scene, Muriel. To-morrow we can think more clearly, and we will know its meaning. Meanwhile, good night."

She rose from her seat, and they came toward each other with outstretched hands. It was strange, but for the first time in all their long acquaintance, their hands passed each other, his arms encircled her, and hers rested on his, with her hands upon his shoulders. A trance seemed to glide upon them. The lighted room was very still ; the sad wind sighed in the hush around the dwelling ; and gazing into each other's faces, with a vague thrill remotely stirring in the peace of their spirits, they stood motionless, as in a dream.

Thus for a little while, which seemed long, lasted their communion. Earthly cares and hopes forgotten, earthly strifes removed and dim, and the sorrow of their hopeless love so chastened and sanctified in the nobleness of mutual sacrifice that it knew no touch of pain.

A long, mysterious sigh of the night-wind breathed around the dwelling, and stole into the peace of their minds. Harrington smiled, and his heart rose in benediction as he silently laid his hands upon the fair and sacred head of his beloved.

"The night deepens on, Muriel, and we must part," he gently murmured.

"Yes, we must part," she answered, in a low tone, "and our parting to-night seems like a type of the greater parting."

"To me the same," he murmured, in a rapt voice. "Never before has it seemed so like parting forever. I might feel thus when passing through the dusks of death, with the dream of all earth's sweet and vanished hours fading in visions of the life to come."

There was a long pause, in which the cadence of his words seemed to linger like the ghost of music on the air.

"But we shall meet there," she said. "We who have passed so many holy and poetic hours here—we shall meet there. The earthly 'good-night' is but the prelude to 'good-morning.' So shall the last farewell of earth prelude the heavenly greeting."

"Yes, we shall meet there," he murmured. "Have we not met there already—friends, true and loving, dwellers in Hea-

12

ven's happy star! Who shall gainsay the alchemist who wrote that 'Heaven hath in it this scene of earth.' The true life is there, and our existence here is but a fleeting hour of absence from our heavenly home. Yes, we shall meet there, reclothed with the divine memory, and keeping the memory of all we wrought and were on earth, that earth might fulfill the large purposes of God—meet there, old friends, true and loving, changed, and yet the same."

Again there was a pause of trancing silence, filled with the floating ghost of visionary music, keeping the sweet tradition of his words, and telling to the soul what music tells. Again around the lonely dwelling swelled the wind's mysterious eolian sigh, rising in inarticulate wild prophecies, and wailing sombrely away.

"Good night, good night," he softly murmured, with a movement of departure.

"Good night," she answered, in a low and fervent voice, "friend, true and loving, good night."

A sense of heavenly tenderness rose trembling in their souls, and with meeting lips they were clasped in each other's arms. Oh, solemn ecstasy of prayer and peace! Oh, mystic passion of a veiled true love!

Was it a dream? She was alone. Standing in the solitary room, her brow bent upon her hand, the dim sweetness of the vision in her mind, she floated away in vague, delicious reverie. Soft light fled pulsing through her spirit; a sacred and passionless perfume floated in her brain; a celestial tenderness tranced her soul. He loved another; his love for her was the love of friend for friend—no more; but she was happier, holier, nobler to have inspired such love, and stronger than ever to resign him now, and to live her life alone. So thinking, like one lost in a blissful dream, she glided away to her pillow.

Was it a dream? How strangely sweet and vague! He was wandering noiselessly down the shadowy street in the wan moonlight, with the cold air blowing on his cheek, as void of coldness as though he had been a phantom, and not a man. When had he left her—how? but his thoughts recalled only the peaceful passion of that moment, and between the lighted room and the moonlit street, there was a blank chasm Dear moment, never to come again, dear magic flower that bloomed in the sad garden of his love, never to be renewed, yet sweetening life and life's submissive sacrifice forever. Dear friend, true friend and sweet, whose clasp, whose sacred kiss—the first, the last—gave tokens of no earthly love, but rich memorials and previsions of the love that makes the hills of heaven more fair! So ran the voiceless music of his thought, while memory kept the phantom form of the beloved one in visioned light and odor. To-morrow he would meet her, and the day after, and on for many a day through months and years to come, but never again on the height of the ideal and intimate communion, where their spirits had met and said farewell. Years hence, and she a happy wife and mother, how softly this hour would glide from the innermost holiest cloister of memory, and lend a more pensive and tender grace to her beauty, and shed a finer and more ethereal essence on her happiness! Consecrating her forever, its consecration would rest on his own life, pledging him more firmly to lofty and generous effort, and sanctifying all low toils and struggles as with the presence of an angel.

Softly, and without noise, he entered his dark and silent house. A moment, and he had lit his shaded lamp, and conscious of the sleepless vigil in his mind, he opened the volume which held for him the rich lore of Verulam, his unfailing pleasure, and the comfort of his saddest hours, and sat down to read the night away. Within all was still. Without, the wind swept drearily through the wan and shadowy street around the silent dwelling, the lilac odors had died, and the pale moonlight shone with the blue glimmer of swords.

CHAPTER XVI.

THE GLIMPSES OF THE MOON.

The gibbous moon hung midway down the zenith over the vast and sleeping city, a lob of spectral light in the cold, blue heavens, over a fantastic brood of dreams. Daniel Webster's liegemen and victims slept, and Black Dan himself, liegeman and victim to a darker power than he, slept also; but the liegemen and victims of Dan Cupid had a more uncertain chance of slumber, and four among them at least had wakeful eyes that night as the moon was going down.

As the moon was going down, its pale gleam fell upon the pallid face and disordered form of Wentworth. He had risen from his bed, and was sitting, half dressed, at his open chamber window, in an upper story of his father's house on Tremont street, and brooding mournfully on the misshapen planet, which hung like a huge, bulging drop of watery lustre above the roofs beyond the Common trees. His bed, all tossed and tumbled, glimmered in white confusion behind him, and faint rays of moonlight touched the lines of the gilt frames upon the walls, the books upon their shelves, the ghostly busts and statuettes around the chamber, and the dark, goblin shapes of the disarranged furniture. Within the chamber all was dusk disorder, and a dusk disorder was within the clouded mind and aching heart of its tenant.

Passion had spent its fury; the frenzy and the fever of his heart were allayed; and something like the wan tranquillity of the night had succeeded. It was all over; the play was played; she had lured him on to love her; she had trampled on his love; he had repaid her with one bitter burst of scorn; he had struck her heartless pride with insult into tears; it was done; he would never see her more.

It was done, but was it well done? The calm, rebuking image of Harrington rose in his mind. Him, too, she was deceiving, or seeking to deceive—but he—would he have answered her so? Oh, idiot that I am, he thought; he would have shamed her even in her triumph by his silence, his compassion, his forgiveness, and made her feel how poor a thing she was; while I have shown her that my wound burns and rankles that she may exult over it, and given her the advantage by an insult which will only bring her sympathy and me shame!

Convulsed for a moment by the turbulent rush of fury that whirled through him, he suddenly controlled himself with a strong effort, and leaning his burning head upon his hands, thought on. How would her wiles prosper on Harrington? Ha! it was joy to think that she would be baffled there! She does not know that he loves Muriel; she will not know it; she will spin her seductive web; she will try every charm, and fail, and fail—and know not why she fails! For he loves Muriel—yes, he loves Muriel. But that thought brought another to the mind of Wentworth. In vivid contrast with his own mean and little jealousy of his friend when he thought him his rival for the love of Emily, came Harrington's selfless generosity to him whom he thought his rival for the love of Muriel. This, too, had led Harrington to attach himself in all their walks and meetings to Emily—he had stood aside, he had waived his claim to the contest for Muriel's love, he had left the field clear and open, with every advantange to him. Brought to the full consciousness of this lofty magnanimity, alive now to his own selfish selfness, hot tears, wrung from him in the agony of his self-abasement, welled from his eyes. But this could be atoned for. To-morrow, yes, to-morrow, he would see Harrington—he would tell him all—he would confess his fault, and ask for pardon. This wrong could be undone—so easily; a little sacrifice of pride—that was all; but Emily—her wrong to him could never be undone—never, oh, never! A ruined heart, a ruined life, love scorned, self-respect crushed; oh, Emily, Emily, his wild thought wailed, loved, idolized, adored still, despite your cruel baseness, your heartless wrong, your life-long injury to me, how can I forget you, how can I forgive you, how can I blot out your image from my life, how be again as in the days of youth and love and hope now gone forever and forever!

Weak, shaken, convulsed with passionate despair, he bowed his head upon his nerveless arms, weeping bitterly in silence, as the moon was going down.

As the moon was going down, its pale light shone into the haunted shadow of a chamber, and on the lovely pallid face and sumptuous form of Emily, dimly projected in the perfumed dusk against the velvet of a cushioned chair, in which she lay reclining like a young empress doomed to die upon the morrow morn. Her eyes were closed; her head rested back almost in profile upon the velvet; and the pale and sculptural features, relieved by the unbound blackness of her hair, were like a dream of death. The white night-robe had fallen away, and clearly outlined against the glorious length of ebon tresses which sloped in thick profusion down behind her, bloomed the polished ivory of one peerless shoulder, melting within the crumpled tissue of the loose sleeve which covered her drooping arm. Still, but for the slow heaving of her bosom, she lay in pallid loveliness—a maiden queen of passional love, love-lorn, discrowned, abandoned and brought low.

She had been warned of this—too late, too late for her own peace—and the warning had come true. How delicately, how gently, yet how clearly, had Witherlee warned her to beware of Wentworth's insidious honey tongue. Kind friend, wise friend, whom they think treacherous and subtle, you were loyal and true to me. But your warning came too late, for I had already given my heart, my life, my peace to him. Had you but spoken earlier, had you but warned me in time—but now, too late, too late, cast off, betrayed, undone! a handsome gallant's sport, his theme for mockery and insult—come Death, best other friend, best friend of all to me, best friend and only friend to me! take me from life to God, for all that made existence sweet is ended!

So ran the silent passion of her thought, with silent-flowing tears. The solemn night was still around her vigil, and the hush of the chamber was like the hush of the tomb. They sleep, she thought, they sleep in peace, while I watch here uncomforted. She sleeps, my noble-hearted Muriel—she who, misled by my proud, spleenful folly, thinks I have given my heart to Harrington. And he! oh, how can he forgive me when I tell him—but he will—that noble nature cannot scorn me; he will understand and pity and pardon. Let me only tell him frankly—let me atone for all my wrong by humbling myself before him; let me crave his compassion and forgiveness, and so be fitter to go from earth to my Savior's rest. To-morrow I will depart from hence, and before I go I will see Harrington and Muriel, and make my peace with them. I who was jealous of her, even her, my sweet, deep-hearted Muriel; I will own it, I will ask her forgiveness. Punished, justly punished, for my wrong to them both, let me be forgiven by them, and then let me go away to die.

So ran the deep contrition of her thought, with mournful-running tears. Sorrowfully weeping, she turned her beautiful and haggard face to the table near her, and took from thence a single faded rose. It had been large and fresh in full-blown crimson beauty, when he had given it to her, a little week ago. Pledge of a love then in its seeming hour of radiant victory, it was the withered token of a love all dead and disenchanted now. Weeping, she pressed it to her lips; she kissed it with gentle and passionate kisses. The sweet, dry odor of the soft petals stole to her brain, with the mournful memory of the vanished and delicious hour when the rose bloomed fresh in the lover's giving hand, and his tender and gallant face was the rose of all the world to her. Dear rose, she murmured, memorial of hours when life was ecstasy, and heaven itself seemed cold and far—you are all that is left me now! I will keep you, I will love you, while life lasts, and when I die, they shall put you in my bosom, under the shroud, and lay us together in the grave. Gift of him I loved—of him I love forever—oh, Richard, Richard, you have wronged me, but I do not scorn you—you have killed me, but I do not hate you; I love you now; I love you, I forgive you, I bless you—with my last breath I shall forgive, and love and bless you!

Murmuring the words, in an ecstasy of passionate fervor, her voice trembling, and the tears streaming from her eyes, she pressed the flower with both hands to her lips, and swooning slowly back upon the cushions, she lay motionless, a shape of glorious pallid beauty, sculptured upon the odorous dusk, as the moon was going down.

As the moon was going down, its pale ray streaming aslant the drooping misty veils that fell in parted festoons from a golden ring above the pure and cloud-like couch of Muriel, threw a tender glory on her Madonna face, sweet in its waven fall of shadowy tresses. She rested, half-reclined upon her side against the broad bank of her pillows, in the soft suffusion of gloomy bloom which insphered her couch from the darkness of the chamber. Her beautiful white arms flowing from an open sleeve, which left them bare nearly to the shoulders, lay along her form upon the silvery grey of the coverlet, and her eyes shone like dim, rich gems. Alone and sleepless, in the still seclusion of her chamber, the phantoms of her many-peopled life thronged her spirit, and the drama of the day lived anew. All the persons she had known from her childhood upward—faces, too, that she had seen and forgotten—came floating in a strange air of dreams upon her vague and pensive musing. All that had passed since morning—the places where she had been, the people she had met, their shapes, their colors, their manners and gestures ; what had been said, what had been done—came in spectral retrospection, singularly minute and circumstantial ; and now and then, some face, some glimpse of a passing form, some room or fragment of sunlit street, half surprised her by softly appearing to the inner visual sense, with the jut and hues and vivid reality of actual life. Amidst the profuse and teeming phantasmagoria of her thought, came often the strong face of her uncle—with the surly scowl she had last seen upon it, melting into an ominous smile she had never seen, which strangely altered it to the sinister face of the negro-holder. And with this—sometimes preceding it, sometimes following it, and mysteriously connected with it, almost as fantastically as in a dream—came the agonized and imploring dark face of Roux, which somehow seemed changed, and not his so entirely, but that it suggested a likeness to some other face which she could not recall. Following these—recurring again and again, a hundred times, and linked with the inexplicable incident of the evening—came Wentworth, pale, and bitterly laughing, passing, with half-turned, scornful head, through one door ; and Emily, melting from haughty scarlet into pallor and tears, and sweeping away, with her face bowed in her hands, through the other. Because it has been played upon—because it has been played upon. The words came with every return of these two figures—came wearily and strangely ; darkly significant, yet wholly meaningless, and leaving her in quiet wonder as to what lurked beneath them. In all this spectral picturing, the form of Harrington was absent ; and, though several times, conscious of the vivid life of her mind that night, she strove to bring him before her, she could not succeed. But again and again the thought of his love for Emily and of hers for him, came to her, never impressing her so singularly as now. The strange reticence of his demeanor to Emily, courteous, frank, kind and loving, it is true, but yet so unlike the abandonment she might have looked for in a lover ; the curious attentions of Emily to him, her lustrous looks into his face, her fond, close leaning on his arm, her form bending so near him, her restless desire to isolate herself with him even when she and Wentworth were present, her low tones and whisperings, and smiles, tokens of love, and yet somehow vaguely unloverlike ; all came to her vividly, and like an ordinary page in a book which yet contained a lurking riddle that distracted the mind from the ostensible reading. Then their strange reserve. Emily had never intimated aught of her love to her, save in the conversation which she herself had instituted to charm down her lover-like jealousy, and the admission then was rather tacit than direct. And Harrington, too—he had never breathed a word, or given the remotest hint of his love to her—not even to her, his adored and trusted friend. Why this secrecy ? What imaginable reason had they for this close conspiracy of reserve ? She could not guess. She could not even invent a plausible supposition to account for it. In the candid and vivid temper of her mind that night, she felt that the mystery of their relation and conduct would be fathomed by her, could she but keep it before her thoughts; but in vain, for as she held it, it would drop away, and be lost in the phantasmagoric population which crowded and faded upon her, and then appear again, and again be lost; and so crowding and fading, and coming again, in quiet and spectral complication, with a vague sense of mystery, and monition and shadowy warning, all mingling indefinitely together, and leaving no result in her mind, her phantom host of useless reminiscence poured ceaselessly around her, as the moon was going down.

As the moon was going down its sad, ray, filtering between a tunnelled lane of roofs and walls across the garden gate of Harrington, touched his drooping forehead, as he sat near his open window, breathing the refreshing coolness of the night air. His night-lamp left the lower part of the room in dusky shadow, but threw a steady radiance on the open volume from which he had risen when he could no longer abstract his mind to the rich pages. He was thinking of his own future—how he should arrange his life for the human service. The dream of love was dissolved; henceforth it could never agitate his heart; now he was wholly and only mankind's. She had receded from him into the farthest distance of memory. He thought of her as of one whom he had known and loved many, many years ago. Now she was gone, and he was alone, and for him there was only the clouded present and the unknown future.

Rising from his seat, he paced the room. A strange and solemn heaviness weighed upon him, and he yearned for the morrow. With the sense of the night, the deep hush of the air, the shadowy quiet of the room, the brooding sentience of the ghostly hour, was mingled a vague, dark, unimaginable portent which hung like lead upon his soul. Pausing in his silent walk, he leaned his head upon his hand, alone in the vast, haunted solitude of his being, and longing to be at rest. Musing on and on, a fleeting gleam of peace, like a ray shining through clouds over a waste of midnight desolation, stole upon his hour of lonely weakness, as across his mind floated the image of Muriel sleeping—her lily face composed to rest in its nimbus of bright hair, and sweet with happy dreams. So had he seen her in her light slumber that day. It came into his mind as he mused—how she had leaped up from her graceful rest, with what ethereal summer lightning of a smile on her awakened face, with what delicious laughter and what gay replies. Her words—'you are the fairy prince that awakened me, and now I am to follow you through all the world.'

He looked up with a throbbing brain. The dream of love was dissolved; henceforth it could never agitate his heart: now he was wholly and only mankind's—Oh, mockery of mockeries!

In the dead stillness there was the sense of mighty pulses madly beating, and the air was flame. All his being rose like the torrent surge and thunder of a heaven-drowning sea, and for one fierce instant the world of life quivered through and through with agony. He gazed before him with tense and burning eyes. A faint radiance cast from the funnel of his lamp, lit the kingly-fronted statue of Verulam on its pedestal. The light lay lucid on the vast and sovereign brow, melting into fainter light below, and the face was as the face of a god rapt in the white peace of Eternity. It grew upon the convulsing storm of his passion with a diffusive calm. Slowly, as he brooded upon the august countenance, tranquil in massive majesty, its sweet serenity, its passionless and regal peace sank upon him: a sad and gentle inflowing tide of feeling lifted him above his agitations, till at length, with clasped hands and bowed head, and all the tempest of his spirit dying down in streaming tears, he rose into communion with the man whose life on earth began new ages.

No words breathed from his lips, no thoughts came to his mind, but in the ideal presence of the soul he loved, raptures of solemn comfort arose within him, and he became composed. A load seemed to lift from his spirit, and turning away, relieved and exalted, he sank into his former seat, and sat in tranquil musing as the moon was going down.

CHAPTER XVII.

NOCTURNAL.

Gradually a desire to be out in the spiritual solitude of the night came upon him. He rose from his seat, closed the window, took his hat from the wall, and setting the night-lamp in the open chimney, turned it down to a faint glimmer, and left the room, locking the door behind him.

A feeble growl reminded him of the dog, and he delayed a moment to go to the kennel of the animal. The creature knew him, and lazily yawning as he approached, pawed feebly in its nest in the packing case, and wagged its tail. Patting it on the head, and murmuring a kind word or two, he turned from it, and abstractedly wandered out at the gate, and away from the house, with his head bent upon his breast, and his arms behind him.

It was the dead of night, and the shadowy streets, wanly lighted by the setting moon, were intensely still. The air was bleak and cold, but the wind, which had been stirring before midnight, had gone down. On that memorable night, as he afterward remembered, he was in such a condition of mental abstraction, that he took no note of the course his steps pursued, nor did he once lift his head to look around him. The strangeness of the moon as he crossed the streets where it was visible, would have roused him to observation, had he chanced to look at it. But he did not, and meeting no person, not even a watchman, and unmindful of the route he took, he wandered mechanically on.

What thoughts engaged him, if any, he never could recall. It seemed to him, however, that his mind must have been in blank vacancy, uncrossed by any shadow of mentality. Yet he was remotely sensible of the echoes of his footfalls in the solitary streets and of his passage under the overshadowing bulks of the dark houses. Remotely sensible, too, that there was moonlight, that the air was ghast and cold, and that he was loitering on, alone, with his head sunk upon his breast, and his hands clasped behind him.

He knew, too, when he had reached Washington street, though he did not look up, but he felt, as it were, the character of the street, and was dimly aware of the great multitude of signs that covered the buildings. He was conscious of wandering up the deserted thoroughfare for some distance, then of returning, still in the same absent mood, of crossing several moonlit spaces formed by the intersecting streets, of passing the grey, towering spire of the Old South Church, and of turning up School street. In all this route, he did not meet a single person, or once arouse even for a moment from his intense abstraction.

But as he turned up School street on the left hand side, the solemn and funereal clang from the Old South steeple startled him from his lethargy, striking with gloomy clangor the hour of two. He stopped, listening to the sombre and heavy blare of the great bell as it tolled the hour, and then died away in ghostly and aërial reverberations. Hearkening till the last faint dinning of the swarming tones seemed to fail into soundless vibratory waves, he waited till these too failed, and the awful silence of the night again descended brooding on the air. Two. The hour when spirits, as some wild seer avers, have power to enter from without, and walk the earth till dawn. Looking up, as the fancy crossed his mind, he saw the street, a lonely vista darkling in blue and melancholy gloom, so strangely litten, so unearthly in its whole appearance, that a sudden and silent diffusion of awe spread softly through his being, and held him still.

Had he been brought there blindfolded, and the bandage removed, he would scarcely have known where he was, so changed was the street from its familiar aspect. The gibbous moon, a huge, misshapen mass of watery light hanging low in the dead, dark blue, poured a flood of wan, metallic brilliance down one side of the vista, bringing out its architectural features in vivid lustre and ebon blackness, while the structures on the side on which he stood, loomed dark and sharp in deep shadow. So lone, so ghast, so supernaturally still, so changed in the weird and frigid glitter, so desolate and splendid in the melancholy light, the haggard darkness, the mournful and marble silence, that the gazer might have dreamed he stood in the demon-city of the Hebrew story, where foot of man hath seldom trod, and the evil night broods eternal.

Tranced with wondering awe, he moved slowly up the pavement, gazing upon the solemn palaces of ebony and silver, with his imagination darkly stirred. Beyond him lay a garden space, breaking the line of the vista, with two chestnut-trees in front on the pavement, whose thick cones of foliage seemed sculptured in metal, and were dimly silvered by the moon. Further on rose the square belfry and high-windowed wall of the Stone Chapel, with its flank gleaming, and its panes glittering in the wan lustre. As his glance rested on this, he saw a gaunt and spectral figure emerge from a shadowed angle, and move slowly, with a strange, uncertain motion, along the base of the chapel wall, with the unearthly light upon its shapeless outlines, and its long, black shadow distinct upon the gleaming pavement. Now creeping on, now halting and appearing to waver, strange in movement, strange and alien in form, it intensified the ghastly and desolate solitude with its presence, and seemed like some lone vagrant fiend slinking abroad from his lair, in the pallor of the waning moon.

Vaguely attracted by the strangeness of its shape and movements, which had something unusual about them he could not define, Harrington kept his eyes fixed upon it, as he moved on. The figure halted and wavered in its shambling walk as he drew nigh, and finally stood still, looking toward him. A secret tremor stirred his blood, for the nearer he approached the figure, the more inexplicable was the gauntness and shapelessness of its outlines. He was still some twenty or thirty yards distant from it, and without well knowing why he did so, for he had no intention of accosting it, he slowly crossed the street, and walked as slowly forward. As he drew nearer, a vague disgust mingled with the faint tremor of his veins, for a horrible and poisonous smell, which grew stronger as he approached, burdened the cold air. What dreadful outcast is this? he thought. Suddenly he stood still, aghast, petrified, filled with an icy affright mixed with unutterable loathing, and his eyes riveted to the awful shape before him. He was within a couple of yards of it, and as it stood trembling in the weird brilliance of the moon, it seemed some terrific scare-crow risen from Hell.

It was the figure of a man, but save for the wild, dark face that glared at him, the long, gaunt hands, like claws, that hung by its side, the thin legs half bare, and gaunt, splay bare feet on which it stood trembling, it seemed liker some monstrous rag. A loathsome and abominable stench exhaled from it. Its clothes were a dark shirt and trowsers, which hung in jagged tatters on its wasted skeleton frame. Wound round and round its neck in a thick sug, which gave it that appearance of shapelessness he had first noticed, was what seemed an old blanket. Above this glared a face of livid swarth, lit by the gloomy moon, the cheek bones protruding, the cheeks horribly sunken, the mouth fallen away from the white teeth, the eyes hollow and staring, the whole face that of some appalling mummy, burst from the leathern sleep of its Egyptian tomb, and endowed with horrid life to make night hideous.

The blood of Harrington seemed turned to ice as he gazed, and his hair rose.

"In the name of God," he gasped, "what manner of man are you?"

The figure did not answer, but stared at him and trembled.

Harrington's heart was stout, and conquering at once his affright and the sickening disgust which the stench gave him, he made one stride nearer to the figure.

"Who are you? Where did you come from?" he demanded.

The figure made no answer, but still stared rigidly at him, and trembled.

Harrington closely scanned the ghastly and hideous face, but could not determine anything concerning it. In the wan light of the moon, its horrible emaciation and livid duskiness of hue, together with the terrific expression the fallen mouth and exposed teeth gave it, made it seem like the face of a ghoul.

"Where do you live? Have you no home?" asked Harrington, shuddering.

"No, Marster."

If a corpse could speak, its voice might be the weak and hollow quaver in which the outcast made this answer. An awful feeling rose in the heart of Harrington, for he knew by the accent of the ghastly stranger that he was a negro, and the title he had bestowed upon him indicated that he was a runaway slave.

"Where do you come from? Where have you been?" he asked quickly.

The outcast trembled violently throughout his lank frame, and his jaws chattered.

"Oh, Marster, don't ask me," he answered in his weak, hollow voice. "I've been in hell, Marster, and I've got away. I've been in hell, Marster, sure. Don't send me back, now don't. Have a little mercy, Marster, and let me go."

So awful were the words in that lone hour; so awful the hollow and sepulchral voice that uttered them; so awful the motion of the face which writhed in speaking, as though in some rending agony; so awful and so dreadful the black skeleton gauntness, the monstrous raggedness, the Druidic filth of the trembling figure, with its swathed neck showing like some enormous circle of wen, and the poisonous stench sickening the whole night with its exhalations, that Harrington instinctively recoiled. Up from the lowest abysses of social wretchedness they swarmed into his mind;—the degraded of every low condition and degree—the neglected, the forgotten, the forlorn, the scum and dregs and ordure of mankind—the thieves, the beggars, the tatterdemalion sots and prostitutes and stabbers—the bloated, brutal, malformed nightmare monsters of a Humanity transformed to shapes more fearful than the foulest beasts;—up from the dark and fetid dens of the filthiest quarter of the city—up from the sinks and stews of the Black Sea—a wild and grisly company—they swarmed upon him. In all their misery, no misery like this—in all their number, no shape to pair with this. Below the lowest abyss of their wretchedness, yawned a lower, new-come from which, in the haggard pallor of the moon, stood a figure from whose ghastly and abominable Pariah shape the foulest and the vilest of them all would have shrunk away. Below the lowest hell wherein, in sunless crime and vice, their ruined natures were immerged, lay, as in the Inferno of Dante, a hell still lower—the hell decreed by avarice for innocent men, new-risen from which, all loathly foul, all awful with long suffering, stood the dark fugitive, afraid to tell his name, afraid to say from whence he had come, afraid to stand in the presence of his fellow, as though he were some frightful felon dreading the vengeance of mankind !

Gasping and shuddering through all his frame, Harrington gazed at him.

"O my country !" he murmured, "that such a thing as this should be ! That such a wrong as this should be wrought by you !"

The fugitive seemed to hear some fragment of his words, for he spoke instantly.

"Marster," he said, "you'll be a friend to me, won't you ? I've gone through a good deal to git away, Marster. I have, indeed, and I've got so fur now, you won't send me back. Oh, Marster, don't send me back !"

He tried to kneel to him on the pavement. The tears sprang to Harrington's eyes, and conquering his disgust, he strode forward, caught the foul form, and raised it to its feet. The fugitive shrank a little at his touch, and stood trembling.

"You poor fellow," sorrowfully said Harrington, "don't be afraid of me. I won't harm you. No, I won't send you back. And if you'll trust in me, you shall be safe and no one shall lay a hand upon you. But it's not safe for you to be out here in the street. Come with me, and I'll give you a place to sleep, and food to eat, and take care of you."

The fugitive hesitated a moment, still trembling.

"Marster, I'll trust in you," he said at length. "I'll trust in you, Marster, and I'll go along with you, if you won't send me back."

"I promise you, before God, that you shall be safe with me," said Harrington, solemnly. "Come."

He grasped, as he spoke, the thin arm of the trembling fugitive, and so assisting him, they moved slowly away together in silence, across Tremont street, and up the slope of Beacon street, with the light of the sinking moon in their faces. The fugitive was very weak, and tottered as he walked, despite the support the arm of his protector gave him. An overmastering pity, mixed with sombre sadness, filled the heart of Harrington as he felt the tottering motion, and heard the faint, stertorous panting of the miserable creature beside him. The slow pace at which they moved, combined with the nauseating odor of the rags which covered the fugitive, was an added trial to him, but he saw there was no help for it, and was patient.

Somewhat apprehensive about meeting a watchman, and not liking to be interrogated with a companion whom it was prudence to hide as much as possible, Harrington took the least public route he could under the circumstances. As they turned into Somerset street, the fugitive faltered, stopped, and began to cough. A terrible cough, weak, hoarse, incessant, which shook his whole frame. It ended at last, and with a faint groan of exhaustion, he sat down on a doorstep, panting, and breathing hard.

Shaken with pity, and doubly anxious lest the noise should attract some wandering night-policeman, Harrington stood over him, impatient to resume the journey.

"Do you feel better now?" he said, gently. "We must get on as fast as we can."

"Oh, Marster," gasped the fugitive, slowly and painfully rising. "I feel as if I couldn't go no further. I'm so powerful weak, Marster."

He tottered as he spoke; and Harrington, thinking he was going to fall, hastily, and somewhat awkwardly, threw up his arms to catch him, and struck his hand against something hard. Confused and startled, he withdrew his hand to rub it, wondering what could have hurt it. He thought it had come in contact with the sug around the fugitive's neck ; but, as that was clearly only a wrappage of cloth, and as the fugitive's head was bent at the time, he fancied he might have struck his hand against the man's teeth."

"Did I hurt you?" he asked, hastily. "Did I hit your teeth?"

"No, Marster," replied the fugitive, fumbling with the folds around his throat.

"Why do you wear that blanket so?" asked Harrington.

"Felt cold, Marster."

He said no more, but stood feebly handling the wrappage, and trembling. Harrington thought it strange that he should thus guard his throat, when his body was so bare, yet admitted to himself that perhaps the cloth could not have been better disposed for comfort, and thinking no more of it, he again grasped the fugitive's arm, and drew him on. They moved as slowly as before over the dark slope of Somerset street, under the shadow of the dwellings. Presently, the fugitive stopped again, and began to cough. This time Harrington formed a desperate resolution.

What was it? There are people who think they love mankind. But among the natural barriers that divide us from our fellows, there is none more impassable than a loathly uncleanliness. How many of the lovers of men could so have conquered nature as to clasp that leprous form in their arms? How many could have borne the test of their love which such an act would impose? For this was the test that proved the mighty heart of Harrington, and this was his resolution.

"Listen to me, friend," he said, when the cough had subsided. "It will never do for us to get on as slowly as this, for we have some distance to go. Now you keep still, for I'm going to carry you."

He quickly took off his coat and vest as he spoke—for he did not wish to spoil them by contact with the filthy body of the fugitive—rolled them up in a close bundle, which he secured with his neckerchief ; then without permitting himself to feel the strong repugnance which the foulness of the poor creature's apparel inspired, he flung his strong arms around him, and lifting him across his breast, with his head above his shoulder, deaf to his feeble remonstrance, set off at a rapid stride. The remonstrance ceased presently, and Harrington, hardly feeling the weight of his burden, strode at a masterly pace over the dark slope of Somerset street, turned into Allston, from thence into Derne, crossed Hancock to Myrtle, wheeled into Belknap, kept the grand stride down the hill to Cambridge street, crossed into Chambers, and set his load down at the garden gate.

A little heated by his exertion, he opened the gate with one hand, rubbing his shoulder with the other, and with a nod of his head invited the fugitive to enter, wondering meanwhile what it was about the man's neck that had pressed so hard against his shoulder all the way. Something as hard as iron, and several times he had even felt a point, like a muffled spike, press upon his flesh, through the folds of his blanket. There was something mysterious under those folds, he thought, as he unlocked his door, and he was curious to know what it could be.

Congratulating himself that he had been so lucky as not to meet a single person during his nocturnal march, he held the door open till the fugitive had entered, and then closing and locking it, he took the glimmering lamp from the chimney, set it on the table, and turned up the flame. The fugitive stood, shaking on his gaunt legs, with his eyes wildly revolving upon the rows of books all around him, and ever returning to rest for a moment on the bust of Lord Bacon on its pedestal. Poor Tom in Lear—that wild figure plucked up from the low gulfs of the Elizabethan wretchedness, and set in Shakspearean light forever—was tame compared to the lank and ghastly figure of the lorn wanderer from slavery. Less unearthly in the light which fell upon his visage from the funnel of the lamp, than in the weird rays of the moon, he was not less hideously pitiable. His façe, which was naturally quite dark, was terribly emaciated, with the skull almost visible through its wasted features, or, at least, suggested by the prominence of the teeth and forehead, the projection of the cheek-bones, the hollow pits of the cheeks, and the cavernousness of the eyes, which were ridged with heavy eye-brows. Harrington took in his aspect with one firm glance, and mindful of his weakness, brought him a chair, and made him sit down ; then opened the windows, to let the fresh air relieve the smell of his rags in the close room.

Going up his ladder the next minute, he lit a lamp above, and turned on the water into his bath-tub. He came down presently, bare to the waist, the light gleaming on his muscular arms and massive chest, and stood fronting the fugitive with his watch in his hand, his head bent toward him on the kingly and beautiful slope of his white shoulders.

"Now, friend," said he, with naïve gravity, "you must be washed. In five minutes the bath-tub will be full, so take off those things, and I'll give you some other clothes."

"Yes, Marster, I'm in need of bein' washed. I ain't fit to be in this nice house," quavered the fugitive abjectly, rising feebly as he spoke.

Harrington, without replying, watched him curiously as he fumbled at the blanket on his neck, and saw that he was loth to remove it.

"O Marster, Marster," he groaned, "I'm afeard to let you see it. But, Marster, you'll be friendly to me, and you won't send me back, Marster ?"

"Come, come, poor fellow, you know you're safe with me," said Harrington, kindly, all alive meanwhile with curiosity. "Come, off with it."

The negro still fumbling at the blanket, without undoing it, and sighing piteously, Harrington laid his watch on the table, and stepping forward, unwound the wrappage from his neck, fold after fold, pulled it off, and disclosed an iron collar with a prong, and the letters distinct upon it—LAFITTE BROTHERS, NEW ORLEANS.

He did not start, nor stagger back, but stood, like a statue struck by thunder, glaring at the collar with parted lips and starting eyes, a pallor like death upon his countenance, and a strong shudder quivering through his bare chest and arms, while the negro cowered with a hideous-piteous imploring face, his form crouching, and his hands clasped before him. In the dead silence, nothing was heard but the loud running of the water in the room overhead, and the faint gasping breath of the fugitive.

"God Almighty!" shouted Harrington, "what is this?"

The fugitive did not answer, but stood faintly gasping. The next instant Harrington started, with a strong muscular convulsion of his frame, and strode a pace forward.

"Who put that collar on your neck!" he demanded with awful anger.

"Marster Lafitte put it on, Marster."

"Master Lafitte? which one? That says Lafitte Brothers," cried Harrington, pointing with outstretched arm and finger straight at the name.

"Marster Torwood Lafitte put it on, Marster," quavered the fugitive, affrighted at Harrington's manner.

Harrington's outstretched arm sank slowly, and dropped by his side. A deep and burning flush mounted to his face, and clenching his hands, he thundered a tremendous oath. Such an oath as Washington swore when Lee chafed him in his legions. Such an oath as had never before passed the calm lips of Harrington, but it burst from his heart's core.

He stood in silence for a moment, the flush dying from his face, and his anger settling down from that explosion into calm.

"Who are you? what's your name?" he demanded.

"Antony, Marster."

Harrington was past surprise, but his brain whirled, and blankness gathered upon it. For a minute, he stood vacantly staring at the fugitive. Then, recovering from his stupefaction, he sighed vaguely, and wiped away the perspiration from his face with the palm of his hand. Glancing presently at his watch, he saw that the five minutes had not expired, and going to a drawer, he produced a bunch of keys.

"We'll have that collar off," said he, approaching the fugitive.

Key after key was tried, but none fitted. Throwing down the bunch, Harrington looked at the watch, and went up-stairs to stop the water. He came back presently, took the shade from the lamp, and holding the light to the collar, inspected its make carefully. He saw that it opened on a hinge behind, and was secured by a lock before. Putting the lamp on the table, he reflected for a moment.

"Lie down on the floor," he said, presently.

The fugitive obeyed, with as much alacrity as his feebleness permitted. He already had the most entire and perfect confidence in his protector.

Bending over him, Harrington turned him on his side. Then taking up the poker, he inserted it between the neck of the fugitive and the under side of the collar, and putting his foot on this for a purchase, thus holding the collar firmly to the floor, he seized the upper side near the lock with both hands.

"Now lie still," he said. "I don't know whether I'm strong enough to break the lock, but, by mankind!" he shouted, "I'll try!"

Slowly, the muscles in Harrington's arms straightened, his bent leg grew firm as iron, the arms became two stiff, white corded bars, the muscles in his back and shoulders tensely trembled, the blood mounted to his face and body, and in the midst of the slow, tremendous strain, there was a faint clicking gride, a sudden snap, a screaking wrench, and one half the collar rose on its rusty hinge in his hands. The deed was done! Harrington stood up, and stepped back, exercising his arms, while the bought thrall of Lafitte scrambled erect, ghastlily grinning, and stood surveying the accursed necklace, which lay open as his neck had abandoned it, with the bent poker lying on its inner surface.

"To-morrow," said Harrington, quietly, "you are to tell me all about this. Now undress yourself."

"Yes, Marster," and the fugitive, with a sort of ghastly joyfulness, hastily divested himself of his foul rags, which Harrington at once threw into the yard.

An awful sight was that black skeleton of a body. As it lankly straddled across the room, and up the ladder, following Harrington, Holbein might have taken it as Death come for the Scholar—a grimmer and grislier figure than any in the Dance Macaber. Few men would have borne to abide even for a moment in the same room with it. The very dog in the yard, himself the Pariah of brutes, would have bayed at it and shrunk into his kennel.

Our free and happy country had been at work upon that form. North and South had wrought together to bring it to perfection. The old scars which covered it, the horny wheals of many a scourging, the thick ring of callosed flesh left by the iron collar around its neck—these were the special tool-marks of the South. The recent cuts and bruises, the swollen contusions left by fist and boot upon it, the raw, blue sores, the general offence and stench it had contracted in the noisome pit of a vessel's noisome hold—these showed the tooling of the North. That ghastly gauntness, that lank emaciation, that livid swarth, those signs and tokens of ferocious abuse, of cold and hunger and sickness and privation—our free and happy country had done it all!

Servant and soldier of mankind, thy menial task of love is set, thy work is here! Purge the pollution from this wasted body, and with thy own hand, tender and skillful as a woman's, bind up these wounds, anoint and dress these sores! For him, the lowest and the loathliest of thy brethren, are these mean toils—the meanest man can do for man. Thy free and happy country would say thou doest ill; and "ill" the snickering whinny and brute scoff from the jaws of her slavers and traders; and "ill" her hell-dog statute dragging thee to the jail and fine for helping the lorn wanderer. Thou call'st the spirit of the ages by another name than ours—thou call'st it Verulam, we call it Christ. Oh, man beloved of Christ and Verulam, thou doest well!

An hour passed on and the solemn task was done. His matted hair cut off, his body clean, his wounds dressed, the fugitive, clad in a shirt and drawers of Harrington's, a world too large for his wasted frame, was placed by the young scholar in his bed, and sitting there was fed with biscuit, and wine and water—the only food and drink accessible then. The repast ended, Harrington washed himself, put on clean clothes, arranged the room, and then turned to go down. The fugitive lay weakly sobbing.

"Good night, Antony," said Harrington, gravely, standing

with the lamp in his hand, its light shining on his beautiful and bearded countenance.

Suddenly, before he could be stopped, the fugitive scrambled from the bed, and flinging himself at Harrington's feet, embraced them with his thin wrists and huge hands, and laid his head upon them.

"The Lord Jesus bless you, Marster," he sobbed in a broken and sepulchral voice, "Oh, Marster, the Lord Jesus bless you, for there's not no such Marster as you, Marster, nowhere—Oh Marster"——

Harrington stopped him by suddenly starting away to lay down the lamp, and returning, lifted him to his feet and got him into bed again.

"I know all you feel, Antony," he said, pulling the clothes over him; "but you musn't talk to-night, poor fellow. Now go to sleep, and have a long rest, and to-morrow or the next day, we'll talk. Good night."

"Good night, Marster," sobbed the submissive negro.

Harrington took from a nail on the wall, an old camlet cloak which had been his father's, and seizing the lamp, went down.

The first thing was to take the collar from the floor, and put it in a drawer; then untying his bundled coat and vest, he shook them out, and hung them up; then opening the door and windows, for the taint of the foul rags was still in the room, he went into the yard, and stood breathing the cool, pure air, and gazing, with a sense of boding at his heart, upon the thick hordes of stars. The night seemed all wild and alive. Something sinister and evil pervaded the atmosphere, and the dark blue spread like an astrologic scroll bright with burning cyphers and diagrams of doom.

Returning to the house with a mind ill at ease, he closed the door and shutters, leaving the windows open. Then taking a revolver from its case in a drawer, he drew the charges, and reloaded the weapon. It was altogether unlikely that the hunters would come to his dwelling; still there was nothing like being ready; and Harrington with his Baconian faith that men without natural good were but a nobler sort of vermin, was quite resolved both to "prevent the fiend and to kill vermin," as the Shakspearean phrase has it, if they crept near the hiding-place of the fugitive.

His pistol loaded, he laid it on the table, and sat a few minutes thinking of the strangeness of his night's adventure. How awful and marvellous it all was! The brother of Roux, whom he had tried to ransom, in his keeping—Roux himself in danger—Lafitte in the city, and master of the secret of his locality! The air seemed thick with peril.

Rising presently, he put the lamp in the fire-place, and turned it low; then taking the cushion of his chair for a pillow, he wrapped himself in the camlet cloak, and lay down on the sofa. A few moments' dazed reflection on the events of the night, and fatigued by his labors, he dropped away into dreamless slumber.

CHAPTER XVIII.

THE PRETTY PASS THINGS CAME TO.

As an iceberg sinks dissolved into the waters of the Southern ocean, so sank the cold, blue night into the golden crystal of a warm, delicious day. Again beneath the hiving roofs of the great city, awoke the complex, many-actioned, myriad-thoughted swarm of life, and again through the grotesque and picturesque crooked streets poured the motley varieties of civic existence, with the municipal clash and rattle, the scurry of driving feet, the blab of many voices, the incessant buzzing roar. The traders went to their trade; the merchants to their stores and wharves; the mechanics to their labor; the little ones to their schools; the women to their household tasks; the lawyers to their courts; the clergy to their conventions; the anti-slavery people to their debate; the dark children of the race of Attucks to their humble toils, and the phantoms of the Reign of Terror with them.

In the fencing-school, Monsieur Bagasse fenced with his

pupils, pausing with curious eyes, and chin levelled at the door whenever a new footstep was heard upon the stairs, and wondering why Wentworth and Harrington, who had seldom failed before, did not arrive. Captain Vukovich, too, with thoughts intent on the cigar-shop he was going to open, and bent on consulting the young men with regard to the best situation, and perhaps invoking a little material aid, waited for them, meditatively stroking his thin moustache, and wandering up and down the fencing-school. But they both waited in vain, for the young men did not appear.

Harrington meanwhile, up after four hours' sleep, was closeted with Captain Fisher, telling him his night's adventure, the astounded Captain swearing tobacco at every pause in the narrative, with his head all askew, like a marine raven who had been taught nothing but imprecations on slavery and slaveholders.

Wentworth, exhausted by his night of suffering, had gone down to his studio, and lay there asleep on a sofa, pale and haggard, in the dim-pictured, shadowy room. Among the paintings and sketches around the chamber, was one canvas with its face turned to the wall. It was the unfinished portrait of Emily. On the easel, illumined by the pale slanting light from the single unshaded window, was the canvas which held, sketched in in dead colors, the Death of Attucks. Vaguely through its confused gloom, loomed one dark figure with arm uplifted in menace and defiance.

Emily had appeared at the breakfast-table, calm and pale, with dark circles around the dimmed lustre of her eyes. To Mrs. Eastman's anxious inquiries, she had simply pleaded indisposition, and after the meal, at which Muriel alone, paler than usual, was chatty and gay, she had retired to her room to collect her thoughts for the coming hour of confession and departure.

Muriel, sinking from her assumed gaiety into sobriety, went to market near by in Mount Vernon street, returned in a few minutes, and, sitting alone in the library, resolutely shut out all thought for the present regarding the mysterious complication of affairs, and resumed the studies she had begun before breakfast, bent on pursuing them till Harrington came to go with her to Southac street.

In the mean time things had come to a pretty pass in the private counting-room of Mr. Atkins's office on Long Wharf.

"Yes, sir, things have come to a pretty pass when such an infernal rascal undertakes to let a black beggar loose from aboard my brig," foamed Captain Bangham, red with passion, and pounding the desk with his fist.

The merchant sat in an arm-chair near the desk, looking at the captain, with iron-clenched jaws, his eyes sparkling with rage in his set blanched face.

"If I ever heard of such a thing in all my life, Bangham!" he exclaimed, slapping both arms of his chair with his palms, and glaring all around the little mahogany-furnished office. "But where were you when this was done?"

"I, sir? Asleep in the cabin, Mr. Atkins. Never knew a thing about it, sir, till this morning. Just for special safety I didn't have the brig hauled up to the dock yesterday, but let her lay in the stream. 'Jones, says I, have you seen the nigger this morning?' 'No I haven't, says he, cool as you please. 'I guess I'll take a look at him,' says I, and so I took a biscuit and a can of water, and toted down to the hole where I had the nasty devil tied up, and begod, he was gone! I tumbled up on deck: 'Jones,' I shouted, 'where's the nigger?' 'I don't know where he is now,' says he, lazy as a ship in the doldrums. 'All I know is,' says he, 'that I rowed him ashore about midnight, and told him to put for it.' By"—— gasped Captain Bangham, with a frightful oath, "I was so mad that I couldn't say a word. I just ran into the cabin, and when I came out, Jones wasn't to be seen.—Hallo, there he is now!" cried the captain, starting to his feet and pointing out of the window to a tall figure lounging along the wharf, and looking at the shipping.

The merchant jumped from his chair, threw up the window, and shouted, "Here, you, Jones! Come in here."

The figure looked up nonchalantly, and lounged across the street toward the office.

"He's coming," said the merchant, purple with excitement, and sinking back into his chair.

They waited in silence, and presently the tall figure of the mate was seen in the outer office, through the glass door, lounging toward them. He opened the door in a minute, and came in carelessly, chewing slowly, and nodding once to Mr. Atkins. A tall man, dressed sailor-fashion, in a blue shirt and pea-jacket, with a straw hat set negligently on his head, and a grave, inscrutable, sunburnt face, with straight manly features and dull blue eyes.

"Mr. Jones," said the merchant, his face a deeper purple, but his voice constrained to the calm of settled rage, "this is a fine liberty you have taken. I want to know what you mean by it?"

"What do you refer to, Mr. Atkins?" returned the mate, stolidly.

"What do I refer to, sir? you know what I refer to. I refer to your taking that man from my brig," roared the merchant.

"Mr. Atkins," replied the mate, phlegmatically, "Bangham, there, was going to take that poor devil back to Orleans. You don't mean to tell me that you meant he should do it?"

"Yes, sir, I *did* mean he should do it," the merchant vociferated.

"Then you're a damned scoundrel," said the mate, with the utmost composure.

Captain Bangham gave a long whistle, and sat mute with stupefaction. Mr. Atkins turned perfectly livid, and stared at the mate with his mouth pursed into an oval hole, perfectly aghast at this insolence, and almost wondering whether he had heard aright.

"You infernal rascal," he howled, springing to his feet the next instant, purple with rage, "do you dare to apply such an epithet to *me*? *You*—to *me*?"

"To you?" thundered the seaman, in a voice that made Mr. Atkins drop into his chair as if he was shot. "To you? And who are you? You damned lubberly, purse-proud aristocrat, do you want me to take you by the heels and throw you out of that window? Call me that name again, and I'll do it as soon as I'd eat. *You*, indeed? You're the Lord High Brown, aint you? You're the Lord Knows Who, you blasted old money-grubber, aint you! *You*, indeed!"

In all his life, Mr. Atkins had never been so spoken to. He sat in a sort of horror, gazing with open mouth and glassy eyes at the sturdy face of the seaman, on which a brown flush had burned out, and the firm, lit eyes of which held him spell-bound. Bangham, too—horror-stricken, wonder-stricken, thunder-stricken—sat staring at Jones for a minute, then burst into a short, rattling laugh, and jumping to his feet, cried, "Oh, he's mad, he's mad, he's mad, he's got a calenture, he's got a calenture, he's mad as a March hare," capering and hopping and prancing, meanwhile, in his narrow confine, as if he would jump out of his skin.

"You, too, Bangham," said the mate, making a step toward him, with a menacing gesture, at which the captain stopped capering, and shrank, while Mr. Atkins slightly started in his chair, "you just clap a stopper on that ugly mug of yours, and stop your monkey capers, or you'll have me afoul of you. I haven't forgot your didoes with the men aboard the Soliman. Just you say another word now, and I'll put in a complaint that'll lay you by the heels in the State Prison, where you ought to have been long ago, you ugly pirate, you!"

The captain evidently winced under this threat, which Mr. Jones delivered with ominous gravity, slowly shaking, meanwhile, his clenched fist at him.

"And now look here, you brace of bloody buccaneers," continued the irreverent seaman, "short words are best words with such as you. I untied that poor old moke of a nigger last night, and rowed him ashore. What are ye going to do about it?"

Evidently a question hard to answer. Merchant and captain, stupefied and staring, gave him no reply.

"Hark you, now, Atkins," he went on. "We found that man half dead in the hold when we were three days out—a sight to make one's flesh crawl. The bloody old pirate he'd run away from, had put a spiked collar on his neck, just as if he was a brute, with no soul to be saved. I'm an old sea-dog—I am ; and I've seen men ill treated in my time, but I'm damned if I ever seen a man ill-treated like that God-forsaken nigger. He'd run away, and no blame to him for running away. He'd been livin' in swamps with snakes and alligators, and if he hadn't no right to his freedom, he'd earned one fifty times over, and it's my opinion that a man who goes through what he did has more right to his freedom than two beggars like you, who never done the first thing to deserve it. Mind that now, both of ye !"

The mate paused a moment, hitching up his trowsers, and rolling his tobacco from one side of his twitching mouth to the other, and then, with his face flushed, and his blue eye gleaming savagely, went on.

"What's the first thing that brute there did to him? Kicked him, and he lyin' half dead. Then in a day or two, when the poor devil got his tongue, he told how he'd got away, and the sort of pirate he'd got away from. God! when we all a'most blubbered like babes, what did that curse there do? Knocked the man down, and beat his head on the deck, till we felt like mutiny and murder, every man of us! And then when we'd got the poor devil below, sorter comfortable, down comes Bangham, and hauls him off to stick him into a nasty hole under hatches, and there he kep' him the whole passage, half-starved, among the rats and cockroaches. Scarce a day of his life aboard, that he didn't go down and kick and maul him. He couldn't keep his hands off him—no, he couldn't. When I took the man ashore in the dead o' night, he was nothin' but a bundle o' bones and nasty rags, and he made me so sick, I couldn't touch him. That's the state he was in. Now, then, look here."

The mate paused again for a moment, turning his quid, with his face working, and laying the fingers of his right hand in the palm of his left, began again in a voice gruff and grum.

"That infernal buccaneer, Bangham," he said, "was bent on takin' the poor devil back to Orleans, after all he'd gone through to get away. Well, he's a brute, and we don't expect nothin' of brutes like him. But you're a Boston merchant, Atkins, and callin' yourself a Christian man, you put in your oar in this dirty business, and was goin' to help Bangham. You thought I was goin' to stand by and see you do it. No!" he thundered, with a tremendous slap of his right hand on the palm of his left, which made both the merchant and the captain start, "no! I wasn't goin' to stand by and see you do it! I'm an old sea-dog and my heart is tough and hard, but I'm damned if it's hard enough to stand by when such a sin as that's afoot, and never lend a hand to stop it. I took that man out of your clutches, you brace of pirates, and I set him adrift! You think I'm afraid to own it? No, I'm not, begod! I did it. Ephraim Jones is my name, and I come from Barnstable. There's where I come from. I'm a Yankee sailor, and, so help me God, I could never see the bunting of my country flying at the truck again, if I let you two bloody Algerine thieves carry off that man to his murder. That's all I've got to say. Take the law of me now, if you like. I won't skulk. You'll find me when you look for me. And if James Flatfoot don't have his harpoon into both of you one of these days, then there's no God, that's all!"

Turning on his heel with this valediction, which consigned the merchant and the captain's future beyond the grave to the Devil, who, under the name of James Flatfoot, occupies a prominent place in marine theology, Mr. Jones carelessly lounged out of the private room, leaving the glass door open, and with a nonchalant glance at the three or four startled clerks and book-keepers who sat and stood at their desks wondering what had been going on within, for they had only caught confused scraps of the stormy colloquy, he went down stairs, with a load off his mind which had been gathering there during the whole voyage of the Soliman.

For a moment after his departure, Mr. Atkins sat mute and still, feeling like one in a horrid dream. Roused presently by a deep-drawn breath from Captain Bangham, he wheeled his chair around to the desk, and taking out his white handkerchief, wiped away the cold sweat which had started out on his face and forehead.

"What are we going to do now, Mr. Atkins ?" said the captain.

"I don't know, Bangham," replied the merchant in a voice like the faint voice of a sick man. "I should like to have that scoundrel arrested. Such insolence I never heard in all my life. My God ! what are we coming to in this country when a low fellow like that can presume to talk so to a man of my standing !"

He murmured these words feebly, and again wiping his face, sat with his eyes glassy and his jaw working.

"Mr. Atkins," said Bangham, after a pause, "this black curse has got off, but he must be somewhere in the city. If I should happen to meet him about town anywhere"——

"Just seize him," cried the merchant, with a start. "Lay hands upon him at once, and carry him aboard the vessel. You can say, if anybody interferes, that he is a thief, and that you're taking him to the police-office."

"I'll do it," exclaimed the captain, with an oath. "I'll hang around Nigger Hill, where he's likely to be, and if I meet him, off he'll go. It'll be horrid if we don't find him, and they should happen to hear of it down in Orleans."

"Indeed it will, Bangham," replied the merchant. "Though, of course, we could explain it satisfactorily. Still, there's the trouble of the explanation, and it would be far better if we could return the rascal. That would settle the whole thing at once."

"By the way, have you told Lafitte anything about this?" inquired the captain, anxiously.

"God bless me, no!" replied Mr. Atkins, hurriedly. "Lafitte musn't know anything about this. We must keep it from him."

"What is it you must keep from me, my dear friends ?" said a smooth, courteous voice.

They both started, and turned around. There stood Mr. Lafitte, smiling a bland sardonic smile. So still—so cool—so unruffled. It almost seemed as if he had outgrown upon them from the air. But he had come softly through the outer office, and stood just within the glass door, which Jones had left open.

"Better not keep anything from me, my dear friends," blandly continued the Southerner, smiling stilly down upon their blank and ghast faces. "Because I am the very devil for finding out things that are kept from me. Besides, frankness is a virtue—a positive virtue."

He closed the glass door behind him, and entering, took a chair, and removed his Panama hat, smiling stilly all the while, with his tawny, blood-specked, glossy eyes slowly and almost imperceptibly roving from one to the other.

"Lafitte," gasped the merchant, feeling as if he was about to faint, "don't blame me. I meant it for the best."

"Blame you, my friend!" returned the Southerner, smoothly, with an air of tender reproach which was atrocious; "blame you! Could I be so cruel? Ah, no! Bangham, my love, how are you? It is long since I have seen you. The last time I saw you, my Bangham, was at the St. Charles Hotel—and oh, my friend, how drunk you were! But you are not drunk to-day, dear captain. Ah, no! To-day we can appeal from Philip Bangham drunk to Philip Bangham sober. Let us then appeal to you to tell us what is the mystery."

The captain reddened under this address, and looking exceedingly nonplused, fidgeted with his necktie as if it choked him.

"Lafitte, don't joke," said Mr. Atkins, nervously. "Don't, I beg of you. I feel ill already, and you disturb me. Listen. Here is the trouble. One of your slaves was found in Bangham's vessel when he was three days out, and came on here to Boston. We kept him bound in the hold, intending to have him sent back to you, and last night the infernal scoundrel of a mate let him go, and we've lost him."

"And you were going to keep this from me, were you?" said Mr. Lafitte, blandly, all the tiger seeming to condense into his glossy, tawny orbs, while his smile remained serene and still. "Really, my dear Atkins, you were not frank."

"Oh, my God!" exclaimed the merchant, "don't talk so! What was the use of disturbing you? We were going to institute a search for the negro, and have him returned to you as quickly and quietly as possible."

"Good friend! good Atkins!" said the Southerner, with gentle approval. "So considerate of you. I really hope you may find the runaway, for if you shouldn't, and it gets noised on the Levee, your house will suffer. Of course, I wouldn't mention it myself, but these things always get out. The sailors, you know! Very indiscreet those sailors—ah, very, very!"

"Depend on my doing everything I can, Lafitte," hurriedly replied the merchant, uncertain whether the Southerner's words held a menace or no. "We will ransack the city. Suppose you get a warrant out for him—how will that do?"

"No," answered Mr. Lafitte, blandly. "I should prefer not. Since you lost him, you ought in justice to find him. If you don't succeed, we may try the police. But, apropos, you do not tell me the boy's name."

"He called himself Antony," replied Bangham.

They almost shuddered to see the silent change that came to the rich brunette visage of the Southerner. His complexion became purple and livid in spots, his nostrils dilated, his eyes were steady orbs of cruel gloss, with the blood-specks distinct upon their tawn. Slowly swaying in his chair for a moment, he stopped in this movement, and spoke.

"It is Antony, is it?" he said, in a low, smooth voice. "Gentlemen, I urge you to find that slave of mine. He is a wretch whom I wish to see once more. When you told me you had a boy of mine, I thought it must be one of my brother's, who ran away the week before I left. I did not imagine it was Antony, for I thought he was done for in the swamp."

"Where, Mr. Lafitte?" asked the merchant.

"In the swamp," repeated Lafitte. "That scoundrel, Mr. Atkins, flew upon me, and left me for dead on the floor of my house. Then he ran for the swamp, half-killing my overseer on the way. We roused the neighbors and hunted for him three days and part of a fourth, and at last finding his clothes near a bayou, we concluded he was food for alligators. Though why we should find his clothes, and not him, was a mystery to me. And so he got to Boston, after all. Now where do you expect to find him, gentlemen?"

"Well, Mr. Lafitte, I don't exactly know," returned the merchant, dubiously; "but Bangham here will look round Nigger Hill, a quarter where the colored people herd together. The best way would be to get out a search warrant, and put the matter in the hands of the city marshal."

"Listen to me, Atkins," said the Southerner. "I've got a clue. Several months ago I received a letter offering to purchase this fellow. Now, eight or nine years ago his brother William ran away from me, and it was clear to me, when I received this letter, that whoever sent it knew where William was, and was probably put up to it by him."

"Well, who did send it?" demanded Mr. Atkins.

"That letter," pursued Lafitte, "was postmarked from Philadelphia, and the answer was to be sent to a Mr. Joseph House, who, it seems, was to act as agent in the matter. I called on House, and was told by him that the person who wrote the letter lived in London. In fact, he showed me the person's name and address in a London Directory, and he was so serious about it, that I swear I was thrown off the track. But I had my misgivings afterward, and the more I thought of it the stronger they grew. Mr. Atkins, that letter was signed John Harrington."

"John Harrington!" exclaimed the merchant, starting and scowling. "You don't mean to say"——

"Mr. Atkins," interrupted Lafitte, "when you told me that fellow's name who came into the Abolition meeting last night with your lovely niece, it flashed upon me at once that he was the man that wrote the letter."

"Upon my word," said the merchant, "this is odd. But this Harrington's poor as poverty. How should he be buying your negro?"

Mr. Lafitte shrugged his shoulders.

"Who knows?" he returned. "Perhaps the dear William has earned the cash, and wants to treat himself to a bit of black brother in his old age. Perhaps," he added, with a sly, sardonic smile, "your lovely niece wants to do a little philanthropy for him. She's rich, you told me. Your Boston ladies are so fond of the philanthropy business, you know. And Harrington's sweet upon her, isn't he? Who knows but that he has put her up to it. He looks just like one of those noble fools we read of. Now, what will you wager he doesn't know this dear William, and hasn't been touched by the sorrows of that black angel? Atkins, keep your eye on Harrington to find William, and finding William, perhaps you'll find Antony."

"Upon my word, Lafitte, you're the very devil," cried the merchant, with a harsh laugh, looking at the visage of the Southerner, which was lit with an infernal smile.

"That's your clue," said the latter. "Just follow it, and you'll find I'm right."

"But how am I to follow it?" returned the merchant. "There's any quantity of black Williams in Boston, probably, and who knows what name your man goes by now?"

"Egad," replied Mr. Lafitte, his face darkening, "I didn't think of that."

"Had your man William any other name?" asked the merchant.

"Name?" scoffed the Southerner. "The black cattle change their names with their masters. This fellow would be called by mine, if he was called anything but William. I bought him and his brother with a lot of others off the estate of old Madame Roux."

"Roux? Hold on!" exclaimed Atkins. "Roux? By George, that's the name of the colored man Serena—that's my sister—recommended to us, and we got him to do some white-washing and window-cleaning this spring!"

"Your sister?" interrogated Lafitte.

"Yes, my sister, Mrs. Eastman. She's the mother of the young lady you saw last night."

Mr. Lafitte leaned back in his chair, and shook with long, silent merriment, outward token of the raging floods of devilish joy which swelled within him.

"There you have it, dear Atkins," he chuckled, at length. "There you have it. Follow up Roux, my boy, follow up

Roux. Set Bangham to look after the dear William. My own Bangham. Whom I love," and Mr. Lafitte ogled the captain in a manner which would have been purely ridiculous if it had not been superlatively infernal.

Bangham reddened, and looked foolish and uncomfortable under these affectionate regards.

"I guess I'll go out and see to the cargo," he said, rising. "The stevedores are unlading, you know, Mr. Atkins."

"That's right, Bangham," returned the merchant. "Come back soon, and we'll make arrangements for this other matter."

"*Au revoir*, Bangham. God bless you," cried the Southerner, after the departing captain. "And now, Atkins," he continued, drawing up his chair, "let's have a talk about business, and get that off our minds, before we follow up that dear William and that dear Antony."

CHAPTER XIX.

THE ROAR OF ST. DOMINGO.

Captain Bangham, with a mortal aversion to Lafitte, hovered about the outside of the glass door, and left the office several times, before the talk on business was concluded. In those beatific days Cotton was King, and His Majesty's concerns required a great deal of mercantile, as well as political, attention.

It was about eleven o'clock when, the talk on business concluded, Mr. Lafitte strolled up State street, with the intention of dropping in at Parker's to lunch. If anything had been needed to complete his elation, the warm and beautiful blue day which shone upon the crowded city, would have done it. Like Sir Ralph the Rover, in Southey's poem, his heart was joyful to excess; and equally true was it that like that Rover, this Rover's mirth was wickedness. He felt, as he himself would have expressed it, refreshingly wicked.

Lunch over, and a drink taken, Mr. Lafitte thought it would be pleasant diversion to visit that Nigger Hill he had heard so much about, and see how the colored brethren were lodged. Enchanted with the idea, he engaged a carriage, and lighting a cigar, got in, and told the driver where to carry him.

The carriage set off, and Mr. Lafitte, lolling back on the cushions, smoked placidly, and indolently gazed out of the window at the passengers. Presently, instead of passengers to gaze at, there were the elegant aristocratic dwellings in the streets on Beacon Hill, and soon after there were the dingy houses of the negro quarter.

His cigar smoked out, Mr. Lafitte enjoyed whatever there was to enjoy in the prospect the carriage window afforded. It was pretty near dinner-time in that region, and most of the people were indoors. A few colored men and women stood at some of the thresholds or looked out at the windows, and colored urchins were playing in the streets. The carriage driving slowly, Belknap street, South Russell street, Butolph street, Garden street, Centre street, May street, Grove street, and all the streets of the quarter, passed in successive review under the interested and inspecting eyes of the gallant Southerner.

In Grove street, a fancy came upon him to walk a few steps and note the effect from the pavement. Stopping the carriage, he got out, and bidding the driver wait there for him, he walked on, and turned the corner into Southac street.

Walking slowly, and contemplatively twirling his moustache, while he softly hummed an air, he gazed with a roving eye at the squalid and sunlit houses of mingled brick and wood which stood in the vertical light on either side of the street. There were few people about, fewer even than he had seen in the streets he had passed through, and beginning to find it a bore, he was turning to go back to the carriage, when his eye chanced to rest on the closed window of a house obliquely opposite to him, and stopping in the midst of his humming, his hand fell from his moustache, and he stood still.

There, behind the closed window of the second story, absently gazing out straight before him, stood William Roux! Mr. Lafitte knew him at the first glance, and an infernal joy bathed his heart. Afraid the next instant that he would be seen, he drew back into a narrow alley near by, still gazing up at the window. But he had no reason for apprehension, for the negro was apparently lost in reverie, and stood with his hands in his pockets, looking straight before him.

The entire abstraction of Roux's manner suggested to Mr. Lafitte that there was no other person up there in the room, and a demoniac idea leaped at once into the brain of the slaveholder and took possession of him. Here was the carriage within fifty paces just round the corner. What was to prevent him from quietly walking up into that room, taking Roux by the arm, and quickly marching him off to it? It flashed into his mind just how Roux would behave. The submissive, docile negro, so different from that sullen, fiery Antony, overcome with fright he would never think of struggling, and with the old servile habit of instant obedience falling again upon him, cowed by the stern mandate, paralyzed by the strong grasp, thunder-stricken by the unexpected appearance of his old master, he would just march along without a word. Quickly he would walk him, cram him into the carriage, pull down the curtains, and drive away like fury. Ha! the moment when he should have him safe, rushed upon his brain like fire. One bold stroke—now for it!

Emerging from the alley, he quickly crossed the street, and mounted the wooden steps which he saw led up to Roux's room. The door was ajar, and pausing for one moment to listen, with torrents of hellish exultation pouring through his being, he recognized by the silence that Roux was alone. Softly pushing open the door, which floated inward without a sound, he saw his victim standing with his back to him at the window, and crossing the floor on noiseless tiptoe, he tapped him on the shoulder.

Roux turned with a start, and with his black face flaring into ashen fright, he would have fallen to the floor, but Lafitte caught him by the throat with both hands, and upheld him.

"Not one word, you dog!" he hissed, glaring into his bulging eyes. "I have you! Stand!"

He released his throat, and Roux stood with a terrific look

of agony on his visage, which seemed at once to have grown thin and grey.

"Oh, Master Lafitte!" he gasped in a horrified whisper, his whole frame shaking as if he had the palsy.

"Silence, cur!" hissed the slaveholder, grasping his arm like a vice. "Come with me! Not a word—not a sign—or I'll dash your brains out."

Roux, though not a strong nature, was no coward, and under ordinary circumstances, he would have fought to the death for his liberty. But this horrible phantom that had risen upon him! It was not a man—it was Fate—it was the anaconda, and he crushed in the vast and muscular gripe of its folds! The deadening ether of utter horror fell upon him, and passive as one falling from a precipice, with the iron clutch of his master on his arm he moved with him to the door.

At the first step, there was a bounce in the entry, and Tugmutton appeared on the threshold. In less than a second, the blobber-cheeked guffaw-grin of glee fell from the fat face of the broad-limbed Puck into a shock-haired white-eyed stare of goblin terror, and with a shrill yell he vanished. His chattering screech outside was heard by Lafitte just as he got within a yard of the door with his victim, and at the same instant, there was a bound, and Harrington bursting into the room like a thunderbolt, dashed the slaveholder with a crash against the wall.

Roux tottered back and fell prone in a dead swoon. Pale as marble, dilated, regnant, terrible, eyes and nostrils open, Harrington stood over his prostrate body, his front turned in war upon his foe, while Muriel, brave and radiant, sprang like flame into the room by his side.

"Spawn of hell!" howled the Southerner, "you die!"

With the hoarse snarl of a tiger, he came rushing at Harrington, bowie-knife in hand. Muriel would have leaped between her lover and the weapon, but Harrington held her back with his left arm, and stood fronting his enemy with terrible and dauntless eyes, which stopped the infuriated wretch in mid-course like a rampart of swords. Lafitte was brave as a brute is brave, but the Bengal tiger will not spring against a man when his godhood is in his eyes, and arrested by the regal prowess of that bright and fearless gaze, the livid fiend stood all acrouch, the knife gleaming in his hand, his wild-beast orbs drained of their bloody fire, and his breath breaking in gasping snarls on the silence. The next instant he slunk back shivering, and stood with the knife in his nerveless grasp, conquered !

Harrington dropped his arm, which had lain like a bar across the bosom of Muriel, and advanced upon the cowering wretch before him.

" Listen !" said he, in a voice like bronze, deep, solemn and awful. " Listen to those murmurs in the street ! Hark !"

In the dead hush, there was a noise like a coming sea, pierced with shrill sounds like the distant screams of the curlew.

" Man !" thundered Harrington, " you came here to rob your fellow of all God gave him ! You dared to risk your life among these plundered and trampled poor—despoiled and outraged daily by you and such as you ! Are you ready to die ?"

Silent, amidst the ominous gathering murmurs and inarticulate shrill sounds, the slaveholder stood, with his livid, ghastly, sweat-bedabbled face turned toward Harrington's. Suddenly the surging ocean swelled and tossed in wild confusion, and sinking into a pouring rush of running feet, rose again in a savage and appalling roar.

" Hark to the coming of your doom !" cried Harrington, his voice pealing up amidst the din, and his arms uplifted like a prophet of ruin. " Hark to the hoarse blood-roar ! Hark to the roar of St. Domingo ! They come, the people you have trodden upon, they come to tear you limb from limb ! In five minutes your head will roll in that street—your body be trampled into bloody mire !"

" My God !" shrieked the trembling wretch, " am I to die here like a rat ! Let me go—let me fight my way through the hounds !"

Brandishing the knife, he rushed with forlorn bravery for the door.

" Back !" thundered Harrington. " That way leads to certain death !"

He sprang upon him as he spoke, wrested the knife from his hand, and hurling it across the room, flung him back to the wall. The wretched man covered his face with his hands!

"They come! they are here!" cried Harrington.

He sprang to the open door, and stood on the threshold, while amidst a tumbling sea of shouts and yells, came a tumultuous rush of feet on the wooden stairs.

"Save me, save me," wailed the miserable creature, rushing forward, and flinging himself on his knees with clasped hands at the feet of Muriel.

"Up, up," she cried, "quick, quick, and stay here."

She dragged him up on his feet as she spoke, and hurrying him into the inner room, closed the door upon him, and flew with the courage of an angel to the side of Harrington, just as the dense and raving mob of negroes poured headlong into the passage-way.

He stood on the threshold, resolute and tranquil, knowing well that his own life was in imminent danger at that moment, as well as the slaveholder's. Muriel stood by him, as calm and brave in that terrible crisis as he. Arrested in their fury by these strong, still presences, the sullen-browed and heavy-lipped grotesque throng hung lowering and swaying for the rush of the next instant. In their front stood the tall and muscular form of Elkanah Brown, with his knife in his hand.

"Mr. Brown," said Harrington, with magnetic dignity, "come here."

The stalwart negro stepped forward, with a face of fearful fierceness, amidst a deep hush in front, while shouts and murmurs still rose behind.

"Mr. Brown," said Harrington, in the same tone, "I want to speak with you a moment in this room, and I want you to ask our friends to remain where they are till you come out to them."

The negro hesitated for a moment, fiercely glaring at Harrington. Then, his glance falling on the sweet and solemn face of Muriel, grew gentler; and slowly turning, with a limber-hipped, insouciant movement, he waved his hand to his fellows.

"Just wait here till I come out," he said with a commanding air ; then turning again, he entered the room, amidst a wild swarming of voices, and Harrington, closing the door, bolted it and faced him.

"Is William Roux dead ?" asked Brown, glancing gloomily at the prostrate body.

"No, he is unharmed—he has only fainted," said Harrington.

"Where's that soul-driving hound of a kidnapper ?" roared the negro, gnashing his teeth, and rolling his fierce and torrid eyes around the room. "The boy said he was in here. Where've you hid him ? Let me at him, till I cut his heart out !"

"Listen to me, Brown," said Harrington, in a solemn and majestic voice, fronting the roused passion of the negro with his soul divinely splendid in his eyes. "You are a brave man and the son of the brave. Your father fought in the black corps with Jackson, at New Orleans. Face to face with the foe, in honorable war. You yourself, walked from slavery in Louisiana to freedom in Massachusetts, knife in hand, through a land of enemies. You slew the hounds that followed you. You struck dead the armed hunters that opposed you. Man to man, in honorable war, with the odds against you, you proved yourself a brave man. Is it for you to stain the bravery of your manhood now, with the blood of a murder ?"

Half-subdued by the electric majesty of Harrington's bearing, for the speech had poured from him as by inspiration, and he stood masterful and dauntless, the centre of magnetic forces such as darted from Rienzi to quell the tempest fury of old Rome ; gratified, too, by the just tribute to his prowess which the young man had paid him, and with his nobler nature dimly rising through the black and bloody seethe of vengeance, the negro remained for a moment in silence, with an irresolute and startled air, while the shouts and murmurs swelled and tossed like a rising sea of sound around the dwelling.

"Murder, Mr. Harrington ?" he faltered.

"Yes, murder," replied Harrington. "This base wretch lies here, helpless and at your mercy. To kill him, and you a thousand to one, is murder. You who never slew a man save in fair fight, will you slaughter him and the helpless in your hands ? Think ! When this hour of passion is over, will you feel proud that this miserable wretch was butchered by you in his helplessness? Think!"

The negro stood glaring at Harrington with parted lips, and sombre and torrid eyes.

"He took the risk himself!" he answered sullenly, with mounting rage. "The soul-driving hound dared to come here where we live, and try to drag off one of us. What right has he to mercy? Look at that man there, scared into a dead faint! He did it"——

"He did worse!" cried Harrington, with stern energy: "he enslaved a hundred of your people! He heaped on them every wrong and outrage worse than death. They were in his power, and he never spared them. Now the power is yours. How will you use it? As basely as he did? Will you degrade yourself by following his example? Will you lower yourself to the level of a brute that has not manhood enough for mercy?"

The negro stood touched, but irresolute. Harrington saw that the crisis had come, and that a feather either way would turn the scale. A desperate inspiration came to him, and with a bound he tore open the door of the inner room, and dragged Lafitte front to front with the negro.

"Look at him!" he cried. "Helpless, miserable, merciless wretch, I cast him on your mercy! Show him what it is to be a man. Teach him the lesson that he never learned—how the brave can spare; and let him crawl home with the shame upon him that he owes his life to the compassion of the people he would destroy!"

The words swept from Harrington's lips like a storm. An awful moment of silence succeeded, disturbed only by the roaring clamor of voices that surged around the dwelling. In that moment, the slaveholder, believing that his hour had come, stood crouching and ahunch, stupefied with terror, his hands clasped, his dead eyes staring on the visage of the negro, his hair bedrenched and limp around his livid, sweat-bedabbled face, his dark moustache hanging dank above his fallen jaw, his breath coming and going in short, thick gasps, and his whole frame shaken like an aspen. Muriel, calm, but still and pallid as a statue, stood gazing on him with a white sparkle in her ashen eyes. The negro, dilated to his full height, like a man in the presence of a wild beast, glared upon him for an instant with a look of frightful ferocity, and then his expression changing to contemptuous pity, he burst into a short, scornful guffaw.

"You damned soul-driving tyrant," he bellowed at him, "I could split your heart with this knife if you wasn't too mis'ably mean for me to look at."

And with this address, and another short, scornful guffaw, he turned away, snorting with contempt, and sheathed his bowie-knife under his waistcoat.

Muriel started from her stillness, and with something of her usual frank and cordial air, advanced and held out her hand to him. The negro, suddenly disturbed, as though just conscious of her presence, took the offered hand, half ashamedly, and bowed low.

"Excuse my language, Miss Eastman," he said, "but I kind o' forgot you were in here. Now, Mr. Harrington," he said, hurriedly turning from her with a look of trouble, "I don't know how we'll get this curse out of here. I'm afeard the folks 'll fly at him when they see him. The women folks 'll be the worst to manage. Hold on there!" he shouted, going to the door, which was straining with the outside pressure, and resounding with kicks and blows, "I'll be out in a minute. The women folks, you see," he resumed, "they'll have red pepper to throw, just as like as not. It'll be skittish business, I tell you."

Harrington lifted Roux, who was recovering from his swoon, from the floor, carried him into the other room, laid him on the bed, and returned.

"Listen, Brown," he said, quickly. "It's a hard matter, but you must use all your influence to keep the people still. Unless you can persuade them to disperse, there's only one thing to be done. You and I must take him between us, and go through the crowd."

Lafitte seemed to catch what was going on, and abjectly slinking near Harrington, gasped out that he had a carriage waiting for him round the corner, if they could only get him to that. Harrington instantly communicated this information to Brown.

"Mr. Brown," said Muriel, "suppose you let in twenty or thirty of the men outside for a body-guard. Then we can take him in the centre. How will that do?"

"That's a good idea," replied Brown. "Mr. Harrington, come and help me to stand the rush."

He moved to the door accompanied by Harrington.

"Hallo, there!" roared Brown. "Stand back. I'm going to open the door."

There was a sudden retrograde rush, with a swarming clamor of voices, and sliding back the bolt, Brown flung the door open, and with Harrington by his side, sprang upon the threshold.

"Back, now!" he shouted. "See here, I want some of you in here. Come in as I call you. The rest wait."

With his eye roving over the crowd, he called about thirty names in succession, the men passing in between him and Harrington, as they were summoned. Toward the end of the roll-call, Tugmutton appeared, and darted into the room between the legs of Harrington, who tried to stop him.

"Now, then, gentlemen," said Brown, in his grandiose way, addressing the gaping crowd of negroes and mulattoes outside, "you wait there, and we'll be out soon."

With that, he and Harrington withdrew, bolting the door again. The first thing Harrington saw, was the infuriated Tugmutton lightly prancing around the wincing and crouching slaveholder, and punching and butting him without mercy, and in perfect silence. Nothing could have more completely indicated Lafitte's utter prostration of spirit than his submission to the pummelling he was receiving. Muriel was in the inner room, bending over Roux, and the body of negroes, all grinning, were the only witnesses, besides Harrington and Brown, of this extraordinary transaction.

"Hallo there, Charles!" cried Harrington, "stop that!"

Tugmutton, who had just lifted his short, knurly leg for a kick, which would have been like the kick of a Shetland pony, let his foot fall, and stood, his broad limbs all dispread, and his blobber-cheeks puffed out with rage under his shocks of wool. Harrington's eye was on him, or he would have given the enemy of his race a parting thump of one sort or another; but as it was, he slunk off in the sulks to the adjoining room.

"See here, gentlemen," said Brown, addressing the motley group of negroes, who now stood fierce and open-mouthed, rolling their eyes upon the slaveholder, "I've got something to say to you. There's a lady here, and what you've got to do is to behave like gentlemen."

There was instantly great confusion of elaborate ducking and bowing to the lady, Muriel having come from the inner room as Brown spoke. She acknowledged their grotesque and extravagant politeness by smiling and curtseying, which set them all going again with the added grace of much good-natured grinning, and some spruce strutting on the part of the younger men, especially the mulattoes. One could not help noticing, as part of the general effect, the contrast between this facile affability and anxious desire to please, and the uncouth and outlandish figures of these courtiers, every one of whom had something singular and nondescript about his apparel or bearing.

"Now gentlemen," pursued Brown, after an embarrassed pause, in which he kept moving his hand over his mouth as one in doubt what to say next, "the reason I've asked you in here is because I've most especial confidence in you. Fact is, gentlemen, we shall all get into trouble and have the police down on us, unless we get that man there off safe. That's got to be done, gentlemen, and you've got to do it. What you've got to do, gentlemen, is to form in a hollow square, and put him in the middle of you, and walk him off handsome, to a carriage round the corner."

They all stood staring open-mouthed with eyes revolving wildly at the speaker. Lafitte, coming to his senses again, was in an agony of apprehension, while both Muriel and Harrington stood with throbbing hearts.

"Deacon Massey," said Brown with some pomposity of

manner, "what's your opinion as to whether this thing can be done?"

Deacon Massey, an elderly colored man of pragmatical aspect, with two bunches of white wool protruding from under an old cap which he wore on the back of his head, and with a general flavor of antiquity in his shabby garments, instantly assumed an air of the profoundest deliberation.

"It my 'pinion, Brother Brown," he said, with a very important air, after a long pause, "that this thing can be done if these yer brethren 'll put their trust in the Lord and stick together."

There was an instant burst of declarations from the entire group that they would trust the Lord and stick together, and do the thing in first rate style.

"All right, gentlemen," said Brown. "Now form."

Amidst much bustle, Harrington directing, and Brown hustling them into place, a hollow square was formed in the centre of the room.

"I will take Mr. Lafitte by one arm," said Muriel, "and you Mr. Brown, will take the other. Mr. Harrington will follow behind."

Harrington looked grave. "You run great danger, Muriel?" he murmured. "I think you'd better stay here."

"No," whispered Muriel, "with a woman on his arm, his risk will be lessened. We must omit nothing that will protect him. Don't fear for me. I'm not afraid."

"Miss Eastman," said Brown, approaching with a bow, "you're the bravest lady I've ever seen by long odds. You can't be beat, Miss Eastman."

"Thank you, Mr. Brown," she said with a curtsey, almost gay. "Now, sir," she added gravely, turning to the shuddering Lafitte, "collect yourself, keep your head down, and don't look around you."

She picked his hat up from the floor, and put it on him. He tried to bow with something of his usual courtesy, but was too much agitated to do so. Taking him firmly by the left arm, she led him into the centre of the square, which closed around them with locked arms. The awful moment was approaching.

"Now, gentlemen," said Brown, firmly, "mind you stick together. Don't march till I give the word."

He went to the door and unbolting it, threw it open.

"Gentlemen," he roared, in a tremendous voice, "this affair is settled. We're going to escort this man away from the neighborhood. Fall back, all of you, and clear the way."

He advanced upon them with waving arms.

There was an instant's hesitation, and then, with a sudden movement, they receded tumultuously, and poured down the wooden steps amidst a chorus of shouts and cries, which was taken up below, and swelled into a ponderous uproar.

Returning hastily to the room, Brown entered the hollow square, and grasped Lafitte by the right arm. Harrington followed him and took his place behind, and the square closed.

"Forward, march!"

As the words burst from the mouth of the negro, they marched from the room, only breaking their order to get through the doorways. The moment they appeared on the steps, the whole wild, tossing, sunlit multitude sent up an appalling and tremendous howling roar. Lafitte almost fainted, but encouraged by Muriel, he rallied, and keeping his head on his breast, without looking at the crowd, he was got down the steps, and the next instant the little phalanx, joining together with locked arms, plunged into the living sea, which closed around them amidst an awful din.

They turned up the sidewalk, stepping quickly, with the mob parting before them, and following on their left flank and behind them, and the tossing and roaring multitude in the middle of the street crowding them hard, and at times driving them to the wall of houses on their left. Amidst the uproarious clamor, Brown's voice pealed incessantly, calling on those before him to clear the way, and to those on his left to stand back. As Muriel had foreseen, her presence was an invaluable aid, for at the sight of the beautiful, calm lady, the foremost of the flanking multitude would crowd back upon those behind them, and driven forward again, would again crowd and struggle backward. Soon, too, the imitative faculty had its way, and the phalanx deepened by the accession of other negroes who locked arms with it, till it filled the sidewalk to the kerb-stone, which in turn opposed a slight barrier to the dense press of the multitude. But the passage through the stifling crush was still arduous, and the heat and foul odors made it more so. Awful, too, were the howls and cries and imprecations which greeted every glimpse of the Southerner. At that moment, Lafitte would have willingly given everything he was worth in the world to be out of the danger which menaced him.

The height of the ordeal was when they reached Grove street, where they had to cross to the carriage, with the multitude on each side of them. It was but a short distance, but the phalanx, struggling and swaying in the dense and roaring press, had to literally tear its way through. There was already hustling and pushing, with angry words flying, and Harrington saw that presently it would come to blows, when all would be lost. Bending forward, he shouted in Brown's ear to take the lead and endeavor to clear the way. The negro instantly dropped Lafitte's arm, which Harrington seized, and gaining the van of the phalanx, he burst upon the crowd with all the strength of his body and the thunder of his voice. They surged back for an instant, leaving a clear space in front.

"Quick step! forward!" pealed the trumpet tones of Harrington.

The phalanx made a desperate rush, Brown flying in the van, and in an instant the carriage was gained. Quick as thought Lafitte was forced into it, and Harrington and Muriel sprang in beside him. The crowd poured around with a clamor of shouts and cries, and while the horses, with the frightened driver at their heads, reared and plunged, the carriage itself, seized by the crowd, began to sway as if it would be overthrown. Lafitte fainted dead away.

"Quick!" vociferated Brown to the driver. "Mount the box, and drive like mad!"

The driver scrambled to his seat, and lashed the horses, while the negro sprang inside. Away they rattled at a furious pace, with the howling multitude surging along on either side and behind them. Muriel and Harrington, flushed and bathed with perspiration, sat, with disordered dresses, holding up the inanimate form of the slaveholder, while Brown, in a reek of sweat, busied himself with beating off the hands that clutched momently at the carriage door. Along Grove street into May, and from thence up West Centre into Myrtle, the frightened horses tore like a whirlwind ; but before they reached Myrtle, the clamor was receding, and the crowd had thinned and fallen behind, unable to keep up with them, but still following in the distance.

"We're safe !" cried Harrington, joyfully.

"Faith, yes," returned Muriel, gaily, her golden eyes glowing in the faint pink flush of her face, "but it was warm work while it lasted."

CHAPTER XX.

EXPLANATIONS.

For a few moments they all were silent.

"Mr. Brown," said Muriel, breaking the pause, "we owe you the most cordial thanks. You have saved this man's life."

"I'm afeard, Miss Eastman, that his life's not worth saving," returned the negro, in an exhausted voice, wiping away, with his shirt-sleeve, as he spoke, the streaming moisture which shone on his swart visage. "He's in a fit, aint he, Mr. Harrington ?" he added, glancing at the slaveholder, who sat, flaccid and inanimate, between the young man and Muriel.

"No, he has only fainted," replied Harrington. "We must revive him."

He removed the Southerner's hat, took off his neckcloth, and opened his shirt, to give him air, while Muriel busied herself with fanning him, using his hat for that purpose. She had dropped her fan and parasol on the steps at the time when Tugmutton had screamed to them what was going on in Roux's room.

"I should just like to know the rights of this matter, Mr. Harrington," said Brown, "for I've got no clar understandin' of it, any way. The fust thing I knew, I heerd a hollerin' in the street, and I caught a sight of that boy of Roux's tearin' like mad from house to house, bawlin' somethin' or other, and the folks comin' out and runnin' in all sorts of ways, shoutin', till the street filled with 'em. I stood a minute, and then I run down to Tug. 'Hullo, you young devil,' says I, 'what's to pay.' 'There's a kidnapper luggin' off father,' he bawls, and off he goes like a shot, hollerin' that into the houses, and dodgin' about like a Ingy rubber ball. I sung out, 'come on, men,' and I put for Roux's, knife in hand, lickedy split. That's all I know."

"Well, I hardly know more myself," replied Harrington. "Miss Eastman and I were going up to see Roux. We met the boy, who ran up the steps before us, and as we were ascending, he came flying back screaming that there was a kidnapper in there carrying off his father, and vanished past us. I didn't know what to make of it, but I rushed up and in, and sure enough there was this person, whom I had seen last night at the Convention, grasping Roux's arm, and leading him to the door. I flew at him, and dashed him to the wall. Then came the noise in the street, and the people poured into the house."

"Who is this man anyway?" said the negro.

"He is named Lafitte, and he was formerly Roux's master," replied Harrington.

The negro threw back his head, and laughed, showing his splendid teeth and pink gums.

"Well, if this don't beat all!" he exclaimed. "You don't mean to tell me that he thought he could carry off Roux alone right out of the midst of us? Why, the man's crazy!"

"Well, it looks insane enough," said Harrington, "and what put such a foolhardy idea into his head, I can't imagine. And yet, Brown, reckless and crazy as this attempt seems, do you know that I think it would have been successful? You should have seen Roux. The man was perfectly helpless with fright. He looked fascinated, like a bird in the jaws of a snake. I verily believe that he would have walked without the slightest resistance to the carriage, and have been taken back into slavery without our ever knowing what had become of him."

"I swear," cried Brown, "I didn't think Bill Roux was such a coward."

"Coward? I don't think he is," returned Harrington. "Just think of the awful and unexpected shock it must have been to suddenly find this man in the room with him!"

Lafitte, at this moment, showed signs of returning consciousness, and the conversation ceased. The carriage, having arrived at Mount Vernon street, was now going at a more moderate pace, the crowd having, in the various turns it had made, lost the track of it. If it had been going on a straight road, those negroes would have followed it till they dropped down.

Shuddering, as he returned to life, the ghastly Southerner, so unlike the smiling and sardonic gentleman of an hour before, looked around him, and his glance falling upon Brown, he cowered.

"You are in safety, sir," said Muriel, gently.

He smiled, or tried to smile, sicklily, and his lips moved in the endeavor to speak, but no sound came from them.

"Where shall we take you, Mr. Lafitte?" said Harrington, after a pause.

After two or three ineffectual efforts, Lafitte contrived to whisper that he was stopping at the Tremont House. Harrington gave the order to the driver, and in a few minutes they arrived at the hotel. By that time Lafitte had recovered, and Harrington assisted him to button up his shirt and vest, resume his neckcloth, and get himself into something like decent trim.

Leaning on Harrington's arm, he got from the carriage, and stood, weak and ghastly, on the sidewalk. The flurried driver, pointing to his horses, which stood reeking, and covered with froth and pasty foam, remarked that "if them animals ain't blown, it's nobody's fault—that's all." Mr. Lafitte gave him a handful of gold and silver, and appeased, he retired with profuse thanks.

"And now, look here," said Brown, fronting the slave-holder. "I don't want to say nothin' ugly to a man in your state, but I'll give you my advice. You've had a taste of Southac street to-day, and if you ain't dead, it's just because this gentleman begged your life of me. You just leave this city now as quick as convenient, for if any of our folks fall afoul of you, you'll get knifed as sure as you're born. That's my advice to you. Just you follow it, and bear in mind that you can't carry on here as you do way down in Louzeana."

"That is good advice, Mr. Lafitte," said Harrington, "and Mr. Brown here means well by you in giving it. After what has passed, you must not remain in Boston."

Harrington spoke with ominous earnestness, and Mr. Lafitte was evidently impressed by him. He stood, looking weak and sick, while these remarks were made to him, with his eyes cast down.

"I'll go," he faltered, "I certainly will. I am indebted to you, Mr. Harrington, for your protection—much indebted, sir. And to this lady also."

"You are far more indebted to Mr. Brown," said Muriel. "Without his friendly aid, we could have done nothing for you."

Mr. Lafitte was silent. Even in his humiliation, his rank and insolent Southern arrogance would not suffer him to make any acknowledgments to a negro, though it was a negro who had preserved him.

"Mr. Harrington," he said after a pause, "I drew my knife on you to-day, and you made a generous return for the injury I tried to do you. Indeed, sir, I am aware that you saved my life."

Harrington's blue eyes flashed fire, and his nostrils lifted.

"Listen to me, sir," he said, with stern solemnity. "The life you live is not human. Nothing is human that forgets the kindness man owes to man. To-day I have helped to save you, for I do not hate you, and I wish you no harm; but understand that a life like yours has small claims on my heart, and I call it love and mercy to kill you when you attack the weak and poor. Go now from this city, and never come here again to lay your hand on one man in it. I do not seek your life; I would guard it if I could; but while I am tender of you personally, I bid you remember that the issues between tyrants and freemen are the broad issues of life and death. Once I have saved you—twice I will not. Go in peace—but come here again on such an errand, and I will slay you with my own hand, for, by the Eternal God, never while I live, shall you nor any one make Boston a hunting-ground for men!"

Lafitte, with his ghastly visage bowed, shook like a leaf while Harrington, with a white face and flaming eyes, and with stern determination in every tone, uttered an admonition which rose to the dignity of the great issue between Liberty and Slavery.

"I regret to say this to you in your present condition," said the young man, after a pause, "but it is necessary that you should hear it, and understand it well. Now I will help you in."

Leaving Muriel on the sidewalk for a minute, he gravely assisted Lafitte up the steps of the hotel, and left him.

"Now, dear fellow-soldier," he said, returning, "we must go back and carry off Roux."

"Decidedly, yes," replied Muriel, taking his arm, "for when the wolf gets well, he may have a hankering for the lamb. Come with us, Mr. Brown."

They took another carriage which was standing there, and drove back to Southac street.

It may be said here, that Harrington had left Antony, soundly sleeping, in the care of Captain Fisher, who sat with the door bolted, and the pistol by him, keeping watch and ward, while the young man fulfilled his appointment with Muriel. Arriving an hour earlier than that assigned, Harington had astonished her and her mother with the wild tale of his nocturnal adventure. That the brother of Roux should have arrived in Boston at this juncture, and that the young man, of all persons on earth, should have come upon him, were coincidences almost too marvellous for conception, and the two ladies dwelt upon them with speechless wonder.

Not less marvellous to Harrington and Muriel, was their fortunate arrival at Roux's house in the critical moment of his dreadful peril. Three minutes later, and the negro would have been a lost man.

Reaching Southac street again, they found Roux weak and haggard with the terrible shock he had received. He was sitting in a chair near the stove as they entered. Tugmutton was frying potatoes in a spider, accompanying his operations with sage reflections on the recent incident, mingled with lofty reproofs to Roux for not having "squashed in," as he phrased it, the head of the slaveholder, together with pompous comments on his own promptness and courage in having first roused the neighborhood, and then assaulted the kidnapper. On this last feat, the fat squab dwelt proudly, as the crown of the whole transaction, and Roux meekly listening, with great admiration, looked upon Tugmutton as more than ever a superior being.

Tugmutton, a little apprehensive lest Harrington should not take the same view of the crowning feat, fried the potatoes in discreet silence, while he and Muriel questioned Roux. It appeared that Roux's wife and the children had been invited to remain a week in Cambridge, at the house of the brother-in-law, who was a well-to-do colored man, Roux himself having come into town, with Tugmutton, to attend to his business. It was at once decided that Roux should take up his abode for the present at Temple street, and that Harrington should write to his family, stating where he was, and the reason for this step. Tugmutton, who was to keep his father company, was to be dispatched with the letter.

This settled, the fire was slaked, and locking the door behind them, they all descended to the carriage. Tugmutton, having objected to so speedy a departure, on the ground that the fried potatoes would be sacrificed, which he regarded as a serious breach of the domestic economy of the establishment, had been prevailed upon to compromise the matter by bestowing those edibles, together with the remnant of the meat and whatever bread there was in the house, on big Ophelia and her elvish husband in the room opposite. "You know,

Charles," Muriel had gaily observed to him, "that these are the days of the Compromise Measures, and you must be in fashion." Touched by this appeal to his statesmanship, the fat Puck had made the donation with the air of one giving away a million of money, and the donation having been graciously received, he had, by way of prudence, loftily added a bouncing fib, to the effect that he and Roux were going out to stay some time at his uncle's country-seat in Cambridge.

Two or three policemen had arrived in Southac street, just after the exit of the Southerner. They had prudently abstained from interfering with the excited crowd ; but the crowd had dispersed, and few of their number remained in the street as the carriage came for Roux and drove away again.

Arrived at Temple street, Roux was installed in an upper chamber ; books and pictures were left him to while away his days of imprisonment, and Harrington and Muriel withdrew to the library, to consult with Mrs. Eastman as to what was to be done with Antony.

It was finally decided that the news of his brother's arrival should be broken to Roux the next morning, and then, that Antony, too, should be conveyed to the house and shut up with Roux. It was also resolved that all of them should take up their future abiding place in Worcester, as soon as it should be judged safe to remove them ; for, with such a man as Lafitte alive, they could no more go at large in safety in Boston, at that period, than Italian patriots could in Naples, among the sbirri of Bomba.

The council over, Mrs. Eastman retired to send up some dinner to Roux, and Harrington, meanwhile, dashed off the letter for Tugmutton to carry to Cambridge.

"Good !" said Muriel, reading what he had written. Harrington rose.

"I must leave you," said he, taking up his hat.

"Oh, but stay and dine with us," she pleaded.

"Indeed, I can't," he replied. "I must go and relieve the Captain, who is watching over Antony, and wondering what has become of me."

"True," she answered. "And I must go make my toilette,

for I am in a state. But, John, when shall I see you again? You know we have this matter of Emily and Wentworth to look into."

"I declare I forgot it. This business quite drove it from my mind," exclaimed Harrington, quickly. "What have you heard?"

"Not a word," she answered. "Emily appeared at breakfast with the story of a sleepless night in her poor lack-lustre eyes. I said nothing, for I had no chance, and since then she has kept herself locked up in her chamber. There is something passing strange in this. Have you seen Wentworth?"

"No, Muriel. It is the first day I have not seen him for I know not how long. I should have gone in search of him to get at the bottom of this matter, but for my strange adventure last night. And Emily—I declare I must see Emily, for I have something to say to her."

"About this, John?"

"No." Harrington colored. "About something else."

Muriel smiled faintly, thinking this the desire of a lover's heart.

"Well, John," she said, "let me tell her you are here."

Harrington hesitated, thinking whether he ought to keep the Captain on duty longer. On the other hand, he felt the need of an immediate understanding with Emily. With this mingled a sense of how painful and embarrassing an interview it would be. Would this time be well chosen for it, when Emily was already in sorrow? No. He concluded that he must wait.

Muriel, while he deliberated, had moved slowly to the door, awaiting his decision, and seeing that he seemed unable to make up his mind, resolved to decide for him.

"I'll call her," she said, vanishing from the room, just as Harrington had made his conclusion.

Harrington sprang forward to stop her, stumbled over a stool, and nearly fell, and when he reached the entry Muriel was not to be seen.

"Good!" he muttered, with some chagrin. "It seems the Fates have decided that the explanation is to ensue now."

He threw down his hat, and tried to think what he should say. As usual in such cases he could think of nothing.

"A pretty plight I'm in to see anybody," he muttered, glancing at his dust-covered garments, and conscious that a bath would improve him.

Suddenly, long before he had expected her, the door opened, and Emily, pale as marble, with her eyes swollen with weeping, came into the library with a movement so unlike in its rapidity, her usual sumptuous and slow stateliness, that Harrington was startled. She came straight up to him with outstretched hands, her lips parted, the tears flowing from her eyes, and so agonized and desperate a look on her face, that it shocked him.

"John," she gasped, seizing his hands convulsively, "hear me! Muriel told me you wanted to see me, but it is I that want to see you—to talk with you—to ask your compassion and forgiveness."

"Emily!—what!—forgiveness!—my forgiveness!"——

She broke in upon his stammered words, wildly, almost fiercely.

"Hush? do not speak! Let me speak," she cried. "Let me atone for my baseness to you by my self-degradation—my confession—my repentance"—

"Emily—Emily—silence!" cried Harrington, shocked beyond expression! "I cannot hear you speak of yourself so. Baseness? In you? Never! All the world would not make me believe it—you yourself"——

"John! hear me! hear me!" she wailed, her face agonized, and the wild tears streaming—"hear me, I implore you! I have deceived you. I have beguiled you. I have misled you —I have made you think I love you"——

"No, Emily, you have not. You have won my affection, but it is the affection of a brother who will be a brother to you forever. You have made me think you love me, but with the love of a friend and sister. No more."

She dropped his hands, and receding a pace, looked at him with a hushed face, on which the tears lay wet, but ceased to flow. The solemn and fond avowal sank like dew on the burning passion of her brain. For a full minute she looked at him.

"Harrington!" she said slowly, in a deep still voice from which the tremor had gone. "Is it possible! Can this be so! My whole attitude to you—my court to you—my words, my looks, my actions—all that misled others—that made them think I loved you—that deceived them utterly."

"They never deceived me, Emily. I looked upon them only as the tokens of your friendship, of your sisterly regard. No more."

She gazed at him in wondering awe. Suddenly a wild light broke upon her face, and she clasped her hands.

"Oh, man without vanity!" she passionately cried, "simple, honorable heart—nature unspotted by the world, and knowing nothing base—how am I worthy to live in your presence! The arts that would have flattered the self-love of the moths that flutter round me, were powerless on you, and untempted, unelated, unsuspecting, you took my treacherous homage as only the token of the love of a sister and a friend!"

The words trembled away in a rapture of fervor. Ceasing, her head sank upon her bosom, and her face was wet with a solemn rain of tears. Moved beyond speech, and sadly understanding all, Harrington stood with his flushed face mute, a sweet thrill melting through his frame, and his eyes were dim.

"It is over," she sorrowfully faltered. "The worst is over. There is more to be said—much more, but I cannot say it now. Not now—not now."

She stood in deep dejection, her head bowed, her hands clasped and drooping, and her eyelids almost closed.

"I am very humble," she slowly murmured, in a voice like the dropping of tears. "I stand in the Valley of Humiliation, and the Valley of the Shadow, lies before me. Alone, I enter it—forsaken—alone."

He heard the words, mournful as the sound of a funeral bell, and he strove to speak, but could not shape his lips to language that did not seem to profane the sanctity of her sorrow. Silently he held out his arms to her.

"O my brother !" She glided near, and laid her head upon his breast, and her voice was weak and low. "Let me rest here a little. Do not speak to me. I am very weary. Let me rest here a little while—let me dream of my childhood—of the old sweet days that are gone—a little while before I go."

He had put his arms silently and tenderly around her, and she leaned upon his breast with closed eyes, pale and still. No sound broke the hush. A sad peace filled the air, and the slow minutes ebbed away.

"Where am I ?" she raised her head slightly, then let it sink again upon his bosom. "I am here—still here. I was gliding away—away. It was very comforting and sweet. I am better now. I think I must have slept a little. I feel so refreshed and light. Thank you, my brother, for this rest and strength. Now I must go. Kiss me, Harrington."

She turned her pale mouth up to his as she whispered the words. Vaguely surprised at the strangeness of her request, and deeply touched by its dreamful and childlike innocence, he bent his head and kissed her. Her lips were not fevered, but cool and dewy, like the lips of a child. Wondering at this, he was about to unclasp his arms to release her, when her eyes closed and her head sank again upon his breast. Holding her so, with his gaze turned far away to the blue sky beyond the windows of the room, he heard her breathe gently, and looking at her face, he saw that a light dew had started out upon it, and that she was asleep. He knew at once that this strange sleep was magnetic, and that its blessed rain of healing would fall deep and long on the arid trouble of her brain. Grateful that so sweet an influence had been shed upon her through him, he held her for a few moments, and then gently lifting her in his arms, he laid her on a couch. The sumptuous pride and passion of her womanhood seemed to have fallen from her, and pale, with her long dark eyelash sleeping on her cheek, she lay in thrilling and exquisite marble beauty, slumbering with the restful innocence of childhood.

He was about to ring and ask for Mrs. Eastman; then reflecting that she might be in the parlor, he chose rather to go down to her on his way out from the house, but stepping on tiptoe to the door for this purpose, he saw Muriel clad in a white wrapper, just ascending to her chamber, and beckoned to her. She came instantly, all lily-fair from her bath, with her bright hair rippling back from a face serious with inquiry, and gazed with some astonishment on the reposing form of Emily. Briefly explaining to her in a whisper the nature of the sleep in which Emily lay, and advising that she should be covered, and left there to slumber undisturbed, Harrington softly quitted the room, promising to return as soon as he could, and tell Muriel more.

"But John," murmured Muriel, in the corridor, "do give me a little information about this before you go. You say she fell asleep leaning on your breast, and that nature was overcome with suffering. What was her trouble? Surely what Wentworth said to her could not have affected her so terribly."

"Muriel," said Harrington, gently, after a pause, "this is a secret, but it is one, I think, you ought to know. Briefly, then—Emily imagined that she had won my heart from me, and was stricken with generous grief to think that she had no love but a sister's to give me in return. It was easy to rectify her painful error, and I have done so."

Muriel stood gazing at him, as if she had turned to stone.

"Good-bye," said Harrington, after an awkward pause.

She slowly bent her head in reply, and stood motionless, with her lips parted in wonder, as he went down-stairs and out at the front door.

"Yes," he murmured, as he strode off down the street, "and she loves Wentworth. That is her heartbreak—that is why she paid her desperate and reckless court to me. Oh, Muriel, I would not have you know it for the world!"

CHAPTER XXI.

THE BREAKING OF THE SPELL.

Recalled to herself by the shutting of the street door, Muriel started from her trance, and flew upstairs into her chamber. Falling on her knees by her bedside, she covered her eyes with her hands, and buried her face in the coverlet, floods of dazzling light pouring upon her brain.

"I see it all!" she cried, springing to her feet, and throwing up her hands, her face radiant, and a smile breaking upon it like March splendors from the wild clouds; "I see it all now! Wentworth and she are lovers. Oh, let me not die with joy!"

Her luminous face upturned, her arms upthrown, she flew across the room, stopped suddenly, and covering her eyes with her hands, stood still, light, perfume, and victory rushing upon her soul and mantling through her veins.

"Yes, I see it all!" she cried, flinging her hands from her eyes, and clasping them before her, "they love—they love. It is a lover's quarrel. To vex Wentworth, she paid court to Harrington. It was on Richard's account that she was jealous of me. And that is why Richard was so devoted to me —yes, to vex her. And I who patronized him, that she and Harrington might be together—ah, that made Harrington think I loved Richard. I see it—I see it! That is what he meant when he asked me to tell him who my fairy prince was! Oh, noble heart, you hid your pain—you sacrificed your love —you tried to be happy in the happiness you dreamed for me! And I, who made you suffer—I, who could be so misled, as to think, even for an instant, that you loved another —Oh, blind, blind!"

Her eyes swam, and her beautiful head drooping like a

flower, she stood motionless, her fallen hands clasped before her, thinking, thinking, thinking of it all. Swiftly, as in the fairy tale at the touch of the prince's wand the tangled floss unravelled, and all the colors lay assorted, so in her musing the whole tangle of misapprehension and illusion unwound and fell into orderly and candid form.

" Ah, Richard, you scamp !" she gaily soliloquized, half to herself and half aloud, "you shall make amends for this! But you, too, must have suffered. Now what could have made them quarrel ? Let's consider. What have I ever seen Richard do to Emily ? Nothing but look cold, and glum, and piqued. All that was clearly in response to her manner. Then that ugly speech he made—but that was the finale. Stand aside, Richard, my friend. Now, Emily. What have I seen Emily do to Richard? Let me see. Why nothing either for a commencement of the trouble. My observations began in the middle of it all. Stay—there was that little affair of the violets for a sample. But that was in the middle, too. And that was due to our sweet friend Fernando. Oho !" she cried, opening her eyes with a comical air, "I have an idea ! Wait, wait, now, my little idea, till I put a pin in you! Let's see. With one subtle speech, one artful tone, one delicate lift of those expressive eyebrows, one curious non-significant, all-significant, anything-significant look, this clever Witherlee contrives to put it into my simple Emily's head to slight and wound her lover. That was a delicious proceeding, and I saw it in all its indescribable beauty. That was a sample of Fernando's method. That was one of his fine touches. Still that is but one. But suppose he has been playing this sort of game with Emily from the first? So gently, so delicately, so skillfully poisoning her mind against Wentworth. Her intimate friend—so close with her, so confidential—ah, ha ! my daughter of Eve, has the serpent been at your ear, too ! Oh, my poor Eveling, has he been putting you up to this mischief? Good ! I'll engage that we shall find Witherlee at the bottom of the whole imbroglio when all is known."

And Muriel, ineffably delighted at her own sagacity, her

nimble mind having glanced from point to point to this conclusion, threw back her charming head, and gave way to a rivulet of low, delicious laughter.

"Shame on me to laugh about it," she resumed, looking very grave. "It has cost too much suffering to laugh about. And yet," she ran on, rippling again into golden laughter, "I can't help it. I'm so happy! And it is such a pleasure to have found the track of the fox that stole the grapes! Well, Fernando! you're a nice young man! And oh, Cupid, Cupid, you weren't painted with the bandaged eyes for nothing, you rogue! But, bless me, here am I chattering to myself, and Emily to be covered, dinner nearly ready, and I not dressed."

She broke off to hasten to a bureau, from a lower drawer of which she took a grey silk coverlet to lay over Emily, and went swiftly from the room.

Emily was sleeping deeply, with a faint color in her pallid and lovely face. Bending over her, Muriel covered her with the quilt, and kissing her forehead softly as a spirit, darkened the room, and left her. Then going down to her mother, and warning her not to disturb the sleeper, she hurried up to her chamber, and finished dressing herself just as Bridget, a comely little Irish girl who waited at table when they dined alone, came up to summon her to dinner.

Charmingly attired in a robe of black silk, with an open corsage of snowy lace, and looking more radiantly fair than ever, Muriel came down to dinner, and during the meal entertained her mother with a circumstantial account of her noon adventure. The story, of course, made a sensation, as the popular phrase goes; but as far as Muriel was concerned, Mrs. Eastman listened without shuddering or chiding. She had such perfect confidence in her daughter's ability to take care of herself, and such a conviction that everything she did befitted her—for, like Shakspeare's Cleopatra, Muriel shed the artistic grace of her nature on all her actions, and compelled them to become her ornaments—that she heard the part she had played in the wild scene not only without discomposure, but with considerable pride and admiration, thinking at the same time how proud Mr. Eastman would have been of the way his child had borne herself. As he would, for his wishes for Muriel were well expressed in the noble lines of Ben Jonson, of which he was very fond :

> "I meant the day-star should not brighter ride,
> Nor shed like influence from his lucent seat :
> I meant she should be courteous, facile, sweet,
> Free from that solemn vice of greatness, pride !
> I meant each softest virtue there should meet,
> Fit in that softer bosom to abide :
> Only a learned and a manly soul
> I purposed her, that should with even powers
> The rock, the spindle, and the shears control
> Of Destiny ; and spin her own free hours.

A piquant incident occurred while they yet lingered at dessert. The chief result, perhaps, of Muriel's narration, was to lend an added blazon, in Mrs. Eastman's mind, to the character of Harrington ; and, by the way, she still firmly believed —his declaration to the contrary notwithstanding—that her daughter loved him.

"I often think," she observed, during the conversation, "how superior John is to all other men I know. The other day I met him in the street, and my first impression was of his superiority in contrast to those around him."

"Yes, that strikes one certainly," returned Muriel, with a nonchalant air.

"Ah, there is none like him, none !" said Mrs. Eastman. "I wish I had the rewarding of him."

Muriel laughed.

"Virtue is its own reward you know, mamma," she said, playfully. "But what other reward would you give him ?"

"You !" quickly said Mrs. Eastman, smiling and coloring.

Muriel looked at her with a twinkling mouth and a demure face.

"You do not mean to say, mamma," she replied, "that you would choose Harrington from the crowd of my adorers for my husband."

"Indeed," said Mrs. Eastman, with some warmth, "if I

had the choosing, Harrington should be your husband to-morrow."

Muriel now looked at her with an indescribable air of bewitching gaiety.

"To-morrow, mamma? So soon?" she said, jestingly.

Mrs. Eastman looked confused, like one who has been betrayed into saying a foolish thing, and blushing deeply, began to laugh.

"Well," she replied, with an air of raillery, "the day after to-morrow."

"The day after to-morrow," repeated Muriel, her countenance beaming with gracious fun. "Well, my dear mamma, I will reflect upon it, and if I decide to oblige you by marrying Harrington the day after to-morrow, I will let you know."

Mrs. Eastman laughed at this pleasantry, and thinking Muriel was evading the subject, said no more, but rose from the dinner-table with her. Their relation as mother and daughter also involved, as is not always the case, the relation of courteous friendship, and this was the nearest approach Mrs. Eastman had ever made to penetrate within the veil of any reservation of Muriel's.

Immediately after dinner, Muriel wrote a note to Wentworth, bidding him come to the house instantly. This she dispatched by Patrick, bidding him find the young artist, if possible, and give it into his own hand; and Patrick, who would have gone through fire and flood for his young mistress, promised to find Wentworth if he was to be found, and started off on his errand.

It was about four o'clock when Wentworth arrived. He was shown up into the studio, where Muriel was waiting for him. Pale and wan, and grave even to coldness, he was the handsome and gallant Wentworth still; a man to be loved at first sight by women and by men, even now, when a storm had blown upon his May.

He bowed coldly and constrainedly to Muriel as he entered, though he was struck by her exceeding beauty as she glided forward with her natural affable smile and curtsey to greet him. But Wentworth was sick of all the world at that moment, and affecting not to see Muriel's outstretched hand, he looked aside and reached her a chair.

"What is it you wished to see me for, Muriel?" he said, half coldly, half carelessly, drawing up another chair for himself.

"Richard?" Her voice carried a soft rebuke, though it was gentle and low. "Not glad to see me, your friend, your sister, Richard."

He kept his gaze fixed upon the floor, but his lip quivered, and the faded colors of the carpet suddenly swam. The next instant he felt her arms around him, and blind with tears, he let his forehead sink upon her shoulder.

"Forgive me, Muriel," he faltered, in a moment, lifting his face to hers, and wanly smiling through his tears. "Indeed I love you, but my heart is half broken, and I am weary of the world."

"Ah, Richard," she said, with tender gaiety, "there is a fairy prince here who mends broken hearts, and makes the world-weary glad again."

Her arms fell from him, and as they fell, he caught her hand and pressed it to his lips.

"Your magic is strong, dear fairy prince," he said, with sad playfulness, "but there are spells no magic can unbind. Come—let us speak of other things."

"Good!" said Muriel, sinking into the chair, while Wentworth also seated himself—"and since we must speak of other things, let us speak of Witherlee."

Wentworth reddened instantly.

"And he *is* a thing!" was his scornful answer. "I abhor him."

"Abhor the good Fernando!" she exclaimed, with a jesting face. "Why Richard, I am astonished at you! Abhor so talented a young gentleman!"

"Talented!" scoffed Wentworth. "What has he a talent for?"

"A talent for poisoning, dear skeptic," she replied, lightly. "A splendid talent for poisoning. No poisoner of the Middle Ages was ever more skillful."

Wentworth looked confused.

"Poisoning? What do you mean?" he murmured.

"Only those old poisoners wrought on life," she pursued, "while he, you know, works on character, minds, hearts. They could add a deadly perfume to a harmless rose. He, now, can do the same with an innocent bunch of violets."

Wentworth looked at her silently, with a strange feeling rising within him.

"Confess, Richard," she went on, "that you scented something deadly to your love after he had dropped a word over those violets!"

"I understand you," he replied, slowly, "he said something which prevented Emily from giving me the violets."

"And that wounded you sorely," she remarked.

"I confess it did," he answered. "It was a very trifling thing, to be sure, but at that time it meant a great deal, and to be frank with you, Muriel, I was hurt. No matter," he added, "there were other things for which he was not responsible, which hurt me far more. I cannot now be hurt again."

"But consider," said Muriel, quietly. "If that morning Emily had given you the flowers, the gift would have gone far to reconcile you to her. Would it not?"

"It would," cried Wentworth, vehemently. "One little act of kindness from her to me at that time, would have made me forget all her former slights, and try to win her to me again. But, Muriel, why dwell on this? It was her intention to trifle with me from the first. Come, I must not talk of her. Let it all go. It amounts to nothing."

"It amounts to just this," she replied, coolly. "That Mr. Witherlee was interested in your affairs to the extent of making fresh dissension between you and Emily, and that he widened a breach already made. Now do you imagine his interest extended no further than that moment? But, Richard, tell me frankly, how did your difference with Emily arise!"

"Muriel," he replied solemnly, "as Heaven is my witness, I do not know. I never did anything to cause it. I left her here one afternoon, and I was happy, for though I thought she loved me before, I was never sure of it till then, when we met in the first embrace, the first kiss, and the last, she ever gave me. Witherlee appeared at the parlor door, and retreated again for a minute or so. Then you came into the parlor from the conservatory, and he entered at the same moment. You will recollect that afternoon—you brought in a bunch of flowers, and as he came in you held out the bouquet to him, which he took from your hand. Do you remember?"

Muriel nodded.

"Well," continued Wentworth, "I felt a little abashed at Witherlee's entrance, for I thought he had seen us, and in fact, it was so awkward for me, that I took my leave in a few minutes."

"And that evening—I remember it well"—interrupted Muriel, "he and Emily talked together in a corner the whole time, while mother and I were busy with a roomful of guests."

"Did they!" said Wentworth, coldly, seeing nothing in the circumstance worthy of notice. "Well, Muriel," he continued, after a moment's consideration, "I called the next morning to see Emily, happy as I could be, and full of love for her, and she met me with such chilling hauteur that I was frozen. It was like an ice-bath. I felt piqued and hurt, and though I thought it only a passing freak, I could not help being cool to her. Indeed, her manner prevented anything but coolness. I thought, however, it would pass over. But the next day it was the same, and the next and the next. I am proud, Muriel, and I was innocent of any fault. Could I do less, and keep my self-respect, than remain cool to a lady who was treating me so? Meanwhile, I saw her attentions to Harrington, and I made up my mind that she had trifled with me for her amusement. So it went on, till last night when she heaped contumely on me, and I repaid her with the speech you heard. There. I did not mean to speak of this, but you have led me on. Now I am quits with her."

There was a moment's silence, and then Wentworth resumed:

"In all this, Muriel, I did, as far as she was concerned, only one wrong thing. When I saw her wooing Harrington, to show her that I could bear her injury, and to spoil her triumph, I was very attentive to you. I knew you would not mistake my assiduities for love, and I knew it would pique her. I ask your pardon. It was wrong. I did another and a greater wrong to Harrington, and I have sought him in vain to-day, to beg his forgiveness. I thought he loved Emily, and I was meanly envious and jealous of him—I was cold and reserved to him—I treated him with hauteur, which I saw he could not understand, and "——

"How did Harrington act to you when you treated him with hauteur?" interrupted Muriel, quickly.

"Like the man he is!" replied Wentworth, with impetuous fervor. "Like the nature too noble for this world! Great, grand heart, he shamed me even in my very treason to him with his unaltered kindness. He came to me frankly, unrepelled by my attitude to him, he came with a look, a word, a generous hand, and he conquered me. My envy and my jealousy arose again, and were wasted on him. I could not alienate him from me. He overlooked—he forgave all. Let me only see him again, let me ask his compassion and his pardon, and then let me go away, and hide my shame in Italy, for I am not worthy to live on the same soil with him—I am not worthy to be his friend."

Two bright tears flowed calmly down the face of Muriel, and her smile was sweet and proud for her lover.

"Ah, Richard," she said, gently, "had you treated Emily's hauteur as Harrington treated yours, you, too, might have conquered her. It was not true love to answer her slights with coldness and silence."

"Perhaps, so, Muriel," he answered with averted eyes, feeling her rebuke. "Perhaps I might. But no. It was not her nature. She meant to play upon me. No matter. Let it pass. And as for Witherlee, I hate him. Chiefly because I believe his insidious words set me against Harrington."

"Ah," said Muriel, coolly, almost carelessly, "he set you against Harrington, did he?"

"He did," replied Wentworth.

"And yet you loved Harrington," she continued, "you loved him truly. But Witherlee could set you against him."

"He could," faltered Wentworth. "I own it to my shame, but he could."

"And now, Richard," she said, gravely, "answer me this. Would Emily be more to blame for having been set against you by Witherlee, than you were to blame for having been set against Harrington by him?"

Wentworth looked at her, and colored.

"No," he faltered. "I could not blame her if her feeling against me arose from anything said by Witherlee. But what right have I to suppose that he has said anything against me?"

"Richard Wentworth," she cried, starting from her chair, and her face lit, and her voice rang clear and free, "never dare to condemn Emily till you know that this is not so. Never condemn any person on any evidence till you have given that person a hearing. Here is a man who goes about, dropping the hint, the innuendo, the shrug, the hum, the ha, the meaning look, for aught I know the downright wicked lie, all the poisons used by calumny, and while you know him to be on terms of intimacy with Emily, you venture to suppose that he is guiltless of having poisoned her mind against you. Permit me to say that you venture to suppose too much. I would not condemn even him unheard, but what we know, though it is not enough for proof, is quite enough to create a presumption. You have found him fomenting strife between you and Harrington; you know him to have widened the breach between you and Emily. These things show him no friend of yours. And between the evening of your happy parting with Emily and the morning of coldness and alienation, he spent several hours conversing with her. Ominous link, Richard! Find out what it means. Do not assume that she meant to trifle with you. I know better. I know Emily Ames better than you do, and I know that a woman more honorable and loyal in her love never breathed. Go, Richard Wentworth! imitate the magnanimity of Harrington and never let me have it to say that the manliness of your friend was more than that you showed to the woman that you love!'

Wentworth rose from his chair, his color flashing and failing, an awful sense of the justice of Muriel's speech mingling with an awful suspicion of Witherlee, and his love for Emily rushing like a torrent on his heart.

"Muriel," he faltered, "you are right. I have been rash. What shall I do? Oh, if after all I have wronged Emily—if she loves me"——

"Richard," said Muriel, solemnly, "I know she loves you. I have been blind till to-day, but now I see. No sleep came to your poor Emily's eyes last night, and all day she has been in agony. A little while ago, Harrington was here, and he has soothed her to rest. She lies now asleep in the library. Come with me, and I will leave you to sit by her. Her wakening eyes must rest first on you, and you must make your peace with her. But you must not awaken her. Promise me you will sit patiently by her till she wakes—promise!"

Wentworth pressed Muriel's hand to his lips, and lifting his blanched face, streaming with tears, to hers, faltered—

"I promise."

"Oh, my brother," she fondly said, affectionately encircling his shoulder with her arm, "all will be well with you now. Said I not that the fairy prince dwelt here? Behold, he gives you back to life and love! Come."

Smiling with her happy and noble smile into his face, she led him forth with her arm in his and downstairs to the library door.

"Remember your promise," she whispered. "Now go in."

He entered softly, softly closed the door behind him, and stood in the dim room with a beating heart. For a moment, he only saw the books in their cases, the sumptuous furniture, the glimmer of the frames upon the walls, the rich, dark color of the room. Stealing to the window, he parted the curtains to let in a little light, and turning, in the faint ray he saw on the low couch, the pale face of his beloved, with the long dark eyelash sleeping on her cheek, and her black hair fallen in a thick, soft tress along the exquisite and melancholy beauty of her countenance. Still, peaceful, void of scorn or pride, lovely and mournful in her marble repose! The tears streamed from his eyes, and gliding near her he knelt by her side, forgetting, forgiving all, and resolved, though she woke upon him in anger, with hate, with contempt, to answer her only with blessings, and love her till his pulses were still forever.

The hours passed by. The room grew dark, and going to the window, he put aside the curtains, and let in the twilight. That twilight was yet early, for the sun had but just set, and the grey light again lit the sleeping face of Emily. As he watched it, he saw the color rise to it—the sunny gold and rose, the bright carnation of the curved lips, behind which glimmered the dim pearls. With his heart wildly throbbing, he kept his eyes fixed upon her countenance. Presently, a faint smile stole upon it, and she murmured softly—"he gave me that rose." A thrill surged through him. He remembered the rose he had given her in the sunrise of their love, and knew that she was dreaming of it and of him. Gazing upon her face, he heard her faint regular breathing pause in a long respiration like a sigh; her form moved slightly under the silken coverlet, and tossing out her beautiful bare arms, they fell along her form, and she lay still. The next moment, her large and lustrous eyes unclosed slowly, and met his. She did not start, but the eyes gradually brightened, and the color rose upon her face and lips in rich suffusion. He did not move—he did not speak—he knelt beside her, gazing into her face, with his heart throbbing, and a still flush in his brain.

"It is a dream," she murmured. "A dream of my love."

He did not speak, but his arms softly stole around her, and hers enfolded him at first so lightly that he scarcely felt them. Lightly and softly at first, till suddenly with a double cry they were clasped together, and the disenchanted Fairyland of love burst and streamed in music and light and odor around them.

"Richard! Is it you?"

Holding him from her, with all her strength, her face impassioned, her eyes like stars, she gazed upon him, with her fervent cry still ringing in the twilight air.

"It is I. Forgive me, Emily. I love you."

She impetuously drew him to her, and locked in each other's arms, they were still.

The fairy prince had triumphed, and Witherlee's work was quite undone!

CHAPTER XXII.

INTERSTITIAL.

That evening, visitor after visitor called, and the parlor was full of talk and music and laughter. Amidst her company, Muriel felt a lonely longing for the face of Harrington. He sometimes dropped in late, for a little while, and this evening, as ten o'clock approached and the guests began to depart, she half-hoped he would come. But he did not, and tired with her last night's vigil, as with the fatigues of the day, she went to rest as soon as the last visitor had said good night.

The next day came bright and beautiful, and Harrington not appearing as he commonly did, Muriel went out to take her early morning walk alone. While she was out, he arrived and at once went up to the chamber where Roux was confined.

It was not more than six o'clock, but Roux was up and dressed. He sat in a chair, and Tugmutton, squatted on a stool by his side, was reading aloud to him from Uncle Tom's Cabin. Tugmutton's reading was a treat to hear. It was, when the text was at all serious, what is called at the theatres, spouting, and spouting of the most grandiloquent order, at that. Accompanied, also, by much and varied action of his big paw, and interspersed not only with explanations and comments of his own, but whenever he came to anything that particularly pleased him, with chirrups and guffaws of goblin laughter, and bobbings and waggings of his big head and blobber cheeks over the page, the effect was, to say the least of it, peculiar. On the present occasion, the fat Puck happened to have arrived at a chapter highly congenial to his special views on the Slavery Question—to wit: that wherein George Harris and his fellow runaways fight the hunters of men ; and Roux was at some trouble to detach the sense of the narrative from the luxurious overgrowth of dissertation, interpolation, exclamation, cachinnation, and general outward limbs and flourishes wherewith Tugmutton was embellishing it. Having got to the point where Phineas topples the slave-hunter down the rocks, the delighted squab leaned back and gave vent to an uproarious guffaw, and in the midst of this, while Roux, with a faint and curious smile on his simple, dark face, was listening, Harrington's knock was heard at the entrance.

Tugmutton instantly grew sober, and sat staring with his great white eyes at the door, as Roux crossed to open it.

"Good morning, Mr. Roux," said Harrington, entering, and shaking hands with him. "How are you?"

"Firs'rate, thank ye, Mr. Harrington," replied the smiling Roux, bowing humbly, and shutting the door again.

The intuitive Tugmutton, instantly gathering from Harrington's slightly distraught air, that something was the matter, remained perfectly motionless, squatting on his low stool with the book in his hands, and staring open-mouthed at him, with a look of preternatural curiosity on his fat face.

"Sit down, Roux," said Harrington, dropping into a chair without noticing the boy, and gazing absently around the room.

Roux resumed his chair, and with his hand fumbling over his mouth as was usual with him, rolled his eyes timidly about the room.

"Roux, I've got news to tell you," faltered Harrington, smiling. "Good news. What would be the best news you could hear?"

Roux smiled faintly, and still fumbling around his mouth with his hand, while his eyes continued to wander, he appeared to hesitate.

"Well, Mr. Harrington," he said, after a pause, "I ruther feel oncertain as to what to say. It would be the most uncommonest best news, if I heerd that my brother Ant'ny was to git away. But I'm afeard that's not likely, Mr. Harrington."

Roux's eyes kept wandering, and Harrington looking hard at the opposite wall, smiled furtively. The next instant both he and Roux were startled by a sudden screech of eldritch mirth, and by the apparition of Tugmutton pitching forward on his hands, and slapping over in a somerset as quick as light, coming up clean on his feet with a sober-staring face, and a low "Hoo!" They both stared at him, Harrington with a stir in his blood, for he had not seen the squab, and he was completely startled by his appearance in this astonishing gymnastic.

"Hi!" exclaimed Tugmutton, standing legs dispread, just as he had landed from his flip-flap, and pointing at Harrington with his thumb, while a jovial grin slowly spread over his fat visage. "Hi! That nigger has arroven! My gosh! Mr. Harrington, I smell a rat as if I was nothin' but nose! Hooraw! Three cheers! Likewise a horse larf! O sing you niggers, sing!" and chanting this line in a shrill voice, Tugmutton stopped to fly into a furious double-shuffle and breakdown, with his shock head bobbing like mad.

"Hallo, you, Tug, now," quavered Roux, looking frightened. "Just you ricollect where you are now, Tug, in this nice house. What's the matter with you, and what you goin' off in that way for now? I don't see what you mean by sech actions, noways."

Tugmutton stopped in his dance at the sound of Roux's voice, and with his short arms akimbo on his ribs, and his short, broad legs dispread, glared up at him with a look of supreme indignation.

"My gosh, father!" he exclaimed, "if you ain't stupid now! Why jus' you look at them liniments of Mr. Harrington!" and he pointed with his thumb at Harrington's face, which was wrinkled into an amused smile. "Now, what's there father, jus' as plain as print?"

Tugmutton ended with a snort, and ineffably disgusted at Roux's unintelligence, dumped down on his stool, and looked at Harrington. Roux meanwhile gazed at the young man with a timid and imploring expression.

"Charles is right, Mr. Roux," said Harrington, cheerfully,

while Tugmutton relapsed into a jovial grin of satisfaction, showing all his ivories, and wagging his bushy head delightedly. "But now, Mr. Roux," continued Harrington, "I want you to keep cool. The good news is that your brother is free. Don't let it overcome you. Be cool."

"I will, Mr. Harrington," stammered Roux, terribly agitated, "I will be cool. I won't let it overcome me."

"That's right—don't," replied Harrington, with an affectation of phlegm. "By the way, how is your wife? How does she bear the letter I sent her?"

"Oh, she's pretty well, Mr. Harrington, and she says she thinks I'll be safe here," said Roux, trembling all over.

Harrington led him on to talk of other subjects, diverting his mind as much as possible from the matter in hand, and in a few minutes got him tranquil again.

"Now, Mr. Roux," he said, "Antony is free as I told you, and I want you to prepare yourself to see him soon."

"Yes, Mr. Harrington, I will," said Roux with a wondering face. "Did Miss Ames buy him, Mr. Harrington?"

"Oh no," returned Harrington, "how could she when it was only a day or two since she knew of him? Antony ran away. I have him at my house."

Roux sprang to his feet, wi.d with joy,.

"Let me go to see him, Mr. Harrington," he cried.

"No," said Harrington, rising and gently pressing Roux into his chair again. "You are not safe out of this room. I will bring him here to stay with you. Keep cool, Roux, and be patient. You must expect to see Antony very thin, for he has been sick. But he will soon recover. Now I must go, and to-night when it is dark, I will bring him here. Good bye. Keep up a good heart. He will soon be with you."

"Oh, I knew it from the very fust," complacently remarked Tugmutton, taking his leg on his knee, and lolling back a little with the most indifferent air in the world, "I ain't astonished. My gosh! no, you can't astonish me. I'm above it."

"That's because you have a great mind, Charles," said Harrington, jestingly. "Now just use your talents in cheering up your father—that's a good boy."

"I'll do it, Mr. Harrington," replied the cheerful youth, jumping up to let Harrington out, with his pear-face shining gleefully. "I'll cheer him up so that nobody 'll ever know him again. Good bye, Mr. Harrington. Call again."

Nodding pleasantly, Harrington departed, while Tugmutton waved his big paw with a lofty air, like a king dismissing his prime-minister after a cabinet council, and closed the door after him.

In the passage below, Harrington met Mrs. Eastman, and mentioned that he intended to bring Antony there that evening after dark.

"Of course," he added, "there is no danger of the servants mentioning that there are colored men in the house. It would not do to have it gossiped about."

"No, indeed," returned Mrs. Eastman, smiling. "They have all, except little Bridget, been with us for years, and are like part of the family. Not the least danger of them. You know, John, we have had fugitives here several times before.

"Yes, I know that," he replied, laughing.

After a minute's further conversation, he departed, and went home to breakfast, without having asked for Emily, or seen Muriel. To tell the truth, a feeling of trepidation—a sense of some gathering mystery which made his heart tremble—had grown upon Harrington since he had left Emily the day before, and he shrank in spirit from meeting her or Muriel. He felt darkly that something of import, closely affecting him, remained undisclosed in the mutual relations of himself and his friends. The words of Wentworth—"because it has been played upon" —rang in his memory like a bell. Undoubtedly, Harrington would have unriddled the mystery almost as quickly as Muriel had done, but the blundering avowal of Wentworth that he was Muriel's betrothed, stood in the way of his sight, and baffled him.

Restless ; ill at ease ; unwilling to think upon the subject, which yet persisted in invading his mind ; and in that state of nervous incertitude, in which mysterious agitations and sudden tinglings of the blood incessantly visit the frame, it was a positive relief to Harrington to get away from himself, among the cheerful, familiar faces around the Captain's table. The family were assembled in the dining-room, which opened off the kitchen. A pleasant, old-fashioned room, looking on the street, and furnished with plain, old-fashioned, homely furniture. Curtains of white dimity to the windows ; a semi-circular stand, holding rows of flower-pots, at one of them, from which the smell of geraniums and roses was shed throughout the apartment ; the floor covered with a woven rag-carpet of soberly gay colors ; a bureau, spread with white linen at one side, with the miniature model of a ship full-rigged, upon it ; straight-backed mahogany chairs, with horsehair seats ; two rocking chairs, with white tidies on their backs ; a looking-glass between the windows, and on the opposite wall, on either side of the mantel, two portraits, fearfully bad, of the Captain and his wife. The Captain, however, regarded these works of art with complacent satisfaction, and held them as chief among his household treasures. The wandering country artist who had executed them, had represented the Captain as a dark-eyed, rosy-cheeked, staring, marine Adonis, preternaturally blooming in complexion, attired in an indigo blue coat with brass buttons, a buff waistcoat, and a frilled shirt-front, and grasping a spy-glass in one hand and a quadrant in the other. To match this artistic triumph, Mrs. Fisher appeared with sky-blue eyes, lily-white complexion, pink cheeks and lips, an azure dress with a huge broach, and a gold chain and pencil-case, on which the artist had spent his finest genius and his brightest chrome. To trace a resemblance between the portrait, and the kind, quiet, pale-eyed, colorless little woman in a gauze cap, who sat at the head of the breakfast-table, would have been more difficult than to establish a similar likeness between the other portrait and the Captain. But the Captain was happy in the belief that the portraits were gems of truth and art, and as he himself was accustomed to observe on various occasions, putting it as a profoundly philosophical conclusion, "What's the odds, so as you're happy!"

A chorus of greetings welcomed Harrington, as he came in and took his seat at the breakfast table.

"We began to think you warn't comin', John," remarked Mrs. Fisher, pouring out his coffee.

"I hurried home as quick as I could, Hannah," replied the young man. "Well, Sophy, you look as bright as gold this morning. The jewellers would put you in a box of pink cotton."

Sophronia, a plump and pretty little miss, with blue eyes, a charming little snub nose, and a dimple in her chin, smiled coquettishly at this compliment, and glanced at the smiling face of the speaker.

"My!" she exclaimed, saucily, "how smart you are, John! I wish I could say such pretty things to you."

"Well, try," jested Harrington. "Compliment me on this beard which you admire so much."

"Beard indeed!" said Sophy, tossing her head, with a playful pout of her ripe cherry lips, "I don't admire it at all. The girls ought to set their faces against it."

"Maybe they do, Sophy," returned Harrington, with sly significance.

Sophy was caught, and tossed her head, coloring and smiling, while the Captain, with his mouth full of bread and butter, burst into a roar of laughter, in which Mrs. Fisher, John H., and Joel James joined, the latter beating the table with the haft of his knife.

"That's all very well for you to say," said Sophy, with another fling of her head, and pout of her lip.

"And that's all very well for the girls to do," bantered Harrington, whereat the merriment burst forth again.

"Gracious! There's no use in me talking. You're as smart as a steel trap, John," she answered.

Joel James, a bluff and burly rosy-cheeked boy, with his father's features and his mother's blue eyes, interrupted this play of repartee, to say, with his mouth full of breakfast, that his kite wouldn't fly nohow.

"She pitches about like as if she was crazy, John," he grumbled, munching between the words.

"That's because she hasn't bob enough. We'll fix that,"

returned Harrington, as much interested in the boy's grievance as if it was an affair of State.

"And I can't make my peg-top spin, John," complained John H., looking dolefully at Harrington with his soft black eyes and chubby countenance.

"Can't? Well, after breakfast I'll show you how," said Harrington, good-naturedly. "The kite shall fly and the top shall spin, as sure as the world goes round. By the way, Eldad, how's our friend out yonder? I haven't seen him this morning."

The Captain glanced out at the open window looking into the yard, before replying.

"He's up, eating his breakfast," he answered. "I've locked your door, and the garden gate too, and here's the keys," he added, pointing to them by the side of his plate.

"Poor forsaken critter!" murmured Hannah compassionately. "It just made my heart ache to see him when I went up there yesterday. He looked so awful lean and sick."

"He looks a great deal better this mornin'," remarked the Captain. The sleep's done him a heap of good. It's astonishin' how much those colored folks can bear. You wunt know that chap in about a week, he'll have fatted up so. I've dressed him out, John, in some of my old clothes, and made him look quite decent."

"That's right, Eldad," said Harrington. "I'll make it up to you."

The Captain laid down his knife, and with his head all askew, looked at Harrington.

"You'll make it up to me, John?" he remarked, blandly, with a great disposition to swear. "By the spoon of horn, I'd like to catch you at it! The best suit of clothes I've got in the house wouldn't be too good for a man that's gone through what he has—leastways, if they was fit for him, which they ain't; and I'm not goin' to be paid for my Christian duty, young man."

"I ask your pardon, Eldad," returned Harrington. "I spoke hastily, and didn't mean to hurt your feelings."

"Of course you didn't," grumbled the Captain, mollified.

"It's only just your plaguy openhandedness that wunt let nobody go to expense but yourself."

"By the way, Eldad," hurriedly replied the young man, steering off the conversation from the approaching commendations, "I'm going to take him off to-night. He'll be safer there."

"All right. So he will," rejoined the Captain, curtly. "That is, if he's safe anywhere in Massachusetts now. It's ebb-tide with us this year with a vengeance. If the people haven't had enough of conservative legislation to sicken 'em this term of the General Court, they never will have. The doin's of the Legislature have been shameful. Half a dozen righteous measures that passed the Senate, those black sheep in the House have defeated.

"Yes," returned Harrington. "The Personal Liberty Bill is lost—the bill to protect the property of married women is lost, too—the bill"——

"Anyhow, we've got the Maine Law," interrupted the Captain, triumphantly.

"And that's tyranny, pure and simple," said Harrington. "Sorry to differ, Eldad. I respect the temperance people, and I would go for a law that would shut up every dram-shop in Massachusetts; but this Maine Law is a downright violation of the doctrines of civil liberty, and I can't sacrifice liberty to temperance or anything else."

Whereupon there was discussion, in which the Captain got the worst of it; and rising, at last, with his head all awry, and his features atwist, took his pipe from the mantel-piece, preparatory to a smoke in the yard. Harrington rose also.

"Why, John," said Mrs. Fisher, "you've made no breakfast at all."

"Oh yes, Hannah," he returned, cheerily. "Plenty. Now, Joel and John, the kite and the top."

The boys scrambled off to fetch the playthings, while Harrington went to his own apartments. The kite and the top put in order, Captain Fisher volunteered to mount guard over Antony if Harrington wanted to go out; and availing himself of this offer, the young man posted off to the fencing-school, and after an hour's vigorous exercise, returned. Wentworth had called in his absence, and had left word that he was going out of town for the day, but wanted to see Harrington for something special to-morrow. Disturbed at this message—he knew not why—and feeling his strange trepidation stronger than ever, Harrington, who, like Goethe, always sought relief from cares and troubles in intense application to his books, immured himself for a long day's study, dreading to see Wentworth, dreading to see Emily, dreading, above all, to see Muriel, and yet he knew not why.

CHAPTER XXIII.

THE BLOOMING OF THE LILY.

Muriel, in the meantime, had returned from her walk, and had a tender and happy hour with Emily. Emily was glorious that morning in her beauty, for the Valley of Humiliation had burst and flamed into roses of life and love, and the Valley of the Shadow lay far withdrawn in radiance upon the verge of life. There were soft showers still in the summer of her sky, but those were tears of contrite gratitude to Muriel. There were mellow thunders rolling in the summer of her sky, but those were words of rich anger and scorn for Witherlee. Muriel had guessed aright. The good Fernando had poisoned Emily's mind against Wentworth, and the deed was done on the evening he had spent with her after her parting with her lover. It would not have appeared at all surprising to a Court of Love that Emily, in blaming Wentworth for his supposed desertion of her, never imputed that desertion to her treatment of him. Quite overlooking her own conduct, she had taken his as proof of Witherlee's assertions regarding him. But now the films had dropped from her eyes, and in her talk with Wentworth the night before, which had lasted late and long, she had awakened to the perception of the game that had been played upon her by the good Fernando. How she raved at him! But Muriel laughed her angers down as they rose, till what might have been sheeting bursts were only momentary jets of flame. For Muriel was optimist and socialist, and, referring the faults of people to mal-organization, mis-education, and the play of adverse influences upon them, her golden charity spread even over Witherlee.

Breakfast came, and after breakfast Wentworth. Another tender and happy hour between the three, in which Wentworth made some revelations, poured out his soul in affection and gratitude to his dear fairy prince, as he called her, and lightened his scorn upon the good Fernando. Then Muriel having, in turn, toned down his meteor wrath, he and Emily set off together to Cambridge to announce their engagement to her parents, who were friends of his family, and very fond of him. They were to return the following day, and Emily was to continue her stay with Muriel.

A little while after they left, Mrs. Eastman went out to spend that day and night at a relative's in Milton, a few miles from Boston, and Muriel was left alone.

No work that day for Muriel; no study, no visiting, no occupation of any kind. She summoned Patrick, and bade him deny her to every one that called, and then shut herself up in the library to pass the day alone.

And all the long bright day—the sweet and beautiful deep-breathing sacred day—while the soft and opulent effulgence of the sun flooded the chamber with a mist of violet and gold, she lay at rest, or glided to and fro, lovely as some incarnate angel from a more ethereal star than ours, and with a mystic change upon her loveliness. For the summer of her life had come to her, and all its virginal and dewy lilies were in bloom. Summer languors filled her; Eden tremors melted through her; and floating in light and perfume through the tender-litten land of reverie and dreams, she heard the impassioned melodies of Paradise. A more bewildering grace had fallen around her form, and every negligent and flowing curve, veiled in the soft and snowy drapery of the robe she wore, seemed rounded to a contour more nobly and magically fair.

Faint with excess of happiness, dreaming upon the sweet and secret purpose of her heart, and musing in a dim oblivion of tenderness on all that had been, and was, and was to be, while ever on and on the lilies of her love grew glowing into magic roses of red hymeneal joy—so passed the cloistered day, and evening fell.

She rose from the couch on which she had sat, half reclining. The sunset light lay within the library, and rested on the luxuriant symmetry of her figure, as she stood with her hands crossed upon her bosom and her exalted face upturned.

"You were right, my Emily," she fervently murmured, "life is indeed life in the greatness and sweetness of love, but life is truliest life in loving and being beloved. And yet had I asked love, could I have felt this stainless flame of joy! Sweet, sweet when the two souls give the mutual undemanding love—sweet, sweet as the sweetness of Paradise! Oh, I am happy, happy!"

She clasped her hands in a calm transport of joy, and with her head bowed upon her bosom, like a flower drooping with its wealth of bloom, she remained still and silent for a little while.

"Ah, lovers who sadden without love, I think of you," she said again, lifting a gay and radiant face, and speaking with tender playfulness. "For you, poor lovers, you who bear love's cross, and may not wear love's crown—for you I pray! Oh, doleful company, would that I could make you happy, too!"

Laughing a little to herself, she let her clasped hands fall, and with a slow, harmonious movement, glided, musing, from the room.

She went up-stairs to the studio, and sitting by her desk, wrote these lines to Harrington.

"Flos equitum!—flower of chevaliers! Be sure to come this evening. A matter of the greatest importance, so do not fail. This is a vermilion edict. Hear and obey! MURIEL."

"Good!" said she, laughing softly, as she folded the note. "A piebald epistle truly. But, like Mercutio's wound, it is enough. And now for some dinner, for no beautifulest poet, as Carlyle says, but must dine, and lovers are subject to the same condition. Indeed, I think love gives one an appetite, for I am quite famished."

Gaily talking to herself in this way, she went down-stairs, dispatched Patrick with the note, and sat down to her solitary dinner, which she had ordered to be served at this hour.

It was well that she had written to Harrington, for the young scholar, his mysterious trepidation increasing as the hour drew near when he was to convey Antony to Temple street, had decided, when the note reached him, to send Captain Fisher with the fugitive instead. Of course he revoked his decision, when he read the missive, and quaking at heart, and wondering what the "matter of the greatest importance" could be, he set out about half-past eight o'clock, with Antony.

He had previously told the poor man that he knew his brother, and was going to take him to him that evening, and Antony was lost between utter astonishment and delighted expectation. To his simple mind, this strong, beautiful, friendly, masterful Harrington, who lived in a house full of books, who treated him as he had never dreamed even of being treated by a white man, and who completed his wonderful benefactions by taking him to see his brother, was little less than a god. Regarding him with actually servile reverence, Antony thought he knew everything and could do anything, and that he was the greatest man in the world.

Arrived at the house, they were let in by Patrick, who, though he had been forewarned of the arrival of another colored man that evening, looked a little frightened as he caught a glimpse under the hall-light of the black cheek-bones and ghastly, hollow eyes of the fugitive. Nothing more could be seen of his face, for Harrington had taken the precaution to muffle it almost to the eyes, and the black felt hat which the fugitive wore, he had bade him keep on till he saw his brother. Assisting his charge, who was still weak, up into the library, Harrington left him sitting there in the dark room, lighted only by the moon, and went up-stairs to announce his arrival to Roux. Returning in a few minutes, he conducted the trembling fugitive up to the door of the room where Roux was, which was ajar, and bidding him push it open, and enter, he retreated.

On the stairs he heard, with a thrill, the rush, the cry, of that meeting, followed by the shrill laughter and hilarious breakdown of Tugmutton. He did not pause, but ran lightly down into the library, and flinging himself into a corner of a cushioned couch, he covered his burning eyes with his hand, and sat still, his heart swelling with compassionate emotion. Harrington had none of those imperfect sympathies of which Charles Lamb speaks with such gentle humor ; and the meeting, after so many years of separation, of those two poor black, uncomely brothers of a despised race, touched his heart as much as if they had been the most beautiful and elegant people in the world.

Recovering in a few moments, he looked up, and the former feeling of mingled anxiety and trepidation flowed back upon his heart. Patrick had said Miss Eastman wished him ushered into the library, but had he not mistaken his instructions ?—for the library was unlighted. Still there was light enough for conversation, for the curtains were withdrawn, and the pale moonlight streamed into the apartment. He watched it for a few minutes wanly glimmering on the glass cases, filled with books, which lined the chamber; on the dim busts of bronze which stood above them; the pictures on the walls; the statuettes of metal and marble on brackets and pedestals; the various ornaments here and there; the dark shapes of the rich furniture, all softly salient in the dim light and vague shadows of the perfumed air. Gradually his mind lost its interest in the phantasmal effects before him, and feeling weary and sad at heart, he leaned his elbow on the arm of the couch, and covering his closed eyes with his hand, sat without moving for a long time.

How still the room was ! Dropping his hand from his eyes, as a ghostly sense of its intense stillness crossed his mind, he saw, with a sudden thrill of surprise, the figure of Muriel in the moonlight before him. She stood serene and motionless, with a certain grave majesty of mien which awed him—her beautiful bare arms lightly laid one upon another, and her white robe falling softly around the perfect outlines of her tall and stately form. The moonlight rested on the shadowy amber of her hair, and on her face, grave and sweet, from which her dimly shining eyes looked calmly upon him. A little surprised at the suddenness of her appearance, as by her mystic beauty he sat for a moment gazing at her.

"Do not rise," she said, quietly, as he made a movement to leave his seat. "Remain where you are. I have sent for you this evening, John, to converse with you on a matter of moment to both of us."

Her voice had never seemed so serenely sweet as now. It thrilled him like the low tones of some exquisite musical instrument. But wondering what she could mean, and filled with strange wonder at her manner, he sat breathlessly gazing at her.

"What is it, Muriel?" he said at length, in a hushed voice.

"It is this, John," she replied, still remaining motionless. "You have not seen Wentworth since I saw you last?"

"I have not, Muriel."

"Nor Emily?"

"No."

"I thought not," she said, after a pause. "John, I talked with Wentworth this morning, and he told me of a conversation that passed recently between Mr. Witherlee and your master-at-arms—Monsieur Bagasse. Wentworth, for certain reasons which he will explain to you to-morrow, told you only a portion of that conversation as it was reported to him. There is a part which I want to tell you now."

Harrington, who thought when she mentioned that she had spoken with Wentworth, that she was about to tell him the meaning of the strange speech the young artist had flung at Emily, looked at her, utterly puzzled to know what possible importance could attach to the conversation between Bagasse and Witherlee.

"The part I want to tell you, relates to you, John," she

continued. "Mr. Witherlee had led the fencing-master to suppose that you loved a lady whom he described as wealthy, of high social position, and much personal beauty."

"Oh, yes," interrupted Harrington, quietly. "I heard that Witherlee has represented me as Emily's lover."

"No," said Muriel, serenely, "it was not Emily he mentioned. It was another lady."

Harrington's heart leaped convulsively, and, even in the shadow where he sat, Muriel saw the color rush to his face.

"Monsieur Bagasse," she continued, "expressed his satisfaction that you were to marry so fine a lady, whereat Witherlee told him he was mistaken, that the lady would as soon marry a man out of the poorhouse, and that it was very odd that he should think a lady who belonged, as he said, to our first society, would wed a man who wears such a plain coat as you do."

Harrington, astonished beyond measure, sat in silence, wondering what object Muriel could have in telling him this, all his being, meanwhile, one burning flush of grief and pain.

"To which," pursued Muriel, "Monsieur Bagasse replied in his French *patois* to this effect: 'Why is it odd that a rich and beautiful lady should love Mr. Harrington. Is it odd because he wears an old coat? Ah, Mr. Witherlee, there are duchesses that love the old coat because it covers the nobility of heart they also love! Listen,' said Monsieur Bagasse, 'to what I would do if I were a beautiful, rich lady, and knew that Mr. Harrington loved me. I would say—you good, gallant, noble man, so like the knightly gentlemen of the heroic time, I know that you love me, and I love you for all you are. I love you with your old coat—I love your old coat because it has covered you. Take me to your heart—take me to your life—share my home, my wealth—I am yours forever! That,' said Monsieur Bagasse, John, 'that is what I would say to Mr. Harrington if I were a beautiful, rich lady, and knew that he loved me.'"

Her voice, in saying all this, was so even, so low and clear and sweet, so calm and unimpassioned, and she stood so motionless in her mystic beauty, with her arms serenely laid upon each other, that Harrington, sadly listening, and gazing at her seraphic face and gem-like eyes, as she bloomed before him in the tender moonlight, had no sense of the climax to which her soul was rushing, no hint of the meaning which her recital concealed. But suddenly a thrill stirred his pulses, for she stepped a pace forward, and her arms fell.

"Hear me, my Paladin," she said, and her voice rose into fuller melody, and a proud and glorious smile kindled her features—"your Frenchman's speech was the voice of a manly heart, and the lady of whom Witherlee spoke, responds to its every word. Knowing that you love her, and hoping she is worthy of a love like yours, she has said—you, in whose frame beat the pulses of gentlemen and chevaliers—you, in whose soul the spirit of the antique chivalry lives anew—take me, for I love you, and I have loved you long. Take me to your heart—take me to your life—for I am yours forever!"

He sprang to his feet, and stood in the moonlight, dilated, his eyes resplendent, and his features still and pallid as the features of the dead. Her arms were stretched toward him, and with all his being yearning to her, he could scarcely restrain the impulse that bade him whirl every consideration to the winds, and clasp her to his heart. But no: there was some mystery here to be made plain; he must be sure that some sudden passion had not made her forgetful of her plighted faith to another; he must not wrong his friend. The thought quelled the tumult of his spirit, and held his struggling heart as a giant holds a giant.

"Oh, I read you well," she exclaimed, her arms sinking slowly, while she still looked at him with her proud and glorious smile. "My soul is clairvoyant to-night, and I read you well. Love is strong, but it is chained by honor. You think me the betrothed of Wentworth. Ah, no! Emily is the betrothed of Wentworth, and when he told you otherwise, it was his hasty blunder—no more. John!" she faltered, and her voice grew sweet and low—"you asked me once to tell you of the fairy prince I was to follow through all the world, and I told you I would tell you of him when I found him. I have found him—here!"

The word rang from her lips in a fervent and adoring cry, and she was in his arms. One wild, delirious instant, and then the tumult of his joy mounted to his brain, and spread into the stillness of a blissful dream. O solemn ecstasy of prayer and peace! O mystic passion of true love unveiled! The moonlight rested on the noble beauty of their forms, with the dark and rich phantasmal room around them. They saw it not—they knew not where they were. Tranced in the temple of the night, they stood, silent, motionless, filled with ethereal light, as if a rosy star had burst within their being, filled with an all-pervading, holy tenderness. Ended now the strange delusion—the restlessness and pain, the hopeless yearning, the generous grief, the alternate hope and doubt and fleeting joy, the sad renunciation, the selfless and submissive sacrifice, were ended; they had passed away like clouds, and the sweet heavens of love remained.

Slowly her head drooped back, and clinging to him yet, her noble face, tranquil and wet with tears, gazed fondly into his.

"Beloved Muriel," he said, and his deep voice was tremulous and low, "I came here sad and dark, and you have filled me with light and life and joy. What am I that I should invoke a love like yours—what am I that it should descend to me so rich in blessing?"

"Not so, not so," she fervently replied. "It is I that am bold, for I have chosen you for my beloved from all living men I know. But I love you. Oh, should I not love you—for you made life sweet to me, you taught me to make life noble! Dear friend so long—my husband now—still help me to make life noble, for I could not love you so much if I did not love the world you live for more. Come; we have much to talk of. Sit here by me."

She sank upon the couch near by, and he took a seat by her side. Silent a little while before their talk began, they sat folded in each other's arms, the hour of wonder sinking slowly like a subsiding sea, and the moonlight resting peacefully upon them.

CHAPTER XXIV.

THE BLOWING OF THE ROSE.

Day, ethereal and splendid, burst up the wide horizon like a hymn, and filled the sacred morning with light and love and joy. A morning ruled by a celestial sun—a morning blue and golden, and throbbing with immortality. To breathe was happiness. To drink the cool aërial wine of the clear, sweet atmosphere, was in itself rapture. In all the lustrous azure there was no cloud, and the heavenly day seemed set apart and consecrate to love.

Its glorious ray streamed through the crystal and purple panes of the rich library, and filled the perfumed air with floating lights of violet and gold. The chamber, decked and fragrant with a profusion of delicate and dewy blush roses, and swimming in the sumptuous colored radiance, had bloomed into a hymeneal bower. But more than all its adornments, was the youthful beauty of Emily and Wentworth. They sat by each other, her hand clasped in his, talking in gay, fond voices, and the sun never shone on lovers more joyous and handsome than they. His face, lit by the blue, sparkling eyes and the proud, brilliant smile, with the thick cluster of auburn locks carelessly curling on the passionate sloping brow and around the florid cheeks, was turned to hers; while she, magnificent in her Spanish beauty, her damask cheeks glowing through the clear gold of her complexion, and heightened by the darkness of her hair, gazed at him with lustrous eyes, the pearls of her curved carnation mouth half shown in her slow and indolent ambrosial smile. So sat they in the gold and violet glory of the room—a sight to make an anchorite forswear his weeds, and pray the saints to send him youth and love.

A bounding step was heard upon the stairs, and Emily turned, while Wentworth looked toward the door. It opened presently, and the martial figure of Harrington appeared. The color flashed upon the face of the superb brunette, and springing to her feet, she ran to him. Then, with her arms around him, she turned to Wentworth with a flushed and laughing face, and ——

"Are you jealous, Richard, are you jealous?" she cried, with riant gaiety.

"Jealous? Jupiter Pluvius!" shouted Wentworth, bounding to his feet, and rushing over to Harrington.

Clasping him with an embrace of steel, Harrington bent his head, and kissed him on each cheek, then pushed him from him, with his hands upon his shoulders.

"That is the kiss of France," he gaily cried. "That is the kiss of the Paris that I love. And here," he added, grasping Wentworth's hand, "here is the hand of the Old England and the New—the hand of love and faith and the oaken heart. Yours, Richard, now and always."

Wringing the generous hand, his face convulsed, and his lip quivering, Wentworth gazed at his friend with humid eyes. A moment, and two bright tears rolled down his cheeks, and his head fell.

"Ah, John," he faltered, "I do not deserve the hand, nor the heart that gives it. I treated you basely, and you" ——

"Hush, Richard! Not a word of that. I know it all," said Harrington, putting his right arm around Wentworth, and drawing him to his breast. "You, too, Emily," and his left arm encircled her.

There was a moment of silence, deep and sweet as prayer. Standing so, with his beautiful and regal bearded face bent down to them, he gazed upon their features, solemn in that moment with the fervor of their love for him.

"Dear Emily—dear Richard," he said, in his strong melodious voice, "we will not cloud the joy of this sacred day with any word of what has passed forever. Let us not look upon it with one regret. Let us think of it rather with gratitude and blessing; for it has bound us together closer than we were before. See, I had but two friends; and now, I, who have no brother or sister of my own, have found a sister and a brother in you. That is worth the mutual pain—that repays it all. Behold, a new heaven and a new earth have come to us, and the former things are passed away."

His voice ceased, and the silence came like a benediction. In a moment, his arms fell, and he turned from them. There was a pause, in which Wentworth and Emily wandered to the windows, wiping their eyes.

"Ah, me," presently sighed Wentworth, breaking into his volatile laugh, "as I always say, I feel as if I'd got religion. In fact, I've got religion several times the last few days."

"So have I," cried Emily, dropping her handkerchief from her eyes, and laughing merrily. "John!" she exclaimed, turning quickly, and sweeping, with a rustle of silks, toward Harrington—"now, Richard, don't be jealous!" she archly said in passing—"John, you restored me to life. I was dying with my long vigil of suffering when you held me in your arms. You lulled me to that sweet sleep, and when I awoke it was to happiness. You gave me back my life, and Muriel gave me back my love. How can I ever thank and love you enough for all you did for me? How can I ever repay you? But I owe you one thing—the kiss you gave me. Oh, I was like an unloved, weary child, dying for affection that hour when I asked you to kiss me. See—I owe you that kiss, and I give it to you."

Wentworth, touched by the simple and tender fervor of her voice, and by the child-like affection of her action, turned away, filled with emotion.

"Good, now!" he exclaimed, in a moment, wheeling around, and playfully assuming an injured air. "Just keep that up all day, will you! Continue! I'm placid. I can stand any amount of laceration. Don't stop for me. I'll bear it."

They laughed gaily, and came toward him, arm in arm.

"Well, you're a handsome couple anyway," pursued the mercurial Wentworth, surveying them with an air of bland admiration—genuine admiration, too, mixed with his affectation of it. "As for Emily, she's just what Muriel calls her—the gorgeous queen-rose of Ispahan. But you, Harrington—what have you been doing to yourself? I never saw you look so finely in my life. Walter Raleigh—the beautiful and tall Sir Walter—must have looked like you, though I don't believe he looked so well."

Emily, leaning on Harrington's arm, looked up into his face, and saw that what Wentworth said was true. A change had fallen upon the masculine bearded countenance—a fine rapture lit its regular features—a faint color lessened its pallor, and the pure blue eyes swam in brilliance.

"Indeed, Richard, you are right," said Emily. "He looks as beautiful as the sun-god."

"Exactly. 'Hyperion's curls, the front of Jove himself'"——

"Oh, come now," interrupted Harrington, blushing. "Is this a meeting of the Mutual Admiration Society? You pair of gross flatterers! Praising my personal pulchritude to my face in this way! But do I look well? No wonder. Last night I slept the sleep of the blessed, and to-day I am happy. You know why. Ah! and you haven't given me joy yet! Yes, and I, too, haven't given you joy."

"We know why? Given you joy? Why, what do you mean, John?" cried Emily.

"Hasn't Muriel told you?" said Harrington.

"No," cried Emily, breathlessly; but Wentworth saw what was coming, and a slow flush crept over his illumined face.

"Muriel and I plighted troth last night," said Harrington, simply.

Wentworth flew across the room with a shout, and with the utmost deliberation began to dance. Emily dropped Harrington's arm, stood for a moment pale, with her hands to her bosom, glowed into bright color again, and burst into tears.

"Oh, John!" she cried, springing back a pace, and seizing his hands, with a smile flashing splendid through the glittering rain on her impassioned face. "Oh, I am so happy! Joy, joy to you! I never dreamed of it—never! Joy, joy, joy!"

She wrung his hands in an ecstasy of delight, while Wentworth, breaking from his dance, came flying across the room, and over a chair that stood in his way, and clutching away the right hand from Emily, shook it as if he meant to shake it off, his face flushed and his lip quivering, and his congratulations breaking from his lips like wildfire.

"Everlasting cornucopias of happiness poured out upon you both for countless quadrillions of never-dying eternities!" he hallooed. "By the Capitolian Jove, John, but I'm too glad to say a syllable. Don't ask me to give you joy, for there's not enough words in the beggarly English language for me to do it with! Oh, thunder! if this is not the tip-top crown and summit of it all, then I'm a Dutchman!"

He burst away, panting, and hurling himself at full length upon a couch, burst into a ringing peal of jubilant laughter.

"Oh, Lord! I shall die!" he gasped, ceasing, and fanning himself with his hand. "Hallelujah! Hallelujah!"

Harrington, faint with mirth, sat down, and Emily, also laughing furiously, scurried over to Wentworth, and shook him till he laughed again, and shook him till, aching with laughter, he implored her to stop.

"Well, Emily," exclaimed Harrington, as she relinquished her hold of her lover, "I declare I never saw you romp before, and I did not think you could."

"'Pon my word, she's as bad as Muriel," cried Wentworth, with a comical look of mock anxiety. "I'm afraid her aristocratic morals are getting corrupted by the company she keeps in this house."

"Well, John," said Emily, a little flushed and panting with her exertions, and laughing in short fits as she spoke, "I believe you are right. Romping is, if not new to me, very unusual. But to-day I am so happy, I hardly know what I am doing. This glad news takes me out of myself completely. Oh, I am so rejoiced! And to think that Muriel never told me! Cunning fox! But I'll be even with her for it. I see now why she has decked the room with such a wilderness of roses. She is going to make it a fete day in honor of her engagement."

"Why, yes," said Harrington, starting up. "I didn't notice all these exquisite flowers before, but I suppose that *is* the reason why she has filled the library with them."

"You suppose," said Emily. "Why, don't you know?"

"Not I," replied Harrington, laughing. "Muriel asked me to come and spend the day with her, and only said she was going to give me an agreeable surprise. She wouldn't tell me what the agreeable surprise was, but I suppose this is it. How exquisite and sweet they are," he murmured, bending over a shallow vase of Parian, filled with the roses, and inhaling their delicate fragrance.

"When are you to be married, John?" asked Emily.

"I declare I don't know," said he naively. "I never thought of asking Muriel."

"Never thought—well, that's a good one!" exclaimed Wentworth. "Why, almost the first thing I asked Emily after our betrothal was"——

"Now, Richard," cried Emily, scampering up to him with a laugh, and sealing his mouth with her hand.

Wentworth struggled to get free, and succeeding in a minute, seized her hands, and held them, she, in turn, endeavoring to get them upon his mouth again.

"Hear me, for I will speak!" he declaimed, with serio-comic dignity. "The first thing I asked Emily, John, was—when are we to be married?"

"And what did she say?" inquired Harrington, amusedly.

"She said October, John," replied Emily, laughing. "He shan't tell you. I'll tell you myself. Yes, John, we are to be married in October. See my betrothal ring. Is it not beautiful?"

He took the fair hand in his, and looked at the exquisite opal, whose soft, clouded flames of iridescent color shone on her finger.

"Beautiful," he assented, pressing the hand to his lips. "I pray for your life-long happiness, dear Emily. Yours and Richard's. And may I be present at your wedding?"

"Indeed you must," she answered. "It would be but half a wedding if you were not there."

"My sentiments," cried Wentworth. "Without you, John, our wedding would be a fiasco. But it is to be a grand affair. In open church, crowds of guests, Emily in full bridal array, with a small army of bridesmaids, and I in gorgeous toggery, with a retinue of grooms which will astonish your Spartan simplicity. Oh, I tell you, we shall blow out in splendid hymeneal flower, amidst overpowering magnificence !"

"Hear the absurd fellow !" exclaimed Emily, smiling at Harrington, who stood listening half-amusedly, half-pensively, as the gay Richard ran on. "Only listen to him. But it is true, John—we are to have a splendid wedding."

"I am glad to hear it," he replied. "You are both splendid, and it is natural and proper for you to put forth splendid rays on such an occasion."

"Nevertheless, I'll bet you won't find Harrington and Muriel flashing out like us, Emily," cried Wentworth, showing his fine teeth in a brilliant laugh. "I wouldn't be afraid to wager that you'll see that young man married in his ordinary clothes, without a rag of a white kid glove, or an ornament of any kind whatever, or wedding cake, or cards, or guests, or anything."

"Why, Richard, I don't know," said Harrington, smiling good-naturedly. "If Muriel were to wish the usual parade I would agree of course. But you are right—my choice would be as little external show as possible. Some simple rites would be more grateful to me than any pomp or display. Marriage to me is so private and spiritual a sacrament that it seems a sort of profanation to make it public—or surround it with factitious embellishments. These flowers for example, this sweet, rich room, Muriel lovely, and clothed as befits her loveliness, I in this plain coat, not very new, but well-fitting and graceful, Mrs. Eastman and you two loving friends here —what more could I desire to decorate my wedding? And less than this—yes, nothing of this—Muriel and I alone in some quiet room, or under the blue sky, or the forest trees, pledging ourselves to each other in spirit and in truth—this of itself would be enough, and would make the most imperial bridals seem gaudy and theatrical."

"Then you object to our fine fashionable wedding, John," said Emily, playfully.

"Oh no—not object," returned Harrington, coloring, with

an embarrassed air. "Have I said too much? Have I cast any personal reflections? I hope not, for I did not mean to. I only meant to say that the ideal nobleness and beauty of marriage are not very well expressed by the usual modish and artificial ceremonials and decorations. The thing itself is holy and poetic. Let the rites and adornments be holy and poetic too. That is all."

Emily turned away, musing, and Wentworth twirled his gay moustache with an abstracted air.

"But where's Muriel, I wonder?" said Harrington, after a pause.

"Here she is—no, it's our dear mamma," exclaimed Wentworth.

"Your mamma it is, children," said Mrs. Eastman, coming into the room, silver-gay, with her bonnet on. "I have just returned from Milton, and heard your voices, or rather John's voice, as I came up-stairs. But, bless me, where did all these flowers come from? Why, the library is turned into fairy-land!"

"Ah, mamma," said Emily, "we are all in fairy-land to-day, and the fairy-prince has done it, with the help of this fairy chevalier," and she bent her head toward Harrington.

"Why, what has happened to you, children?" asked Mrs. Eastman, laughing softly, as she removed her bonnet.

"Now, mamma," said Wentworth, fronting her with Emily on his arm, "I'm going to surprise you. Prepare to be surprised."

"Well, I'm ready," said Mrs. Eastman, gaily.

"Emily and I are to be married in October," said Wentworth, suddenly.

"My dear children, I am more glad to hear this than I can say," fondly replied Mrs. Eastman, kissing both of them. "But, children, you don't surprise me at all," she added, with smiling equability. "I saw that you were lovers some time since, and was expecting this."

Mrs. Eastman might have also said that she saw they had quarrelled, and knew what was the matter with Emily during her night and day of sorrow, but she was discreet and did not.

"There!" exclaimed Wentworth, with a grimace, "there's my surprise now? Mamma, you're a witch, and there's no keeping anything from you!"

"Stop, Richard!" cried Emily. "Let John try his hand at a surprise."

Mrs. Eastman was well named Serena, she was so sweetly calm, but the color rose to her face, and she trembled, as Harrington came toward her with outstretched arms.

"Mother," he fervently said, holding her in his embrace, "you have your wish. I was mistaken. Last night, Muriel and I"——

Her eyes filled, and without a word she flew from his arms and out of the room. Harrington covered his humid eyes with his hand, and stood still. Wentworth and Emily moved silently away, with hushed faces.

It was but a moment, and she came back with a swift, free step, her calm face lighted between its silver tresses, the tears upon her cheeks, and put her arms around him.

"Hush!" she whispered. "Do not speak to me. Let me dream of this. I am too happy."

His arms had enfolded her, and with his eyes closed, and his lips pressed to her beautiful silver hair, while her face lay upon his bosom, they stood still.

"Yes," she murmured, after a long pause, looking up with a still and radiant face into his noble countenance, "yes, I have my wish, and I am happy."

She placed her arm in his, and moved with him across the library.

"Well, mamma," said Emily, with her ambrosial smile, "We did surprise you, after all."

"Yes and no, dear Emily," replied Mrs. Eastman, fondly looking at Harrington. "Yes and no. It was the evening star of my life; a cloud obscured it, but I still had faith that my evening star was there."

There was a pause, filled by the pensive memory of her voice. Suddenly Wentworth and Emily uttered a low exclamation, and Mrs. Eastman and Harrington turned, started, and stood still. It was Muriel, but Muriel transfigured in resplendent beauty. A robe of rich, ethereal vivid crimson, at once soft and glowing, like the color of the rose, cut low, and encircling the shoulders by only a narrow gathered band, spread loosely around her bosom, and descending in many light folds, expressed her perfect form, and heightened the dazzling fairness of her complexion. Color faint as the hues of the blush roses whose ecstatic odors filled the room, bloomed on her cheeks and lips ; her amber hair, encircled by a slender fillet of myrtle, bright green, small leaved, and terminating on either side with a rose, drooped low in rippling tresses around her radiant and hymn-like face ; and her mouth rosy-pale against its milk-white teeth, was parted in an enchanting smile. Gliding forward, with her noble harmony of movement, the floating gold and violet glory that filled the chamber resting on her beauteous face and figure, and her sumptuous drapery falling around her faultless limbs, she seemed some wondrous vision of incarnate joy. So sacred, so transcendent was her bewildering loveliness, that they gazed upon her with strange awe, as in the presence of her in her immortality.

Harrington looked at her, rapt, and passion-pale ; then with a thrill of melting tenderness, as if his soul was dissolving in his frame, he closed his giddy eyes and bowed his head upon his clasped hands.

" Harrington, my beloved !"

He started at the deep eolian music of her voice, and holding her in his arms, gazed with an impassioned face into her clear lambent eyes.

" Ah, Muriel, Muriel !" he fervently murmured, " I tremble lest you make life too sweet for me. Oh, dear friends," he cried, " you can bear to see the dance, for you hear the music ! Look at her ; is she not beautiful ?"

A low murmur of admiration ran from lip to lip, and Emily, breaking from her trance, embraced Muriel and kissed her fervently. Then her mother, with tender and pathetic words of endearment, folded her to her heart.

" Oh, my daughter," she said, gently and mournfully, " what would I give if your father could see you now ! He who hung over your cradle so often in your infancy, and called you so fondly his glorious little child, what would I give if he could see you now in your glorious womanhood !"

"Dear mother, he sees me," answered Muriel, her face lit with a celestial smile, and her clear eyes upturned. "In this the best and brightest hour of my life, he sees me ! He is alive and well, and he sees me !"

In the solemn pause which followed, while they stood with dim eyes and heads bowed, it seemed as if some silent spirit stood among them in the rich glory of the room.

The thrilling feeling slowly died away like failing music, and timidly looking up, Wentworth saw the eyes of Muriel sink from their celestial height and rest kindly and lovingly on him.

"Come to me, Richard," she said. "You alone have not spoken to me—you alone have not expressed your joy."

"Muriel," he answered, moving near her, with a timid and tardy step, "if so bad a boy as I am"——

"Bad? oh, no ! You are not a bad boy," she said with tender playfulness, caressing him as she spoke. "You are my own dear brother Richard, gallant, and fond, and true. Could I love you if you were not ? Could I kiss you thus, and thus, and thus, with magic kisses three ?" she said, kissing him each time as she said the word, and smiling at him with bewitching gaiety. "Ah ! I am very happy this morning ! That is the reason you all admire me so. See : my joy has burst into its fullest flower, and this is its color and its symbol."

Smiling upon them, she laid her hand on her gorgeous crimson robe.

"I see," said Emily, "Madame de Staël said the color of the trumpet-sound was crimson, and the sound of the golden trumpet is the sound of joy. Oh, Muriel, I never saw you dressed so admirably. You are splendid as the sun !"

"Yes, and mark you now," said Wentworth, gaily, "there is another symbol here. This is the color of the dress of the fairy prince. Ah, it is the same dress, too, if you only knew it. The fairy prince wove a spell of weird, gave one touch of the magic wand, and lo ! the crimson cymar changed into a crimson robe, and the fairy prince stands before you transformed into a fairy princess !"

"Bravo, Richard!" said Harrington, "that is ingenious, now."

"And then," continued Wentworth, "the gold embroidery on the cymar melted into gold lustre, and passed into Muriel's eyes. See how golden her eyes are this morning. Their clear grey looks through a transparent sheen of gold."

"They are golden with love, then," said Muriel, laughingly, "for the cymar is up-stairs, with all its embroidery intact. It is Harrington who is the fairy prince, and I am the Sleeping Beauty whom he waked from her sleep of twenty years, and now I am to follow him through all the world. But come, John, I promised you an agreeable surprise this morning, you know."

"Well, and have you not given it to me?" said Harrington, smiling at her. "This beautiful room, all bedecked with roses, and then yourself in your miraculous beauty—why, I am in receipt of two agreeable surprises!"

"Ah, John," she replied, with enchanting gaiety, "but I have a third more wonderful than those."

"What is it?" asked Harrington, amusedly.

"I'll tell you," she answered. "Friends, attention! My dear mother, do you remember the little conversation we had at dinner the day before yesterday?"

"Perfectly," replied Mrs. Eastman, coloring slightly, and looking at her charming daughter with some wonder.

"Well, my dear mother," returned Muriel, with bewitching playfulness, "I reflected seriously all day yesterday on what you said, and I decided to oblige you. John, come here to me."

Harrington, curious to know what was meant by this preface, approached, and stood before her with a sweetly smiling countenance. Slowly her beautiful white arms stole around him, clasped him lightly, and drew him to her. It seemed in that moment as if, in the noble features upturned to his, all the versatile expressions of which they were capable darted magically together in a bewildering and harmonious play, like the soft floating and intermingling of evanescent, tender rainbow hues on a clear and delicate air. But slowly through

16*

their indecisive enchantment broke a dazzling smile, a fairy tremor lifted her fine nostril, the color bloomed deeplier on her cheeks and lips, and her eyes glowed.

"John!" said she, in a clear, melodious voice, "this is our marriage morn."

A splendid scarlet flamed on the face of Harrington, and with a start he clasped her to his breast, gazing into her face with eyes like wondering stars. Mrs. Eastman, ineffably astonished, but more ineffably amused, that Muriel had taken her at her word, sank into a chair, with her countenance flushed, and burst into low laughter; while Emily, with the rich color suffusing her features and her eyes and mouth orbed in wonder, pressed her folded hands to her bosom; and Wentworth stared vacantly, with his face as red as fire.

"This the morning of our marriage!" exclaimed Harrington. "This!"

"This it is, John," she replied, gaily, "and this is my third agreeable surprise. How do you like it?"

Harrington, with a sudden motion, bent his head and kissed her.

"Muriel, Muriel!" he laughingly cried, "you are indeed a fairy princess! You touch the moment, and it bursts into the unexpected miracle-flower of joy."

"Now by all the gods at once!" exclaimed the volatile Wentworth, and bounding up with three distinct pigeon-wings into the air, he came down again erect and gallant, and burst into a peal of mellow laughter.

"Well I declare!" ejaculated Emily. "Of all the splendid freaks I ever heard of, this is the most splendid. To be married this morning! But who's to marry you? where's the minister?"

"Oh, he's coming," returned Muriel, smiling. "I wrote a note to Mr. Parker this morning, and he is to be here at ten."

"Good!" exclaimed Harrington. "If I am to have any minister to marry me, let it be Mr. Parker. It will be an added consecration."

"I knew you would think so," replied Muriel.

"To be sure," he answered. "He would consider me a heathen, looking at me theologically, but that's no matter."

Muriel looked at his smiling countenance, and shook her finger at him.

"Oh, you Verulamian heretic !" she exclaimed, gaily.

"Well, Muriel," laughed Emily, "I'm sure you're very obliging to have even Mr. Parker. With your invincible hostility to Madame la Grundy, it is positively a remarkable concession."

"Ah, dear Emily," replied Muriel, smiling tenderly, "can the words of a clergyman make more holy the union of lovers, who love in spirit and in truth ! Were Mr. Parker not in the world, and were we in Pennsylvania to-day, and not in Massachusetts, I would rather choose to stand up with John before our friends, avowing our love in the sweet and beautiful old simple Quaker fashion, and sparing every other rite beside. To have the spiritual marriage publicly recognized would be enough. But then," she added, with gentle gaiety, "on this point, Mrs. Grundy has the law on her side, so I curtsey and submit, hoping to atone for the submission by a long series of flagrant rebellions, against which there is no statute ! For while it is both proper and necessary, as things stand, that Mrs. Grundy should be obeyed, it is also proper and necessary as things stand, that the dear old woman should be defied. So there's a paradox for you !"

"Bravo !" cried Wentworth. "Centripetality and centrifugality for ever !"

"Exactly so," replied Muriel, with a frolic curtsey. "Now, mother, there you sit without saying a word, and you haven't told me yet whether you are going to lend the light of your countenance to my extraordinary proceedings."

"Of course I am, dear," cried Mrs. Eastman, starting up to kiss her bewitching daughter, while they all rippled off into lively talk and the hilarity of the immortals.

"Come," said Muriel in a few moments, "let us have music till Mr. Parker comes. Gluck and Mendelssohn and the divine Mozart and Beethoven, shall speak for us to-day. Color and fragrance, and dancing, and silence can express deep joy, but music expresses it as nothing else can, and to-day is the flower of my existence."

She moved as she spoke to the organ, and the gorgeous tones of golden bronze rolled forth in sunset clouds of heavenly harmony, with her seraph voice singing sweet among them. Pass, hour of noble raptures, hour of the spirit, hour of celestial love and hope and joy, pass, fitting prelude for his coming—the valiant soul and tender, now blest among the blessed, whose disenchanted dust lies in the holy soil of Florence, and lends one hallowed memory more to the land of Dante's grave!

It was like a sacred dream in which he came—the mighty, the well-beloved, the lion-hearted Theodore; he of the domed brow, the Socratic features, resolute and tender, and stern at times with the long battle he waged for Christian liberty; he of the beautiful and dove-like eyes whose clear sweetness the roaring hatred of his foes could never stain or change. It was like a sacred dream in which they heard the noble language of his charge inspiring them to lives of holiest and highest humanhood, and then while the dream deepened into an interval of unutterable calm, and a stiller glory seemed to swim, a more celestial fragrance seemed to flow, upon the quiet of the room, the pledges of the nuptials were spoken, and his voice arose in tender and fervent supplication to the Heavenly Father of the world—Father and Mother, too—Father of Love and Freedom and all that makes the world more fair—Lover of lovers, and Lover of the world He made—that the eternal spring-time of His Presence might rest upon their wedded lives, greenness and strength and beauty to them forevermore.

It was still a sacred dream, when he had gone. But the very air seemed to tremble with an ecstasy of painful happiness, and Muriel, pale with a joy which was insupportable, because voiceless, glided to the organ.

Softly again upon the glory of the air, drifted the molten bronze of the rich music and her clear soprano, sweet and low, arose and blended with the heavenly anthem. Sweet and low as the mother's cradle hymn, and tender as the remembered songs of childhood, it floated on above the mellow murmur of the instrumental flow; and rising like a thrilling gush of perfume into more celestial melody, it rose again in rapturous ascension, intermingled with the surging and dilating swell of the organ-tones, and rang in pealing hallelujahs, draining the soul of every earthly thought and feeling, and lifting it pale and throbbing on the burning wings of seraphs into the light and odor of the Life Divine. Then sinking slowly, voice and music failed upon the palpitating air, failed from the spirits throbbing with the blended sweetness, and the room was still.

She rose from the organ with her face inspired, and turned to be folded in the arms of Harrington.

"Ah, Muriel," he fervently murmured, "your songs are more than 'the benediction that follows after prayer!'"

She did not answer, but stood silently in his embrace, with her face bent upon his breast. Lifting it to his at length, she looked upon him with glowing eyes.

"We are married," she said. "Do you realize it?"

"Hardly," he replied. "But it is true. We are one. One in love for liberty."

"One in love for liberty," she echoed. "One in love for all mankind."

They stood in silence for a few moments. Then turning with their arms around each other, they saw Emily and Wentworth sitting together in deep abstraction.

"Well, Richard and Emily, what are you thinking of?" Muriel playfully demanded.

"I was thinking," returned Wentworth more gravely than was usual with him, "that is before your singing, Muriel, lifted me out of my mind, as it always does—I was thinking what a man Mr. Parker is. How great and noble—how beautiful were his words and manner. Ah, that was a true marriage service!"

"And so was I," cried Emily, who had been weeping a little. "I was thinking the same thing. I shall never hear our own minister with comfort again."

"Oh, flower of Episcopalians, are you turning Parkerite?" gaily exclaimed Muriel.

"I declare I believe I am," sighed Emily, so dolefully that Wentworth began to laugh, and she herself followed his example.

"Come," cried Wentworth, starting to his feet, "this won't do. Here are John and Muriel married. Do you realize that fact, Emily?"

"Yes, I do," she answered, bounding up, and rushing over to the lovers to pour out the joy of her heart upon them.

Mrs. Eastman and Wentworth followed, and in a moment the room rang with gay talk and frolic hilarity.

"And just take notice," cried Wentworth, amidst the affluent fun, "take notice that Harrington has his wish. He was wishing, Muriel, or rather in a little discussion we had as to the proper mode of doing the marriage ceremony up golden brown, he was observing that to be married in this room, just as he is, with never a ghost of a kid glove on him, or any wedding embellishments, and nobody present but us, would be the height of his ambition. So you see, his Spartan soul is gratified!"

"So it is!" laughed Harrington. "I had forgotten it amidst the excitement; but that is what I said, and you, dear fairy princess, have gratified me."

"Hold on now," burst in the mercurial Wentworth, interrupting Muriel in the gay reply she was about to make. "Hold on! An idea strikes me. To wit, that nobody has called this lady by her new name. Sweet Muriel Eastman, *vale, vale, vale.* Adieu forevermore! Vanish, flower of spinsters, vanish into the fragrant twilight of memory. Mrs. Harrington, appear! All hail, Mrs. Harrington!"

"Bravo!" exclaimed Emily, clapping her hands, and undulating backward into a low curtsey. "All hail, Mrs. Harrington!"

Muriel, still clasping her husband, looked at them in their mirth with a pensive smile.

"I had forgotten it," she said gently, and almost dreamfully, "for I feel like Muriel Eastman, still, with unmerged individuality."

"And Muriel Eastman you shall be," laughingly said Harrington; "and with unmerged individuality, too."

"Nay," said Muriel, with tender gaiety. "My new, sweet name, John—Muriel Harrington. I accept it. At least to the world I will be Muriel Harrington, and you shall think of me, and call me Muriel Eastman, still."

"As I will ever," responded Harrington.

"Bravo!" cried Wentworth. "An amicable adjustment of a serious difficulty. And now, what next?"

"Next, music," laughingly said Emily, moving to the organ.

Her rich contralto voice rose with the instrumental surge into a trumpet pæan, and so, amidst music and laughter, and many-colored festal talk, the golden banquet of the day passed by, and as they stood together at the single western window of the library, the evening overspread them with a sky of deepest azure, filled with vast clouds of purple and amber flame, like the wings of seraphim.

Slowly the burning magnificence of the celestial pageant faded from the sky, and the enchanted twilight came with soft and odorous southwind breathings. All the long evening, in the dim bloom of moonlight, too faint to veil the brightness of the stars, the long wafts of balmy odor hung swaying with the airy poise of spirits around the dwelling, rising in low whisperings, and slowly swooning away in sweetness. Gradually the sounds of life died away, the moon sank low, the shadows slept within the street, and the silence was unbroken save by the passionate whispers of the fragrant wind. Far above the dark roofs, the bright stars were throbbing in the divine blue gloom, and over the vast night brooded the infinite presence of the triune Love and Life and Joy.

CHAPTER XXV.

WITHERLEE.

The next day the announcement of the marriage appeared in the newspapers, and falling soft as a rose-leaf on the tail of that great Chicken Little, Society, Society ran round clucking as if the sky had fallen. Great was the sensation—especially among the score or so of lovers who for a long time had been vainly endeavoring to get sufficiently intimate with Muriel to make their love manifest, and whose fate was now sealed.

Not having been invited to the wedding, Society expected the cards to arrive inviting it to the conventional reception. But Society hearing presently, through some intimate friends of the family, that Muriel and her husband had decided to dispense with conventionalities, took it kindly, as just what might have been expected of that lady, and began to pour in a stream of congratulatory callers at the house in Temple street. Among the callers, the startled and enraged Atkinses were missing, which was melancholy. Amidst the family wrath, Horatio kept contemptuously cool, remarking, like the fine young American he was, that a social mesalliance always brought its own punishment, as she (Muriel) would find to her sorrow; while Thomas, on all occasions, when the subject of the marriage came up in conversation, observed, that that's what comes of letting girls have too much head, be Jove!

Great was the sensation the next morning when Muriel and Harrington appeared at Captain Fisher's, announcing their espousals, and great was the joy, and immense the satisfaction.

Greater than all or anything was the large and lustrous happiness of the wedded lovers. The deep change that had come upon their lives gave them a new and statelier beauty. So might have looked the beautiful and tall Sir Walter, and so the fair Elizabeth Throgmorton, his bright Elizabethan flower of wifely womanhood, in their happiest hour of wedded love.

At home in Temple street the day after their wedding, in the new and fresh enjoyment of a marriage whose perfect nobleness might have gladdened the pure soul of Swedenborg, they laid their little plans for the future. It was first agreed that Harrington should permit himself a vacation, free from the toil of study, in this the golden crescent of their eternal honeymoon. It was next resolved that Harrington should keep his house in Chambers street, and live there when he so chose. Both he and Muriel thought that married people are too intimate with each other, see too much of each other, push too far and frequently into the sacred privacy which Nature sets around the individual soul, and so lose the charm of freshness which is at once the crowning delight and most potent safeguard of love. If, in married life, they thought, familiarity does not breed contempt, it commonly breeds a sort of humdrum unappreciating indifference which makes the wedded lovers seem less beautiful and noble to each other than in the matin prime of their early passion. And as Muriel and Harrington designed to be lovers forevermore, they resolved to maintain the relations which make love ever magical and ever new. Counting himself fortunate, therefore, that he had a house of his own to retire to in those golden-valleyed intervals which Nature prescribes to checquer and enhance the tender and holy beauty of the mountain land of love, and sadly wishing that his fortune might be shared by all, as it might in a nobler order of society, Harrington agreed with Muriel, and she with him, to use their new freedom of intercourse wisely, he spending his studious days as heretofore in his own house, she passing her happy life as in her maidenhood in hers, both coming together whenever their souls drew, or their duties bade, freely, attractively, in mutual ministration and communion, living for each other and for the world's great family of souls.

The next thing that came under discussion was a proposition from Muriel to settle half her fortune on her husband, which Harrington would not listen to on any condition. It was finally compromised, amidst much gaiety, by his agreeing to let no want of his go untold, and to always accept from her whatever money he needed, instead of interrupting his studies with compositions to supply his deficiencies. Which bargain Muriel closed with a frolic threat of banishment from her presence if she ever discovered him infringing the terms of the compact, until he made atonement by accepting a double sum for his disobedience.

Other matters talked of, and the business conference ended, they were sitting together in the library, when Wentworth arrived, handsome as usual, and full of gay greetings. Presently Emily came in from a shopping excursion, and sat with them.

"And why is Raffaello out of his studio this morning?" she said, in a gay tone, to Wentworth.

"Well," he returned, "fact is, I couldn't paint for thinking of our recent blind-man's buff game. Now, look here, friends, let's have a grand confession. Here we are together, and what I want to know is this: How is it that we four people, of tolerably good wits, contrived in our love affairs to be so mistaken in regard to each other? Grant Witherlee's share in the matter, and our own duplicity—that is, yours and mine, Emily dear—but after all, is it not singular that we didn't see through it?"

They sat pensively smiling, with their eyes bent upon the floor, while he, smiling also, with his brilliant teeth displayed, looked at them.

"Just think," he continued. "Just think of the slightness of the evidence which set every Jack of us against his true Jill, and every Jill against her true Jack. Such evidence wouldn't have misled us if any other matter but love was involved. How is this? Now, Emily, perhaps it's not wonderful that you should have thought that I loved Muriel, for who wouldn't love her? but how could you for a moment imagine that she—so manifestly my superior every way, so evidently made for a nobler man than I am—could possibly love me?"

"I don't know," naively replied Emily, while Muriel and Harrington, coloring at the compliment Wentworth so frankly paid them, laughed amusedly. "It was very foolish in me, I'm sure, and it seems like a strange dream."

"Good," continued Wentworth. "The next question is, how could I imagine that Harrington, with his heaven-fated wife before his eyes, could possibly love my Emily? And that I don't know either, and can't explain, except on the theory that I'm a complete fool, which I'm not."

They all laughed merrily, Wentworth louder than any.

"And you, Muriel," he pursued. "How could you imagine for a moment that Harrington loved anybody but you? Both of you in constant communion, in the fullest, and broadest, and closest sympathy with each other, how could you think that he loved Emily better than you?"

"Why, Richard," returned Muriel, with bewitching gaiety, "since this is the hour of confession, let me confess that I don't know."

Wentworth laughed uproariously, and the rest joined him in his mirth.

"Well, Harrington," he continued, in a minute, "you now. It's not singular, of course, that you should have thought I loved Muriel; but in the name of all the gods at once, how could you think that she loved me? Where was your insight, Harrington?"

"Well, Richard," said Harrington, jocosely, "this whole matter may be solved on the theory that we are not the wisest people in the world."

"No, John, that won't do," returned Wentworth, "we're not the wisest, but we're wise enough not to be made fools of in anything but a love affair."

"Well then, let us concede our wisdom," replied Harrington, in the same jocose vein, "and solve the whole riddle with that deep maxim of my beloved Verulam, 'Love is the folly of the wise.'"

"Good! I rest there," said Wentworth, laughing. "Yes, my Lord Bacon, you're right, love is the folly of the wise."

"But it is the highest wisdom, too," observed Muriel.

"Of course," replied Harrington. "Verulam would be the last to gainsay that. I understand him to only mean that the mortal reason most exempt from the clouds of the other passions, is subject to the obscurations of this. It is one side of his tribute to the potency of love, and all human experience justifies it. Particularly ours," he jestingly added.

At this moment a tap was heard at the library door. It was Patrick, who, all in smiles for the new-married couple, announced that Mr. Witherlee was in the parlor below.

"Jupiter!" exclaimed Wentworth. "Let's have him up here, and give him a rowing."

"Yes, do," said Emily nervously. "Let's hear what he has to say for himself."

Muriel looked dubiously at Harrington.

"I really think," said Harrington, in answer to her look, "that Fernando ought to have a lesson on the danger and folly of such detraction and mischief-making as he practises. It would be salutary."

"Well then—but, Richard, you must promise me that you won't get angry at Mr. Witherlee—that you'll talk to him calmly," said Muriel.

"Oh, indeed I will!" declared Wentworth, rubbing his hands gleefully, and all alive with eagerness. "Only have him up here. I promise sacredly that I'll be as gentle as a sucking dove."

"And you, Emily, you must engage to be calm," said Muriel.

"Oh, I'll be calm. I despise him too much to be anything but calm," returned Emily with an air of indolent scorn.

"Very well. Patrick, show Mr. Witherlee up here," said Muriel.

Patrick bowed, and departed.

"Now for a scene!" cried the gleeful Wentworth. "His impudence won't get him out of this scrape."

"Take care, Richard," remarked Harrington, "for in my opinion you'll find it difficult to convict him of any misconduct."

"We'll see!" exclaimed Wentworth with a confident air.

Presently the door opened, and the good Fernando came in, bowing low with an almost cringe in his courtesy, and smiling with his usual constrained smile of elegance. He was very fashionably dressed, and looked, as he commonly did, handsome.

"Good morning," he said with courteous *empressement*, as he came bowing forward. "All together, as usual."

"Yes, all together," said Harrington, good-naturedly, giving him his hand as he spoke, and taking no notice of the covert sneer which lurked rather in the tone of his last remark than in the words.

Muriel also gave him her hand, Wentworth his rather distantly, though he smiled, and Emily bent her head with a sumptuous negative politeness, without rising from her chair.

In a minute or so, the good Fernando was seated, and gazing at them with opaque glittering eyes which restlessly flickered and seemed not so much to look at them, as toward them. He began to feel, magnetically, that there was something mysterious and menacing in their manner, and his plump, colorless, morbid face grew marble-cool and immobile, with the lips a little parted and rigid, as the lips usually are when there is an attempt at the concealment of emotion or purpose.

"Well, Fernando, have you heard the news," said Wentworth, alluding to Harrington and Muriel's marriage.

"No," drawled Witherlee, with a face discharged of all expression. "What is it?"

"Haven't you seen the papers this morning?" said Wentworth.

"No; I rose rather late this morning," was the equable answer, "and didn't breakfast at home. I went down to Parker's and had a lunch with a bottle of Sotairne, and it never occurred to me to glance at the paper. What is the news?"

Wentworth paused a moment, conscious that Witherlee had not heard of the marriage, and filled with an amused disgust, especially at the affected drawl with which the young fop had pronounced the word Sauterne, and generally at his ostentatious and unnecessary mention of his epicurean breakfast.

"The news is," replied Wentworth, changing his intention, "that Emily and I are engaged to be married in October."

Witherlee looked at him for a moment with his eyes more opaque, his lips more rigid, his face more expressionless than before, and slightly lifted his handsome eyebrows; then smiled with immense cordiality.

"I am *very* glad to hear it," he exclaimed, with tender *empressement*, "very glad indeed. But you surprise me. I hadn't the remotest idea that such a thing would happen"——

"And you didn't mean it should, if you could help it," interrupted Emily, with bland tranquillity.

Witherlee looked at her with an astonishment so admirably counterfeited, that she almost thought it genuine, and her heart faltered in its purpose. Wentworth, with a strong disposition to laugh, bit his lip, and looked at the floor. Muriel wore an air of sunny laziness, and Harrington, sitting a little apart, kept his searching blue eyes fixed intently on Witherlee's countenance, unnoticed by him.

"Why, Emily," said Fernando, slowly, after a long pause, "what do you mean! If I could help it? Why how could I hinder it, even if I wished to? How could I be supposed to know anything about it?"

"You knew Richard and I loved each other," stammered Emily, losing her self-possession as she thought how intangible was all her evidence against her colloquist. "You knew it, and you tried to prejudice me against him."

"I knew it?" repeated Fernando. "Miss Ames, you must pardon me for saying it—but you are very unjust to me." And he assumed an injured air, which was really touching. "It is utterly impossible that I could have known it, for neither you nor Wentworth, nor anybody, ever told me. As for prejudicing him, I do not know what you refer to—but if you mean our conversation one evening more than a week ago, you must permit me to observe that that is only a proof that I knew nothing whatever of this matter. For if I had, is it likely that I would be so foolish as to injure myself in your good opinion by saying anything against a man you loved? Even if I were ungenerous enough to do so, would I be so unwise? I am sorry, very sorry that you can think so meanly of my good sense, not to speak of anything higher."

He said it all so mildly, so sadly, with such an injured

air, that Emily was confounded, and felt unable to deny the apparent justice of his plausible plea. Yet a desperate sense that he had tampered with her feelings, and maligned her lover, still lingered in her mind.

"It may be as you say, Fernando," she faltered, "but at any rate, you know that you made remarks affecting Richard's character, which could not but make me think hardly of him."

"What did I say?" inquired Fernando, lifting his eyebrows in utter astonishment.

Emily, at that moment, could not for the life of her recall a single disparaging sentence. All the delicate poisoned phrases which had interspersed his lavish praise of Wentworth, were as invisible to the eye of her mind, as would be the deadly fragrance of some exquisite poisonous flower.

"Did I not speak of Mr. Wentworth in the warmest terms?" he demanded. "Did I not pay the warmest tributes to his character and talents?"

"I admit that you did," replied Emily, painfully coloring; "but you, nevertheless, contrived to throw a shadow on his constancy and purity as a lover, and what could have been worse to me who loved him?"

"I contrived!" exclaimed Fernando, lifting his head with an air of proud and disdainful injured innocence, which Harrington and Muriel alone saw was theatrically assumed and overdone. "I contrived! Miss Ames, I might answer this charge with simple silence, and conscious of its untruth, might bear it as a gentlemen should bear all injuries, with forgiveness But, since you were so unfortunate as to receive a wrong impression from remarks which were made only in candor, and which were not intended to injure any one, let me say this: Did you not yourself ask me to tell you candidly what I thought of Mr. Wentworth?"

"I own I did," replied poor Emily, wishing she had not said a word, and sorry that she had so rashly blamed the good Fernando for what was, she thought, her own fault after all.

"And when you asked me that, in the mutual confidence of friendship," pursued Witherlee, "can you blame me for having answered you with the candor you requested?"

Emily, with the tears very near her eyes, and her face glowing, was silent.

"If I had imagined what your feelings for Mr. Wentworth were," continued Witherlee, with touching mildness, "I would never have uttered anything but praise of him, though you asked it ever so much. But I never even suspected that. As for throwing a shadow on Mr. Wentworth's constancy, I never did it. I simply said, believing it to be true, and I'm very sorry if it's not true, that he had had a great many love affairs, and fell in love easily, and got out of it lightly, and so forth; but I'm sure that's nothing uncommon with a handsome young man whom all the young ladies are after, and no blame to anybody."

Wentworth colored up to the roots of his hair at the latter part of this speech, which the good Fernando delivered with a nonchalant, jocose air, very different from the wicked significance of manner with which, in speaking the words he avowed, and others of the same nature, he had given Emily to understand that her lover was a gay Lothario.

"You're mistaken, Fernando," stammered Wentworth, "if you think I ever fell seriously in love with any woman, and outlived it. I've had my fancy touched by a number of pretty girls, it is true, and I've been uncommonly amiable to them, no doubt, but they always disappointed me when I came to know them a little, and there never was any heart-injury done anywhere."

"I never supposed or said there was," replied Fernando, coolly. "It is Emily's misfortune to have exaggerated the simple meaning of what I did say, and what you, Richard, have confirmed. As for throwing any suspicion on Wentworth's moral character, Emily, I do not know what you can mean, and I must ask you to explain, for this is the most serious part of the whole misapprehension."

"You made no charge of that nature against Richard," said Emily terribly embarrassed, "but you told me of that young lady's betrayal—I forget her name—by young Whittemore, and dwelt on the insidiousness of his addresses to women in such a way, that I thought you were thinking of

Richard, or withholding something similar you knew of him, and—Oh, I have acted like a fool!" she passionately exclaimed, dashing away the tears which sprang to her eyes.

Witherlee saw his triumph with an exulting heart, while his face was, save for a little dejection, perfectly immobile.

"I am very, very sorry," he remarked in a slow, kind voice. "It is unaccountable to me that you should connect my narration, which was simply true, with Mr. Wentworth. I never heard of anything so singular."

"Let it go, Fernando," said Emily, "and do forgive"——

"What is the young lady's name of whom you speak in connection with Mr. Whittemore, Fernando?" interrupted Muriel, with an air of phlegm which she had caught from Harrington, who occasionally wore it. Muriel put the question, at once because she wanted to know, and because she was anxious to save Emily from the disgrace of asking Witherlee's forgiveness, when, as she saw, he had only adroitly juggled away his subtle slanders.

"Why it's Susan Hollingsworth," returned Witherlee, "you know her."

"That pretty Susan Hollingsworth!" exclaimed Muriel. "To be sure I know her. But I hadn't heard of this. How strange that I had not!"

"It is, certainly," replied Witherlee, lifting his eyebrows, "for it's town talk, and Miss Hollingsworth's position in society is perfectly ruined. She's taboo forever. I was at a party last night at Mrs. Binghampton's and you should have heard the way the ladies cut her up. It was a treat to hear it"—and Witherlee laughed with his turtle-husky chuckle. "That young Mr. Mill undertook to defend her, and it was perfectly ludicrous to see the scrape he got himself into. Miss Bean wanted to know instantly if he was going to come out in favor of Mormonism, and Mill was completely dumbfoundered, and covered with disgrace in a moment." And again Witherlee laughed with his turtle-husky chuckle.

"Have you seen Susan lately?" asked Muriel, abstractedly, with a face of sadness.

"No, I haven't called there since I heard of this affair,"

replied Witherlee with a sort of stolid importance. "The Hollingsworths have been sent to Coventry, and no decent person visits them."

Muriel colored, but very slightly, and only for a moment.

"*I* shall visit them," she said, quietly, "and I would have visited them before if I had heard of this. What is more, Susan is as good a girl as ever breathed, and I shall make it a point to invite her to come and spend a month at my house."

Witherlee looked perfectly immobile, but secretly stung by the rebuke Muriel's words conveyed to him, he felt the necessity of defending his attitude toward the Hollingsworths.

"I should be glad to still visit Miss Hollingsworth, if I could conscientiously," he said, with an air of cold and lofty virtue. "But when a young lady lets herself be led astray by an *ignis fatuus* light, from the paths of Christian morality"——

The generous color flashed to the calm face of Muriel, and her golden eyes glowed on him so suddenly that he stopped in the middle of his sentence.

"Fernando Witherlee," said she, in a slow and steady voice, and with a dignity that abashed even him, "if there is anything that could make me despise a fellow-creature, it would be such a speech as you have just made. *Ignis fatuus* light! I answer you with Robert Burns, and I accept it in a profounder sense than he did, that even the light that leads astray is light from Heaven. Christian morality! Who was the friend even of the Magdalen?—who was the friend and companion of publicans and sinners—the taboo men and women of old Jerusalem? Oh, shame upon you! A poor girl loving with the whole fervor of the sacred nature God gave her, guilty, at the most, only of a too absolute confidence in the traitor she had cast her heart upon, deceived now and abandoned, and suffering not only from her own private anguish, the greatest a human heart can know, but from the insolent and infamous scorn of society—and it is at such a time that you can have the soul to avoid her! And worse—you can tell the cruel treatment she receives from her sex, and laugh. Those graceless women—but I may well spare my indignation at the inhuman way women treat any of their number who have fallen from what they call virtue. Shut out by the impudent assumptions of mankind from public life—shut out from that experience which widens the understanding, and thus, as the statesman said, corrects the heart—theirs may well be twilight judgments! Well may they have constricted minds and narrow souls, with life's best culture denied them! Treated as vassals, theirs are vassals' vices. But you—a man! And society! Society whose mutual voice should peal consolation and encouragement to this poor forlorn one, howling her off into social exile, and, were she poor, to a life of shame—howling her self-respect, her very womanhood out of her. Oh, what can I say of such a society! No matter. You can do as you think best; but I, for one, will never taboo Susan Hollingsworth, and she shall visit me if I can persuade her."

Wincing secretly under this rebuke, which Muriel uttered calmly, but with impressive energy, Witherlee sat in silence, with his opaque eyes fixed on vacancy, and his handsome eyebrows lifted very high. Harrington, without taking his gaze from him, expressed his gratification at what Muriel had said by laying his large hand over hers, as it rested on the arm of her chair. Emily sat with a dazed look, and her lover was biting his lip all through the episode, to suppress any signs of the satisfaction he felt at Witherlee's discomfiture.

"My sentiments exactly, Muriel," said Wentworth. "But now, Fernando, to resume. You appear to have cleared yourself of any blame in the construction Emily put upon your words, and so far so good. But there are some other things I want to talk with you about."

"Proceed," said Witherlee, coolly. "Though I really think Emily ought to be permitted to make the apologies she was about to make to me for so grievous an injury to my feelings as I have sustained."

It is utterly impossible to describe the exquisite titillation of insult which, despite his subdued manner, these words of Witherlee conveyed. Wentworth reddened like fire instantly, and was only checked in a tremendous retort by a glance from the quiet eye of Muriel. But poor Emily, filled with contrition, started and colored, and was about to pour forth a profuse apology, when—

"Pardon me, Fernando," broke in the calm, deep voice of Harrington, "but let me suggest that Miss Ames' apologies will be in better place when you are entirely clear from the accusations connected with her, which Wentworth has to bring against you."

Witherlee turned very pale, though he showed no other signs of emotion, and fixed his impassible eyes on Harrington's, but unable, with all his stone opacity of outlook, to sustain their broad blue gaze, he carelessly lifted his eyebrows and looked away. Emily, meanwhile, having noticed Harrington's determined face, suddenly felt a suspicion that all was not so clear with Fernando as it seemed, and resolved to say nothing till she saw the end.

"What I have to say, Fernando, is this," began Wentworth, having choked down his rage into smiling calm. "It seems to me that on one occasion, at least, you did make mischief, if you'll excuse the word, between Emily and me. You said something that prevented Emily from giving me a bunch of violets last Tuesday morning."

"I did not," returned Witherlee, coolly. "I simply made a playful remark to Emily—the most innocent remark imaginable—which I'm perfectly willing to repeat now."

"Nevertheless," said Wentworth, "your innocent remark, or the manner in which you made it, incensed Emily against me."

"Am I to blame for her misapprehensions, Richard?" mildly asked Fernando. "You are aware now that Emily was in an unusually sensitive state of mind at that time. You see how she mistook the sense of other things I said, and yet you yourself have admitted that I am blameless in respect to those. Why, then, may she not have mistaken the sense of the playful remark I made about the flowers, and if so, why do you hold me to an account for it?"

Wentworth could not get over this. He was fairly checked in the very outset. The devil take it, he said to himself, I believe that Emily and I have been to blame after all!

"I was as much astonished as you were, Richard, at Emily's conduct about the violets," continued Fernando. "But I never imagined till this moment, that she was influenced by my remark. How could I? I thought she was rude to you, and I felt sorry. You must remember that I expressed my friendly regret to you at the time. Surely, I wouldn't have done that, if I had instigated her to offend you."

"Well, well," said Wentworth, hastily, "I pass that. I own that Emily was in a mood to misunderstand things; but see here. There were things you said to me in the fencing-school that morning which, to my shame, made me think unkindly of Harrington. Now"——

"Pardon me, Richard," interrupted Witherlee, with an air of great concern, "but this is the unkindest thing yet, and I do not understand what has got into you people's minds this morning. Now, what in the world did I ever say to you against Harrington? Just tell me candidly—were not you at that time incensed with Harrington for something or other—I don't know what?"

"I own I was," replied Wentworth, twirling his moustache and blushing.

"Very well. And did I ever express anything more than sympathy with you in your irritation?" demanded Witherlee.

"Well, I admit," replied Wentworth, "that what you said was in the form of sympathy with me. But then it led me to think more hardly of Harrington than I would have done."

Witherlee laughed as if his throat was full of turtle at this.

"You'll excuse me for laughing, Wentworth," he remarked, "but this is exceedingly absurd. Here were you in a state of nervous resentment at Harrington, and because your fiery temper took my kindly-meant attempts at consolation as fresh fuel, you blame me! Now I put it to you, as a reasonable man, was I to blame because you wrong-headedly twisted my consolations against your friend?"

Wentworth colored deeply, and did not answer. The deuce take it, he thought: I am making myself ridiculous in all this: the fact is, I was in such a miserably jealous and irritable state, that, as he says, I turned everything topsy-turvy.

"Ah, me!" sighed Witherlee, sadly lifting his eyebrows, as one who thus expressed that this was the fate of friendship, loyalty, virtue of all sorts, in this wicked, wicked, wicked world.

"Well, Fernando," said Wentworth, "I'm truly sorry—but stay, there's another thing, and that's not so easily explained. John Todd told me of a talk you had with Bagasse that same morning, about us four."

Wentworth paused to look at Witherlee, expecting to see him start and change color at this. Nothing of the sort. Witherlee's eyebrows were up, and his eyes were their opaquest, and his face was perfectly discharged of all expression. But in his soul was the first shock of alarm, for he had not counted on his conversation with Bagasse being reported to Wentworth.

"Well," said he, imperturbably, "what did John Todd say? You will first allow me to observe that it is not very creditable in him to have played the eavesdropper on a private conversation. And you will pardon me for remarking, Richard, that had I been in your place, my sense of honor would not have permitted me to listen to any gossip from him."

Wentworth blushed deeply. Gallant, honorable fellow that he was, he half-mistrusted that he had not done right in letting John Todd make his report, and what Witherlee said, certainly seemed in the most punctilious spirit of chivalry. Witherlee, meanwhile, satisfied with having dealt Wentworth's case a telling blow at the outset, rested in injured innocence, nervously impatient in spirit at the same time, to have the worst over with.

"I won't excuse myself, Fernando," said Wentworth, hurriedly. "But here is what the boy told me. In the first place, you mentioned the names of these two ladies to Bagasse. Now, that was not decorous"——

"Why not?" demanded Witherlee. "Just consider that what I said to Bagasse was in the confidence of familiar friendship, and the proof is, that Bagasse himself never spread it abroad—only that sneak of a boy."

"Familiar friendship with Bagasse!" exclaimed Wentworth, amazed. "I did not imagine you would be so intimate with the old fellow."

"And why not?" demanded Witherlee, with an air of noble disdain. "A gallant old soldier of the Empire—a brave old Frenchman, who wears the cross of the Legion! Do you think I'm such a snob as to shun his friendship because he's poor and plebeian, and all that? Indeed, no! Bagasse and I," he added, lying desperately, "are on very intimate terms, and I therefore felt justified in talking freely to him—which I wouldn't have done if I had noticed the presence of that reptile of a boy."

"Well," said Wentworth, beginning to despair, "but that does not excuse your making fun of my dress, or of"——

"It's not true," interrupted Witherlee. "I simply said, jestingly, that you looked bizarre with your long curls and your Rubens hat, and so you do. But it was harmless joking enough, I'm sure."

"I don't think, at anyrate, it was harmless joking for you to jeer at Harrington's coat, and say he looked like a ragpicker," remarked Wentworth.

"Well, if I ever heard of such malice and misrepresentation as that little serpent has been guilty of!" exclaimed Fernando, with virtuous indignation. "I never said anything of the sort. I simply remarked that Emily looked all the more gorgeous in contrast to the plain attire of Harrington, which was the simple truth. And as for the rest, my remark was that if she was dressed like a ragpicker, she would still be beautiful. Upon my word, I will chastise that boy the next time I see him!"

Wentworth looked perfectly confounded as Witherlee, with an air of indisputable veracity, told these bold lies.

"By Jupiter!" he exclaimed, "Johnny must have mistaken what you said, Fernando, with a vengeance! Well—but see here, you certainly gave Bagasse to understand that Harrington and I were in love with Muriel and Emily. Since you are a friend of his, I won't blame you for what you say you said in confidence; but still that doesn't excuse you for saying contemptuously that Muriel would as soon marry a man out of the alms-house as Harrington, and scornfully calling attention, as you did in that connection, to Harrington's apparel. You must have said that, for Johnny told me circumstantially what Bagasse said in reply, and he seemed to remember that better than what you had said. And by the way, your representing that John and I were these ladies' lovers, doesn't square with your assertion just now to Emily, that you had no idea of any feeling between her and me. By Jupiter, Fernando!" cried Wentworth at this point, elated to think that he had really caught Witherlee in a contradiction, "you can't make that square!"

"Mr. Wentworth," replied Fernando with dignified severity, "you go too far when you impugn my veracity, and you are perfectly reckless in your assertions. I told Emily that I had no idea there was any feeling between you two, and I told her the truth."

"Who did you think I had a feeling for?" demanded Wentworth.

"Since you force me to say, I thought it was Muriel—and Harrington can bear me witness," said Witherlee, severely.

"Yes," said Harrington, laconically. "Fernando told me so."

"Now, then!" exclaimed Witherlee, triumphantly, "where doesn't it square?"

Wentworth looked completely flabbergasted, as the sailors say, and colored painfully.

"As for the rest," pursued Witherlee, "it is just one tissue of misstatements. I never told Bagasse you and Harrington were in love with these ladies. On the contrary, when he got the notion into his head, I scouted it, as your own statement shows, for I did not wish him to believe what, though I supposed it, I did not absolutely *know* was the case. It is true that in endeavoring to convey to Bagasse that there was no foundation for his belief, I did say, rather splenetically, for his pertinacity irritated me, that it was just as likely Muriel would wed a man out of the poor-house as Harrington. But I protest against the construction of those words which would make it seem that I compared Harrington to a pauper, or insulted him in any way. I was only endeavoring to indicate the distance between his social position and Muriel's. You must bear in mind that I was talking to an illiterate man and a foreigner, and I only adapted my language to his illiteracy and to his imperfect knowledge of English, and used coarser terms than I would to a different person, which explains my use of that phrase, and the allusion to Harrington's plain coat. All I meant, and all I would have said to a person of culture, was that Muriel would not marry beneath her station."

"You were right, Fernando," said Muriel, coldly. "I never would, and Harrington knows it."

"So I thought," complacently replied Witherlee, thinking, oddly enough, that she concurred with him. "I knew that you and Harrington were only friends."

"But this Bagasse, I am told, thought it would not be beneath me to marry Harrington," remarked Muriel, with an air of contemptuous hauteur which Witherlee had never seen her wear before, and which surprised him. Whew! he thought, Harrington is catching it now for his presumption with a vengeance! I wouldn't sit there, and have that said to my face, for anything.

"Why yes," he replied, glancing at Harrington, who sat with his face buried in his hand, and what was visible of it so red that Witherlee thought he was smitten with agonizing shame, as he was, but it was for Witherlee. "Yes, Bagasse went into a fit of eloquence about it, and told what he would do if he was 'vair fine ladee,' and thought Harrington loved him." And Witherlee laughed turtle-husky at the reminiscence, without any more regard for Harrington's feelings than if he were a post.

"Well, Wentworth, are you satisfied?" asked Muriel, quietly.

Wentworth, who had gone off into deep abstraction, and lost the conversation between Muriel and Witherlee (which would have convulsed him, and which had sorely tried Emily's power to suppress her mirth), started and colored.

"Why, yes," he replied, "I am bound to own that Fernando's explanation puts a different look upon the matter, though I think he did wrong to speak to Bagasse in such terms of Harrington, and I think he owes Harrington an apology for language at the best too ungentlemanly—I must say it, Fernando—to be passed over in silence. There is no excuse for it. It was shameful."

"Do you really think so, Richard?" said Muriel, with such a contemptuous tone and expression that Wentworth turned red, and stared at her, wondering what she could mean; while Emily moved away to the window, and hid herself behind a curtain, that she might give some vent to her agony of mirth.

"Well, Fernando," said Muriel, after a pause, "what do you think about making Mr. Harrington an apology?"

Witherlee, emboldened to intense insolence by his monstrously silly supposition that Muriel was showering contempt on her lover, curved a supercilious lip and curled a contumelious nose to that extent, that the fiery Wentworth positively ached to knock him down.

"I do not think about it at all," drawled the good Fernando.

"Very well," said Muriel, holding Wentworth with her eye. "Now, Fernando, since we are explaining things, let me ask you how you came to say that you saw Wentworth and I one afternoon more than a week ago, folded in each other's arms in the parlor, and kissing each other?"

Muriel's tactics were capital. By diverting his mind from the main subject of conversation, she had thrown him completely off his guard, and then suddenly sprung this question upon him. Fernando positively changed color, and then turned deadly pale. If a bomb-shell had quietly fallen into his lap, with the fuze just fizzing into the powder, he could not have been much more astounded.

There was a pause, in which Emily came gliding back to her seat, all alive with curiosity at this unexpected turn in affairs, while Wentworth stared blankly, and Harrington sat with his face buried in his hand, watching Witherlee, as the marine phrase has it, out of the tail of his eye.

"Well, Fernando, you turn red, and then you turn pale," remarked Muriel, quietly. "What do those two colors mean?"

"They mean astonishment," said Witherlee, recovering his self-possession instantly, and looking at her with his most brazen face, conscious that the tug of war had come, and with an antagonist of another sort than Wentworth or Emily.

Oho, thought Muriel, surveying his admirably dissimulated face. I wonder if I'm going to lose this move. Let's see.

"You don't mean to deny that I did see you in such a position with Wentworth?" said Witherlee.

"Most assuredly," was Muriel's quiet reply.

"Most inevitably," said Wentworth, like an Irish echo.

"Why, this is perfectly unaccountable," murmured Witherlee, with superbly acted astonishment. "I certainly did see you both, as I told Mr. Harrington in a rash moment, which I can never too much regret. I was entering the parlor when I saw you, and drew back instantly. I came in again in a minute, and Emily had just entered the room, through the door leading from the conservatory."

"It can't be," said Muriel.

"Can't possibly be," said the Irish echo, ineffably delighted at Witherlee's fix.

"But how could I be mistaken," persisted Witherlee. "There you evidently were, both of you, in that position. You, Muriel, had on the lilac dress you so often wear. It was the first thing I saw, and I knew you by it instantly."

"Utterly impossible," said Muriel.

"Tee-totally impossible," said the gleeful echo.

Witherlee was silent, and gazed at them with admirable dubiety, wishing in his heart that they would only say more, for with these brief denials, he found it difficult to gracefully gain the point he was driving at.

"It was I you saw, Fernando; I had on a lilac dress that evening," said the innocent Emily, blushing.

Muriel winced, for her game was weakened by this avowal, which had brought up the point Fernando was waiting for, and which she did not mean he should have. Fernando, meanwhile, was delighted, for he saw his clear way out.

"You had on a lilac dress that evening!" he said, with an air of surprise, to Emily. "Well, I declare I didn't notice it. But how does that alter the matter? Oh, I see!" he exclaimed, his face lighting. "It was the lilac dress misled me, for you wore your lilac dress that evening, Muriel. That's it. My eye caught sight of the dress, and I mistook you for Emily, and retreated before my eye could rectify the error. What an unlucky blunder! I'm very, very sorry. But in the confusion of the moment, I was naturally deceived. Well, well! Muriel, I humbly beg your pardon, not only for having mentioned what I thought I saw to Mr. Harrington—but you won't blame me for that, for it foolishly came out in the heat of conversation—but for this unfortunate mistake of mine. It was natural, under the circumstances, but it is not the less humiliating. Say that you forgive me, now, do!"

"Oh, well, Fernando," she replied, nonchalantly laughing, "I must, of course, give weight to your plea of its naturalness under the circumstances. Still, you perceive it was a rather awkward blunder, and it ought to make you more careful for the future."

"Indeed, it will—I'll be very careful not to make such a mistake again," said Fernando, laughing turtle, and quite exhilarated by his lucky escape.

"That's right," said Muriel, gaily. "For such a mistake, Fernando, might break up our long acquaintance. At all events," she pursued, with a laugh, "it might prevent your being honored with such a theatrical reception as I gave you that evening."

"Theatrical?" said he, smiling; "what do you mean?"

"Why, don't you remember," she lightly responded, "how suddenly I struck an attitude, and held out the bunch of flowers to you?"

"Yes, indeed," replied the jocund Witherlee. "I had forgotten it, but I remember it now. Just as I came in at one door, and you"——

He paused blankly, but he was in the trap, and there was no escape now.

"And I came in at the other," continued Muriel, finishing his sentence.

He gazed at her, pale, with opaquest eyes; she at him, with clear eyes aglow, and a solemn look upon her countenance. Wentworth and Emily stared at both of them, not comprehending the point at all.

"And now, Fernando," said Muriel, calmly, "the question for you to answer is—How could you think you saw me with Wentworth, when you saw me come in from the conservatory, holding out the bunch of flowers to you?"

A posing question! There was a long pause, in which Witherlee kept his rigid face fixed upon her. Then, unable to bear her clear gaze, he meanly trembled, and his head fell.

"Ah!" said Wentworth, in a low voice, "catch the first! A decided catch. Fernando, my boy, we have you in a pure and simple lie."

At this terrible speech, Witherlee lifted his livid and rigid face with a forlorn attempt at dignity, but he could not sustain it. His glittering and unsteady eyes flickered away from the open and gallant countenance of Wentworth; from Emily, gazing at him with lustrous scorn; from Muriel, looking at him with solemn pity; from Harrington, sitting with his head bowed in his hand, and fell. He could not bear to look at them. Mischief-makers, like other criminals, usually mix folly with their crime, and in the commission of their wickedness, commonly leave the clue to its discovery. Thus had Witherlee done. And now he was found out. To tattle and lie and slander was nothing to him; but to be discovered, was death.

"Fernando," said Emily, with indignant composure, "this wicked falsehood you have told makes it impossible to believe a word you have said. I do not now credit a single syllable of your explanation—not one."

At the sound of her voice, Witherlee seemed to recover a

little self-possession, for he turned quickly to her, though his unsteady eyes did not rest upon her face.

"You have no right to say that," he replied in a querulous and tremulous voice, "no right whatever. I am willing to own my fault, but it is not fair to argue from one fault to another. I have told you the truth, and you saw its reasonableness, and acquitted me of blame. It is not fair to take it back, not at all fair."

He rose to his feet with a look of received injury, which even then touched Emily, and made her hesitate in her verdict. But at that moment Harrington left his chair, and came toward him with tears flowing from his eyes. Witherlee cowered at the sight of this solemn and compassionate emotion, and his head fell. In that moment he remembered the hard and cruel insult he had so lately flung upon the man before him, and he trembled in an agony of shame.

"Fernando," said Harrington, calmly and tenderly, "I pity you from the bottom of my heart. I could almost die with pity for you. Do not, I beg of you, do not degrade your soul by persisting in what you know to be falsehoods. You know you are not telling Emily the truth now, and you know there is not a word of truth in all you have told her."

"I do not see what right you have to say that, Harrington," faltered Witherlee.

"Fernando!" exclaimed Harrington, solemnly, "Alas, alas! you poor fellow, I do not blame you! there is some virtue still in this forlorn attempt to clothe the nakedness of your falsehood in the semblance of truth. But it is useless, and it only does your nature a more grievous harm. Do you not see that you have already confessed all? You have admitted that you knew it was Emily and Wentworth you saw together. You knew, therefore, that they were lovers. How can you say then, that in your conversation with Emily that very evening, you did not know of their feeling for each other? How can you say that you did not know your terrible dispraise of Wentworth, so artfully clothed in praise, would shock and grieve the woman who loved him? How can you say you did not know your story of Susan Hollingsworth would throw its shadow on the thoughts with which you had filled Emily? How can you say you thought your aggravating word a week later over the violets, was harmless? Ah, Fernando! how could you so coldly and cruelly drop this subtle poison into the hearts of two lovers? You gave Richard and Emily hours of terrible suffering. You nearly alienated them from each other—you almost murdered their love. How could you do it? You knew they loved each other—you knew I loved Muriel; and yet you wantonly saddened my heart by virtually telling me that Wentworth and Muriel were betrothed. At the same time when you knew that Emily loved Wentworth, you gave Captain Fisher to understand that she was engaged to me. Fernando, you are entirely discovered. Your talk with Bagasse is just as transparent, and just as disgraceful to your better nature, as all the rest. Alas, alas! I can only pity you!"

The deep voice was gentle, and tears still flowed from the calm eyes. Emily sat with her handkerchief to her face, touched by the majestic sorrow of Harrington into compassion, and weeping silently. Muriel had covered her eyes with her hand. Wentworth stood with folded arms, his face pale, and fixed on Witherlee. Witherlee, completely unmasked even to himself, stood with bowed head, livid and trembling, and there was a long pause.

"Harrington," faltered the poor rogue, in a weak, querulous voice, "I am very sorry—I am indeed. I know I've done wrong—very wrong, and I'm sorry. I feel very miserable. I haven't a friend in the world now, and I know I don't deserve to have. But I hope you'll forgive me, Harrington, though I did you harm. I didn't quite mean"——

His faltering voice broke, and apparently unconscious of any but the presence of the young man before him, he sunk his head a little lower, and stood trembling.

"Forgive you!" exclaimed Harrington, in a voice so sudden and sonorous that Witherlee started, and fell a pace away. "Fernando, give me your hand!"

Tremblingly, as Harrington strode straight up to him, with a frank outstretched arm, Witherlee put his nerveless hand in his, looked up for an instant into the masculine and noble face, dropped his head and burst into tears.

A surge of emotion overswept them all, and for a minute there was no sound but the thick sobs of Witherlee.

"Fernando," said Harrington, solemnly, clasping his hand, and putting his arm tenderly around him, "let the past be with the past, and live nobler for the future. See: your repentance cancels all, and lifts you into better life. You are not friendless—not forsaken. We are your friends, all of us, and we will stand by you. Forgive you? I do with all my soul, fully, heartily, cordially."

"And I, too, Fernando," cried Muriel, bounding up, and gliding swiftly toward him, with humid eyes and outstretched hand. "Well I may, for you did me the greatest service ever done to me, and I owe you much gratitude."

"I don't understand," faltered poor Witherlee, trembling all over, and smiling, with an effort, a thin, gelid, arctic smile through his abject tears, as he tremulously shook her hand.

"You introduced me, three years ago, to Harrington," she smilingly replied, "and now he is my husband. We were married yesterday."

Fernando stopped trembling, and lifted his handsome eyebrows a hair's breadth, with something of his old manner, then fell a-trembling again, and tried to smile.

"I am very glad to hear this," he wanly faltered, "very glad indeed. I wish you much happiness. If you'll please to excuse me, I'll—I'll take my leave."

He bowed with the ghost of his former affected elegance of manner, and gelidly smiling, backed toward the door.

"Hold on, Fernando," exclaimed Wentworth, flying over to him. "Tip us your flipper, my boy. There isn't a speck of me that's not friendly to you—not a speck. Come and see me as often as you can—that's a good fellow."

And Wentworth, smiling, shook his hand up and down with great cordiality, as he rattled off this address.

"And I, Fernando," said Emily, with her slow, ambrosial smile, sweeping over to him as she spoke, and also taking his hand, "I am more your friend than I have ever been. I felt terribly at what you said, but I don't now, so let it all go. Come to see me soon, won't you ?"

"Thank you. You are both very kind," faltered Witherlee.

"Let us see you as often as you can, Fernando," said Harrington, shaking hands with him.

"Yes, do, Fernando," said Muriel, also giving him her hand. "Let us forget all this, and when we next meet, let it be happily."

He bowed, with his face full of forlorn emotion, and backing to the door, bowed himself out of the room. They stood in silence. Presently they heard the shutting of the street-door. He was gone.

"Good !" exclaimed Wentworth, with a deep respiration. "Fernando's cured for life !"

"I believe he is," murmured Muriel. "But he almost missed his salvation, poor fellow !"

"That he did," replied Wentworth. "He got clear of Emily, and he got clear of me. I never saw anything like it. But you nailed him, Muriel, and Harrington finished him."

"Ah, me !" said Harrington, with a deep sigh, "it was an awful lesson to give a fellow-being. But it was for his good. Yes, he will be a better man for the future."

Emily sat in silence, wiping the fast-springing tears from her eyes.

"I wonder how he will look when we next see him," said Wentworth, musingly. "And I wonder how soon he will call here after this"——

"Nay," interrupted Muriel, her drooping hands clasped before her, and her head bowed in pensive reverie, "he will never call here again."

She was right. He never did—but once.

CHAPTER XXVI.

A MAN OF RUINED BLOOD.

WHERE was Mr. Lafitte all this time? Had he returned to the sunny South, and to that particular part of its sunniness in which sweltered his negroes at their miserable toil?

Mr. Lafitte had not. He was still in the city, at the Tremont House, and for the last three days he had kept his room, sick and shattered with the terrible shock he had received, and raging like a devil in his impotent fury. That he should owe his life to the man he hated was bad enough; but to a woman, and worse still, to a negro—oh, to his rank and insolent pride this was the humiliation of humiliations! It had not come to him at first, but several hours after Harrington had left him, when he began to recover from the paralysis of spirit in which he lay, it outgrew upon him, and increased in intensity, till he raved in a phrenetic agony of infernal shame and rage.

In this delightful mood he had continued for three days. Exhausted on the night of the third by the violence of his frenzy, he had slept heavily, and awakened late on the morning of the fourth, calmer in spirit, and though still somewhat weak, stronger and in better health than he had been. The Atkinses, father and sons, had called severally three times, during his illness, but he had left orders that he would see nobody, and they had not been admitted to his presence.

Up now and dressed, his breakfast eaten, two juleps imbibed and a cigar finished, he began to feel more like himself, and look more like the handsome brunette devil he usually was. A little less rich in color, to be sure, but still sufficiently so for good appearance's sake; and as he walked up and down the plainly-furnished chamber, in the space between his bed and the window, he even felt something of his usual fiendish jocundity revive sullenly within him.

Three letters had arrived for him during his illness. He had not even looked at them, but let them lie unopened on the table where the servant had laid them. Now, however, when his mind was able to attend to their contents, he paused in his walk as his eye rested on them, and approaching the table, took them up, and gazed at their superscriptions and post-marks.

"That's from my brother," he muttered, "and that also, and this—'Mobile—forwarded'—who can this be from?"

He tore it open, and ran his eye over the contents.

"Oh, pshaw!" he snarled, flinging it down. "Business. Business be cursed! I'm in no mood for business. Let's see what Joseph has to say for himself. Which is the first—Oh, this is it."

He opened the letter, deliberately smoothed it out, and caressing his moustache with one hand, while he held the sheet in the other, began to read with a face that flushed into a horrid and tigerish smile as he read on. This was the letter:

New Orleans, La., *May 20th*, 1852.

Dear Torwood:

There's been the devil to pay up on your plantation, and no mistake, and poor Tassle has gone the way of all flesh. On the 15th, Tassle lashed that mulatto wench Sally three or four times for falling down in the rows—the yellow beast pretending of course that she was sick, as they always do. Precious little work, at all events, was got out of her that day, and when night came, Tassle staked her down for a good flogging. That black Jim of yours, her husband, tried to beg her off the flogging, but Tassle wasn't to be wheedled out of it, and struck Jim, so they tell me, across the face with the whip. Whereupon, Jim flew at him with an axe, and in a second it was all up with poor Tassle. The boy actually cut him to pieces, and then ran for the swamp. The planters were roused, however, got out the dogs, hunted him down, and in less than no time, I may say, a fire was lit by the bayou, and the black scoundrel trussed up and burned alive, screeching like mad, with all the niggers looking on. They'll profit by the example, I reckon, and learn that it won't do to murder a white man—the cursed brutes.

I am hurrying up to fix business, so that I can go up river, and attend to the plantation for you, till you get back. But you'd better hurry home as quick as you can, for it's a busy season with us here, and I can't well be away. In haste, your aff.,

JOSEPH LAFITTE.

P.S. By the way, the wench Sally gave birth to a fine piccaninny, a boy, that night—somewhat prematurely, I'm told. So you see there's no small loss without some great gain. As for Tassle, he's no loss at all, for you can easily replace him, and I've got my eye on a capital overseer for you. J. L.

The smile on the sardonic visage of Mr. Lafitte expanded more and more tigerish, and as he came to the end of the letter, he burst into a smooth, soft roar of merriment, while floods of devilish delight raged within him.

"And so William Tassle's food for worms," he soliloquized, shaking with internal laughter. "Poor Tassle, that's the end of you. And Jim's roasted. Good! I hope they made the fire slow. Infernal scoundrel! I wish I'd been there to hear him screech the soul out of him. That's the way to keep the black devils under. God! if it wasn't for a good fire round some of them when they lift their hands against us, I believe that they'd be up in insurrection, and give us St. Domingo. But that they never can do while the Union lasts. Ah, the glorious Union! Rise on us if you dare, my black angels, and see the short work the muskets of the Union will make with you. Liberty and Union, now and forever, one and inseparable! That's the ticket for you, my black cherubs!"

And again Mr. Lafitte burst into raging laughter.

"Ah, me, ah me!" he sighed, subsiding. "I feel refreshingly wicked to-day, spite of all. This news has done me good. But let's see what Joseph has to say again," he added, deliberately opening the other letter, and smoothing it out as he had done the first, with a sardonic smile on his brunette face.

Ah, Mr. Lafitte! What is this? As he began to read the color of his face vanished, like the flame of a blown-out lamp, his complexion became livid, with dark spots on its ghastliness, his eyes grew glassy, and his jaw fell. He did not drop the letter, but read slowly and steadily on—and this is what he read:

LAFITTE PLANTATION, AVOYELLES, LA.,
May 23d, 1852.

TORWOOD, come home for God's sake as quick as you can. There's worse news here than I wrote you on the 20th. Josephine has eloped with young Raynal. I'm sorry to tell you so abruptly, but I don't know how to break it to you. This is evidently a preconcerted affair, for Raynal, you know, was retiring from business just about the time you left, and has since been turning all his property into money. Anyhow, they're gone—gone to Italy—and they're out of the country by this time.

I've just arrived here, and I never was so horrified in my life as when I discovered this. I half suspected that there was something wrong when I heard that Raynal had been in the neighborhood, for I knew that he loved her before her marriage to you. But I didn't get any idea of it till just now, when I came up to the house and inquiring for Josephine, was told by your cook that Raynal came there the night of Jim's barbecue, and that she had left with him, taking only a single trunk with her. Which way they went, up river or down, nobody knows. But I went up-stairs into her chamber, and found a sheet of note paper lying on her writing-desk, addressed to you, on which was written just these words and no more: "Lafitte, I go away to-night to Italy, never to return." That was every word.

Torwood, I'm devilish sorry for you. I had no idea that Josephine would do such a thing as this, for everybody knows and says you've been a good husband to her, and down in Orleans you were talked of as a model couple, and your constant courtesy and kindness to her was in everybody's mouth. Well, women are the devil, and no mistake.

But come home as soon as you can. Nobody but me knows what has happened, and I think we can keep this matter private, and save you the disgrace. Of course her family must know it, but they'll feel terribly cut up about it, and be willing to keep dark. I've spread it around that Raynal has taken her up North to you, so the wonder of her absence is explained. Then, perhaps, you can say that she died suddenly up North, and put on the bereaved dodge, and so cover it up for good.

Anyhow, come right along, and we'll consult together about it.

In great haste, your aff.,

JOSEPH LAFITTE.

He slowly laid the letter down, and stood still. Livid and spotted as a corpse when decomposition has begun, his glassy orbs fixed on vacancy, his jaw fallen and rigid, his whole form motionless. Thus for a full minute. Then, his fallen jaw slowly lifted, his lips came together, and a still and frightful smile glided upon his features.

"God !" he exclaimed, in a low, clear, distinct voice, "it's over. Josephine has escaped from holy matrimony."

He said no more, but with the still and frightful smile upon his face, stood motionless for some minutes. Slowly his color returned, his glossy, blood-specked, tawny orbs outgrew again from the glassiness, and opening his tiger mouth, he burst into a long fit of smooth, soft, sardonic laughter.

"Yes," he soliloquized, subsiding from his fiendish mirth into a fiendish smile—"yes, indeed, Josephine has escaped from holy matrimony. Oh, what a blow to the interests of morality ! What a shock to the foundations of society! What a rupture of the sacred bonds of wedlock ! What a profanation of the sacrament of marriage ! And Joseph proposes to keep it dark. Oh, Joseph, Joseph, how can you? As a good Christian, as a friend of morality, and religion, and society, and, above all, holy matrimony, could I do it? Ah, never, never ! And Joseph wants to save me the disgrace. The disgrace !"—and with a negrine *ptchih*, Mr. Lafitte went off into a fit of chuckling merriment.

"No, indeed, Joseph," he resumed, "we must spread it, and spread it wide. We must get it into the papers, my beloved brother. We must get it into the New Orleans papers, and the Western papers, and the New York papers. Josephine must have the disgrace as my last love-touch, and I must have the sympathy of the Friends of Virtue, sweet Joseph. Oh, Lord !" and he chuckled, "what fun I shall have in my affliction reading the homilies of the moral editors ! Let's see, how will they go. . . . Melancholy Case of Conjugal Infidelity. . . . Yes, that's pretty good. . . . Free Love Invading the Family Circle. . . . And that's magnificent. . . . The Results of Free Love Teachings. . . . That's magnificent, too. Let's see. . . . Another Base Violation of the Marriage Tie. . . . Shocking Case of Seduction, Elopement, and Crime. . . . . Another Blow at the Foundations of Morality. . . . Ruin of a Home and a Husband. . . . . Oh, they're all good—capital ! Then the articles. Lord, but won't they be luscious! How I shall weep over the tender sympathy; how I shall mourn, yet say, it is just, over the stern condemnation of Josephine; what a moral glow I shall feel through all my being at the severe rectitude and fidelity to the best interests of morality which will pervade those high-toned editorials! Now let's see. Let's compose an appropriate one. It must be a piece of ignorant, stupid, brutal, sentimental twaddle, mal-apropos and blundering, and stuck full of stale quotations, or it won't be in style. Hold on now," and in a declamatory voice he went on as follows: ". . . . . We chronicle in another column a mournful case of conjugal perfidy, of which a too tender and confiding husband is the heart-broken victim. To what vortex are we rushing? Well may we say, in the language of the immortal dramatist, that such a deed as this—

—'makes marriage vows
As false as dicers' oaths. Oh! such a deed
As from the body of contraction plucks
The very soul; and sweet religion makes
A rhapsody of words! Rebellious hell,
If thou canst mutine in a matron's bones,
To flaming youth let virtue be as wax,
And melt in her own fire!'

Capital, capital!" roared Mr. Lafitte, with a spasm of chuckling merriment, rubbing his hands gleefully, as he spoke, "that's the stock quotation, and doesn't it come in gloriously! Rebellious hell in the matron Josephine's bones—Oh, upon my soul, but that's decidedly neat! Fire away, my boy. . . . In this melancholy tragedy which has laid low the Lares and Penates of a once happy home, and brought the severest affliction on the fond and trusting heart of a highly respectable and estimable citizen, we trace the pernicious influence of those detestable and licentious doctrines which have become, alas! too prevalent throughout the land. We allude of course to the doctrines of Free Love, and let every man in his sober senses look upon this domestic tragedy, the legitimate result of those vile teachings whose poison is spread abroad through the very air, and ask what is to be the end, when such tenets are openly disseminated? Here was a woman—we call her woman, but every true woman's heart will rise in just indignation to clutch away the name from such a moral monster! a female fiend rather, who could defile the inviolable sanctuary of wedded life, listen to the insidious honeyed words of a base seducer, fly from the tender endearments of home, ruthlessly abandon her fond and trusting husband and innocent children—Oh, damn it," broke in Mr. Lafitte, "that won't do! I've got no children. Ah, me! what a pity. It would be so pathetic if the children could be in it—the dear, little innocent children! No matter: . . . . abandon her fond and trusting husband, with whom she had lived so many happy years, and who had lavished on her his wealth, his good name, and all the priceless riches of a generous and affectionate nature, surrounding her with every comfort and ministering with the tenderest assiduity to her lightest want—abandon all this, and depart with her paramour to a life of shame on the voluptuous and luxurious shores of Italy. Ah, well may this modern Messalina go to Italy!

> ''Tis the land of the East, 'tis the clime of the sun,
> Can he smile on the deeds that his children have done?'

. . . Capital!" again roared Mr. Lafitte, rubbing his gleeful hands, "Italy the land of the East! That's a regular blunderbuss of a quotation, and therefore in exquisite keeping. Oh, upon my soul, that comes in finely! But fire away, Lafitte, you delicious dog. Let's see now. . . . . What makes the criminality of this shameful woman's conduct more inexcusable and inexplicable is the fact that she had lived for years in the most perfect harmony with her amiable and estimable husband, receiving from him the most unvarying tenderness, and to the eye of every person most familiar with their domestic life, evidently the happiest of the happy. We have it from the most reliable sources that no cloud ever appeared to mar the horizon of their home, and among their intimate friends, the courtesy and almost uxorious tenderness of his demeanor toward her, was absolutely proverbial. But why seek to trace the causes of this base and ungrateful treachery? Alas! since

Eve listened to the temptings of the serpent, how many of the sex have sacrificed their conjugal Eden for the bleak wilderness of illicit love! Frailty, thy name is woman!" . . .

Mr. Lafitte stopped, and with another *ptchih*, went off into a fit of infernal merriment, wagging his head from side to side in the frenzy of his glee.

"That's the way they do it!" he exclaimed, resuming. "Lord, I ought to be an editor! I was cut out for a high-pressure moral editor of the purest water! The blasted idiots—that's the way they roll it out whenever one of these inexcusable and inexplicable cases of shameful criminality on the woman's side, and heavenly love and tenderness on the man's side, or vice versâ, come to their confounded eyes! The owls—the bats—the insufferable fraternity of asses! Lord, Lord! how often I've laughed till I ached over their moral gabble, thinking all the while of the sweet little hell the women or the men they were pitching into had cut away from, and which the witless ninnies hadn't brains enough to fancy! And then their tender sympathy to the bereaved one—hold on—let me fancy how they'll touch me off? . . . We proffer to the bereaved husband, in his sad affliction, our tenderest sympathy, and may God who tempers the wind to the shorn lamb, give him strength to bear this terrible trial which has thus desolated the sanctuary of his lonely and forsaken home. . . . and so forth, and so forth, and so forth. Yes, that's the way they'll pour the oil of healing into my aching wounds! Oh, but it'll be touching. And then society—what sympathy I'll have from society. I must be in New Orleans a few weeks to enjoy my affliction. How melancholy I'll look—how interesting! And all the old ladies flocking around me with such doleful and tender faces, and oh, Mr. Lafitte, we feel so sorry for you, and oh, Mr. Lafitte, we read that beautiful article in the paper this morning, and it was so sweet and so noble and so high-toned, and so this, that, and the other. And the young ladies ogling me with melancholy eyes, and whispering to each other, oh, isn't he handsome, and oh, isn't he interesting, and oh, doesn't he bear it beautifully, and how much did you say he was worth? —and dying to become Mrs. Lafitte, number two, every fool of them. And then the Friends of Virtue, men and women, young and old, in solid column, pitching into Josephine, and scandalizing her sky-high, and raking up everything she ever said or did, and twisting it against her. Oh, but it will be sweet! Sweeter than to have Raynal's blood on my hands—the dog! Then when the grand hallali begins to die out, I'll apply for my divorce, and revive it all once more. Ah, delicious! And then by and by, perhaps, I'll marry again—some queen of a girl dead in love with the rich Mr. Lafitte, the handsome Mr. Lafitte, the gentle and courteous Mr. Lafitte, with the steel claw in the velvet paw. Ah! and if Fatima isn't docile, Bluebeard will take her into the Blue Chamber where Josephine had a little private experience. Good, good! Lafitte, you gay dog, you are positively witty!"

Wagging his wicked head to himself, he walked slowly up and down, laughing softly and smoothly, with his face bent toward the carpet. He stopped his walk in a minute or two, and the smile on his visage faded slowly into a look of sullen and evil moodiness.

"The revenge is sweet," he muttered, "but there is gall in it. She has escaped from her hell with me, and she will be happy with Raynal. Yes, there in that lovely Italy, far away from all the howls of the slandering curs, she will be happy with Raynal. For he loves her, and they are both young still, and she is beautiful, and will be fond and sweet, and he is tender to women, and manly—bah! I hate him!"

He walked up and down in silence for a few minutes, with an evil and moody face, and finally paused with his gloomy eyes fixed on vacancy.

"People will rave at them," he muttered, "but what matter is it what people will say! Fools! Look at it. What was she? The prey of my lust—the victim of my cruelty. God! I will not lie to myself whoever else I lie to! That is just what she was. I won her, a young, inexperienced, innocent girl—she lived with me as she did, and they call it holy matrimony. She flies now from lust and cruelty to love and tenderness, and they call it adultery. Oh, world, world, world! Should I have been what I am, if you had not been what you are ! Damn you ! you have ruined me !—from my very cradle you have ruined me ! I hate you—I despise you —I have grown up hating and despising you—soured, and corrupted, and depraved by you—and I shall be glad when this wretched candle of a life goes out in the blackness of darkness forever. Well, well ! Be happy, Josephine, with your Raynal. I hate you both, and what I can do to harm you I will."

He sat down near the table, and leaned his head on his hand. As he did so, a tap came to the door.

" Come in," he snarled.

It was a servant, who said a gentleman wanted to see him.

" What's his name ? No matter. Show him up."

With an uneasy, furtive glance at him, the man departed, and in two or three minutes appeared again with Captain Bangham.

" Well, what do you want ?" snarled Lafitte, the moment he appeared. " Have you found that curse, Antony ?"

The captain looked savage and sullen at this reception, and hated Lafitte ten times worse than ever, while, at the same time, he was afraid of him.

"No, I haven't found him," he said, snappishly. " I've been two or three times up where that Roux lives, and he's not there, and nobody knows where he is ; and as for the other, I can't get any clue to him."

Mr. Lafitte rose from his chair, and with glossy, tigerish eyes, and a ferocious face, advanced upon Bangham, who winced a little as he came, as if he would like to run from the room but for the shame of it. Bullies are not always cowards, but this bully was.

" Hark you, Bangham," said Mr. Lafitte, in a low, smooth voice, " I'm going home in the first train, and you may tell Atkins I've gone, for I shan't see him again. That Roux I don't want, so let him alone. But you find Antony for me, or look out. You're in a fix, my captain, and you know it. You can't bring any evidence against the presumption of the law that you willfully refused to return that slave. Where are your witnesses to the contrary ? Your mate has left Atkins's employ—your sailors don't go back to New Orleans with you.

You know the penalty for not bringing back a slave you find on board your brig—from three to seven years in prison, and the payment of the full value of the slave ; and I'll set that value high, Bangham, you may depend. Let your brig touch the Levee again and he not on board, and I'll make you suffer to the full extent of my power, and spread stories around which will ruin Atkins in New Orleans for good. Mind what I say to you. Now go."

At the haughty mandate of the Southerner, spoken with an outstretched finger, as though he was ordering away his meanest slave, Bangham slunk from the room without a word.

"Whelp," snarled Lafitte, walking away from the door with a shrug of contempt. "Yes, I'll let Roux go. I owe so much to that good fool, Harrington, I suppose. Curse me, if I don't almost hate myself for liking that fellow ! There's another happy pair. He and that bright creature will be marrying presently, and going in for domestic felicity with a rush. Blast them, I hope they'll be miserable together through life, and I wish I could make them so ! Well—now to pack up and leave this cursed city for home. I burn to get at my black cattle again, and ease my heart of its hatred on them. I hate them and they hate me, and life is thick and sweet with hate. Oh, but I'll work, and flog, and torture them worse than ever now ! Thanks to the blessed laws of Louisiana, I can do it, as long as the glorious Union lasts. Till these northern curs dissolve that, my rule is secure, but when they do, if they ever do, 'ware Lafitte, 'ware my Southern brethren, for the black worm will turn, and hey for St. Domingo !"

CHAPTER XXVII.

REVELATIONS.

Witherlee had not left the house in Temple street but a little while, when a couple of ladies, intimate with the family.

who had seen the news of the marriage in the morning paper, called, on a visit of congratulation. Presently more came, and up to one o'clock there was a dropping shower of callers. Last of all arrived Miss Bean, a fat and spectacled childish old maiden lady, with a prude's face—the same who, when poor Susan Hollingsworth was being flayed alive at Mrs. Binghampton's party, had brought ignominy on her defender, young Mr. Mill, by inquiring if he was going to come out in favor of Mormonism. Received graciously, and having found out all she could about Mr. Harrington, and that the newly married couple were not going on a bridal tour, and that there was to be no reception, but that everybody was expected to call without formality, Miss Bean waddled off, and, as Muriel expected she would do, never rested till she had gone the entire round of her acquaintance, and spread the information she had received to the remotest borders of society.

Left alone, Harrington and Muriel, accompanied by Wentworth and Emily, went to call on the tabooed Hollingsworths, and returned in about an hour in great satisfaction. None but Muriel, however, knew the sweetest part of that visit ; for poor Susan not appearing in the parlor, Muriel had begged to see her, and at last had been admitted to the sad chamber of her humiliation and anguish. And there, with all fond endearment, and sweet, wise words of sympathy and counsel, Muriel had cheered and comforted her, and prevailed on her to make the visit. It was not a deed that the lofty rectitude of a Bean or a Binghampton could approve ; but alas, the beautiful blonde was not a Friend of Virtue !

That Susan was to make the visit, and that she was to come some time next week, was all that anybody but Susan and Muriel knew, but that was enough to set the party in a state of great gratification, and in that state they arrived again at Temple street.

Wentworth had been prevailed upon to spend the day, and after dinner, Harrington having said to him, "Richard, you are interested in Hungarian fugitives, come with us and see some fugitives of another color," they had all gone up-stairs, Mrs. Eastman included, to listen to the story of Antony.

It was a story till then untold to any of them, even to Harrington; for in Antony's weak health, and amidst the thick-crowding excitements and interests of the four preceding days, time and opportunity had been wanting. Now, however, they had come, and the story was told.

A touching and an awful story. The story of a man who had fled for Liberty or Death through the malignant horrors of a Southern fen, with the hounds and hunters of a pirate civilization on his trail, and who had lain for weeks like years, in cold, and stench, and hunger, with rats and vermin swarming over him, in the black and filthy antre of a Northern vessel's hold, with a Northern ruffian to maltreat him daily in his wasting torture; earning thus, with pangs and fears that freemen never know, his right to the freedom Nature gave him for his own.

A touching and an awful story, whose dread reality had a haggard, haunting shadow, more dreadful than itself. For the man's childish imagination had been unnaturally wrought upon, and his tale involved a flickering and ghostly sense that he had been in Hell, and that his tormentors were not men but devils. He did not aver it, but it was strangely and indefinably implied in his grotesque narration, and reached the minds of his auditors. Was he wrong? He had suffered much; his reason had been a little shaken by his awful experiences; his superstitious, childish fancy had been insanely stirred. And yet—was he wrong?

As people emerging from some dark cavern into the glad light of day, so from the room of the fugitive, came the five again into the cheerful library. Muriel's face was grave and dreamful; Harrington was sad and silent; Mrs. Eastman wore a disturbed look; Emily seemed a little frightened, and Wentworth was red with indignation.

They took their seats again without speaking, and for a minute or two nothing was said.

"Well, Richard," said Harrington, at length, "what do you think now of Hungarian fugitives as objects of sympathy, compared with fugitives like that up-stairs?"

"Oh bother Hungarian fugitives!" blurted Wentworth.

"Here's Hungarians, as John Randolph said of the Greeks, at our very doors. After hearing that man's story, I can't help losing my admiration for Kossuth. You know he censured the editor Gyurman, his countryman, for writing against slavery, and I thought once he was right; but, by Jupiter, a man who knows anything about slavery, as I do now, and doesn't become a red-hot Abolitionist, has a stone in the place where his heart ought to be, or I'm a Dutchman."

"Well," returned Harrington, laughing at Richard's vehemence, "don't go too far the other way, dear Raffaello. We must feel for the Hungarians too, you know. As for Kossuth, his only fault is, that he's so much of a patriot, that he's willing to flatter American tyranny to serve Hungary. It's wrong and weak, but let us still aspire for Hungarian independence as for American liberty."

"I agree," replied Wentworth. "But how did you come across this poor fellow, Harrington?"

"I was out on a nocturnal ramble," replied Harrington, "and I found him in the street, just escaped from the brig, and took him home with me."

"Yes, Richard," said Mrs. Eastman, quickly; "but you don't know all John did for him. He"——

"Now, mother," pleaded Harrington, coloring, "don't mention that—please don't."

"I'll tell you, Richard, sometime when John is out of the way," said Muriel, archly confidential. "No objections, John! We'll spare your modesty, and satisfy Richard's curiosity, and you are to know nothing about it."

"And my curiosity, too," said Emily, laughing.

"And yours too," replied Muriel.

"Well, I must say that that was very noble in John," said Wentworth. "But he's always"——

"No nobler than you're giving poor Vukovich house-room till he found another friend in Bagasse," broke in Harrington, laughing and coloring.

"Peuh!" said Wentworth, blushing. "How did you find that out? No matter—he was only a Hungarian. But this poor fellow—oh, what an account for a man to have to give of himself! It actually made my blood boil."

"By the way," said Harrington, "we must try and discover the name of that captain, and have this piece of infamy properly made public. I can't help fancying that Antony is wrong about the name of the brig. The brig Solomon. Isn't Solomon an odd or unusual name for a vessel? Solomon—Solomon. But still—I don't know; she may be named for her owner. I wonder who he is—for this rascality must have been known to him, and we must hold him responsible to the public for it, too."

Muriel, who was abstractedly thinking, suddenly started, then closed her parted lips, and reflected again, with a painful color stealing over her countenance.

"John," said she in a low voice, "an idea occurs to me. You remember that stevedore, Driscoll. Wasn't it on a brig that he broke his leg?"

"Yes," returned Harrington, wondering what she meant. "It was on one of your uncle's vessels."

"And don't you remember the name of that brig? It was the brig Soliman."

Mrs. Eastman started violently, and turned pale, while the color came like red fire to the face of Harrington.

"Heavens!" exclaimed the pale lady, clasping her hands. "Oh, I hope you are wrong! I hope Lemuel has not been lending himself to such work as this."

"Wait a minute," said Harrington, springing up and leaving the room.

He went up-stairs to the chamber of the fugitives. Roux and Antony were sitting near each other, and Tugmutton was reading to them in his usual grandiloquent way.

"Antony," said Harrington, "what did you say the name of that brig was?"

The fugitive, still lean and haggard, but wonderfully improved in aspect, stared at him with his hollow eyes and skull-like visage for a moment.

"Brig Solomon, Marster Harrington," he replied, quickly.

"You say you read the name of the brig when you were in the water, before you boarded her?"

"Yes, Marster."

"Can you spell the name you read? Spell it for me."

"Yes, Marster. S-o-l, sol, i, solo, m-a-n mon, Solomon."

"You're sure that was the way it was spelled."

"Yes, Marster."

"Very well," and Harrington turned to go.

"But that's not the way to spell Solomon," bawled Tugmutton.

No more it's not, thought Harrington, as he slowly went down-stairs—but that's the spelling. O Lemuel Atkins!

He entered the library with a face so grave that they all saw what he had to tell.

"You are right, Muriel," he said, sinking heavily into his chair. "It is the Soliman."

Mrs. Eastman burst into tears.

"My dear mother!" cried Muriel, flying to her side, and folding her in her arms, while the astonished and agitated Emily also came to her.

"No matter," said Mrs. Eastman, suddenly recovering, and gently pushing them from her, while her pale face became severe. "It was but a moment's pain, and I am now filled with indignation. To think that Lemuel, my own brother, would join in oppressing that poor creature—oh, I cannot bear to think of it! I feel it as if it were my own sin. I am disgraced by it. Every action of his, in his pro-slavery mania, rests on me like a disgrace that I cannot bear. But this is the worst of all."

"My dear mother," said Harrington, approaching, and taking her hands in his, "let it all go. Fortunately, Antony has escaped from their clutches, and the worst is over. We will do nothing more about it, but let it rest in silence. You cannot help your brother's misconduct, and are not in any way responsible for it, though I can well understand how it should grieve you."

"It ought to be made public, John," she answered tremulously, with the tears in her eyes, "and it would be for his good if he were taught, by the indignation of at least a portion of the people, that such things cannot be done with impunity. Heaven forgive me, if I fail in my duty, but I cannot help shrinking from the public outcry, and he my own brother."

She covered her eyes with her hand, as Harrington sadly withdrew to his chair.

"But, look here, now," said Wentworth, "aren't you all too fast? There may be another brig Soliman, you know."

"Perhaps," replied Harrington; "but I fear not. It is unlikely, I think, that two vessels of the same name would be in the New Orleans cotton trade."

"Who is this Driscoll, John?" asked Emily.

"Driscoll is a stevedore," he replied, "who fell into the hold of the Soliman, last winter, as they were unlading, and broke his leg. I heard of the accident through Captain Fisher, who happened to be on the spot and knew the man, and as he had a family who were thus deprived of their means of support till he got well, I made bold to call on them, and Muriel and Mrs. Eastman took care of the poor people till Driscoll got well, and was able to work again. Of course, I recollected him, but the name of the vessel on which he met with his accident, though I knew Mr. Atkins was her owner, had slipped my mind."

"Oh, John," said Emily, impetuously, "how like you!"

"What? To forget the name?" said Harrington, innocently, misled by her tone. "Indeed, no. I usually remember names very well"——

"'Psha! no," replied Emily, laughing at his simplicity. "But to visit the poor man, and have his family taken care of. You, a perfect stranger to them all. Now, I should like to know who beside you would have felt called upon to interest himself in such a matter?"

"Oh, pooh! A mere trifle," said Harrington, reddening, and looking extremely uncomfortable. "Hundreds of people would have done the same thing. It was Mrs. Eastman and Muriel who did the real work in this case. So, you see, there are more more willing hearts and hands than mine in the world."

"I wonder if my grand Lord Bacon, Baron Verulam, and Viscount St. Albans would have interested himself in the plebeian Driscolls," said Wentworth, slily, aiming a hit at Harrington's favorite.

"Indeed he would," replied Harrington, with great animation. "It is recorded of him that no case of distress ever came under his notice without being promptly relieved. Verulam played Providence well, till the bloat king, and the pack of Conservatives ruined him. Yes, till then, and afterward, till he left the globe. Bacon was the Theodore Parker of his time, plus the Verulamio-Shakspearean intellect—so don't you say one word in his dispraise, Master Wentworth, or you and I shall quarrel."

Wentworth laughed at the gay threat, and said no more.

"*Revenons à nos moutons*—let us return to our Southdowns," said Muriel, playfully. "I had a talk with Roux, John, of which I was going to tell you when our company came this morning, and I haven't had a chance since. The sum and substance of which is, that Roux is alive to his danger in Boston, and consents to go to Worcester. So on Monday, John, you must transport him and Antony there, find them a boarding-house, see Mr. Higginson about them, and let them be looking out for a house and occupation, while we arrange to send on the wife and children after them. So there's work laid out for you, my husband!"

"Bravo!" cried Harrington, joyfully. "I'll attend to it."

"In the meantime," pursued Muriel, "we'll put Roux on salary sufficient to cover all expenses till he gets settled again. Then, there's his shop to be closed up, and his furniture to be removed, all which is on your broad shoulders, my Atlas."

"I'll bear the load!" said Harrington, gaily.

"For it won't do to have Roux burdened with it," she continued, "lest in his removing he should be removed."

"See here. Can't I help?" put in Wentworth. "I burn with ardor."

"Oh, Raffaello! bantered Muriel, with a gay and charming smile—"you? Flower of painters, I fear me that you will not find such anti-slavery service to your taste! However, we will see. Yes, Richard, seriously, you shall help if you want to."

"Good!" said Wentworth, laughingly. "What a nest of traitors to the blessed old granny of a Government we are!"

"My faith!" said Muriel, with bewitching levity, "if they will have their Fugitive Slave Law, they shall also have their traitors to balance. But there was once a time," she fervently added, "when a poor man could earn his bread in the city which I love, with none to molest him or make him afraid, and may that good time come again."

"Amen!" cried Wentworth. "And, apropos, have any of you seen the papers to-day? Have you heard the great news?"

"I have not," said Muriel.

"Nor I," said Harrington. "What is it?"

"It came yesterday," replied Wentworth, "but to-day's paper has a fuller account of it. Charles Sumner has announced in the Senate that he is going to speak on the Fugitive Slave Law! Hurrah!"

"Io triumphe!" cried Muriel, flying from the room to get the paper, amidst a general chorus of delight.

She came back presently with the "Commonwealth," and read aloud Mr. Sumner's brief remarks on presenting the petition of the New England Quakers for the repeal of the Fugitive Slave Law—remarks which were the prelude to one of the ablest and noblest speeches ever heard in the American Congress.

"Bravo!" cried Harrington, when she had finished. "Now we shall hear the old New England voice!"

"By Jupiter, yes," said Wentworth. "Charles Sumner's going in. It'll be like a giant slinging up an elephant by the tail, and whacking the enemy with it."

They all laughed uproariously at this novel symbol of aggressive eloquenee.

"Come now," said Wentworth, when the laughter had subsided, "this news calls upon us to round up Saturday night with music. Sing, you pair of seraphs, sing. Let's have Theodore Körner's 'Battle-Hymn of the Berlin Landsturm.'"

Muriel and Emily moved to the organ, and on the rich and passionate clouds of Weber's music, their noble voices stormed in melody. But as the first exalting tones arose, Mrs. Eastman, sad and sick at heart, withdrew to her chamber, to think with sorrow of her brother's baseness, to think and think and think, and weep alone.

CHAPTER XXVIII.

THE SABBATH MORNING.

THE Sabbath dawned calm and peaceful and beautiful, and filled with Sabbatic stillness. Such a Sabbath as would have waked the holy muse of Donne or Herbert, of Keble or Heber, to celebrate its restful sanctity in sacred song. But its sweetest hymn was the gracious face of Muriel, as she sat at the organ in the library, singing in a low voice a psalm that breathed from heaven into the soul of David three thousand years ago.

The spirit of the music lived in her countenance as she sang, and lingered there when the tender and regal chant had failed. Too happy for even music to express, she rose from the instrument, and rapt in heavenly reverie, wandered to and fro about the room.

But a little while, however, for presently the bounding foot of Harrington was heard upon the stairs, and he came in.

"Ah, truant!" she playfully exclaimed, gliding to his arms, and gazing up into his smiling face, "where have you been. I woke this morning to find myself a widow. Now give me the morning kiss of which I was defrauded."

He folded her in his arms, and fondly kissed her again and again.

"I have been to my house," he said, "and do you know

why? To see after my dog. Positively, I had almost forgotten the existence of that delectable animal, and my conscience smote me this morning lest he should have been neglected, which he has not been, for the boys have been his guardians. So I stole from your side like a thief of the night. You were sleeping so sweetly, and looked so beautiful in your sleep, that I did not dare to disturb you. Strange feeling I had in leaving you—it was almost like going never to return."

"And I, too," she replied, melting from her blushing smile into musing. "I woke from a singular dream of you. I dreamed that I was going about alone in the house and in the streets and among all sorts of people, and you were at an immeasurable distance above me, looking at me constantly from behind the air, as it were. The strangest thing was that I could not see you, though at the same time I knew you were there just as if I saw you. But we were separated. And yet I was not sad—indeed, the dream was happy. Presently I unclosed my eyes, and for a moment," she said, laughing, "I really felt as if I were a widow, which I have no ambition to be, I assure you."

Harrington laughed gaily, and pressed his lips to her forehead.

"Dreams are strange," he said, lightly. "But how exquisite you are this morning! Every time I see you you look new. Stand back a pace, and let me admire you!"

She danced back a couple of yards, and stood playfully regarding him, with her beautiful and noble head bent a little on one side, while his eyes dwelt on her delicately tinted features, and wandered over the stately elegance of her form. She was robed that morning in pale rose-colored silk, with lace corsage and lace open sleeves. About her hung that indefinable and delicious patrician odor which we sometimes perceive around the persons of fair women, and which touches the imagination like the aroma of a poetic nobility of soul. A thrill fled through the veins of Harrington as he gazed on her, and then his eyes grew sad, and the smile on his face died slowly away.

"Ah, Muriel," he said, in a low, rapt voice, "the beauty

that my eyes see in you is the token of the beauty my soul knows in you. How could I bear to leave you! Once it was a joy to think of death, but now heaven could not tempt me from earth with you."

She came quickly to him, with an agitated face, and passionately clung to him. He folded her to his breast, and felt, as his face drooped upon her forehead, a vague sense, as of some luminous shadow resting on them. In a moment, she lifted her face to his, serene, though the clear eyes were dim, and gazed ardently into his countenance.

"Do not speak of leaving me, John," she said. "It was my foolish dream put that into your mind. Ah, we shall neither of us leave each other. Life is before us, and love. Come, let us not dwell on this, but speak of other things."

"So be it," he replied. "Well, what shall we do with ourselves to-day?"

"I don't know," she gaily answered, swinging around from his breast to his side, and putting her arm about him, while he encircled her waist. "Suppose we vary the general impiety of our proceedings by going to church."

"Agreed. To Mr. Parker's, of course."

"Most assuredly. There's the breakfast bell."

And, arm in arm, they descended to the breakfast-room.

Church-time came, with the aërial pealing of bells, and with it came Wentworth, in gallant and perfumed attire, to convoy Emily to her devotions. Emily, however, had decided to go with Harrington and Muriel, and presently they all set out together, Mrs. Eastman, who had recovered her serenity, accompanying them.

The streets were full of church-goers, some of them haply wending their way to be regaled with exhortations to obey all laws, right or wrong, especially the Fugitive Slave Law, and to consent, if need be, to have their brothers go into slavery to save the Union. In that blissful period, it was agreed, among all respectable people, that ministers must not meddle with politics, unless they were pro-slavery politics, which were considered perfectly orthodox, *doulos* of Christ having been ascertained to mean, not servant, but slave of Christ, and Paul having been proved to have sent back Onesimus, not at all as a brother beloved, but as a runaway Thomas Sims. The sedulous inculcation of these soul-elevating views and this cheering exegesis of Scripture, was understood to be in perfect harmony with the dictum that ministers musn't meddle with politics, and many ministers conducted themselves accordingly.

Debarred by their own hardness and frowardness of heart from the holy solace of these ministrations, our little party held their perverse way to the Melodeon. The choir was singing as they entered, and the church was crowded as usual, for no minister in Boston gathered such a concourse as the mighty Theodore. A little movable pulpit, on which bloomed a vase of flowers, occupied the platform, and behind it, with clasped hands, musing, sat he who shall heave his noble thought in massive mountain-chains of strength and beauty never any more. Living, his presence was the magic spell that evoked and commanded Freedom. Oh, dying, was it less strong—less strong when he had died? Lo! he drew nigh the shores of Italy, and she rose, in the red storm of Magenta, from the bondage of ten centuries, free! He laid him down to sleep in the soil of her Florence, and pale and radiant from her long agony, all disenchanted of her doom, she stands above his dust, bastioned with hearts and swords, free! Free, and free forever, and secure of ever-broadening freedom, for the land can never rest in tyranny that holds within its bosom Parker's grave!

There are thousands who remember those Sabbaths in his presence; but who shall paint them in hues that will not seem faint and unfaithful in the light of memory? What words shall revive his image as he stood behind the little pulpit—Socratic-featured, strong, earnest, reverend—the large volume of old Scripture open before him, the tinted flowers blooming by his side, the faces of thousands all mutely turned toward him, as once toward Luther, Savonarola, Abelard? What words shall tell of the firm eyes holding all those faces, the resolute features stirring, the orotund and fervent deep voice sounding, as he read from the sacred pages, lifting the verses into their fullest significance and life, and flooding the soul with all that is loftiest and sweetest in the old saints and prophets' lore? Who shall bring back the hours when, as in that hour, the deep voice rose in the tender and gorgeous prayer, filled with the affluent sunshine, the flowers, the greenery, the wild-bird melodies, the living glory of the spring, all music-rich with reverential thought and feeling, all overflowed with gratitude and praise to the Giver, with faith, and piety, and aspiration, all throbbing with immortal longings, and raising the soul to the mystic's vision of God, and kindling the heart with the hero's hope of the ideal future of man? A streaming altar-flame, uprising rich with incense from hills and valleys lovely in the blue day and pomps of spring-time, thronged with the saints and saviors of all time, and echoing with the supplications and hosannas of mankind, might be the symbol of that prayer. But what symbol shall gather within it the strong and salient intellections of the following sermon—its massive breadth and scope of statement, its valiant dealing with the public sins and sinners of the time, its learning that swept all history, its knowledge that swept all life, the broad illumination of its eloquence, the prowess of its virtue, the sweetness of its piety? A torch of burning splendor upheld by Greatheart, and flashing on his brand and mail in the crash of combat with Apollyon—its blaze poured strong and definite upon the open midnight landscape of our mortal life, illumining the path of nobleness, lighting every danger, darting its ray upon the secret pitfall, and into the ambush of the foe, and streaming forward over all the perilous track to the gates of God—such might be the visioned symbol of a speech which yet no symbol can describe. Closed now in death that glorious eloquence, nor in a hundred years may such a bloom unfold again; but the continents shall remember how in an evil time burst forth its flower of flame, and its fragrance shall fill the world from age to age.

Every high heart has felt the sense of renewal and reconsecration which follows the words of a great pulpit orator; and with this sense strong within them, the little party left the church when the service was ended. On their way home, Wentworth stopped the others to announce that Emily was to dine at his father's house, and return to Temple street late in the afternoon. A few moments passed in exchanging warm eulogiums on the sermon, and then Mrs. Eastman, Muriel, and Harrington left the other two and walked across the beautiful sunlit Common.

"Now, John," said Muriel, gaily, "of course you have some criticism to make on Mr. Parker."

"I declare no," he responded; "I haven't the conscience to criticise him. He makes one's heart glow so with his manhood, that criticism must be dumb. I pass his theology, everything in fact, I might differ on, and rest only on his magnificent public service, and the inspiration of his example."

"Still," she returned, "you would differ, if you could."

"To be sure," he replied, smilingly. "If I could criticise, I would own to a divine dissatisfaction. For the sermon implied no theory that adequately accounts for the scheme of things, as my own theory does, at least to me. However, I won't grumble. I have Emerson still for my refuge. All the modern thinkers cramp me in a cell, more or less spacious, but in Emerson, chiefly in his poems, I escape into the vast of space and stars, and breathe blithely like the self-existent soul I am."

"Oh, heretic!" she gaily exclaimed. "But I agree with all you say, and especially about the poems. They are incomparably beyond all else the Muse has vouchsafed to our American bards."

"Now, John," said Mrs. Eastman, "I should really like to know what your theory of things is. Come, define your position."

"My dear mother," replied Harrington, laughing, "will it do to give it voice? The tell-tale birds might hear me, and carry the news to the orthodox, and then I should have a grand auto-da-fe, with all the great wits and little wits dancing around me in my expiring agonies."

"Oh, but John," she banteringly answered, "this is the age and land of free thought, you know."

"Yes, indeed. Free thought meaning your freedom to think as the mass of your fellow-citizens do. Go beyond that, and they'll melt up Judas Iscariot and Cæsar Borgia, and all the rascals, little and big, for colors, as Allston's Paint-King melted up the lady, and paint your portrait in hues of earthquake and eclipse, as Shelley's phrase has it. Political liberty with us includes the right to wallop your own nigger, and howl into Coventry, or hang to a tree, any humane person who objects. Social liberty means the right to make you submit to the ordinances of Mrs. Grundy, be they the prescriptions of a French tailor or milliner in regard to your dress, or the fancies of some conclave of bigots in regard to your actions, and if taste or conscience rises in revolt, Mrs. Grundy raps them on the head with a stick, as Lear's cockney did the eels when she put them in the pie alive, and cries, 'Down, wantons, down!' Religious liberty involves the right to fling theological mud and fire on the good name of anybody who ventures beyond the notions of clergymen, and liberty in general means your privilege to say and do what moderate and immoderate intellects concede you may. Socially speaking, the very essential principle of liberty, toleration, is tucked away in Roger Williams' grave. The people of this country think they love liberty. They don't. They don't know what liberty means. If they did they'd love tyranny. It is my deliberate conviction that if the people of this country understood what the doctrine of liberty involves and comprehends, as it lies in the pages of the scholars who conceived it, they would deny it utterly, and set up the despotism of the Middle Ages as their idol."

Muriel laughed heartily at this outburst.

"Bravo, John!" she cried. "Methinks I hear you thundering that from the rostrum into the startled hearts of your fellow-citizens."

"Yes, amidst groans and hisses," returned the smiling Harrington. "But I should flash a bolder speech than that if I were to address the public. That is weak rose-water compared to what I would say when I came to recite the special instances of the civil or social abuses of which I complain."

"Heaven save the sinners from your sprinkling then if that is only rose-water," jested Muriel. "But here is mamma bursting with impatience for your theory of the Universe."

"My dear mother," said Harrington, laughingly, "another time, when I can collect my vagrant ideas, I will confide to you all I saw when I put my eye to a chink of this mortal prison, and looked out on the True. Meanwhile, you will find some slight hint of my notions in Goethe's poem of 'The Festival.'"

"Which I shall read when I get home," replied Mrs. Eastman.

And talking in this strain, they reached the house in Temple street.

CHAPTER XXIX.

HELL ON HEAVEN IMPINGING.

As Mr. Parker only preached in the forenoon, they did not go to church again, but after dinner sat together all the afternoon in the library, reading aloud, and talking, and supremely happy.

So the sweet and peaceful day wore slowly on to sunset, and as the declining beams gilded the rich room, the trio sank, as if by mutual consent, into a lapse of silence, and sat enjoying the luxury of the happy hour, and glad in their own society. Mrs. Eastman reclined in a fauteuil, her cheek pensively resting on her hand, and her serene, poetic face musing between its graceful silver tresses on the lovers. The clouds had melted from her mind, and she only thought with tranquil joy of the beautiful change that had come so silently upon her daughter's life, sundering no tie and marring no relation, and her soul was filled with gratitude to know that the love of her child was anchored on a heart so noble.

Unconscious that she was the subject of such sweet reflection, Muriel sat in reverie, and Harrington, sitting at a little distance, fondly dreamed upon her vision-like beauty. So exquisite in her delicate clear color, with the silken amber tresses rippling low around her cheeks, and the perfection of her form tenderly told by the pale, rose-hued robe, that she touched his imagination with a strange sense of faëry. He was so happy, as he gazed on her, that he could scarcely believe in his happiness. Mixed with his ethereal pleasure in her loveliness, was a dim feeling as of one who had wedded a princess in his dream, and knew that he dreamed, and would awaken soon to find himself unwedded and alone. Strange—strange to think that this surpassing woman was his wife. But it was true; it was indeed reality, and not a dream; it was indeed reality, and it had flooded life with the tranquil ecstasy of heaven.

Gazing upon her in deep abstraction, he became aware that her sweet eyes were fixed upon his face, and saw, by the suffusion on her countenance, as of the rosy color of the morning, that she was conscious of his ardent gaze. Confused a little at being thus detected in his admiration, he started, blushing, and then laughed, as she archly shook her finger at him.

"I caught you," she said. "Now, John, what were you thinking of?"

"Of you, Muriel. Of our happiness. I am strangely happy to-night. Were not you conscious, and you, mother, of a singular happiness as we all sat here in silence together? The Sabbath peace of the evening was like the peace of heaven."

They did not answer, but bowed their heads in assent, and lulled by the sweet influences of the hour, remained in silence It was but a few moments, and the sunset light died from the room; and as it faded away, and the first grey of twilight filled the air, Muriel and Harrington both rose, as if its departure was the dissolution of a spell that had held them, and approached each other with loving faces and outstretched arms.

They were within a yard's distance, when suddenly the door-bell rang with such a violent and furious clanging clatter, that they stood still. It was like the scream of a fury warning them asunder. The love-look dropped from their faces, and their arms fell. Only a second's pause, and again the bell rang and rang and rang, clashing and clanging without intermission, like the startling peal of an alarum from a chamber where murder was being done, and the struggling victim had seized the bell-rope. Utterly amazed at this frightful clamor, and wondering who could be ringing in such a manner as this, they stood with a shock in their blood, blankly gazing at each other. Suddenly they recovered, as Mrs. Eastman flew past them with an indignant face, and flung open the library door.

"Who dares"——

She stopped in the midst of her incensed exclamation, for at that moment the hall-door was opened, and with a wild clatter of angry words from Patrick below, something bounced in and up-stairs, and rushed panting to fall before them.

It was Tugmutton. They gazed upon him in utter amazement. He fell prone, then rose suddenly on his knees as if a spring in the floor had shot him up, and knelt gasping and speechless before them, a fat open-mouthed face of ashen fright glaring with white saucer-eyes upon them from its great shocks of wool, and the two huge hands lifted like the paws of a begging dog, in an agony of supplication. For a moment, they looked at him astounded. Suddenly Harrington saw his cap lying on the floor—staggered back with a reeling brain, dashed forward with a spring up to Roux's room, and flung open the door.

Roux was lying on the bed asleep, and did not waken. For an instant Harrington's eye swept the chamber, then became fixed. He heard the voices down-stairs. He heard the regular breathings of the sleeping man. He heard the dinning of his own brain. Then all seemed to grow still, and with a dreadful feeling in his mind, he slowly turned and went down.

Tall, erect, terrible, white as death, he entered the library. They gazed upon his face with draining eyes. He looked at them for a moment in silence. The boy still knelt gasping and shuddering on the floor. But they were motionless—motionless as marble.

"Mother," His voice was clear and low. He paused. "Mother—collect yourself. Be calm. Has he told you?"

There was silence, intense and awful. He did not look at

his wife, but he felt that she turned away. He looked only at the pallid face gazing at him with parted lips and mute eyes between its silver tresses, as if it had turned to stone. Suddenly her voice rang.

"He has not told me. Speak! I can bear anything but this."

"Mother, the poor wanderer to whom you gave shelter is gone. He went out with the boy. He has been kidnapped in the streets of Boston."

She stood for a moment, ghastly, rigid, immovable. Suddenly a low cry wailed from her lips and she fell. He sprang and caught her, lifted her in his arms and bore her to a couch. Muriel glanced from the room. Flying to the windows, he flung them open to let in the fresh air. Then, back to the lady in her swoon, and kneeling beside her, his quick hands snapped the silken strings of her bodice, unclasped her belt, and loosened her clothes. The boy softly sank on his face, and lay gasping on the floor.

A light touch: Muriel, calm, self-possessed, pale, was beside him. He took from her hands the glass of water, and sprinkled the pallid face, while she drenched her handkerchief with cologne and bathed the still brow and nostrils. The evening wind blew freshly into the room, and gradually a quiver of life came to the marble features. Harrington silently pointed to the loosened bodice, moved away, and stood with his brow resting on his hand.

Minute after minute passed on and all was silent save the fainter gaspings of the boy. Gradnally, low rustling movements and faint murmurs, mixed with the sweet and soothing whispers of Muriel, came to him from the couch. He remained motionless, his mind blank and cold. In a minute or two Muriel spoke to him.

"She has recovered, John."

His hand fell from his brow as he heard her words, and lifting his white face, he moved noiselessly across the room, closed the windows, and came to the pale lady's side.

"Mother," he said, kneeling by her, and tenderly folding her in his arms, "I would not have told you if I could have kept it from you."

"Hush!" she murmured. "You did well. It was terrible, but I had to know it. Come, I am ready now for the rest. Bring Charles here, and let me know all. I will lie here and listen. Do not fear. I can bear everything now."

Rising to his feet, he crossed the room, lifted the boy from the floor as lightly as though he were a baby, and held him face to face at arms' length before him. The hapless Tugmutton, dangling broad-limbed and big-footed between the strong supporting hands, stared with blobber visage, ashen with fright and grief, and with mouth, eyes, and nostrils wildly open, into the white face smiling into his, with a smile gentle even in its ghastliness.

"Charles," said Harrington, in a low, consoling voice, "don't be frightened, poor boy. See, I am not angry with you. I feel badly for what has happened, but I am not angry with you, Charles."

The miserable Tugmutton, inert in his suspension, opened his big mouth wide, and burst into a roar of tears.

"My gosh! Mr. Harrington," he howled, amidst his grief, "there aint a more mis'able young nigger this side of Jordan than me. He's took off, and I'm the guilty party, Mr. Harrington, when I didn't mean it. Oh, Lord A'mighty, I can't provide for that family never no more, and the man that won't provide for his family, is just wus than an infidel, and that's in the Holy Bible, Mr. Harrington, and father's the victim of misplaced confidence, and oh, my gosh, I wish I was in Canada, as sure as you're born."

With which outburst, the wretched Tugmutton let his head droop on the blue-striped shirt which covered his fat chest, and with his grey-jacketed, short fat arms hanging over Harrington's hands, and his grey-trowsered, short broad legs dangling motionless, he sobbed as if his big heart was breaking. Harrington, filled with compassion for his uncouth sorrow, took him in his arms like an infant, and held him still, not even smiling at the odd ideas and odd phrases which he had poured forth, and which, even in that painful hour, might well have moved a smile.

"Hush, Charles," murmured the young man. "Don't cry

any more. Come, I want you to tell us all that has happened. I want you to tell the whole truth, and perhaps we can find Antony again."

At this, Tugmutton started in his arms, and stopped crying instantly.

"Let me down, Mr. Harrington, let me down," he excitedly vociferated, wriggling like a conger eel from Harrington's hold, and dumping upon the floor. "My gosh! if you'll on'y find that Antony, I'll tell you every word of the truth and the whole truth, and nothing but the truth, so help you God."

Harrington pushed a chair up to the couch for Muriel, and seating himself in another, drew the boy near him, and at once, in rapid and excited tones, Tugmutton began his confession, telling everything even to the most irrelevant details.

It appeared from what he said that his empire over Roux had extended also over Antony, and that the latter, completely subjugated by his grand airs and assumption of superior knowledge, had in his simplicity come to look upon him as one of the most powerful of his guardians. In this mood, Tugmutton had regaled him with glowing accounts of the attractions of the city, every inch of which, from Roxbury Line to Salutation Alley, and further in all directions, was as familiar to the Bedouin feet of the fat Puck as his own abode in Southac street. Especially had he dwelt upon the glories of Boston Common, and that day he had expatiated upon them till Antony, filled with wonderment, almost imagined the place some unheard of Eden. Roux falling asleep in the afternoon, Tugmutton had continued his ecstatic panegyric on the Common, and finally wound up by proposing a short tour to that romantic region during the repose of his father. After some demurring on the part of Antony, and considerable domineering on that of Tugmutton, the former yielded, and they stole softly down-stairs and out at the street door, while their hosts were in the library. Reaching the Common, rich in the sunset light, and its malls filled with gaily-dressed promenaders, the enchanted Antony wandered with his pigmy guide across the inclosure, and emerged with him on the Park street corner. There they stood on the pavement, while Tugmutton descanted on the magnificence of the Park street church, with especial reference to the height of the steeple, loftiness of spire being in his view the chief end and crowning perfection of all church architecture. As he was talking, a hack drove up and stood at a little distance from them, and at the same time his eye fell upon a gentleman standing near a side entrance of the church, and smilingly beckoning to him. A little astonished at first, and then a little flattered at this affability, he turned with a lofty and vain-glorious air to Antony, as much as to say, you see the immense consideration paid me by the aristocracy, and bidding him wait there a moment, crossed the street to the stranger, who, with a smiling nod, retreated into the passage, which happened to be open. Thither Tugmutton followed him. What the stranger said, his subsequent fright drove out of his memory, and he could only recollect that he held him lightly by the arm as he spoke to him ; but in the midst of the interview, happening to glance around, he saw a man rush, pushing Antony before him, crowd him into the hack, and spring in after him, while the vehicle rattled away down Winter street. Of course Tugmutton sprang to follow, but the stranger seized him by the throat, and shook him so that he could neither speak nor cry. Released presently, the wretched boy rushed into the street, and after the carriage. But it was out of sight, and running back to the church, the stranger was gone. Too much horrified to make any outcry, Tugmutton had instantly run with all his speed back to Temple street, where he had arrived as we have related.

All this, involving details which under ordinary circumstances he would have suppressed as disgraceful to himself, but which he now frankly disclosed in the full conviction that a knowledge of the entire truth would enable Harrington to recapture Antony from the kidnappers, Tugmutton poured forth in his own way to his pale and silent auditors, and ending, sat eagerly staring first at one and then the other, as wondering what was to be done now that he had told all.

" Charles," said Harrington, " what kind of a looking man was it you saw seize Antony !"

"My gosh! it was so quick that I scase got a sight of him, Mr. Harrington," returned Tugmutton, staring into the white face of his questioner. "I on'y saw he had on a straw hat an' a sorter light coat, an' was tanned consid'ble."

"Tanned," mused Harrington. "That must have been the captain of the Soliman."

He was right in his conviction. It was Bangham.

"I see how it was done," he pursued. "They were together, and came on Antony and Charles standing there. One hailed the carriage—probably some passing hack—the other decoyed the boy away to prevent his outcries—and the rest we know. O Boston, Boston! I loved you once—every stone in your pavement was dear to me; but I sicken of you now, and I shall never walk your streets with joy again! A poor, helpless, harmless man—a fugitive from the worst tyranny that deforms the world—and in the streets of this free city, in open daylight, on the Sabbath, with a crowd standing around, he can be stolen, as a horse could not be stolen, and not one person lifts a hand to prevent it, or asks why! Not one—not one!"

He covered his burning eyes with his hand, and sat still. The doleful boy gazed piteously at the pale, mute faces of the two ladies, his fat, ashen visage quivering with the feeling that he had done a mischief which not even Harrington could undo.

"John." It was Mrs. Eastman that spoke. "You have not asked who the man was that decoyed Charles."

He looked with mortal sadness into her agitated face.

"Need I ask, mother?" he drearily replied. "A gentleman. It was not Lafitte, for him Charles knows. There is but one other person that wears the attire of a gentleman who could be a party to this deed."

The tears flowed on her face, and as they flowed she wiped them away.

"You are right," she faltered. "It is the last, the worst disgrace I can ever know. A brother of my own blood, the son of the mother that bore me—and with his own hands, not preserving even the miserable decorum of an agent, with his own hands he commits this crime. It almost kills me to think of it."

"John," said Muriel, "listen to me."

He started from his lethargy of sorrow, and gazed into her face. She was pale, collected, calm ; her eyes firm and clear, and her voice and manner full of quiet energy.

"John," she pursued, "we must not waste these hours. All is not lost yet. We have the clues to this infamy in our hands. That man has no doubt been taken on board the Soliman. You must at once procure a writ of habeas corpus and get"——

She paused, arrested by the strange and ghastly smile that changed his countenance.

"I have thought of it," he said. "If it were not for this Fugitive Slave Law, we might have a chance of success. But see—perjury would be nothing to the men that could do this deed. When the writ is served on them, they will swear that the man is not in their possession. Then a warrant will be procured for his arrest, and after a pretended search, he will be found, dragged before a commissioner, and sent into slavery. And if I get a writ, who will I get to serve it? From the sheriff to the lowest catchpoll is there one of them that can be depended upon to do his duty in such a case? Justice is drugged with slavery. Law winks at kidnapping."

She looked at him with a still face, touched for a moment by what he said, then refluent to its purpose.

"It must be tried, nevertheless," she said firmly. "You yourself, John, can serve the writ, or accompany the officer."

He gazed at her with eyes that filled with tears, as they wandered from her countenance to her mother's. Mrs. Eastman shrank and covered her face with her hands. In an instant Muriel comprehended the deeper reason which had made him hopeless of a rescue, and with a feeling as nearly like despairing agony as her nature, organized for faith and hope and joy, could feel, she sank back in her chair.

"Muriel," said he, in a solemn voice, "I have thought of all, and I see no way open to us. Under other circumstances,

I would get the writ, and though he probably could not be found, endeavor to save this man. But I cannot take the first step without involving Lemuel Atkins. Can I do it? Think how mother feels this already. Think how she would feel it then. Think of the position we are in."

"Tell me, John, tell me," faltered Mrs. Eastman, weeping, "tell me what I ought to do. Ought I to have this made public? What would you do if he were your brother, as he is mine?"

"Mother," said he, solemnly, "I cannot guide you. Were he my brother, though it might break my heart to do it, I would never keep this wrong secret and silent. But my conscience cannot give the law to yours."

"I cannot do it," she sobbed. "You will despise me, but I cannot bear to think of the disgrace my consent would bring upon him."

"Despise you?" he quickly answered. "Never. Your feeling is sacred to me. I appreciate it. I respect it."

"At least," she cried, "give me time to think. Let me first go to him—let me implore him to undo what he has done. He does not know that the man was sheltered here. Oh, perhaps I can prevail with him. Think of the shame it will be one day to his wife and children. When this slavery madness ends, as it may soon, think of the awful shame his family will feel if this act lives against him. How can I bear to have it brought on them! At least for their sake let me try every other effort, and then if I fail, perhaps"——

She faltered—her voice choked with emotion. She could not bring herself to say, that perhaps she would consent to publish her brother's shame, and bring the fury of anti-slavery rebuke, and the scorn of the coming years of freedom upon him.

They sat in silence thinking with hopeless sadness of the terrible cloud that had rushed so suddenly upon their peaceful and happy day, and the twilight began to darken around them. Mrs. Eastman rose.

"I will go at once to see him," she said.

"Let me attend you," said Harrington, rising.

"No, John. Thank you. I will go alone," she replied, and left the room.

"You must stay here, Charles," said Harrington, turning to Tugmutton. "On no account must you go to your father after what has happened, until we decide what to do."

Tugmutton said nothing, but sat down on a low stool in a corner of the room, and leaned against the wall in deep despondency.

"And what are we to do, Muriel?" murmured Harrington. "How are we to tell Roux of this? It will kill him. Even now, perhaps he is wondering where his brother is. Poor, poor man! Oh, misery, misery!"

He turned away and walked the dim library with an aching heart. Muriel, silent, her mind in its fullest activity, was vainly striving to think of some plan by which this sad stroke of fortune could be retrieved. Presently, Harrington rang for lights, and Patrick came in and lighted the chandelier, whose moony globes of ground glass filled the library with mellow radiance.

Alone again, Harrington turned to Muriel; she rose from her seat, and gliding swiftly toward him, clasped him in her arms. Holding her to him, he gazed, sadly smiling, into her face, exquisite in its pale beauty.

"Beloved," he murmured mournfully, "it is the first sorrow of our wedded life."

"The first," she calmly answered. "But, oh, my husband, let us be grateful that it is a sorrow that we feel for others, and not for ourselves."

The tears ran down his face, and he fondly bent his head and pressed his lips to her forehead.

"We were so happy," he faltered. "Never was my spirit lulled in so deep and sweet a happiness as when this dreadful tidings rushed upon me. Strange, strange to think this heavenly day should end thus, in this blackness of darkness. It quite unmans me."

Folded in each other's arms, they remained for a little while in silence, while his agitation gradually subsided into sorrowful calm.

"Do you remember, Muriel," he resumed, "the description in the last chapter of the Revelations of St. John, of the heavenly city where there is no night, nor sun, nor moon, but the glory of God lightens it, and the Lamb is the light thereof? And without, you remember, the Evangelist says is the horrible abode of the wicked. You remember?"

"Yes, I remember," she answered, gazing into his abstracted and sorrowing face.

"When I was a boy," he continued, "I used to have a dream, unspeakably awful, derived, I think from my reading of that part of the Revelations. In my dream, I was in heaven—a strangely beautiful dim land, filled with a still, mystic glory. I cannot tell you the ineffable hush that pervaded the happy region, and there I wandered tranced in an indescribable tranquil ecstasy. But in this dream, which I frequently had, I always came to a spot which seemed the confines of the place. The glory of the region ran to a point there, in a shape like the apex of a triangle, and on either side a railing of rich fretted gold separated it from the region beyond. Suddenly, as I stood, a dreadful perception of the outer region would overwhelm me. I saw a horrid realm of black and grisly twilight, strangely mixed with black darkness—I heard the savage baying of dogs, the confused jargon of unhuman blasphemies and demon laughter, and the hideous faces of devils gnashed at me through the golden pales. It is impossible to tell you the ghastly affright that suddenly struck through my ecstasy when this came to me, nor can I say how fearfully it was intensified by the contrast between the ecstatic stillness and glory of the place, and the hideous and discordant sights and sounds beyond. I always awoke in horror, drenched with perspiration, and afraid to be alone in the darkness."

"What a dreadful dream?" she murmured, shivering slightly, and clinging a little closer to him.

"Yes," he responded, his voice low, and his white face frigidly fixed on vacancy. "Yes. It was like a spiritual symbol. And now it has come to me."

His countenance suddenly grew livid and convulsed with

writhing anguish, and dark circles started out around his tear-filled eyes.

"It has come to me," he gasped, tremulously, shaken with strong agony. "I have wandered to the confines of my happy heaven of love, and through the glory and the stillness, and through my sacred ecstasy, the grisly land of slavery strikes upon me, with its jargonic blasphemies and revelries of hate, the gnashing of its devils, and the baying of the dogs that hunt men. It has come to me. The dream of my boyhood was its true symbol. A dreadful dream of reality, and I wake from it in despair and agony and horror."

His low voice shuddered into silence, and convulsed through all his frame, he tore himself from her, and covered his face with his hands. Sad as she had never been before, she turned away and stood in her wonted attitude, her clasped hands drooping before her, and her head bent upon her bosom. Squatting on his stool in the corner of the room, the horrified Tugmutton glared at them, with his white eyes bulging from his blobber face under his great shocks of wool, like some lubber imp of darkness risen to work them bane.

In a few moments Harrington's hands fell heavily from his face, and agile as lightning, Muriel flashed into his arms, and clung to him, with a smile brilliant and tender as the morning on her impassioned features.

"Oh, my beloved!" she cried, "do not sink from yourself into despair—do not lose the immortal in the mortal! Think of the briefness of this life—think of the endless golden reaches of the life of which all our earthly experience is but a moment. Heaven knows my sympathies are not imperfect; I could die myself—ah, more, I could see you die—to save to a life of human use this poor spirit, whom his fellow spirits, in their incarnate madness, have dragged away from us to wreak their insanity of hate upon. But it is greater pain than my death or yours, to see you mourn his fate with a mourning that forgets the godhood within you. You told me once the divine sentence of the alchemist—'Heaven hath in it this scene of earth.' Oh, remember it now—think how brief, how fleeting is this term of grief and wrong—think of the eternal heaven in which the grief and wrong melt away forever, and be sustained and comforted !"

As at the harpings of the young shepherd of Israel, the dark spirit sank from Saul, so at the clear, fervent music of her voice, the agony and horror passed from him, and he grew calm. Fondly and sadly, with the tears still wet upon his cheeks, he gazed into her exalted face, lit with a smile of auroral tenderness.

"You are wise," he said mournfully, "and I know that my sorrow is weak and unworthy. I sink from my faith—I lose myself in this dark hour of trouble. A poor, helpless, despised, rejected man, more forlorn and wretched than the most loathed outcast—I found him in the friendless streets, I took him to my home, I nourished his feeble life—and they have clutched him from me, and dragged him back to outrage and torment and murder. If it were the act of some solitary ruffian, I could bear it ; terrible as it is, I could bear it ; but to think that society in all its structure makes it possible for deeds like this to be done ! Oh, sleep of civilization ! Justice, honor, compassion, love, have you gone from earth forever ! Is human brotherhood a Bedlam dream, vanishing from the mind of man, and leaving him to the dark sanity of one life-long mutual murder ! Is this civil-suited swarm of sordid devils and furies the vanguard of the new civilization that is to oversweep the world ! Let me not think of it—let my sick heart swoon from the misery of it ! Oh, that I were dead this night, if death could hide from me this tremendous shame ! Better to be dead than stand here, tied hand and foot, unable to lift a finger to prevent the commission of this ghastly outrage. Better death than to live poisoned to my heart's core with the knowledge that society is one fell league against the weak and poor."

The words which had begun in sorrow, rose into low tempestuous agony and ended in a tone of heart-broken desolate sadness which language cannot tell. Muriel gazed at him mournfully, and the tears silently welled from her eyes.

"My beloved," she said in a tremulous voice, sadly smiling

as she spoke, "it grieves me more than all other grief, to see you overmastered thus. What can I say to calm you? Alas! that I who love you so deeply, am powerless to lift you from this dread sorrow!"

He looked at her with a spasm of self-control in his sad face, and seemed to struggle into calm.

"Let me not grieve you," he faltered. "See, it is over. It shall not master me. There: I am strong again. For your sake I will crush it down. I love you—I will not pain you. I will strive to forget it, and be again as in our happy hours of love and peace before this"——

The faltering voice failed, and the mighty struggle to be calm again wrought in his features.

"Courage, courage," she cried, tenderly smiling upon him. "Courage! All is not ended yet. At worst we can say, with King Francis, that everything is lost but honor. But everything is not lost. We shall devise some means to retrieve this stroke. Oh, my poor mother, if it were not for your unlucky weakness, the victory would not be so difficult! We would sound a blast in Master Lemuel's ears that would bring down his ambition for kidnapping like Jericho. But there's no leaven of the Roman in poor mother's composition, and we are fatally hampered by her feeling."

"Yes," said Harrington, mournfully, "the necessity for keeping this matter private is our ruin. I know not what to do, or which way to turn."

"At all events," she replied, "let us not despair. Nothing palsies one's faculties and energies like despair. Come, sit here by me, and let us coolly review our position, and see what we can do."

She sat down on the couch, and he took his seat by her side.

CHAPTER XXX.

THE HEARTS OF CHEVALIERS.

THEY were about to commence conversation, when footsteps and voices were heard upon the stairs, and presently Emily and Wentworth, joyous and smiling, came into the library.

"Here we are again!" cried Wentworth, in his hearty voice, flinging his hat on the table, and running his hand through his clustering curls. "Here we are, in the height of felicity. Hallo, who's that?" he exclaimed, catching sight of Tugmutton squatting in the corner. "Why, you ineffable young goblin, what are you doing there?"

Emily, who was laying off her bonnet and shawl, turned quickly in the direction he was apostrophizing, and laughed half-amusedly and half-wonderingly at the doleful visage of the boy.

"Why, what's the matter with you, Charles?" she inquired.

"Well put," cried Wentworth. "He looks as if he had a bad attack of the mulligrubs."

"Now, Richard!" exclaimed Emily. "I do wish that you wouldn't talk slang. You artists are perfectly incorrigible in your use of slang."

"All due to the artistic faculty, Emily dear," he gaily returned. "Slang is the picturesque of language, and we must talk picturesquely, or die. But, conscience alive! Why, Harrington! And you, Muriel! What's the matter? You look as if you had a touch of the ebony lamb's complaint too."

"Don't jest, Richard," said Harrington. "We have had an awful experience since we saw you."

"Awful!" exclaimed Wentworth, turning pale. "Why, what's happened?"

Emily came flying over to them, with her cheeks blanched, and her lips parted in frightened inquiry.

"What is it?" she cried. "Is anything the matter with Mrs. Eastman?"

"No, Emily; she is well," replied Harrington. "Richard, the Hungarian fugitive is safe in the streets of Boston. No hound of Vienna can track him here. But the American fugitive is not safe here from the Vienna of the Union. The poor man, whose tale of suffering so moved you—he has been kidnapped in the streets of our city this evening."

"My God!" shouted Wentworth, stamping his foot on the floor, and turning livid.

Emily burst into tears, and dropped into a chair.

"Kidnapped this evening!" pursued the young artist. "Why, you had him here. How could this happen?"

"Listen, and I will tell you," replied Harrington.

Wentworth and Emily drew up their chairs, and sat facing their friends. There was a moment's silence, and then in a few clear, direct words, Harrington told them all.

Wentworth sat still and silent till he had finished, and then turned with a face of wrath upon Tugmutton, who immediately began to cry.

"Hush, Richard!" exclaimed Harrington, stopping Wentworth in the furious speech he was about to pour upon the miserable squab. "Don't use one word of reproach to him. Poor boy! He suffers enough as it is. See," he whispered, "it is a loving creature, and you have hurt his poor heart. Now say something to soothe him."

Wentworth choked down his rage, and sat still for an instant. Then, forcing himself to smile, he rose, and went over to Tugmutton, who was roaring in a muffled undertone of heart-broken grief.

"There, Tuggy, my boy, don't cry," he said soothingly, patting him on the shoulder. "I'm sorry I looked at you so, but I didn't mean anything."

"My gosh, Mr. Wentworth, I feel as if the light of other

days was fled," howled Tugmutton, reminiscent in his anguish of a line from the song he had picked up somewhere.

Wentworth, mad as he was, felt a strong disposition to laugh.

"Never mind, Tuggy," he said lightly. "Cheer up. It'll be all right."

"If I could on'y see Brudder Baby in my affliction," sobbed Tugmutton, "'pears to me, it would be a reviver. But I can't, an' I'm wus off than a bob-tail horse in fly-time."

"Cheer up, Charles," said Harrington, "you shall see Brother Baby soon. Don't cry."

"Yes, don't cry, whatever you do," said Wentworth, "for crying's bad for the liver. Here's something to remember me by," and he gave him a half dollar.

Tugmutton, with a feeling that his liver was in immediate peril, and touched by Wentworth's munificence, took the money with a duck of his head, and immediately knuckled away his tears with his big paws.

"The young devil," muttered Wentworth, walking back to his chair. "Ought to have a sound flogging for his mischief, instead of a half dollar; but that's Harrington all over, and he just makes a fool of me."

"What are you saying to yourself, Richard?" asked Harrington, with a wan smile.

"Nothing, nothing," said Wentworth, hurriedly. "But now what's to be done with Roux?"

"I don't know," sadly responded Harrington; "when he hears of his brother's capture, I fear it will kill him or drive him crazy."

"Oh, by Jupiter! but he musn't hear of it," replied Wentworth—"at least not yet a while, till we see if this mischief can't be remedied someway. We may get hold of Antony again, you know, for he's not out of Boston yet. Meanwhile, you must go up and tell Roux that while he was asleep you sent Antony off to Worcester."

"No, Richard," returned Harrington, "I can't tell a lie. If I could, how could I bear to go up, and look into that poor man's face, and say that? I can't do it."

"You can't, eh?" returned Wentworth, reddening. "Then I can. Hark you, Harrington: I may have told fibs in my life, but I can say, with Alfieri, that I'm a man of as few lies as anybody. Still, when the time comes for a bouncer, let it be a big one, I say, and handsomely done. In my judgment, the time has come now, and up-stairs I'm going to do the deed. After which, if I don't grab Antony back again, even if I have to go all the way to Louisiana to do it, then Emily Ames will never be Emily Wentworth. So!"

And with his handsome face flushed and kindled, Wentworth walked out of the library and up-stairs to Roux's room.

"Where's my brother Ant'ny," cried Roux, with a wild face, the minute he saw him. "I waked up, and he's not here, and I'm afeard of my life for him."

"My dear Mr. Roux, don't be at all alarmed, for Antony is perfectly safe," said Wentworth, blandly, with an air of the most perfect smiling composure.

Roux put his dark hand over his mouth as was his wont, and looked at Wentworth with a wistful dubiety, as wondering if he spoke the truth. But there was truth in every lineament of Wentworth's smiling countenance, and Roux's gaze wandered downward to the floor.

"I've been mighty skeered, Mr. Wentworth," he said, timidly. "I was afeard all wasn't right somehow."

"Perfectly right, Mr. Roux," pursued Wentworth. "You know we were going to send you up to Worcester on Monday or Tuesday. But we had a chance this evening to send Antony on by private conveyance, and as we thought that safer than the cars, we let him go. You were asleep, and as you were to see him again so soon, we thought we wouldn't waken you. Tugmutton's gone on with him, and to-morrow or next day, you are to follow. I thought I'd just come up and tell you, lest you should be anxious."

"I'm very much obleeged to you, Mr. Wentworth," said Roux, smiling and bowing, "and I feel mighty relieved to hear this, sir, for I begun to be proper skeered."

"Indeed?" said Wentworth, blandly, "I'm sorry. But it's all right. Good evening."

"Good evening, Mr. Wentworth," returned the joyful Roux, bending himself double in response to the easy and graceful bow with which Wentworth took leave.

They were all sitting in silence when he entered the library.

"There," said he, seating himself with an air of grave satisfaction, "I've told the biggest whopper I ever told in my life, and if you only knew the virtuous glow and elevation of spirit I feel, you'd all go and tell one apiece to get your souls in the same condition. I've saved poor Roux from awful suffering, maybe death or madness, and I'd do it again if it was necessary. I never told a thundering lie before, but now I've done it, and done it well, and, when Sterne's Accusing Angel bears it up to Heaven's Chancery, if the Recording Angel doesn't drop the biggest tear upon it his lachrymal glands can furnish, and blot it out forever, then I trust the Lord will turn him out of office for not understanding his duty, that's all. I'm sorry if you blame me, Harrington, but there's a happy man up-stairs to balance my side of the ledger."

"I am not your conscience, Richard," said Harrington, simply. "There are some truths that come from hell, and there are some lies that savor of heaven. I believe such falsehoods as yours to be among the latter. I sometimes almost wish I could tell them."

The tears sprang to Richard's eyes.

"Ah, Harrington," said he, dejectedly, "it's all very well for me to talk, but I feel poorer in spirit, for having said, even at such an urging, what was not true. You are a nobler man than I, for you would not lie for the man you would die for. No matter," he added, recklessly, "I could not do otherwise."

Harrington covered his eyes with his hand, and sat silent. Emily, in a dazed condition, looked slowly from one to the other. But Muriel, after a moment's pause, rose from her seat, put her arms around Richard, and kissed him.

"I kiss away the good sin, dear Raffaello," she said, with sad playfulness, caressing his curly head. "The brave and generous good sin."

She stood by him a minute, with her hands resting on his

head, and her beautiful, exalted face upturned, then noiselessly glided to her seat, and slowly sank down.

"Now, Harrington, what are we to do?" said Wentworth, drying the tears from his eyes. "My good sin, as Muriel calls it, staves off Roux's trouble for a couple of days, but if we can't get hold of Antony, it will be terrible."

"I have only one thought, and that is a forlorn one," replied Harrington. "I am waiting for Mrs. Eastman to return. If her brother does not consent to liberate this man, or if she cannot bring herself to bear public action on this matter, I shall go at once to my house, get my pistols, and search the Soliman for Antony."

At this astonishing declaration, which Harrington made very quietly, they all stared. Even Muriel looked amazed. But Harrington, unconscious of their wondering looks, sat in sad abstraction, brooding on his forlorn determination.

"That will compromise no one but the captain of the brig," he said presently. "A writ of habeas corpus would involve Atkins, but a rescue of this sort concerns only myself and that captain."

"But, dear John," said Emily, with a slight shiver, "there will be men on board the vessel, and they will never permit this."

Harrington's broad nostrils quivered in the marble stillness of his face, and his blue eyes gleamed.

"It will go hard with any men who step between me and my purpose to-night," he said, in a low, quiet voice, which made their blood thrill. "The strength of ten is in me now, and I will cripple whoever undertakes to oppose me. If they outnumber these naked hands, I have my pistols. I will not be balked. If Antony is on board the Soliman, I will take him away with me, or leave my body beside him. Gladly would I respect the law and order of society, but it is the day of slavers and traders, and civilization sleeps."

"Yes," impetuously cried Wentworth, "and when civilization sleeps, up, gentlemen and chevaliers, for it is the hour of chivalry!"

Harrington looked calmly into his glowing and electric face.

"You say well, Richard," he replied. "When civilization lies inert, and the organized mass either helps or does not hinder the daily outrage to humanity, it is time for every gentleman to take upon himself the vow which bound the antique chevaliers to suffer no injustice, and to succor the oppressed and helpless. That is the time to try what redress lies in the individual arm. That is the hour of chivalry."

There was a long pause, in which a subtle flame of enthusiasm, born from the colloquy, beat in the veins of all but Harrington. In him there was no enthusiasm, but cold and sad determination.

"But, John," said Emily, at length, "you will not go on this desperate adventure alone?"

"Yes. Alone," he replied.

"You shall not!" she exclaimed, with flashing eyes and her lit face aglow, stopping the fiery answer just bursting from the lips of Wentworth. "Richard shall go with you, and I wish I had twenty lovers to send on such an errand."

Harrington looked at her with a faint color on his melancholy countenance. As for Wentworth, he sank back in his chair, flushed and throbbing with boundless pride in Emily.

"Emily," said Harrington, "think! You yourself suggested the danger of this expedition, and there is danger, for if we are opposed, it will be by sailors, who are not slow to handle knives in a quarrel. Now think coolly. It would be dreadful if Richard were brought home to you dead."

She looked at him with a paling countenance, proud, though the tears gathered in her lustrous eyes.

"If he died in trying to save a poor man from a life worse than the worst death," she answered with a quivering lip, "I would think of him as gone to our Savior's rest, and bear my sorrow like a joy till I died and found him with God. Say no more, Harrington. He shall go with you."

"That I will," cried Wentworth, as springing to his feet, and leaping to the large fauteuil in which sat Emily, he threw himself by her side, and clasped her in his arms. "Ay, marry will I go, and wo to the nautical mind that shall conceive the idea of assaulting me, after the speech I have heard from you, Emily, for on that depraved and abandoned sailor will I execute, with Berserker fury, all that Bagasse has taught me, and I swear it by this kiss!"

And with a kiss on her carnation mouth, that brought the rich blood to her face like fire, he sprang up gaily with an exulting countenance, and flung himself into his chair.

"Bravo!" cried Muriel, with a flash of her usual gaiety, "Cupid and Mars in arms! Richard," she added more seriously, "you have my thanks. And you, too, flower of Episcopalians, bright battle-rose of womankind. Yes, John, you must take Richard with you."

"I will, I will," he impetuously cried. "Oh, why should I despond when there are hearts like these! Would to God, that I could sow the world with such as you, Emily; with such as you, Richard! Yes, Richard, you shall go. And you, Muriel," he added, sinking into mournful playfulness, "you, too, give me leave of what may prove eternal absence from you."

"Not eternal," she answered, with a radiant smile; "not in the worst event eternal. Go, then, and even were it eternal, still go!"

A vapor of fire mounted to his brain, and his heart beat thick and fast. He did not reply, but sat motionless, with his eyes covered by his hand, and all his being pulsing in solemn sweetness.

"Hark!" whispered Muriel, "she is coming. I hear her step on the stairs."

Her ear must have been fine indeed, for listening they could hear nothing.

"No, I am not mistaken," she said, seeing their incredulous faces. "Well I know that soft, slow step. She is coming, and she has failed. Oh, Lemuel Atkins, I pity you!"

There was a moment's pause, and then the library door swung slowly open, and with a face severe and ashen, and a decrepit step, Mrs. Eastman came in. They all rose.

"I have seen him," she said, in a low, frigid, desolate voice. "I have told him everything. I have knelt to him in supplication. Useless—useless. He refused me."

"What did he say, mother?" murmured Muriel.

"Do not ask me," she replied. "I am heart-sick. Ask me nothing. I told him that it was in our house the man had found shelter. And he said he was glad to hear it, for it was a guaranty that he would not be disturbed in the execution of his purpose. He has a power of attorney from Lafitte, he told me, to act as his agent in the matter, and if we presumed to interfere further, he said, he would immediately bring the case before a Commissioner, and have the man returned by law. That was all."

They remained silent a little while, looking with pity on the frozen desolation of her still and pallid features.

"Mother," said Muriel, "what shall we do? Are you willing to let us act publicly in this matter now?"

"Do not ask me," she faltered. "Give me a little time to think. I am going to my chamber. Don't disturb me. I want to be alone. I will think, and to-morrow I will let you know."

They stood with bowed heads, touched by the solemn winter of her sorrow, and she feebly glided from the room. Emily, after a moment's hesitation, followed her.

"Ah, me, I fear the case is hopeless," sighed Muriel. "Everything depends now on your success in finding Antony on board the Soliman."

"Everything," replied Harrington. "Yet, Muriel, on reflection, it is, perhaps, as well that we should not seek a public redress. For if the writ of habeas corpus failed in its execution, as it probably would, Mr. Atkins would at once get out a warrant for Antony, and then he would be lost, indeed. Yes, lost—but by the Eternal God!" he vehemently cried, lifting his arms to heaven, "never should he, never shall any fugitive, be taken from Boston without a desperate effort to prevent it. I have seen one slave dragged hence, and that sent my brains to my hands. Never while I live will I see another. The hour that sees the next man haled before a Commissioner, will see me burst into their court-room, armed to the teeth, and I will take him from them, if I have to do it through a lane of corpses, or leave my body beside him. Then, if I live, let them try me for treason, and if I die, let them put a traitor's stone upon my grave !"

His arms fell heavily, and he strode away toward the door,

"Think, Muriel," he cried, turning suddenly, "think of the baseness of this uncle of yours. To refuse his own sister the man her charity had sheltered ! If he had found refuge in the house of a stranger, I could conceive it ; but to take him from here ! And she knelt to him. Knelt to him in her agony, and he could deny her ! Oh, avarice, avarice ! His wretched cotton-trade is affected, and to that he sacrifices the ties of blood, the feelings of a sister, honor, pity, charity, manhood, everything. Let me not think of it. Come, Richard, come ; let us try our fortune."

At that moment Emily returned.

"I have prevailed upon Mrs. Eastman," she said, "to sleep with me to-night. I could not bear to think of her being alone in this affliction."

"Kind Emily," said Muriel, fondly embracing her. "You anticipated me. Alas ! poor mother ! But, come, Emily, say good bye to Richard, for he is going."

Emily ran to Wentworth's arms, and kissed him.

"You'll come back safe, I know," she said, cheerfully.

"That I will," he returned, with a gay laugh ; "and wo to the man of the tarry trowsers who interferes with my safe return."

"Adieu, Muriel," said Harrington, embracing and kissing her. "We will not part forever," he added, with a sad smile, "for I feel that I am to come back again."

"So do I," she replied. "Good bye. We will wait tea for you, gentlemen."

They departed, and Muriel and Emily sat down, under the eyes of the silent Tugmutton, to await their return.

In two hours they came back disconsolate, for they had not found Antony. They had found the Soliman lying at Long Wharf, and had boarded her. Nobody happened to be in the vessel but a stupid sailor, half drunk, who, when Harrington told him, very simply, that he came to look for a man hidden on board, imagined that he was a policeman, and got him a lantern. With this Harrington and Wentworth searched every hole and corner of the vessel, but Antony was not there. In fact, Bangham had him tied hand and foot, and stowed away in the back room of a low boozing ken on Commercial street, whose landlord was a friend of the captain's. On leaving the vessel, the young men found the sailor lying in a sottish sleep, and as they were certain that he would remember nothing on the morrow of his visitors, they left him without buying his secrecy, as they had intended, and returned with heavy hearts to Temple street.

"And so," said Harrington, concluding his narration, "as there is nothing more to be done till to-morrow, if then, let us try to forget it all as much as we can. The Soliman sails on Tuesday night, the sailor told us. I shall not abandon the hope of finding the man on board of her till she has gone."

He took a revolver from his breast pocket as he ended, and laid it on the mantel, then wearily sat down.

"Come," said Muriel, "let us go to tea. We shall all feel better for a little refreshment. Come, Charles."

Tugmutton, whose grief had not injured his appetite, which was not the case with the others, bounced up nimbly, and followed them.

After tea, the doleful Puck was charged not to go near his father, and was provided with a separate room. Slowly and sadly the evening deepened on, till at last the hour of slumber spread its dove's wings over all their sorrows.

CHAPTER XXXI.

WRECK AND RUIN.

The next day arose in the dazzling effulgence of a fervid sun. It was the thirty-first of May—the last day of spring—but the light and heat of June filled the streets of the crowded city under a cloudless and resplendent blue.

Anticipating a crowd of callers, Muriel, unwilling to see them with this trouble on her mind, gave Patrick orders to admit no one but Wentworth and Captain Fisher, Harrington having sent for the latter.

The Captain arrived about ten o'clock, and his features grew all atwist, and his head all awry, the moment he laid eyes on Harrington. There is no knowing the unimaginable screw he would have got himself into could he have seen the ghastly face the young man had worn the evening before. To-day Harrington was only intensely pallid, and his face was resolute, stern, and calm. While the Captain yet stared at him, and before he could express his astonishment, Harrington bade him sit down, and at once told him the whole story.

The moment he had done, the Captain rose in awful wrath, and began to swear. Such oaths! No spruce-gum imprecations then, but tobacco of every conceivable brand, did the infuriated old seaman pour forth in a steady stream. The army that swore terribly in Flanders, never swore worse than he in his wrath. Lafitte, Atkins, Boston, Boston merchants, kidnappers, slaveholders, and slavery in the abstract and in the concrete, did he shower with curses. Never had the Captain such a backsliding before. Harrington, who perhaps thought of Sterne's Recording Angel, with his disposition to blot out with tears the record of what Muriel called good sins, let him rip away till, as the man in the play says, he got all the bad stuff out of him, and tumbled into his seat exhausted with his rage.

The interview lasted about an hour, and without result. Harrington had thought it best to let the Captain know what had happened, and did not hope that he could suggest any action, as under the circumstances he could not. Profoundly depressed with the knowledge that Mrs. Eastman's invincible feeling shut out even the forlorn hope of legal or anti-slavery effort, the old man departed with a self-imposed promise to remain all day on the wharf and watch the Soliman.

Mrs. Eastman's feeling was indeed invincible. She said nothing, but as they saw her moving about the house like a ghost, they understood from her austere and ashen features that she could not bring her heart to consent to her brother's public dishonor, and her own related disgrace. The family *esprit de corps* was mighty in her.

Muriel, meanwhile, thinking that the true disgrace and dishonor would be to have Antony sacrificed to any private feeling, however sacred, was holding busy audience with her teeming brain, as to the duty of disregarding her mother's feeling, and resolutely taking matters into her own hands. The chief consideration that withheld her decision now, was that the captain of the Soliman might deny, when the writ was served on him, that the man was in his possession, and that then, in the interim of delay, Mr. Atkins would procure a regular warrant, which would be fatal to Antony. Besides, she well knew that the moment the fugitive was brought before a Commissioner, the dauntless Harrington, thoroughly trained in the use of arms, and with the might of ten men in him, would burst into the court-room like a thunderbolt of war, and slay every man that stood between him and the rescue, or be himself slain. There was good blood in the veins of young Muriel —the old red blood of the Achaian women who sent their dear ones to Platea with the cry of "return with your shields or upon them"—the old red blood of the New England women who armed their husbands for Lexington ; and strong in her faith of the deathlessness of life, she did not shrink from the thought of his death in such a cause ; but still she preferred that every peaceful means of obtaining the end should be employed before the last stern issue should be made.

While she yet debated with herself, Wentworth arrived. A hasty council was at once held between the three, and it was resolved that Harrington should wait on Mr. Atkins, with a proposition to buy Antony at any price within reason.

Accompanied by Wentworth, Harrington at once set out for Long Wharf. It was then nearly noon, and the crowded streets through which they passed were salient and swarming in the vertical splendor. A few minutes' walk brought them to the place of their destination, and Wentworth agreeing to wait outside, wandered across the street to the shipping, while Harrington turned in to the counting-room.

He paused a moment in the dusky ware-room opening on

the street, and surveyed its contents. Amongst other merchandise was visible a pile of dirty cotton-bales, burst here and there with their fullness, and the white staple bulging from the rents. The thick, musty, stifling smell of cotton choked the air of the ware-room. It was the same smell that had stifled the conscience of the merchant, the conscience of his fellows, the conscience of the nation—yes, honor, duty, courage, compassion, manhood, independence, all that was truly American.

Pausing only for a moment, Harrington went up-stairs into the office, and glancing at the clerks by the desks, looked away and saw the merchant sitting with his back to him in the little inner counting-room, and by his side Driscoll, the stevedore. He at once passed forward, noticing, as he entered the counting-room that Driscoll had a twenty-dollar gold piece in his hand. Without thinking anything of this, Harrington nodded to the stevedore, and bowed gravely to Mr. Atkins as the latter turned with a sudden flush and a half scowl toward him.

"Mr. Atkins," said the young man, courteously, "will you favor me with a few minutes' conversation with you?"

The merchant's first impulse was to order him out of the office, but Harrington's manner was at once so courteous and so dignified that he found it difficult to treat him with incivility.

"Driscoll," said he, "just wait outside a few minutes. Now, Mr. Harrington, what is it?"

Driscoll withdrew just outside of the open door, where he remained standing, while Harrington took a chair beside the merchant, who turned his obstinate, energetic face straight to the wall before him, and linked his fingers, with the air of one who was resolved to hear patiently all that could be said, and not be moved by anything.

"Mr. Atkins," began Harrington, "I have called to see you about this man Antóny. I am aware that he escaped from New Orleans in one of your vessels, and I fully appreciate the difficulties of the position in which his escape has placed you. If it should happen to become known, it not only injures the credit and character of your house in New Orleans, but it renders your captain liable to imprisonment. Is it not so, Mr. Atkins?"

"It is, Mr. Harrington," replied the merchant, somewhat disconcerted by the gentle suavity of Harrington's manner, and by his fair statement of the matter, which were not what he had anticipated.

"On the other hand, Mr. Atkins," pursued Harrington, "is the fact that this negro escaped, as there is no reason to doubt, from a master of unusual hardness, and only after being very cruelly treated. Furthermore, he chanced to find shelter with your sister, who feels a deep sympathy for his misfortunes, and would be very seriously injured both in health and spirits if he were returned to the unhappy life from which he has fled. Now I assume of course that you do not wish to unnecessarily afflict this poor fellow, still less to grieve Mrs. Eastman. All that you wish is to be rid of the unfortunate consequences which his escape is likely to entail upon you in New Orleans. Is not that the case?"

Mr. Atkins stared at the wall with an uneasy look, and twiddled his thumbs.

"Something of that sort, Mr. Harrington, something of that sort," he nervously replied.

"Exactly," returned Harrington. "Now I take the liberty to suggest that this matter can be readily arranged to the satisfaction of all parties, and every unpleasant consequence be avoided. I am commissioned to say that the value of this man, and even twice or three times his value, will be paid to his owner. It will be easy for you to state this in a card in the New Orleans papers, and also to state the circumstances under which he got to Boston in your vessel. Everybody will see at once that you and your captain were not at all responsible for his escape, and this frank statement, conjoined with your avowed willingness to reimburse the owner for his loss, will not only free you from all suspicion of complicity in his flight, but will raise your credit as an honorable man in New Orleans, and also with the conservative portion of the community at the North. Besides, this compromise will spare your sister and niece the real distress they will feel if the man is returned, and this I think you will be willing to do if you can in justice to all other parties concerned. This arrangement will not only cost you nothing, but benefit you materially, besides satisfying every person involved in the matter. Now, candidly, is not this a fair and reasonable proposition?"

Mr. Atkins fidgeted in his chair for a minute, unable to deny the force of what Harrington had said.

"Well, Mr. Harrington," he replied, "I admit that your plan is feasible enough, and not unfair, certainly. But there is one difficulty in the way. Mr. Lafitte is unwilling to lose this man. His value is not more than twelve hundred dollars, but I am convinced that Mr. Lafitte would not take five thousand for him."

"Mr. Atkins, we will give him five thousand," said Harrington.

"But I tell you he wouldn't take it," replied the merchant.

"Well, then, we will give him ten thousand," said Harrington.

Mr. Atkins stared at him.

"Pshaw! Mr. Harrington, you surely wouldn't be such a fool as to give that sum for a worthless nigger," he contemptuously answered.

Harrington's blood grew hot, but externally he kept cool as ice.

"My dear sir," he said, affably, "we will not mention the negro. It is Mrs. Eastman who is concerned. Your niece will willingly give ten thousand dollars out of her fortune to spare her mother's feelings. And surely you would not deny her the privilege of comforting her mother, even were this a mere matter of prejudice."

Mr. Atkins really felt cornered. He could not but see the various solid advantages of this proposition. But Mr. Atkins had considerable of the mule in his composition.

"Mr. Harrington," said he, after an embarrassed pause, "suppose Lafitte wouldn't be willing to take even ten thousand."

"My dear Mr. Atkins," replied Harrington, laughing—alas!

he found it hard to laugh, poor gentleman—" do you not see that if Mr. Lafitte refuses to take so extravagant a sum, he will only make himself ridiculous in the eyes of the New Orleans people. Why, they will hoot at him! And besides, they will extol your public spirit to the skies. It will give you a name there no other merchant possesses. Just think of it! Why, Lafitte would be forced to accept out of pure shame, even were he indifferent to the advantage of having the round sum of ten thousand dollars."

"I declare, sir, this is too preposterously absurd," said the merchant, growing red with vexation at being thus tempted out of his plan. "To think of wasting so much money as that for such a purpose."

"But, Mr. Atkins," replied Harrington, "large as the sum is, what is it compared with your sister's peace of mind? If you only knew the dreadful state of distress she is in, you would not think so. True her distress may be nonsensical, but still as a practical man you will be willing to allow that we must take human nature as we find it. Besides, we need not give so large a sum. We only wish to give enough to repair matters, and set you right with the New Orleans folks. Lafitte can appraise his slave, and regard for public opinion will make him keep within reason. Still we are ready to do anything rather than have you prejudiced in your business, or your sister injured as, at her time of life, this matter would injure her."

"I don't see why you should interest yourself so much in this affair, Mr. Harrington," grumbled the merchant.

"Pardon me, I am only an agent," replied Harrington, with a sweet civility which not even Atkins could resist. "I hope you will excuse me if I have said anything to offend your sense of propriety, but I only meant to suggest a way out of this unpleasant embroilment, which I thought might not have occurred to you, and which I am sure will commend itself to your judgment as a practical business man, and one who only desires fair play to all parties. I trust there is no offence in this Mr. Atkins."

"Oh, no sir, no sir," said the merchant hastily, with an awkward bow, his jaw working meanwhile with his embarrassment at the deferential politeness with which Harrington presented what he could not but admit was an unexceptionable way of settling the whole matter. "No offence at all, sir. But—well —what I—well the fact is, Mr. Harrington, you know my political views, which of course you don't agree with."

"We will not differ about politics, sir," replied Harrington with gracious affability.

"No, of course not, of course not," fidgeted Mr. Atkins. "But this is the point: There has been too much tampering with slave property in this country, sir, and I wanted to send that man back that Southern men might see that we are devoted to their interests, and can promptly return their property without putting them to the trouble of legal formalities."

"My dear sir," put in Harrington, "in what better way could you prove your devotion to the interests of Southern men than by the plan I mention? Consider how inferior the return of the man would be to the magnificent offer to pay ten times his value, publicly made, and promptly accomplished. The one would be the theme of limited complimentary mention, but the other would be blazoned far and wide, and loud and long. A Northern merchant willing to sacrifice ten thousand dollars even, rather than loosen one bond of political or business fellowship between the North and South! Why, it is impossible that you should not see the superiority of this measure to accomplish the very end you have in view."

Mr. Atkins thrust his hands into his pockets, and working his jaw convulsively, struggled between the temptation to yield, and the obstinate desire to carry out his original purpose. Harrington saw that the crisis had come, and fearing to irritate the merchant into refusal by his presence, he rose.

"Permit me to leave you to think of it," he said courteously. "Just give it candid consideration, solely as a business matter, and with regard to your own interests and political feelings, and let me call again, if it is not asking too much, at any time you may mention."

It is perfectly impossible to describe the fine tact of bearing, the sweet and winning courtesy and delicacy with which

Harrington conducted himself during this difficult interview. If Lemuel Atkins had not been more stubborn than the unwedgeable and gnarled oak, he would have soon opened to that subtle charm, and as it was, he began to open to it.

"Well, Mr. Harrington," he said after a pause, "I'll think of it, and you can call in about—no you needn't," he cried, with a sudden revulsion, turning red in the face with passion. "I'll be damned if I'll do it! There. It's cursed folly, and I won't consent to it."

Harrington's trembling heart froze, but he did not yet abandon hope.

"Nay," said he, gently, "I trust you will not decide hastily. I know it may strike you unfavorably in one view of it, but if after careful consideration you do not approve the course I mention, why then I will submit to your maturer judgment. Only consider it calmly and candidly, and I do not fear the result."

"I won't," snarled the merchant. "I won't consider it at all."

"But Mr. Atkins"——

"I tell you I won't. Come, bother me no more with it."

"At least, sir, give one moment's consideration to the suffering your sister is in."

"Oh, damn my sister! What do I care for her suffering. Let her suffer. I tell you, I'll send that black scoundrel back in spite of her and you, and the whole pack of you," he roared, purple with rage, and shaking his fist at Harrington.

"Mr. Atkins," said Harrington, with an impressive solemnity which cooled the merchant even in the mad heat of his fury—"you know the nature of Mr. Lafitte as well as I, for you have had dealings with him. I pray you to consider that if you send that man back, you send him to his murder. Murder by the most merciless torture, Mr. Atkins. Can you bear the responsibility of that? Now think of it coolly."

"I don't care for his murder," sullenly growled the merchant. "I'll send him, whether or no."

Harrington saw that the case was hopeless.

"Mr. Atkins," he said, with touching gentleness, "do not

decide this matter in anger. Pardon me, if I have said anything to offend you, and pray think of this again."

"I've heard enough," returned Atkins. "Let me hear no more. You have my final decision."

"At least," replied Harrington, mournfully, "think of the future. The day may come when public opinion will change. The old New England opposition to slavery may arise again even in Boston. Do not commit yourself by such an act as this, so that a few years hence men may judge you harshly. Think of what your children will say of you if you leave them a name spotted with disgrace. Think of that."

"It is a matter of perfect indifference to me what my children will say of me," coolly replied the merchant, with a yawn. "Hark you, Mr. Harrington," he cried, rising to his feet, and sternly facing the young man. "I'll just give you my idea of this slavery question, and one which involves my whole action in this matter. When any nation concludes that it is for the best interests and prosperity of the country to make men slaves—I don't care whether those slaves are white or black—no man nor body of men, nor any other nation, has a right to interfere with, or in any way prevent that nation's making them slaves, and keeping them in slavery. White or black, it makes no difference. This nation or any other nation, it's all the same. Statesmen have settled that—older heads than yours or mine. That principle of national right has come up, as a question of national right, before the sober, sound, conservative statesmanship of the American Union, and that statesmanship has answered it."

"How has it answered it?" put in Harrington, quickly, fixing his stern and searching eyes on the flushed face of the merchant.

"How has it answered it?" repeated Mr. Atkins, with a sarcastic air. "Well, sir, how has it answered it?"

"It has answered it with the roar of Decatur's guns under the walls of Algiers!" thundered Harrington, with a look of fire.

Mr. Atkins, at this stunning demolition of his position, turned red, and then pale, and then all sorts of colors, and finally sat down with a working jaw, and a face of utter confusion.

"That is the way the sober, sound, conservative statesmanship of the Union answered that question of national right," sternly continued Harrington. "It answered from the blazing muzzles of Decatur's cannon, that the nation that undertakes to hold innocent men in slavery is a nation of pirates. By its own answer it stands condemned. Every State in this Union, that holds innocent men in slavery, is an organized piracy. The Union that sanctions the crime, and makes it possible, is another. And you, Lemuel Atkins, trampling on your sister's heart, in your scoundrel zeal to thrust an innocent and wretched man into that pirate hell from whence his own bravery freed him, you are the vilest, because the meanest, pirate of them all. The most degraded slaveholder is white beside such a wretch as you. Never let me hear again of Southern infamy. You, a Northern merchant, kidnapping your brother—kidnapping a man whose right it is to say with you, in his prayers to Heaven, 'Our Father'—not respecting even the miserable forms of pirate law in your infernal zeal for wickedness—what wretch is there, however black, that does not whiten into virtue beside you! Lafitte himself sees in you a depth of mean vice to which his self-respect will not permit him to descend. God forgive me, that I lowered myself to prune my speech, and curb my heart, and strain my conscience, in the effort to win and bribe you from your ghastly crime against mankind. Go on with it now. Blacken down into your pit of iniquity. Wrench from the world of living men to which he yet clings, the poor victim of your accursed avarice, and send him back as you and your muck-rake tribe sent Sims, to shriek his life away under the bloody scourge. So live your life, and gorging on your miserable gains till you drop into your grave, may you never know the fate it is to feel the curses of the poor!"

Gazing aghast, with glassy eyes, like one fascinated, into the white and terrible countenance of Harrington, with a horrible, blind look on his own visage, Atkins sat petrified under the low, magnetic voice in which, like wind and rain and fire and hail, these words burst upon him. A moment, and Harrington had gone ; and rising to his feet, and shaking all over as in an ague fit, with that horrible blind look upon his furious face, and a mad-dog slaver gathering on his loose and livid lips, his sick-man's voice strained and gasped into speech, such as might unnaturally tear its way in agonizing rage from the throat of one organically dumb.

"B-y G-a-ud, I'd sa-end him ba-eck," he drawled agasp, "e-ff I-i ha-ed t-a be sa-ent t-a ha-ell!"

I would send him back if I had to be sent to hell. With these words, which sounded as if they were torn from him, as the fabled mandrake was said to be torn from the earth, with low shrieks and dripping blood ; and which seemed to cling as they were wrenched away, as the demon vegetable was said to cling when dragged from the soil, he tottered backward, and fell with a heavy slump into his chair. There he sat gasping, with his face turned to the wall.

Driscoll had slunk away into the outer office as Harrington left the counting-room, and the young man passed down into the street without seeing him, and crossed to where Wentworth was standing. The young artist gazed with a shocked expression into his colorless face as he approached him.

"Heavens! Harrington, how white you are!" he murmured.

"I have failed, Richard," returned Harrington in a deep and quiet voice. "He has no heart, no reason even. Trade has eaten the one and the other out of him. I made my plea as well as I could. I appealed to his mean self-interest, so that even he felt the force of my appeal, and wavered. But he refused me, and I flung upon him the bitterest words that ever passed my lips, and left him."

Wentworth looked in silence on the marble countenance, white in the shadow of the slouched hat, with the vertical sunlight just touching the beard below.

"I am glad, Harrington," he said, after a pause, "that you flung bitter words upon him."

"No," replied Harrington, mournfully, "do not be glad,

for it cannot gladden me. Yet I do not regret what I said to him, nor do I think it were better unsaid. Let him pass. He lies, the saddest wreck I know, stranded on the shores of my pity. Mal-organized, miseducated, the imperfect infant taken from his cradle, and every imperfection developed by the hap-hazard social culture, and all else undeveloped ; you have him at last, what he is—at once the product and the victim of a half-barbarous state of society. Pity him. He might have been better had he lived in a better day and among better men."

"Well, no doubt," musingly replied Wentworth. "Like Dr. Johnson's Scotchmen—caught young, something might have been made of him. In the mean time, blast his eyes !"

They wandered on a few steps together. Suddenly Harrington stood still.

"There's no use in the Captain watching the Soliman," he said. "The man is secreted somewhere, and will probably not be taken on board till the vessel is ready to sail. Besides, it may awaken suspicion if anybody should happen to know Eldad's connection with me, and see him hanging about the brig. Let's go down to him."

They turned and went down the wharf.

"What do you think of boarding the Soliman again ?" asked Wentworth.

"Better not," Harrington returned. "Antony is not there. It would only put them on their guard. The sole chance now is the writ of habeas corpus."

"And how about Mrs. Eastman ?" said Wentworth.

"We must disregard her," Harrington replied. "She will thank us by and by for doing so, especially if we succeed in saving poor Antony. The Soliman does not sail till Tuesday night, so there is plenty of time. We will return presently, see Muriel, and then I will at once procure the writ. If I fail with it, the last thing is to search the Soliman as she is on the point of leaving the wharf, opposition or no opposition."

"Good," exclaimed Wentworth, with a proud thrill.

They went on in silence, and presently reached the Soliman. The stevedores were busy lading her, and all was activity on board and on the wharf. Looking about, Harrington presently caught sight of Captain Fisher on the opposite pavement, and at once went over to him. The two joined Wentworth in a couple of minutes, and they all went up the wharf together.

"Now, Captain," said Harrington, as they walked on, "I am going on to Temple street, and I will be at your house soon. Then you and I will go together for the writ—so wait for me."

"All right, John," returned the Captain, who had been previously told by Harrington that Mrs. Eastman was to be disregarded.

Half way up, the Captain stopped and fixed an admiring gaze on a pretty little sail-boat, sloop-rigged, which lay alongside, and which belonged to him.

"Pooty, aint she?" he remarked, ogling his property.

"Yes, indeed," returned Harrington, "we've had many a pleasant sail in her in the old days."

He sighed vaguely, and they went on, up the busy wharf, and into the noise and bustle of State street. It was the great mercantile street of the city, the old street of solemn memories, the proud street of Sam Adams and Paul Revere, the brave street of the Boston Massacre, the dark street of the rendition of Sims. Over those stones once wet with the sacramental blood of Attucks, under the solemn eye of the morning star, the child of his race, surrounded by sabres, had gone to the vessel a Boston merchant volunteered to take him to his murder. Side by side, amidst the weeds and rubble of traffic, burst the black slaver flower and bloomed the bright historic rose.

The merchants were thick on 'Change as the three companions came up the street, and there was much lifting of hats and fluttering and swarming, which for a moment they could not account for. But presently, as they entered the crowd, they met a figure which explained that decorous commotion, and involuntarily made them start and for a second pause. It was Webster. Not, alas! the dark Hyperion, splendid in statued majesty, of a younger day, when those stern lips thundered the speech of freemen; but him grown old, his leonine and massive features austere and sullen-grim, fire-scarred in swarthy grain with base ambition and battered by the storms of state, yet kingly still in ruin, and with some relic of their former sombre beauty. He lifted his hat to a gentleman as they came up, and for an instant they gazed upon the rugged and malignant grandeur of that imposing countenance, with its vast brow and iron majesty of mouth, and its cavernous and torrid eyes. A moment, and they had gone by. Wentworth looked awed, the Captain's face was rigid and atwist, and Harrington was blind with tears.

"To meet him at such an hour as this!" he gasped. "He who has done it all! He with the seventh of March upon his face, and you and I and all of us with its shadow on our lives. One speech for freedom then, and the cloud of this anguish and dishonor would have passed away. That speech, half-written in his desk, never spoken, but in its stead the speech for slavery, which has made kidnapping a law. And he, fallen forever, standing there amidst those muck-rake rogues, fallen from all he was, fallen from all he might have been, sunk to herd among the thieves of men! Oh, wreck of wrecks—grief of griefs—ashes and dust and ruin!"

Touched by the solemn passion of his sorrow, they did not speak, but went on in brooding silence, regardless of the passing crowds around them. In a few minutes they reached the head of State street, where the Captain silently nodded and left them, and turning in the opposite direction, they went on to Temple street.

CHAPTER XXXII.

HERALD SHADOWS.

It was about one o'clock when they arrived. After a hasty dinner, Muriel withdrew to argue matters with her mother, while Harrington went into the library, and Wentworth. who was suffering from the heat, started for home to change his clothes, promising to meet his friend soon at the house in Chambers street.

The conference with Mrs. Eastman lasted nearly an hour, failed of result of course, and without telling her mother of her purpose, Muriel went into the library, and gave her decision in favor of instant action.

Harrington immediately put his revolver in his pocket, and took, in case of need, a hundred dollars in bills, which Muriel, with her usual foresight, had drawn from the bank that morning. Then receiving her fervent hopes for his success, he folded her in his arms and kissed her, and sallied forth upon his mission.

He was resolute and calm, yet nervously alive with incertitudes and apprehensions, which fled like strange shadows across his burning brain. The day was still brilliant and sultry, but in the stainless blue of the morning masses of bright wild clouds had gathered, and lay fantastically changing from shape to shape in densely huddled concourse. He watched them as he strode along, finding in their tottering transformations and flaring brightness, as in the mutable shapes they assumed, some weird expression of his own mood. Here they were unclimbable alps of cloudy snow, upreared in a glittering mass of mountainous giddiness, and toppling from their bases. There they stretched in a carded drift of fierce white fire, smouldering in the resplendent blue, and consumed by its own intensity. In one place they had heaped into the form of a defying giant, impotently melting away in fantastic dissolution. In another they were a long cohort of crouching lions looking out of their manes. Below the zenith, before him, a solitary cloud shaped itself into a vapory hydra ; beyond, another wore the semblance of some mongrel dragon of the air ; and all were sphinxine, monstrous, dazzling, wonderful—a phantasmagoric rack of intervolved chimeras.

With such a pageant bright and wild above his head, and with a feeling corresponsive to it all within his mind, he strode on through the quiet streets of the neighborhood, and arrived at his house in Chambers street. For some reason or other, the Captain had not yet arrived, and, expecting him presently, after a minute's kindly chat with Hannah and Sophy, he went into his own apartment.

The afternoon sun lay bright and cheerful within the room where he had spent so many sweet and studious hours, but the first thing he saw on entering, brought night and winter on his heart. Below the empty pedestal, the bust of the beloved Verulam lay shattered to fragments on the floor. His head sunk upon his breast, and he stood sadly gazing upon the ruin. He did not grieve for the loss of the treasured statue ; he did not even remember to think how the accident could have occurred ; all considerations were lost in the feeling of mournful significance which swept over his burning brain, as he brooded on the broken image of the majestic Lord of Civilization.

A few moments he gazed upon the wreck with a face of marble; then, suddenly, his features became convulsed, and his eyes filled with tears.

"It is well, it is well !" he cried, in a transport of passionate sorrow. "Oh image, why should you stand there when the shamed land has lost her breed of noble blood, and civilization sleeps, and tyranny darkens back upon the world ! Well may you lie shattered, for all that is human and holy is shattered too. Why should I keep you in this base city, where all that is noble rests in the grave, or lives a dying life in the forlorn grapple with hell ! Fade, fade, large memories of saints and martyrs—drop, statues of heroes—melt, phantoms of old honor from the pictured wall—away, and yield your places to the forms of clowns and knaves ! Come, you artists," he raved, in passionate bitterness—"come, you dilettante bastards—come, you anatomies, whom the ghost of Angelo mocks and scorns—here is work for you. God ! the serpentry and maggotry of Power are all before you ! Choose from them—choose from them—mould us statues of slavers, paint us pictures of kidnappers, to fill the vacant places ! Down with the just and great—up with the small and vile !"

Quivering with the tempest of his agony, he tottered away, and flinging himself into his chair, covered his face with his hands.

A few minutes trailed by in deep stillness. Gradually he

became calm, and his hands dropped from his white and sorrowful features.

"I waste my heart in grief," he mournfully murmured. "It will pass, it will pass. Oh, winter of Slavery you will pass, and the spring-time of Freedom will emerge. It is but a season—only a season. Patience, patience, patience."

He sat for a little while, then rose, gathered up and laid out of sight the fragments of the statue, bore the pedestal upstairs, and returning resumed his chair.

The minutes were wearing on in deep silence when a low knock came to the door.

"Enter," cried Harrington, looking up from his mournful musing.

The door opened and revealed the grotesque and sloven figure of Bagasse. He had on an old swallow-tailed coat, and wore his usual dingy cap, with the visor turned down, under which his swarthy, upturned face, with the mustachioed, lion mouth open in a curious smile, and the nose adorned with the horn-rimmed goggles, pointed with suave inquiry at Harrington, while the hand performed a military salute.

"Why, Bagasse!" cried Harrington, smiling, and rising from his chair to cross over and shake hands—"how are you? Come in. I'm glad to see you."

"Ah, Missr Harrington," returned the old soldier, entering and bowing low with a quick motion, over the hand he grasped in his, "I am vair glad to see you. I haf not see you for so long. Zen I fancee you are seek, and I call zoo be vair sure zat it is not zat keep you from ze acadamee. How is you helt? Br-r-r! *Sacrebleu!* but you haf been seek, eh?" he cried, with a sudden commiseration, expressed by a shrug of his shoulders, a lift of his eyebrows, and a startled grimace of his features, as he noticed the whiteness of Harrington's countenance. "*Mon Dieu!* you is vair pale wis you eye circle wis ze dark color! O my fren' Missr Harrington, was is ze mattair wis you?"

A little moisture gathered in Harrington's eyes at the pathetic anxiety of the old man's look and voice, but he smiled cheerfully, and shook his head.

"No, Bagasse," he replied, "I am not sick. I am as well as I have ever been. Come, take a seat."

Bagasse removed his cap, and sitting on the sofa, kept his upturned visage pointed in dubious inquiry at Harrington, who had resumed his chair.

"You know I have been married," said Harrington smilingly.

"Marry! No! *Mon Dieu*, no! I haf not hear zat!" exclaimed Bagasse, with a start, and his bright eye glowing from a flushed visage.

"Yes," replied Harrington. "To that beautiful rich lady Mr. Witherlee told you of."

Bagasse turned the color of heated iron, partly with joy at this intelligence, partly with wonder at Harrington's knowledge of what had passed between himself and Witherlee.

"By dam!" he exclaimed suddenly, "I am so glad I haf ze desire zoo dance like ze vair devail! But how you know what zat pup Witterly—ex-cuse me, Missr Harrington, but zat is vair bad young man—ah, vair bad!—how you know what he say zoo me?"

"No matter, Bagasse," returned Harrington, smiling, "we won't talk of that. But my wife heard of what you said to him—you remember?—what you said you would tell me if you were her—and she said that to me. Yes, she did."

Bagasse, with his grotesque ferruginous face all aglow with a dozen emotions, sprang up with a stamp which shook the room, dropped into his seat again, and slapped his heart with his hand.

"Hah!" he hoarsely cried, "it is superb! By dam! I sall fly. My heart is too big for his box. And zat beautifool, rich, vair, fine ladee say zat? Sublime! She is great, she is grand, she is more zan ze great Empress Josephine of ze great Nap-oleon. Ah, Hypolite Bagasse my frien', you haf ze biggest compliment I sall evair hear!"

"You must see my wife, Bagasse," continued Harrington. "She feels very grateful to you, first for defending me from poor Witherlee's talk"——

"*Sacre!*" growled Bagasse, interrupting, "I catch zat pup

Witterly in my acadamee once more, and I break him in two pieces ovair my knee !"

"No," said Harrington, gently, "for my sake, don't touch him. He has been punished enough already. Say that you won't touch him, Bagasse."

"Missr Harrington, I do evairysing you want," replied the pacified fencing-master. "You say let Witterly off, I let him off. I treat him wis civilitee."

"That's right," returned Harrington; "do. But as I was saying, my wife feels especially grateful to you for having given her the charming idea of making that speech to me, and she wants to see you, and know you, and thank you herself. So the first opportunity I get, I am going to take you to her house."

Bagasse turned swarthy-red at this, and looked embarrassed.

"Pardon me, Missr Harrington—ex-cuse me, sir, please," he said, with suave shamefacedness, bowing low as he sat. "But it is too mush honor—vair many too mush. You beautifool, vair, fine, ladee wife, she is so high, she is so *distingué*, she is ze count-ess, ze duch-ess, ze queen. She is so far up like ze beautifool sun. I am so low down like ze paving-stone ze sun shine on. You zink now! I am ze poor old fencing-mastair—ze man zat eat ze garleek and drink ze brandee-bottel—ze ugly old devail Bagasse, so low down. Br-r-r-r! It is not propair zat I make ze viseet zoo ze vair, fine, beautifool rich ladee-wife—I, zee poor way low down child of ze people. *Sacrebleu*, no!"

"Oh, Bagasse, Bagasse," said Harrington, in a tone of good natured chiding, "fie upon you to talk in that way! Suppose my wife is the sun, as you say. Well, the sun is a democrat. The sun shines as sweetly on you as on the emperor. Now my wife is like the sun in that particular at least. Ah, Bagasse, she, too, is a child of the people, and she will be proud to know a man who could make the manly speech you made! She is not a lady who respects coats and bank-stock, but heart, honor, manhood. Come, now, you fancy her a bit of a Marie Antoinette. Not at all, Bagasse. Think of that dear child of the people whom Frenchmen love—Josephine. That is a better image of her. Don't say a word—you shall visit her, and then you'll see how much at home she'll make you feel."

All which Harrington said in French that Bagasse might perfectly understand him. The old man sat, with a touched face, looking at the floor for some time after the young scholar had ceased to speak. Looking up, at length, with an unsteady eye, he saw that the sad, introverted expression had returned to the pallid features before him. In fact, Harrington's thoughts had dropped away to the trouble on his mind, and he was wondering why the Captain did not come.

"Missr Harrington," said Bagasse, in a voice, a little lower and hoarser than usual, "you make me vair proud—you do me vair mush honor. But ah, my joay haf mush melancolee wis him, for you look so pale, so bad. Ex-cuse me, Missr Harrington—but was is ze mattair wis you? Why, you look so white, so sorrowfool? Ah, tell you old Bagasse zat he may say ze leetel word wis comfort in him! You marry ze beautifool, dear ladee wife—*mon Dieu!* zat sall make you so happy zan evairybody. Why zen you haf zat face? Zat is not ze face for ze new husband—*sacrebleu,* no! Now why is zat?"

Harrington paused a moment before replying, struggling to repress the agitation he felt not only at the rude tenderness of the old Frenchman's words and manner, but at the aching sense it brought him of the grief that had clouded his sweet and perfect happiness.

"Don't ask me, Bagasse," he faltered. "Kind old friend, I wish I could tell you, but there are reasons"——

A low knock at the door made him break off in the midst of his sentence.

"No, don't go," he said to the fencing-master, who had moved to rise. "Come in," he cried.

The door opened slowly, and to the astonishment of Harrington, Driscoll the stevedore entered. Harrington smiled vaguely, and bent his head with an absent and wondering air in reply to the abashed and awkward bow the Irishman made as he came in.

"Why, Mr. Driscoll," he said, slowly, "I didn't expect to

see you, though I'm glad you came. Take a chair. How are you?"

"Purty well, thank ye kindly, Mr. Harrington," replied Driscoll, taking off his old straw hat, and wiping his forehead with his coat sleeve, without looking at the young man.

Harrington, wondering at his curious air of awkward bashfulness, and beginning to feel a rising perturbation, as he remembered that he had seen the man in Atkins' office not long before, blankly stared at him. He was a strong, thick-set, stooping man, dressed in coarse canvas trowsers, all stained with pitch and dirt; a soiled red flannel shirt; and a short frowsy old coat with large horn buttons. He had what is commonly called a thoroughly Irish face—which means not the Irish face of Jeremy Taylor or Edmund Burke, but the face of an Irish peasant after despotism, political, social, and religious, has wrought on him and his ancestry for a certain period, giving him some abjectness, some lawlessness, some clownishness, some stupidity, some insensibility, an aspect of hard work and poor fare and low condition, and degrading his forehead, clouding his eye, lowering his nose, making his lips loose, his gums prominent, his cheeks scrawny, his throat scraggy, and barbarizing the manhood of him generally. Such, with the addition of tan and freckles got from labor in the sun, and also the grime and sweat of that labor, was the visage of Driscoll. The only other thing Harrington noticed about him was that he kept his left hand tightly clenched while he wiped his face with the rough sleeve of his right arm.

"Well," continued Harrington, after a pause, "how goes it, Mr. Driscoll? How is your wife? And the children? And how is the broken leg? Won't you sit down?"

"They're all purty well, sur, thank ye kindly," returned Driscoll, ducking his head continuously as he spoke, and moving up to the table. "And the leg's sthrong as a post, glory be to God, sur. Sorra the word o'lie in it, but it's yerself that it's owin' to, and divil a leg I'd have to stand on this minit widout you, Mr. Harrington."

"Oh, well," said Harrington, smiling; "I'm glad you're

over that trouble. But you came up to tell me something, I suppose. Did—did Mr. Atkins send you?"

"Deed he did not, sur," replied Driscoll. "I kem up to make bowld to ask ye something, Mr. Harrington, if ye wouldn't think it an offince, sur," he added, with a furtive sidelook at Bagasse, who sat with an upturned face of curious interrogation levelled at him.

"Certainly not," replied Harrington. "No offence at all. Ask away. Never mind my friend, there."

"Bad scran to me if I wor to mind a frind o' yours, sur," returned Driscoll, coming close up to the edge of the table, and looking uneasily at Harrington. "It's a quistion I'll make bowld to ask ye, sur."

"Well, ask on," said Harrington, blankly gazing at him, with a mounting color, and his heart beating painfully with a blind clairvoyant sense of what was coming.

"Are ye," confidentially asked the stevedore, with considerable burr on the "are"—"are ye opposed, sur, to it's bein' done?"

Harrington started so violently, and turned so pale, that Bagasse sprang to his feet, and Driscoll's face grew stupid with surprise.

"To what being done?" gasped Harrington. "Speak quick. Tell me what you mean?"

"Are ye opposed, sur, to ould Atkins sendin' off the durty negur? That's what I mane," said Driscoll.

"I am!" cried Harrington, with a lightning look at Bagasse, and a wish that he was out of the room.

Driscoll looked at the table, and looking at it, slowly swung up his clenched left fist like one pelting a pool, and hurled a twenty dollar gold piece ringing on the cloth.

"Then I'm dommed if I'll do it," he exultingly howled, with a thump of his fist on the money. "Hurroo for the bridge that carries us over, and it's you that wor the bridge of goold to me and the ould woman and the childher in the black hour, Mr. Harrington. Ould Atkins and his money to the divil, and bad scran to him and his for an ould robber, for I'm dommed if I'll do wan thing that ye are opposed to, sur. Arrah, bad look to him, and may he niver know glory, for the black thafe o' the world that he is ; but it's yerself that dhressed him down thremindous this blissed day, Mr. Harrington. Troth, but it's the good blood that's in the Harringtons, and kings and imperors they wor in the ould country wanst, and sorra the word o' lie in it !"

With which highly apocryphal assertion, Driscoll's excited outburst ceased, and he fell to wiping his heated face, first with one coat-sleeve and then with the other.

Harrington rose from his seat, white as death, his nostrils heaving and his eyes aflame.

"Bagasse," he said, "will you be kind enough to leave me"—— He stopped, touched by the look of tender sympathy on the grotesque face of the fencing-master. "No," he cried, "don't go. Stay with me. You shall know it—you shall know what it is that is killing me. But tell me," he pursued, speaking in French, "tell me, on the honor of a soldier, that you will never breathe one word of this to any living being, for it is a secret which must be kept close as the grave."

Bagasse struck hands with him with passionate and martial energy.

"I swear it," he hoarsely cried in French. "Let me know it, for I cannot bear to see you suffer, and if I can help you, I will !"

"Good !" exclaimed Harrington. "Driscoll, attend to me. Where is that negro ?"

"They've got him, sur, in the cuddy of a boat down on Spectacle Island," replied the stevedore, frightened into conciseness by the stern voice and flaming eyes of Harrington.

"Who are they that have him ? Men employed by Atkins ?"

"Yes, sur. Siven o' thim, sur. It's me that wor to be eight."

"Seven men paid by Atkins. Who are they ? Stevedores ?"

"Stevedores and sailors, sur. Twinty dollars apiece they get for it, sur."

"What are they doing with him there?"

"Howlding on to him, sur, till the Soliman sails. She's to heave to, and take him on board, sur."

"When does the Soliman sail?"

"To-morrow morning at break o' day, sur."

"To-morrow morning? No—you mean Tuesday night."

"'Deed I don't, sur. She sails to-morrow morning, if there's a breath o' wind."

Harrington drew his breath. Lucky I found this out, he said to himself; to-morrow I should have been too late.

"Driscoll," he continued, "are those men armed?"

"They've got their knives, sur."

"No pistols?"

"Sorra the wan, sur."

"Do they stay in the boat all the time?"

"'Deed they don't, sur. Wan or two o' thim stays in her turn and turn about, and the rist o' thim plays cards in the little room o' the house on the island."

"The house? Oh, it's a hotel. Does the owner of the house know they have a negro in the boat?"

"'Deed he don't, sur. The negur's tied hand and fut, and kep' in the cuddy."

"What does the owner of the house think those men are there for?"

"I don't know, sur. Captain Bangham paid him well for the room they have, and he niver comes nigh thim at all."

"How long were you there?"

"This morning early, I wint down with thim, sur."

"How came you to be up in the city this noon?"

"I kem up, sur, with Captain Bangham. He wint down to the island in a boat of his own, along wid us this morning early, and stayed wid us a while, dhrinkin' like a fish, till he got purty dhrunk. So I kem back wid him to help him manage the boat lest he'd get dhrowned, sur."

"How came you to come up with him, and not a sailor?"

"We dhrew lots for it, sur, and I was the wan."

"And you were going down to the island again?"

"Yis, sur. I was goin' in the first boat that wint down the

harbor. I wint in to ould Atkins to take the pay, for the others had got theirs, and there wasn't enough in his pocket for me when he paid thim, so he tould me to come in whin I kem up from the island, and begorra, I tuk him at his word."

"Did Atkins pay those men himself?"

"Deed he did, sur. Early in the mornin' when they wint down, he was there, and paid thim."

"This Captain Bangham is the captain of the Soliman, I suppose?"

"Yis, sur."

"Where does the boat lie that has the negro on board."

"At the wharf o' the island, sur."

"This room in which the men stay—where is it?"

"It's in the outbuilding, sur. A little room nixt to the kitchen, low down, wid the doore openin' on the ground, an' wan step for the stairs, sur."

"Good. Now, Driscoll, you are not going to help these men any more?"

"I'm dommed if I'll do it, whin you're opposed to me doin' it, sur. Troth, I heard ivery word ye said to the ould thafe, and says I to meself, if I do wan thing that Mr. Harrington's set aginst, and he the gintleman that befrinded me and mine in the black throuble, may the divil fly away wid me."

"Driscoll, take that gold piece back to Mr. Atkins, and tell him you've thought better of it. Don't say another word to him but that. Have no quarrel with him. Say that, put the money on his desk, and leave his office. Do you understand?"

"Yis, sur. I'll do it."

"Good. You shall not lose by it. Take this from me."

Harrington drew from his pocket the money he had received from Muriel, and counted him out twenty-five dollars.

"Here, Driscoll," he said, holding out the bills to him.

"Oh, begorra, Mr. Harrington, but I'll niver take it from you. Plaise don't offer it to me."

"Driscoll, I insist upon your taking it. You shall."

He seized the stevedore's hand, and put the money into it.

"There. Don't thank me, but attend to what I say. Driscoll, that negro is a poor laboring man like you. He has as good a right to his freedom as you have. When you joined those men to keep him in that boat, you were guilty of a great sin. Never do such a thing again! You say you are grateful to me. Then be kind to negroes for my sake. Be kind to them for your own sake. You are a poor man, and you ought to be kind to the poor."

Driscoll looked abashed and touched. Perhaps the words moved him less than the solemn and gentle voice which uttered them.

"Sorra the harm I'll ever work wan o' thim, sir," he murmured. "Deed, I didn't know it was a sin."

"And now, Driscoll," pursued Harrington, "I have reasons for wishing this matter kept secret, and I want you to swear to me that you will never speak of this to any person whatever. Never tell anybody that you were in that boat—that Mr. Atkins hired you—or that you came here and told me. Never speak of this at all in any way."

"I'll swear it, sur. Deed I will."

Harrington turned to his shelves, and took down a Douai Bible, its covers blazoned with a golden cross.

"Driscoll," said he, "you are a Catholic. Here is the Catholic Bible. It is opposed to slavery. There have been great men of your church who hated slavery. The Pope himself has cursed slavery. See, here is the cross of your church on the cover. Take this book in your hands, and swear that you will never speak to any person, man or woman, of what you have done, of what passed between Mr. Atkins and you, of what has passed between us here. Swear it."

Driscoll reverently received the Bible in his hands, took the oath, and kissed the cross.

"That is all," said Harrington, receiving the Bible, and restoring it to its place. "I am very grateful to you for having told me of this, Driscoll. You have done me the greatest good that any man could do me."

Driscoll stood in silence, awed and wonder-stricken at what

had passed, and subdued by the majestic gentleness of Harrington's demeanor. In a moment he took the gold piece from the table, and moved to the door.

"God save ye kindly, sur," he faltered, ducking his head.

"Good bye, Driscoll. Shake hands."

He awkwardly took the frank hand Harrington outstretched as he came over to him, felt it grasp his own as never gentleman's had grasped it before, and with a wild and woful enthusiasm heaving within him, and repressed by shame and awe, he turned away, and stole out at the door the young man opened for him.

Harrington closed the door, and, all unmindful of Bagasse, turned away with clasped hands, and a face of solemn ecstasy.

"Oh, bread cast upon the waters," he murmured, "is it thus I find you after many days? I helped him in his trouble, and he pays me back with life!"

His head sunk upon his breast, and he stood with closed eyes, rapt and still, his heart swelling with gratitude and thanksgiving.

Suddenly, from the barrel-organ in the street, a strain of martial music arose and flowed in upon the dreaming silence. It was the thrilling tonal glory of the Marseillaise. The thought of his heart came like flame to the broad-nostrilled countenance of Harrington, and he stood with kindled features and dilated form, while the proud and mournful music swept like the march of an army around him. On and on in burning measure, rolled the sad and conquering lilt of liberty, and darkening down in fire and tears, voice of the passion of mankind, voice of the wrongs and woes that redden earth while the good cause lies bleeding, the weird strain arose and rang in the clear cry for the sword, and wailed in the mournful glory of those final tones whose melody is like a hymn for the dead who die for Man.

Harrington rushed from the room. The Frenchman, left alone, stood with a dark glow on his iron visage, and the red light of battle in his eye, thinking of the old days of military ardor, the old wars in which he had stormed on Europe, the old Paris folding in her bosom the ashes of the Emperor, the old France he himself would never see again.

The flush of memory the music brought him was paling into sadness, when Harrington returned from the street.

"I have paid him, and sent him away, Bagasse," said the young man. "After that air, I wanted to hear no more. Now sit down, and I will tell you the meaning of all this."

Bagasse took his seat on the sofa, and Harrington sitting beside him, in a few words told him all.

"And now," he joyfully said, in conclusion, "everything begins to lighten, since I know where this poor Antony is to be found."

"Ah, Missr Harrin'ton," returned the old man, smilingly regarding him over an upturned chin, "zat face you haf is now ze face of ze new husband! Ze dear ladee wife will lof zat face so gay. Missr Harrin'ton, you are ze most grand zhentilman I sall evair see. You feel kind for ze vair old devail himself. You get white, you get ze dark round you eye for zat neeger man so mush as he was you own self. Nobody, not ze white man, not ze neeger man, not no man at all, feel so bad for you like you feel for evairy ozzer man. Why is zat?"

Harrington's maxillary muscles wrinkled, and his teeth flashed in an amused laugh, while his face grew scarlet at this complimentary recognition of the human kindness that was so mighty in him.

"Bagasse," said he, "don't praise me for having the feelings of a man. If you could have seen the poor fellow when I found him in the street, and if you could have heard his account of the life he had been living, you would feel as badly as I did. But here's Wentworth and the Captain at last," he added, catching sight of them from the window near him, as they entered the garden gate.

They came in presently, and for a moment there was a confusion of salutations. Then the Captain, having been introduced to Bagasse, turned to Harrington.

"John," said he, "I'm awful exercised about keepin' you waitin', but" ——

"Never mind," interrupted Harrington. "I shan't try to get the habeas corpus writ now. Let me tell you what's happened."

"By Jupiter!" cried Wentworth, reddening at the sight of Harrington's kindled face. "Antony's got off! Good! Hurrah!"

"Hold on. Not so fast, Richard," returned Harrington. "Antony's not off yet, but he's going to be. Now listen."

And in a few words he gave them an account of the interview with Driscoll.

"So Antony's in the cuddy of a boat at Spectacle Island," he added, concluding. "And now, see here. Thank fortune Mrs. Eastman's feelings can be spared, Antony saved, and yet the whole affair be kept strictly private. I shall wait, Captain, till the dead of night, when those fellows will all be asleep, and I hope drunk—all except the one in the boat—and then I shall run down in your craft, land, and capture the captured."

"Bravo!" shouted Wentworth. "By Jove! I shall laugh fit to kill when we get hold of Antony."

"We?" said Harrington, jestingly. "Why, are you going?"

"Am I going!" roared Wentworth. "Of course I am. Do you think I'd let you go alone?"

Captain Fisher, who had been sitting in silence, with his winter pippin face agrin, burst into hearty laughter.

"By the spoon of horn!" he exclaimed, "but this is a leetle the richest idee I ever heern tell on. But, John, look a-here. Siven of them fellers, you know. Sposin you find them in the boat all together, like Brown's cows, when he had but one? What'll you do then?"

"It's not likely," replied Harrington. "Men love their ease too much to be out in the night when it's not necessary. For my own part, I think Atkins has managed this matter like a fool. Two men would have answered his purpose perfectly, and he puts eight there. I can't imagine what he was thinking of."

Mr. Atkins was thinking of Harrington, if Harrington could but have known it. The moment Mrs. Eastman had told him that Antony had been sheltered in her house, a feeling had come to him that the young scholar, whose dauntless temper he had some notion of, might possibly attempt a rescue, and he took his measures accordingly. This accounted, too, for Antony not being on board the Soliman.

"But look a-here, John," pursued the Captain. "Satan's niver onready to play ye a trick, an' there's no countin' on what's likely with him. Now sposin you find them siven fellers in the boat when you git down?"

"In that case," replied Harrington, gravely, "there's nothing for it but a desperate fight. I shall tell them of the illegality of their proceeding, and try to frighten them into giving up Antony. If they refuse, I shall fall on them like a fury. Here's Bagasse has been training me for years, and I think I should do credit to his training even with seven men.

"Missr Harrin'ton," said Bagasse, with a grimace, "you do me one favor. No, *pardieu*, I take zat favor. Look. I go wis you. Zat is settle. Zen if ze seven men wish zoo fight, zey sall fight wis you and me, and zey find out, by dam, zat we is fourteen!"

"Bravo, you old Gascon!" cried Wentworth, slapping him on the shoulder. "Let him go, Harrington. Don't refuse."

"But, Bagasse," said Harrington, "you have a wife, and I can't consent that you should put your life in danger on my affair."

"Chut! poo, poo!" answered the fencing-master. "Ex-cuse me, Missr Harrin'ton, but zat is feedelstick! You haf ze beautifool, dear ladee wife, and I take care of you for her. Good. Zat is well. Now I go wis you."

"Don't deny him, Harrington," pleaded Wentworth. "Come, let's arrange the rest of this matter. Where do we start from?"

"Long Wharf, at about twelve o'clock," replied Harrington. "Whoever gets to the boat first will wait for the rest. Then about landing. Faith, it won't do to land at Long Wharf, if any of us gets hurt. We shall have the night police asking questions if they see one of us limp. Besides, the less seen of Antony the better. We must land at South Boston, where it's lonely as a desert."

"And walk over to the city!" asked Wentworth, with a laugh.

"No, we must have a carriage," replied Harrington. "Now who's going to drive the carriage out and wait there with it? I can't, for I must go in the boat."

"And I must go wis you," said Bagasse.

"So must I," added Wentworth.

"It's me then," said the Captain, getting all awry. "Now, that's a pity, for I want to be with you. And sposin there's a fight. Then you're one able-bodied man the less."

"See," put in Bagasse. "I tell you. We get John Todd for to drive. You pay him money. Zen he go. Zat John Todd lof money."

"Bravo!" cried Wentworth. "That's an idea. I'll give Johnny ten dollars for the job."

"I hardly like to have another party in a matter so private," demurred Harrington.

"But he needn't know anything about it," said Wentworth. "He needn't even see Antony. When we land, I'll go up and get the carriage, letting him stay behind, put Antony in, drive up again, take Johnny on the box, drive in town, set him down, and go on to Temple street."

"Well," said Harrington, "that may do. Now who'll get the carriage? We want a close carriage."

"I'll get it," returned Wentworth. "I know a man who'll let me have one. I'll attend to all that, and to engaging Johnny. Where shall we have the carriage stand? Say Q street, Good. We'll all go armed, of course."

"Certainly," replied Harrington, "I will take my revolver."

"And I my pistols," said Wentworth.

"I sall carree ze good cavalree sabre wis my pistol," said Bagasse.

"And I'll take that hickory stick of mine with the lead knob, and that'll give any feller a headache that wants one," said the Captain, with his head ominously askew.

"Good, everything's settled," said Harrington. "Now, gentlemen, to-night at twelve. We shall get there by two at the latest, if there's any breeze at all, and probably at one.

You'd better all meet here, and go down together. I will meet you at the boat."

"Agreed," said Wentworth. "Now, Bagasse, you and I will go after Johnny."

"And I home," said Harrington. "I'll meet you again at twelve."

He lingered a few moments after they had gone, musing with a kindled and exulting face, and then with a sudden yearning to pour out his gladness to Muriel, he seized his hat and left the room. In the yard he happened to think of the dog, and he went for a moment to the kennel. The animal was lying on its side, apparently asleep, and Harrington was just about to turn away, when he chanced to notice that its eyes were partly open. Surprised a little, he bent down, and laid his hand on the animal. It did not move. The old dog was dead.

He arose, and stood for a moment with a vacant and reeling brain; then turned, and with a dazed feeling, went into the street and on his way. The clouds were still bright and wild in the afternoon sky, and tottering fantastically into ever mutable strange shapes, fierce, dazzling, sphinxine, wonderful. He gazed at them for a little while as he strode on, until oppressed by their instability, and with a dark sense that they were like an untranslatable hieroglyphic of something that had been, or was, or was to be, and that could not be defined, he turned his eyes from them, his heart throbbing thick and fast, and his burning brain giddy with a fullness of life which, like the clouds, seemed to reel in dissolution, and yet, like them, did not dissolve away.

CHAPTER XXXIII.

THE OLD ACHAIAN HOUR.

A LOW and melancholy melody was dreaming from the organ through the corridors, as Harrington entered the still and darkened dwelling. He was about to ascend to the library, when the parlor door opened, and Mrs. Eastman, severe and ashen, beckoned him, with a ghostly motion, to come in. He entered at once. Closing the door behind him, and folding her in his arms, he looked tenderly into her still and grief-worn face, while the low music brooded above them in aërial and solemn lamentation.

"John," she whispered, "where have you been? John, an awful feeling has been with me since you left the house—a feeling that you are doing that which I cannot bring my heart to have done—that you have already done it."

She stopped to pore with a ghastly gaze into his countenance. In the dead stillness, tranced into deeper stillness, as it seemed, by the low creeping music, he came into rapport with the cold, dark terror that froze her soul, and he felt his blood curdle and his hair stir.

"If you have done this," she whispered in a tone that thrilled him, "it will kill me. I cannot survive it. Tell me that you whom I love so dearly—tell me that you have not been so cruel to me. Have you done it?"

"Mother," he said sadly, "be at ease. I have not, and I never will. But, oh! my mother, you who dread this disgrace and dishonor, think of the disgrace and dishonor it would be if that wretched fugitive were sacrificed by us! How can you bear to think of that?"

She shuddered and clung to him, wildly agitated, but smiling ghastlily with the joy she felt at the assurance of her brother's safety from public obloquy; and still the low, lamenting strain above them dreamed sombrely in hollow murmurs through the darkened air.

"I know it; it is terrible," she whispered. "But it must be. Yes, it must be. Hate me—despise me—never look at me again; but it must be so, and I am glad—very glad. Glad in my grief; full of grief, but glad. I am weak, I am degraded, but it is for his sake, for my brother's sake. Oh, I bless you, I bless you that you have spared him, and me through him; I bless you. Hate me, despise me, if you must. But he is safe; the little child I played with once is safe; my brother whose sins are many and grievous, he is safe, and I am glad—I am glad!"

"Peace, peace, my mother! Let it go," he cried. "Do not speak so to me. Do not load yourself with reproach. Oh, I feel with you, and I am not removed from you. There there—let it all be forgotten. Time will efface these sad hours, and we will be happy again."

She gently withdrew from his embrace, weeping, and turned away; and gazing at her for a moment, full of mournful pity, he left the room, and went slowly up-stairs, with the sad music deepening around him.

It stopped as he entered the room, and Muriel rose from the organ, and came swiftly toward him, clad all in white, and noble in her beauty. He clasped her in his arms as if he had not seen her for a year.

"Joy!" she cried, looking at him with brilliant eyes, and a faint color mantling her face, "you come back to me with a changed look! You have succeeded."

"Not yet," he replied, proudly smiling, "but we are going to succeed. Come, let us sit together, and let me tell you what has occurred, and my plan."

They sat down, with their arms around each other, and he told her all, and what he was going to do. She listened to the end in dreamful silence, smiling faintly, and occasionally bending her graceful head in assent to his designs.

"Now, what do you think?" he asked in conclusion. "How does the enterprise strike you?"

"I like it," she replied, half gaily. "It is bold, simple, and I think you cannot fail of success. Go manfully then to the little battle for the good cause, and come back with your shield, or upon it. My soul goes with you."

He folded her to his heart, proudly smiling.

"Dear friend, brave wife," he said, fondly. "Thank heaven that we are wedded for life's duties and life's ends! Oh, blessed love that has not shut us in a private luxury, careless of liberty and justice and the tears of man! Yes—I will go on this enterprise of mercy, and I feel I shall succeed."

They sat in fervent communion till the twilight fell. Emily

came in as it began to darken, and they had just finished telling her what was to be done, and were charging her to say nothing of it to Mrs. Eastman, when Wentworth arrived in great spirits.

"All right," he cried, upon entering. "The deed is done, and I feel like Benvenuto Cellini when he drew his rapier, and fought the whole gang of the Pope's soldiers, single-handed, pinking a couple of dozen of the rascals. Ha! that was an artist for you! Oh, Benvenuto was a regular brick, he was."

"Now, Richard! Slang again," chided Emily.

"Slang? I deny it," returned Wentworth, impudently. "Now what did I say?"

"You said Cellini was a brick," said Emily, laughing.

"So he was," retorted Wentworth, gaily. "A regular brick. Call brick slang? Why, it's one of the finest epithets in the English language! What other term could you use that is half as expressive? And what was language made for but to express our ideas with adequacy, propriety, and elegance? Oh, by Jupiter! but I'll stick to brick like mortar!"

"So you have Johnny," observed Harrington, laughing.

"Yes. He's to start from the stable at about half-past twelve and drive over to Q street to bring home a small fishing-party," replied Wentworth, with a satirical air. "A party that goes down the harbor to catch black-fish."

"I hope the party won't catch a tartar," said Emily, jestingly.

"Nor a cold," added Muriel. "But there's the tea-bell."

They arose and went down to the tea-room, talking and laughing gaily.

After tea they returned for a short time to the library. Presently, Mrs. Eastman, feeling unwell, left them, and retired for the night, attended by Muriel, who, filled with compassion for her poor mother, went with her to her chamber and stayed till she was asleep.

She was gone about half an hour, and returning to the lighted library at the expiration of that time, found the three chatting together.

"Now, I am going to leave you two," said Harrington,

rising, and addressing Wentworth and Emily. "Muriel, I feel weary with the excitements of this day, and as I shall want all my freshness and vigor for this adventure, I am going up-stairs to sleep an hour or two. Richard, I'll see you at the boat."

"Good," responded Wentworth. "Au revoir."

Harrington bent his head smilingly to them both, and putting his arm around Muriel's waist, drew her with him from the room.

"Sleep will be twice sleep with you near me," he tenderly murmured, bending his face down to hers, as they went up the stairs together.

"Ah," she said, with pensive playfulness, "I was afraid you were going to leave me in exile while you slept, and I do not wish to be away from you now."

He did not answer, but clasped her a little closer to him, and they ascended in silence to their chamber.

She silently lighted a sconce upon the wall, which shed through its ground-glass globe a mellow moony light upon the pure and virginal room, with its furniture of white and gold, and its cloudlike couch, overhung with a drooping fall of filmy gauze. Then going to a closet, she took from thence a slender crystal flask covered with golden arabesques, and brought it to him.

"See," she said, "My Greek friend, Kestor, made me a present of this more than a year ago. It is Greek wine. Yes—the vine that gave us this grew from the soil of the antique heroes. I have kept it for some great occasion, and to-night before you go, you and I will drink it."

Smiling, he took the flask from her hand and held it to the light, looking at the clear rosy-golden glow of the fine liquid.

"It is beautiful," he said. "Too beautiful to drink. One might fancy this such wine as Leonidas and the Three Hundred drank at the last banquet before they sallied from the immortal pass and fell upon the hosts of Xerxes. It looks fit for the veins of heroes."

"And heroes' wives," she playfully added, with a charming smile. "Therefore, you and I will drink it, pledging the enterprise. But we must have some glasses."

She rang, and presently one of the maids came up, went, and returned again with half a dozen small goblets on a tray.

"Well," said Muriel, laughing as she looked at the tray, "with six glasses we can drink pledges. Good. Now let us sleep."

Turning the light low, she unbound her tresses, and lying down with him, kissed his eyelids with soft and dewy kisses.

"Sleep sweetly, my beloved," she murmured. "It is the fourth night. A very little night, but the fifth night will be sweet and long, and full of rest."

He did not reply, but gently kissed her, and with their souls stilled with ineffable tenderness they sank away together in a slumber, innocent and sweet as that of childhood.

The room was dim around that tranquil rest, and the faint light softly showed the forms of the reposing lovers. Locked in each other's arms, with the snowy films drooping from the golden ring in the ceiling in long and flowing festoons around them, they lay like some fair picture of immortal love and peace shadowed within the clear depths of a magic mirror in a light of darkling dawn.

An hour melted slowly by, and during that hour, folded to her bosom, and breathing the balm of her parted lips, the rest of Harrington was sweet and deep. Then a strange dream outgrew upon his brain from the oblivion of his slumber.

He was running cautiously along a vaulted archway of the rude Saxon architecture, toward a flight of five or six stone steps, which led up into the open air. It was in Saxon England, in some time of trouble, and he was a young Saxon. He saw himself clothed in a short, brown tunic, belted at the waist, and reaching nearly to the knees, which were bare, and with leather buskins on his feet. As it often happens in dreams, he both was that figure, and saw it. It was himself, but utterly unlike himself both in aspect and character. The head was uncovered, save by short, dark, curling hair; the face was youthful, unbearded, mild and timid in expression, with the cheeks rather wan; and the figure was that of a slight and strengthless stripling. A sense of general carnage was in the air of the dream, and it seemed as if in that form, he was seeking to escape from enemies. Too gentle and weak in nature to feel violent fear, he had only a timorous and innocent apprehension of his danger ; and in this mood, running on to the steps, and ascending, suddenly the opening of the archway filled with armed warriors, and as he shrank on the point of turning to flee, their long axes fell upon him, and he was slain.

He awoke instantly, not with a start, but by simply unclosing his eyes. The dream was vivid, but not frightful, and waking without alarm, his first and only thought was that it was a memory of an old avatar in which he had lived on earth in a different organization than he had now, and had been killed young. For a moment this feeling came clearly to him, and then sensible of where he was, and of the sweet face breathing balm so near his own, his eyelids closed with an irresistible drowsiness, and he slept on.

His sleep was undisturbed for about half an hour when another strange dream slid upon his mind. He was sitting up awake in a bed alone by himself, and though the bed was in a room, it was yet, by some singular ubiquity, which still was not incongruous or wonderful, on the sidewalk of some unfamiliar street. Sitting upright in it in his night-clothes in a broad, grey daylight, and looking over his shoulder, he saw far, far away an illimitable waste of snow, out of which thousands upon thousands of piteous and imploring negro faces looked toward him. He had the feeling that these were the faces of the thirty thousand fugitives who at that period had fled to Canada. While he gazed at them, he beheld coming down the street on the pavement, a long procession of the Boston merchants, all familiar to him, respectable and cosy citizens whom he often saw about town, or on 'Change. They all wore their usual garb and aspect, but as they passed by his bed they all changed, yet without seeming to change, into medieval Jews, with long avaricious faces and drooping beards and stooping shoulders, and eyes bent obliquely upon the ground before them. Every hand clutched a money-bag, and every form wore the conical hat and the long Jewish gaberdine of Shylock. So they passed him, and when they had passed they were Boston merchants again, while the rest coming on changed, yet did not seem to change, into money-greedy Jews as they went by, and resumed their previous forms, though without seeming to resume them, when they had reached a certain vague limit. All this did not in the least surprise him, or seem extraordinary, or unusual, but wearying at last of the interminable and monotonous procession, he sighed and awoke.

Her dreaming face was still near him, and the cool balm of her breath touched his sense with sweet and sad ecstasy. There was a moment of unutterable weary sorrow, in which the bitter symbolism of his vision lingered with him, and then, with a feeling of melancholy comfort, his heavy eyelids drooped, and he slept again.

He had a consciousness that he had slept long, and with this in his mind, his sleeping soul awoke in a third dream. He had left his body and was in the air of the chamber. Spiritually light and poised, with the delicious sense of being able to float upward at will, he was looking down upon the couch, with the quiet room around him. He saw his body lying folded in her arms, the face sleeping close to her own. He saw how that face looked to others, and felt a dim wonder at its strangeness to his own eyes. His gaze dwelt with calm and holy tenderness, undisturbed by any regret, upon the beautiful and noble face of his beloved, sleeping in its shadowy tresses, its curved lips slightly parted, and all its clear and graceful lines composed in slumber. A thrill of silent blessing and farewell stole softly through his being, and with the feeling that he must go, he slowly floated backward through the wall, which made no more resistance than air. A trance fell upon him as he passed through, and seemed to last, though he had no sense of time, till he found himself alone in a rich and holy garden. The strange flowers were thick and deep, and wonderful in mystic beauty, and though of many rare and lovely colors, the still and tender living glory that brooded on all, gave them something of the rich pallor of flowers seen in some imaginary pearl and purple moonlight stiller and fairer than melts from any moon of ours. Or rather, they seemed pale with their own ecstasy of heavenly odor, for they filled the soft, self-luminous air with a fragrance which dissolved through all his being in ethereal and tranquil rapture. Filled with celestial bliss, he wandered on through the purpureal glory of the garden, under the holy shadow of strange trees, and amidst the myriad-blowing clusters of the flowers, while the songs of birds sounded in liquid melody around him, and yet did not break the divine silence of the solemn Paradise. And wandering on, he turned a curve of the path, and came upon the gracious presence of the man he loved. He knew the majestic front, the vast brow, the sweet and piercing eye of Verulam, and like a younger brother yearning with affection, he drew nigh and laid his head upon his breast. The arms gently enfolded him ; the regal face bent over his with a tender and benignant smile ; and thrilling with the slow sweetness of an unutterable ecstasy, he seemed to sink into the swoon of the soul, and the vision was gone.

Her arms had fallen away from him in her slumber, and noiselessly rising as he awoke, he sat on the edge of the couch, and leaned his damp brow on his hand, his brain light and clear, his frame drenched in the renewing dew of sleep, and throbbing with the remembered bliss of his dream, and one still solemn thought distinct in his mind. He was to die ! The meaning of that dream was death ! A slow thrill ran through his veins as he thought of it. Yes, that was its meaning. He was to die !

He sat still for some minutes, with that thought in his mind. Gradually the sweetness of the dream failed from him, merged in a ghostly sense of the quietude around him. He looked up with a feeling of awe. The dim lamplight faintly lit the pure and shadowy chamber. All was vague, motionless, indefinite. Nothing seemed distinct or living, but that strange and awful conviction, too strong for any doubt, that he was to die.

Turning slowly, he gazed upon the face of Muriel. The last lingering relic of the sweetness of his dream failed from him as he looked upon her. His young wife. How could he bear to leave her! Four days of heavenly joy with her—heavenly even in the sorrow that had lain upon the last; four little days—the divine dawn of a long life of happiness—only four, and this was to be the end! The golden gates of a beautiful existence, affluent of use and influence and fame, just opened to him with her, and now to close forever. To lay down all the deliciousness, the joys, the hopes, the ambitions of life, for the happiness of two poor negro brothers. For their poor trampled rights to abandon life—oh, above all, to resign her! To die, and leave her on earth alone, her bursting day-spring of happy and noble love quenched in the black and blotting cloud of death. To die—to die and leave her.

Icy cold, yet with a burning brain, and slow thrills creeping through the horror of his veins, he turned away, and sat still. Hark! In the silence came the distant sound from a steeple striking the hour. He counted the slow strokes. Eleven. He looked at his watch. It was eleven o'clock. In one hour more he was to go.

He looked around the quiet room. Life never seemed to him so sweet as then. In contrast to the stillness and seclusion, the peaceful comfort and warm luxury of the restful chamber, came the vision of the bare and open night upon the bleak waste of waters, and he in the lonely boat with those rude men, thinking of the gentle being he had left behind him. A sense as of one who shivers out under the winter stars, and turns to the warm firelight and the cheerful faces of friends in the cosy glow of home, came to him, and with it came temptation like a voice. Turn from this purpose—turn to love and life! You have been staunch and true in human kindness to its uttermost demand, but your life belongs to her, and not to another. Well to save this man from his doom, but not to fling away your life for a single service, when ampler service needs you. Think of her suffering, think of her mother's grief for your loss, think, too, of the friends you are leading into peril. Perhaps your warning includes them—think of those who will mourn them, and for their sakes turn from this hopeless purpose. Turn, for this is warning and not fate—or go, still in safety, and plead with those men for the fugitive's release—threaten them, menace them with civil penalties, and perchance they will yield him. But if they do not, all is done that you are called to do, and life is more than you are called to give ; so turn away from them, and tell your friends you cannot risk their safety, and come back here to long years of happiness with her.

Sitting in icy silence, the temptings rose within his brain, clear as if a still and gentle voice had breathed them, and mingled with a siren sense of honeyed music that seemed to circle round and round him like an airy coil. Suddenly he sprang up with a spasm of heroic grief and agony, and stood quivering with his eyes covered by his hands. Her eyelids unclosed, and lying still, she looked at him. The next instant, she leaped from the couch and clasped him in her arms.

There was a long pause of awful silence, in which he stood with head uplifted and his eyes covered with his hands, while she clung to him, her face still between its thick length of waven tresses, and gazed with dilated eyes into his half-hid features.

"My beloved! My own beloved, what is this? Was it a dream? Be calm—be strong. I am with you. I hold you in my arms. No evil thing can come to you when I am near. Love clasps you, my dear and gentle lover, and nothing can harm you."

At the full, tender silver of her voice, the shadows and the terrors rushed from his soul. His hands fell from his still and pallid features, and putting his arms around her, he gazed into her face.

"Hush!" he murmured. "A moment! I will tell you in a moment."

They stood in silence gazing at each other.

Presently his arms fell from her, and swiftly gliding away she turned up the light, which at once filled the room with mellow radiance. Hurriedly, he bound on his shoes, put his pistol in his breast, and sat on the couch beside her.

"Muriel," said he, "you were right ; I have had dreams. Listen."

In a low, clear voice, he told her all. The narration occupied several minutes, and during that time she listened with a still face and lips parted. He ceased at length, and there was a long pause.

"What does this mean?" she murmured. "Do you take these dreams as augury?"

"Muriel," said he with solemn and passionate tenderness, "do you remember what you said when we lay down to slumber? It comes again to me now. You said: 'It is the fourth night; a very little night; but the fifth night will be sweet and long, and full of rest.' Oh, my beloved, sweet and long, and full of rest may it be to you! Sweet and long, and full of rest, it will be to me. To-night I go from you. Can you bear that I should go when I am not to return? For the dream meant death, and I am going away to die."

One spasm of overmastering pain convulsed her features, and vanished. The next instant her face was calm, between its fall of shadowy tresses; her lips were lightly closed; her eyes were fixed on his. But a torrent rush of memories overswept her—memories of omens and presentiments that had mysteriously foreshadowed this; and a mighty feeling rose within her, and told her that this was the voice of the prescient soul. Not for an instant did she think he was deceived, and the calmness that sank upon her spirit was the shadow of eternity.

"To die!" she answered, in a slow, rapt voice. "Going away from me to die."

Her lips closed, and pressing one hand to her bosom, she lifted her clear, still eyes to heaven, and her countenance became pale and radiant as though it gazed upon the face of God.

There was a long interval of terrible silence.

"It is true," she said at length, in low, abstracted tones, "he is to leave me. Our happiness foreran the ages. The world could not sustain it. The music was too divinely sweet to last, and it melts back from earth! Well, well, I know it now. The days have been filled with tokens and prophecies of this, and now I understand them. Yes—he is to die!"

Slowly her eyes grew back to him. He sat motionless, his face pallid in shadow, gazing with mournful awe upon her clear, pale features.

"Have you had presentiments of this, Muriel?" he asked.

"Yes," she answered, in a hushed voice; "there have been many. They crowd upon me now. You remember what I told you of that morning when I thought you loved Emily—how strangely your face smiled on me in my reverie from that immeasurable distance. I know now what it meant. That was a veiled prevision. Oh, my beloved, you smiled upon my soul from the depths of Eternity!"

A slow, cold thrill went through him at the solemn tenderness of her voice, and for a few moments his mind gathered blankness. Gradually the prefigurations of this hour which had filled his life for days past, came to him.

"I, too, have had spiritual warnings of this," he murmured. "My soul has told me much lately. You remember my sad fancy when I left you on Sunday morning, that I was not to return. And on the evening of that day the event occurred which separates us."

"Yes," she responded, "and that was the morning when I dreamed that you were gone from earth, and were looking at me as I moved through life alone."

Again a long silence succeeded.

"To wake from our happy sleep thus," she said, suddenly, "is it not strange! Is it not awful! And yet I realize it all. I realize that these are our last moments together. To deny these presentiments is impossible. Yes—it is destiny. Is it not? Is there any escape for us?"

"It rests with my will, Muriel," he answered. "I believe this dream is only a warning. If I stay here with you I am safe. It rests with me to decide whether I will go or stay."

"Can nothing be done?" she hurriedly asked. "Is there no other way of saving this man?"

"None," he answered. "It is too late now. The ship sails in a few hours. There is nothing but for me to go at midnight and rescue Antony, or leave him to his fate, and Roux to death or madness. One thing alone shakes me."

"What?" she asked.

"The suffering my death will give your mother," he answered. "It may kill her."

"And if you die her brother's infamy will become known," she replied. "Public inquiry will follow, and all she wishes kept secret will be exposed with the added guilt of your death upon it."

He did not answer, and she remained silent for a few moments, with her soul wildly stirred.

"Oh, Lemuel Atkins," she exclaimed at length, "if you only knew the harm you have done us!"

"Pity him, Muriel," answered Harrington. "Both he and Lafitte are the cause of this disaster. Let us pity and forgive them. They are the victims, and not we."

"I do," she responded, clasping her hands; "I pity and forgive them."

"It only remains for me to decide," he said, after a pause. "If I go to-night I feel I shall save Antony. But I think it will not be done without a struggle, and I shall be killed. On the other hand is your mother's grief, and all the consequences of my death, and if I stay these will be spared."

"What do you decide?" she said, quickly.

"Muriel," said he, tenderly, "I have not spoken once of what you lose in losing me, for I know your nobleness, my wife, and I know that you can resign me to duty."

She flung her arms around him, her eyes glowing and her features kindling into flushed and exalted loveliness.

"Do not think of me," she said in a clear and fervent voice. "Oh, my husband, we were wedded in love for liberty, in love for all mankind, and we cannot be divided. Think alone of duty—for death can only separate us a little while, and we are wedded in love forever."

He gazed at her with lit eyes.

"I will be worthy of you," he answered, with proud fervor. "The Hereafter is ours. Many an earthly marriage is but a tent of the night, folded by death, and never to be raised again ; but ours is a temple eternal in the heavens."

Drawing her to his bosom, he pressed his lips to hers ; then rose to his feet, and stood before her.

"My duty is clear, Muriel," he said, in firm, determined tones. "What is all suffering that will follow my death, compared with the suffering and the wrong my death will prevent? Think of the scene we saw at Roux's house, when Emily wished to buy his brother. Think of Antony being dragged back to torture and murder. Think of that poor brother's agony when he learns that Antony has been recaptured. Think of all the misery and the outrage now impending. It must not be. And beyond it all is the duty I owe my country and mankind. I have sworn to balk tyrants—I have sworn to stand up for the helpless and the poor. Never yet has a man suffered wrong that I could prevent, or gone unsuccored when I could succor him. Not now shall the weak and friendless find me a dastard in their cause. So then"——

He paused, stifled with sudden emotion.

"So then"— she repeated, looking at him with a still countenance.

A rapture of color blazed upon his pallid face, and he flung up his arms.

"So then," he cried, in a ringing voice, "I must say like him of the old Commonwealth, 'To heaven, my love, to heaven, and leave you in the storm!'"

Her eyes flashed, and she rose to her feet with the rich blood glowing in her kindled features.

"Brave heart!" she passionately cried, "one hour of life with you is worth annihilation! Away with grief—let it never come nigh me! I swear to you, Harrington, never, when you are gone, shall one pulse of sorrow stir within me—never shall one tear stain the lustre of my soul's pride in you! You die—die?—no!—it is not death, but life! It is the life of life to die for man!"

"Ay!" he exclaimed, with rapturous fervor, "I feel it so. It is life to live for man. It is the life of life to die for him. It is sweet to die for one's country, and to-night I die for mine. Far in the future I see it—my own dear land, my America, the land where all shall be free and equal, the land of lovers and of friends. Oh, my land, of you I dream, for you I have lived, for you I die!"

She stood gazing at him as he poured forth these words—her face white and radiant, her eyes brilliant, her hands pressed to her bosom, which rose and fell in quick pulsations.

"And for you," he cried, as his eyes rested upon her, "for my love of you I die. Oh, my wife, I love you greatly, or I could not leave you! I could not love you truly if I failed in love for liberty and justice. Dying for them, I prove my love for you."

With a low, adoring cry she was in his arms, and clasping each other, they moved to the centre of the chamber, with sweet and passionate words of affection and farewell. The burning moments of that last sublime communion sped swiftly by, and the time for the earthly parting drew near.

"It is the last banquet," she said, with a bright smile. "To-night is your Thermopylæ."

"Ours," he quickly answered. "Ours, for you, too, die. Your death is to be divided from me—a sterner and loftier death than mine."

"Yes," she answered, with solemn fervor, "it is indeed my death. My heart is proud, my soul is filled with joy, but I die, for life will never be truly life again till I meet you in the land of the asphodel. So be it. I do not quail. For you, for me, it is the old Achaian hour."

"For you, for me," he fervently responded. "I await you in the Hereafter. My life will be but half divine until you come. Now we must part."

She clung to him for a moment, then withdrew from his arms.

"Come," she said, taking up the flask, "the last pledge. Ah, wine of the land of Leonidas, little did I dream we should pour you to the pledge of the immortals! But the old Greek hour—the festal hour of death has dawned.

With a quick, deft blow on a marble console, she smote the top from the flask, and filled the six goblets with the rosy-golden wine. Each took one. Holding up the glass, her pale face lit with a dazzling smile, her fine nostrils quivering, and the long, bright locks flowing over her white vesture, her noble figure, in its debonair abandon, wore the old Greek Bacchanal grace and glow.

"The wine from the land of the Three Hundred is fit to pledge liberty's defence," she gaily said. "Come, let our first pledge be—In Liberty's Defence!"

"Good!" he answered. "In Liberty's Defence!"

The goblets clanged, the pledge was drank, and the glasses were flung down. They took up two more.

"And now?" she said.

He looked at her with a sweet and solemn face.

"And now," he answered, "forgiveness and compassion. For all injuries, for all baseness, for all trampling of the rich upon the poor, for all trampling of the strong upon the weak—forgiveness and compassion!"

"With my whole soul," she solemnly and gently replied. "For the sordid and the cruel—forgiveness and compassion!"

The goblets softly clanged, the tender pledge was drank, and the glasses were flung down.

"Now," said he, as they took up the last two, "the first pledge was in wine from the land of Leonidas. But the second was in wine from the land of Socrates. Let the third be drank in wine from the land of both—the saint and the hero; for the pledge is mighty."

"Speak it, my beloved," she said, in clear and thrilling tones.

"Drink," his deep voice sounded, "drink the deep pledge in the wine from the bright ideal shore, to the Spirit whose wings span the world, whose life pulses through the universe—the Spirit for whom we live and die!"

"I know, I know!" she cried. "Spirit, we drink to thee in the wine from the holy shore! Spirit of every noble thought and deed and passion, whose breath is life to liberty and justice, and the soul of man—to thee, for whom we live and die—True Love, we drink to thee!"

They quaffed the fiery and aërial wine, and dashing the goblets ringing and shivering on the floor, they sprang into each other's arms. One long and close embrace—one long and passionate clinging kiss—and they withdrew.

"Hereafter!"

Their voices rang together by a common impulse in the word: and with one long dreaming gaze of impassioned tenderness upon her proud and radiant face, he rushed away to his death like a bridegroom to his bride.

CHAPTER XXXIV.

IN LIBERTY'S DEFENCE.

A LOW, guttural mutter of distant thunder shuddered through the air as Harrington rushed into the night, and turning at the head of the street, he saw the knotted snakes of the lightning flash and writhe, and vanish, inextricable, on the slow-heaving wall of heavy thunder-cloud that filled the western sky. Black poisonous vapors, the flying couriers of the coming tempest, fled swiftly up the zenith, and half obscured the livid and tottering moon; and projected in the yet unclouded purple east before him, redly glimmered the large few stars. He did not pause, but strode rapidly on, while the fitful gusts of the rising wind swept the dim, deserted streets into storms of dust around him. It was a wild night, and heaven and earth seemed to reel in the gathering darkness; but his soul was unshaken, and he was strong to die.

The moon was hid before he had reached Beacon street, and a solid blackness, lit only at intervals by wild, bright flashes of still distant lightning, filled the lampless streets. Behind him, as he sped on, the low ominous thunder shuddered through the black vast, and the dust swept around him in rustling storms through the darkness. He met no one—every person was safely housed, and even the watchmen had crept away into sheltered nooks from the tempest.

A melancholy and funereal sound of bells tolled vaguely through the thick air, striking the midnight hour, as he reached the head of State street. The streaming gusts had lulled, and in dead silence, broken only by the hollow tramp of his quick footfalls, and by an occasional muffled shudder of rolling thunder, he sped over the deserted pavement, while ever and anon the sudden blue of the lightning lit for a moment the dark bulks of the looming buildings, and gleamed ghastfully on their multitude of gilded signs to vanish into sightless darkness.

Soon he reached the wharf, and saw beyond the dim wilderness of masts and yards, far out at sea, under the heavy canopy of cloud, a broad half-sphere of clear purple sky with the moonlit level of the distant ocean shining in lustrous silver beneath it. Again the lightning quivered, bluely irradiating for an instant the dark vault into livid violet, and as it vanished, and the darkness closed, a long, staggering roll of heavy thunder resounded above him, and a few large drops of rain fell.

Breaking into a run, he sped along the pier, and presently saw a vague figure standing and looking toward him. It was Captain Fisher, dressed in an oil-skin coat and tarpaulin, on which the sprinkling rain was pattering.

"Here I am," whispered Harrington. "Have they arrived?"

"Yes," returned the Captain in a low voice. "We're all here."

"In then, and away at once," returned Harrington, rushing along the pier in advance of him to the boat.

They came upon it presently, and in a faint shimmer of blue lightning Harrington saw Wentworth and Bagasse standing below him in the little vessel. Letting himself down from the pier, he dropped lightly into it, followed by the Captain.

"By Jove!" murmured Wentworth, with a low laugh, while the Captain was unhampering the sails, "this is a bad night for our work."

"No, it's a good night," whispered Harrington, glancing up at the hulls of the two vessels between which the boat lay, to be sure that no one was listening. "The storm is a real godsend, for it will be sure to drive those fellows in doors, and I hope every man of them."

"Ah, ze dam rain," growled Bagasse. "She will wet our jacket for us."

Harrington turned away, cast off the painter, and the boat moved out a little way from her moorings.

"How'll you have her, John?" whispered the Captain, referring to the arrangement of the sails.

"There'll be a streaming wind presently," replied Harrington, with a glance at the sky. "We'd better have two reefs in the mainsail and one in the jib. Then she'll drive."

The Captain and Wentworth seized the halyards, and up went the sails. Harrington took the tiller, and while they busied themselves at the reefing nettles, the boat moved silently through the black water between the long vista made by the dark hulls of the vessels on either side. The wind was in the lull preceding the tempest, but it was sufficient to belly the sail, and push them with silent swiftness before it. Large drops of rain plashed on the little vessel and in the dark water as they went on. Presently, Bagasse, with a Frenchman's aversion to wet, went forward muttering, and crept into the cuddy. The Captain sat on the thwart with the mainsheet in his hand, and Wentworth beside him. Harrington, with one hand on the tiller, was silently brooding on the ghostly effect of the dark hulls and piers on either side, which made the place seem like the black wharves of Acheron.

Silently, amidst the soft plashing of the sprinkling rain, they glided out into the salt smell of the open harbor, and as the blue lightning shook over the broad vault and dark sea, they saw a boat with several rowers shoot across their bows at a distance of about thirty yards. It was the harbor police, and their boat at once hove to.

"Hallo there," roared a rough voice over the waters—"who's that, and where are you bound such a night as this?"

"It's me, Belcher," shouted the Captain. "Eldad Fisher and the Polly Ann. Goin' down on business."

The Polly Ann glided past the police boat as he spoke.

"All right," returned Belcher, with a laugh. "Great night though to go on business, 'Dad. Row, men."

The oars at once fell with a roll in the rullocks, as the Captain would have phrased it, and the police boat shot away.

Nothing was said in the Polly Ann, and she moved on with a steady motion, the drawing wind pulling her bulging sail. The Captain had lit his short pipe, and had turned with his face to the west, watching for the breeze. Harrington sat in silence solemnly brooding on the strange scene around him. Overhead a rack of solid darkness; underneath the inky swells of the wide sea, like a sea of weltering shadow, which broke as the boat clove its silent way into a flow of soft gloomy phosphorescent fire from her prow and in her wake; before him the uncouth crouching figure of the Captain, with the red glow of his pipe momently lighting his cheek in little flashes, and giving his face the grim, leathern look of some weird Charon piloting them over the sullen lake of Death; and beyond in the far distance, below the sombre canopy, that shape of clear sky, smaller now, with the silver level of the sea beneath it, calm and lustrous as the ocean of Eternity. A sense of sombre sweetness melted into the young man's heart, as he gazed over the solemn and awful flood of shadow to that melancholy glory far away. He thought of that last hour with her; of their proud and exulting parting; he thought of her standing now, graceful and radiant as a Greek goddess, and noble in her widowhood, dreaming of him with the mellow light of the holy room around her, while he drifted on over the sullen water toward that bright line of jasper, like one drifting from eternal Night to the ocean of eternal Day.

A moment, and the heavy canopy closed down over the clear horizon, and all was impenetrable darkness. The wind freshened with a long, mysterious sigh, the sails swelled and strained, and the boat began to rush with the water gurgling and brattling around her bows, and flowing swiftly past her sides and from her stern in a brighter gloom of phosphorescent fire. Except that strange senescent light, and the red glow of the revolving beacon far down the harbor, which every little while glared in the darkness like a sombre eye, there was no glimmer on all the black expanse under the vast and hollow vault of sooty cloud.

Suddenly, while the broad blue shuttle of the lightning shook over the wild and livid sea, the solid darkness of the rack split with a crash in a long, bright jagged crack of fire, and closed again with a tremendous trampling roar. At once through the blackness, the headlong torrent dropped hissing and seething on the water, the heavy wind streamed staggering down, shook the craft, stopped and reeled, rose howling in a mighty forward gale, and amidst the cataract rushing of the rain, the heeling boat tore like a fury through the level sea with the spray flying over her bows, and the wash rippling in at her gunnel. On she fled, leaning down with her bulging sails strained as though they would burst from the bolt-ropes, the water swishing swiftly past her side and rushing from her stern in phosphorescent gloom, the rain plashing in clattering riot on her planks and canvas, and the whole inky flood beaten into myriad-millioned jets of springing flame around her. Again shook the broad blue shuttle of the lightning, illuminating the darkness for an instant with a ghastly bloom, and showing the wild shapes of the clouds, and again through the following blackness burst the roar of the tumbling thunder, dying away in the sweeping rush of the headlong wind, and the voluminous plash and clatter of the falling torrent. Not a word was spoken on board the flying boat. The Captain sat grimly holding the tail of the mainsheet, ready to let fly at a moment's warning ; and Wentworth, with a tin-pail in his hands, baled out the water as fast as it came in, while Harrington, bare-headed, for he had taken off his felt-hat to wrap around his pistol that it might be kept dry, and tucked both into his bosom, sat grasping the tiller, drenched, like every one on board, save the mackintoshed Captain and Bagasse, to the skin, his soul throbbing with stern glory in the splendid terrors of the storm. So, amidst wind and rain and darkness, and the incessant bursts of lightnings, rosy-purple now, and the tumbling roll of thunder, the boat held her flying course through seething flood and showering spray.

At the headlong velocity with which she flew, with the wind

right abaft and a level sea beneath her hull, it could not take her long to reach the port to which the hand of Harrington steered her. It was perhaps hardly half an hour before, in a sheeting flood of rose and purple lightning, he saw the large, humpy mass of the island loom up from the sea before him. The darkness fell, followed by the thunder, and the boat sped on. Soon came another sheet of lightning, and this time, much nearer the island now, he saw the house upon it, and caught a glimpse of two boats lying at the wharf on the southern side of the shore. The rain had begun to slacken, and the wind to abate its violence. He waited a moment till the thunder had rolled away, and then called the Captain to him.

"Captain," said he, "settle away the sails, call Bagasse, and out with the oars. I am going to run the boat to the northwestern side of the island, out of sight of the fellow we're after."

The captain sprang away, cast off the main-sheet, while Wentworth seized the jib, and amidst the clank and rattle of hoops and halyards, the sails were settled and clewed, and the boat swung masterless upon the brine. Bagasse came creeping out of the cuddy at the call of Wentworth, and Harrington securing the tiller rose and came forward.

"Hah!" said the Frenchman, hoarsely, "I haf my jacket dry! Br-r-r! It is ze night of ze old devail wis his tonnerre and light and rain watair." And with a shrug, he looked out on the black expanse around him, and held out his hand to see how much rain was falling.

"The rain is nearly over," said Harrington, observing his motion, as he stooped to take up an oar. "Can you row, Bagasse?"

"Oh, yes; I row vair fine," returned the fencing-master, taking up another, and seating himself.

They all took their places, Harrington at the stroke-oar, the blades fell into the water, and the boat turned and shot to the northwestern side of the island. A few minutes' rowing brought them to the shore, and at the word of command they rested, backing water, and keeping within about ten yards' distance from the strand. At that moment the lightning blazed, showing them the little beach covered with a mass of huge pebbles, and the steep acclivity just beyond which led to the grassy summit of the island.

A few moments' discussion ensued, Harrington having suggested that perhaps it would be better to make the attack by rowing up to the boat of the kidnappers, instead of going across the island as he had intended. Presently it was decided to carry out the original plan, as if the guard saw a boat approaching, he might summon his fellows, and thus necessitate a conflict.

"Now, friends, attention," said Harrington. "Captain, take my oar."

The Captain who sat by his side with one oar, took the other, and Harrington stepping past the other two, turned and faced them all.

"Listen," said he. "I am now going on shore to reconnoitre, which can be best done by one person. If there is only one man in the boat, I can easily handle him. If there are more, I will return and we will all go up together; for though I am loth to imperil your lives, we must not put success at hazard. Stay here, and wait for me. On no account leave the boat, till I come to you. Remember now, for if you come on shore when I have left you, it may cost me my life. Bagasse, I trust you, old soldier, to see that I am obeyed."

He uttered the last sentence in French, that Bagasse might not mistake him.

"It shall be so, my captain, since you command it," returned the Frenchman, in the same language.

"Good," said Harrington. "Now row me in."

They bent to the oars in silence, and with one stroke the boat shot in five yards, and with a vigorous leap from the prow, Harrington sprang the other five, landed safely, and ran swiftly up the acclivity. The lightning blazed as he reached the summit, and they saw him sink down. The next instant the darkness fell with a peal of thunder, and he had vanished. So thick was the night, that he could not be seen after the lightning failed.

Left to himself, Harrington, with his body bent low, ran swiftly over the wet, coarse grass, past the dark bulk of the silent house, in the outbuilding of which a dim lamp glimmered, and toward the wooden pier. The lightning blazed rosy-purple as he was midway, and fearful of being seen, he dropped prone. The next instant he rose in darkness, and ran on. Presently he approached the pier, and dropping on his hands and knees, he crept down to it, and vaguely saw the two boats, schooner-rigged, and both secured to the wharf at the foot of a short ladder running down to the water. Sinking still lower, he crept to the edge of the wharf, lay flat, and gazed at the boats, through the dense darkness, with straining eyes. In a moment the lightning flashed again, and he saw a single man standing in one of the vessels, looking out to sea, with his back to him, and his hands in the pockets of a sou'wester. At a glance, Harrington knew, by the look of his figure, that he was a sailor, and overjoyed that he had but one to deal with, he instantly rose, drew his pistol from his breast, put on his hat, and with a noiseless step glided down the pier to the ladder.

The man turned just as he was within two or three yards of it, and saw him.

"Oh, it's one o' ye at last," he growled, mistaking him for a comrade. "Egod, it's about time for some o' ye to bear a hand in this dog's watch I've had of it."

Harrington's answer was to swing himself from the top of the ladder into the boat, which rocked beneath him. At that instant the lightning shook out in vivid rose and purple, illuminating his stern bearded face and stalwart form, and the man, burly fellow though he was, started violently.

"Who are you? What d'ye want here?" he demanded.

"I want that negro in the cuddy. Hurry!" said Harrington, abruptly.

The man clapped his hand to his waist for his knife. Harrington clutched his throat, and held the pistol to his temple.

"Take your hand from that knife or I'll shoot you," he said, sternly.

Aghast at the terrible gripe on his throat, and the touch of the cold pistol-barrel on his brow, the man let his hand drop, and would have sunk upon his knees only that Harrington upheld him.

"Mercy !" he gasped.

"Stand up," said Harrington, releasing him.

The man stood up with shaking knees, trembling with terror.

"Go forward and take that negro from the cuddy," ordered Harrington.

The man paused an instant, then went forward, followed by Harrington, and sprang for the ladder. But the long arm clutched him by the throat, and again the terrified wretch felt the pistol-barrel on his brow.

"Attempt that again and you die," said Harrington. "Now take out the negro. Quick !"

Shaking with affright, the man stooped, opened the cuddy doors, and dragged out Antony, feet bound together, and arms lashed above the elbows to his side.

"Oh, Marster Harrington," cried the delighted fugitive ; "oh, I knowed you was comin' right along. Never guv it up, Marster Harrington."

"Silence, Antony," said his savior. "Take your knife and cut those cords," he added, to the other.

The man instantly obeyed, and the fugitive scrambled to his feet. The lightning blazed, and showed his lank figure, and his skull-like face wildly lighted with joy.

"Put up your knife, and sit down in the bottom of the boat where you are," said Harrington to the man.

The man obeyed without a moment's hesitation. He was almost frightened out of his wits by this terrible armed apparition.

"Now, Antony, can you walk ?" asked Harrington.

"Yes, Marster ; fus'rate," returned the fugitive, with a ghostly caper, which proved that the ropes on his ankles, and his cramped position in the cuddy, had not materially impaired his circulation.

"Very well," replied Harrington. "Now go up that ladder, and wait on the wharf till I come to you."

The man groaned, but Antony, with a chuckle, instantly grasped the steps, crept up the ladder, and stood on the pier.

"Now," said Harrington, turning to the squatting wretch, "you follow him."

The man rose, trembling, and began to ascend, but he had only gone three steps when he felt the vice-like hand gripe his leg.

"Turn round and sit down on the ladder," said Harrington, standing on the deck of the cuddy.

The man obeyed, and in the flash of purple lightning that came at that instant, sat livid, with glaring eyes, palsied with terror.

Harrington stuck his pistol between the buttoned lapels of his coat, clutched the man's thigh with one hand, thus pinning him to the seat, and held out the other hand to him.

"Give me your knife," he said, imperatively.

"You're not going to murder me," gasped the sailor.

"No," said Harrington, curtly.

The man panted hard, and gave him the knife. Still holding him by the thigh, Harrington grasped the ladder with the hand in which he held the knife, put one foot on the lower step, drew the boat round broadside to with the other, and bore heavily on the gunnel.

"What are ye doin'?" stammered the sailor. "She's takin' in water with your bearin' on her."

"I am capsizing your boat so that you can't follow me," coolly replied Harrington, amidst the gurgling rush of the water with which the boat was nearly full.

The man stared, breathing hard and trembling. Presently the boat toppled softly and slowly over and her masts splashed on the water. Harrington at once cut the rope which secured her, and she began to recede on the weltering swells.

Changing his position, Harrington put out his foot and drawing the other boat to him, began to press on the gunnel.

"You're not goin' to capsize that boat, too," gasped the man.

Harrington did not answer, but bore down heavily, and the boat filled and toppled down with a splash. As it went over, the man gave a smothered yell, frantically dashed both hands on his tarpaulin, and with a sudden desperate effort tore himself free from the gripe which held him, scrambled up the ladder, and with loud shouts ran madly for the house.

Harrington nearly fell from his hold into the water, and in the endeavor to save himself, his pistol dropped from the lappel and was gone. Recovering, he cut the rope which secured the capsized boat to the pier, and in his haste thoughtlessly flinging away the knife, sprang up the ladder.

"Quick Antony," he cried, "fly, for they'll be after us."

They rushed together up the pier, and fled past the house, just as the entire gang poured from the outbuilding. At that moment the vivid lightning blazed broad, and the wild yells and the sudden furious thudding of feet behind them told them that they were seen.

"Run, Antony, run for your life!" cried Harrington.

Spurred by his fear of being retaken, the fugitive ran by Harrington's side as fast as he did. Had he fallen behind, the young man would instantly have caught him up, and ran with him, but he did not. Together they reached the steep sloping edge of the island and plunged furiously down. But to the sudden horror of Harrington, Antony, impelled by some strange confusion of fear, instead of heading down with him to the left toward the boat, swerved in his descent obliquely away to the right and sped at a frantic pace in that direction toward the water. It was a moment before Harrington could stop in his headlong velocity, wheel, and rush after him, and in that moment Antony got the start of him at least thirty yards, and ran like a race-horse. Flying after him, Harrington heard the feet of the pursuers tearing down the slope, and close behind. Suddenly down went Antony on the large pebbles close to the edge of the water. The next instant Harrington reached him, turned, and through the darkness saw his enemies coming fast, and not more than forty yards distant. With one rapid glance to the right, he looked through the thick darkness for the boat, saw it not, and knew that the battle was now with him, and with him alone.

"Lie still, Antony; don't move," he cried, stepping close to the prone body and standing with his back to the sea, like a lion at bay.

They were coming. Had it been, not on those loose stones, or in the night, but in broad daylight or on a fair field, not those seven, no, nor twice their number, could have stood unvanquished before that agile vigor, that dauntless spirit of assault, that roused and terrible magnetic front of war. For this was one of those rare men whose presence in a battle is worth a thousand brands, and who carry death in their arm, and victory in their eye. This was the Cid Rodrigo Diaz, at the wind of whose sword-sweep ranks fled and fell. This was Roland, storm of dread with the pine-branch in his grasp among the cloven swarms at Ronceval. This was Tancred, arm of fate among a thousand foes at Dosylæum. This was Gaston when with forty knights at his back he drove before him one hundred thousand weaponed Jacqueric. All that ever Paladin did in blazing powess was in him to do. But there, on the brink of the salt flood, unarmed, in the murk night, on the rough ground, with seven knived hands to conquer—oh, hopeless hour of doom and ruin!—oh, forlorn death-grapple of the brave!

They came in a body—they spread from right to left in an arc of murder—they poised for the simultaneous rush—he swayed back for the cleaving spring. But at that instant, with a tremendous staggering clap of thunder, which rent the sky with fifty glittering cracks of fire, and stunned them all, the whole heaven, deep and vast and broad, and earth and air and sea, upburst in a long and lingering rosy flood of living flame. In that instant, as in a magic dream, he saw the boat far down the beach, rise with a peal of cries and a silent lift of oars, and shoot in silence to the shore—he saw the great sea sink and swell in vast and weltering lustrous shadow—he saw the seven assassins standing crouched with gleaming knives around him—he saw the deep heavens open up in rosy light to God. The next instant the darkness fell like the shutting of an eye; a surge of strength rushed like the blood of the whole race to his heart—and with a terrific bound he fell upon his foes.

Brief and awful was that battle. At the first leap he went through them like a thunderbolt, and two went down crashing senseless on the pebbles. Turning with a flying spring, he charged them as they huddled in a fierce knot of five, and dead thumped the sluff of the French kick, and the thud of the English blow. It was not more than a quarter of a minute in which he raged among their astounded junto, but in that quarter of a minute something like a sense that this was a statue of solid iron, preternaturally endowed with animate life, and flying among them with limbs of agile destruction, burst through their terrified souls. Down they went in swift succession, kicked and dashed and whirled hither and thither in crashing overthrow, and not a man rose more than to crawl, after he once fell. The last of the seven was a brawny wretch, who made a headlong rush and found no man in the place where there was one a second before, but instead two crushing hands that jarred the marrow in his bones as they fell from behind around his bull neck, and swung him off his feet to dash him howling a dozen paces distant on the rocky strand. Not more than a quarter of a minute, and at the tail of it came Bagasse with cries of fury, and the leaps of a Zouave, brandishing his cavalry sabre ; and fast behind him Wentworth, springing like a panther, with a pistol in each hand ; and behind him the Captain, with his loaden stave. But the field was won ! Groans and curses of anguish resounding from it in all directions. One bruised assassin feebly tottering away from it through the darkness ; three more weakly crawling over the stones on their hands and knees ; and the other three lying half senseless where the mighty limbs of Harrington had hurled them.

Yes, the field was won, but after the battle there was going to be massacre. For the fierce Celtic blood of Bagasse was up, and standing only for an instant, he swung up his sabre and dashed with a yell upon a wretch who was essaying to rise. Harrington sprang and caught him by the wrist.

" No, Bagasse," he cried. " Spare them. They are hurt enough already."

Bagasse stood for an instant, panting, then turned sullenly away.

At that moment the Captain, who had stood looking in blank stupefaction on the prostrate bodies, burst into screams of eldritch merriment, brandishing his stave, and capering like mad.

Wentworth, meanwhile, was hugging the panting Harrington, almost wild with exulting joy.

"By all the gods!" he shouted, bursting away and roaring with laughter, "was there ever the like of this! Seven to one, and he flogs the life out of them! Oh, Froissart, where are you! Sieur Jehan Froissart, why did you die! Come back, you old clerk of chivalry, and write it down! Seven to one, and there they lie!" And Wentworth bent himself double in a fresh convulsion of merriment.

"He fit 'em," hooted the Captain, prancing deliriously, "he fit 'em all. Glory hallelujah, world without end, amen." And with a halloo, he subsided, and walked from body to body, bending curiously over each, and dropping cheerful suggestions to the sufferers, as to the sort of medical treatment they would better employ.

"Bagasse," panted Harrington, grasping the Frenchman's hand, "I owe you this victory. Your training stood me in good stead with these fellows."

"Ah, Missr Harrington," returned Bagasse, tapping him on the chest with the hilt of the sabre, "you do me mush credit. Zat was done vair brown."

"I'll bet it was," corroborated Wentworth. "They'll remember it to their graves, the cowardly ruffians. Had they knives? They had, eh?" he continued, as Harrington bent his head in assent. "But why didn't you shoot them?"

"I lost my pistol," replied Harrington, breathing hard.

"And fought them bare-handed," said Wentworth. "You infernal dastards," he roared, turning toward the crawling wretches, "you deserve to be slaughtered, every hound of you. Yes, crawl off, you jackals of slavery. Curse you! I hate you."

"Richard, Richard," said Harrington, feebly, "don't talk

so. It's enough to have half-killed the poor fellows, without abusing them. Heaven knows I wouldn't have harmed them if it hadn't been necessary. But let us not stain victory with insulting them in their misery."

"Insulting them!" snapped Wentworth. "Come, I like that. Insulting kidnappers! By Jove, it's not possible! Suppose they had killed you. I swear, Harrington, it was the merest chance that we came—though, to be sure, our coming was coming too late. We heard the running and shouting, and didn't dare to leave the boat till we knew what it meant, and where you were. But if I'd only heard your pistol, I tell you I'd have been on shore, orders or no orders. Then the next thing, we saw you in the flash, with the scoundrels around you, and we put for the spot at once. The infernal ruffians!"

"Come, come," murmured Harrington, ending this hasty colloquy, which had not occupied more than three or four minutes, "let's be off. I am breathed a little, and I feel exhausted, and want to lie down."

"But where's Antony?" said Wentworth.

"Oh, here he is," replied Harrington, turning to the fugitive, who in blind obedience to his unrevoked command, still lay upon the stones near the sea. "Get up, Antony. You're safe forever, I hope, poor fellow."

The fugitive instantly rose, and followed the little party over the shingle, delightedly sniffing in the salt air.

"There's no possibility of those wretches following us in the condition they're in, and that's a comfort," said Wentworth.

"None, whatever," replied Harrington, in an exhausted voice. "Besides, I capsized all the boats on the island."

"By Jupiter!" exclaimed Wentworth. "Bagasse—Captain—do you hear that? He has capsized all the boats on the island! Oh, well, there's no use in saying another word, for of all the trumps in this world you're the trumpiest, Harrington!"

Bagasse and the Captain joined in with excited questions as to how he did it, and Harrington gave them a hasty account of the whole procedure as they went together along the shingle. Soon amidst great hilarity they reached the Polly Ann, lying bound to the rocks by a grapnel, which the Captain had flung as he rushed from her to Harrington's rescue. Antony got in first and squatted down forward on the deck of the cuddy, then the others, and last Harrington, who went aft to the tiller and sat down. For a minute all was activity, then amidst the clank and rattle of hoops and halyards up went the mainsail and jib, the reefing nettles were unclewed, the canvas filled languidly, and the boat moved away from the shore with a faint brattle over the dark, lifting swells.

CHAPTER XXXV.

PALLIDA MORS.

For a few minutes they all sat in silence, all but Harrington flushed and throbbing with the excitement of the adventure, and joyous with their success. The storm had broken with that last thunder-clap, the clouds were rolling away, and already the moon appeared in the west in a clear sky, and threw its still lustre upon the drowsy mass of the far distant city, with its dim multitude of spars, and over the vast and wild expanse of lifting and falling water which filled all the open void with its invigorating odor. Low in the east the golden lightnings flashed fitfully, lighting up fairy grottoes in the sullen clouds, and overhead the stars bloomed large and lambent through braided shadows, which were rapidly fleeting away. Far in the distance over the flood, the red revolving beacon glowed a steady ruby, and failed, and glowed again. But the wind had almost died from the magic night, and hardly bellied the sails as it flowed gently from the slumbrous west, and the boat, gliding with a faint wash and ripple through the swells, went but slowly.

"We shall have a long voyage tacking up to South Boston at this rate," murmured Wentworth.

The Captain grunted assent, and for a few minutes they all were silent.

"How white you look, Harrington," said Wentworth again, looking at the noble, straight-featured face of his friend, as he sat, bare-headed, leaning against the stern grasping the tiller, with the moonlight resting on his pallid countenance.

Harrington did not answer for a minute, but sat looking at them with still eyes.

"Friends," said he at length, in a sweet and hollow voice, "come here to me. I want to tell you something."

A little startled at his tone and manner, they rose and sat near him.

"Promise me that you will not let Antony know what I am going to tell you," he said. "I don't want to grieve the poor creature, and besides, it is necessary to the preservation of our secret. I do not know whether the secret can be preserved now, but it is possible, and we must try. But promise me that you will not tell Antony."

"Why, certainly, we will not," returned Wentworth, vacantly. "What is it?"

"When we get back, Richard," pursued his friend, "you must take Antony up at once to Charles's room; then, in the morning, take him in to his brother, and tell Roux what has happened to him, and why you concealed it from him, charging him, at the same time, to say nothing to anybody of this matter. Then you must take both of them to Worcester in the first train. But you must tell neither of them of what I am now going to tell you. Promise me all this."

"I do," responded Wentworth, tranced with wonder. "But what is it?"

"Dear Richard," said Harrington, in the same voice of hollow sweetness—"dear friends all, I am going to leave you."

They gazed at him.

"What do you mean?" faltered Wentworth, in a hushed voice.

"Look," murmured Harrington.

They stared aghast at the hand he held out to them. The tips of the fingers were red with blood.

A slow horror sank upon them with an icy chill, and the hair of the three rose as though they were one.

"I am hurt to the life," said Harrington. "Here."

He laid the bloody hand upon his left side just over the heart, as he uttered the last word.

Bagasse fell upon his knees before him with a yell, and flung open the coat and vest, which were unbuttoned, while Wentworth and the Captain burst into tears. There was a little blood on the white shirt—very little. Bagasse stared at it for an instant, with a look of livid horror. Then, with a fierce and sudden motion, he rent the shirt in two, put in his hand to the slit of the undershirt, tore it down, and pulling the clothes asunder with both hands, gazed. A little blot of thin red on the silver skin—in the centre a short dark line—a little red blood thinly oozing from it. They all gazed upon the wound.

"He is stab," said Bagasse, in a low, hoarse voice of heart-breaking pathos. "He is stab, and he bleed inside him. Ah, my fren' is stab, and he die, die, die. Oh my old, old vair seek heart, what will I do wis you? My fren', Missr Harrin'ton, so good, so kind, so brave, so tendair as ze woman, zat nurse me like ze littel babe in my seekness, zat come to me when evairy ozzer one stay off, zat look at me and I was glad, zat take my hand and I was glad, zat make my old life glad wis ze lof of him, he is go away out of zis dam world to die, die, die. Oh, miseree, miseree!"

"Hush, hush, Bagasse!" faltered Harrington, hardly able to speak for emotion. "Hush, old friend. We must all die sometime. Don't grieve. There, there. It will soon be over. Richard, dear Richard, don't weep so. Captain, friend, father, do not break my heart. Come, come, bear up, bear up."

"Oh, Harrington," sobbed Wentworth, throwing himself upon his breast, "what will life be to me if you die! And Muriel—my God, this will kill her! To lose you in this way, three days after her wedding. She never can survive it."

"No, Richard," said Harrington, calmly. "Muriel will

bear her loss with a brave heart. Both she and I knew that we were not to meet again when I parted from her to-night. We had spiritual warning of this."

"You had spiritual warning of this?" said Wentworth, awed from his wild grief into calm.

"Yes," murmured Harrington, "in presentments and in dreams. Both of us. We were both prepared for it. I came here expecting to die, and I was surprised when the conflict was over to find myself, as I believed, unharmed. I felt strangely weak, but I thought it the exhaustion of excitement, and it was not till I entered the boat that I became conscious of a heavy feeling and a little smarting in my breast, and discovered that I was stabbed."

"Haven't ye no idee when it was done, John?" gasped the Captain, weeping.

"Not the least," replied Harrington, hollowly. "I was not aware that any of the men touched me during the whole fray."

Bagasse rose from his knees, and turning away, stood in a stupor of despair, with his head bent upon his chest and his arms tightly folded.

"Oh, Harrington, Harrington!" cried Wentworth, "how could you go on this accursed enterprise! How could you leave Muriel, loving her so much, when you knew that you were to die! Your love for her should have kept you" ——

"No, Richard," interrupted Harrington, in his sweet, faint tones. "My love for her sent me. I could not love her so much if I did not love mankind more. No—I might well doubt the worth and truth of my love for Muriel if it made me unwilling to lose my life for the rights of the humblest slave."

Wentworth rose to his feet.

"Dying, dying before our eyes," he wailed, in a low voice. "Oh, it cannot be. Bagasse, is there no hope? The wound does not bleed much."

Bagasse shook his head.

"I haf see many wound, Missr Wentwort'," he sombrely replied. "Nevair one in zat place where ze man will not die. He bleed inside him."

"Bleeding internally," gasped Wentworth, wringing his hands. "Oh, if we could only get home to a physician. No wind—the boat dawdling along—and he dying! Look here, Captain, down with the sails, and let's row. We must go faster than this.

Captain Fisher rose quickly, and as he did so, Bagasse suddenly caught up his sabre and faced him.

"See, Capitaine Fisser," he howled hoarsely, "you turn ze boat to zat dam island. You let me go zere after zose rascail for my revenge. Zey haf kill ze man I lof—zey haf kill me —zey have kill ze whole world, when zey kill ze man zat haf lof in his heart for evairybody. Now I kill zem. See, Missr Harrin'ton will die. Ze doctair haf not skill to make him well —no nevair. Good: you let me go for zose murdair devail, and chop zem into small fragment wis my sabre. You give me zat sweet revenge, zen I go home and cry wis my old eye into my grave. You do zat now."

"Bagasse," said the hollow voice of Harrington, "that must not be. If you love me, do not think of harming those men. No, let us go on. I want to get home. I am dying slowly, but I hope to live till I get home."

Bagasse lifted his knee, snapped the sabre in two across it, and flung the pieces into the sea.

"I nevair fight nobody no more," he said hoarsely. "I haf not zat revenge, and I care for nossing. Zey do to me evairy insult—zey keek me, zey jump on me, zey roll me in ze mud, I will not fight zem, for I haf not my revenge."

"Come, Captain," cried Wentworth, "let's settle away the sails, and out with the oars."

He flew to the jib halyards, and the Captain to the mainsail. In a minute, both sails were clewed down, and the mainsail boom lashed one side to the cleat. Wentworth and the Captain, followed by Bagasse, threw off coats and waistcoats, and seized the oars. The Captain drew up the sliding-keel, and took the stroke-oars. Bagasse and Wentworth had the other two. In a moment the blades fell, and the boat foamed through the moonlit swells.

Of all this colloquy, conducted for the most part in low

voices, Antony, perched upon the cuddy-deck, and hid from sight by the mainsail, heard little or nothing, and had no idea that Harrington was in any way injured. Now that the sail was down, Harrington saw him, and beckoned him aft. He came instantly, grotesquely sidling between the two front rowers, and skipping over Captain Fisher's oars, looking, with the gleam of the moonlight on his dark, skull-like face, something as he did on the night when Harrington found him.

"Sit down here by me, Antony," said the young man, in his sweet, feeble voice.

Antony squatted beside him, and Harrington put his left arm around his shoulder, feeling, in his dying hours, a mild and compassionate affection for the poor creature for whom he had laid down his life.

For a little while there was silence, broken only by the regular roll of the oars in the rowlocks, the plash and dip of the blades, and the steady, seething, effervescing sound of the water foaming from the bows and stern of the boat as she shot through the lifting flood. The clouds had rolled down the east, and Harrington sat weak and suffering, with his white and beautiful face upturned to the millioned host of lambent stars—a solemn and tremendous glory of golden rain that seemed descending slowly under the frosted nebulæ and vaulted blue.

Soon his face drooped from the midnight sky, and he smiled palely on the fugitive, who was wistfully looking at him.

"How do you feel, Antony?" said the hollow and gentle voice.

"Fus' rate, Marster Harrin'ton. Right glad to git away from them soul-drivers, Marster. Hope you'll scuse me, Marster Harrin'ton, for goin' out that Sunday, an' givin' you such a heap o' trouble, Marster. I aint wuth much trouble, Marster."

"Did you think I would find you again, Antony?"

"Yes, Marster."

"What made you think so?"

"Thought you'd git it out o' some o' them books in your house, Marster."

"You can read, Antony?"

"Ruther p'orly, Marster. Never had much chance at books. Often felt as if I'd like to git a chance, but couldn't git none. Had a hard time in this world, an' been kep' down awful, Marster."

Harrington did not reply, and for a few minutes there was silence.

"Feel tired, Marster Harrin'ton?" asked Antony.

"What makes you think so?" was the reply.

"Voice sounds tired, Marster. Rather curis voice, an' not zactly like yours, Marster. 'Spect you fout them soul-drivers oncommon hard to-night. I'd liked to fout, too, but fight's most out o' me, Marster. How do you feel, Marster Harrin'ton?"

"Are you ever ashamed of yourself, Antony, when you think of all you don't know, and can't do?"

"Yes, Marster."

"You know you are a very poor man, Antony."

"Yes, Marster."

"Very humble, very low, very ignorant, perhaps wicked."

"Yes, Marster."

"Well, did you ever, for a little while even, feel that you were greater and wiser and better than you had thought you were?"

"Yes, Marster. Had that feelin' come over me once awful. It was 'long back when I was chokin' with no air, an' most gone for somethin' to eat, lyin' on the cotton in the hold of the Solomon, Marster. Tried to make a noise to be let out, Marster, and couldn't. Then I guv up for good, an' felt as if I was dyin', an' all on a sudden like, when I was sort o' sailin' away, that feelin' come over me awful, Marster. Oncommon grand feelin', an' I can't account for it nohow, but it was oncommon grand, Marster."

Harrington slowly lifted his tranced and peaceful face to the sky, and gazed upon the solemn and awful golden rain of stars.

"That is the way I feel to-night, Antony," he said in his sweet and hollow dying voice. "That was your true self, your soul. That was God in you."

There was a long silence.

"Do you understand, Antony?" said Harrington.

"No, Marster."

"It will be made clear to you," answered Harrington, after a pause. "When you are dying it will begin to be made clear to you. It will grow clearer and clearer as you leave the world, and when you are dead you will understand."

The voice was thrilling, tender and low. Awed by its hollow music, the fugitive sat silently revolving the strange words in his simple mind. Gradually his thoughts went from him, melted in the vast peace of the brooding night, and soon, lulled by the regular sound of the rowing, he sank away in a sort of waking doze. Harrington sat motionless, dreaming upon the stars, his tranquil soul ebbing in suffering from his dying frame. No word was said—no sound was heard but the regular plash and drip of the rolling oars, and the steady and continuous seethe of the sea.

A long and weary hour went by, and through the lonely darkness, weirdly lit by the wan gleam of the low crescent moon, the dark shore and dim houses began to loom over the weltering flood. The rowers redoubled their energy, and the boat flew seething through the brine. Half an hour more, and her keel grated on the sand.

Wentworth and Bagasse sprang up hot and panting, flung down their oars, and leaped ashore. The Captain waited till they had seized the painter, then shipped his oars, and left the boat followed by Antony. Dropping the painter, and hauling all together on the boat, they drew it up high and dry upon the sands.

"Take Antony on with you, Captain," whispered Harrington.

The Captain silently put on his clothes, and taking the fugitive by the arm, led him up the dark lane. Bagasse and Wentworth hurriedly resumed their garments, and assisted Harrington to rise and leave the leaning boat. He was very weak, his noble masculine vigor nearly drained away, but his resolute soul still upbore him, and he could walk feebly, though with heavy and tottering knees. Upheld by the strong hold around him, and leaning on their shoulders with clasping arms, he advanced with them up the lane. They wanted to carry him, but not wishing to let Antony know his condition, he refused.

The cool air was full of delicious summer fragrance, as they went on through the glimmering darkness. In a few minutes they heard the snorting and pawing of horses, and looking up the road, saw the carriage at some little distance. Leaving Harrington to the charge of Bagasse, Wentworth ran forward, told John Todd to stay where he was, and mounting the box, turned the horses and drove the hack down. Antony and the Captain got in, then Bagasse and Harrington coming up, entered also, and Wentworth turning the horses again drove up the street, stopped for an instant to take up John Todd on the box beside him, and away they rolled rapidly over the smooth road.

It was then between two and three o'clock. Everything had been successfully managed, and to his dying day John Todd never knew who the occupants of the carriage were. Wentworth was taciturn, and after a few remarks, finding he got no answer, John left off talking, and they went on in silence.

Through the dark, deserted streets of South Boston they rolled rapidly, and over the long bridge they rapidly rumbled, silent within the carriage and without. Then over the rattling pavements into Dover, and up Tremont street to Park, and into Mount Vernon to Temple, where Wentworth reined in the smoking and pawing horses.

"Get down, John," said he, "wait here for five minutes, then walk down Temple street, where you'll find the carriage, and drive it back to the stables. I'll see you to-morrow. Now do exactly as I tell you."

"Just as you say, Mr. Wentworth," returned the boy, getting down, and wondering what all this meant anyway.

Wentworth at once drove the horses down the declivity of Temple street, drew them up at the door of the lighted house, and with a bursting heart, leaped from the box, and went up the steps. He laid his hand on the bell-knob to ring, but shook so in his nerveless agony, that he had to pause.

Suddenly the door opened, and Muriel appeared standing within the lighted entry, clad all in white, calm, beautiful and radiant. Wentworth burst into tears, and staggering forward, fell into her arms.

"Hush, dear Richard," she said, in a serene and tender voice, "I know it all. Be calm, as I am. Bring him to me."

Blind with tears, he tottered down the steps to the carriage, and threw open the door.

"Richard," said the faint voice from within, "take Antony up at once."

Antony got out from the carriage, wondering why his protector spoke in such a weak voice, and followed Wentworth in.

"Welcome back, Antony," said Muriel, with a grave smile. "Go up with Mr. Wentworth."

She turned her face to the carriage, as the fugitive, cringing low, with his dark, skull-like face hideous with a reverential smile, passed her, dragged hastily up-stairs by Wentworth.

In a moment Bagasse sprang from the carriage, and turning, reached in for Harrington, who crept down presently, supported from behind by the Captain, and before by the fencing-master. The moment he touched the pavement, Muriel flew down the steps, clasped him in her arms, and gazed for an instant, with a pale, bright smile, into his dying face.

The two men gazed at her for a moment, their haggard and weeping faces stilled with wonder at her seraphic smile of calm, and the soft vision of her beauty in the darkness. Then starting from their pause, they lifted Harrington from his feet, bore him up into the library, laid him half reclining on a couch, and as they did so, she came quickly with water and wine, and knelt beside him.

Wentworth entered behind them, drenched and draggled with the rain and spray, with his hair dishevelled, and his face livid and haggard with grief, and went at once to Emily, who lay on a couch in a dead swoon. The two men stood forlornly weeping, Bagasse with his face buried in his hands, the Captain with his head bent on one side, his visage white with dark circles around the eyes, and the tears streaming on his cheeks. Save for their low, hoarse sobs, the lighted room was intensely still.

"Beloved Muriel," murmured Harrington, "I thank the kind fate that suffers me to see you again, and to die in your arms."

"And I, my husband," she replied, in a subdued and tender voice, "I am happier that it has been ordered so. You return to me, as I knew you would, living or dead, a victor."

"Yes," he replied, "we have triumphed. All is retrieved, and I can pass away in peace. I was alone; I lost my weapon, and they were seven to one; but I mastered them all with only one wound. Only one—here—but it is fatal."

She quickly undid his neckerchief and collar, laid bare his massive breast, and gazed upon the stab. Then rising, she went over to Wentworth, who was bending over Emily, she having just recovered from her swoon.

"Richard," said she, "I do not think there is any hope for John, but it is best to call in Dr. Winslow. Will you go for him?"

Wentworth at once left the room.

"Dear Emily, be calm," said Muriel, gently. "I told you of this beforehand, that you might be saved the shock. Try to be calm. Try, for my sake, to meet this sorrow bravely."

"Oh, Muriel," replied Emily, with the tears flowing upon her blanched and agitated face, "is he hurt? Don't tell me he is killed! Don't tell me that! Where is he? Let me see him."

"Come here, dear Emily," said Harrington, faintly.

Tremblingly rising, assisted by Muriel, and weeping bitterly, she crossed the floor, supported by her, and sinking down by Harrington, who had covered his breast, she laid her head on his shoulder, while he, in low murmurs, tried to comfort her. Muriel knelt beside them with one arm around Harrington, and his hand held to her bosom. In a minute or two Emily had stilled her grief, and nothing was heard but the low, hoarse sobs of the two men. Watching Harrington's face, amidst the sobbing, Muriel saw a faint expression of weary pain flit across it. She instantly rose, and turned to the two mourners.

"Mr. Bagasse," said she, sadly smiling, as she laid her hands on his arm. "I am glad to see you, though I did not think our first meeting would be at such a time as this."

He dropped his hands from his uncouth and martial features,

swarthy-white with grief, and bowed low, with the tears running from his eyes.

"Ah, madame," he faltered, hoarsely, "ze honor and ze joay I haf to see ze beautifool ladee wife is all covair ovair wis my sorrow. My old vair seek heart is cut all up wis my des-pair."

"Nay, do not grieve so," she tenderly replied. "We shall all see the man we love again. Ah, Mr. Bagasse, you could bear to see men die for France. Can you not bear to see one die for humanity.

"Yes, I haf see vair many men die," he answered, slowly moving his head up and down. "I was conscrip' wis Nap-oleon. I see men die in big heap wis cannon an sabre and bayonet at Ligny and Waterloo, an' I bear it. I see my two brozzer kill dead at Ligny, an' I bear it. Not Missr Harrin'ton. No. I see him kill—I see ze lof of my heart, so kind, so good, so brave, so tendair wis evairbody, kill by zose murdair devail, and I nevair bear it. Ah, madame, nevair, nevair!"

She smiled sadly with dim eyes, and held out her beautiful white hands to him. He caught them quickly in his, pressed them to his lips, and with a convulsive flush darkly reddening his grotesque and martial features, drew himself up, and looked for an instant at her solemn festal loveliness.

"I bear it, madame," he cried hoarsely, with passionate vehemence. "You lof him so mush, and you bear it. You learn me zat lesson, and I will bear it wis you. Ah, madame, you are ze brave, beautifool soldier wife. You was fit for his great lof. I res-pect, I ad-mire, I wor-ship you."

He dropped her hands, bowed low, and falling back a pace, tightly folded his arms, and stood sombre and calm, with his one eye glowing like a coal.

She looked at him for a moment, and then her still eyes wandered slowly to the weeping Captain, and she glided over to him.

"Mr. Fisher," she said, in a calm, compassionate voice, "let us endure this trial with fortitude. I grieve to see you suffer. Try to be calm."

"I can't endoor it," moaned the Captain. "He's everything to us. What'll Hannah and the children say when I tell 'em he's gone! It'll be the house of mournin' foriver. Here's the workin's of slavery. If John H., or Joel James, was in his coffin this minute, it wouldn't compare with this bereavement. I don't see how you can endoor it. I can't."

"He is the light of life to me," she answered, gently, "but I yield him up with joy and pride. Can I feel one pulse of grief when I think that he dies for the inalienable rights of man? Can I remember that he dies to save a fellow-creature from cruelty and wrong, and mourn? Think! He was rich, and he dies for the poor; he was strong, and he dies for the weak; he was a freeman, and he dies for the slave. Is that a death to mourn? No! My soul is glad in him—my heart covers him with glory."

The Captain looked at her calm and radiant face with a startled visage, while a thrill ran through his veins.

"Well, that's noble," said he. "Yis, that's high-minded. Don't say another word, Mrs. Harrington. I'm done. Yis, John dies in the Lord. His father died in the Lord, an' so he will. It's hard to bear, but it's for libaty."

He turned from her, sobbing, with his head on one side, and sat down. She looked at him compassionately, and then glided away to Harrington. He lay half-reclining, with the mellow lamplight resting on his face, sculptural now with the pallor of dissolution, the eyes clear and still in their shadows, the brow lit with the dews of suffering, and a sweet, faint smile palely irradiating all. Emily, white as marble, sat by him with her hands clasping one of his, magnetically calmed by his tender words, and by the peaceful and noble passion of his dying. Motioning to her not to move, Muriel pushed a footstool near the couch, and kneeling upon it beside him, put one arm around his neck, and the other across his bosom over his shoulder, and clasping him so, gazed with adoring tenderness into his eyes.

Kneeling in silence thus, and holding his soul to hers, a few minutes passed away, and the sound of the shutting door announced the arrival of the physician. Muriel and Emily arose, and the former opened the door of the library. Presently the doctor, a courteous, elderly gentleman, with a shining bald head, entered bowing, with his hands folded together.

"My dear Mrs. Harrington," said he, "what is this? Your husband stabbed! I am shocked to hear it."

He did not seem at all shocked, however, but was simply kind, professional and affable, with a little approval and admiration of Muriel's beauty visible in his manner as he looked at her.

"Yes, doctor," she replied, calmly. "Will you look at the wound?"

She turned toward Harrington as she spoke, and the physician at once passed her, bowing, with his lips pursed up, and laying aside the young man's clothes, looked at the stab. Every eye was fixed upon him, and every heart, save Muriel's, throbbed painfully in expectancy. In a few moments, he turned away, and came toward them with a silent look on his face, which filled them with cold despair.

"How did this happen, Mrs. Harrington?" he asked, with affable gravity.

"Briefly, doctor, thus," she replied. "Mr. Harrington interfered to-night in behalf of a poor man, and was wounded by some unknown hand in the contest."

The doctor made a clicking sound with his tongue against his teeth.

"What a pity!" he added. "Have you no clue to the perpetrator of this outrage. The police should be set on the track at once."

"Doctor," said she, "I will tell you of this hereafter. Let me only say now that I wish this matter to remain unknown if possible. The mischief is done, and it would only be painful to us to have it given to the public. If you can serve me in this way, I will be deeply grateful to you."

"Oh, certainly, Mrs. Harrington," he replied. "I can appreciate your feeling under these distressing circumstances. You may depend on me. There is nothing to be done, I am sorry to say. Probably one of the small coronary arteries has been severed. The wound will not bleed, externally. Give him water and a little wine occasionally, and plenty of air. I will come in again in the morning; but I regret to say that I can do nothing, and as I unfortunately cannot, I will not intrude further."

She bent her head in response to his affable bow, and he backed bowing out of the library, and was gone.

Muriel opened the windows, then glided over to Harrington, and knelt, murmuring inaudibly beside him, while the rest stood in a common stupor of cold, blank sorrow. Presently she arose, and gave him wine; then laying down the glass, she turned to the dejected group:

"Friends," said she, with calm solemnity, "come here!"

They all approached slowly, and stood with bent heads, gazing with mute and mournful faces on the white majestic features of Harrington. He lay, half reclined, his head supported by the cushions, and rising with something of its old martial carriage from the massive breast, while he looked upon them, sweet and regnant, with bright, dying eyes.

"Dear friends," said he, in a voice hollow and low, but firm and clear, "you will remember to keep all that has happened secret. It is my last request."

There was a brief interval of silence.

"Come close to me," he said, looking at the Captain.

The old man knelt down beside him, weeping, and put his arms around him.

"Kind father," said the low, sweet voice, "my own father's friend, the true friend of my mother, so good and faithful to me, I love you dearly, and I bless you. Give my fond love to the poor wife and the children, and tell them we shall all meet hereafter. I wish I could have seen them, but it has been ordered otherwise. No matter: we shall meet again."

There was a long silence. Then rising, still weeping bitterly, and unable to speak a word, the old man grasped for a moment the cold hands of him he loved like his own children, and turned away sobbing.

"Come, Bagasse," said Harrington, trying to lift his arms to him.

With a sudden movement, the Frenchman threw himself

upon one knee beside him, clasped him in his arms, and kissed him on each cheek.

"Hah! I lof you," he cried hoarsely, with a visage of glowing iron, and an eye of fire. "I lof you wis my heart, my life. See: I die vair soon. It is sixtee year old wis me. Soon I die and come to you. Ah, brave, kind, tendair zhentil-man, you go off vair young! You lof evairybody so much zat ze dam world will not haf no place for you. You go to ze good God. Ask Him zoo par-don ze vair bad life of old Bagasse zat he may come stay wis you. Zen I am happy, happy."

"Fear not—soon you will see me," murmured Harrington, calmly smiling. "It is but a little while. Bend your face down to me."

Bagasse did so, and Harrington gently pressed his lips to each cheek.

"There. It is the kiss of France," he said. "Take it with my love. Farewell."

"Farewell, brave zhentilman, farewell," the Frenchman replied. "Farewell, till I meet wis you. I lay ze immortelle on you grave."

He sprang back, erect and martial, and folded his arms. Emily sank down beside Harrington, calm, though with a face of marble, and Wentworth, white and stern with despairing grief, knelt on the footstool, with one arm around his neck and the other grasping his hand.

"Dear lovers," said Harrington, smiling with pale tenderness, "when the wedding comes think of me as there. Do not think that you will be lost to my love, when I am lost to your eyes. I will be happy in your happiness; and my memory will be part of your joy. In all the good sweet hours, in all the hours of earthly trial and sorrow, I will be with you. Our happy days together are not ended—they will be ours again hereafter."

"Oh, we have lost all in losing you," wailed Emily, with the tears flowing from her eyes. "I wish that I had died before this sorrow could come to me."

"And I," gasped Richard; "my heart is broken!"

The fleeting soul rallied in the feeble frame of Harrington, and with a convulsive effort he raised his arms, and clasped them to his breast. They clung to him, silently weeping, and for a little while all were still.

"This is the grief of dying," he faltered, at length. "Oh, dear ones, death is bitter to me when I see you grieve."

"No, no, it shall not be," cried Wentworth, lifting his streaming eyes to Harrington's. "We will not pain you. Emily, dear Emily, let us be calm—let us not make him suffer whom we love."

"I will not," she answered, lifting her beautiful agonized face, and controlling herself with a strong effort. "I will be calm. For your sake, John, for I love you as I never dreamed I could love."

"Thanks, thanks," faltered Harrington. "Dear Emily, dear Richard, think of Muriel. She is here, she you love so fondly remains to make life beautiful to you. Oh, think of that, and be filled with gladness and gratitude! There. I have much to say to you, but my strength fails me. Live happy. Love much. Now farewell till we meet in the bright land."

Emily bent down, folding him in her arms, and pressed her mouth to his cold lips in a long, fervent kiss, whose memory never left her life. Rising presently, she swept away to the extremity of the room, and sank on her knees by a chair. Wentworth remained for a little while, his arms around his friend, his head resting upon his bosom. Then raising his sorrowful and haggard face, he kissed him on the forehead, grasped his hand and held it to his heart, and with one lingering, mournful look upon the noble and peaceful countenance which smiled upon him, reverently laid the hand down, and slowly wandering away, knelt beside Emily.

Harrington looked at Muriel, with his white face kindled.

"Come to me now, my beloved," he said, in a faint and fervid voice. "The shadows have passed. Come, and share my dying hour of joy."

Pale, and glorious in her festal beauty, she moved to the folding-doors.

"I will stay with him till he is gone," she said, calmly. "Wait here till I come out to you."

She withdrew, closing the doors behind her, leaving the mourners together. The Captain and Bagasse seated themselves in silence. Presently Emily and Wentworth arose from their knees, and sat on a couch, clasped in each other's arms. An intense stillness succeeded, and the quiet light shone lonelily on the four bowed and moveless forms.

CHAPTER XXXVI.

IO TRIUMPHE.

THE solemn time slowly wore away. Gradually the twilight began to glimmer through the slats of the western window. Wentworth rose noiselessly, opened the window, put back the blinds, and withdrew the curtains; then extinguishing the light, resumed his seat again beside Emily.

The glimmering twilight slowly melted into pale dawn with a deep violet sky; and the few vague noises of reawakening life began to sound in the streets of the quiet neighborhood. Soon the violet of the sky changed into the light blue of early morning, touched by the unrisen sun, and the pure pallor of the daylight, lay within the chamber, and on its bowed and silent occupants.

Day broadened, and the first fresh beams of the sunrise reddened on the tops of the chimneys. A faint stir came to them from the inner room, and the folding-doors unclosed a little, and remained slightly ajar. They all rose, and stood in silence. Looking through the aperture, they saw that the lamps were extinguished within, and that a brighter day than theirs flushed with light the silent room. Suddenly the folding-doors swung wide open, and Muriel appeared, with a face of cloudless radiance. For a moment she stood in silence, exalted, dazzling, a presence like intoxicating music ; her snowy drapery falling around her in holy bacchanal folds, her amber hair rippling goldenly and low, and her features kindled with a smile like morning.

"It is over," she said, her voice thrilling with a rapture of tenderness. "He has gone."

They stood in silence, gazing with awe upon her pure and lovely face, and the light of her immortal joy and peace floated in upon their cold and desolate sorrow, like heavenly rays upon a winter sea. Her sacred and auroral beauty interblended with their sense of the solemn presence of the dead, and the feelings that arose within them were like the prayers and hymns of resurrection.

Standing with bowed heads, the passing perfume of her robes told them that she moved, and they silently followed her into the room where all that was mortal of the hero lay. The curtains were drawn aside, and the light of the morning, warmed by the coming gold of the sunrise, streamed tenderly upon the white and noble features. He lay reclined, the head resting upon a cushion, the hands crossed upon the bosom, the bearded face beautiful in grand and sweet serenity, with the lips and eyelids closed. So peaceful and unchanged was his countenance, save in its marble pallor, that it might have been thought he slept. But he was dead. Nerveless now the limbs so mighty in liberty's defence ; pulseless now the strong heart whose generous currents beat for man ; the busy brain that had wrought with such divine ambitions for the race, was stilled ; and all the godhood that had given that body its majesty and beauty, was gone from it forever.

They gazed calmly upon the deserted form. Grief had had its hour. It would but have profaned the sanctuary of that holy and grand repose. The beauteous peace of death was there, and it made them still. Silently, for a little while, they looked with mournful and chastened spirits upon the clear and lovely features, and as they turned away, Emily bent and kissed the sacred forehead.

"Sleep sweetly, gallant and gentle heart," she said in a voice like fervid music. "Sleep, folded in the rest of Heaven, folded in our Savior's arms. Well for us if we had died like you."

She rose with a rapt and pallid face, and moved away encircled by Wentworth's arm, with her own around him.

"I love you, Richard," she said. "I love you with my whole nature! But far above me, I saw a nobler love than mine. It was a love too great and sweet for me—a love to which I never could attain; and with that love I loved him."

He did not reply, but clasped her closer to him, and they all went out into the other section of the room.

While they stood in silence, a loud and violent ring, like the jar of devils breaking in upon their solemn peace, came at the hall entrance. Muriel paused a moment, then shut the folding doors, and stepped into the passage. Patrick was up, and was already shuffling along the entry below to answer the summons. Presently the hall-door opened, and Muriel, leaning over the banister, heard a harsh and angry voice say:

"Where's Mr. Harrington? I want to see him immediately."

It was Lemuel Atkins.

"Patrick," said Muriel, before the servant could reply, "show that person up here."

She retired into the library, and trampling rudely up-stairs came Mr. Atkins, and strode into the library with his hat on, livid with passion.

"Where's that ruffian husband of yours?" he brawled, fronting Muriel. "I want to see him instantly. Where is he? Where have you hidden him?"

"Mr. Atkins," said Wentworth, stepping forward, with a stern white face, "permit me to remind you that you are speaking to a lady, and that you have your hat on in her presence. Take your hat off at once, sir."

Mr. Atkins took his hat by the rim with both hands, pulled it down more firmly on his head, and swelling out his chest with vulgar insolence, fronted Wentworth with a blustering air.

"There, sir," said he.

"And there, sir," replied Wentworth, knocking the hat from his head clear across the room.

Mr. Atkins, frightened a little at this decisive action, glared at him with glassy eyes, but Wentworth, with a cold, stern face, retired a few paces, with his gaze fixed on Muriel. Bagasse, meanwhile, the hat having fallen near him, crushed it beneath his feet, and stood on it, with an eye like a red coal.

"Well, sir," said Muriel, quietly, "you were asking after my husband. What do you want with him? What is the matter?"

"The matter is this, madam," roared the merchant, bending his livid and brutal face down to hers, with his horse-jaws wide open. "I send a damned runaway scoundrel down the harbor for safe-keeping, and your ruffianly husband goes down there, and not only takes him away, but nearly kills the men I put in charge of him. Don't you deny it, madam, and say it was some one else, for one of those men heard the runaway rascal call him by his name. Now, where is he? Out with him at once! Here's one of those men just come up to me with the news; yes, and there's another thing. He had to hail a boat that was passing to take him up to the city, for your robber of a husband upset every boat that was at the wharf. Yes, madam, upset them! And then when the men endeavored to retake their prisoner, he fell upon them with his fists and feet, and nearly killed them. There they are, seven of them, all mangled, and bruised, and battered, and ——. Where is he, I say? Produce him at once!"

There was no change in Muriel's serene face while the merchant belched all this into it, save only a close contraction of her delicate nostrils; and this was not caused by emotion but by the fetor of his breath, which was abominable.

"How many men did you say, sir?" she asked quietly, the moment he had done speaking.

"I said seven, madam; seven men all bruised and"——

He stopped, arrested and confused nearly to choking, by her still smile of scorn.

"Seven men, Lemuel Atkins," said she, derisively. "Seven men with knives in their hands. Seven armed ruffians, and my husband, bare-handed, crushed them all! Oh, my husband, but I am proud of you! And you, Lemuel Atkins, you have the face to come here, and blazon the shame of your seven hired assassins. Well done!"

Brutal and impudent as he was, Mr. Atkins could not but be abashed at this sarcastic exposure of his inglorious complaint, and stood working his jaw in the effort to collect himself.

"And you want to see my husband?" pursued Muriel. "Good. You shall see him. Richard, throw open those doors."

Wentworth immediately flung the folding-doors asunder, and Muriel, grasping the merchant by the wrist, drew him into the room, and up to the couch.

"There he is," said she, "murdered! By you!"

The merchant's visage instantly changed to a frightful and ghastly blue, his jaw dropped, his hair rose bristling, and, petrified with horror, he stood glaring at the corpse. Like many coarse natures, he had a natural vulgar dread of a dead body, but added to that was the terrific shock of being brought suddenly before the slaughtered corpse of his niece's husband, the dreadful consciousness that he himself was morally responsible for this ruin, and the soul-sickening fear that now the law would pursue its authors, and that his own wicked and illegal act, with the blood of a murder on it, would be exposed to the public view. The simple illegal kidnapping, at a time when Boston had gone for kidnapping, was nothing; his tribe would wink at that; but with this crime upon it, he never could survive the consequences.

"See," said Muriel, laying bare the breast, "there is the wound of the knife that slew him. You, Lemuel Atkins, through your agent, struck that blow."

She looked at him with clear and glowing eyes, but he did not heed her, nor did the ghastly aspect of his visage change. Transfixed with horror, he stood immovable, his gaze bound by a dreadful fascination to the short purple line in an orb of red suffusion on the white breast. But at last, his glassy eyes wandered to her face.

"It'll kill her," he murmured in a horrible, low voice, talking to himself as though she were not present. "She'll die of grief for him."

Muriel smiled—a clear, still smile that made him shiver.

"You think so!" she replied, in firm and steady tones. "You think I will die of grief for my slain husband? Well you may, for I loved him with a love of whose strength and fervency a nature like yours knows, and can know, nothing. Well may you think so, for he was the light of life to me. But see—" she seized the merchant's hand, and laid it on her wrist—"the pulse beats calm! Feel"—she placed his hand upon her heart—"there is no throb of anguish there! Look at my face—it is not the face of grief! Kill me? No, it will not kill me! Grieve me? No it can never grieve me! Sorrow nor death can come not nigh me—for he lies dead in the divinest death a man can die, and I am filled with gladness and with pride! Should I not be glad and proud? The most forsaken of mankind, the Pariah of a despised and trampled race, came from long years of misery to his charge, and when you stole that most wretched being that you might send him back to the hourly murder from which he had emerged, my spotless hero went from this house knowing that he never would return alive, and willingly laid down his life to save him. Yes—he knew that the price of that man's liberty was his own life, and he paid it. Alone he did it—alone he took your victim from his captors—alone and naked-handed he crushed the seven assassins who dared to front him in his manhood—and with that red star of honor on his breast he came home here to die in my exulting arms. There he lies—dead in the noblest death a man can suffer—death in the service of the weak and poor. Dead—and on all his life the splendor of that heroic devotion; dead—and on his breast that red blazon of glory immortal; and I could rifle earth of its roses to deck this hour, and break up heaven for the music of my joy!"

The clear and fiery silver of her voice rang through him like a hundred swords, and staggering back a pace, he fairly crouched before the stormy effulgence of her beauty. For she flamed upon him, dilated, with a terrible enthusiasm quivering through her flushed and kindled features and an electric aureole of victory darting from her like a sense of rays. Not him alone did she overwhelm—the air of the room was deluged with the torrent magnetism of her spirit, as if it had been flooded with a rushing ether of light flame, and every heart beat as with the wings of eagles, and every cheek was pale with the draining rapture of her ardor. Not him alone, but him chiefly, and only him with dread. Had she flashed hate and scorn upon him, he could have better borne it. But this supernatural exultation over an event which he thought would have bowed her in pallid agonies of grief—this sublime and haughty glory in her husband's fate—astounded and terrified him. It mingled with his sense of her pæan tones and words, the patrician nobility of her figure in its snowy odor-breathing raiment, all the fiery beauty and dazzling enchantments of her presence—and it rushed into a consciousness worse than the consciousness of her hate and scorn—the consciousness of the thing he was contrasted with her. The very sight of her was the insupportable verdict of his own utter baseness, and he stood crouching and shuddering, with his glassy eyes bound to her face, as if some judgment angel, dreadful in loveliness, had burst upon him from the woman he knew.

She turned away, and his gaze slowly reverted to the corpse. At once, with tenfold vehemence, his former fear and horror rose within him.

"My God!" he gasped, "this is an awful tragedy!"

Sudden as lightning she wheeled around, and the first slanting beam of the sunrise smote her forehead, and lit her noble features with a new resplendence!

"It is not!" she cried, in a proud and ringing voice. "It is a triumph! You threw the interests of your party and your trade into the scale against a man's liberty. He threw the rich, red blood of his heart into the other side, and weighed you down. It is a triumph! Call it no tragedy which breaks one fetterlock, even at the cost of a sweet life! Oh, brother of the despised and the rejected, well for earth's proudest if he went to God like you, the savior of a poor spirit from the curse of bonds, and bearing up to heaven the trophy of one broken chain! Pass me, sorrow, pass, and come not nigh me—for oh, my husband, you laid down your life for a weak and lowly slave, and there is morning in my heart forever!"

Her pealing voice, proud and ringing while she spoke to him, melted into clear and noble pathos as she turned to the visioned image of her hero, and the words breathed in tones of illimitable ecstasy upon an air that seemed to beat and swim in rapture. The swiftly ascending sunlight rested upon her as she stood with clasped hands, her tresses shining in golden glory around her divinely kindled face, her soft, white drapery flowing and trembling around her, and gazing upon her from the inner room as through a veil of fire and tears, she seemed to them like some splendid seraph of the morning, dilated with holy and heroic joy.

A low groan heaved from the chest of the wretched Atkins. She looked at him. He was gazing with a face of abject horror and despair on the majestic figure of the dead.

"Come away," she said, solemnly, taking the passive wretch by the arm, and leading him into the other room. "I pity you from the depths of my soul. You are the tragedy—you and the social order that has ruined you. Would that I could do you good! I cannot. You are made, and only death can unmake you. Well will it be for you when your sad failure of an earthly life is ended, and you can resume that you were before you were born."

He turned toward her, dreadfully agitated, with the foul tears flowing on his convulsed and livid visage.

"Spare me," he hoarsely faltered, clasping his hands, "spare me the exposure! For the love of God, let it be hushed up! It'll ruin me and my family, and—Oh, I beg of you let it"——

"Listen to me," said Muriel, interrupting him. "My mother has not yet left her chamber, and therefore does not know of what has happened. Spare her the anguish of seeing you here with the body of her beloved son lying there. I have already kept you too long. But hear this: the persons present, and one other, are the only persons who know of this transaction, and they are pledged never to divulge it. Keep it secret then yourself. It ends here."

"Oh, thank you, thank you; I'm very grateful indeed I am," he hurriedly replied, showing in his agitation a mean relief at his escape from the consequences of his wickedness: "I'll go at once."

He looked around for his hat. Bagasse kicked it over to him, with an eye that flashed red fire. Atkins did not show the least resentment at the insult, but hastily picking up the crushed castor, hurriedly left the library straightening it out, and presently they heard the hall-door close behind him.

Muriel went to the body of Harrington, and arranged the clothes over the bosom. In a moment or two the others followed her, and as they approached, she turned toward them.

"I must go up to tell mother of this," she said. "It is better that she should hear it in her own chamber."

"We ought to have called her, that she might see John before he died," said Emily.

"No," replied Muriel; "I thought of it, but I feared to have her here for her own sake. And I fear the shock it will give her now. I must go at once."

She moved to the entrance, but at that moment Mrs. Eastman entered the library in the section beyond the folding doors. Muriel sprang, caught her in her arms, and gazed with all her soul in her eyes, into her pale countenance. Mrs. Eastman had not caught sight of the body, but she saw Bagasse and the Captain, and knew at once that something unusual had happened, and with a startled glance at the averted faces of the group, she looked with ashen features at Muriel.

"Mother," said Muriel, in a firm, proud voice, "look at me. Am I not happy?"

Mrs. Eastman gazed with a wan smile at the radiant countenance of her daughter.

"Yes, dear," she wonderingly murmured; "I never saw you look more so. But why are you joyful?"

"Because this is a day of joy, mother," replied Muriel. "It is the joy of joys to-day. Heaven touches earth with me, and I am happy. Mother, the poor man who was stolen from us is saved ! John has ransomed him !"

"Why!" exclaimed Mrs. Eastman, starting, with a bright smile, in her daughter's arms. "This is indeed good news. But what do you mean—how did John ransom him ?"

"With a great price, my mother," cried Muriel, a brilliant smile irradiating her inspired features. "A price which I am willing and proud to pay. Are you ?"

"I would pay any price for such a good as this," replied Mrs. Eastman, with some wonder visible in her joy.

"Any, mother ?"

"Yes, any."

"Ah, mother, let me try you. Suppose the price was your whole fortune. Would you give it ?"

"I would give it all," answered Mrs. Eastman, fervently. "I would give everything rather than go through life with the shame and agony of Lemuel's sin and that poor man's murder upon me."

"But, mother, suppose Heaven asked of you a greater price than that. Suppose it asked, as the price of a poor man's liberty, your daughter's life, or the life of your son. Would you give it ? Answer me yes," she cried, with flashing eyes. "Tell me that yours is not a cheap devotion to the old New England honor—the old New England liberty—the old New England justice ! Tell me that you are willing to offer up to Heaven the dearest and the proudest sacrifice a soul can offer, that I may love you with the love of love forevermore !"

To stand before that impassioned and magnetic face, to hear those burning and electric tones, and not be kindled by their enthusiasm, was not in human nature. The flame thrilled through the mother's soul, and with a pale, proud countenance, and quivering nostrils, while a vague and awful consciousness of what had happened arose within her, she looked steadily into the flushed and exalted features of Muriel.

"I have not your spirit, Muriel," she tremulously answered, "and such a sacrifice would be hard for me to make, but I would strive to make it—I would strive to be worthy of my daughter."

"Mother of my heart!" cried Muriel, with passionate fervor. "Behold, the hour has come for you to strive with every mortal weakness. Lean on me now—let me fill you with my strength—let me dilate you with my joy. Rouse up your soul to fortitude—nerve it to bear as only a woman's soul can bear—for Heaven has asked the great sacrifice of us all. Oh, my mother, Heaven has said to him we love—the price of the ransom is your own life—and with his life he has paid it."

The mother looked at her with a pale, still countenance. She did not swoon, she did not shriek, she did not weep nor tremble. The strong sustaining spell of Muriel's spirit was upon her; her clear magnetic eyes upheld her; and she breathed in the mighty ether of that electrifying sphere of pride and joy. Left to herself she might have dropped dead or mad; but interpenetrated with that effluent will, and moved and kindled by the grandeur of her daughter's nobleness, she rose in courage like the courage of a spirit when it leaves the serene regions to dare the doom of dark avatars.

"I hear you," she said, in a low, full, equal voice, sounding more like Muriel's than her own. "I hear you, and I am filled with your life. You wish me to be calm and strong. I am calm and strong. I understand you perfectly. You tell me that he is dead."

"Mother," replied Muriel, with solemn fervor, "his earthly life is ended, but he lives forever. He died a hero's death, and all who made earth noble with their living and their dying, rise up to welcome him."

There was a moment's pause, in which their eyes remained bound to each other. Then the low, full, equal voice spoke on.

"Tell me more, Muriel. Tell me how he died. I am calm. I can bear to hear it all."

"I will tell you, my mother," Muriel replied. "He heard that the man was a prisoner in a boat at an island wharf in the bay. Last night he sailed through the tempest, and captured him. Seven to one, they followed him to the beach, and fell upon him. He crushed them every one, received a death-wound in the fray, returned in victory, and died here at sunrise. That is all."

The pale face flushed slowly.

"I drove him to this," was the low reply. "Did I not? Have not I killed him?"

"No, mother," answered Muriel, calmly. "It is not so. I had determined to disregard your wishes, but this plan was surer, and he and I chose it."

The pale face lightened, and the flush died away in marble pallor.

"No, it was not I that killed him," she said, slowly. "It was another, and him I renounce forever. Lemuel" ——

"Hush, mother," said Muriel. "Not a word of him. Let us pity and pardon him—but do not utter his name again. Let him pass in peace."

There was a brief interval of silence before the mother spoke again.

"Where is he, Muriel? Let me see him. Do not hold me from him. Do not fear for me. I am calm and strong. I can bear to see him now, though he is dead."

The pleading and pathetic voice touched Muriel to her heart's core, though there was no sign of emotion on her face. Her clasp tightened around her mother, and for a moment her clear eyes dwelt upon the pallid countenance.

"Can you bear to look upon him now?" she replied. "Be calm—be strong. Look into that room. He is there."

The mother, strongly held by Muriel's arms, slowly turned her head, and gazed. A broad ray of sunlight rested on the couch, and the sculptured face shone in white splendor. Long and breathlessly she gazed upon it.

"Come," murmured Muriel.

Clasped in each other's arms, they moved slowly to the side of the couch, and stood gazing on the white and noble features, clear-cut and glorious in the dazzling stream of light which fell upon them, and relieved by the violet velvet on which the body lay. It was death, but death in the lustrous beauty of a vision. The rich magic splendor that irradiated the majestic countenance, seemed issuant from it—a blazing halo, in which it would rest forever.

"He is beautiful," murmured Mrs. Eastman, in a hushed

and mournful voice. "Beautiful as a dream. My dead son !"

Three little words, but in them what a large world of affection and sorrow found room ! A thrill of emotion came to the silent group as her low, distinct voice, awful in its pathos, gave those words utterance. Noiselessly and slowly she sank from Muriel's arms to her knees, and laid her head upon the pulseless breast ; for a little while she remained there, with the strong glory lending a brighter silver to her tresses ; and rising again, her calm face was wet with tears.

"It is a great grief," she said, as Muriel again encircled her in her arms. "It is a greater grief, Muriel, than when your father died. I wonder that I can bear it as I do. And you, my poor child, widowed now like me, how can you endure your loss—how can you look so beautiful and happy, and he lying dead beside you ?"

"Look, mother," cried Muriel, "look at that sky !"

She drew her to the casement as she spoke, and flinging it open, they stood, with the blithe, fresh air of the brilliant morning around them, gazing together on the transcendent pomp of the sunrise. Far up the blue zenith, the sky was bannered with floating clouds of gold and purple and crimson, and burst on burst of splendor streamed through them from the dazzling orb which filled the broad day with haughty and majestic glory.

"Is this a day for grief ?" said Muriel. "Behold, it throbs with victory—it trembles with immortality ! See how its colors and its splendors deck the sky ! They glow and burn in beauty and in triumph for the return of a conqueror. Dead soldier of Democracy, the beautiful and bannered sky is for you ! Burst high, flash far, float wide, oh divine resplendence, and fill the vast with the gorgeous colors of victory, for to-day all Heaven holds jubilee, and welcomes back one saint and savior more !"

Her low voice trembled with fervor as it uttered the passionate words, and her sunlit face shone like an angel's. Still holding her mother in her arms, she turned with her to the illuminated form of her lover.

"Think, mother, how he lived," she said; "think how he died. In a city whose vice it is that its valor and compassion run to brains, he was an arm. A mind trained for the human service, and an arm. An arm swift, and loving-swift to smite the robbers of the poor; a heart that could feel tenderly and gently even for them; a life which beat, in its every artery, with the blood of his love for mankind. Oh, never can I mourn him! The question that shakes the land and age came to him—in the person of that forlorn wanderer it came, saying, shall it be slavery or liberty for such as me—and not with a word, but with a deed he answered, liberty! Ay, with his life he answered, liberty! Look on him with joy as I do, for grief is insult to the dead who die for man. Proud, proud death! Sweet, sweet to die for liberty, and sweet to look in life on him who has so died. Mourn him? Oh, never! My own dear love, my friend, my husband, angel of my heart and of my life, I do not mourn you—I think of you with joy and pride. You smile upon me still, you wait for me in the Hereafter, you see my life all festal with your memory, you see my earthly years flow forward beautiful with your presence and rich with the light of your Paradise. Oh, still be with me—let me never lose the dear consciousness that you see me—let it endure to make my solitude divine, until I meet you in the world of souls!"

Awed and thrilled by her tender and fervent ecstasy, Mrs. Eastman slowly withdrew from her arms, and sank into a chair. A deep and solemn silence tranced the rich room. Muriel glided near her dead lover, and stood with the soft summershine of June tenderly splendid on her golden hair and noble features, her soul rapt in exultant joy and peace, and her thoughts sweeping through Eternity. And as she mused, Emily, with the color in her face and her eyes like stars, went to the organ, and the deep surge of music fit for the buriel of champions, rose and rolled in ravishing triumphal grandeur, and swelled in a burning dream of joy immortal, and endless glory for the brave.

Loud rolled and soared the pæan of the music. Burst on burst, the rays of haughty splendor streamed through the bannered pomps that flamed and glowed against the dazzling sapphire of the day. Tide on tide the effulgence poured around the heavenly-hearted heroine; and kindling on the violet velvet of the couch, as on the bier of an emperor, into a softer rapture of triumphant flame, it lay in a blazing halo on the folded hands, the broad heroic breast, the martial and noble features of the dead soldier of Democracy.

EPILOGUE.

THAT morning, at eight o'clock, Wentworth took Roux and Antony, with the elfin Tugmutton, to Worcester, and delivered them, with a note from Muriel, to the care of a friend. A week later, and Roux's family followed him. Safe in the uncorrupted heart of the Commonwealth, where, even in that dark period, the old New England honor fortressed the rights of the lowly—happy, because they knew not what had befallen their strong friend—thenceforth their humble fortunes flowed in peace.

Wentworth returned in the afternoon of that day, but even before his return, the news of Harrington's death had spread abroad among all who knew the family, and already a number of friends had called. Mrs. Eastman and Muriel, however, unwilling to be questioned, had decided to excuse themselves to every one, and nobody was admitted. Harrington had lived rather a reclusive life—at least, he went but little into what is called society, and except to a number of poor and humble people, he was little known. To most of the friends and acquaintance of Muriel, he was a stranger, and to the neighborhood only a stately figure, sometimes seen alone from the windows, sometimes walking with her. Hence the interest the neighborhood felt in his death was, as far as he personally was concerned, vague, and keen only on account of Muriel, whose loss, so soon after her marriage, excited a great deal of sympathy and comment.

The funeral was to be strictly private, and Wentworth returned to find the beauteous body already prepared for the grave. It lay in its casket in the library, garbed in the clothes it had worn in life. The young man gazed upon it a little while, then turned to Muriel.

"Of course," he said, "the burial permit has been attended to."

"Yes," she answered. "Dr. Winslow gave the certificate."

"What cause could he have assigned for the death?" he asked, with a startled air.

Muriel looked at him for a moment with a strange, faint smile.

"Enlargement of the heart," she answered.

Wentworth's pale face became convulsed, and his eyes filled with tears.

"Yes," he murmured, clasping his hands, "that was the cause indeed!"

It was a day of grief to all but Muriel. The servants moved about the house with eyes red with weeping. Patrick seemed ten years older with his forlorn sorrow. Hannah and the children came to the house, and remained for a couple of hours, crying bitterly. Gracious and calm and sweet amidst the mortal anguish, Muriel soothed and strengthened and consoled them all.

The next day was the day of the funeral. The library where the body lay was decked as on the day of the wedding, with a profusion of roses. All the windows were open, and the rich, dark room swam in clear radiance.

In the morning, Mrs. Eastman, Emily, Wentworth, and Captain Fisher, being present, Muriel produced a brief will which Harrington had made the day after his marriage. The few engravings which decorated his room, and a portion of his books, he had bequeathed to Emily and Wentworth. The bulk of his library was given to Muriel. His house to Captain Fisher, with the provision that the two rooms in which he had lived should be kept for the refuge of any fugitive, exile, houseless or outcast person of any description who might stand in need of succor. His little income he had also given in charge to the Captain to be expended for the relief of any human distresses that might fall within his knowledge, or to be used at his discretion for any charitable end.

The old man bent his head, silently weeping, and the rest sat mute and still, thinking with swelling hearts of the kind spirit that had left earth forever.

A little while, and they were gone from the room—all save Muriel and Wentworth. The latter stood bending over the coffin and looking mournfully on the beautiful dead face of his friend, and Muriel sat at the organ dreaming in music, which brooded in sweet and glorious surges on the sunlit air.

As the melody died away, Wentworth stole slowly to her side.

"I forgot to ask you," he murmured, "about the burial service. Have you sent for a clergyman?"

"No, Richard," she replied. "He needs none. Our thoughts and memories are the fittest burial rites for him. He was a type and harbinger of the day when religion shall be the tender love and reverence of every soul for all. In the vision of that day let us lay his dead form in the grave, hallowed by our remembrance."

He bent his head in silence and moved away.

An hour passed by, and a low tap came to the door. It was Patrick come up to say that Mr. Witherlee was below, and begged to see her. Muriel paused a moment, with a strange feeling of surprise at this unexpected visit, and then went down into the parlor.

Witherlee was there, standing hat in hand, in the middle of the floor. He did not bow as she came in, but looked at her with a rigid and wan face, and sad opaque eyes. For a moment, Muriel, usually so collected and calm, lost herself in wonder at his aspect, and blankly gazed at him. He was singularly changed. All the affected elegance of manner was gone; the contumeliousness, the superciliousness, the morbidity of the face were gone too; the handsome brown hair was brushed flat; the handsome eyebrows seemed as if their expressive lift was lost forever. He was attired in deep black, with not a line of white visible, and his colorless and rigid countenance wore a strange expression of wan, ascetic abstraction.

"Why, Fernando," said Muriel, in a slow, wondering voice,

recovering from her momentary pause, and approaching him with an outstretched hand, "I am surprised to see you."

He took her hand and bowed slightly, with an abstracted air.

"I ask your pardon for calling," he replied, looking vacantly at her, and speaking as if in dreaming soliloquy. "I heard of his death."

He paused, looking at her with his rigid lips slightly parted, and his eyes like sad stone.

"Yes," said she, slowly, wondering more and more at his strange manner. "It is true. He died yesterday morning at sunrise."

There was another long pause, in which she looked blankly at his abstracted gazing face.

"I am going to join the Catholic church," he said presently, looking vacantly at the wall, though his eyes had not seemed to turn from her countenance.

"Indeed!" she replied.

"Yes," said he, "in two or three days I am going to Baltimore. I intend to prepare myself for holy orders."

"Do you mean that you are going to become a priest?" she wonderingly asked.

"Yes," he replied, "in the Catholic church.

She blankly looked at him, marvelling at what he had told her.

"Would you be kind enough to let me see him?" said he, vacantly. "Only for a moment. I would be very grateful."

So great was her wonderment at the strange alteration in him, and so potent the deadening influence that radiated from him, that for a few moments she remained still and silent, fixedly looking at his face.

"Certainly, Fernando," she suddenly replied, starting from her amazement. "Certainly, you shall see him. Come with me."

She went quickly from the room and upstairs, almost doubting that he was following her, so noiseless was his movement. But as she entered the library and turned, he was there, and moving slowly to the casket on the table, with his lips parted, and his eyes fixed upon it. He laid his hat down as he reached it, and gazed intently on the face of the dead. For a moment, Muriel's eyes sank from him to the floor, and when she looked up again, she saw that his hands were folded, his eyes closed, and his lips moving in prayer. She turned away, with a touched heart.

A few minutes went slowly by, and a dim sense of motion, as if the air stirred, came to her. He was standing near her, hat in hand. His face was mute, and sad, and very pale.

"Thank you," said he, in a low voice. "I am very grateful. It has done me great good to see him once more. I feel better for it."

Her heart rose to him, and with a sudden movement she reached out her hand. He took it instantly, and his lip trembled.

"You were very good to me," he faltered—"you and Richard and Emily. I do not feel fit to come here, and I would not have come again if I had not heard he was dead. I did not feel fit to see him while he lived, but I wanted to see him when I heard he was no more. He was the best friend I had in the world. He did me good. I think I really never loved any one but him."

"Fernando," said Muriel, tenderly, "can you not let the past be forgotten? Do not go away from us. Stay here, for we are your friends, and you need to be sustained and comforted. Let us forget all that has happened, and meet happily together now."

"Thank you," he replied, sadly. "You are very kind, and I am grateful to you. But I do not feel fit to live near you. I do not deserve your friendship."

Her lips parted to answer him, but he retreated shaking his head mournfully, and stepping noiselessly from the room, went down-stairs like a phantom, and was gone. Muriel's head drooped, and with her hands clasped together, she stood musing for a long time.

The hours wore on, and as the time drew near to three o'clock, which was the hour at which they were to bear the dead to Mount Auburn, Muriel went to her chamber to attire herself for the sacred journey. When she came down into the library, all who were to go were there. Her mother, Captain Fisher and his family, Emily and Wentworth, Bagasse, and with him a new comer—his wife, a little middle-aged, brown Frenchwoman, whose eyes were swollen and red with hours of weeping for the dead gentleman who had nursed her husband in his sickness, and helped him and her to meet life as they had never been helped before. Muriel paused a few moments to greet her kindly in her own language, and then went to the body of Harrington.

As she reached the coffined form, illumined by the bright light which filled the room, she saw something on the dark-garbed breast, which brought to her golden eyes the first tears they had known since her hero died. It was the Cross of the Legion of Honor! She knew at once who had placed it there, and a mighty wave of emotion swept through her as she gazed on the old soldier's great-hearted tribute to the valor of her dead.

For a few moments she stood still, then turning with a sun-flash in her dewy eyes, and her features flushed with generous color, she saw the old Frenchman standing near her, looking with a reverent and sombre visage, and an eye of dark brilliance, on the cross of the Legion.

"It is mush bettair zere zan here," he said, laying his hand upon his heart, as his eye met hers. "Mon Empereur, he gif me zat wis his own hand, madame. I was young conscrip' at Ligny, and I take ze standard from ze Prussian. Zen he put on my breast zat cross. I lof it wis vair mush lof, and I will keep it for vair many year till I die. Zen he die—zat is my ozzer self, and I put it on him. It is his right. Ze brave zhentilman, wis his gallantree, his goodness, his mush lof, he lie in ze grave wis ze cross of ze Legion on his breast. Zat is well. It is his right, madame."

She pressed his hand in both of hers, looking fervently into his uncouth and martial visage.

"Thanks," she replied, speaking in French. "You fill me with gratitude. I accept for him the great and noble tribute of your love. It is, as you say, his right, for he belonged to the Legion of Honor. He was a soldier of the Guard—the old Guard which dies, but never surrenders!"

The dark eye blazed as he took in the proud significance of her words, and silent with emotion, he bowed, and retired.

Two hours later, and, the burial over, they stood in the green and tender sunlit shadows of Mount Auburn. A still peace filled the sweet sequestered shades. The birds sang in the murmuring leaves; the soft warm odors of the flowers and greenery breathed around them; the blue June sky was cloudless and calm; and the descending sunlight shone sweetly on the quiet graves.

For a little while after the others were gone, Muriel and Wentworth lingered looking at the gentle light which floated with the shadows of the oak-leaves overhead, on the new-made mound.

"It is all over," said Wentworth mournfully. "Alas! I never thought I would stand by his grave! He realized the noblest dreams of chivalry—he was the last grand chevalier—and he is gone. What is left us now!"

"Memories," she calmly answered, "memories of a life of love. Love beat through all his life, love nerved him in the strife in which he fell. He smote like Socrates at Delium—like the divine old Greek who clove his country's foe, and blessed him as he died. So smote he with stern love, and in all the wealth of memories he leaves me, that memory too, is mine. Sweet memories, I treasure you in my heart of hearts! Sweet blossoms of True Love, I fold you all. Stern blossom of True Love, I fold you too."

He gazed with mournful tenderness at her noble features, which were lit with a brilliant and fervent smile.

"True Love, indeed!" he answered. "Who but he could leave his beautiful Muriel, his adored wife, and go away to die for one of the lowliest of God's creatures! Ah, were there a thousand such as he, this land would be purged of every wrong! But he was alone in nobleness."

"No, not alone," she said with sudden spirit. "Not alone. This is America—America, forming and emerging, with martyrs and heroes such as no land has seen. The Greek could die for freemen ; but when died he for the helot? Oh, I see the heroes of all lands and times ! They live and die for country, for ideas, for religions, but in America they live and die for man. Land of Lovejoy's grave, land of Torrey's grave, land of the graves obscure and countless, graves of the lovers for whose love the lowest was not too low, I read your golden augury ! You prophecy the future ; you herald the America uprising—the beautiful divine land of lovers and of friends ! Shall it not come ? Oh, graves of all who die that it may be, answer, answer, answer !"

Her thrilling voice ceased, and as they silently moved away, a long and sea-like swell of wind arose, and all the leaves tossed and swept in an aspiration of innumerable rushing voices, holier than ever murmured in the dim groves of Dodona.

Answer, answer, answer ! Oh, grave at Auburn, green with summer beauty, folding beneath the oak-tree shadows the ashes of the dead chevalier, answer, answer, fading as I gaze ! Answer, lone grave in the Adirondacks, fadeless and immortal above the dust of the True Lover who tried to save his country from her slaves, and died that the land of lovers and of friends might be ! Answer, graves of the strong score of heroes who flung themselves with the true-loving sword upon the Jacquerie of slavery, and perished for the hope that makes America divine ! Answer, graves of all that made the country holy with the passion of their living and their dying for mankind—answer, and tell us that America emerges, the land of lovers and of friends !

It comes ! It comes ! Clear and sweet are your voices, oh, graves ! Raging clamors drown the voices of the living, but clear and sweet are the voices of the dead, and it comes —the bright land comes—the land of lovers and of friends, it comes !

THE END.

NOTE.

I AM indebted for the sketch of the flight of a fugitive through the Great Pacoudrie (or Cacodrie) Swamp, in the introductory portion of this volume, to a couple of pages in the graphic and affecting narrative entitled "Twelve Years a Slave," by Mr. Solomon Northup, a free citizen of New York, who was kidnapped in that State, and sold into bondage in Louisiana, from which he was fortunately rescued and restored to his wife and children, after a dozen years of enforced servitude.

Another acknowledgment remains to be made. The reader of the twelfth chapter of this book may already have observed that Harrington, if he had lived, would have been a believer in the theory regarding the origin and purpose of the Shakspeare Drama, as developed in the admirable work by Miss Delia Bacon, entitled "The Philosophy of Shakspeare's Plays Unfolded," in which belief I should certainly agree with Harrington. I wish it were in my power to do even the smallest justice to that mighty and eloquent volume, whose masterly comprehension and insight, though they could not save it from being trampled upon by the brutal bison of the British literary press, yet lift it to the dignity, whatever may be its faults, of being the best work ever composed upon the Baconian or Shakspearean writings. It has been scouted by the critics as the product of a distempered ideality. Perhaps it is. But there is a prudent wisdom, says Goethe, and there is a wisdom which does not remind us of prudence; and, in like manner, I may say that there is a sane sense, and there is a sense that does not remind us of sanity. At all events, I am assured that the candid and ingenuous reader Miss Bacon wished for, will find it more to his profit to be insane with her on the subject of Shakspeare, than sane with Dr. Johnson.

I am aware that in even making this acknowledgment, I do something to excite the rancor of the stupid and senseless prejudice which finds no difficulty in assigning the noblest works of the human genius to the fat peasant of Stratford—a man who, as Emerson justly says, lived a profane and vulgar life, and whose biography, collected after the painful labors of more than a century, does not present a single point which bears any relation to, or correspondence with, the holy and heroic pages which bear his name; while, at the same time, this prejudice derides as a mad and monstrous impossibility, the theory which ascribes those pages to Lord Bacon and his compeers—men in whose lives and careers all the Shakspearean conditions are fulfilled, and all the Shakspearealities included. But since I have decided, for reasons, to advance again, though even thus slightly, the theory I refer to, it is only fair to render due credit to its true author. I do so, earnestly wishing that her work might receive the respectful attention it undoubtedly merits; and, though the hand which wrote that glowing iliad of the glory and the genius of the Elizabethan men, will write no more, that justice might be done to the great dead scholar in her grave.

W. D. O'C.

ANTI-SLAVERY WORKS.

I.

THE PUBLIC LIFE OF CAPTAIN JOHN BROWN,

BY JAMES REDPATH.

With an Autobiography of his Childhood and Youth.

With a Steel Portrait and Illustrations. pp. 408.

This volume has been the most successful of the season, — having already reached its FORTIETH THOUSAND, and the demand still continuing very large. It has also been republished in England, and widely-noticed by the British press. The *Autobiography* (of which no reprint will be permitted) has been universally pronounced to be one of the most remarkable compositions of the kind in the English language. In addition to being *the* authentic biography of John Brown, and containing a complete collection of his celebrated prison letters — which can nowhere else be found — this volume has also the only correct and connected history of Kansas, — from its opening for settlement till the close of the struggle for Freedom there, — to be found in American literature, whether periodical or standard. It treats, therefore, of topics which must be largely discussed in political life for many years. A handsome percentage, *on every copy sold,* is secured by contract to the family of Capt. Brown. Price ONE DOLLAR. Copies mailed to any address, post paid, on receipt of the retail price.

☞ Agents wanted.

II.

SOUTHERN NOTES FOR NATIONAL CIRCULATION.

EDITED BY JAMES REDPATH.

This is a volume of *facts* of recent Southern life, as narrated by the Southern and Metropolitan press. It is a history of the Southern States for six months subsequent to John Brown's Invasion of Virginia. The diversity of its contents may be judged from the titles of its Chapters, — Key Notes, Free Speech South, Free Press South, Law of the Suspected, Southern Gospel Freedom, Southern Hospitality, Post Office South, Our Adopted Fellow Citizens South, Persecutions of Southern Citizens, The Shivering Chivalry, Sports of Heathen Gentlemen, &c., &c., &c. As a manual for Anti-Slavery and Republican orators and editors it is invaluable.

A HANDSOME PAMPHLET OF 128 PAGES. PRICE 25 CENTS.

☞ Copies mailed to any address on receipt of price. Agents wanted.

III.

ECHOES OF HARPER'S FERRY.

This volume is a collection of the greatest Speeches, Sermons, Lectures, Letters, Poems, and other Utterances of the leading minds of America and Europe, called forth by John Brown's Invasion of Virginia. They are all given — mostly for the first time — *unabridged;* and they have all been corrected by their authors for this edition, or re-printed with their permission from duly authorized copies. That this volume is justly entitled to the claim of being the *first* collection of worthy specimens of American Eloquence, the following brief summary of its contents will show: It contains *Speeches* and *Sermons* — by Wendell Phillips (two), Ralph Waldo Emerson (two), Edward Everett, Henry D. Thoreau, Dr. Cheever (two), Hon. Charles O'Conor, Henry Ward Beecher, Theodore Tilton, Col. Phillips, Rev. Gilbert Haven, James Freeman Clarke, Fales Henry Newhall, M. D., Conway (of Cincinnati), and Edwin M. Wheelock; *Letters* — by Theodore Parker (two), Victor Hugo (two), Mrs. Mason of Virginia, and Lydia Maria Child; *Poems* and other *Contributions* — by William Allinghame, John G. Whittier, William Lloyd Garrison, Judge Tilden, F. B. Sanborn, Hon. A. G. Riddle, Richard Realf, C. K. Whipple, Rev. Mr. Belcher, Rev. Mr. Furness, Rev. Mr. Sears, Edna Dean Proctor, L. M. Alcott, Wm. D. Howells, Elizur Wright, &c., &c., &c. Also, all the Letters sent to John Brown when in prison at Charlestown by Northern men and women, and his own relatives: "one of the most tenderly-pathetic and remarkable collections of letters in all Literature." Also, the Services at Concord, or "Liturgy for a Martyr;" composed by Emerson, Thoreau, Alcott, Sanborn, &c.: "unsurpassed in beauty even by the Book of Common Prayer." With an Appendix, containing the widely-celebrated Essays of Henry C. Carey on the value of the Union to the North.

Appended to the various contributions are the autographs of the authors.

EDITED BY JAMES REDPATH.

1 volume, 514 pages, handsomely bound in muslin. Price $1.25.

☞ Sample copies mailed to any address on receipt of the retail price, postage paid.

For Circular of Terms address the Publishers.

www.ingramcontent.com/pod-product-compliance
Lightning Source LLC
LaVergne TN
LVHW021238110826
845150LV00002B/350

* 9 7 8 1 4 2 5 5 6 1 7 2 7 *